# DRACULA

Collect all 5 titles in this Classic Horror series and experience each cover coming to life through Augmented Reality!

Available from Amazon on Kindle, Hardback or Paperback.

Frankenstein
Mary Shelley

Dracula
Bram Stoker

The Picture of Dorian Gray
Oscar Wilde

Jekyll and Hyde
Robert Louis Stevenson

Phantom of the Opera
Gaston Leroux

Keep up to date with the latest titles, offers and other Augmented Reality genres by visiting:

www.augmentedclassics.com

Instagram: @augmentedclassics

# How to Experience the Augmented Reality Book Cover

*Dracula QR code*

- **Open the camera** on your Smartphone and ensure you have **Internet connectivity.**
- Ensure the **volume is turned** up on your Smartphone.
- **Scan the QR code** above (or on the back cover or spine) by placing your camera over the QR image.
- **Click the new link** that appears on your Smartphone.
- A welcome page will appear, click **LAUNCH.**
- If you are asked for access to your camera and motion and orientation click **ALLOW.**
- Wait as the augmented reality cover loads.
- Close this book and hold the Smartphone screen above this cover to bring it to life.
- **Enjoy** the Augmented Reality experience.

If you have any questions or need support visit:

**www.augmentedclassics.com**

# Dracula - Fan Reviews

"Chilling from the off, Bram Stoker's Dracula truly feels like the father of the Gothic Genre!
**Youtube : Ciara Foster / Instagram: @ciarascorner_**

"The character of Count Dracula has crossed oceans of time, inspiring literature, film, and scores of other dark delights with good reason. Seeing the book come to life in a new way is exciting when handled with such creativity and care. Terrifying even now, the fight for love and life against a horrifying monster feels all too real when told through the eyes of those whose lives and sanity he draws down into hell, like so much blood."
**Youtube: Typical Books - Horror Fiction**
**Instagram: @typicallydia**

"This well known tale of the most popular vampire deserves its spot as one of the best horror classics that is not only horrifying but allows readers to reflect on good and evil. Stoker wrote an extremely captivating story that held up and influenced many other authors. Anyone who loves a good creature tale has to read about the most notable and notorious vampire out there."
**Instagram: @classicsandhorror**

"Dracula has become one of my favourite classics since studying it in depth at university and what draws me in most is Stoker's use of figurative language.
I'm excited to see such a modern, unique edition of this novel being published - it's the perfect book to add to your 'Halloween Hopefuls' to-be-read list."
**Instagram: @allthegenres**

"Bram Stoker's *Dracula* has tormented the minds of readers for over a century. Count Dracula has become the figure that haunts our nightmares, faced with the curse of immortal life and feeding on our very souls. Although not the first ever vampire tale, the blood thirsty

creation of Stoker has set the archetype for the vampire narrative, inspiring countless media representations portraying the demonic Count, however, nothing can really compare to the frightening and possessive story of the original text. *Dracula* will make you challenge your own fears and confront your worst nightmares, accumulating into a dramatic and climactic end."
**Instagram: @gothicbookworm**

# Foreword

When a brand name becomes the description for an entire product category or is adopted as a new adjective in popular culture, it has transcended into something more than a product name it has become an idea! Hoover is used in the UK to describe a vacuum cleaner or 'to hoover up'; Ping Pong is actually a brand name for table tennis and we 'google it' when we want to search for something online. Likewise, Dracula and 'vampire' have become interchangeable. Despite vampire myths predating Bram Stoker's fictional character, most people use the world Dracula and vampire as one.

So, why of all the horror protagonists has Dracula resonated so deeply within our culture? Why rather than the mummy or the werewolf has Dracula towered above all other creatures of the night?

Perhaps, it's the potent idea that a supernatural being maintains its strength by preying on helpless human victims, sucking their blood and infecting them with a curse, that has attached Dracula to a deep primordial fear inside our collective imagination. The disease-spreading mosquito; the plague-ridden rat; even a coronavirus are real-life terrors which parallel the malevolent habits of Dracula!

Could it be the seductive Gothic descriptions of castles, candles and concubines that has erected a blood-soaked gallery of evocative images in our minds? Or is it the promise of eternal life that abides with us? What makes Dracula such an enduring figure?

I would like to offer something much less obvious, as to why Dracula is the best selling Halloween costume of all time and why there have been so many vampire movies made... It's not the message of the story but the medium of the storytelling that established Dracula as the OG of horror!

The novel Dracula is an epistolary, a collection of documents, letters, diaries and newspaper clippings. Move over Blair witch project! The first found-footage horror story was Dracula! This type of storytelling is as uncommon as writing in the second person. You will agree no doubt ;-)

Encountering Dracula through found-footage gave the first readers in 1897 a new perspective, a sort of breaking down of the fourth wall which let Dracula jump off the page to shock the literary audiences of the time! When reading diary entries and newspaper articles the reader is moved away from being spoon-fed a narrative, invited instead to become the narrator themselves.

Likewise in 1922 when the silent movie Nosferatu: A symphony of horror was released, the terrifying shadow of a vampire burnt through audiences retinas leaving a permanent pointy-toothed imprint in horror cinematography and pop culture. Vampires had crossed from paper to celluloid and they had only just begun!

Computer games; audiobooks; graphic novels; teenage romantic fiction; role-playing. Dracula crossed time and space to be with you and with every medium-metamorphosis the nightmarish legend and his global brand grew, reaching the minds of each successive generation.

When the storytelling medium is new, it can engage people in fresh ways, taking them out of their comfort zones away from their expectations and familiarity. Creating a new and unsettling landscape in which horror above all genres loves to thrive.

The emergence of augmented reality is in my view another one of these storytelling transformations, where the medium itself can communicate stories in a totally new way. Merging video and 3D graphics in 'real world' space, augmented reality is set to enhance our lives in ways we are only just imagining.

I founded Augment Classics to bring the novelty, fun and awe of augmented reality to classic fiction with the aim of introducing a tech-savvy generation to the beauty and majesty of the printed word. By mixing augmented reality experiences with physical print and paper it is my hope that books remain a relevant and beloved part of modern culture.

It had to therefore be Dracula himself who received the augmented reality treatment first. Inviting this eternal shape-shifting character to come freely off the page once again and leave something of the happiness he brings in your house.

"I want you to believe... to believe in things that you cannot."

Nik Maguire
Augmented Classics

# DRACULA
## By
## Bram  Stoker

Colophon
NEW YORK
GROSSET & DUNLAP
Publishers

Copyright, 1897, in the United States of America, according
to Act of Congress, by Bram Stoker
[All rights reserved.]
PRINTED IN THE UNITED STATES
AT
THE COUNTRY LIFE PRESS, GARDEN CITY, N.Y.

# Contents

*JONATHAN HARKER'S JOURNAL* .................................................................. *12*

*JONATHAN HARKER'S JOURNAL— continued* ........................................... *25*

*JONATHAN HARKER'S JOURNAL— continued* ........................................... *38*

*JONATHAN HARKER'S JOURNAL— continued* ........................................... *51*

*Letter from Miss Mina Murray to Miss Lucy Westenra.* ............................... *65*

*MINA MURRAY'S JOURNAL* ....................................................................... *74*

*CUTTING FROM "THE DAILYGRAPH," 8 AUGUST* .................................... *87*

*MINA MURRAY'S JOURNAL* ..................................................................... *102*

*Letter, Mina Harker to Lucy Westenra* ......................................................... *118*

*Letter, Dr. Seward to Hon. Arthur Holmwood* .......................................... *132*

*Lucy Westenra's Diary.* ............................................................................... *146*

*DR. SEWARD'S DIARY* ............................................................................... *158*

*DR. SEWARD'S DIARY— continued.* ........................................................... *175*

*MINA HARKER'S JOURNAL* ...................................................................... *191*

*DR. SEWARD'S DIARY— continued.* ........................................................... *206*

*DR. SEWARD'S DIARY— continued.* ........................................................... *220*

*DR. SEWARD'S DIARY— continued.* ........................................................... *232*

*DR. SEWARD'S DIARY* ............................................................................... *245*

*JONATHAN HARKER'S JOURNAL* ............................................................. *261*

*JONATHAN HARKER'S JOURNAL* ............................................................. *274*

*DR. SEWARD'S DIARY* ............................................................................... *289*

*JONATHAN HARKER'S JOURNAL* ............................................................. *303*

*DR. SEWARD'S DIARY* ............................................................................... *316*

*DR. SEWARD'S PHONOGRAPH DIARY, SPOKEN BY VAN HELSING* ...... *328*

*DR. SEWARD'S DIARY* ............................................................................... *343*

*DR. SEWARD'S DIARY* ............................................................................... *357*

*MINA HARKER'S JOURNAL* ...................................................................... *375*

# CHAPTER I
# JONATHAN HARKER'S JOURNAL

## (Kept in shorthand.)

**3** May. Bistritz.— Left Munich at 8:35 P. M., on 1st May, arriving at Vienna early next morning; should have arrived at 6:46, but train was an hour late. Buda-Pesth seems a wonderful place, from the glimpse which I got of it from the train and the little I could walk through the streets. I feared to go very far from the station, as we had arrived late and would start as near the correct time as possible. The impression I had was that we were leaving the West and entering the East; the most western of splendid bridges over the Danube, which is here of noble width and depth, took us among the traditions of Turkish rule.

We left in pretty good time, and came after nightfall to Klausenburgh. Here I stopped for the night at the Hotel Royale. I had for dinner, or rather supper, a chicken done up some way with red pepper, which was very good but thirsty. (Mem., get recipe for Mina.) I asked the waiter, and he said it was called "paprika hendl," and that, as it was a national dish, I should be able to get it anywhere along the Carpathians. I found my smattering of German very useful here; indeed, I don't know how I should be able to get on without it.

Having had some time at my disposal when in London, I had visited the British Museum, and made search among the books and maps in the library regarding Transylvania; it had struck me that some foreknowledge of the country could hardly fail to have some importance in dealing with a nobleman of that country. I find that the district he named is in the extreme east of the country, just on the borders of three states, Transylvania, Moldavia and Bukovina, in the midst of the Carpathian mountains; one of the wildest and least known portions of Europe. I was not able to light on any map or work giving the exact locality of the Castle Dracula, as there are no maps of this country as yet to compare with our own Ordnance Survey maps; but I found that Bistritz, the post town named by Count Dracula, is a fairly well-known place. I shall enter here some of my notes, as they may refresh my memory when I talk over my travels with Mina.

In the population of Transylvania there are four distinct nationalities: Saxons in the South, and mixed with them the Wallachs, who are the descendants of the Dacians; Magyars in the West, and Szekelys in the East and North. I am going among the latter, who claim to be descended from Attila and the Huns. This may be so, for when the Magyars conquered the country in the eleventh century they found the Huns settled in it. I read that every known superstition in the world is gathered into the horseshoe of the Carpathians, as if it were the centre of some sort of imaginative whirlpool; if so my stay may be very interesting. (Mem., I must ask the Count all about them.)

I did not sleep well, though my bed was comfortable enough, for I had all sorts of queer dreams. There was a dog howling all night under my window, which may have had something to do with it; or it may have been the paprika, for I had to drink up all the water in my carafe, and was still thirsty. Towards morning I slept and was wakened by the continuous knocking at my door, so I guess I must have been sleeping soundly then. I had for breakfast more paprika, and a sort of porridge of maize flour which they said was "mamaliga," and egg-plant stuffed with forcemeat, a very excellent dish, which they call "impletata." (Mem., get recipe for this also.) I had to hurry breakfast, for the train started a little before eight, or rather it ought to have done so, for after rushing to the station at 7:30 I had to sit in the carriage for more than an hour before we began to move. It seems to me that the further east you go the more unpunctual are the trains. What ought they to be in China?

All day long we seemed to dawdle through a country which was full of beauty of every kind. Sometimes we saw little towns or castles on the top of steep hills such as we see in old missals; sometimes we ran by rivers and streams which seemed from the wide stony margin on each side of them to be subject to great floods. It takes a lot of water, and running strong, to sweep the outside edge of a river clear. At every station there were groups of people, sometimes crowds, and in all sorts of attire. Some of them were just like the peasants at home or those I saw coming through France and Germany, with short jackets and round hats and home-made trousers; but others were very picturesque. The women looked pretty, except when you got near them, but they were very clumsy about the waist. They had all full white sleeves of some kind or other, and most of them had big belts with a lot of strips of something fluttering from them like the dresses in a ballet, but of course there were petticoats under them. The strangest figures we saw were the Slovaks, who were more barbarian than the rest, with their big cow-boy hats, great baggy dirty-white trousers, white linen shirts, and enormous heavy leather belts, nearly a foot wide, all studded over with brass nails. They wore high boots, with their trousers tucked into them, and had long black hair and heavy black moustaches. They are very picturesque, but do not look prepossessing. On the stage they would be set down at once as some old Oriental band of brigands. They are, however, I am told, very harmless and rather wanting in natural self-assertion.

It was on the dark side of twilight when we got to Bistritz, which is a very interesting old place. Being practically on the frontier— for the Borgo Pass leads from it into Bukovina— it has had a very stormy existence, and it certainly shows marks of it. Fifty years ago a series of great fires took place, which made terrible havoc on five separate occasions. At the very beginning of the seventeenth century it underwent a siege of three weeks and lost 13,000 people, the casualties of war proper being assisted by famine and disease.

Count Dracula had directed me to go to the Golden Krone Hotel, which I found, to my great delight, to be thoroughly old-fashioned, for of course I wanted to see all I could of the ways of the country. I was evidently expected, for when I got near the door I faced a cheery-looking elderly woman in the usual peasant dress— white undergarment with long double apron, front, and back, of coloured stuff fitting almost too tight for modesty. When I came close she bowed and said, "The Herr Englishman?" "Yes," I said, "Jonathan Harker." She smiled, and gave some message to an elderly man in white shirt-sleeves, who had followed her to the door. He went, but immediately returned with a letter:—

"My Friend.— Welcome to the Carpathians. I am anxiously expecting you. Sleep well to-night. At three to-morrow the diligence will start for Bukovina; a place on it is kept for you. At the Borgo Pass my carriage will await you and will bring you to me. I trust that your journey from London has been a happy one, and that you will enjoy your stay in my beautiful land.

"Your friend,

"Dracula."

4 May.— I found that my landlord had got a letter from the Count, directing him to secure the best place on the coach for me; but on making inquiries as to details he seemed somewhat reticent, and pretended that he could not understand my German. This could not be true, because up to then he had understood it perfectly; at least, he answered my questions exactly as if he did. He and his wife, the old lady who had received me, looked at each other in a frightened sort of way. He mumbled out that the money had been sent in a letter, and that was all he knew. When I asked him if he knew Count Dracula, and could tell me anything of his castle, both he and his wife crossed themselves, and, saying that they knew nothing at all, simply refused to speak further. It was so near the time of starting that I had no time to ask any one else, for it was all very mysterious and not by any means comforting.

Just before I was leaving, the old lady came up to my room and said in a very hysterical way:

"Must you go? Oh! young Herr, must you go?" She was in such an excited state that she seemed to have lost her grip of what German she knew, and mixed it all up with some other language which I did not know at all. I was just able to follow her by asking many questions. When I told her that I must go at once, and that I was engaged on important business, she asked again:

"Do you know what day it is?" I answered that it was the fourth of May. She shook her head as she said again:

"Oh, yes! I know that! I know that, but do you know what day it is?" On my saying that I did not understand, she went on:

"It is the eve of St. George's Day. Do you not know that to-night, when the clock strikes midnight, all the evil things in the world will have full sway? Do you know where you are going, and what you are going to?" She was in such evident distress that I tried to comfort her, but without effect. Finally she went down on her knees and implored me not to go; at least to wait a day or two before starting. It was all very ridiculous but I did not feel comfortable. However, there was business to be done, and I could allow nothing to interfere with it. I therefore tried to raise her up, and said, as gravely as I could, that I thanked her, but my duty was imperative, and that I must go. She then rose and dried her eyes, and taking a crucifix from her neck offered it to me. I did not know what to do, for, as an English Churchman, I have been taught to regard such things as in some measure idolatrous, and yet it seemed so ungracious to refuse an old lady meaning so well and in such a state of mind. She saw, I suppose, the doubt in my face, for she put the rosary round my neck, and said, "For your mother's sake," and went out of the room. I am writing up this part of the diary whilst I am waiting for the coach, which is, of course, late; and the crucifix is still round my neck. Whether it is the old lady's fear, or the many ghostly traditions of this place, or the crucifix itself, I do not know, but I am not feeling nearly as easy in my mind as usual. If this book should ever reach Mina before I do, let it bring my good-bye. Here comes the coach!

5 May. The Castle.— The grey of the morning has passed, and the sun is high over the distant horizon, which seems jagged, whether with trees or hills I know not, for it is so far off that big things and little are mixed. I am not sleepy, and, as I am not to be called till I awake, naturally I write till sleep comes. There are many odd things to put down, and, lest who reads them may fancy that I dined too well before I left Bistritz, let me put down my dinner exactly. I dined on what they called "robber steak"— bits of bacon, onion, and beef, seasoned with red pepper, and strung on sticks and roasted over the fire, in the simple style of the London cat's meat! The wine was Golden Mediasch, which produces a queer sting on the tongue, which is, however, not disagreeable. I had only a couple of glasses of this, and nothing else.

When I got on the coach the driver had not taken his seat, and I saw him talking with the landlady. They were evidently talking of me, for every now and then they looked at me, and some of the people who were sitting on the bench outside the door— which they call by a name meaning "word-bearer"— came and listened, and then looked at me, most of them pityingly. I could hear a lot of words often repeated, queer words, for there were many nationalities in the crowd; so I quietly got my polyglot dictionary from my bag and looked them out. I must say they were not cheering to me, for amongst them were "Ordog"— Satan, "pokol"— hell, "stregoica"— witch, "vrolok" and "vlkoslak"— both of which mean the same thing, one being Slovak and the other Servian for something that is either were-wolf or vampire. (Mem., I must ask the Count about these superstitions)

When we started, the crowd round the inn door, which had by this time swelled to a considerable size, all made the sign of the cross and pointed two fingers towards me. With some difficulty I got a fellow-passenger to tell me what they meant; he would not answer at first, but on learning that I was English, he explained that it was a charm or guard against the evil eye. This was not very pleasant for me, just starting for an unknown place to meet an unknown man; but every one seemed so kind-hearted, and so sorrowful, and so sympathetic that I could not but be touched. I shall never forget the last glimpse which I had of the inn-yard and its crowd of picturesque figures, all crossing themselves, as they stood round the wide archway, with its background of rich foliage of oleander and orange trees in green tubs clustered in the centre of the yard. Then our driver, whose wide linen drawers covered the whole front of the box-seat— "gotza" they call them— cracked his big whip over his four small horses, which ran abreast, and we set off on our journey.

I soon lost sight and recollection of ghostly fears in the beauty of the scene as we drove along, although had I known the language, or rather languages, which my fellow-passengers were speaking, I might not have been able to throw them off so easily. Before us lay a green sloping land full of forests and woods, with here and there steep hills, crowned with clumps of trees or with farmhouses, the blank gable end to the road. There was everywhere a bewildering mass of fruit blossom— apple, plum, pear, cherry; and as we drove by I could see the green grass under the trees spangled with the fallen petals. In and out amongst these green hills of what they call here the "Mittel Land" ran the road, losing itself as it swept round the grassy curve, or was shut out by the straggling ends of pine woods, which here and there ran down the hillsides like tongues of flame. The road was rugged, but still we seemed to fly over it with a feverish haste. I could not understand then what the haste meant, but the driver was evidently bent on losing no time in reaching Borgo Prund. I was told that this road is in summertime excellent, but that it had not yet been put in order after the winter snows. In this respect it is different from the general run of roads in the Carpathians, for it is an old tradition that they are not to be kept in too good order. Of old the Hospadars would not repair them, lest the Turk should think that they were preparing to bring in foreign troops, and so hasten the war which was always really at loading point. Beyond the green swelling hills of the Mittel Land rose mighty slopes of forest up to the lofty steeps of the Carpathians themselves. Right and left of us they towered, with the afternoon sun falling full upon them and bringing out all the glorious colours of this beautiful range, deep blue and purple in the shadows of the peaks, green and brown where grass and rock mingled, and an endless perspective of jagged rock and pointed crags, till these were themselves lost in the distance, where the snowy peaks rose grandly. Here and there seemed mighty rifts in the mountains, through which, as the sun began to sink, we saw now and again the white gleam of falling water. One of my companions touched my arm as we swept round the base of a hill and opened up the lofty, snow-covered peak of a mountain, which seemed, as we wound on our serpentine way, to be right before us:—

"Look! Isten szek!"— "God's seat!"— and he crossed himself reverently.

As we wound on our endless way, and the sun sank lower and lower behind us, the shadows of the evening began to creep round us. This was emphasised by the fact that the snowy mountain-top still held the sunset, and seemed to glow out with a delicate cool pink. Here and there we passed Cszeks and Slovaks, all in picturesque attire, but I noticed that goitre was painfully prevalent. By the roadside were many crosses, and as we swept by, my companions all crossed themselves. Here and there was a peasant man or woman kneeling before a shrine, who did not even turn round as we approached, but seemed in the self-surrender of devotion to have neither eyes nor ears for the outer world. There were many things new to me: for instance, hay-ricks in the trees, and here and there very beautiful masses of weeping birch, their white stems shining like silver through the delicate green of the leaves. Now and again we passed a leiter-wagon— the ordinary peasant's cart— with its long, snake-like vertebra, calculated to suit the inequalities of the road. On this were sure to be seated quite a group of home-coming peasants, the Cszeks with their white, and the Slovaks with their coloured, sheepskins, the latter carrying lance-fashion their long staves, with axe at end. As the evening fell it began to get very cold, and the growing twilight seemed to merge into one dark mistiness the gloom of the trees, oak, beech, and pine, though in the valleys which ran deep between the spurs of the hills, as we ascended through the Pass, the dark firs stood out here and there against the background of late-lying snow. Sometimes, as the road was cut through the pine woods that seemed in the darkness to be closing down upon us, great masses of greyness, which here and there bestrewed the trees, produced a peculiarly weird and solemn effect, which carried on the thoughts and grim fancies engendered earlier in the evening, when the falling sunset threw into strange relief the ghost-like clouds which amongst the Carpathians seem to wind ceaselessly through the valleys. Sometimes the hills were so steep that, despite our driver's haste, the horses could only go slowly. I wished to get down and walk up them, as we do at home, but the driver would not hear of it. "No, no," he said; "you must not walk here; the dogs are too fierce"; and then he added, with what he evidently meant for grim pleasantry— for he looked round to catch the approving smile of the rest— "and you may have enough of such matters before you go to sleep." The only stop he would make was a moment's pause to light his lamps.

When it grew dark there seemed to be some excitement amongst the passengers, and they kept speaking to him, one after the other, as though urging him to further speed. He lashed the horses unmercifully with his long whip, and with wild cries of encouragement urged them on to further exertions. Then through the darkness I could see a sort of patch of grey light ahead of us, as though there were a cleft in the hills. The excitement of the passengers grew greater; the crazy coach rocked on its great leather springs, and swayed like a boat tossed on a stormy sea. I had to hold on. The road grew more level, and we appeared to fly along. Then the mountains seemed to come nearer to us on each side and to frown down upon us; we were entering on the Borgo Pass. One by one several of the passengers offered me gifts, which they pressed upon me with an earnestness which would take no denial; these were certainly of an odd and varied kind, but each was given in simple good faith, with a kindly word, and a blessing, and that strange mixture of fear-meaning movements which I had seen outside the hotel at Bistritz— the sign of the cross and the guard against the evil eye. Then, as we flew along, the driver leaned forward, and on each side the passengers, craning over the edge of the coach, peered eagerly into the darkness. It was evident that something very exciting was either happening or expected, but though I asked each passenger, no one would give me the slightest explanation. This state of excitement kept on for some little time; and at last we saw before us the Pass opening out on the eastern side. There were dark, rolling clouds overhead, and in the air the heavy, oppressive sense of thunder. It seemed as though the mountain range had separated two atmospheres, and that now we had got into the thunderous one. I was now myself looking out for the conveyance which was to take me to the Count. Each moment I expected to see the glare of lamps through the blackness; but all was dark. The only light was the flickering rays of our own lamps, in which the steam from our hard-driven horses rose in a white cloud. We could see now the sandy road lying white before us, but there was on it no sign of a vehicle. The passengers drew back with a sigh of gladness, which seemed to mock my own disappointment. I was already thinking what I had best do, when the driver, looking at his watch, said to the others something which I could hardly hear, it was spoken so quietly and in so low a tone; I thought it was "An hour less than the time." Then turning to me, he said in German worse than my own:—

"There is no carriage here. The Herr is not expected after all. He will now come on to Bukovina, and return to-morrow or the next day; better the next day." Whilst he was speaking the horses began to neigh and snort and plunge wildly, so that the driver had to hold them up. Then, amongst a chorus of screams from the peasants and a universal crossing of themselves, a calèche, with four horses, drove up behind us, overtook us, and drew up beside the coach. I could see from the flash of our lamps, as the rays fell on them, that the horses were coal-black and splendid animals. They were driven by a tall man, with a long brown beard and a great black hat, which seemed to hide his face from us. I could only see the gleam of a pair of very bright eyes, which seemed red in the lamplight, as he turned to us. He said to the driver:—
"You are early to-night, my friend." The man stammered in reply:—
"The English Herr was in a hurry," to which the stranger replied:—
"That is why, I suppose, you wished him to go on to Bukovina. You cannot deceive me, my friend; I know too much, and my horses are swift." As he spoke he smiled, and the lamplight fell on a hard-looking mouth, with very red lips and sharp-looking teeth, as white as ivory. One of my companions whispered to another the line from Burger's "Lenore":—
"Denn die Todten reiten schnell"—
("For the dead travel fast.")
The strange driver evidently heard the words, for he looked up with a gleaming smile. The passenger turned his face away, at the same time putting out his two fingers and crossing himself. "Give me the Herr's luggage," said the driver; and with exceeding alacrity my bags were handed out and put in the calèche. Then I descended from the side of the coach, as the calèche was close alongside, the driver helping me with a hand which caught my arm in a grip of steel; his strength must have been prodigious. Without a word he shook his reins, the horses turned, and we swept into the darkness of the Pass. As I looked back I saw the steam from the horses of the coach by the light of the lamps, and projected against it the figures of my late companions crossing themselves. Then the driver cracked his whip and called to his horses, and off they swept on their way to Bukovina. As they sank into the darkness I felt a strange chill, and a lonely feeling came over me; but a cloak was thrown over my shoulders, and a rug across my knees, and the driver said in excellent German:—

"The night is chill, mein Herr, and my master the Count bade me take all care of you. There is a flask of slivovitz (the plum brandy of the country) underneath the seat, if you should require it." I did not take any, but it was a comfort to know it was there all the same. I felt a little strangely, and not a little frightened. I think had there been any alternative I should have taken it, instead of prosecuting that unknown night journey. The carriage went at a hard pace straight along, then we made a complete turn and went along another straight road. It seemed to me that we were simply going over and over the same ground again; and so I took note of some salient point, and found that this was so. I would have liked to have asked the driver what this all meant, but I really feared to do so, for I thought that, placed as I was, any protest would have had no effect in case there had been an intention to delay. By-and-by, however, as I was curious to know how time was passing, I struck a match, and by its flame looked at my watch; it was within a few minutes of midnight. This gave me a sort of shock, for I suppose the general superstition about midnight was increased by my recent experiences. I waited with a sick feeling of suspense.

Then a dog began to howl somewhere in a farmhouse far down the road— a long, agonised wailing, as if from fear. The sound was taken up by another dog, and then another and another, till, borne on the wind which now sighed softly through the Pass, a wild howling began, which seemed to come from all over the country, as far as the imagination could grasp it through the gloom of the night. At the first howl the horses began to strain and rear, but the driver spoke to them soothingly, and they quieted down, but shivered and sweated as though after a runaway from sudden fright. Then, far off in the distance,from the mountains on each side of us began a louder and a sharper howling-that of wolves-which affected both the horses and myself in the same way-for I was minded to jump from the calèche and run, whilst they reared again and plunged madly, so that the driver had to use all his great strength to keep them from bolting. In a few minutes, however, my own ears got accustomed to the sound, and the horses so far became quiet that the driver was able to descend and to stand before them. He petted and soothed them, and whispered something in their ears, as I have heard of horse-tamers doing, and with extraordinary effect, for under his caresses they became quite manageable again, though they still trembled. The driver again took his seat, and shaking his reins, started off at a great pace.This time, after going to the far side of the Pass, he suddenly turned down a narrow roadway which ran sharply to the right.

Soon we were hemmed in with trees, which in places arched right over the roadway till we passed as through a tunnel; and again great frowning rocks guarded us boldly on either side. Though we were in shelter, we could hear the rising wind, for it moaned and whistled through the rocks, and the branches of the trees crashed together as we swept along. It grew colder and colder still, and fine, powdery snow began to fall, so that soon we and all around us were covered with a white blanket. The keen wind still carried the howling of the dogs, though this grew fainter as we went on our way. The baying of the wolves sounded nearer and nearer, as though they were closing round on us from every side. I grew dreadfully afraid, and the horses shared my fear. The driver, however, was not in the least disturbed; he kept turning his head to left and right, but I could not see anything through the darkness.

Suddenly, away on our left, I saw a faint flickering blue flame. The driver saw it at the same moment; he at once checked the horses, and, jumping to the ground, disappeared into the darkness. I did not know what to do, the less as the howling of the wolves grew closer; but while I wondered the driver suddenly appeared again, and without a word took his seat, and we resumed our journey. I think I must have fallen asleep and kept dreaming of the incident, for it seemed to be repeated endlessly, and now looking back, it is like a sort of awful nightmare. Once the flame appeared so near the road, that even in the darkness around us I could watch the driver's motions. He went rapidly to where the blue flame arose— it must have been very faint, for it did not seem to illumine the place around it at all— and gathering a few stones, formed them into some device. Once there appeared a strange optical effect: when he stood between me and the flame he did not obstruct it, for I could see its ghostly flicker all the same. This startled me, but as the effect was only momentary, I took it that my eyes deceived me straining through the darkness. Then for a time there were no blue flames, and we sped onwards through the gloom, with the howling of the wolves around us, as though they were following in a moving circle.

At last there came a time when the driver went further afield than he had yet gone, and during his absence, the horses began to tremble worse than ever and to snort and scream with fright. I could not see any cause for it, for the howling of the wolves had ceased altogether; but just then the moon, sailing through the black clouds, appeared behind the jagged crest of a beetling, pine-clad rock, and by its light I saw around us a ring of wolves, with white teeth and lolling red tongues, with long, sinewy limbs and shaggy hair. They were a hundred times more terrible in the grim silence which held them than even when they howled. For myself, I felt a sort of paralysis of fear. It is only when a man feels himself face to face with such horrors that he can understand their true import.

All at once the wolves began to howl as though the moonlight had had some peculiar effect on them. The horses jumped about and reared, and looked helplessly round with eyes that rolled in a way painful to see; but the living ring of terror encompassed them on every side; and they had perforce to remain within it. I called to the coachman to come, for it seemed to me that our only chance was to try to break out through the ring and to aid his approach. I shouted and beat the side of the calèche, hoping by the noise to scare the wolves from that side, so as to give him a chance of reaching the trap. How he came there, I know not, but I heard his voice raised in a tone of imperious command, and looking towards the sound, saw him stand in the roadway. As he swept his long arms, as though brushing aside some impalpable obstacle, the wolves fell back and back further still. Just then a heavy cloud passed across the face of the moon, so that we were again in darkness.

When I could see again the driver was climbing into the calèche, and the wolves had disappeared. This was all so strange and uncanny that a dreadful fear came upon me, and I was afraid to speak or move. The time seemed interminable as we swept on our way, now in almost complete darkness, for the rolling clouds obscured the moon. We kept on ascending, with occasional periods of quick descent, but in the main always ascending. Suddenly, I became conscious of the fact that the driver was in the act of pulling up the horses in the courtyard of a vast ruined castle, from whose tall black windows came no ray of light, and whose broken battlements showed a jagged line against the moonlit sky.

## CHAPTER II
## JONATHAN HARKER'S JOURNAL— continued

5 May.— I must have been asleep, for certainly if I had been fully awake I must have noticed the approach of such a remarkable place. In the gloom the courtyard looked of considerable size, and as several dark ways led from it under great round arches, it perhaps seemed bigger than it really is. I have not yet been able to see it by daylight.

When the calèche stopped, the driver jumped down and held out his hand to assist me to alight. Again I could not but notice his prodigious strength. His hand actually seemed like a steel vice that could have crushed mine if he had chosen. Then he took out my traps, and placed them on the ground beside me as I stood close to a great door, old and studded with large iron nails, and set in a projecting doorway of massive stone. I could see even in the dim light that the stone was massively carved, but that the carving had been much worn by time and weather. As I stood, the driver jumped again into his seat and shook the reins; the horses started forward, and trap and all disappeared down one of the dark openings.

I stood in silence where I was, for I did not know what to do. Of bell or knocker there was no sign; through these frowning walls and dark window openings it was not likely that my voice could penetrate. The time I waited seemed endless, and I felt doubts and fears crowding upon me. What sort of place had I come to, and among what kind of people? What sort of grim adventure was it on which I had embarked? Was this a customary incident in the life of a solicitor's clerk sent out to explain the purchase of a London estate to a foreigner? Solicitor's clerk! Mina would not like that. Solicitor— for just before leaving London I got word that my examination was successful; and I am now a full-blown solicitor! I began to rub my eyes and pinch myself to see if I were awake. It all seemed like a horrible nightmare to me, and I expected that I should suddenly awake, and find myself at home, with the dawn struggling in through the windows, as I had now and again felt in the morning after a day of overwork. But my flesh answered the pinching test, and my eyes were not to be deceived. I was indeed awake and among the Carpathians. All I could do now was to be patient and to wait the coming of the morning.

Just as I had come to this conclusion I heard a heavy step approaching behind the great door, and saw through the chinks the gleam of a coming light. Then there was the sound of rattling chains and the clanking of massive bolts drawn back. A key was turned with the loud grating noise of long disuse, and the great door swung back.

Within, stood a tall old man, clean shaven save for a long white moustache, and clad in black from head to foot, without a single speck of colour about him anywhere. He held in his hand an antique silver lamp, in which the flame burned without chimney or globe of any kind, throwing long quivering shadows as it flickered in the draught of the open door. The old man motioned me in with his right hand with a courtly gesture, saying in excellent English, but with a strange intonation:—

"Welcome to my house! Enter freely and of your own will!" He made no motion of stepping to meet me, but stood like a statue, as though his gesture of welcome had fixed him into stone. The instant, however, that I had stepped over the threshold, he moved impulsively forward, and holding out his hand grasped mine with a strength which made me wince, an effect which was not lessened by the fact that it seemed as cold as ice— more like the hand of a dead than a living man. Again he said:—

"Welcome to my house. Come freely. Go safely; and leave something of the happiness you bring!" The strength of the handshake was so much akin to that which I had noticed in the driver, whose face I had not seen, that for a moment I doubted if it were not the same person to whom I was speaking; so to make sure, I said interrogatively:—

"Count Dracula?" He bowed in a courtly way as he replied:—

"I am Dracula; and I bid you welcome, Mr. Harker, to my house. Come in; the night air is chill, and you must need to eat and rest." As he was speaking, he put the lamp on a bracket on the wall, and stepping out, took my luggage; he had carried it in before I could forestall him. I protested but he insisted:—

"Nay, sir, you are my guest. It is late, and my people are not available. Let me see to your comfort myself." He insisted on carrying my traps along the passage, and then up a great winding stair, and along another great passage, on whose stone floor our steps rang heavily. At the end of this he threw open a heavy door, and I rejoiced to see within a well-lit room in which a table was spread for supper, and on whose mighty hearth a great fire of logs, freshly replenished, flamed and flared.

The Count halted, putting down my bags, closed the door, and crossing the room, opened another door, which led into a small octagonal room lit by a single lamp, and seemingly without a window of any sort. Passing through this, he opened another door, and motioned me to enter. It was a welcome sight; for here was a great bedroom well lighted and warmed with another log fire,— also added to but lately, for the top logs were fresh— which sent a hollow roar up the wide chimney. The Count himself left my luggage inside and withdrew, saying, before he closed the door:—

"You will need, after your journey, to refresh yourself by making your toilet. I trust you will find all you wish. When you are ready, come into the other room, where you will find your supper prepared."

The light and warmth and the Count's courteous welcome seemed to have dissipated all my doubts and fears. Having then reached my normal state, I discovered that I was half famished with hunger; so making a hasty toilet, I went into the other room.

I found supper already laid out. My host, who stood on one side of the great fireplace, leaning against the stonework, made a graceful wave of his hand to the table, and said:—

"I pray you, be seated and sup how you please. You will, I trust, excuse me that I do not join you; but I have dined already, and I do not sup."

I handed to him the sealed letter which Mr. Hawkins had entrusted to me. He opened it and read it gravely; then, with a charming smile, he handed it to me to read. One passage of it, at least, gave me a thrill of pleasure.

"I must regret that an attack of gout, from which malady I am a constant sufferer, forbids absolutely any travelling on my part for some time to come; but I am happy to say I can send a sufficient substitute, one in whom I have every possible confidence. He is a young man, full of energy and talent in his own way, and of a very faithful disposition. He is discreet and silent, and has grown into manhood in my service. He shall be ready to attend on you when you will during his stay, and shall take your instructions in all matters."

The Count himself came forward and took off the cover of a dish, and I fell to at once on an excellent roast chicken. This, with some cheese and a salad and a bottle of old Tokay, of which I had two glasses, was my supper. During the time I was eating it the Count asked me many questions as to my journey, and I told him by degrees all I had experienced.

By this time I had finished my supper, and by my host's desire had drawn up a chair by the fire and begun to smoke a cigar which he offered me, at the same time excusing himself that he did not smoke. I had now an opportunity of observing him, and found him of a very marked physiognomy.

His face was a strong— a very strong— aquiline, with high bridge of the thin nose and peculiarly arched nostrils; with lofty domed forehead, and hair growing scantily round the temples but profusely elsewhere. His eyebrows were very massive, almost meeting over the nose, and with bushy hair that seemed to curl in its own profusion. The mouth, so far as I could see it under the heavy moustache, was fixed and rather cruel-looking, with peculiarly sharp white teeth; these protruded over the lips, whose remarkable ruddiness showed astonishing vitality in a man of his years. For the rest, his ears were pale, and at the tops extremely pointed; the chin was broad and strong, and the cheeks firm though thin. The general effect was one of extraordinary pallor.

Hitherto I had noticed the backs of his hands as they lay on his knees in the firelight, and they had seemed rather white and fine; but seeing them now close to me, I could not but notice that they were rather coarse— broad, with squat fingers. Strange to say, there were hairs in the centre of the palm. The nails were long and fine, and cut to a sharp point. As the Count leaned over me and his hands touched me, I could not repress a shudder. It may have been that his breath was rank, but a horrible feeling of nausea came over me, which, do what I would, I could not conceal. The Count, evidently noticing it, drew back; and with a grim sort of smile, which showed more than he had yet done his protuberant teeth, sat himself down again on his own side of the fireplace. We were both silent for a while; and as I looked towards the window I saw the first dim streak of the coming dawn. There seemed a strange stillness over everything; but as I listened I heard as if from down below in the valley the howling of many wolves. The Count's eyes gleamed, and he said:—

"Listen to them— the children of the night. What music they make!" Seeing, I suppose, some expression in my face strange to him, he added:—

"Ah, sir, you dwellers in the city cannot enter into the feelings of the hunter." Then he rose and said:—

"But you must be tired. Your bedroom is all ready, and to-morrow you shall sleep as late as you will. I have to be away till the afternoon; so sleep well and dream well!" With a courteous bow, he opened for me himself the door to the octagonal room, and I entered my bedroom....

I am all in a sea of wonders. I doubt; I fear; I think strange things, which I dare not confess to my own soul. God keep me, if only for the sake of those dear to me!

7 May.— It is again early morning, but I have rested and enjoyed the last twenty-four hours. I slept till late in the day, and awoke of my own accord. When I had dressed myself I went into the room where we had supped, and found a cold breakfast laid out, with coffee kept hot by the pot being placed on the hearth. There was a card on the table, on which was written:—

"I have to be absent for a while. Do not wait for me.— D." I set to and enjoyed a hearty meal. When I had done, I looked for a bell, so that I might let the servants know I had finished; but I could not find one. There are certainly odd deficiencies in the house, considering the extraordinary evidences of wealth which are round me. The table service is of gold, and so beautifully wrought that it must be of immense value. The curtains and upholstery of the chairs and sofas and the hangings of my bed are of the costliest and most beautiful fabrics, and must have been of fabulous value when they were made, for they are centuries old, though in excellent order. I saw something like them in Hampton Court, but there they were worn and frayed and moth-eaten. But still in none of the rooms is there a mirror. There is not even a toilet glass on my table, and I had to get the little shaving glass from my bag before I could either shave or brush my hair. I have not yet seen a servant anywhere, or heard a sound near the castle except the howling of wolves. Some time after I had finished my meal— I do not know whether to call it breakfast or dinner, for it was between five and six o'clock when I had it— I looked about for something to read, for I did not like to go about the castle until I had asked the Count's permission. There was absolutely nothing in the room, book, newspaper, or even writing materials; so I opened another door in the room and found a sort of library. The door opposite mine I tried, but found it locked.

In the library I found, to my great delight, a vast number of English books, whole shelves full of them, and bound volumes of magazines and newspapers. A table in the centre was littered with English magazines and newspapers, though none of them were of very recent date. The books were of the most varied kind— history, geography, politics, political economy, botany, geology, law— all relating to England and English life and customs and manners. There were even such books of reference as the London Directory, the "Red" and "Blue" books, Whitaker's Almanac, the Army and Navy Lists, and— it somehow gladdened my heart to see it— the Law List.

Whilst I was looking at the books, the door opened, and the Count entered. He saluted me in a hearty way, and hoped that I had had a good night's rest. Then he went on:—

"I am glad you found your way in here, for I am sure there is much that will interest you. These companions"— and he laid his hand on some of the books— "have been good friends to me, and for some years past, ever since I had the idea of going to London, have given me many, many hours of pleasure. Through them I have come to know your great England; and to know her is to love her. I long to go through the crowded streets of your mighty London, to be in the midst of the whirl and rush of humanity, to share its life, its change, its death, and all that makes it what it is. But alas! as yet I only know your tongue through books. To you, my friend, I look that I know it to speak."

"But, Count," I said, "you know and speak English thoroughly!" He bowed gravely.

"I thank you, my friend, for your all too-flattering estimate, but yet I fear that I am but a little way on the road I would travel. True, I know the grammar and the words, but yet I know not how to speak them."

"Indeed," I said, "you speak excellently."

"Not so," he answered. "Well, I know that, did I move and speak in your London, none there are who would not know me for a stranger. That is not enough for me. Here I am noble; I am boyar; the common people know me, and I am master. But a stranger in a strange land, he is no one; men know him not— and to know not is to care not for. I am content if I am like the rest, so that no man stops if he see me, or pause in his speaking if he hear my words, 'Ha, ha! a stranger!' I have been so long master that I would be master still— or at least that none other should be master of me. You come to me not alone as agent of my friend Peter Hawkins, of Exeter, to tell me all about my new estate in London. You shall, I trust, rest here with me awhile, so that by our talking I may learn the English intonation; and I would that you tell me when I make error, even of the smallest, in my speaking. I am sorry that I had to be away so long to-day; but you will, I know, forgive one who has so many important affairs in hand."

Of course I said all I could about being willing, and asked if I might come into that room when I chose. He answered: "Yes, certainly," and added:—

"You may go anywhere you wish in the castle, except where the doors are locked, where of course you will not wish to go. There is reason that all things are as they are, and did you see with my eyes and know with my knowledge, you would perhaps better understand." I said I was sure of this, and then he went on:—

"We are in Transylvania; and Transylvania is not England. Our ways are not your ways, and there shall be to you many strange things. Nay, from what you have told me of your experiences already, you know something of what strange things there may be."

This led to much conversation; and as it was evident that he wanted to talk, if only for talking's sake, I asked him many questions regarding things that had already happened to me or come within my notice. Sometimes he sheered off the subject, or turned the conversation by pretending not to understand; but generally he answered all I asked most frankly. Then as time went on, and I had got somewhat bolder, I asked him of some of the strange things of the preceding night, as, for instance, why the coachman went to the places where he had seen the blue flames. He then explained to me that it was commonly believed that on a certain night of the year— last night, in fact, when all evil spirits are supposed to have unchecked sway— a blue flame is seen over any place where treasure has been concealed. "That treasure has been hidden," he went on, "in the region through which you came last night, there can be but little doubt; for it was the ground fought over for centuries by the Wallachian, the Saxon, and the Turk. Why, there is hardly a foot of soil in all this region that has not been enriched by the blood of men, patriots or invaders. In old days there were stirring times, when the Austrian and the Hungarian came up in hordes, and the patriots went out to meet them— men and women, the aged and the children too— and waited their coming on the rocks above the passes, that they might sweep destruction on them with their artificial avalanches. When the invader was triumphant he found but little, for whatever there was had been sheltered in the friendly soil."

"But how," said I, "can it have remained so long undiscovered, when there is a sure index to it if men will but take the trouble to look?" The Count smiled, and as his lips ran back over his gums, the long, sharp, canine teeth showed out strangely; he answered:—

"Because your peasant is at heart a coward and a fool! Those flames only appear on one night; and on that night no man of this land will, if he can help it, stir without his doors. And, dear sir, even if he did he would not know what to do. Why, even the peasant that you tell me of who marked the place of the flame would not know where to look in daylight even for his own work. Even you would not, I dare be sworn, be able to find these places again?"

"There you are right," I said. "I know no more than the dead where even to look for them." Then we drifted into other matters.

"Come," he said at last, "tell me of London and of the house which you have procured for me." With an apology for my remissness, I went into my own room to get the papers from my bag. Whilst I was placing them in order I heard a rattling of china and silver in the next room, and as I passed through, noticed that the table had been cleared and the lamp lit, for it was by this time deep into the dark. The lamps were also lit in the study or library, and I found the Count lying on the sofa, reading, of all things in the world, an English Bradshaw's Guide. When I came in he cleared the books and papers from the table; and with him I went into plans and deeds and figures of all sorts. He was interested in everything, and asked me a myriad questions about the place and its surroundings. He clearly had studied beforehand all he could get on the subject of the neighbourhood, for he evidently at the end knew very much more than I did. When I remarked this, he answered:—

"Well, but, my friend, is it not needful that I should? When I go there I shall be all alone, and my friend Harker Jonathan— nay, pardon me, I fall into my country's habit of putting your patronymic first— my friend Jonathan Harker will not be by my side to correct and aid me. He will be in Exeter, miles away, probably working at papers of the law with my other friend, Peter Hawkins. So!"

We went thoroughly into the business of the purchase of the estate at Purfleet. When I had told him the facts and got his signature to the necessary papers, and had written a letter with them ready to post to Mr. Hawkins, he began to ask me how I had come across so suitable a place. I read to him the notes which I had made at the time, and which I inscribe here:—

"At Purfleet, on a by-road, I came across just such a place as seemed to be required, and where was displayed a dilapidated notice that the place was for sale. It is surrounded by a high wall, of ancient structure, built of heavy stones, and has not been repaired for a large number of years. The closed gates are of heavy old oak and iron, all eaten with rust.

"The estate is called Carfax, no doubt a corruption of the old Quatre Face, as the house is four-sided, agreeing with the cardinal points of the compass. It contains in all some twenty acres, quite surrounded by the solid stone wall above mentioned. There are many trees on it, which make it in places gloomy, and there is a deep, dark-looking pond or small lake, evidently fed by some springs, as the water is clear and flows away in a fair-sized stream. The house is very large and of all periods back, I should say, to mediæval times, for one part is of stone immensely thick, with only a few windows high up and heavily barred with iron. It looks like part of a keep, and is close to an old chapel or church. I could not enter it, as I had not the key of the door leading to it from the house, but I have taken with my kodak views of it from various points. The house has been added to, but in a very straggling way, and I can only guess at the amount of ground it covers, which must be very great. There are but few houses close at hand, one being a very large house only recently added to and formed into a private lunatic asylum. It is not, however, visible from the grounds."

When I had finished, he said:—

"I am glad that it is old and big. I myself am of an old family, and to live in a new house would kill me. A house cannot be made habitable in a day; and, after all, how few days go to make up a century. I rejoice also that there is a chapel of old times. We Transylvanian nobles love not to think that our bones may lie amongst the common dead. I seek not gaiety nor mirth, not the bright voluptuousness of much sunshine and sparkling waters which please the young and gay. I am no longer young; and my heart, through weary years of mourning over the dead, is not attuned to mirth. Moreover, the walls of my castle are broken; the shadows are many, and the wind breathes cold through the broken battlements and casements. I love the shade and the shadow, and would be alone with my thoughts when I may." Somehow his words and his look did not seem to accord, or else it was that his cast of face made his smile look malignant and saturnine.

Presently, with an excuse, he left me, asking me to put all my papers together. He was some little time away, and I began to look at some of the books around me. One was an atlas, which I found opened naturally at England, as if that map had been much used. On looking at it I found in certain places little rings marked, and on examining these I noticed that one was near London on the east side, manifestly where his new estate was situated; the other two were Exeter, and Whitby on the Yorkshire coast.

It was the better part of an hour when the Count returned. "Aha!" he said; "still at your books? Good! But you must not work always. Come; I am informed that your supper is ready." He took my arm, and we went into the next room, where I found an excellent supper ready on the table. The Count again excused himself, as he had dined out on his being away from home. But he sat as on the previous night, and chatted whilst I ate. After supper I smoked, as on the last evening, and the Count stayed with me, chatting and asking questions on every conceivable subject, hour after hour. I felt that it was getting very late indeed, but I did not say anything, for I felt under obligation to meet my host's wishes in every way. I was not sleepy, as the long sleep yesterday had fortified me; but I could not help experiencing that chill which comes over one at the coming of the dawn, which is like, in its way, the turn of the tide. They say that people who are near death die generally at the change to the dawn or at the turn of the tide; any one who has when tired, and tied as it were to his post, experienced this change in the atmosphere can well believe it. All at once we heard the crow of a cock coming up with preternatural shrillness through the clear morning air; Count Dracula, jumping to his feet, said:—

"Why, there is the morning again! How remiss I am to let you stay up so long. You must make your conversation regarding my dear new country of England less interesting, so that I may not forget how time flies by us," and, with a courtly bow, he quickly left me.

I went into my own room and drew the curtains, but there was little to notice; my window opened into the courtyard, all I could see was the warm grey of quickening sky. So I pulled the curtains again, and have written of this day.

8 May.— I began to fear as I wrote in this book that I was getting too diffuse; but now I am glad that I went into detail from the first, for there is something so strange about this place and all in it that I cannot but feel uneasy. I wish I were safe out of it, or that I had never come. It may be that this strange night-existence is telling on me; but would that that were all! If there were any one to talk to I could bear it, but there is no one. I have only the Count to speak with, and he!— I fear I am myself the only living soul within the place. Let me be prosaic so far as facts can be; it will help me to bear up, and imagination must not run riot with me. If it does I am lost. Let me say at once how I stand— or seem to.

I only slept a few hours when I went to bed, and feeling that I could not sleep any more, got up. I had hung my shaving glass by the window, and was just beginning to shave. Suddenly I felt a hand on my shoulder, and heard the Count's voice saying to me, "Good-morning." I started, for it amazed me that I had not seen him, since the reflection of the glass covered the whole room behind me. In starting I had cut myself slightly, but did not notice it at the moment. Having answered the Count's salutation, I turned to the glass again to see how I had been mistaken. This time there could be no error, for the man was close to me, and I could see him over my shoulder. But there was no reflection of him in the mirror! The whole room behind me was displayed; but there was no sign of a man in it, except myself. This was startling, and, coming on the top of so many strange things, was beginning to increase that vague feeling of uneasiness which I always have when the Count is near; but at the instant I saw that the cut had bled a little, and the blood was trickling over my chin. I laid down the razor, turning as I did so half round to look for some sticking plaster. When the Count saw my face, his eyes blazed with a sort of demoniac fury, and he suddenly made a grab at my throat. I drew away, and his hand touched the string of beads which held the crucifix. It made an instant change in him, for the fury passed so quickly that I could hardly believe that it was ever there.

"Take care," he said, "take care how you cut yourself. It is more dangerous than you think in this country." Then seizing the shaving glass, he went on: "And this is the wretched thing that has done the mischief. It is a foul bauble of man's vanity. Away with it!" and opening the heavy window with one wrench of his terrible hand, he flung out the glass, which was shattered into a thousand pieces on the stones of the courtyard far below. Then he withdrew without a word. It is very annoying, for I do not see how I am to shave, unless in my watch-case or the bottom of the shaving-pot, which is fortunately of metal.

When I went into the dining-room, breakfast was prepared; but I could not find the Count anywhere. So I breakfasted alone. It is strange that as yet I have not seen the Count eat or drink. He must be a very peculiar man! After breakfast I did a little exploring in the castle. I went out on the stairs, and found a room looking towards the South. The view was magnificent, and from where I stood there was every opportunity of seeing it. The castle is on the very edge of a terrible precipice. A stone falling from the window would fall a thousand feet without touching anything! As far as the eye can reach is a sea of green tree tops, with occasionally a deep rift where there is a chasm. Here and there are silver threads where the rivers wind in deep gorges through the forests. But I am not in heart to describe beauty, for when I had seen the view I explored further; doors, doors, doors everywhere, and all locked and bolted. In no place save from the windows in the castle walls is there an available exit.

The castle is a veritable prison, and I am a prisoner!

## CHAPTER III
## JONATHAN HARKER'S JOURNAL— continued

W HEN I found that I was a prisoner a sort of wild feeling came over me. I rushed up and down the stairs, trying every door and peering out of every window I could find; but after a little the conviction of my helplessness overpowered all other feelings. When I look back after a few hours I think I must have been mad for the time, for I behaved much as a rat does in a trap. When, however, the conviction had come to me that I was helpless I sat down quietly— as quietly as I have ever done anything in my life— and began to think over what was best to be done. I am thinking still, and as yet have come to no definite conclusion. Of one thing only am I certain; that it is no use making my ideas known to the Count. He knows well that I am imprisoned; and as he has done it himself, and has doubtless his own motives for it, he would only deceive me if I trusted him fully with the facts. So far as I can see, my only plan will be to keep my knowledge and my fears to myself, and my eyes open. I am, I know, either being deceived, like a baby, by my own fears, or else I am in desperate straits; and if the latter be so, I need, and shall need, all my brains to get through.

I had hardly come to this conclusion when I heard the great door below shut, and knew that the Count had returned. He did not come at once into the library, so I went cautiously to my own room and found him making the bed. This was odd, but only confirmed what I had all along thought— that there were no servants in the house. When later I saw him through the chink of the hinges of the door laying the table in the dining-room, I was assured of it; for if he does himself all these menial offices, surely it is proof that there is no one else to do them. This gave me a fright, for if there is no one else in the castle, it must have been the Count himself who was the driver of the coach that brought me here. This is a terrible thought; for if so, what does it mean that he could control the wolves, as he did, by only holding up his hand in silence. How was it that all the people at Bistritz and on the coach had some terrible fear for me? What meant the giving of the crucifix, of the garlic, of the wild rose, of the mountain ash? Bless that good, good woman who hung the crucifix round my neck! for it is a comfort and a strength to me whenever I touch it. It is odd that a thing which I have been taught to regard with disfavour and as idolatrous should in a time of loneliness and trouble be of help. Is it that there is something in the essence of the thing itself, or that it is a medium, a tangible help, in conveying memories of sympathy and comfort? Some time, if it may be, I must examine this matter and try to make up my mind about it. In the meantime I must find out all I can about Count Dracula, as it may help me to understand. To-night he may talk of himself, if I turn the conversation that way. I must be very careful, however, not to awake his suspicion.

Midnight.— I have had a long talk with the Count. I asked him a few questions on Transylvania history, and he warmed up to the subject wonderfully. In his speaking of things and people, and especially of battles, he spoke as if he had been present at them all. This he afterwards explained by saying that to a boyar the pride of his house and name is his own pride, that their glory is his glory, that their fate is his fate. Whenever he spoke of his house he always said "we," and spoke almost in the plural, like a king speaking. I wish I could put down all he said exactly as he said it, for to me it was most fascinating. It seemed to have in it a whole history of the country. He grew excited as he spoke, and walked about the room pulling his great white moustache and grasping anything on which he laid his hands as though he would crush it by main strength. One thing he said which I shall put down as nearly as I can; for it tells in its way the story of his race:—

"We Szekelys have a right to be proud, for in our veins flows the blood of many brave races who fought as the lion fights, for lordship. Here, in the whirlpool of European races, the Ugric tribe bore down from Iceland the fighting spirit which Thor and Wodin gave them, which their Berserkers displayed to such fell intent on the seaboards of Europe, ay, and of Asia and Africa too, till the peoples thought that the were-wolves themselves had come. Here, too, when they came, they found the Huns, whose warlike fury had swept the earth like a living flame, till the dying peoples held that in their veins ran the blood of those old witches, who, expelled from Scythia had mated with the devils in the desert. Fools, fools! What devil or what witch was ever so great as Attila, whose blood is in these veins?" He held up his arms. "Is it a wonder that we were a conquering race; that we were proud; that when the Magyar, the Lombard, the Avar, the Bulgar, or the Turk poured his thousands on our frontiers, we drove them back? Is it strange that when Arpad and his legions swept through the Hungarian fatherland he found us here when he reached the frontier; that the Honfoglalas was completed there? And when the Hungarian flood swept eastward, the Szekelys were claimed as kindred by the victorious Magyars, and to us for centuries was trusted the guarding of the frontier of Turkey-land; ay, and more than that, endless duty of the frontier guard, for, as the Turks say, 'water sleeps, and enemy is sleepless.' Who more gladly than we throughout the Four Nations received the 'bloody sword,' or at its warlike call flocked quicker to the standard of the King? When was redeemed that great shame of my nation, the shame of Cassova, when the flags of the Wallach and the Magyar went down beneath the Crescent? Who was it but one of my own race who as Voivode crossed the Danube and beat the Turk on his own ground? This was a Dracula indeed! Woe was it that his own unworthy brother, when he had fallen, sold his people to the Turk and brought the shame of slavery on them! Was it not this Dracula, indeed, who inspired that other of his race who in a later age again and again brought his forces over the great river into Turkey-land; who, when he was beaten back, came again, and again, and again, though he had to come alone from the bloody field where his troops were being slaughtered, since he knew that he alone could ultimately triumph! They said that he thought only of himself. Bah! what good are peasants without a leader? Where ends the war without a brain and heart to conduct it? Again, when, after the battle of Mohács, we threw off the Hungarian yoke, we of the Dracula blood were amongst their leaders, for our spirit would not brook that we were not free. Ah, young sir, the

Szekelys- and the Dracula as their heart's blood, their brains,and their swords- can boast a record that mushroom growths like the Hapsburgs and the Romanoffs can never reach. The warlike days are over. Blood is too precious a thing in these days of dishonourable peace; and the glories of the great races are as a tale that is told."

It was by this time close on morning, and we went to bed. (Mem., this diary seems horribly like the beginning of the "Arabian Nights," for everything has to break off at cockcrow— or like the ghost of Hamlet's father.)

12 May.— Let me begin with facts— bare, meagre facts, verified by books and figures, and of which there can be no doubt. I must not confuse them with experiences which will have to rest on my own observation, or my memory of them. Last evening when the Count came from his room he began by asking me questions on legal matters and on the doing of certain kinds of business. I had spent the day wearily over books, and, simply to keep my mind occupied, went over some of the matters I had been examining at Lincoln's Inn. There was a certain method in the Count's inquiries, so I shall try to put them down in sequence; the knowledge may somehow or some time be useful to me.

First, he asked if a man in England might have two solicitors or more. I told him he might have a dozen if he wished, but that it would not be wise to have more than one solicitor engaged in one transaction, as only one could act at a time, and that to change would be certain to militate against his interest. He seemed thoroughly to understand, and went on to ask if there would be any practical difficulty in having one man to attend, say, to banking, and another to look after shipping, in case local help were needed in a place far from the home of the banking solicitor. I asked him to explain more fully, so that I might not by any chance mislead him, so he said:—

"I shall illustrate. Your friend and mine, Mr. Peter Hawkins, from under the shadow of your beautiful cathedral at Exeter, which is far from London, buys for me through your good self my place at London. Good! Now here let me say frankly, lest you should think it strange that I have sought the services of one so far off from London instead of some one resident there, that my motive was that no local interest might be served save my wish only; and as one of London residence might, perhaps, have some purpose of himself or friend to serve, I went thus afield to seek my agent, whose labours should be only to my interest. Now, suppose I, who have much of affairs, wish to ship goods, say, to Newcastle, or Durham, or Harwich, or Dover, might it not be that it could with more ease be done by consigning to one in these ports?" I answered that certainly it would be most easy, but that we solicitors had a system of agency one for the other, so that local work could be done locally on instruction from any solicitor, so that the client, simply placing himself in the hands of one man, could have his wishes carried out by him without further trouble.

"But," said he, "I could be at liberty to direct myself. Is it not so?"

"Of course," I replied; and "such is often done by men of business, who do not like the whole of their affairs to be known by any one person."

"Good!" he said, and then went on to ask about the means of making consignments and the forms to be gone through, and of all sorts of difficulties which might arise, but by forethought could be guarded against. I explained all these things to him to the best of my ability, and he certainly left me under the impression that he would have made a wonderful solicitor, for there was nothing that he did not think of or foresee. For a man who was never in the country, and who did not evidently do much in the way of business, his knowledge and acumen were wonderful. When he had satisfied himself on these points of which he had spoken, and I had verified all as well as I could by the books available, he suddenly stood up and said:—

"Have you written since your first letter to our friend Mr. Peter Hawkins, or to any other?" It was with some bitterness in my heart that I answered that I had not, that as yet I had not seen any opportunity of sending letters to anybody.

"Then write now, my young friend," he said, laying a heavy hand on my shoulder: "write to our friend and to any other; and say, if it will please you, that you shall stay with me until a month from now."

"Do you wish me to stay so long?" I asked, for my heart grew cold at the thought.

"I desire it much; nay, I will take no refusal. When your master, employer, what you will, engaged that someone should come on his behalf, it was understood that my needs only were to be consulted. I have not stinted. Is it not so?"

What could I do but bow acceptance? It was Mr. Hawkins's interest, not mine, and I had to think of him, not myself; and besides, while Count Dracula was speaking, there was that in his eyes and in his bearing which made me remember that I was a prisoner, and that if I wished it I could have no choice. The Count saw his victory in my bow, and his mastery in the trouble of my face, for he began at once to use them, but in his own smooth, resistless way:—

"I pray you, my good young friend, that you will not discourse of things other than business in your letters. It will doubtless please your friends to know that you are well, and that you look forward to getting home to them. Is it not so?" As he spoke he handed me three sheets of note-paper and three envelopes. They were all of the thinnest foreign post, and looking at them, then at him, and noticing his quiet smile, with the sharp, canine teeth lying over the red underlip, I understood as well as if he had spoken that I should be careful what I wrote, for he would be able to read it. So I determined to write only formal notes now, but to write fully to Mr. Hawkins in secret, and also to Mina, for to her I could write in shorthand, which would puzzle the Count, if he did see it. When I had written my two letters I sat quiet, reading a book whilst the Count wrote several notes, referring as he wrote them to some books on his table. Then he took up my two and placed them with his own, and put by his writing materials, after which, the instant the door had closed behind him, I leaned over and looked at the letters, which were face down on the table. I felt no compunction in doing so, for under the circumstances I felt that I should protect myself in every way I could.

One of the letters was directed to Samuel F. Billington, No. 7, The Crescent, Whitby, another to Herr Leutner, Varna; the third was to Coutts & Co., London, and the fourth to Herren Klopstock & Billreuth, bankers, Buda-Pesth. The second and fourth were unsealed. I was just about to look at them when I saw the door-handle move. I sank back in my seat, having just had time to replace the letters as they had been and to resume my book before the Count, holding still another letter in his hand, entered the room. He took up the letters on the table and stamped them carefully, and then turning to me, said:—

"I trust you will forgive me, but I have much work to do in private this evening. You will, I hope, find all things as you wish." At the door he turned, and after a moment's pause said:—

"Let me advise you, my dear young friend— nay, let me warn you with all seriousness, that should you leave these rooms you will not by any chance go to sleep in any other part of the castle. It is old, and has many memories, and there are bad dreams for those who sleep unwisely. Be warned! Should sleep now or ever overcome you, or be like to do, then haste to your own chamber or to these rooms, for your rest will then be safe. But if you be not careful in this respect, then"— He finished his speech in a gruesome way, for he motioned with his hands as if he were washing them. I quite understood; my only doubt was as to whether any dream could be more terrible than the unnatural, horrible net of gloom and mystery which seemed closing around me.

Later.— I endorse the last words written, but this time there is no doubt in question. I shall not fear to sleep in any place where he is not. I have placed the crucifix over the head of my bed— I imagine that my rest is thus freer from dreams; and there it shall remain.

When he left me I went to my room. After a little while, not hearing any sound, I came out and went up the stone stair to where I could look out towards the South. There was some sense of freedom in the vast expanse, inaccessible though it was to me, as compared with the narrow darkness of the courtyard. Looking out on this, I felt that I was indeed in prison, and I seemed to want a breath of fresh air, though it were of the night. I am beginning to feel this nocturnal existence tell on me. It is destroying my nerve. I start at my own shadow, and am full of all sorts of horrible imaginings. God knows that there is ground for my terrible fear in this accursed place! I looked out over the beautiful expanse, bathed in soft yellow moonlight till it was almost as light as day. In the soft light the distant hills became melted, and the shadows in the valleys and gorges of velvety blackness. The mere beauty seemed to cheer me; there was peace and comfort in every breath I drew. As I leaned from the window my eye was caught by something moving a storey below me, and somewhat to my left, where I imagined, from the order of the rooms, that the windows of the Count's own room would look out. The window at which I stood was tall and deep, stone-mullioned, and though weatherworn, was still complete; but it was evidently many a day since the case had been there. I drew back behind the stonework, and looked carefully out.

What I saw was the Count's head coming out from the window. I did not see the face, but I knew the man by the neck and the movement of his back and arms. In any case I could not mistake the hands which I had had so many opportunities of studying. I was at first interested and somewhat amused, for it is wonderful how small a matter will interest and amuse a man when he is a prisoner. But my very feelings changed to repulsion and terror when I saw the whole man slowly emerge from the window and begin to crawl down the castle wall over that dreadful abyss, face down with his cloak spreading out around him like great wings. At first I could not believe my eyes. I thought it was some trick of the moonlight, some weird effect of shadow; but I kept looking, and it could be no delusion. I saw the fingers and toes grasp the corners of the stones, worn clear of the mortar by the stress of years, and by thus using every projection and inequality move downwards with considerable speed, just as a lizard moves along a wall.

What manner of man is this, or what manner of creature is it in the semblance of man? I feel the dread of this horrible place overpowering me; I am in fear— in awful fear— and there is no escape for me; I am encompassed about with terrors that I dare not think of....

15 May.— Once more have I seen the Count go out in his lizard fashion. He moved downwards in a sidelong way, some hundred feet down, and a good deal to the left. He vanished into some hole or window. When his head had disappeared, I leaned out to try and see more, but without avail— the distance was too great to allow a proper angle of sight. I knew he had left the castle now, and thought to use the opportunity to explore more than I had dared to do as yet. I went back to the room, and taking a lamp, tried all the doors. They were all locked, as I had expected, and the locks were comparatively new; but I went down the stone stairs to the hall where I had entered originally. I found I could pull back the bolts easily enough and unhook the great chains; but the door was locked, and the key was gone! That key must be in the Count's room; I must watch should his door be unlocked, so that I may get it and escape. I went on to make a thorough examination of the various stairs and passages, and to try the doors that opened from them. One or two small rooms near the hall were open, but there was nothing to see in them except old furniture, dusty with age and moth-eaten. At last, however, I found one door at the top of the stairway which, though it seemed to be locked, gave a little under pressure. I tried it harder, and found that it was not really locked, but that the resistance came from the fact that the hinges had fallen somewhat, and the heavy door rested on the floor. Here was an opportunity which I might not have again, so I exerted myself, and with many efforts forced it back so that I could enter. I was now in a wing of the castle further to the right than the rooms I knew and a storey lower down. From the windows I could see that the suite of rooms lay along to the south of the castle, the windows of the end room looking out both west and south. On the latter side, as well as to the former, there was a great precipice. The castle was built on the corner of a great rock, so that on three sides it was quite impregnable, and great windows were placed here where sling, or bow, or culverin could not reach, and consequently light and comfort, impossible to a position which had to be guarded, were secured. To the west was a great valley, and then, rising far away, great jagged mountain fastnesses, rising peak on peak, the sheer rock studded with mountain ash and thorn, whose roots clung in cracks and crevices and crannies of the stone. This was evidently the portion of the castle occupied by the ladies in bygone days, for the furniture had more air of comfort than any I had seen. The windows were curtainless, and the yellow moonlight, flooding in through the diamond panes, enabled one to see even colours, whilst it softened the wealth of dust which lay over all and disguised in some measure the ravages of time

and the moth. My lamp seemed to be of little effect in the brilliant moonlight, but I was glad to have it with me, for there was a dread loneliness in the place which chilled my heart and made my nerves tremble. Still, it was better than living alone in the rooms which I had come to hate from the presence of the Count, and after trying a little to school my nerves, I found a soft quietude come over me. Here I am, sitting at a little oak table where in old times possibly some fair lady sat to pen, with much thought and many blushes, her ill-spelt love-letter, and writing in my diary in shorthand all that has happened since I closed it last. It is nineteenth century up-to-date with a vengeance. And yet, unless my senses deceive me, the old centuries had, and have, powers of their own which mere "modernity" cannot kill.

Later: the Morning of 16 May.— God preserve my sanity, for to this I am reduced. Safety and the assurance of safety are things of the past. Whilst I live on here there is but one thing to hope for, that I may not go mad, if, indeed, I be not mad already. If I be sane, then surely it is maddening to think that of all the foul things that lurk in this hateful place the Count is the least dreadful to me; that to him alone I can look for safety, even though this be only whilst I can serve his purpose. Great God! merciful God! Let me be calm, for out of that way lies madness indeed. I begin to get new lights on certain things which have puzzled me. Up to now I never quite knew what Shakespeare meant when he made Hamlet say:—
"My tablets! quick, my tablets!
'Tis meet that I put it down," etc.,
for now, feeling as though my own brain were unhinged or as if the shock had come which must end in its undoing, I turn to my diary for repose. The habit of entering accurately must help to soothe me.
The Count's mysterious warning frightened me at the time; it frightens me more now when I think of it, for in future he has a fearful hold upon me. I shall fear to doubt what he may say!

When I had written in my diary and had fortunately replaced the book and pen in my pocket I felt sleepy. The Count's warning came into my mind, but I took a pleasure in disobeying it. The sense of sleep was upon me, and with it the obstinacy which sleep brings as outrider. The soft moonlight soothed, and the wide expanse without gave a sense of freedom which refreshed me. I determined not to return to-night to the gloom-haunted rooms, but to sleep here, where, of old, ladies had sat and sung and lived sweet lives whilst their gentle breasts were sad for their menfolk away in the midst of remorseless wars. I drew a great couch out of its place near the corner, so that as I lay, I could look at the lovely view to east and south, and unthinking of and uncaring for the dust, composed myself for sleep. I suppose I must have fallen asleep; I hope so, but I fear, for all that followed was startlingly real— so real that now sitting here in the broad, full sunlight of the morning, I cannot in the least believe that it was all sleep. I was not alone. The room was the same, unchanged in any way since I came into it; I could see along the floor, in the brilliant moonlight, my own footsteps marked where I had disturbed the long accumulation of dust. In the moonlight opposite me were three young women, ladies by their dress and manner. I thought at the time that I must be dreaming when I saw them, for, though the moonlight was behind them, they threw no shadow on the floor. They came close to me, and looked at me for some time, and then whispered together. Two were dark, and had high aquiline noses, like the Count, and great dark, piercing eyes that seemed to be almost red when contrasted with the pale yellow moon. The other was fair, as fair as can be, with great wavy masses of golden hair and eyes like pale sapphires. I seemed somehow to know her face, and to know it in connection with some dreamy fear, but I could not recollect at the moment how or where. All three had brilliant white teeth that shone like pearls against the ruby of their voluptuous lips. There was something about them that made me uneasy, some longing and at the same time some deadly fear. I felt in my heart a wicked, burning desire that they would kiss me with those red lips. It is not good to note this down, lest some day it should meet Mina's eyes and cause her pain; but it is the truth. They whispered together, and then they all three laughed— such a silvery, musical laugh, but as hard as though the sound never could have come through the softness of human lips. It was like the intolerable, tingling sweetness of water-glasses when played on by a cunning hand. The fair girl shook her head coquettishly, and the other two urged her on. One said:—

"Go on! You are first, and we shall follow; yours is the right to begin."
The other added:—
"He is young and strong; there are kisses for us all." I lay quiet, looking out under my eyelashes in an agony of delightful anticipation. The fair girl advanced and bent over me till I could feel the movement of her breath upon me. Sweet it was in one sense, honey-sweet, and sent the same tingling through the nerves as her voice, but with a bitter underlying the sweet, a bitter offensiveness, as one smells in blood.

I was afraid to raise my eyelids, but looked out and saw perfectly under the lashes. The girl went on her knees, and bent over me, simply gloating. There was a deliberate voluptuousness which was both thrilling and repulsive, and as she arched her neck she actually licked her lips like an animal, till I could see in the moonlight the moisture shining on the scarlet lips and on the red tongue as it lapped the white sharp teeth. Lower and lower went her head as the lips went below the range of my mouth and chin and seemed about to fasten on my throat. Then she paused, and I could hear the churning sound of her tongue as it licked her teeth and lips, and could feel the hot breath on my neck. Then the skin of my throat began to tingle as one's flesh does when the hand that is to tickle it approaches nearer— nearer. I could feel the soft, shivering touch of the lips on the super-sensitive skin of my throat, and the hard dents of two sharp teeth, just touching and pausing there. I closed my eyes in a languorous ecstasy and waited— waited with beating heart.

But at that instant, another sensation swept through me as quick as lightning. I was conscious of the presence of the Count, and of his being as if lapped in a storm of fury. As my eyes opened involuntarily I saw his strong hand grasp the slender neck of the fair woman and with giant's power draw it back, the blue eyes transformed with fury, the white teeth champing with rage, and the fair cheeks blazing red with passion. But the Count! Never did I imagine such wrath and fury, even to the demons of the pit. His eyes were positively blazing. The red light in them was lurid, as if the flames of hell-fire blazed behind them. His face was deathly pale, and the lines of it were hard like drawn wires; the thick eyebrows that met over the nose now seemed like a heaving bar of white-hot metal. With a fierce sweep of his arm, he hurled the woman from him, and then motioned to the others, as though he were beating them back; it was the same imperious gesture that I had seen used to the wolves. In a voice which, though low and almost in a whisper seemed to cut through the air and then ring round the room he said:—

"How dare you touch him, any of you? How dare you cast eyes on him when I had forbidden it? Back, I tell you all! This man belongs to me! Beware how you meddle with him, or you'll have to deal with me." The fair girl, with a laugh of ribald coquetry, turned to answer him:—

"You yourself never loved; you never love!" On this the other women joined, and such a mirthless, hard, soulless laughter rang through the room that it almost made me faint to hear; it seemed like the pleasure of fiends. Then the Count turned, after looking at my face attentively, and said in a soft whisper:—

"Yes, I too can love; you yourselves can tell it from the past. Is it not so? Well, now I promise you that when I am done with him you shall kiss him at your will. Now go! go! I must awaken him, for there is work to be done."

"Are we to have nothing to-night?" said one of them, with a low laugh, as she pointed to the bag which he had thrown upon the floor, and which moved as though there were some living thing within it. For answer he nodded his head. One of the women jumped forward and opened it. If my ears did not deceive me there was a gasp and a low wail, as of a half-smothered child. The women closed round, whilst I was aghast with horror; but as I looked they disappeared, and with them the dreadful bag. There was no door near them, and they could not have passed me without my noticing. They simply seemed to fade into the rays of the moonlight and pass out through the window, for I could see outside the dim, shadowy forms for a moment before they entirely faded away.

Then the horror overcame me, and I sank down unconscious.

## CHAPTER IV
## JONATHAN HARKER'S JOURNAL— continued

I AWOKE in my own bed. If it be that I had not dreamt, the Count must have carried me here. I tried to satisfy myself on the subject, but could not arrive at any unquestionable result. To be sure, there were certain small evidences, such as that my clothes were folded and laid by in a manner which was not my habit. My watch was still unwound, and I am rigorously accustomed to wind it the last thing before going to bed, and many such details. But these things are no proof, for they may have been evidences that my mind was not as usual, and, from some cause or another, I had certainly been much upset. I must watch for proof. Of one thing I am glad: if it was that the Count carried me here and undressed me, he must have been hurried in his task, for my pockets are intact. I am sure this diary would have been a mystery to him which he would not have brooked. He would have taken or destroyed it. As I look round this room, although it has been to me so full of fear, it is now a sort of sanctuary, for nothing can be more dreadful than those awful women, who were— who are— waiting to suck my blood.

18 May.— I have been down to look at that room again in daylight, for I must know the truth. When I got to the doorway at the top of the stairs I found it closed. It had been so forcibly driven against the jamb that part of the woodwork was splintered. I could see that the bolt of the lock had not been shot, but the door is fastened from the inside. I fear it was no dream, and must act on this surmise.

19 May.— I am surely in the toils. Last night the Count asked me in the suavest tones to write three letters, one saying that my work here was nearly done, and that I should start for home within a few days, another that I was starting on the next morning from the time of the letter, and the third that I had left the castle and arrived at Bistritz. I would fain have rebelled, but felt that in the present state of things it would be madness to quarrel openly with the Count whilst I am so absolutely in his power; and to refuse would be to excite his suspicion and to arouse his anger. He knows that I know too much, and that I must not live, lest I be dangerous to him; my only chance is to prolong my opportunities. Something may occur which will give me a chance to escape. I saw in his eyes something of that gathering wrath which was manifest when he hurled that fair woman from him. He explained to me that posts were few and uncertain, and that my writing now would ensure ease of mind to my friends; and he assured me with so much impressiveness that he would countermand the later letters, which would be held over at Bistritz until due time in case chance would admit of my prolonging my stay, that to oppose him would have been to create new suspicion. I therefore pretended to fall in with his views, and asked him what dates I should put on the letters. He calculated a minute, and then said:—

"The first should be June 12, the second June 19, and the third June 29."

I know now the span of my life. God help me!

28 May.— There is a chance of escape, or at any rate of being able to send word home. A band of Szgany have come to the castle, and are encamped in the courtyard. These Szgany are gipsies; I have notes of them in my book. They are peculiar to this part of the world, though allied to the ordinary gipsies all the world over. There are thousands of them in Hungary and Transylvania, who are almost outside all law. They attach themselves as a rule to some great noble or boyar, and call themselves by his name. They are fearless and without religion, save superstition, and they talk only their own varieties of the Romany tongue.

I shall write some letters home, and shall try to get them to have them posted. I have already spoken them through my window to begin acquaintanceship. They took their hats off and made obeisance and many signs, which, however, I could not understand any more than I could their spoken language....

I have written the letters. Mina's is in shorthand, and I simply ask Mr. Hawkins to communicate with her. To her I have explained my situation, but without the horrors which I may only surmise. It would shock and frighten her to death were I to expose my heart to her. Should the letters not carry, then the Count shall not yet know my secret or the extent of my knowledge....

I have given the letters; I threw them through the bars of my window with a gold piece, and made what signs I could to have them posted. The man who took them pressed them to his heart and bowed, and then put them in his cap. I could do no more. I stole back to the study, and began to read. As the Count did not come in, I have written here....

The Count has come. He sat down beside me, and said in his smoothest voice as he opened two letters:—
"The Szgany has given me these, of which, though I know not whence they come, I shall, of course, take care. See!"— he must have looked at it— "one is from you, and to my friend Peter Hawkins; the other"— here he caught sight of the strange symbols as he opened the envelope, and the dark look came into his face, and his eyes blazed wickedly— "the other is a vile thing, an outrage upon friendship and hospitality! It is not signed. Well! so it cannot matter to us." And he calmly held letter and envelope in the flame of the lamp till they were consumed. Then he went on:—
"The letter to Hawkins— that I shall, of course, send on, since it is yours. Your letters are sacred to me. Your pardon, my friend, that unknowingly I did break the seal. Will you not cover it again?" He held out the letter to me, and with a courteous bow handed me a clean envelope. I could only redirect it and hand it to him in silence. When he went out of the room I could hear the key turn softly. A minute later I went over and tried it, and the door was locked.
When, an hour or two after, the Count came quietly into the room, his coming awakened me, for I had gone to sleep on the sofa. He was very courteous and very cheery in his manner, and seeing that I had been sleeping, he said:—
"So, my friend, you are tired? Get to bed. There is the surest rest. I may not have the pleasure to talk to-night, since there are many labours to me; but you will sleep, I pray." I passed to my room and went to bed, and, strange to say, slept without dreaming. Despair has its own calms.

31 May.— This morning when I woke I thought I would provide myself with some paper and envelopes from my bag and keep them in my pocket, so that I might write in case I should get an opportunity, but again a surprise, again a shock!

Every scrap of paper was gone, and with it all my notes, my memoranda, relating to railways and travel, my letter of credit, in fact all that might be useful to me were I once outside the castle. I sat and pondered awhile, and then some thought occurred to me, and I made search of my portmanteau and in the wardrobe where I had placed my clothes.

The suit in which I had travelled was gone, and also my overcoat and rug; I could find no trace of them anywhere. This looked like some new scheme of villainy....

17 June.— This morning, as I was sitting on the edge of my bed cudgelling my brains, I heard without a cracking of whips and pounding and scraping of horses' feet up the rocky path beyond the courtyard. With joy I hurried to the window, and saw drive into the yard two great leiter-wagons, each drawn by eight sturdy horses, and at the head of each pair a Slovak, with his wide hat, great nail-studded belt, dirty sheepskin, and high boots. They had also their long staves in hand. I ran to the door, intending to descend and try and join them through the main hall, as I thought that way might be opened for them. Again a shock: my door was fastened on the outside.

Then I ran to the window and cried to them. They looked up at me stupidly and pointed, but just then the "hetman" of the Szgany came out, and seeing them pointing to my window, said something, at which they laughed. Henceforth no effort of mine, no piteous cry or agonised entreaty, would make them even look at me. They resolutely turned away. The leiter-wagons contained great, square boxes, with handles of thick rope; these were evidently empty by the ease with which the Slovaks handled them, and by their resonance as they were roughly moved. When they were all unloaded and packed in a great heap in one corner of the yard, the Slovaks were given some money by the Szgany, and spitting on it for luck, lazily went each to his horse's head. Shortly afterwards, I heard the cracking of their whips die away in the distance.

24 June, before morning.— Last night the Count left me early, and locked himself into his own room. As soon as I dared I ran up the winding stair, and looked out of the window, which opened south. I thought I would watch for the Count, for there is something going on. The Szgany are quartered somewhere in the castle and are doing work of some kind. I know it, for now and then I hear a far-away muffled sound as of mattock and spade, and, whatever it is, it must be the end of some ruthless villainy.

I had been at the window somewhat less than half an hour, when I saw something coming out of the Count's window. I drew back and watched carefully, and saw the whole man emerge. It was a new shock to me to find that he had on the suit of clothes which I had worn whilst travelling here, and slung over his shoulder the terrible bag which I had seen the women take away. There could be no doubt as to his quest, and in my garb, too! This, then, is his new scheme of evil: that he will allow others to see me, as they think, so that he may both leave evidence that I have been seen in the towns or villages posting my own letters, and that any wickedness which he may do shall by the local people be attributed to me.

It makes me rage to think that this can go on, and whilst I am shut up here, a veritable prisoner, but without that protection of the law which is even a criminal's right and consolation.

I thought I would watch for the Count's return, and for a long time sat doggedly at the window. Then I began to notice that there were some quaint little specks floating in the rays of the moonlight. They were like the tiniest grains of dust, and they whirled round and gathered in clusters in a nebulous sort of way. I watched them with a sense of soothing, and a sort of calm stole over me. I leaned back in the embrasure in a more comfortable position, so that I could enjoy more fully the aërial gambolling.

Something made me start up, a low, piteous howling of dogs somewhere far below in the valley, which was hidden from my sight. Louder it seemed to ring in my ears, and the floating motes of dust to take new shapes to the sound as they danced in the moonlight. I felt myself struggling to awake to some call of my instincts; nay, my very soul was struggling, and my half-remembered sensibilities were striving to answer the call. I was becoming hypnotised! Quicker and quicker danced the dust; the moonbeams seemed to quiver as they went by me into the mass of gloom beyond. More and more they gathered till they seemed to take dim phantom shapes. And then I started, broad awake and in full possession of my senses, and ran screaming from the place. The phantom shapes, which were becoming gradually materialised from the moonbeams, were those of the three ghostly women to whom I was doomed. I fled, and felt somewhat safer in my own room, where there was no moonlight and where the lamp was burning brightly.

When a couple of hours had passed I heard something stirring in the Count's room, something like a sharp wail quickly suppressed; and then there was silence, deep, awful silence, which chilled me. With a beating heart, I tried the door; but I was locked in my prison, and could do nothing. I sat down and simply cried.

As I sat I heard a sound in the courtyard without— the agonised cry of a woman. I rushed to the window, and throwing it up, peered out between the bars. There, indeed, was a woman with dishevelled hair, holding her hands over her heart as one distressed with running. She was leaning against a corner of the gateway. When she saw my face at the window she threw herself forward, and shouted in a voice laden with menace:—

"Monster, give me my child!"

She threw herself on her knees, and raising up her hands, cried the same words in tones which wrung my heart. Then she tore her hair and beat her breast, and abandoned herself to all the violences of extravagant emotion. Finally, she threw herself forward, and, though I could not see her, I could hear the beating of her naked hands against the door.

Somewhere high overhead, probably on the tower, I heard the voice of the Count calling in his harsh, metallic whisper. His call seemed to be answered from far and wide by the howling of wolves. Before many minutes had passed a pack of them poured, like a pent-up dam when liberated, through the wide entrance into the courtyard.

There was no cry from the woman, and the howling of the wolves was but short. Before long they streamed away singly, licking their lips.

I could not pity her, for I knew now what had become of her child, and she was better dead.

What shall I do? what can I do? How can I escape from this dreadful thing of night and gloom and fear?

25 June, morning.- No man knows till he has suffered from the night how sweet and how dear to his heart and eye the morning can be. When the sun grew so high this morning that it struck the top of the great gateway opposite my window, the high spot which it touched seemed to me as if the dove from the ark had lighted there. My fear fell from me as if it had been a vaporous garment which dissolved in the warmth. I must take action of some sort whilst the courage of the day is upon me.Last night one of my post-dated letters went to post, the first of that fatal series which is to blot out the very traces of my existence from the earth.

Let me not think of it. Action!

It has always been at night-time that I have been molested or threatened, or in some way in danger or in fear. I have not yet seen the Count in the daylight. Can it be that he sleeps when others wake, that he may be awake whilst they sleep? If I could only get into his room! But there is no possible way. The door is always locked, no way for me. Yes, there is a way, if one dares to take it. Where his body has gone why may not another body go? I have seen him myself crawl from his window. Why should not I imitate him, and go in by his window? The chances are desperate, but my need is more desperate still. I shall risk it. At the worst it can only be death; and a man's death is not a calf's, and the dreaded Hereafter may still be open to me. God help me in my task! Good-bye, Mina, if I fail; good-bye, my faithful friend and second father; good-bye, all, and last of all Mina!

Same day, later.— I have made the effort, and God, helping me, have come safely back to this room. I must put down every detail in order. I went whilst my courage was fresh straight to the window on the south side, and at once got outside on the narrow ledge of stone which runs around the building on this side. The stones are big and roughly cut, and the mortar has by process of time been washed away between them. I took off my boots, and ventured out on the desperate way. I looked down once, so as to make sure that a sudden glimpse of the awful depth would not overcome me, but after that kept my eyes away from it. I knew pretty well the direction and distance of the Count's window, and made for it as well as I could, having regard to the opportunities available. I did not feel dizzy— I suppose I was too excited— and the time seemed ridiculously short till I found myself standing on the window-sill and trying to raise up the sash. I was filled with agitation, however, when I bent down and slid feet foremost in through the window. Then I looked around for the Count, but, with surprise and gladness, made a discovery. The room was empty! It was barely furnished with odd things, which seemed to have never been used; the furniture was something the same style as that in the south rooms, and was covered with dust. I looked for the key, but it was not in the lock, and I could not find it anywhere. The only thing I found was a great heap of gold in one corner— gold of all kinds, Roman, and British, and Austrian, and Hungarian, and Greek and Turkish money, covered with a film of dust, as though it had lain long in the ground. None of it that I noticed was less than three hundred years old. There were also chains and ornaments, some jewelled, but all of them old and stained.

At one corner of the room was a heavy door. I tried it, for, since I could not find the key of the room or the key of the outer door, which was the main object of my search, I must make further examination, or all my efforts would be in vain. It was open, and led through a stone passage to a circular stairway, which went steeply down. I descended, minding carefully where I went, for the stairs were dark, being only lit by loopholes in the heavy masonry. At the bottom there was a dark, tunnel-like passage, through which came a deathly, sickly odour, the odour of old earth newly turned. As I went through the passage the smell grew closer and heavier. At last I pulled open a heavy door which stood ajar, and found myself in an old, ruined chapel, which had evidently been used as a graveyard. The roof was broken, and in two places were steps leading to vaults, but the ground had recently been dug over, and the earth placed in great wooden boxes, manifestly those which had been brought by the Slovaks. There was nobody about, and I made search for any further outlet, but there was none. Then I went over every inch of the ground, so as not to lose a chance. I went down even into the vaults, where the dim light struggled, although to do so was a dread to my very soul. Into two of these I went, but saw nothing except fragments of old coffins and piles of dust; in the third, however, I made a discovery.

There, in one of the great boxes, of which there were fifty in all, on a pile of newly dug earth, lay the Count! He was either dead or asleep, I could not say which— for the eyes were open and stony, but without the glassiness of death— and the cheeks had the warmth of life through all their pallor; the lips were as red as ever. But there was no sign of movement, no pulse, no breath, no beating of the heart. I bent over him, and tried to find any sign of life, but in vain. He could not have lain there long, for the earthy smell would have passed away in a few hours. By the side of the box was its cover, pierced with holes here and there. I thought he might have the keys on him, but when I went to search I saw the dead eyes, and in them, dead though they were, such a look of hate, though unconscious of me or my presence, that I fled from the place, and leaving the Count's room by the window, crawled again up the castle wall. Regaining my room, I threw myself panting upon the bed and tried to think....

29 June.— To-day is the date of my last letter, and the Count has taken steps to prove that it was genuine, for again I saw him leave the castle by the same window, and in my clothes. As he went down the wall, lizard fashion, I wished I had a gun or some lethal weapon, that I might destroy him; but I fear that no weapon wrought alone by man's hand would have any effect on him. I dared not wait to see him return, for I feared to see those weird sisters. I came back to the library, and read there till I fell asleep.

I was awakened by the Count, who looked at me as grimly as a man can look as he said:—

"To-morrow, my friend, we must part. You return to your beautiful England, I to some work which may have such an end that we may never meet. Your letter home has been despatched; to-morrow I shall not be here, but all shall be ready for your journey. In the morning come the Szgany, who have some labours of their own here, and also come some Slovaks. When they have gone, my carriage shall come for you, and shall bear you to the Borgo Pass to meet the diligence from Bukovina to Bistritz. But I am in hopes that I shall see more of you at Castle Dracula." I suspected him, and determined to test his sincerity. Sincerity! It seems like a profanation of the word to write it in connection with such a monster, so asked him point-blank:—

"Why may I not go to-night?"

"Because, dear sir, my coachman and horses are away on a mission."

"But I would walk with pleasure. I want to get away at once." He smiled, such a soft, smooth, diabolical smile that I knew there was some trick behind his smoothness. He said:—

"And your baggage?"

"I do not care about it. I can send for it some other time."

The Count stood up, and said, with a sweet courtesy which made me rub my eyes, it seemed so real:—

"You English have a saying which is close to my heart, for its spirit is that which rules our boyars: 'Welcome the coming; speed the parting guest.' Come with me, my dear young friend. Not an hour shall you wait in my house against your will, though sad am I at your going, and that you so suddenly desire it. Come!" With a stately gravity, he, with the lamp, preceded me down the stairs and along the hall. Suddenly he stopped.

"Hark!"

Close at hand came the howling of many wolves. It was almost as if the sound sprang up at the rising of his hand, just as the music of a great orchestra seems to leap under the bâton of the conductor. After a pause of a moment, he proceeded, in his stately way, to the door, drew back the ponderous bolts, unhooked the heavy chains, and began to draw it open.

To my intense astonishment I saw that it was unlocked. Suspiciously, I looked all round, but could see no key of any kind.

As the door began to open, the howling of the wolves without grew louder and angrier; their red jaws, with champing teeth, and their blunt-clawed feet as they leaped, came in through the opening door. I knew then that to struggle at the moment against the Count was useless. With such allies as these at his command, I could do nothing. But still the door continued slowly to open, and only the Count's body stood in the gap. Suddenly it struck me that this might be the moment and means of my doom; I was to be given to the wolves, and at my own instigation. There was a diabolical wickedness in the idea great enough for the Count, and as a last chance I cried out:—

"Shut the door; I shall wait till morning!" and covered my face with my hands to hide my tears of bitter disappointment. With one sweep of his powerful arm, the Count threw the door shut, and the great bolts clanged and echoed through the hall as they shot back into their places. In silence we returned to the library, and after a minute or two I went to my own room. The last I saw of Count Dracula was his kissing his hand to me; with a red light of triumph in his eyes, and with a smile that Judas in hell might be proud of.

When I was in my room and about to lie down, I thought I heard a whispering at my door. I went to it softly and listened. Unless my ears deceived me, I heard the voice of the Count:—

"Back, back, to your own place! Your time is not yet come. Wait! Have patience! To-night is mine. To-morrow night is yours!" There was a low, sweet ripple of laughter, and in a rage I threw open the door, and saw without the three terrible women licking their lips. As I appeared they all joined in a horrible laugh, and ran away.

I came back to my room and threw myself on my knees. It is then so near the end? To-morrow! to-morrow! Lord, help me, and those to whom I am dear!

30 June, morning.— These may be the last words I ever write in this diary. I slept till just before the dawn, and when I woke threw myself on my knees, for I determined that if Death came he should find me ready.

At last I felt that subtle change in the air, and knew that the morning had come. Then came the welcome cock-crow, and I felt that I was safe. With a glad heart, I opened my door and ran down to the hall. I had seen that the door was unlocked, and now escape was before me. With hands that trembled with eagerness, I unhooked the chains and drew back the massive bolts.

But the door would not move. Despair seized me. I pulled, and pulled, at the door, and shook it till, massive as it was, it rattled in its casement. I could see the bolt shot. It had been locked after I left the Count.

Then a wild desire took me to obtain that key at any risk, and I determined then and there to scale the wall again and gain the Count's room. He might kill me, but death now seemed the happier choice of evils. Without a pause I rushed up to the east window, and scrambled down the wall, as before, into the Count's room. It was empty, but that was as I expected. I could not see a key anywhere, but the heap of gold remained. I went through the door in the corner and down the winding stair and along the dark passage to the old chapel. I knew now well enough where to find the monster I sought.

The great box was in the same place, close against the wall, but the lid was laid on it, not fastened down, but with the nails ready in their places to be hammered home. I knew I must reach the body for the key, so I raised the lid, and laid it back against the wall; and then I saw something which filled my very soul with horror. There lay the Count, but looking as if his youth had been half renewed, for the white hair and moustache were changed to dark iron-grey; the cheeks were fuller, and the white skin seemed ruby-red underneath; the mouth was redder than ever, for on the lips were gouts of fresh blood, which trickled from the corners of the mouth and ran over the chin and neck. Even the deep, burning eyes seemed set amongst swollen flesh, for the lids and pouches underneath were bloated. It seemed as if the whole awful creature were simply gorged with blood. He lay like a filthy leech, exhausted with his repletion. I shuddered as I bent over to touch him, and every sense in me revolted at the contact; but I had to search, or I was lost. The coming night might see my own body a banquet in a similar way to those horrid three. I felt all over the body, but no sign could I find of the key. Then I stopped and looked at the Count. There was a mocking smile on the bloated face which seemed to drive me mad. This was the being I was helping to transfer to London, where, perhaps, for centuries to come he might, amongst its teeming millions, satiate his lust for blood, and create a new and ever-widening circle of semi-demons to batten on the helpless. The very thought drove me mad. A terrible desire came upon me to rid the world of such a monster. There was no lethal weapon at hand, but I seized a shovel which the workmen had been using to fill the cases, and lifting it high, struck, with the edge downward, at the hateful face. But as I did so the head turned, and the eyes fell full upon me, with all their blaze of basilisk horror. The sight seemed to paralyse me, and the shovel turned in my hand and glanced from the face, merely making a deep gash above the forehead. The shovel fell from my hand across the box, and as I pulled it away the flange of the blade caught the edge of the lid which fell over again, and hid the horrid thing from my sight. The last glimpse I had was of the bloated face, blood-stained and fixed with a grin of malice which would have held its own in the nethermost hell.

I thought and thought what should be my next move, but my brain seemed on fire, and I waited with a despairing feeling growing over me. As I waited I heard in the distance a gipsy song sung by merry voices coming closer, and through their song the rolling of heavy wheels and the cracking of whips; the Szgany and the Slovaks of whom the Count had spoken were coming. With a last look around and at the box which contained the vile body, I ran from the place and gained the Count's room, determined to rush out at the moment the door should be opened. With strained ears, I listened, and heard downstairs the grinding of the key in the great lock and the falling back of the heavy door. There must have been some other means of entry, or some one had a key for one of the locked doors. Then there came the sound of many feet tramping and dying away in some passage which sent up a clanging echo. I turned to run down again towards the vault, where I might find the new entrance; but at the moment there seemed to come a violent puff of wind, and the door to the winding stair blew to with a shock that set the dust from the lintels flying. When I ran to push it open, I found that it was hopelessly fast. I was again a prisoner, and the net of doom was closing round me more closely.

As I write there is in the passage below a sound of many tramping feet and the crash of weights being set down heavily, doubtless the boxes, with their freight of earth. There is a sound of hammering; it is the box being nailed down. Now I can hear the heavy feet tramping again along the hall, with many other idle feet coming behind them.

The door is shut, and the chains rattle; there is a grinding of the key in the lock; I can hear the key withdraw: then another door opens and shuts; I hear the creaking of lock and bolt.

Hark! in the courtyard and down the rocky way the roll of heavy wheels, the crack of whips, and the chorus of the Szgany as they pass into the distance.

I am alone in the castle with those awful women. Faugh! Mina is a woman, and there is nought in common. They are devils of the Pit!

I shall not remain alone with them; I shall try to scale the castle wall farther than I have yet attempted. I shall take some of the gold with me, lest I want it later. I may find a way from this dreadful place.

And then away for home! away to the quickest and nearest train! away from this cursed spot, from this cursed land, where the devil and his children still walk with earthly feet!

At least God's mercy is better than that of these monsters, and the precipice is steep and high. At its foot a man may sleep— as a man. Good-bye, all! Mina!

CHAPTER V
## Letter from Miss Mina Murray to Miss Lucy Westenra.

9 May.
"My dearest Lucy,—

"Forgive my long delay in writing, but I have been simply overwhelmed with work. The life of an assistant schoolmistress is sometimes trying. I am longing to be with you, and by the sea, where we can talk together freely and build our castles in the air. I have been working very hard lately, because I want to keep up with Jonathan's studies, and I have been practising shorthand very assiduously. When we are married I shall be able to be useful to Jonathan, and if I can stenograph well enough I can take down what he wants to say in this way and write it out for him on the typewriter, at which also I am practising very hard. He and I sometimes write letters in shorthand, and he is keeping a stenographic journal of his travels abroad. When I am with you I shall keep a diary in the same way. I don't mean one of those two-pages-to-the-week-with-Sunday-squeezed-in-a-corner diaries, but a sort of journal which I can write in whenever I feel inclined. I do not suppose there will be much of interest to other people; but it is not intended for them. I may show it to Jonathan some day if there is in it anything worth sharing, but it is really an exercise book. I shall try to do what I see lady journalists do: interviewing and writing descriptions and trying to remember conversations. I am told that, with a little practice, one can remember all that goes on or that one hears said during a day. However, we shall see. I will tell you of my little plans when we meet. I have just had a few hurried lines from Jonathan from Transylvania. He is well, and will be returning in about a week. I am longing to hear all his news. It must be so nice to see strange countries. I wonder if we— I mean Jonathan and I— shall ever see them together. There is the ten o'clock bell ringing. Good-bye.
"Your loving
"Mina.
"Tell me all the news when you write. You have not told me anything for a long time. I hear rumours, and especially of a tall, handsome, curly-haired man???"
Letter, Lucy Westenra to Mina Murray.
"17, Chatham Street,
"Wednesday.
"My dearest Mina,—

"I must say you tax me very unfairly with being a bad correspondent. I wrote to you twice since we parted, and your last letter was only your second. Besides, I have nothing to tell you. There is really nothing to interest you. Town is very pleasant just now, and we go a good deal to picture-galleries and for walks and rides in the park. As to the tall, curly-haired man, I suppose it was the one who was with me at the last Pop. Some one has evidently been telling tales. That was Mr. Holmwood. He often comes to see us, and he and mamma get on very well together; they have so many things to talk about in common. We met some time ago a man that would just do for you, if you were not already engaged to Jonathan. He is an excellent parti, being handsome, well off, and of good birth. He is a doctor and really clever. Just fancy! He is only nine-and-twenty, and he has an immense lunatic asylum all under his own care. Mr. Holmwood introduced him to me, and he called here to see us, and often comes now. I think he is one of the most resolute men I ever saw, and yet the most calm. He seems absolutely imperturbable. I can fancy what a wonderful power he must have over his patients. He has a curious habit of looking one straight in the face, as if trying to read one's thoughts. He tries this on very much with me, but I flatter myself he has got a tough nut to crack. I know that from my glass. Do you ever try to read your own face? I do, and I can tell you it is not a bad study, and gives you more trouble than you can well fancy if you have never tried it. He says that I afford him a curious psychological study, and I humbly think I do. I do not, as you know, take sufficient interest in dress to be able to describe the new fashions. Dress is a bore. That is slang again, but never mind; Arthur says that every day. There, it is all out. Mina, we have told all our secrets to each other since we were children; we have slept together and eaten together, and laughed and cried together; and now, though I have spoken, I would like to speak more. Oh, Mina, couldn't you guess? I love him. I am blushing as I write, for although I think he loves me, he has not told me so in words. But oh, Mina, I love him; I love him; I love him! There, that does me good. I wish I were with you, dear, sitting by the fire undressing, as we used to sit; and I would try to tell you what I feel. I do not know how I am writing this even to you. I am afraid to stop, or I should tear up the letter, and I don't want to stop, for I do so want to tell you all. Let me hear from you at once, and tell me all that you think about it. Mina, I must stop. Good-night. Bless me in your prayers; and, Mina, pray for my happiness.

"LUCY.

"P.S.— I need not tell you this is a secret. Good-night again.

"L."
Letter, Lucy Westenra to Mina Murray.
"24 May.
"My dearest Mina,—
"Thanks, and thanks, and thanks again for your sweet letter. It was so nice to be able to tell you and to have your sympathy.

"My dear, it never rains but it pours. How true the old proverbs are. Here am I, who shall be twenty in September, and yet I never had a proposal till to-day, not a real proposal, and to-day I have had three. Just fancy! THREE proposals in one day! Isn't it awful! I feel sorry, really and truly sorry, for two of the poor fellows. Oh, Mina, I am so happy that I don't know what to do with myself. And three proposals! But, for goodness' sake, don't tell any of the girls, or they would be getting all sorts of extravagant ideas and imagining themselves injured and slighted if in their very first day at home they did not get six at least. Some girls are so vain! You and I, Mina dear, who are engaged and are going to settle down soon soberly into old married women, can despise vanity. Well, I must tell you about the three, but you must keep it a secret, dear, from every one, except, of course, Jonathan. You will tell him, because I would, if I were in your place, certainly tell Arthur. A woman ought to tell her husband everything— don't you think so, dear?— and I must be fair. Men like women, certainly their wives, to be quite as fair as they are; and women, I am afraid, are not always quite as fair as they should be. Well, my dear, number One came just before lunch. I told you of him, Dr. John Seward, the lunatic-asylum man, with the strong jaw and the good forehead. He was very cool outwardly, but was nervous all the same. He had evidently been schooling himself as to all sorts of little things, and remembered them; but he almost managed to sit down on his silk hat, which men don't generally do when they are cool, and then when he wanted to appear at ease he kept playing with a lancet in a way that made me nearly scream. He spoke to me, Mina, very straightforwardly. He told me how dear I was to him, though he had known me so little, and what his life would be with me to help and cheer him. He was going to tell me how unhappy he would be if I did not care for him, but when he saw me cry he said that he was a brute and would not add to my present trouble. Then he broke off and asked if I could love him in time; and when I shook my head his hands trembled, and then with some hesitation he asked me if I cared already for any one else. He put it very nicely, saying that he did not want to wring my confidence from me, but only to know, because if a woman's heart was free a man might have hope. And then, Mina, I felt a sort of duty to tell him that there was some one. I only told him that much, and then he stood up, and he looked very strong and very grave as he took both my hands in his and said he hoped I would be happy, and that if I ever wanted a friend I must count him one of my best. Oh, Mina dear, I can't help crying: and you must excuse this letter being all blotted. Being proposed to is all very nice and all that sort of thing, but it isn't at all a happy thing when you have to see a poor fellow, whom you know loves you honestly, going away and looking all broken-hearted, and to know that, no matter what he may say at the moment, you are passing quite out of his life. My dear, I must stop here at present, I feel so miserable, though I am so happy.

"Evening.

"Arthur has just gone, and I feel in better spirits than when I left off, so I can go on telling you about the day. Well, my dear, number Two came after lunch. He is such a nice fellow, an American from Texas, and he looks so young and so fresh that it seems almost impossible that he has been to so many places and has had such adventures. I sympathise with poor Desdemona when she had such a dangerous stream poured in her ear, even by a black man. I suppose that we women are such cowards that we think a man will save us from fears, and we marry him. I know now what I would do if I were a man and wanted to make a girl love me. No, I don't, for there was Mr. Morris telling us his stories, and Arthur never told any, and yet— — My dear, I am somewhat previous. Mr. Quincey P. Morris found me alone. It seems that a man always does find a girl alone. No, he doesn't, for Arthur tried twice to make a chance, and I helping him all I could; I am not ashamed to say it now. I must tell you beforehand that Mr. Morris doesn't always speak slang— that is to say, he never does so to strangers or before them, for he is really well educated and has exquisite manners— but he found out that it amused me to hear him talk American slang, and whenever I was present, and there was no one to be shocked, he said such funny things. I am afraid, my dear, he has to invent it all, for it fits exactly into whatever else he has to say. But this is a way slang has. I do not know myself if I shall ever speak slang; I do not know if Arthur likes it, as I have never heard him use any as yet. Well, Mr. Morris sat down beside me and looked as happy and jolly as he could, but I could see all the same that he was very nervous. He took my hand in his, and said ever so sweetly:—

" 'Miss Lucy, I know I ain't good enough to regulate the fixin's of your little shoes, but I guess if you wait till you find a man that is you will go join them seven young women with the lamps when you quit. Won't you just hitch up alongside of me and let us go down the long road together, driving in double harness?'

"Well, he did look so good-humoured and so jolly that it didn't seem half so hard to refuse him as it did poor Dr. Seward; so I said, as lightly as I could, that I did not know anything of hitching, and that I wasn't broken to harness at all yet. Then he said that he had spoken in a light manner, and he hoped that if he had made a mistake in doing so on so grave, so momentous, an occasion for him, I would forgive him. He really did look serious when he was saying it, and I couldn't help feeling a bit serious too— I know, Mina, you will think me a horrid flirt— though I couldn't help feeling a sort of exultation that he was number two in one day. And then, my dear, before I could say a word he began pouring out a perfect torrent of love-making, laying his very heart and soul at my feet. He looked so earnest over it that I shall never again think that a man must be playful always, and never earnest, because he is merry at times. I suppose he saw something in my face which checked him, for he suddenly stopped, and said with a sort of manly fervour that I could have loved him for if I had been free:—

" 'Lucy, you are an honest-hearted girl, I know. I should not be here speaking to you as I am now if I did not believe you clean grit, right through to the very depths of your soul. Tell me, like one good fellow to another, is there any one else that you care for? And if there is I'll never trouble you a hair's breadth again, but will be, if you will let me, a very faithful friend.'

"My dear Mina, why are men so noble when we women are so little worthy of them? Here was I almost making fun of this great-hearted, true gentleman. I burst into tears— I am afraid, my dear, you will think this a very sloppy letter in more ways than one— and I really felt very badly. Why can't they let a girl marry three men, or as many as want her, and save all this trouble? But this is heresy, and I must not say it. I am glad to say that, though I was crying, I was able to look into Mr. Morris's brave eyes, and I told him out straight:—

" 'Yes, there is some one I love, though he has not told me yet that he even loves me.' I was right to speak to him so frankly, for quite a light came into his face, and he put out both his hands and took mine— I think I put them into his— and said in a hearty way:—

" 'That's my brave girl. It's better worth being late for a chance of winning you than being in time for any other girl in the world. Don't cry, my dear. If it's for me, I'm a hard nut to crack; and I take it standing up. If that other fellow doesn't know his happiness, well, he'd better look for it soon, or he'll have to deal with me. Little girl, your honesty and pluck have made me a friend, and that's rarer than a lover; it's more unselfish anyhow. My dear, I'm going to have a pretty lonely walk between this and Kingdom Come. Won't you give me one kiss? It'll be something to keep off the darkness now and then. You can, you know, if you like, for that other good fellow— he must be a good fellow, my dear, and a fine fellow, or you could not love him— hasn't spoken yet.' That quite won me, Mina, for it was brave and sweet of him, and noble, too, to a rival— wasn't it?— and he so sad; so I leant over and kissed him. He stood up with my two hands in his, and as he looked down into my face— I am afraid I was blushing very much— he said:—

" 'Little girl, I hold your hand, and you've kissed me, and if these things don't make us friends nothing ever will. Thank you for your sweet honesty to me, and good-bye.' He wrung my hand, and taking up his hat, went straight out of the room without looking back, without a tear or a quiver or a pause; and I am crying like a baby. Oh, why must a man like that be made unhappy when there are lots of girls about who would worship the very ground he trod on? I know I would if I were free— only I don't want to be free. My dear, this quite upset me, and I feel I cannot write of happiness just at once, after telling you of it; and I don't wish to tell of the number three until it can be all happy.

"Ever your loving

"Lucy.

"P.S.— Oh, about number Three— I needn't tell you of number Three, need I? Besides, it was all so confused; it seemed only a moment from his coming into the room till both his arms were round me, and he was kissing me. I am very, very happy, and I don't know what I have done to deserve it. I must only try in the future to show that I am not ungrateful to God for all His goodness to me in sending to me such a lover, such a husband, and such a friend.

"Good-bye."

Dr. Seward's Diary.

(Kept in phonograph)

25 May.— Ebb tide in appetite to-day. Cannot eat, cannot rest, so diary instead. Since my rebuff of yesterday I have a sort of empty feeling; nothing in the world seems of sufficient importance to be worth the doing.... As I knew that the only cure for this sort of thing was work, I went down amongst the patients. I picked out one who has afforded me a study of much interest. He is so quaint that I am determined to understand him as well as I can. To-day I seemed to get nearer than ever before to the heart of his mystery.

I questioned him more fully than I had ever done, with a view to making myself master of the facts of his hallucination. In my manner of doing it there was, I now see, something of cruelty. I seemed to wish to keep him to the point of his madness— a thing which I avoid with the patients as I would the mouth of hell.

(Mem., under what circumstances would I not avoid the pit of hell?) Omnia Romæ venalia sunt. Hell has its price! verb. sap. If there be anything behind this instinct it will be valuable to trace it afterwards accurately, so I had better commence to do so, therefore—

R. M. Renfield, ætat 59.— Sanguine temperament; great physical strength; morbidly excitable; periods of gloom, ending in some fixed idea which I cannot make out. I presume that the sanguine temperament itself and the disturbing influence end in a mentally-accomplished finish; a possibly dangerous man, probably dangerous if unselfish. In selfish men caution is as secure an armour for their foes as for themselves. What I think of on this point is, when self is the fixed point the centripetal force is balanced with the centrifugal; when duty, a cause, etc., is the fixed point, the latter force is paramount, and only accident or a series of accidents can balance it.

Letter, Quincey P. Morris to Hon. Arthur Holmwood.

"25 May.

"My dear Art,—

"We've told yarns by the camp-fire in the prairies; and dressed one another's wounds after trying a landing at the Marquesas; and drunk healths on the shore of Titicaca. There are more yarns to be told, and other wounds to be healed, and another health to be drunk. Won't you let this be at my camp-fire to-morrow night? I have no hesitation in asking you, as I know a certain lady is engaged to a certain dinner-party, and that you are free. There will only be one other, our old pal at the Korea, Jack Seward. He's coming, too, and we both want to mingle our weeps over the wine-cup, and to drink a health with all our hearts to the happiest man in all the wide world, who has won the noblest heart that God has made and the best worth winning. We promise you a hearty welcome, and a loving greeting, and a health as true as your own right hand. We shall both swear to leave you at home if you drink too deep to a certain pair of eyes. Come!

"Yours, as ever and always,

"Quincey P. Morris."

Telegram from Arthur Holmwood to Quincey P. Morris.

"26 May.

"Count me in every time. I bear messages which will make both your ears tingle.

"Art."

## CHAPTER VI
## MINA MURRAY'S JOURNAL

2 4 July. Whitby.— Lucy met me at the station, looking sweeter and lovelier than ever, and we drove up to the house at the Crescent in which they have rooms. This is a lovely place. The little river, the Esk, runs through a deep valley, which broadens out as it comes near the harbour. A great viaduct runs across, with high piers, through which the view seems somehow further away than it really is. The valley is beautifully green, and it is so steep that when you are on the high land on either side you look right across it, unless you are near enough to see down. The houses of the old town— the side away from us— are all red-roofed, and seem piled up one over the other anyhow, like the pictures we see of Nuremberg. Right over the town is the ruin of Whitby Abbey, which was sacked by the Danes, and which is the scene of part of "Marmion," where the girl was built up in the wall. It is a most noble ruin, of immense size, and full of beautiful and romantic bits; there is a legend that a white lady is seen in one of the windows. Between it and the town there is another church, the parish one, round which is a big graveyard, all full of tombstones. This is to my mind the nicest spot in Whitby, for it lies right over the town, and has a full view of the harbour and all up the bay to where the headland called Kettleness stretches out into the sea. It descends so steeply over the harbour that part of the bank has fallen away, and some of the graves have been destroyed. In one place part of the stonework of the graves stretches out over the sandy pathway far below. There are walks, with seats beside them, through the churchyard; and people go and sit there all day long looking at the beautiful view and enjoying the breeze. I shall come and sit here very often myself and work. Indeed, I am writing now, with my book on my knee, and listening to the talk of three old men who are sitting beside me. They seem to do nothing all day but sit up here and talk.

The harbour lies below me, with, on the far side, one long granite wall stretching out into the sea, with a curve outwards at the end of it, in the middle of which is a lighthouse. A heavy sea-wall runs along outside of it. On the near side, the sea-wall makes an elbow crooked inversely, and its end too has a lighthouse. Between the two piers there is a narrow opening into the harbour, which then suddenly widens.

It is nice at high water; but when the tide is out it shoals away to nothing, and there is merely the stream of the Esk, running between banks of sand, with rocks here and there. Outside the harbour on this side there rises for about half a mile a great reef, the sharp edge of which runs straight out from behind the south lighthouse. At the end of it is a buoy with a bell, which swings in bad weather, and sends in a mournful sound on the wind. They have a legend here that when a ship is lost bells are heard out at sea. I must ask the old man about this; he is coming this way....

He is a funny old man. He must be awfully old, for his face is all gnarled and twisted like the bark of a tree. He tells me that he is nearly a hundred, and that he was a sailor in the Greenland fishing fleet when Waterloo was fought. He is, I am afraid, a very sceptical person, for when I asked him about the bells at sea and the White Lady at the abbey he said very brusquely:—

"I wouldn't fash masel' about them, miss. Them things be all wore out. Mind, I don't say that they never was, but I do say that they wasn't in my time. They be all very well for comers and trippers, an' the like, but not for a nice young lady like you. Them feet-folks from York and Leeds that be always eatin' cured herrin's an' drinkin' tea an' lookin' out to buy cheap jet would creed aught. I wonder masel' who'd be bothered tellin' lies to them— even the newspapers, which is full of fool-talk." I thought he would be a good person to learn interesting things from, so I asked him if he would mind telling me something about the whale-fishing in the old days. He was just settling himself to begin when the clock struck six, whereupon he laboured to get up, and said:—

"I must gang ageeanwards home now, miss. My grand-daughter doesn't like to be kept waitin' when the tea is ready, for it takes me time to crammle aboon the grees, for there be a many of 'em; an', miss, I lack belly-timber sairly by the clock."

He hobbled away, and I could see him hurrying, as well as he could, down the steps. The steps are a great feature on the place. They lead from the town up to the church, there are hundreds of them— I do not know how many— and they wind up in a delicate curve; the slope is so gentle that a horse could easily walk up and down them. I think they must originally have had something to do with the abbey. I shall go home too. Lucy went out visiting with her mother, and as they were only duty calls, I did not go. They will be home by this.

1 August.— I came up here an hour ago with Lucy, and we had a most interesting talk with my old friend and the two others who always come and join him. He is evidently the Sir Oracle of them, and I should think must have been in his time a most dictatorial person. He will not admit anything, and downfaces everybody. If he can't out-argue them he bullies them, and then takes their silence for agreement with his views. Lucy was looking sweetly pretty in her white lawn frock; she has got a beautiful colour since she has been here. I noticed that the old men did not lose any time in coming up and sitting near her when we sat down. She is so sweet with old people; I think they all fell in love with her on the spot. Even my old man succumbed and did not contradict her, but gave me double share instead. I got him on the subject of the legends, and he went off at once into a sort of sermon. I must try to remember it and put it down:—

"It be all fool-talk, lock, stock, and barrel; that's what it be, an' nowt else. These bans an' wafts an' boh-ghosts an' barguests an' bogles an' all anent them is only fit to set bairns an' dizzy women a-belderin'. They be nowt but air-blebs. They, an' all grims an' signs an' warnin's, be all invented by parsons an' illsome beuk-bodies an' railway touters to skeer an' scunner hafflin's, an' to get folks to do somethin' that they don't other incline to.It makes me ireful to think o' them. Why, it's them that, not content with printin' lies on paper an' preachin' them out of pulpits, does want to be cuttin' them on the tombstones. Look here all around you in what airt ye will; all them steans, holdin' up their heads as well as they can out of their pride, is acant- simply tumblin' down with the weight o' the lies wrote on them,'Here lies the body' or 'Sacred to the memory' wrote on all of them, an' yet in nigh half of them there bean't no bodies at all; an' the memories of them bean't cared a pinch of snuff about, much less sacred. Lies all of them,nothin' but lies of one kind or another! My gog,but it'll be a quare scowderment at the Day of Judgment when they come tumblin' up in their death-sarks, all jouped together an' tryin' to drag their tombsteans with them to prove how good they was; some of them trimmlin' and ditherin', with their hands that dozzened an' slippy from lyin' in the sea that they can't even keep their grup o' them."

I could see from the old fellow's self-satisfied air and the way in which he looked round for the approval of his cronies that he was "showing off," so I put in a word to keep him going:—

"Oh, Mr. Swales, you can't be serious. Surely these tombstones are not all wrong?"

"Yabblins! There may be a poorish few not wrong, savin' where they make out the people too good; for there be folk that do think a balm-bowl be like the sea, if only it be their own. The whole thing be only lies. Now look you here; you come here a stranger, an' you see this kirk-garth." I nodded, for I thought it better to assent, though I did not quite understand his dialect. I knew it had something to do with the church. He went on: "And you consate that all these steans be aboon folk that be happed here, snod an' snog?" I assented again. "Then that be just where the lie comes in. Why, there be scores of these lay-beds that be toom as old Dun's 'bacca-box on Friday night." He nudged one of his companions, and they all laughed. "And my gog! how could they be otherwise? Look at that one, the aftest abaft the bier-bank: read it!" I went over and read:—

"Edward Spencelagh, master mariner, murdered by pirates off the coast of Andres, April, 1854, æt. 30." When I came back Mr. Swales went on:—

"Who brought him home, I wonder, to hap him here? Murdered off the coast of Andres! an' you consated his body lay under! Why, I could name ye a dozen whose bones lie in the Greenland seas above"— he pointed northwards— "or where the currents may have drifted them. There be the steans around ye. Ye can, with your young eyes, read the small-print of the lies from here. This Braithwaite Lowrey— I knew his father, lost in the Lively off Greenland in '20; or Andrew Woodhouse, drowned in the same seas in 1777; or John Paxton, drowned off Cape Farewell a year later; or old John Rawlings, whose grandfather sailed with me, drowned in the Gulf of Finland in '50. Do ye think that all these men will have to make a rush to Whitby when the trumpet sounds? I have me antherums aboot it! I tell ye that when they got here they'd be jommlin' an' jostlin' one another that way that it 'ud be like a fight up on the ice in the old days, when we'd be at one another from daylight to dark, an' tryin' to tie up our cuts by the light of the aurora borealis." This was evidently local pleasantry, for the old man cackled over it, and his cronies joined in with gusto.

"But," I said, "surely you are not quite correct, for you start on the assumption that all the poor people, or their spirits, will have to take their tombstones with them on the Day of Judgment. Do you think that will be really necessary?"

"Well, what else be they tombstones for? Answer me that, miss!"

"To please their relatives, I suppose."

"To please their relatives, you suppose!" This he said with intense scorn. "How will it pleasure their relatives to know that lies is wrote over them, and that everybody in the place knows that they be lies?" He pointed to a stone at our feet which had been laid down as a slab, on which the seat was rested, close to the edge of the cliff. "Read the lies on that thruff-stean," he said. The letters were upside down to me from where I sat, but Lucy was more opposite to them, so she leant over and read:—

"Sacred to the memory of George Canon, who died, in the hope of a glorious resurrection, on July, 29, 1873, falling from the rocks at Kettleness. This tomb was erected by his sorrowing mother to her dearly beloved son. 'He was the only son of his mother, and she was a widow.' Really, Mr. Swales, I don't see anything very funny in that!" She spoke her comment very gravely and somewhat severely.

"Ye don't see aught funny! Ha! ha! But that's because ye don't gawm the sorrowin' mother was a hell-cat that hated him because he was acrewk'd— a regular lamiter he was— an' he hated her so that he committed suicide in order that she mightn't get an insurance she put on his life. He blew nigh the top of his head off with an old musket that they had for scarin' the crows with. 'Twarn't for crows then, for it brought the clegs and the dowps to him. That's the way he fell off the rocks. And, as to hopes of a glorious resurrection, I've often heard him say masel' that he hoped he'd go to hell, for his mother was so pious that she'd be sure to go to heaven, an' he didn't want to addle where she was. Now isn't that stean at any rate"— he hammered it with his stick as he spoke— "a pack of lies? and won't it make Gabriel keckle when Geordie comes pantin' up the grees with the tombstean balanced on his hump, and asks it to be took as evidence!"

I did not know what to say, but Lucy turned the conversation as she said, rising up:—

"Oh, why did you tell us of this? It is my favourite seat, and I cannot leave it; and now I find I must go on sitting over the grave of a suicide." "That won't harm ye, my pretty; an' it may make poor Geordie gladsome to have so trim a lass sittin' on his lap. That won't hurt ye. Why, I've sat here off an' on for nigh twenty years past, an' it hasn't done me no harm. Don't ye fash about them as lies under ye, or that doesn' lie there either! It'll be time for ye to be getting scart when ye see the tombsteans all run away with, and the place as bare as a stubble-field. There's the clock, an' I must gang. My service to ye, ladies!" And off he hobbled.

Lucy and I sat awhile, and it was all so beautiful before us that we took hands as we sat; and she told me all over again about Arthur and their coming marriage. That made me just a little heart-sick, for I haven't heard from Jonathan for a whole month.

The same day. I came up here alone, for I am very sad. There was no letter for me. I hope there cannot be anything the matter with Jonathan. The clock has just struck nine. I see the lights scattered all over the town, sometimes in rows where the streets are, and sometimes singly; they run right up the Esk and die away in the curve of the valley. To my left the view is cut off by a black line of roof of the old house next the abbey. The sheep and lambs are bleating in the fields away behind me, and there is a clatter of a donkey's hoofs up the paved road below. The band on the pier is playing a harsh waltz in good time, and further along the quay there is a Salvation Army meeting in a back street. Neither of the bands hears the other, but up here I hear and see them both. I wonder where Jonathan is and if he is thinking of me! I wish he were here.

Dr. Seward's Diary.

5 June.— The case of Renfield grows more interesting the more I get to understand the man. He has certain qualities very largely developed; selfishness, secrecy, and purpose. I wish I could get at what is the object of the latter. He seems to have some settled scheme of his own, but what it is I do not yet know. His redeeming quality is a love of animals, though, indeed, he has such curious turns in it that I sometimes imagine he is only abnormally cruel. His pets are of odd sorts. Just now his hobby is catching flies. He has at present such a quantity that I have had myself to expostulate. To my astonishment, he did not break out into a fury, as I expected, but took the matter in simple seriousness. He thought for a moment, and then said: "May I have three days? I shall clear them away." Of course, I said that would do. I must watch him.

18 June.— He has turned his mind now to spiders, and has got several very big fellows in a box. He keeps feeding them with his flies, and the number of the latter is becoming sensibly diminished, although he has used half his food in attracting more flies from outside to his room.

1 July.— His spiders are now becoming as great a nuisance as his flies, and to-day I told him that he must get rid of them. He looked very sad at this, so I said that he must clear out some of them, at all events. He cheerfully acquiesced in this, and I gave him the same time as before for reduction. He disgusted me much while with him, for when a horrid blow-fly, bloated with some carrion food, buzzed into the room, he caught it, held it exultantly for a few moments between his finger and thumb, and, before I knew what he was going to do, put it in his mouth and ate it. I scolded him for it, but he argued quietly that it was very good and very wholesome; that it was life, strong life, and gave life to him. This gave me an idea, or the rudiment of one. I must watch how he gets rid of his spiders. He has evidently some deep problem in his mind, for he keeps a little note-book in which he is always jotting down something. Whole pages of it are filled with masses of figures, generally single numbers added up in batches, and then the totals added in batches again, as though he were "focussing" some account, as the auditors put it.

8 July.— There is a method in his madness, and the rudimentary idea in my mind is growing. It will be a whole idea soon, and then, oh, unconscious cerebration! you will have to give the wall to your conscious brother. I kept away from my friend for a few days, so that I might notice if there were any change. Things remain as they were except that he has parted with some of his pets and got a new one. He has managed to get a sparrow, and has already partially tamed it. His means of taming is simple, for already the spiders have diminished. Those that do remain, however, are well fed, for he still brings in the flies by tempting them with his food.

19 July.— We are progressing. My friend has now a whole colony of sparrows, and his flies and spiders are almost obliterated. When I came in he ran to me and said he wanted to ask me a great favour— a very, very great favour; and as he spoke he fawned on me like a dog. I asked him what it was, and he said, with a sort of rapture in his voice and bearing:—

"A kitten, a nice little, sleek playful kitten, that I can play with, and teach, and feed— and feed— and feed!" I was not unprepared for this request, for I had noticed how his pets went on increasing in size and vivacity, but I did not care that his pretty family of tame sparrows should be wiped out in the same manner as the flies and the spiders; so I said I would see about it, and asked him if he would not rather have a cat than a kitten. His eagerness betrayed him as he answered:—

"Oh, yes, I would like a cat! I only asked for a kitten lest you should refuse me a cat. No one would refuse me a kitten, would they?" I shook my head, and said that at present I feared it would not be possible, but that I would see about it. His face fell, and I could see a warning of danger in it, for there was a sudden fierce, sidelong look which meant killing. The man is an undeveloped homicidal maniac. I shall test him with his present craving and see how it will work out; then I shall know more.

10 p. m.— I have visited him again and found him sitting in a corner brooding. When I came in he threw himself on his knees before me and implored me to let him have a cat; that his salvation depended upon it. I was firm, however, and told him that he could not have it, whereupon he went without a word, and sat down, gnawing his fingers, in the corner where I had found him. I shall see him in the morning early.

20 July.— Visited Renfield very early, before the attendant went his rounds. Found him up and humming a tune. He was spreading out his sugar, which he had saved, in the window, and was manifestly beginning his fly-catching again; and beginning it cheerfully and with a good grace. I looked around for his birds, and not seeing them, asked him where they were. He replied, without turning round, that they had all flown away. There were a few feathers about the room and on his pillow a drop of blood. I said nothing, but went and told the keeper to report to me if there were anything odd about him during the day.

11 a. m.— The attendant has just been to me to say that Renfield has been very sick and has disgorged a whole lot of feathers. "My belief is, doctor," he said, "that he has eaten his birds, and that he just took and ate them raw!"

11 p. m.— I gave Renfield a strong opiate to-night, enough to make even him sleep, and took away his pocket-book to look at it. The thought that has been buzzing about my brain lately is complete, and the theory proved. My homicidal maniac is of a peculiar kind. I shall have to invent a new classification for him, and call him a zoöphagous (life-eating) maniac; what he desires is to absorb as many lives as he can, and he has laid himself out to achieve it in a cumulative way. He gave many flies to one spider and many spiders to one bird, and then wanted a cat to eat the many birds. What would have been his later steps? It would almost be worth while to complete the experiment. It might be done if there were only a sufficient cause. Men sneered at vivisection, and yet look at its results to-day! Why not advance science in its most difficult and vital aspect— the knowledge of the brain? Had I even the secret of one such mind— did I hold the key to the fancy of even one lunatic— I might advance my own branch of science to a pitch compared with which Burdon-Sanderson's physiology or Ferrier's brain-knowledge would be as nothing. If only there were a sufficient cause! I must not think too much of this, or I may be tempted; a good cause might turn the scale with me, for may not I too be of an exceptional brain, congenitally?

How well the man reasoned; lunatics always do within their own scope. I wonder at how many lives he values a man, or if at only one. He has closed the account most accurately, and to-day begun a new record. How many of us begin a new record with each day of our lives?

To me it seems only yesterday that my whole life ended with my new hope, and that truly I began a new record. So it will be until the Great Recorder sums me up and closes my ledger account with a balance to profit or loss. Oh, Lucy, Lucy, I cannot be angry with you, nor can I be angry with my friend whose happiness is yours; but I must only wait on hopeless and work. Work! work!

If I only could have as strong a cause as my poor mad friend there— a good, unselfish cause to make me work— that would be indeed happiness.

Mina Murray's Journal.

26 July.— I am anxious, and it soothes me to express myself here; it is like whispering to one's self and listening at the same time. And there is also something about the shorthand symbols that makes it different from writing. I am unhappy about Lucy and about Jonathan. I had not heard from Jonathan for some time, and was very concerned; but yesterday dear Mr. Hawkins, who is always so kind, sent me a letter from him. I had written asking him if he had heard, and he said the enclosed had just been received. It is only a line dated from Castle Dracula, and says that he is just starting for home. That is not like Jonathan; I do not understand it, and it makes me uneasy. Then, too, Lucy, although she is so well, has lately taken to her old habit of walking in her sleep. Her mother has spoken to me about it, and we have decided that I am to lock the door of our room every night. Mrs. Westenra has got an idea that sleep-walkers always go out on roofs of houses and along the edges of cliffs and then get suddenly wakened and fall over with a despairing cry that echoes all over the place. Poor dear, she is naturally anxious about Lucy, and she tells me that her husband, Lucy's father, had the same habit; that he would get up in the night and dress himself and go out, if he were not stopped. Lucy is to be married in the autumn, and she is already planning out her dresses and how her house is to be arranged. I sympathise with her, for I do the same, only Jonathan and I will start in life in a very simple way, and shall have to try to make both ends meet. Mr. Holmwood— he is the Hon. Arthur Holmwood, only son of Lord Godalming— is coming up here very shortly— as soon as he can leave town, for his father is not very well, and I think dear Lucy is counting the moments till he comes. She wants to take him up to the seat on the churchyard cliff and show him the beauty of Whitby. I daresay it is the waiting which disturbs her; she will be all right when he arrives.

27 July.— No news from Jonathan. I am getting quite uneasy about him, though why I should I do not know; but I do wish that he would write, if it were only a single line. Lucy walks more than ever, and each night I am awakened by her moving about the room. Fortunately, the weather is so hot that she cannot get cold; but still the anxiety and the perpetually being wakened is beginning to tell on me, and I am getting nervous and wakeful myself. Thank God, Lucy's health keeps up. Mr. Holmwood has been suddenly called to Ring to see his father, who has been taken seriously ill. Lucy frets at the postponement of seeing him, but it does not touch her looks; she is a trifle stouter, and her cheeks are a lovely rose-pink. She has lost that anæmic look which she had. I pray it will all last.

3 August.— Another week gone, and no news from Jonathan, not even to Mr. Hawkins, from whom I have heard. Oh, I do hope he is not ill. He surely would have written. I look at that last letter of his, but somehow it does not satisfy me. It does not read like him, and yet it is his writing. There is no mistake of that. Lucy has not walked much in her sleep the last week, but there is an odd concentration about her which I do not understand; even in her sleep she seems to be watching me. She tries the door, and finding it locked, goes about the room searching for the key.

6 August.— Another three days, and no news. This suspense is getting dreadful. If I only knew where to write to or where to go to, I should feel easier; but no one has heard a word of Jonathan since that last letter. I must only pray to God for patience. Lucy is more excitable than ever, but is otherwise well. Last night was very threatening, and the fishermen say that we are in for a storm. I must try to watch it and learn the weather signs. To-day is a grey day, and the sun as I write is hidden in thick clouds, high over Kettleness. Everything is grey— except the green grass, which seems like emerald amongst it; grey earthy rock; grey clouds, tinged with the sunburst at the far edge, hang over the grey sea, into which the sand-points stretch like grey fingers. The sea is tumbling in over the shallows and the sandy flats with a roar, muffled in the sea-mists drifting inland. The horizon is lost in a grey mist. All is vastness; the clouds are piled up like giant rocks, and there is a "brool" over the sea that sounds like some presage of doom. Dark figures are on the beach here and there, sometimes half shrouded in the mist, and seem "men like trees walking." The fishing-boats are racing for home, and rise and dip in the ground swell as they sweep into the harbour, bending to the scuppers. Here comes old Mr. Swales. He is making straight for me, and I can see, by the way he lifts his hat, that he wants to talk....

I have been quite touched by the change in the poor old man. When he sat down beside me, he said in a very gentle way:—

"I want to say something to you, miss." I could see he was not at ease, so I took his poor old wrinkled hand in mine and asked him to speak fully; so he said, leaving his hand in mine:—

"I'm afraid, my deary, that I must have shocked you by all the wicked things I've been sayin' about the dead, and such like, for weeks past; but I didn't mean them, and I want ye to remember that when I'm gone. We aud folks that be daffled, and with one foot abaft the krok-hooal, don't altogether like to think of it, and we don't want to feel scart of it; an' that's why I've took to makin' light of it, so that I'd cheer up my own heart a bit. But, Lord love ye, miss, I ain't afraid of dyin', not a bit; only I don't want to die if I can help it. My time must be nigh at hand now, for I be aud, and a hundred years is too much for any man to expect; and I'm so nigh it that the Aud Man is already whettin' his scythe. Ye see, I can't get out o' the habit of caffin' about it all at once; the chafts will wag as they be used to. Some day soon the Angel of Death will sound his trumpet for me. But don't ye dooal an' greet, my deary!"— for he saw that I was crying— "if he should come this very night I'd not refuse to answer his call. For life be, after all, only a waitin' for somethin' else than what we're doin'; and death be all that we can rightly depend on. But I'm content, for it's comin' to me, my deary, and comin' quick. It may be comin' while we be lookin' and wonderin'. Maybe it's in that wind out over the sea that's bringin' with it loss and wreck, and sore distress, and sad hearts. Look! look!" he cried suddenly. "There's something in that wind and in the hoast beyont that sounds, and looks, and tastes, and smells like death. It's in the air; I feel it comin'. Lord, make me answer cheerful when my call comes!" He held up his arms devoutly, and raised his hat. His mouth moved as though he were praying. After a few minutes' silence, he got up, shook hands with me, and blessed me, and said good-bye, and hobbled off. It all touched me, and upset me very much.

I was glad when the coastguard came along, with his spy-glass under his arm. He stopped to talk with me, as he always does, but all the time kept looking at a strange ship.

"I can't make her out," he said; "she's a Russian, by the look of her; but she's knocking about in the queerest way. She doesn't know her mind a bit; she seems to see the storm coming, but can't decide whether to run up north in the open, or to put in here. Look there again! She is steered mighty strangely, for she doesn't mind the hand on the wheel; changes about with every puff of wind. We'll hear more of her before this time to-morrow."

## CHAPTER VII
## CUTTING FROM "THE DAILYGRAPH," 8 AUGUST

(Pasted in Mina Murray's Journal.)

From a Correspondent.
Whitby.ONE greatest and suddenest storms on record has just been experienced here, with results both strange and unique. The weather had been somewhat sultry, but not to any degree uncommon in the month of August. Saturday evening was as fine as was ever known, and the great body of holiday-makers laid out yesterday for visits to Mulgrave Woods, Robin Hood's Bay, Rig Mill, Runswick, Staithes, and the various trips in the neighbourhood of Whitby. The steamers Emma and Scarborough made trips up and down the coast, and there was an unusual amount of "tripping" both to and from Whitby. The day was unusually fine till the afternoon, when some of the gossips who frequent the East Cliff churchyard, and from that commanding eminence watch the wide sweep of sea visible to the north and east, called attention to a sudden show of "mares'-tails" high in the sky to the north-west. The wind was then blowing from the south-west in the mild degree which in barometrical language is ranked "No. 2: light breeze." The coastguard on duty at once made report, and one old fisherman, who for more than half a century has kept watch on weather signs from the East Cliff, foretold in an emphatic manner the coming of a sudden storm.

The approach of sunset was so very beautiful, so grand in its masses of splendidly-coloured clouds, that there was quite an assemblage on the walk along the cliff in the old churchyard to enjoy the beauty. Before the sun dipped below the black mass of Kettleness, standing boldly athwart the western sky, its downward way was marked by myriad clouds of every sunset-colour— flame, purple, pink, green, violet, and all the tints of gold; with here and there masses not large, but of seemingly absolute blackness, in all sorts of shapes, as well outlined as colossal silhouettes. The experience was not lost on the painters, and doubtless some of the sketches of the "Prelude to the Great Storm" will grace the R. A. and R. I. walls in May next. More than one captain made up his mind then and there that his "cobble" or his "mule," as they term the different classes of boats, would remain in the harbour till the storm had passed. The wind fell away entirely during the evening, and at midnight there was a dead calm, a sultry heat, and that prevailing intensity which, on the approach of thunder, affects persons of a sensitive nature. There were but few lights in sight at sea, for even the coasting steamers, which usually "hug" the shore so closely, kept well to seaward, and but few fishing-boats were in sight. The only sail noticeable was a foreign schooner with all sails set, which was seemingly going westwards. The foolhardiness or ignorance of her officers was a prolific theme for comment whilst she remained in sight, and efforts were made to signal her to reduce sail in face of her danger. Before the night shut down she was seen with sails idly flapping as she gently rolled on the undulating swell of the sea,

"As idle as a painted ship upon a painted ocean."

Shortly before ten o'clock the stillness of the air grew quite oppressive, and the silence was so marked that the bleating of a sheep inland or the barking of a dog in the town was distinctly heard, and the band on the pier, with its lively French air, was like a discord in the great harmony of nature's silence. A little after midnight came a strange sound from over the sea, and high overhead the air began to carry a strange, faint, hollow booming.

Then without warning the tempest broke. With a rapidity which, at the time, seemed incredible, and even afterwards is impossible to realize, the whole aspect of nature at once became convulsed. The waves rose in growing fury, each overtopping its fellow, till in a very few minutes the lately glassy sea was like a roaring and devouring monster. White-crested waves beat madly on the level sands and rushed up the shelving cliffs; others broke over the piers, and with their spume swept the lanthorns of the lighthouses which rise from the end of either pier of Whitby Harbour. The wind roared like thunder, and blew with such force that it was with difficulty that even strong men kept their feet, or clung with grim clasp to the iron stanchions. It was found necessary to clear the entire piers from the mass of onlookers, or else the fatalities of the night would have been increased manifold. To add to the difficulties and dangers of the time, masses of sea-fog came drifting inland- white, wet clouds,which swept by in ghostly fashion, so dank and damp and cold that it needed but little effort of imagination to think that the spirits of those lost at sea were touching their living brethren with the clammy hands of death, and many a one shuddered as the wreaths of sea-mist swept by. At times the mist cleared, and the sea for some distance could be seen in the glare of the lightning, which now came thick and fast, followed by such sudden peals of thunder that the whole sky overhead seemed trembling under the shock of the footsteps of the storm.

Some of the scenes thus revealed were of immeasurable grandeur and of absorbing interest— the sea, running mountains high, threw skywards with each wave mighty masses of white foam, which the tempest seemed to snatch at and whirl away into space; here and there a fishing-boat, with a rag of sail, running madly for shelter before the blast; now and again the white wings of a storm-tossed sea-bird. On the summit of the East Cliff the new searchlight was ready for experiment, but had not yet been tried. The officers in charge of it got it into working order, and in the pauses of the inrushing mist swept with it the surface of the sea. Once or twice its service was most effective, as when a fishing-boat, with gunwale under water, rushed into the harbour, able, by the guidance of the sheltering light, to avoid the danger of dashing against the piers. As each boat achieved the safety of the port there was a shout of joy from the mass of people on shore, a shout which for a moment seemed to cleave the gale and was then swept away in its rush.

Before long the searchlight discovered some distance away a schooner with all sails set, apparently the same vessel which had been noticed earlier in the evening. The wind had by this time backed to the east, and there was a shudder amongst the watchers on the cliff as they realized the terrible danger in which she now was. Between her and the port lay the great flat reef on which so many good ships have from time to time suffered, and, with the wind blowing from its present quarter, it would be quite impossible that she should fetch the entrance of the harbour. It was now nearly the hour of high tide, but the waves were so great that in their troughs the shallows of the shore were almost visible, and the schooner, with all sails set, was rushing with such speed that, in the words of one old salt, "she must fetch up somewhere, if it was only in hell." Then came another rush of sea-fog, greater than any hitherto— a mass of dank mist, which seemed to close on all things like a grey pall, and left available to men only the organ of hearing, for the roar of the tempest, and the crash of the thunder, and the booming of the mighty billows came through the damp oblivion even louder than before. The rays of the searchlight were kept fixed on the harbour mouth across the East Pier, where the shock was expected, and men waited breathless. The wind suddenly shifted to the north-east, and the remnant of the sea-fog melted in the blast; and then, mirabile dictu, between the piers, leaping from wave to wave as it rushed at headlong speed, swept the strange schooner before the blast, with all sail set, and gained the safety of the harbour. The searchlight followed her, and a shudder ran through all who saw her, for lashed to the helm was a corpse, with drooping head, which swung horribly to and fro at each motion of the ship. No other form could be seen on deck at all. A great awe came on all as they realised that the ship, as if by a miracle, had found the harbour, unsteered save by the hand of a dead man! However, all took place more quickly than it takes to write these words. The schooner paused not, but rushing across the harbour, pitched herself on that accumulation of sand and gravel washed by many tides and many storms into the south-east corner of the pier jutting under the East Cliff, known locally as Tate Hill Pier.

There was of course a considerable concussion as the vessel drove up on the sand heap. Every spar, rope, and stay was strained, and some of the "top-hammer" came crashing down. But, strangest of all, the very instant the shore was touched, an immense dog sprang up on deck from below, as if shot up by the concussion, and running forward, jumped from the bow on the sand. Making straight for the steep cliff, where the churchyard hangs over the laneway to the East Pier so steeply that some of the flat tombstones— "thruff-steans" or "through-stones," as they call them in the Whitby vernacular— actually project over where the sustaining cliff has fallen away, it disappeared in the darkness, which seemed intensified just beyond the focus of the searchlight.

It so happened that there was no one at the moment on Tate Hill Pier, as all those whose houses are in close proximity were either in bed or were out on the heights above. Thus the coastguard on duty on the eastern side of the harbour, who at once ran down to the little pier, was the first to climb on board. The men working the searchlight, after scouring the entrance of the harbour without seeing anything, then turned the light on the derelict and kept it there. The coastguard ran aft, and when he came beside the wheel, bent over to examine it, and recoiled at once as though under some sudden emotion. This seemed to pique general curiosity, and quite a number of people began to run. It is a good way round from the West Cliff by the Drawbridge to Tate Hill Pier, but your correspondent is a fairly good runner, and came well ahead of the crowd. When I arrived, however, I found already assembled on the pier a crowd, whom the coastguard and police refused to allow to come on board. By the courtesy of the chief boatman, I was, as your correspondent, permitted to climb on deck, and was one of a small group who saw the dead seaman whilst actually lashed to the wheel.

It was no wonder that the coastguard was surprised, or even awed, for not often can such a sight have been seen. The man was simply fastened by his hands, tied one over the other, to a spoke of the wheel. Between the inner hand and the wood was a crucifix, the set of beads on which it was fastened being around both wrists and wheel, and all kept fast by the binding cords. The poor fellow may have been seated at one time, but the flapping and buffeting of the sails had worked through the rudder of the wheel and dragged him to and fro, so that the cords with which he was tied had cut the flesh to the bone. Accurate note was made of the state of things, and a doctor— Surgeon J. M. Caffyn, of 33, East Elliot Place— who came immediately after me, declared, after making examination, that the man must have been dead for quite two days. In his pocket was a bottle, carefully corked, empty save for a little roll of paper, which proved to be the addendum to the log. The coastguard said the man must have tied up his own hands, fastening the knots with his teeth. The fact that a coastguard was the first on board may save some complications, later on, in the Admiralty Court; for coastguards cannot claim the salvage which is the right of the first civilian entering on a derelict. Already, however, the legal tongues are wagging, and one young law student is loudly asserting that the rights of the owner are already completely sacrificed, his property being held in contravention of the statutes of mortmain, since the tiller, as emblemship, if not proof, of delegated possession, is held in a dead hand. It is needless to say that the dead steersman has been reverently removed from the place where he held his honourable watch and ward till death— a steadfastness as noble as that of the young Casabianca— and placed in the mortuary to await inquest.

Already the sudden storm is passing, and its fierceness is abating; crowds are scattering homeward, and the sky is beginning to redden over the Yorkshire wolds. I shall send, in time for your next issue, further details of the derelict ship which found her way so miraculously into harbour in the storm.

Whitby

9 August.— The sequel to the strange arrival of the derelict in the storm last night is almost more startling than the thing itself. It turns out that the schooner is a Russian from Varna, and is called the Demeter. She is almost entirely in ballast of silver sand, with only a small amount of cargo— a number of great wooden boxes filled with mould. This cargo was consigned to a Whitby solicitor, Mr. S. F. Billington, of 7, The Crescent, who this morning went aboard and formally took possession of the goods consigned to him. The Russian consul, too, acting for the charter-party, took formal possession of the ship, and paid all harbour dues, etc. Nothing is talked about here to-day except the strange coincidence; the officials of the Board of Trade have been most exacting in seeing that every compliance has been made with existing regulations. As the matter is to be a "nine days' wonder," they are evidently determined that there shall be no cause of after complaint. A good deal of interest was abroad concerning the dog which landed when the ship struck, and more than a few of the members of the S. P. C. A., which is very strong in Whitby, have tried to befriend the animal. To the general disappointment, however, it was not to be found; it seems to have disappeared entirely from the town. It may be that it was frightened and made its way on to the moors, where it is still hiding in terror. There are some who look with dread on such a possibility, lest later on it should in itself become a danger, for it is evidently a fierce brute. Early this morning a large dog, a half-bred mastiff belonging to a coal merchant close to Tate Hill Pier, was found dead in the roadway opposite to its master's yard. It had been fighting, and manifestly had had a savage opponent, for its throat was torn away, and its belly was slit open as if with a savage claw.

Later.— By the kindness of the Board of Trade inspector, I have been permitted to look over the log-book of the Demeter, which was in order up to within three days, but contained nothing of special interest except as to facts of missing men. The greatest interest, however, is with regard to the paper found in the bottle, which was to-day produced at the inquest; and a more strange narrative than the two between them unfold it has not been my lot to come across. As there is no motive for concealment, I am permitted to use them, and accordingly send you a rescript, simply omitting technical details of seamanship and supercargo. It almost seems as though the captain had been seized with some kind of mania before he had got well into blue water, and that this had developed persistently throughout the voyage. Of course my statement must be taken cum grano, since I am writing from the dictation of a clerk of the Russian consul, who kindly translated for me, time being short.

LOG OF THE "DEMETER."

Varna to Whitby.

Written 18 July, things so strange happening, that I shall keep accurate note henceforth till we land.

On 6 July we finished taking in cargo, silver sand and boxes of earth. At noon set sail. East wind, fresh. Crew, five hands ... two mates, cook, and myself (captain).

On 11 July at dawn entered Bosphorus. Boarded by Turkish Customs officers. Backsheesh. All correct. Under way at 4 p. m.

On 12 July through Dardanelles. More Customs officers and flagboat of guarding squadron. Backsheesh again. Work of officers thorough, but quick. Want us off soon. At dark passed into Archipelago.

On 13 July passed Cape Matapan. Crew dissatisfied about something. Seemed scared, but would not speak out.

On 14 July was somewhat anxious about crew. Men all steady fellows, who sailed with me before. Mate could not make out what was wrong; they only told him there was something, and crossed themselves. Mate lost temper with one of them that day and struck him. Expected fierce quarrel, but all was quiet.

On 16 July mate reported in the morning that one of crew, Petrofsky, was missing. Could not account for it. Took larboard watch eight bells last night; was relieved by Abramoff, but did not go to bunk. Men more downcast than ever. All said they expected something of the kind, but would not say more than there was something aboard. Mate getting very impatient with them; feared some trouble ahead.

On 17 July, yesterday, one of the men, Olgaren, came to my cabin, and in an awestruck way confided to me that he thought there was a strange man aboard the ship. He said that in his watch he had been sheltering behind the deck-house, as there was a rain-storm, when he saw a tall, thin man, who was not like any of the crew, come up the companion-way, and go along the deck forward, and disappear. He followed cautiously, but when he got to bows found no one, and the hatchways were all closed. He was in a panic of superstitious fear, and I am afraid the panic may spread. To allay it, I shall to-day search entire ship carefully from stem to stern.

Later in the day I got together the whole crew, and told them, as they evidently thought there was some one in the ship, we would search from stem to stern. First mate angry; said it was folly, and to yield to such foolish ideas would demoralise the men; said he would engage to keep them out of trouble with a handspike. I let him take the helm, while the rest began thorough search, all keeping abreast, with lanterns: we left no corner unsearched. As there were only the big wooden boxes, there were no odd corners where a man could hide. Men much relieved when search over, and went back to work cheerfully. First mate scowled, but said nothing.

22 July.— Rough weather last three days, and all hands busy with sails— no time to be frightened. Men seem to have forgotten their dread. Mate cheerful again, and all on good terms. Praised men for work in bad weather. Passed Gibralter and out through Straits. All well.

24 July.— There seems some doom over this ship. Already a hand short, and entering on the Bay of Biscay with wild weather ahead, and yet last night another man lost— disappeared. Like the first, he came off his watch and was not seen again. Men all in a panic of fear; sent a round robin, asking to have double watch, as they fear to be alone. Mate angry. Fear there will be some trouble, as either he or the men will do some violence.

28 July.— Four days in hell, knocking about in a sort of maelstrom, and the wind a tempest. No sleep for any one. Men all worn out. Hardly know how to set a watch, since no one fit to go on. Second mate volunteered to steer and watch, and let men snatch a few hours' sleep. Wind abating; seas still terrific, but feel them less, as ship is steadier.

29 July.— Another tragedy. Had single watch to-night, as crew too tired to double. When morning watch came on deck could find no one except steersman. Raised outcry, and all came on deck. Thorough search, but no one found. Are now without second mate, and crew in a panic. Mate and I agreed to go armed henceforth and wait for any sign of cause.

30 July.— Last night. Rejoiced we are nearing England. Weather fine, all sails set. Retired worn out; slept soundly; awaked by mate telling me that both man of watch and steersman missing. Only self and mate and two hands left to work ship.

1 August.— Two days of fog, and not a sail sighted. Had hoped when in the English Channel to be able to signal for help or get in somewhere. Not having power to work sails, have to run before wind. Dare not lower, as could not raise them again. We seem to be drifting to some terrible doom. Mate now more demoralised than either of men. His stronger nature seems to have worked inwardly against himself. Men are beyond fear, working stolidly and patiently, with minds made up to worst. They are Russian, he Roumanian.

2 August, midnight.— Woke up from few minutes' sleep by hearing a cry, seemingly outside my port. Could see nothing in fog. Rushed on deck, and ran against mate. Tells me heard cry and ran, but no sign of man on watch. One more gone. Lord, help us! Mate says we must be past Straits of Dover, as in a moment of fog lifting he saw North Foreland, just as he heard the man cry out. If so we are now off in the North Sea, and only God can guide us in the fog, which seems to move with us; and God seems to have deserted us.

3 August.— At midnight I went to relieve the man at the wheel, and when I got to it found no one there. The wind was steady, and as we ran before it there was no yawing. I dared not leave it, so shouted for the mate. After a few seconds he rushed up on deck in his flannels. He looked wild-eyed and haggard, and I greatly fear his reason has given way. He came close to me and whispered hoarsely, with his mouth to my ear, as though fearing the very air might hear: "It is here; I know it, now. On the watch last night I saw It, like a man, tall and thin, and ghastly pale. It was in the bows, and looking out. I crept behind It, and gave It my knife; but the knife went through It, empty as the air." And as he spoke he took his knife and drove it savagely into space. Then he went on: "But It is here, and I'll find It. It is in the hold, perhaps in one of those boxes. I'll unscrew them one by one and see. You work the helm." And, with a warning look and his finger on his lip, he went below. There was springing up a choppy wind, and I could not leave the helm. I saw him come out on deck again with a tool-chest and a lantern, and go down the forward hatchway. He is mad, stark, raving mad, and it's no use my trying to stop him. He can't hurt those big boxes: they are invoiced as "clay," and to pull them about is as harmless a thing as he can do. So here I stay, and mind the helm, and write these notes. I can only trust in God and wait till the fog clears. Then, if I can't steer to any harbour with the wind that is, I shall cut down sails and lie by, and signal for help....

It is nearly all over now. Just as I was beginning to hope that the mate would come out calmer— for I heard him knocking away at something in the hold, and work is good for him— there came up the hatchway a sudden, startled scream, which made my blood run cold, and up on the deck he came as if shot from a gun— a raging madman, with his eyes rolling and his face convulsed with fear. "Save me! save me!" he cried, and then looked round on the blanket of fog. His horror turned to despair, and in a steady voice he said: "You had better come too, captain, before it is too late. He is there. I know the secret now. The sea will save me from Him, and it is all that is left!" Before I could say a word, or move forward to seize him, he sprang on the bulwark and deliberately threw himself into the sea. I suppose I know the secret too, now. It was this madman who had got rid of the men one by one, and now he has followed them himself. God help me! How am I to account for all these horrors when I get to port! When I get to port! Will that ever be?

4 August.— Still fog, which the sunrise cannot pierce. I know there is sunrise because I am a sailor, why else I know not. I dared not go below, I dared not leave the helm; so here all night I stayed, and in the dimness of the night I saw It— Him! God forgive me, but the mate was right to jump overboard. It was better to die like a man; to die like a sailor in blue water no man can object. But I am captain, and I must not leave my ship. But I shall baffle this fiend or monster, for I shall tie my hands to the wheel when my strength begins to fail, and along with them I shall tie that which He— It!— dare not touch; and then, come good wind or foul, I shall save my soul, and my honour as a captain. I am growing weaker, and the night is coming on. If He can look me in the face again, I may not have time to act.... If we are wrecked, mayhap this bottle may be found, and those who find it may understand; if not, ... well, then all men shall know that I have been true to my trust. God and the Blessed Virgin and the saints help a poor ignorant soul trying to do his duty....

Of course the verdict was an open one. There is no evidence to adduce; and whether or not the man himself committed the murders there is now none to say. The folk here hold almost universally that the captain is simply a hero, and he is to be given a public funeral. Already it is arranged that his body is to be taken with a train of boats up the Esk for a piece and then brought back to Tate Hill Pier and up the abbey steps; for he is to be buried in the churchyard on the cliff. The owners of more than a hundred boats have already given in their names as wishing to follow him to the grave.

No trace has ever been found of the great dog; at which there is much mourning, for, with public opinion in its present state, he would, I believe, be adopted by the town. To-morrow will see the funeral; and so will end this one more "mystery of the sea."

Mina Murray's Journal.

8 August.— Lucy was very restless all night, and I, too, could not sleep. The storm was fearful, and as it boomed loudly among the chimney-pots, it made me shudder. When a sharp puff came it seemed to be like a distant gun. Strangely enough, Lucy did not wake; but she got up twice and dressed herself. Fortunately, each time I awoke in time and managed to undress her without waking her, and got her back to bed. It is a very strange thing, this sleep-walking, for as soon as her will is thwarted in any physical way, her intention, if there be any, disappears, and she yields herself almost exactly to the routine of her life.

Early in the morning we both got up and went down to the harbour to see if anything had happened in the night. There were very few people about, and though the sun was bright, and the air clear and fresh, the big, grim-looking waves, that seemed dark themselves because the foam that topped them was like snow, forced themselves in through the narrow mouth of the harbour— like a bullying man going through a crowd. Somehow I felt glad that Jonathan was not on the sea last night, but on land. But, oh, is he on land or sea? Where is he, and how? I am getting fearfully anxious about him. If I only knew what to do, and could do anything!

10 August.— The funeral of the poor sea-captain to-day was most touching. Every boat in the harbour seemed to be there, and the coffin was carried by captains all the way from Tate Hill Pier up to the churchyard. Lucy came with me, and we went early to our old seat, whilst the cortège of boats went up the river to the Viaduct and came down again. We had a lovely view, and saw the procession nearly all the way. The poor fellow was laid to rest quite near our seat so that we stood on it when the time came and saw everything. Poor Lucy seemed much upset. She was restless and uneasy all the time, and I cannot but think that her dreaming at night is telling on her. She is quite odd in one thing: she will not admit to me that there is any cause for restlessness; or if there be, she does not understand it herself. There is an additional cause in that poor old Mr. Swales was found dead this morning on our seat, his neck being broken. He had evidently, as the doctor said, fallen back in the seat in some sort of fright, for there was a look of fear and horror on his face that the men said made them shudder. Poor dear old man! Perhaps he had seen Death with his dying eyes! Lucy is so sweet and sensitive that she feels influences more acutely than other people do. Just now she was quite upset by a little thing which I did not much heed, though I am myself very fond of animals. One of the men who came up here often to look for the boats was followed by his dog. The dog is always with him. They are both quiet persons, and I never saw the man angry, nor heard the dog bark. During the service the dog would not come to its master, who was on the seat with us, but kept a few yards off, barking and howling. Its master spoke to it gently, and then harshly, and then angrily; but it would neither come nor cease to make a noise. It was in a sort of fury, with its eyes savage, and all its hairs bristling out like a cat's tail when puss is on the war-path. Finally the man, too, got angry, and jumped down and kicked the dog, and then took it by the scruff of the neck and half dragged and half threw it on the tombstone on which the seat is fixed. The moment it touched the stone the poor thing became quiet and fell all into a tremble. It did not try to get away, but crouched down, quivering and cowering, and was in such a pitiable state of terror that I tried, though without effect, to comfort it. Lucy was full of pity, too, but she did not attempt to touch the dog, but looked at it in an agonised sort of way. I greatly fear that she is of too super-sensitive a nature to go through the world without trouble. She will be dreaming of this to-night, I am sure. The whole agglomeration of things— the ship steered into port by a dead man; his attitude, tied to the wheel with a crucifix and beads; the touching funeral; the dog, now furious and now in

terror— will all afford material for her dreams.

I think it will be best for her to go to bed tired out physically, so I shall take her for a long walk by the cliffs to Robin Hood's Bay and back. She ought not to have much inclination for sleep-walking then.

## CHAPTER VIII
## MINA MURRAY'S JOURNAL

*Same day, 11 o'clock p. m.—* Oh, but I am tired! If it were not that I had made my diary a duty I should not open it to-night. We had a lovely walk. Lucy, after a while, was in gay spirits, owing, I think, to some dear cows who came nosing towards us in a field close to the lighthouse, and frightened the wits out of us. I believe we forgot everything except, of course, personal fear, and it seemed to wipe the slate clean and give us a fresh start. We had a capital "severe tea" at Robin Hood's Bay in a sweet little old-fashioned inn, with a bow-window right over the seaweed-covered rocks of the strand. I believe we should have shocked the "New Woman" with our appetites. Men are more tolerant, bless them! Then we walked home with some, or rather many, stoppages to rest, and with our hearts full of a constant dread of wild bulls. Lucy was really tired, and we intended to creep off to bed as soon as we could. The young curate came in, however, and Mrs. Westenra asked him to stay for supper. Lucy and I had both a fight for it with the dusty miller; I know it was a hard fight on my part, and I am quite heroic. I think that some day the bishops must get together and see about breeding up a new class of curates, who don't take supper, no matter how they may be pressed to, and who will know when girls are tired. Lucy is asleep and breathing softly. She has more colour in her cheeks than usual, and looks, oh, so sweet. If Mr. Holmwood fell in love with her seeing her only in the drawing-room, I wonder what he would say if he saw her now. Some of the "New Women" writers will some day start an idea that men and women should be allowed to see each other asleep before proposing or accepting. But I suppose the New Woman won't condescend in future to accept; she will do the proposing herself. And a nice job she will make of it, too! There's some consolation in that. I am so happy to-night, because dear Lucy seems better. I really believe she has turned the corner, and that we are over her troubles with dreaming. I should be quite happy if I only knew if Jonathan.... God bless and keep him.

11 August, 3 a. m.— Diary again. No sleep now, so I may as well write. I am too agitated to sleep. We have had such an adventure, such an agonising experience. I fell asleep as soon as I had closed my diary.... Suddenly I became broad awake, and sat up, with a horrible sense of fear upon me, and of some feeling of emptiness around me. The room was dark, so I could not see Lucy's bed; I stole across and felt for her. The bed was empty. I lit a match and found that she was not in the room. The door was shut, but not locked, as I had left it. I feared to wake her mother, who has been more than usually ill lately, so threw on some clothes and got ready to look for her. As I was leaving the room it struck me that the clothes she wore might give me some clue to her dreaming intention. Dressing-gown would mean house; dress, outside. Dressing-gown and dress were both in their places. "Thank God," I said to myself, "she cannot be far, as she is only in her nightdress." I ran downstairs and looked in the sitting-room. Not there! Then I looked in all the other open rooms of the house, with an ever-growing fear chilling my heart. Finally I came to the hall door and found it open. It was not wide open, but the catch of the lock had not caught. The people of the house are careful to lock the door every night, so I feared that Lucy must have gone out as she was. There was no time to think of what might happen; a vague, overmastering fear obscured all details. I took a big, heavy shawl and ran out. The clock was striking one as I was in the Crescent, and there was not a soul in sight. I ran along the North Terrace, but could see no sign of the white figure which I expected. At the edge of the West Cliff above the pier I looked across the harbour to the East Cliff, in the hope or fear— I don't know which— of seeing Lucy in our favourite seat. There was a bright full moon, with heavy black, driving clouds, which threw the whole scene into a fleeting diorama of light and shade as they sailed across. For a moment or two I could see nothing, as the shadow of a cloud obscured St. Mary's Church and all around it. Then as the cloud passed I could see the ruins of the abbey coming into view; and as the edge of a narrow band of light as sharp as a sword-cut moved along, the church and the churchyard became gradually visible. Whatever my expectation was, it was not disappointed, for there, on our favourite seat, the silver light of the moon struck a half-reclining figure, snowy white. The coming of the cloud was too quick for me to see much, for shadow shut down on light almost immediately; but it seemed to me as though something dark stood behind the seat where the white figure shone, and bent over it. What it was, whether man or beast, I could not tell; I did not wait to catch another glance, but flew down the steep steps to the pier and

along by the fish-market to the bridge, which was the only way to reach the East Cliff. The town seemed as dead, for not a soul did I see; I rejoiced that it was so, for I wanted no witness of poor Lucy's condition. The time and distance seemed endless, and my knees trembled and my breath came laboured as I toiled up the endless steps to the abbey. I must have gone fast, and yet it seemed to me as if my feet were weighted with lead, and as though every joint in my body were rusty. When I got almost to the top I could see the seat and the white figure, for I was now close enough to distinguish it even through the spells of shadow. There was undoubtedly something, long and black, bending over the half-reclining white figure. I called in fright, "Lucy! Lucy!" and something raised a head, and from where I was I could see a white face and red, gleaming eyes. Lucy did not answer, and I ran on to the entrance of the churchyard. As I entered, the church was between me and the seat, and for a minute or so I lost sight of her. When I came in view again the cloud had passed, and the moonlight struck so brilliantly that I could see Lucy half reclining with her head lying over the back of the seat. She was quite alone, and there was not a sign of any living thing about.

When I bent over her I could see that she was still asleep. Her lips were parted, and she was breathing— not softly as usual with her, but in long, heavy gasps, as though striving to get her lungs full at every breath. As I came close, she put up her hand in her sleep and pulled the collar of her nightdress close around her throat. Whilst she did so there came a little shudder through her, as though she felt the cold. I flung the warm shawl over her, and drew the edges tight round her neck, for I dreaded lest she should get some deadly chill from the night air, unclad as she was. I feared to wake her all at once, so, in order to have my hands free that I might help her, I fastened the shawl at her throat with a big safety-pin; but I must have been clumsy in my anxiety and pinched or pricked her with it, for by-and-by, when her breathing became quieter, she put her hand to her throat again and moaned. When I had her carefully wrapped up I put my shoes on her feet and then began very gently to wake her. At first she did not respond; but gradually she became more and more uneasy in her sleep, moaning and sighing occasionally. At last, as time was passing fast, and, for many other reasons, I wished to get her home at once, I shook her more forcibly, till finally she opened her eyes and awoke. She did not seem surprised to see me, as, of course, she did not realise all at once where she was. Lucy always wakes prettily, and even at such a time, when her body must have been chilled with cold, and her mind somewhat appalled at waking unclad in a churchyard at night, she did not lose her grace. She trembled a little, and clung to me; when I told her to come at once with me home she rose without a word, with the obedience of a child. As we passed along, the gravel hurt my feet, and Lucy noticed me wince. She stopped and wanted to insist upon my taking my shoes; but I would not. However, when we got to the pathway outside the churchyard, where there was a puddle of water, remaining from the storm, I daubed my feet with mud, using each foot in turn on the other, so that as we went home, no one, in case we should meet any one, should notice my bare feet.

Fortune favoured us, and we got home without meeting a soul. Once we saw a man, who seemed not quite sober, passing along a street in front of us; but we hid in a door till he had disappeared up an opening such as there are here, steep little closes, or "wynds," as they call them in Scotland. My heart beat so loud all the time that sometimes I thought I should faint. I was filled with anxiety about Lucy, not only for her health, lest she should suffer from the exposure, but for her reputation in case the story should get wind. When we got in, and had washed our feet, and had said a prayer of thankfulness together, I tucked her into bed. Before falling asleep she asked— even implored— me not to say a word to any one, even her mother, about her sleep-walking adventure. I hesitated at first to promise; but on thinking of the state of her mother's health, and how the knowledge of such a thing would fret her, and thinking, too, of how such a story might become distorted— nay, infallibly would— in case it should leak out, I thought it wiser to do so. I hope I did right. I have locked the door, and the key is tied to my wrist, so perhaps I shall not be again disturbed. Lucy is sleeping soundly; the reflex of the dawn is high and far over the sea....

Same day, noon.— All goes well. Lucy slept till I woke her and seemed not to have even changed her side. The adventure of the night does not seem to have harmed her; on the contrary, it has benefited her, for she looks better this morning than she has done for weeks. I was sorry to notice that my clumsiness with the safety-pin hurt her. Indeed, it might have been serious, for the skin of her throat was pierced. I must have pinched up a piece of loose skin and have transfixed it, for there are two little red points like pin-pricks, and on the band of her nightdress was a drop of blood. When I apologised and was concerned about it, she laughed and petted me, and said she did not even feel it. Fortunately it cannot leave a scar, as it is so tiny.

Same day, night.— We passed a happy day. The air was clear, and the sun bright, and there was a cool breeze. We took our lunch to Mulgrave Woods, Mrs. Westenra driving by the road and Lucy and I walking by the cliff-path and joining her at the gate. I felt a little sad myself, for I could not but feel how absolutely happy it would have been had Jonathan been with me. But there! I must only be patient. In the evening we strolled in the Casino Terrace, and heard some good music by Spohr and Mackenzie, and went to bed early. Lucy seems more restful than she has been for some time, and fell asleep at once. I shall lock the door and secure the key the same as before, though I do not expect any trouble to-night.

12 August.- My expectations were wrong, for twice during the night I was wakened by Lucy trying to get out. She seemed, even in her sleep, to be a little impatient at finding the door shut, and went back to bed under a sort of protest. I woke with the dawn, and heard the birds chirping outside of the window. Lucy woke, too, and, I was glad to see, was even better than on the previous morning. All her old gaiety of manner seemed to have come back, and she came and snuggled in beside me and told me all about Arthur. I told her how anxious I was about Jonathan, and then she tried to comfort me. Well, she succeeded somewhat, for, though sympathy can't alter facts, it can help to make them more bearable.

13 August.— Another quiet day, and to bed with the key on my wrist as before. Again I awoke in the night, and found Lucy sitting up in bed, still asleep, pointing to the window. I got up quietly, and pulling aside the blind, looked out. It was brilliant moonlight, and the soft effect of the light over the sea and sky— merged together in one great, silent mystery— was beautiful beyond words. Between me and the moonlight flitted a great bat, coming and going in great whirling circles. Once or twice it came quite close, but was, I suppose, frightened at seeing me, and flitted away across the harbour towards the abbey. When I came back from the window Lucy had lain down again, and was sleeping peacefully. She did not stir again all night.

14 August.— On the East Cliff, reading and writing all day. Lucy seems to have become as much in love with the spot as I am, and it is hard to get her away from it when it is time to come home for lunch or tea or dinner. This afternoon she made a funny remark. We were coming home for dinner, and had come to the top of the steps up from the West Pier and stopped to look at the view, as we generally do. The setting sun, low down in the sky, was just dropping behind Kettleness; the red light was thrown over on the East Cliff and the old abbey, and seemed to bathe everything in a beautiful rosy glow. We were silent for a while, and suddenly Lucy murmured as if to herself:—

"His red eyes again! They are just the same." It was such an odd expression, coming apropos of nothing, that it quite startled me. I slewed round a little, so as to see Lucy well without seeming to stare at her, and saw that she was in a half-dreamy state, with an odd look on her face that I could not quite make out; so I said nothing, but followed her eyes. She appeared to be looking over at our own seat, whereon was a dark figure seated alone. I was a little startled myself, for it seemed for an instant as if the stranger had great eyes like burning flames; but a second look dispelled the illusion. The red sunlight was shining on the windows of St. Mary's Church behind our seat, and as the sun dipped there was just sufficient change in the refraction and reflection to make it appear as if the light moved. I called Lucy's attention to the peculiar effect, and she became herself with a start, but she looked sad all the same; it may have been that she was thinking of that terrible night up there. We never refer to it; so I said nothing, and we went home to dinner. Lucy had a headache and went early to bed. I saw her asleep, and went out for a little stroll myself; I walked along the cliffs to the westward, and was full of sweet sadness, for I was thinking of Jonathan. When coming home— it was then bright moonlight, so bright that, though the front of our part of the Crescent was in shadow, everything could be well seen— I threw a glance up at our window, and saw Lucy's head leaning out. I thought that perhaps she was looking out for me, so I opened my handkerchief and waved it. She did not notice or make any movement whatever. Just then, the moonlight crept round an angle of the building, and the light fell on the window. There distinctly was Lucy with her head lying up against the side of the window-sill and her eyes shut. She was fast asleep, and by her, seated on the window-sill, was something that looked like a good-sized bird. I was afraid she might get a chill, so I ran upstairs, but as I came into the room she was moving back to her bed, fast asleep, and breathing heavily; she was holding her hand to her throat, as though to protect it from cold.

I did not wake her, but tucked her up warmly; I have taken care that the door is locked and the window securely fastened.

She looks so sweet as she sleeps; but she is paler than is her wont, and there is a drawn, haggard look under her eyes which I do not like. I fear she is fretting about something. I wish I could find out what it is.

15 August.— Rose later than usual. Lucy was languid and tired, and slept on after we had been called. We had a happy surprise at breakfast. Arthur's father is better, and wants the marriage to come off soon. Lucy is full of quiet joy, and her mother is glad and sorry at once. Later on in the day she told me the cause. She is grieved to lose Lucy as her very own, but she is rejoiced that she is soon to have some one to protect her. Poor dear, sweet lady! She confided to me that she has got her death-warrant. She has not told Lucy, and made me promise secrecy; her doctor told her that within a few months, at most, she must die, for her heart is weakening. At any time, even now, a sudden shock would be almost sure to kill her. Ah, we were wise to keep from her the affair of the dreadful night of Lucy's sleep-walking.

17 August.— No diary for two whole days. I have not had the heart to write. Some sort of shadowy pall seems to be coming over our happiness. No news from Jonathan, and Lucy seems to be growing weaker, whilst her mother's hours are numbering to a close. I do not understand Lucy's fading away as she is doing. She eats well and sleeps well, and enjoys the fresh air; but all the time the roses in her cheeks are fading, and she gets weaker and more languid day by day; at night I hear her gasping as if for air. I keep the key of our door always fastened to my wrist at night, but she gets up and walks about the room, and sits at the open window. Last night I found her leaning out when I woke up, and when I tried to wake her I could not; she was in a faint. When I managed to restore her she was as weak as water, and cried silently between long, painful struggles for breath. When I asked her how she came to be at the window she shook her head and turned away. I trust her feeling ill may not be from that unlucky prick of the safety-pin. I looked at her throat just now as she lay asleep, and the tiny wounds seem not to have healed. They are still open, and, if anything, larger than before, and the edges of them are faintly white. They are like little white dots with red centres. Unless they heal within a day or two, I shall insist on the doctor seeing about them.

Letter, Samuel F. Billington & Son, Solicitors, Whitby, to Messrs. Carter, Paterson & Co., London.

"17 August.

"Dear Sirs,—

"Herewith please receive invoice of goods sent by Great Northern Railway. Same are to be delivered at Carfax, near Purfleet, immediately on receipt at goods station King's Cross. The house is at present empty, but enclosed please find keys, all of which are labelled.

"You will please deposit the boxes, fifty in number, which form the consignment, in the partially ruined building forming part of the house and marked 'A' on rough diagram enclosed. Your agent will easily recognise the locality, as it is the ancient chapel of the mansion. The goods leave by the train at 9:30 to-night, and will be due at King's Cross at 4:30 to-morrow afternoon. As our client wishes the delivery made as soon as possible, we shall be obliged by your having teams ready at King's Cross at the time named and forthwith conveying the goods to destination. In order to obviate any delays possible through any routine requirements as to payment in your departments, we enclose cheque herewith for ten pounds (£10), receipt of which please acknowledge. Should the charge be less than this amount, you can return balance; if greater, we shall at once send cheque for difference on hearing from you. You are to leave the keys on coming away in the main hall of the house, where the proprietor may get them on his entering the house by means of his duplicate key.

"Pray do not take us as exceeding the bounds of business courtesy in pressing you in all ways to use the utmost expedition.

"We are, dear Sirs,

"Faithfully yours,

"Samuel F. Billington & Son."

Letter, Messrs. Carter, Paterson & Co., London, to Messrs. Billington & Son, Whitby.

"21 August.

"Dear Sirs,—

"We beg to acknowledge £10 received and to return cheque £1 17s. 9d, amount of overplus, as shown in receipted account herewith. Goods are delivered in exact accordance with instructions, and keys left in parcel in main hall, as directed.

"We are, dear Sirs,

"Yours respectfully.

"Pro Carter, Paterson & Co."

Mina Murray's Journal.

18 August.— I am happy to-day, and write sitting on the seat in the churchyard. Lucy is ever so much better. Last night she slept well all night, and did not disturb me once. The roses seem coming back already to her cheeks, though she is still sadly pale and wan-looking. If she were in any way anæmic I could understand it, but she is not. She is in gay spirits and full of life and cheerfulness. All the morbid reticence seems to have passed from her, and she has just reminded me, as if I needed any reminding, of that night, and that it was here, on this very seat, I found her asleep. As she told me she tapped playfully with the heel of her boot on the stone slab and said:—

"My poor little feet didn't make much noise then! I daresay poor old Mr. Swales would have told me that it was because I didn't want to wake up Geordie." As she was in such a communicative humour, I asked her if she had dreamed at all that night. Before she answered, that sweet, puckered look came into her forehead, which Arthur— I call him Arthur from her habit— says he loves; and, indeed, I don't wonder that he does. Then she went on in a half-dreaming kind of way, as if trying to recall it to herself:—

"I didn't quite dream; but it all seemed to be real. I only wanted to be here in this spot— I don't know why, for I was afraid of something— I don't know what. I remember, though I suppose I was asleep, passing through the streets and over the bridge. A fish leaped as I went by, and I leaned over to look at it, and I heard a lot of dogs howling— the whole town seemed as if it must be full of dogs all howling at once— as I went up the steps. Then I had a vague memory of something long and dark with red eyes, just as we saw in the sunset, and something very sweet and very bitter all around me at once; and then I seemed sinking into deep green water, and there was a singing in my ears, as I have heard there is to drowning men; and then everything seemed passing away from me; my soul seemed to go out from my body and float about the air. I seem to remember that once the West Lighthouse was right under me, and then there was a sort of agonising feeling, as if I were in an earthquake, and I came back and found you shaking my body. I saw you do it before I felt you."

Then she began to laugh. It seemed a little uncanny to me, and I listened to her breathlessly. I did not quite like it, and thought it better not to keep her mind on the subject, so we drifted on to other subjects, and Lucy was like her old self again. When we got home the fresh breeze had braced her up, and her pale cheeks were really more rosy. Her mother rejoiced when she saw her, and we all spent a very happy evening together.

19 August.— Joy, joy, joy! although not all joy. At last, news of Jonathan. The dear fellow has been ill; that is why he did not write. I am not afraid to think it or say it, now that I know. Mr. Hawkins sent me on the letter, and wrote himself, oh, so kindly. I am to leave in the morning and go over to Jonathan, and to help to nurse him if necessary, and to bring him home. Mr. Hawkins says it would not be a bad thing if we were to be married out there. I have cried over the good Sister's letter till I can feel it wet against my bosom, where it lies. It is of Jonathan, and must be next my heart, for he is in my heart. My journey is all mapped out, and my luggage ready. I am only taking one change of dress; Lucy will bring my trunk to London and keep it till I send for it, for it may be that ... I must write no more; I must keep it to say to Jonathan, my husband. The letter that he has seen and touched must comfort me till we meet.

Letter, Sister Agatha, Hospital of St. Joseph and Ste. Mary, Buda-Pesth, to Miss Wilhelmina Murray.

"12 August.

"Dear Madam,—

"I write by desire of Mr. Jonathan Harker, who is himself not strong enough to write, though progressing well, thanks to God and St. Joseph and Ste. Mary. He has been under our care for nearly six weeks, suffering from a violent brain fever. He wishes me to convey his love, and to say that by this post I write for him to Mr. Peter Hawkins, Exeter, to say, with his dutiful respects, that he is sorry for his delay, and that all of his work is completed. He will require some few weeks' rest in our sanatorium in the hills, but will then return. He wishes me to say that he has not sufficient money with him, and that he would like to pay for his staying here, so that others who need shall not be wanting for help.

"Believe me,

"Yours, with sympathy and all blessings,

"Sister Agatha.

"P. S.— My patient being asleep, I open this to let you know something more. He has told me all about you, and that you are shortly to be his wife. All blessings to you both! He has had some fearful shock— so says our doctor— and in his delirium his ravings have been dreadful; of wolves and poison and blood; of ghosts and demons; and I fear to say of what. Be careful with him always that there may be nothing to excite him of this kind for a long time to come; the traces of such an illness as his do not lightly die away. We should have written long ago, but we knew nothing of his friends, and there was on him nothing that any one could understand. He came in the train from Klausenburg, and the guard was told by the station-master there that he rushed into the station shouting for a ticket for home. Seeing from his violent demeanour that he was English, they gave him a ticket for the furthest station on the way thither that the train reached.

"Be assured that he is well cared for. He has won all hearts by his sweetness and gentleness. He is truly getting on well, and I have no doubt will in a few weeks be all himself. But be careful of him for safety's sake. There are, I pray God and St. Joseph and Ste. Mary, many, many, happy years for you both."

Dr. Seward's Diary.

19 August.— Strange and sudden change in Renfield last night. About eight o'clock he began to get excited and sniff about as a dog does when setting. The attendant was struck by his manner, and knowing my interest in him, encouraged him to talk. He is usually respectful to the attendant and at times servile; but to-night, the man tells me, he was quite haughty. Would not condescend to talk with him at all. All he would say was:—

"I don't want to talk to you: you don't count now; the Master is at hand."

The attendant thinks it is some sudden form of religious mania which has seized him. If so, we must look out for squalls, for a strong man with homicidal and religious mania at once might be dangerous. The combination is a dreadful one. At nine o'clock I visited him myself. His attitude to me was the same as that to the attendant; in his sublime self-feeling the difference between myself and attendant seemed to him as nothing. It looks like religious mania, and he will soon think that he himself is God. These infinitesimal distinctions between man and man are too paltry for an Omnipotent Being. How these madmen give themselves away! The real God taketh heed lest a sparrow fall; but the God created from human vanity sees no difference between an eagle and a sparrow. Oh, if men only knew!

For half an hour or more Renfield kept getting excited in greater and greater degree. I did not pretend to be watching him, but I kept strict observation all the same. All at once that shifty look came into his eyes which we always see when a madman has seized an idea, and with it the shifty movement of the head and back which asylum attendants come to know so well. He became quite quiet, and went and sat on the edge of his bed resignedly, and looked into space with lack-lustre eyes. I thought I would find out if his apathy were real or only assumed, and tried to lead him to talk of his pets, a theme which had never failed to excite his attention. At first he made no reply, but at length said testily:—

"Bother them all! I don't care a pin about them."

"What?" I said. "You don't mean to tell me you don't care about spiders?" (Spiders at present are his hobby and the note-book is filling up with columns of small figures.) To this he answered enigmatically:—

"The bride-maidens rejoice the eyes that wait the coming of the bride; but when the bride draweth nigh, then the maidens shine not to the eyes that are filled."

He would not explain himself, but remained obstinately seated on his bed all the time I remained with him.

I am weary to-night and low in spirits. I cannot but think of Lucy, and how different things might have been. If I don't sleep at once, chloral, the modern Morpheus— $C_2HCl_3O$. $H_2O$! I must be careful not to let it grow into a habit. No, I shall take none to-night! I have thought of Lucy, and I shall not dishonour her by mixing the two. If need be, to-night shall be sleepless....

Later.— Glad I made the resolution; gladder that I kept to it. I had lain tossing about, and had heard the clock strike only twice, when the night-watchman came to me, sent up from the ward, to say that Renfield had escaped. I threw on my clothes and ran down at once; my patient is too dangerous a person to be roaming about. Those ideas of his might work out dangerously with strangers. The attendant was waiting for me. He said he had seen him not ten minutes before, seemingly asleep in his bed, when he had looked through the observation-trap in the door. His attention was called by the sound of the window being wrenched out. He ran back and saw his feet disappear through the window, and had at once sent up for me. He was only in his night-gear, and cannot be far off. The attendant thought it would be more useful to watch where he should go than to follow him, as he might lose sight of him whilst getting out of the building by the door. He is a bulky man, and couldn't get through the window. I am thin, so, with his aid, I got out, but feet foremost, and, as we were only a few feet above ground, landed unhurt. The attendant told me the patient had gone to the left, and had taken a straight line, so I ran as quickly as I could. As I got through the belt of trees I saw a white figure scale the high wall which separates our grounds from those of the deserted house.

I ran back at once, told the watchman to get three or four men immediately and follow me into the grounds of Carfax, in case our friend might be dangerous. I got a ladder myself, and crossing the wall, dropped down on the other side. I could see Renfield's figure just disappearing behind the angle of the house, so I ran after him. On the far side of the house I found him pressed close against the old ironbound oak door of the chapel. He was talking, apparently to some one, but I was afraid to go near enough to hear what he was saying, lest I might frighten him, and he should run off. Chasing an errant swarm of bees is nothing to following a naked lunatic, when the fit of escaping is upon him! After a few minutes, however, I could see that he did not take note of anything around him, and so ventured to draw nearer to him— the more so as my men had now crossed the wall and were closing him in. I heard him say:—

"I am here to do Your bidding, Master. I am Your slave, and You will reward me, for I shall be faithful. I have worshipped You long and afar off. Now that You are near, I await Your commands, and You will not pass me by, will You, dear Master, in Your distribution of good things?"

He is a selfish old beggar anyhow. He thinks of the loaves and fishes even when he believes he is in a Real Presence. His manias make a startling combination. When we closed in on him he fought like a tiger. He is immensely strong, for he was more like a wild beast than a man. I never saw a lunatic in such a paroxysm of rage before; and I hope I shall not again. It is a mercy that we have found out his strength and his danger in good time. With strength and determination like his, he might have done wild work before he was caged. He is safe now at any rate. Jack Sheppard himself couldn't get free from the strait-waistcoat that keeps him restrained, and he's chained to the wall in the padded room. His cries are at times awful, but the silences that follow are more deadly still, for he means murder in every turn and movement.

Just now he spoke coherent words for the first time:—

"I shall be patient, Master. It is coming— coming— coming!"

So I took the hint, and came too. I was too excited to sleep, but this diary has quieted me, and I feel I shall get some sleep to-night.

## CHAPTER IX
## Letter, Mina Harker to Lucy Westenra.

Buda-Pesth, 24 August.

"My dearest Lucy,—

"I know you will be anxious to hear all that has happened since we parted at the railway station at Whitby. Well, my dear, I got to Hull all right, and caught the boat to Hamburg, and then the train on here. I feel that I can hardly recall anything of the journey, except that I knew I was coming to Jonathan, and, that as I should have to do some nursing, I had better get all the sleep I could.... I found my dear one, oh, so thin and pale and weak-looking. All the resolution has gone out of his dear eyes, and that quiet dignity which I told you was in his face has vanished. He is only a wreck of himself, and he does not remember anything that has happened to him for a long time past. At least, he wants me to believe so, and I shall never ask. He has had some terrible shock, and I fear it might tax his poor brain if he were to try to recall it. Sister Agatha, who is a good creature and a born nurse, tells me that he raved of dreadful things whilst he was off his head. I wanted her to tell me what they were; but she would only cross herself, and say she would never tell; that the ravings of the sick were the secrets of God, and that if a nurse through her vocation should hear them, she should respect her trust. She is a sweet, good soul, and the next day, when she saw I was troubled, she opened up the subject again, and after saying that she could never mention what my poor dear raved about, added: 'I can tell you this much, my dear: that it was not about anything which he has done wrong himself; and you, as his wife to be, have no cause to be concerned. He has not forgotten you or what he owes to you. His fear was of great and terrible things, which no mortal can treat of.' I do believe the dear soul thought I might be jealous lest my poor dear should have fallen in love with any other girl. The idea of my being jealous about Jonathan! And yet, my dear, let me whisper, I felt a thrill of joy through me when I knew that no other woman was a cause of trouble. I am now sitting by his bedside, where I can see his face while he sleeps. He is waking!...

"When he woke he asked me for his coat, as he wanted to get something from the pocket; I asked Sister Agatha, and she brought all his things. I saw that amongst them was his note-book, and was going to ask him to let me look at it— for I knew then that I might find some clue to his trouble— but I suppose he must have seen my wish in my eyes, for he sent me over to the window, saying he wanted to be quite alone for a moment. Then he called me back, and when I came he had his hand over the note-book, and he said to me very solemnly:—

" 'Wilhelmina'— I knew then that he was in deadly earnest, for he has never called me by that name since he asked me to marry him— 'you know, dear, my ideas of the trust between husband and wife: there should be no secret, no concealment. I have had a great shock, and when I try to think of what it is I feel my head spin round, and I do not know if it was all real or the dreaming of a madman. You know I have had brain fever, and that is to be mad. The secret is here, and I do not want to know it. I want to take up my life here, with our marriage.' For, my dear, we had decided to be married as soon as the formalities are complete. 'Are you willing, Wilhelmina, to share my ignorance? Here is the book. Take it and keep it, read it if you will, but never let me know; unless, indeed, some solemn duty should come upon me to go back to the bitter hours, asleep or awake, sane or mad, recorded here.' He fell back exhausted, and I put the book under his pillow, and kissed him. I have asked Sister Agatha to beg the Superior to let our wedding be this afternoon, and am waiting her reply....

"She has come and told me that the chaplain of the English mission church has been sent for. We are to be married in an hour, or as soon after as Jonathan awakes....

"Lucy, the time has come and gone. I feel very solemn, but very, very happy. Jonathan woke a little after the hour, and all was ready, and he sat up in bed, propped up with pillows. He answered his 'I will' firmly and strongly. I could hardly speak; my heart was so full that even those words seemed to choke me. The dear sisters were so kind. Please God, I shall never, never forget them, nor the grave and sweet responsibilities I have taken upon me. I must tell you of my wedding present. When the chaplain and the sisters had left me alone with my husband— oh, Lucy, it is the first time I have written the words 'my husband'— left me alone with my husband, I took the book from under his pillow, and wrapped it up in white paper, and tied it with a little bit of pale blue ribbon which was round my neck, and sealed it over the knot with sealing-wax, and for my seal I used my wedding ring. Then I kissed it and showed it to my husband, and told him that I would keep it so, and then it would be an outward and visible sign for us all our lives that we trusted each other; that I would never open it unless it were for his own dear sake or for the sake of some stern duty. Then he took my hand in his, and oh, Lucy, it was the first time he took his wife's hand, and said that it was the dearest thing in all the wide world, and that he would go through all the past again to win it, if need be. The poor dear meant to have said a part of the past, but he cannot think of time yet, and I shall not wonder if at first he mixes up not only the month, but the year.

"Well, my dear, what could I say? I could only tell him that I was the happiest woman in all the wide world, and that I had nothing to give him except myself, my life, and my trust, and that with these went my love and duty for all the days of my life. And, my dear, when he kissed me, and drew me to him with his poor weak hands, it was like a very solemn pledge between us....

"Lucy dear, do you know why I tell you all this? It is not only because it is all sweet to me, but because you have been, and are, very dear to me. It was my privilege to be your friend and guide when you came from the schoolroom to prepare for the world of life. I want you to see now, and with the eyes of a very happy wife, whither duty has led me; so that in your own married life you too may be all happy as I am. My dear, please Almighty God, your life may be all it promises: a long day of sunshine, with no harsh wind, no forgetting duty, no distrust. I must not wish you no pain, for that can never be; but I do hope you will be always as happy as I am now. Good-bye, my dear. I shall post this at once, and, perhaps, write you very soon again. I must stop, for Jonathan is waking— I must attend to my husband!

"Your ever-loving

"Mina Harker."

Letter, Lucy Westenra to Mina Harker.

"Whitby, 30 August.

"My dearest Mina,—

"Oceans of love and millions of kisses, and may you soon be in your own home with your husband. I wish you could be coming home soon enough to stay with us here. The strong air would soon restore Jonathan; it has quite restored me. I have an appetite like a cormorant, am full of life, and sleep well. You will be glad to know that I have quite given up walking in my sleep. I think I have not stirred out of my bed for a week, that is when I once got into it at night. Arthur says I am getting fat. By the way, I forgot to tell you that Arthur is here. We have such walks and drives, and rides, and rowing, and tennis, and fishing together; and I love him more than ever. He tells me that he loves me more, but I doubt that, for at first he told me that he couldn't love me more than he did then. But this is nonsense. There he is, calling to me. So no more just at present from your loving

"Lucy.

"P. S.— Mother sends her love. She seems better, poor dear.

"P. P. S.— We are to be married on 28 September."

Dr. Seward's Diary.

20 August.— The case of Renfield grows even more interesting. He has now so far quieted that there are spells of cessation from his passion. For the first week after his attack he was perpetually violent. Then one night, just as the moon rose, he grew quiet, and kept murmuring to himself: "Now I can wait; now I can wait." The attendant came to tell me, so I ran down at once to have a look at him. He was still in the strait-waistcoat and in the padded room, but the suffused look had gone from his face, and his eyes had something of their old pleading— I might almost say, "cringing"— softness. I was satisfied with his present condition, and directed him to be relieved. The attendants hesitated, but finally carried out my wishes without protest. It was a strange thing that the patient had humour enough to see their distrust, for, coming close to me, he said in a whisper, all the while looking furtively at them:—

"They think I could hurt you! Fancy me hurting you! The fools!"

It was soothing, somehow, to the feelings to find myself dissociated even in the mind of this poor madman from the others; but all the same I do not follow his thought. Am I to take it that I have anything in common with him, so that we are, as it were, to stand together; or has he to gain from me some good so stupendous that my well-being is needful to him? I must find out later on. To-night he will not speak. Even the offer of a kitten or even a full-grown cat will not tempt him. He will only say: "I don't take any stock in cats. I have more to think of now, and I can wait; I can wait."

After a while I left him. The attendant tells me that he was quiet until just before dawn, and that then he began to get uneasy, and at length violent, until at last he fell into a paroxysm which exhausted him so that he swooned into a sort of coma.

... Three nights has the same thing happened— violent all day then quiet from moonrise to sunrise. I wish I could get some clue to the cause. It would almost seem as if there was some influence which came and went. Happy thought! We shall to-night play sane wits against mad ones. He escaped before without our help; to-night he shall escape with it. We shall give him a chance, and have the men ready to follow in case they are required....

23 August.— "The unexpected always happens." How well Disraeli knew life. Our bird when he found the cage open would not fly, so all our subtle arrangements were for nought. At any rate, we have proved one thing; that the spells of quietness last a reasonable time. We shall in future be able to ease his bonds for a few hours each day. I have given orders to the night attendant merely to shut him in the padded room, when once he is quiet, until an hour before sunrise. The poor soul's body will enjoy the relief even if his mind cannot appreciate it. Hark! The unexpected again! I am called; the patient has once more escaped.

Later.— Another night adventure. Renfield artfully waited until the attendant was entering the room to inspect. Then he dashed out past him and flew down the passage. I sent word for the attendants to follow. Again he went into the grounds of the deserted house, and we found him in the same place, pressed against the old chapel door. When he saw me he became furious, and had not the attendants seized him in time, he would have tried to kill me. As we were holding him a strange thing happened. He suddenly redoubled his efforts, and then as suddenly grew calm. I looked round instinctively, but could see nothing. Then I caught the patient's eye and followed it, but could trace nothing as it looked into the moonlit sky except a big bat, which was flapping its silent and ghostly way to the west. Bats usually wheel and flit about, but this one seemed to go straight on, as if it knew where it was bound for or had some intention of its own. The patient grew calmer every instant, and presently said:—

"You needn't tie me; I shall go quietly!" Without trouble we came back to the house. I feel there is something ominous in his calm, and shall not forget this night....

Lucy Westenra's Diary

Hillingham, 24 August.— I must imitate Mina, and keep writing things down. Then we can have long talks when we do meet. I wonder when it will be. I wish she were with me again, for I feel so unhappy. Last night I seemed to be dreaming again just as I was at Whitby. Perhaps it is the change of air, or getting home again. It is all dark and horrid to me, for I can remember nothing; but I am full of vague fear, and I feel so weak and worn out. When Arthur came to lunch he looked quite grieved when he saw me, and I hadn't the spirit to try to be cheerful. I wonder if I could sleep in mother's room to-night. I shall make an excuse and try.

25 August.— Another bad night. Mother did not seem to take to my proposal. She seems not too well herself, and doubtless she fears to worry me. I tried to keep awake, and succeeded for a while; but when the clock struck twelve it waked me from a doze, so I must have been falling asleep. There was a sort of scratching or flapping at the window, but I did not mind it, and as I remember no more, I suppose I must then have fallen asleep. More bad dreams. I wish I could remember them. This morning I am horribly weak. My face is ghastly pale, and my throat pains me. It must be something wrong with my lungs, for I don't seem ever to get air enough. I shall try to cheer up when Arthur comes, or else I know he will be miserable to see me so.

Letter, Arthur Holmwood to Dr. Seward.

"Albemarle Hotel, 31 August.

"My dear Jack,—

"I want you to do me a favour. Lucy is ill; that is, she has no special disease, but she looks awful, and is getting worse every day. I have asked her if there is any cause; I do not dare to ask her mother, for to disturb the poor lady's mind about her daughter in her present state of health would be fatal. Mrs. Westenra has confided to me that her doom is spoken— disease of the heart— though poor Lucy does not know it yet. I am sure that there is something preying on my dear girl's mind. I am almost distracted when I think of her; to look at her gives me a pang. I told her I should ask you to see her, and though she demurred at first— I know why, old fellow— she finally consented. It will be a painful task for you, I know, old friend, but it is for her sake, and I must not hesitate to ask, or you to act. You are to come to lunch at Hillingham to-morrow, two o'clock, so as not to arouse any suspicion in Mrs. Westenra, and after lunch Lucy will take an opportunity of being alone with you. I shall come in for tea, and we can go away together; I am filled with anxiety, and want to consult with you alone as soon as I can after you have seen her. Do not fail!

"Arthur."

Telegram, Arthur Holmwood to Seward.

"1 September.

"Am summoned to see my father, who is worse. Am writing. Write me fully by to-night's post to Ring. Wire me if necessary."

Letter from Dr. Seward to Arthur Holmwood.

"2 September.

"My dear old fellow,—

"With regard to Miss Westenra's health I hasten to let you know at once that in my opinion there is not any functional disturbance or any malady that I know of. At the same time, I am not by any means satisfied with her appearance; she is woefully different from what she was when I saw her last. Of course you must bear in mind that I did not have full opportunity of examination such as I should wish; our very friendship makes a little difficulty which not even medical science or custom can bridge over. I had better tell you exactly what happened, leaving you to draw, in a measure, your own conclusions. I shall then say what I have done and propose doing.

"I found Miss Westenra in seemingly gay spirits. Her mother was present, and in a few seconds I made up my mind that she was trying all she knew to mislead her mother and prevent her from being anxious. I have no doubt she guesses, if she does not know, what need of caution there is. We lunched alone, and as we all exerted ourselves to be cheerful, we got, as some kind of reward for our labours, some real cheerfulness amongst us. Then Mrs. Westenra went to lie down, and Lucy was left with me. We went into her boudoir, and till we got there her gaiety remained, for the servants were coming and going. As soon as the door was closed, however, the mask fell from her face, and she sank down into a chair with a great sigh, and hid her eyes with her hand. When I saw that her high spirits had failed, I at once took advantage of her reaction to make a diagnosis. She said to me very sweetly:—

" 'I cannot tell you how I loathe talking about myself.' I reminded her that a doctor's confidence was sacred, but that you were grievously anxious about her. She caught on to my meaning at once, and settled that matter in a word. 'Tell Arthur everything you choose. I do not care for myself, but all for him!' So I am quite free.

"I could easily see that she is somewhat bloodless, but I could not see the usual anæmic signs, and by a chance I was actually able to test the quality of her blood, for in opening a window which was stiff a cord gave way, and she cut her hand slightly with broken glass. It was a slight matter in itself, but it gave me an evident chance, and I secured a few drops of the blood and have analysed them. The qualitative analysis gives a quite normal condition, and shows, I should infer, in itself a vigorous state of health. In other physical matters I was quite satisfied that there is no need for anxiety; but as there must be a cause somewhere, I have come to the conclusion that it must be something mental. She complains of difficulty in breathing satisfactorily at times, and of heavy, lethargic sleep, with dreams that frighten her, but regarding which she can remember nothing. She says that as a child she used to walk in her sleep, and that when in Whitby the habit came back, and that once she walked out in the night and went to East Cliff, where Miss Murray found her; but she assures me that of late the habit has not returned. I am in doubt, and so have done the best thing I know of; I have written to my old friend and master, Professor Van Helsing, of Amsterdam, who knows as much about obscure diseases as any one in the world. I have asked him to come over, and as you told me that all things were to be at your charge, I have mentioned to him who you are and your relations to Miss Westenra. This, my dear fellow, is in obedience to your wishes, for I am only too proud and happy to do anything I can for her. Van Helsing would, I know, do anything for me for a personal reason, so, no matter on what ground he comes, we must accept his wishes. He is a seemingly arbitrary man, but this is because he knows what he is talking about better than any one else. He is a philosopher and a metaphysician, and one of the most advanced scientists of his day; and he has, I believe, an absolutely open mind. This, with an iron nerve, a temper of the ice-brook, an indomitable resolution, self-command, and toleration exalted from virtues to blessings, and the kindliest and truest heart that beats— these form his equipment for the noble work that he is doing for mankind— work both in theory and practice, for his views are as wide as his all-embracing sympathy. I tell you these facts that you may know why I have such confidence in him. I have asked him to come at once. I shall see Miss Westenra to-morrow again. She is to meet me at the Stores, so that I may not alarm her mother by too early a repetition of my call.
"Yours always,
"John Seward."

Letter, Abraham Van Helsing, M. D., D. Ph., D. Lit., etc., etc., to Dr. Seward.

"2 September.

"My good Friend,—

"When I have received your letter I am already coming to you. By good fortune I can leave just at once, without wrong to any of those who have trusted me. Were fortune other, then it were bad for those who have trusted, for I come to my friend when he call me to aid those he holds dear. Tell your friend that when that time you suck from my wound so swiftly the poison of the gangrene from that knife that our other friend, too nervous, let slip, you did more for him when he wants my aids and you call for them than all his great fortune could do. But it is pleasure added to do for him, your friend; it is to you that I come. Have then rooms for me at the Great Eastern Hotel, so that I may be near to hand, and please it so arrange that we may see the young lady not too late on to-morrow, for it is likely that I may have to return here that night. But if need be I shall come again in three days, and stay longer if it must. Till then good-bye, my friend John.

"Van Helsing."

Letter, Dr. Seward to Hon. Arthur Holmwood.

"3 September.

"My dear Art,—

"Van Helsing has come and gone. He came on with me to Hillingham, and found that, by Lucy's discretion, her mother was lunching out, so that we were alone with her. Van Helsing made a very careful examination of the patient. He is to report to me, and I shall advise you, for of course I was not present all the time. He is, I fear, much concerned, but says he must think. When I told him of our friendship and how you trust to me in the matter, he said: 'You must tell him all you think. Tell him what I think, if you can guess it, if you will. Nay, I am not jesting. This is no jest, but life and death, perhaps more.' I asked what he meant by that, for he was very serious. This was when we had come back to town, and he was having a cup of tea before starting on his return to Amsterdam. He would not give me any further clue. You must not be angry with me, Art, because his very reticence means that all his brains are working for her good. He will speak plainly enough when the time comes, be sure. So I told him I would simply write an account of our visit, just as if I were doing a descriptive special article for The Daily Telegraph. He seemed not to notice, but remarked that the smuts in London were not quite so bad as they used to be when he was a student here. I am to get his report to-morrow if he can possibly make it. In any case I am to have a letter.

"Well, as to the visit. Lucy was more cheerful than on the day I first saw her, and certainly looked better. She had lost something of the ghastly look that so upset you, and her breathing was normal. She was very sweet to the professor (as she always is), and tried to make him feel at ease; though I could see that the poor girl was making a hard struggle for it. I believe Van Helsing saw it, too, for I saw the quick look under his bushy brows that I knew of old. Then he began to chat of all things except ourselves and diseases and with such an infinite geniality that I could see poor Lucy's pretense of animation merge into reality. Then, without any seeming change, he brought the conversation gently round to his visit, and suavely said:—

" 'My dear young miss, I have the so great pleasure because you are so much beloved. That is much, my dear, ever were there that which I do not see. They told me you were down in the spirit, and that you were of a ghastly pale. To them I say: "Pouf!" ' And he snapped his fingers at me and went on: 'But you and I shall show them how wrong they are. How can he'— and he pointed at me with the same look and gesture as that with which once he pointed me out to his class, on, or rather after, a particular occasion which he never fails to remind me of— 'know anything of a young ladies? He has his madams to play with, and to bring them back to happiness, and to those that love them. It is much to do, and, oh, but there are rewards, in that we can bestow such happiness. But the young ladies! He has no wife nor daughter, and the young do not tell themselves to the young, but to the old, like me, who have known so many sorrows and the causes of them. So, my dear, we will send him away to smoke the cigarette in the garden, whiles you and I have little talk all to ourselves.' I took the hint, and strolled about, and presently the professor came to the window and called me in. He looked grave, but said: 'I have made careful examination, but there is no functional cause. With you I agree that there has been much blood lost; it has been, but is not. But the conditions of her are in no way anæmic. I have asked her to send me her maid, that I may ask just one or two question, that so I may not chance to miss nothing. I know well what she will say. And yet there is cause; there is always cause for everything. I must go back home and think. You must send to me the telegram every day; and if there be cause I shall come again. The disease— for not to be all well is a disease— interest me, and the sweet young dear, she interest me too. She charm me, and for her, if not for you or disease, I come.'

"As I tell you, he would not say a word more, even when we were alone. And so now, Art, you know all I know. I shall keep stern watch. I trust your poor father is rallying. It must be a terrible thing to you, my dear old fellow, to be placed in such a position between two people who are both so dear to you. I know your idea of duty to your father, and you are right to stick to it; but, if need be, I shall send you word to come at once to Lucy; so do not be over-anxious unless you hear from me."

Dr. Seward's Diary.

4 September.— Zoöphagous patient still keeps up our interest in him. He had only one outburst and that was yesterday at an unusual time. Just before the stroke of noon he began to grow restless. The attendant knew the symptoms, and at once summoned aid. Fortunately the men came at a run, and were just in time, for at the stroke of noon he became so violent that it took all their strength to hold him. In about five minutes, however, he began to get more and more quiet, and finally sank into a sort of melancholy, in which state he has remained up to now. The attendant tells me that his screams whilst in the paroxysm were really appalling; I found my hands full when I got in, attending to some of the other patients who were frightened by him. Indeed, I can quite understand the effect, for the sounds disturbed even me, though I was some distance away. It is now after the dinner-hour of the asylum, and as yet my patient sits in a corner brooding, with a dull, sullen, woe-begone look in his face, which seems rather to indicate than to show something directly. I cannot quite understand it.

Later.— Another change in my patient. At five o'clock I looked in on him, and found him seemingly as happy and contented as he used to be. He was catching flies and eating them, and was keeping note of his capture by making nail-marks on the edge of the door between the ridges of padding. When he saw me, he came over and apologised for his bad conduct, and asked me in a very humble, cringing way to be led back to his own room and to have his note-book again. I thought it well to humour him: so he is back in his room with the window open. He has the sugar of his tea spread out on the window-sill, and is reaping quite a harvest of flies. He is not now eating them, but putting them into a box, as of old, and is already examining the corners of his room to find a spider. I tried to get him to talk about the past few days, for any clue to his thoughts would be of immense help to me; but he would not rise. For a moment or two he looked very sad, and said in a sort of far-away voice, as though saying it rather to himself than to me:—
"All over! all over! He has deserted me. No hope for me now unless I do it for myself!" Then suddenly turning to me in a resolute way, he said: "Doctor, won't you be very good to me and let me have a little more sugar? I think it would be good for me."
"And the flies?" I said.
"Yes! The flies like it, too, and I like the flies; therefore I like it." And there are people who know so little as to think that madmen do not argue. I procured him a double supply, and left him as happy a man as, I suppose, any in the world. I wish I could fathom his mind.

Midnight.— Another change in him. I had been to see Miss Westenra, whom I found much better, and had just returned, and was standing at our own gate looking at the sunset, when once more I heard him yelling. As his room is on this side of the house, I could hear it better than in the morning. It was a shock to me to turn from the wonderful smoky beauty of a sunset over London, with its lurid lights and inky shadows and all the marvellous tints that come on foul clouds even as on foul water, and to realise all the grim sternness of my own cold stone building, with its wealth of breathing misery, and my own desolate heart to endure it all. I reached him just as the sun was going down, and from his window saw the red disc sink. As it sank he became less and less frenzied; and just as it dipped he slid from the hands that held him, an inert mass, on the floor. It is wonderful, however, what intellectual recuperative power lunatics have, for within a few minutes he stood up quite calmly and looked around him. I signalled to the attendants not to hold him, for I was anxious to see what he would do. He went straight over to the window and brushed out the crumbs of sugar; then he took his fly-box, and emptied it outside, and threw away the box; then he shut the window, and crossing over, sat down on his bed. All this surprised me, so I asked him: "Are you not going to keep flies any more?"

"No," said he; "I am sick of all that rubbish!" He certainly is a wonderfully interesting study. I wish I could get some glimpse of his mind or of the cause of his sudden passion. Stop; there may be a clue after all, if we can find why to-day his paroxysms came on at high noon and at sunset. Can it be that there is a malign influence of the sun at periods which affects certain natures— as at times the moon does others? We shall see.

Telegram, Seward, London, to Van Helsing, Amsterdam.

"4 September.— Patient still better to-day."

Telegram, Seward, London, to Van Helsing, Amsterdam.

"5 September.— Patient greatly improved. Good appetite; sleeps naturally; good spirits; colour coming back."

Telegram, Seward, London, to Van Helsing, Amsterdam.

"6 September.— Terrible change for the worse. Come at once; do not lose an hour. I hold over telegram to Holmwood till have seen you."

## CHAPTER X
## Letter, Dr. Seward to Hon. Arthur Holmwood.

6 September.
"My dear Art,—

"My news to-day is not so good. Lucy this morning had gone back a bit. There is, however, one good thing which has arisen from it; Mrs. Westenra was naturally anxious concerning Lucy, and has consulted me professionally about her. I took advantage of the opportunity, and told her that my old master, Van Helsing, the great specialist, was coming to stay with me, and that I would put her in his charge conjointly with myself; so now we can come and go without alarming her unduly, for a shock to her would mean sudden death, and this, in Lucy's weak condition, might be disastrous to her. We are hedged in with difficulties, all of us, my poor old fellow; but, please God, we shall come through them all right. If any need I shall write, so that, if you do not hear from me, take it for granted that I am simply waiting for news. In haste

Yours ever,

"John Seward."

Dr. Seward's Diary.

7 September.— The first thing Van Helsing said to me when we met at Liverpool Street was:—

"Have you said anything to our young friend the lover of her?"

"No," I said. "I waited till I had seen you, as I said in my telegram. I wrote him a letter simply telling him that you were coming, as Miss Westenra was not so well, and that I should let him know if need be."

"Right, my friend," he said, "quite right! Better he not know as yet; perhaps he shall never know. I pray so; but if it be needed, then he shall know all. And, my good friend John, let me caution you. You deal with the madmen. All men are mad in some way or the other; and inasmuch as you deal discreetly with your madmen, so deal with God's madmen, too— the rest of the world. You tell not your madmen what you do nor why you do it; you tell them not what you think. So you shall keep knowledge in its place, where it may rest— where it may gather its kind around it and breed. You and I shall keep as yet what we know here, and here." He touched me on the heart and on the forehead, and then touched himself the same way. "I have for myself thoughts at the present. Later I shall unfold to you."

"Why not now?" I asked. "It may do some good; we may arrive at some decision." He stopped and looked at me, and said:—

"My friend John, when the corn is grown, even before it has ripened—while the milk of its mother-earth is in him, and the sunshine has not yet begun to paint him with his gold, the husbandman he pull the ear and rub him between his rough hands, and blow away the green chaff, and say to you: 'Look! he's good corn; he will make good crop when the time comes.' " I did not see the application, and told him so. For reply he reached over and took my ear in his hand and pulled it playfully, as he used long ago to do at lectures, and said: "The good husbandman tell you so then because he knows, but not till then. But you do not find the good husbandman dig up his planted corn to see if he grow; that is for the children who play at husbandry, and not for those who take it as of the work of their life. See you now, friend John? I have sown my corn, and Nature has her work to do in making it sprout; if he sprout at all, there's some promise; and I wait till the ear begins to swell." He broke off, for he evidently saw that I understood. Then he went on, and very gravely:—

"You were always a careful student, and your case-book was ever more full than the rest. You were only student then; now you are master, and I trust that good habit have not fail. Remember, my friend, that knowledge is stronger than memory, and we should not trust the weaker. Even if you have not kept the good practise, let me tell you that this case of our dear miss is one that may be— mind, I say may be— of such interest to us and others that all the rest may not make him kick the beam, as your peoples say. Take then good note of it. Nothing is too small. I counsel you, put down in record even your doubts and surmises. Hereafter it may be of interest to you to see how true you guess. We learn from failure, not from success!"

When I described Lucy's symptoms— the same as before, but infinitely more marked— he looked very grave, but said nothing. He took with him a bag in which were many instruments and drugs, "the ghastly paraphernalia of our beneficial trade," as he once called, in one of his lectures, the equipment of a professor of the healing craft. When we were shown in, Mrs. Westenra met us. She was alarmed, but not nearly so much as I expected to find her. Nature in one of her beneficent moods has ordained that even death has some antidote to its own terrors. Here, in a case where any shock may prove fatal, matters are so ordered that, from some cause or other, the things not personal— even the terrible change in her daughter to whom she is so attached- do not seem to reach her. It is something like the way Dame Nature gathers round a foreign body an envelope of some insensitive tissue which can protect from evil that which it would otherwise harm by contact. If this be an ordered selfishness, then we should pause before we condemn any one for the vice of egoism, for there may be deeper root for its causes than we have knowledge of.

I used my knowledge of this phase of spiritual pathology, and laid down a rule that she should not be present with Lucy or think of her illness more than was absolutely required. She assented readily, so readily that I saw again the hand of Nature fighting for life. Van Helsing and I were shown up to Lucy's room. If I was shocked when I saw her yesterday, I was horrified when I saw her to-day. She was ghastly, chalkily pale; the red seemed to have gone even from her lips and gums, and the bones of her face stood out prominently; her breathing was painful to see or hear. Van Helsing's face grew set as marble, and his eyebrows converged till they almost touched over his nose. Lucy lay motionless, and did not seem to have strength to speak, so for a while we were all silent. Then Van Helsing beckoned to me and we went gently out of the room. The instant we had closed the door he stepped quickly along the passage to the next door, which was open. Then he pulled me quickly in with him and closed the door. "My God!" he said; "this is dreadful. There is no time to be lost. She will die for sheer want of blood to keep the heart's action as it should be. There must be transfusion of blood at once. Is it you or me?"

"I am younger and stronger, Professor. It must be me."

"Then get ready at once. I will bring up my bag. I am prepared."

I went downstairs with him, and as we were going there was a knock at the hall-door. When we reached the hall the maid had just opened the door, and Arthur was stepping quickly in. He rushed up to me, saying in an eager whisper:—

"Jack, I was so anxious. I read between the lines of your letter, and have been in an agony. The dad was better, so I ran down here to see for myself. Is not that gentleman Dr. Van Helsing? I am so thankful to you, sir, for coming." When first the Professor's eye had lit upon him he had been angry at his interruption at such a time; but now, as he took in his stalwart proportions and recognised the strong young manhood which seemed to emanate from him, his eyes gleamed. Without a pause he said to him gravely as he held out his hand:—

"Sir, you have come in time. You are the lover of our dear miss. She is bad, very, very bad. Nay, my child, do not go like that." For he suddenly grew pale and sat down in a chair almost fainting. "You are to help her. You can do more than any that live, and your courage is your best help."

"What can I do?" asked Arthur hoarsely. "Tell me, and I shall do it. My life is hers, and I would give the last drop of blood in my body for her." The Professor has a strongly humorous side, and I could from old knowledge detect a trace of its origin in his answer:—

"My young sir, I do not ask so much as that— not the last!"

"What shall I do?" There was fire in his eyes, and his open nostril quivered with intent. Van Helsing slapped him on the shoulder. "Come!" he said. "You are a man, and it is a man we want. You are better than me, better than my friend John." Arthur looked bewildered, and the Professor went on by explaining in a kindly way:—

"Young miss is bad, very bad. She wants blood, and blood she must have or die. My friend John and I have consulted; and we are about to perform what we call transfusion of blood— to transfer from full veins of one to the empty veins which pine for him. John was to give his blood, as he is the more young and strong than me"— here Arthur took my hand and wrung it hard in silence— "but, now you are here, you are more good than us, old or young, who toil much in the world of thought. Our nerves are not so calm and our blood not so bright than yours!" Arthur turned to him and said:—

"If you only knew how gladly I would die for her you would understand— — "

He stopped, with a sort of choke in his voice.

"Good boy!" said Van Helsing. "In the not-so-far-off you will be happy that you have done all for her you love. Come now and be silent. You shall kiss her once before it is done, but then you must go; and you must leave at my sign. Say no word to Madame; you know how it is with her! There must be no shock; any knowledge of this would be one. Come!"

We all went up to Lucy's room. Arthur by direction remained outside. Lucy turned her head and looked at us, but said nothing. She was not asleep, but she was simply too weak to make the effort. Her eyes spoke to us; that was all. Van Helsing took some things from his bag and laid them on a little table out of sight. Then he mixed a narcotic, and coming over to the bed, said cheerily:—

"Now, little miss, here is your medicine. Drink it off, like a good child. See, I lift you so that to swallow is easy. Yes." She had made the effort with success.

It astonished me how long the drug took to act. This, in fact, marked the extent of her weakness. The time seemed endless until sleep began to flicker in her eyelids. At last, however, the narcotic began to manifest its potency; and she fell into a deep sleep. When the Professor was satisfied he called Arthur into the room, and bade him strip off his coat. Then he added: "You may take that one little kiss whiles I bring over the table. Friend John, help to me!" So neither of us looked whilst he bent over her.

Van Helsing turning to me, said:

"He is so young and strong and of blood so pure that we need not defibrinate it."

Then with swiftness, but with absolute method, Van Helsing performed the operation. As the transfusion went on something like life seemed to come back to poor Lucy's cheeks, and through Arthur's growing pallor the joy of his face seemed absolutely to shine. After a bit I began to grow anxious, for the loss of blood was telling on Arthur, strong man as he was. It gave me an idea of what a terrible strain Lucy's system must have undergone that what weakened Arthur only partially restored her. But the Professor's face was set, and he stood watch in hand and with his eyes fixed now on the patient and now on Arthur. I could hear my own heart beat. Presently he said in a soft voice: "Do not stir an instant. It is enough. You attend him; I will look to her." When all was over I could see how much Arthur was weakened. I dressed the wound and took his arm to bring him away, when Van Helsing spoke without turning round— the man seems to have eyes in the back of his head:—

"The brave lover, I think, deserve another kiss, which he shall have presently." And as he had now finished his operation, he adjusted the pillow to the patient's head. As he did so the narrow black velvet band which she seems always to wear round her throat, buckled with an old diamond buckle which her lover had given her, was dragged a little up, and showed a red mark on her throat. Arthur did not notice it, but I could hear the deep hiss of indrawn breath which is one of Van Helsing's ways of betraying emotion. He said nothing at the moment, but turned to me, saying: "Now take down our brave young lover, give him of the port wine, and let him lie down a while. He must then go home and rest, sleep much and eat much, that he may be recruited of what he has so given to his love. He must not stay here. Hold! a moment. I may take it, sir, that you are anxious of result. Then bring it with you that in all ways the operation is successful. You have saved her life this time, and you can go home and rest easy in mind that all that can be is. I shall tell her all when she is well; she shall love you none the less for what you have done. Good-bye."

When Arthur had gone I went back to the room. Lucy was sleeping gently, but her breathing was stronger; I could see the counterpane move as her breast heaved. By the bedside sat Van Helsing, looking at her intently. The velvet band again covered the red mark. I asked the Professor in a whisper:—

"What do you make of that mark on her throat?"

"What do you make of it?"

"I have not examined it yet," I answered, and then and there proceeded to loose the band. Just over the external jugular vein there were two punctures, not large, but not wholesome-looking. There was no sign of disease, but the edges were white and worn-looking, as if by some trituration. It at once occurred to me that this wound, or whatever it was, might be the means of that manifest loss of blood; but I abandoned the idea as soon as formed, for such a thing could not be. The whole bed would have been drenched to a scarlet with the blood which the girl must have lost to leave such a pallor as she had before the transfusion.

"Well?" said Van Helsing.

"Well," said I, "I can make nothing of it." The Professor stood up. "I must go back to Amsterdam to-night," he said. "There are books and things there which I want. You must remain here all the night, and you must not let your sight pass from her."

"Shall I have a nurse?" I asked.

"We are the best nurses, you and I. You keep watch all night; see that she is well fed, and that nothing disturbs her. You must not sleep all the night. Later on we can sleep, you and I. I shall be back as soon as possible. And then we may begin."

"May begin?" I said. "What on earth do you mean?"

"We shall see!" he answered, as he hurried out. He came back a moment later and put his head inside the door and said with warning finger held up:—

"Remember, she is your charge. If you leave her, and harm befall, you shall not sleep easy hereafter!"

Dr. Seward's Diary— continued.

8 September.— I sat up all night with Lucy. The opiate worked itself off towards dusk, and she waked naturally; she looked a different being from what she had been before the operation. Her spirits even were good, and she was full of a happy vivacity, but I could see evidences of the absolute prostration which she had undergone. When I told Mrs. Westenra that Dr. Van Helsing had directed that I should sit up with her she almost pooh-poohed the idea, pointing out her daughter's renewed strength and excellent spirits. I was firm, however, and made preparations for my long vigil. When her maid had prepared her for the night I came in, having in the meantime had supper, and took a seat by the bedside. She did not in any way make objection, but looked at me gratefully whenever I caught her eye. After a long spell she seemed sinking off to sleep, but with an effort seemed to pull herself together and shook it off. This was repeated several times, with greater effort and with shorter pauses as the time moved on. It was apparent that she did not want to sleep, so I tackled the subject at once:—

"You do not want to go to sleep?"

"No; I am afraid."

"Afraid to go to sleep! Why so? It is the boon we all crave for."

"Ah, not if you were like me— if sleep was to you a presage of horror!"

"A presage of horror! What on earth do you mean?"

"I don't know; oh, I don't know. And that is what is so terrible. All this weakness comes to me in sleep; until I dread the very thought."

"But, my dear girl, you may sleep to-night. I am here watching you, and I can promise that nothing will happen."

"Ah, I can trust you!" I seized the opportunity, and said: "I promise you that if I see any evidence of bad dreams I will wake you at once."

"You will? Oh, will you really? How good you are to me. Then I will sleep!" And almost at the word she gave a deep sigh of relief, and sank back, asleep.

All night long I watched by her. She never stirred, but slept on and on in a deep, tranquil, life-giving, health-giving sleep. Her lips were slightly parted, and her breast rose and fell with the regularity of a pendulum. There was a smile on her face, and it was evident that no bad dreams had come to disturb her peace of mind.

In the early morning her maid came, and I left her in her care and took myself back home, for I was anxious about many things. I sent a short wire to Van Helsing and to Arthur, telling them of the excellent result of the operation. My own work, with its manifold arrears, took me all day to clear off; it was dark when I was able to inquire about my zoöphagous patient. The report was good; he had been quite quiet for the past day and night. A telegram came from Van Helsing at Amsterdam whilst I was at dinner, suggesting that I should be at Hillingham to-night, as it might be well to be at hand, and stating that he was leaving by the night mail and would join me early in the morning.

9 September.— I was pretty tired and worn out when I got to Hillingham. For two nights I had hardly had a wink of sleep, and my brain was beginning to feel that numbness which marks cerebral exhaustion. Lucy was up and in cheerful spirits. When she shook hands with me she looked sharply in my face and said:—

"No sitting up to-night for you. You are worn out. I am quite well again; indeed, I am; and if there is to be any sitting up, it is I who will sit up with you." I would not argue the point, but went and had my supper. Lucy came with me, and, enlivened by her charming presence, I made an excellent meal, and had a couple of glasses of the more than excellent port. Then Lucy took me upstairs, and showed me a room next her own, where a cozy fire was burning. "Now," she said, "you must stay here. I shall leave this door open and my door too. You can lie on the sofa for I know that nothing would induce any of you doctors to go to bed whilst there is a patient above the horizon. If I want anything I shall call out, and you can come to me at once." I could not but acquiesce, for I was "dog-tired," and could not have sat up had I tried. So, on her renewing her promise to call me if she should want anything, I lay on the sofa, and forgot all about everything.

Lucy Westenra's Diary.

9 September.— I feel so happy to-night. I have been so miserably weak, that to be able to think and move about is like feeling sunshine after a long spell of east wind out of a steel sky. Somehow Arthur feels very, very close to me. I seem to feel his presence warm about me. I suppose it is that sickness and weakness are selfish things and turn our inner eyes and sympathy on ourselves, whilst health and strength give Love rein, and in thought and feeling he can wander where he wills. I know where my thoughts are. If Arthur only knew! My dear, my dear, your ears must tingle as you sleep, as mine do waking. Oh, the blissful rest of last night! How I slept, with that dear, good Dr. Seward watching me. And to-night I shall not fear to sleep, since he is close at hand and within call. Thank everybody for being so good to me! Thank God! Good-night, Arthur.

Dr. Seward's Diary.

10 September.— I was conscious of the Professor's hand on my head, and started awake all in a second. That is one of the things that we learn in an asylum, at any rate.

"And how is our patient?"

"Well, when I left her, or rather when she left me," I answered.

"Come, let us see," he said. And together we went into the room.

The blind was down, and I went over to raise it gently, whilst Van Helsing stepped, with his soft, cat-like tread, over to the bed.

As I raised the blind, and the morning sunlight flooded the room, I heard the Professor's low hiss of inspiration, and knowing its rarity, a deadly fear shot through my heart. As I passed over he moved back, and his exclamation of horror, "Gott in Himmel!" needed no enforcement from his agonised face. He raised his hand and pointed to the bed, and his iron face was drawn and ashen white. I felt my knees begin to tremble.

There on the bed, seemingly in a swoon, lay poor Lucy, more horribly white and wan-looking than ever. Even the lips were white, and the gums seemed to have shrunken back from the teeth, as we sometimes see in a corpse after a prolonged illness. Van Helsing raised his foot to stamp in anger, but the instinct of his life and all the long years of habit stood to him, and he put it down again softly. "Quick!" he said. "Bring the brandy." I flew to the dining-room, and returned with the decanter. He wetted the poor white lips with it, and together we rubbed palm and wrist and heart. He felt her heart, and after a few moments of agonising suspense said:—

"It is not too late. It beats, though but feebly. All our work is undone; we must begin again. There is no young Arthur here now; I have to call on you yourself this time, friend John." As he spoke, he was dipping into his bag and producing the instruments for transfusion; I had taken off my coat and rolled up my shirt-sleeve. There was no possibility of an opiate just at present, and no need of one; and so, without a moment's delay, we began the operation. After a time— it did not seem a short time either, for the draining away of one's blood, no matter how willingly it be given, is a terrible feeling— Van Helsing held up a warning finger. "Do not stir," he said, "but I fear that with growing strength she may wake; and that would make danger, oh, so much danger. But I shall precaution take. I shall give hypodermic injection of morphia." He proceeded then, swiftly and deftly, to carry out his intent. The effect on Lucy was not bad, for the faint seemed to merge subtly into the narcotic sleep. It was with a feeling of personal pride that I could see a faint tinge of colour steal back into the pallid cheeks and lips. No man knows, till he experiences it, what it is to feel his own life-blood drawn away into the veins of the woman he loves.

The Professor watched me critically. "That will do," he said. "Already?" I remonstrated. "You took a great deal more from Art." To which he smiled a sad sort of smile as he replied:—

"He is her lover, her fiancé. You have work, much work, to do for her and for others; and the present will suffice."

When we stopped the operation, he attended to Lucy, whilst I applied digital pressure to my own incision. I laid down, whilst I waited his leisure to attend to me, for I felt faint and a little sick. By-and-by he bound up my wound, and sent me downstairs to get a glass of wine for myself. As I was leaving the room, he came after me, and half whispered:—

"Mind, nothing must be said of this. If our young lover should turn up unexpected, as before, no word to him. It would at once frighten him and enjealous him, too. There must be none. So!"

When I came back he looked at me carefully, and then said:—

"You are not much the worse. Go into the room, and lie on your sofa, and rest awhile; then have much breakfast, and come here to me."

I followed out his orders, for I knew how right and wise they were. I had done my part, and now my next duty was to keep up my strength. I felt very weak, and in the weakness lost something of the amazement at what had occurred. I fell asleep on the sofa, however, wondering over and over again how Lucy had made such a retrograde movement, and how she could have been drained of so much blood with no sign anywhere to show for it. I think I must have continued my wonder in my dreams, for, sleeping and waking, my thoughts always came back to the little punctures in her throat and the ragged, exhausted appearance of their edges— tiny though they were.

Lucy slept well into the day, and when she woke she was fairly well and strong, though not nearly so much so as the day before. When Van Helsing had seen her, he went out for a walk, leaving me in charge, with strict injunctions that I was not to leave her for a moment. I could hear his voice in the hall, asking the way to the nearest telegraph office.

Lucy chatted with me freely, and seemed quite unconscious that anything had happened. I tried to keep her amused and interested. When her mother came up to see her, she did not seem to notice any change whatever, but said to me gratefully:—

"We owe you so much, Dr. Seward, for all you have done, but you really must now take care not to overwork yourself. You are looking pale yourself. You want a wife to nurse and look after you a bit; that you do!" As she spoke, Lucy turned crimson, though it was only momentarily, for her poor wasted veins could not stand for long such an unwonted drain to the head. The reaction came in excessive pallor as she turned imploring eyes on me. I smiled and nodded, and laid my finger on my lips; with a sigh, she sank back amid her pillows.

Van Helsing returned in a couple of hours, and presently said to me: "Now you go home, and eat much and drink enough. Make yourself strong. I stay here to-night, and I shall sit up with little miss myself. You and I must watch the case, and we must have none other to know. I have grave reasons. No, do not ask them; think what you will. Do not fear to think even the most not-probable. Good-night."

In the hall two of the maids came to me, and asked if they or either of them might not sit up with Miss Lucy. They implored me to let them; and when I said it was Dr. Van Helsing's wish that either he or I should sit up, they asked me quite piteously to intercede with the "foreign gentleman." I was much touched by their kindness. Perhaps it is because I am weak at present, and perhaps because it was on Lucy's account, that their devotion was manifested; for over and over again have I seen similar instances of woman's kindness. I got back here in time for a late dinner; went my rounds— all well; and set this down whilst waiting for sleep. It is coming.

11 September.— This afternoon I went over to Hillingham. Found Van Helsing in excellent spirits, and Lucy much better. Shortly after I had arrived, a big parcel from abroad came for the Professor. He opened it with much impressment— assumed, of course— and showed a great bundle of white flowers.

"These are for you, Miss Lucy," he said.

"For me? Oh, Dr. Van Helsing!"

"Yes, my dear, but not for you to play with. These are medicines." Here Lucy made a wry face. "Nay, but they are not to take in a decoction or in nauseous form, so you need not snub that so charming nose, or I shall point out to my friend Arthur what woes he may have to endure in seeing so much beauty that he so loves so much distort. Aha, my pretty miss, that bring the so nice nose all straight again. This is medicinal, but you do not know how. I put him in your window, I make pretty wreath, and hang him round your neck, so that you sleep well. Oh yes! they, like the lotus flower, make your trouble forgotten. It smell so like the waters of Lethe, and of that fountain of youth that the Conquistadores sought for in the Floridas, and find him all too late."

Whilst he was speaking, Lucy had been examining the flowers and smelling them. Now she threw them down, saying, with half-laughter, and half-disgust:—

"Oh, Professor, I believe you are only putting up a joke on me. Why, these flowers are only common garlic."

To my surprise, Van Helsing rose up and said with all his sternness, his iron jaw set and his bushy eyebrows meeting:—

"No trifling with me! I never jest! There is grim purpose in all I do; and I warn you that you do not thwart me. Take care, for the sake of others if not for your own." Then seeing poor Lucy scared, as she might well be, he went on more gently: "Oh, little miss, my dear, do not fear me. I only do for your good; but there is much virtue to you in those so common flowers. See, I place them myself in your room. I make myself the wreath that you are to wear. But hush! no telling to others that make so inquisitive questions. We must obey, and silence is a part of obedience; and obedience is to bring you strong and well into loving arms that wait for you. Now sit still awhile. Come with me, friend John, and you shall help me deck the room with my garlic, which is all the way from Haarlem, where my friend Vanderpool raise herb in his glass-houses all the year. I had to telegraph yesterday, or they would not have been here."

We went into the room, taking the flowers with us. The Professor's actions were certainly odd and not to be found in any pharmacopœia that I ever heard of. First he fastened up the windows and latched them securely; next, taking a handful of the flowers, he rubbed them all over the sashes, as though to ensure that every whiff of air that might get in would be laden with the garlic smell. Then with the wisp he rubbed all over the jamb of the door, above, below, and at each side, and round the fireplace in the same way. It all seemed grotesque to me, and presently I said:—

"Well, Professor, I know you always have a reason for what you do, but this certainly puzzles me. It is well we have no sceptic here, or he would say that you were working some spell to keep out an evil spirit."

"Perhaps I am!" he answered quietly as he began to make the wreath which Lucy was to wear round her neck.

We then waited whilst Lucy made her toilet for the night, and when she was in bed he came and himself fixed the wreath of garlic round her neck. The last words he said to her were:—

"Take care you do not disturb it; and even if the room feel close, do not to-night open the window or the door."

"I promise," said Lucy, "and thank you both a thousand times for all your kindness to me! Oh, what have I done to be blessed with such friends?"

As we left the house in my fly, which was waiting, Van Helsing said:—

"To-night I can sleep in peace, and sleep I want— two nights of travel, much reading in the day between, and much anxiety on the day to follow, and a night to sit up, without to wink. To-morrow in the morning early you call for me, and we come together to see our pretty miss, so much more strong for my 'spell' which I have work. Ho! ho!"

He seemed so confident that I, remembering my own confidence two nights before and with the baneful result, felt awe and vague terror. It must have been my weakness that made me hesitate to tell it to my friend, but I felt it all the more, like unshed tears.

## CHAPTER XI
## Lucy Westenra's Diary.

12 September.— How good they all are to me. I quite love that dear Dr. Van Helsing. I wonder why he was so anxious about these flowers. He positively frightened me, he was so fierce. And yet he must have been right, for I feel comfort from them already. Somehow, I do not dread being alone to-night, and I can go to sleep without fear. I shall not mind any flapping outside the window. Oh, the terrible struggle that I have had against sleep so often of late; the pain of the sleeplessness, or the pain of the fear of sleep, with such unknown horrors as it has for me! How blessed are some people, whose lives have no fears, no dreads; to whom sleep is a blessing that comes nightly, and brings nothing but sweet dreams. Well, here I am to-night, hoping for sleep, and lying like Ophelia in the play, with "virgin crants and maiden strewments." I never liked garlic before, but to-night it is delightful! There is peace in its smell; I feel sleep coming already. Good-night, everybody.

Dr. Seward's Diary.

13 September.— Called at the Berkeley and found Van Helsing, as usual, up to time. The carriage ordered from the hotel was waiting. The Professor took his bag, which he always brings with him now.

Let all be put down exactly. Van Helsing and I arrived at Hillingham at eight o'clock. It was a lovely morning; the bright sunshine and all the fresh feeling of early autumn seemed like the completion of nature's annual work. The leaves were turning to all kinds of beautiful colours, but had not yet begun to drop from the trees. When we entered we met Mrs. Westenra coming out of the morning room. She is always an early riser. She greeted us warmly and said:—

"You will be glad to know that Lucy is better. The dear child is still asleep. I looked into her room and saw her, but did not go in, lest I should disturb her." The Professor smiled, and looked quite jubilant. He rubbed his hands together, and said:—

"Aha! I thought I had diagnosed the case. My treatment is working," to which she answered:—

"You must not take all the credit to yourself, doctor. Lucy's state this morning is due in part to me."

"How you do mean, ma'am?" asked the Professor.

"Well, I was anxious about the dear child in the night, and went into her room. She was sleeping soundly— so soundly that even my coming did not wake her. But the room was awfully stuffy. There were a lot of those horrible, strong-smelling flowers about everywhere, and she had actually a bunch of them round her neck. I feared that the heavy odour would be too much for the dear child in her weak state, so I took them all away and opened a bit of the window to let in a little fresh air. You will be pleased with her, I am sure."

She moved off into her boudoir, where she usually breakfasted early. As she had spoken, I watched the Professor's face, and saw it turn ashen grey. He had been able to retain his self-command whilst the poor lady was present, for he knew her state and how mischievous a shock would be; he actually smiled on her as he held open the door for her to pass into her room. But the instant she had disappeared he pulled me, suddenly and forcibly, into the dining-room and closed the door.

Then, for the first time in my life, I saw Van Helsing break down. He raised his hands over his head in a sort of mute despair, and then beat his palms together in a helpless way; finally he sat down on a chair, and putting his hands before his face, began to sob, with loud, dry sobs that seemed to come from the very racking of his heart. Then he raised his arms again, as though appealing to the whole universe. "God! God! God!" he said. "What have we done, what has this poor thing done, that we are so sore beset? Is there fate amongst us still, sent down from the pagan world of old, that such things must be, and in such way? This poor mother, all unknowing, and all for the best as she think, does such thing as lose her daughter body and soul; and we must not tell her, we must not even warn her, or she die, and then both die. Oh, how we are beset! How are all the powers of the devils against us!" Suddenly he jumped to his feet. "Come," he said, "come, we must see and act. Devils or no devils, or all the devils at once, it matters not; we fight him all the same." He went to the hall-door for his bag; and together we went up to Lucy's room.

Once again I drew up the blind, whilst Van Helsing went towards the bed. This time he did not start as he looked on the poor face with the same awful, waxen pallor as before. He wore a look of stern sadness and infinite pity.

"As I expected," he murmured, with that hissing inspiration of his which meant so much. Without a word he went and locked the door, and then began to set out on the little table the instruments for yet another operation of transfusion of blood. I had long ago recognised the necessity, and begun to take off my coat, but he stopped me with a warning hand. "No!" he said. "To-day you must operate. I shall provide. You are weakened already." As he spoke he took off his coat and rolled up his shirt-sleeve.

Again the operation; again the narcotic; again some return of colour to the ashy cheeks, and the regular breathing of healthy sleep. This time I watched whilst Van Helsing recruited himself and rested.

Presently he took an opportunity of telling Mrs. Westenra that she must not remove anything from Lucy's room without consulting him; that the flowers were of medicinal value, and that the breathing of their odour was a part of the system of cure. Then he took over the care of the case himself, saying that he would watch this night and the next and would send me word when to come.

After another hour Lucy waked from her sleep, fresh and bright and seemingly not much the worse for her terrible ordeal.

What does it all mean? I am beginning to wonder if my long habit of life amongst the insane is beginning to tell upon my own brain.

Lucy Westenra's Diary.

17 September.— Four days and nights of peace. I am getting so strong again that I hardly know myself. It is as if I had passed through some long nightmare, and had just awakened to see the beautiful sunshine and feel the fresh air of the morning around me. I have a dim half-remembrance of long, anxious times of waiting and fearing; darkness in which there was not even the pain of hope to make present distress more poignant: and then long spells of oblivion, and the rising back to life as a diver coming up through a great press of water. Since, however, Dr. Van Helsing has been with me, all this bad dreaming seems to have passed away; the noises that used to frighten me out of my wits— the flapping against the windows, the distant voices which seemed so close to me, the harsh sounds that came from I know not where and commanded me to do I know not what— have all ceased. I go to bed now without any fear of sleep. I do not even try to keep awake. I have grown quite fond of the garlic, and a boxful arrives for me every day from Haarlem. To-night Dr. Van Helsing is going away, as he has to be for a day in Amsterdam. But I need not be watched; I am well enough to be left alone. Thank God for mother's sake, and dear Arthur's, and for all our friends who have been so kind! I shall not even feel the change, for last night Dr. Van Helsing slept in his chair a lot of the time. I found him asleep twice when I awoke; but I did not fear to go to sleep again, although the boughs or bats or something napped almost angrily against the window-panes.

"The Pall Mall Gazette," 18 September.

THE ESCAPED WOLF.

PERILOUS ADVENTURE OF OUR INTERVIEWER.

Interview with the Keeper in the Zoölogical Gardens.

After many inquiries and almost as many refusals, and perpetually using the words "Pall Mall Gazette" as a sort of talisman, I managed to find the keeper of the section of the Zoölogical Gardens in which the wolf department is included. Thomas Bilder lives in one of the cottages in the enclosure behind the elephant-house, and was just sitting down to his tea when I found him. Thomas and his wife are hospitable folk, elderly, and without children, and if the specimen I enjoyed of their hospitality be of the average kind, their lives must be pretty comfortable. The keeper would not enter on what he called "business" until the supper was over, and we were all satisfied. Then when the table was cleared, and he had lit his pipe, he said:—

"Now, sir, you can go on and arsk me what you want. You'll excoose me refoosin' to talk of perfeshunal subjects afore meals. I gives the wolves and the jackals and the hyenas in all our section their tea afore I begins to arsk them questions."

"How do you mean, ask them questions?" I queried, wishful to get him into a talkative humour.

" 'Ittin' of them over the 'ead with a pole is one way; scratchin' of their hears is another, when gents as is flush wants a bit of a show-orf to their gals. I don't so much mind the fust— the 'ittin' with a pole afore I chucks in their dinner; but I waits till they've 'ad their sherry and kawffee, so to speak, afore I tries on with the ear-scratchin'. Mind you," he added philosophically, "there's a deal of the same nature in us as in them theer animiles. Here's you a-comin' and arskin' of me questions about my business, and I that grumpy-like that only for your bloomin' 'arf-quid I'd 'a' seen you blowed fust 'fore I'd answer. Not even when you arsked me sarcastic-like if I'd like you to arsk the Superintendent if you might arsk me questions. Without offence did I tell yer to go to 'ell?"

"You did."

"An' when you said you'd report me for usin' of obscene language that was 'ittin' me over the 'ead; but the 'arf-quid made that all right. I weren't a-goin' to fight, so I waited for the food, and did with my 'owl as the wolves, and lions, and tigers does. But, Lor' love yer 'art, now that the old 'ooman has stuck a chunk of her tea-cake in me, an' rinsed me out with her bloomin' old teapot, and I've lit hup, you may scratch my ears for all you're worth, and won't git even a growl out of me. Drive along with your questions. I know what yer a-comin' at, that 'ere escaped wolf."

"Exactly. I want you to give me your view of it. Just tell me how it happened; and when I know the facts I'll get you to say what you consider was the cause of it, and how you think the whole affair will end."

"All right, guv'nor. This 'ere is about the 'ole story. That 'ere wolf what we called Bersicker was one of three grey ones that came from Norway to Jamrach's, which we bought off him four years ago. He was a nice well-behaved wolf, that never gave no trouble to talk of. I'm more surprised at 'im for wantin' to get out nor any other animile in the place. But, there, you can't trust wolves no more nor women."

"Don't you mind him, sir!" broke in Mrs. Tom, with a cheery laugh. " 'E's got mindin' the animiles so long that blest if he ain't like a old wolf 'isself! But there ain't no 'arm in 'im."

"Well, sir, it was about two hours after feedin' yesterday when I first hear my disturbance. I was makin' up a litter in the monkey-house for a young puma which is ill; but when I heard the yelpin' and 'owlin' I kem away straight. There was Bersicker a-tearin' like a mad thing at the bars as if he wanted to get out. There wasn't much people about that day, and close at hand was only one man, a tall, thin chap, with a 'ook nose and a pointed beard, with a few white hairs runnin' through it. He had a 'ard, cold look and red eyes, and I took a sort of mislike to him, for it seemed as if it was 'im as they was hirritated at. He 'ad white kid gloves on 'is 'ands, and he pointed out the animiles to me and says: 'Keeper, these wolves seem upset at something.'

" 'Maybe it's you,' says I, for I did not like the airs as he give 'isself. He didn't git angry, as I 'oped he would, but he smiled a kind of insolent smile, with a mouth full of white, sharp teeth. 'Oh no, they wouldn't like me,' 'e says.

" 'Ow yes, they would,' says I, a-imitatin' of him. 'They always likes a bone or two to clean their teeth on about tea-time, which you 'as a bagful.'

"Well, it was a odd thing, but when the animiles see us a-talkin' they lay down, and when I went over to Bersicker he let me stroke his ears same as ever. That there man kem over, and blessed but if he didn't put in his hand and stroke the old wolf's ears too!

" 'Tyke care,' says I. 'Bersicker is quick.'

" 'Never mind,' he says. 'I'm used to 'em!'

" 'Are you in the business yourself?' I says, tyking off my 'at, for a man what trades in wolves, anceterer, is a good friend to keepers.

" 'No' says he, 'not exactly in the business, but I 'ave made pets of several.' And with that he lifts his 'at as perlite as a lord, and walks away. Old Bersicker kep' a-lookin' arter 'im till 'e was out of sight, and then went and lay down in a corner and wouldn't come hout the 'ole hevening. Well, larst night, so soon as the moon was hup, the wolves here all began a-'owling. There warn't nothing for them to 'owl at. There warn't no one near, except some one that was evidently a-callin' a dog somewheres out back of the gardings in the Park road. Once or twice I went out to see that all was right, and it was, and then the 'owling stopped. Just before twelve o'clock I just took a look round afore turnin' in, an', bust me, but when I kem opposite to old Bersicker's cage I see the rails broken and twisted about and the cage empty. And that's all I know for certing."

"Did any one else see anything?"

151

"One of our gard'ners was a-comin' 'ome about that time from a 'armony, when he sees a big grey dog comin' out through the garding 'edges. At least, so he says, but I don't give much for it myself, for if he did 'e never said a word about it to his missis when 'e got 'ome, and it was only after the escape of the wolf was made known, and we had been up all night-a-huntin' of the Park for Bersicker, that he remembered seein' anything. My own belief was that the 'armony 'ad got into his 'ead."

"Now, Mr. Bilder, can you account in any way for the escape of the wolf?"

"Well, sir," he said, with a suspicious sort of modesty, "I think I can; but I don't know as 'ow you'd be satisfied with the theory."

"Certainly I shall. If a man like you, who knows the animals from experience, can't hazard a good guess at any rate, who is even to try?"

"Well then, sir, I accounts for it this way; it seems to me that 'ere wolf escaped— simply because he wanted to get out."

From the hearty way that both Thomas and his wife laughed at the joke I could see that it had done service before, and that the whole explanation was simply an elaborate sell. I couldn't cope in badinage with the worthy Thomas, but I thought I knew a surer way to his heart, so I said:—

"Now, Mr. Bilder, we'll consider that first half-sovereign worked off, and this brother of his is waiting to be claimed when you've told me what you think will happen."

"Right y'are, sir," he said briskly. "Ye'll excoose me, I know, for a-chaffin' of ye, but the old woman here winked at me, which was as much as telling me to go on."

"Well, I never!" said the old lady.

"My opinion is this: that 'ere wolf is a-'idin' of, somewheres. The gard'ner wot didn't remember said he was a-gallopin' northward faster than a horse could go; but I don't believe him, for, yer see, sir, wolves don't gallop no more nor dogs does, they not bein' built that way. Wolves is fine things in a storybook, and I dessay when they gets in packs and does be chivyin' somethin' that's more afeared than they is they can make a devil of a noise and chop it up, whatever it is. But, Lor' bless you, in real life a wolf is only a low creature, not half so clever or bold as a good dog; and not half a quarter so much fight in 'im. This one ain't been used to fightin' or even to providin' for hisself, and more like he's somewhere round the Park a-'idin' an' a-shiverin' of, and, if he thinks at all, wonderin' where he is to get his breakfast from; or maybe he's got down some area and is in a coal-cellar. My eye, won't some cook get a rum start when she sees his green eyes a-shining at her out of the dark! If he can't get food he's bound to look for it, and mayhap he may chance to light on a butcher's shop in time. If he doesn't, and some nursemaid goes a-walkin' orf with a soldier, leavin' of the hinfant in the perambulator— well, then I shouldn't be surprised if the census is one babby the less. That's all."

I was handing him the half-sovereign, when something came bobbing up against the window, and Mr. Bilder's face doubled its natural length with surprise.

"God bless me!" he said. "If there ain't old Bersicker come back by 'isself!"

He went to the door and opened it; a most unnecessary proceeding it seemed to me. I have always thought that a wild animal never looks so well as when some obstacle of pronounced durability is between us; a personal experience has intensified rather than diminished that idea.

After all, however, there is nothing like custom, for neither Bilder nor his wife thought any more of the wolf than I should of a dog. The animal itself was as peaceful and well-behaved as that father of all picture-wolves— Red Riding Hood's quondam friend, whilst moving her confidence in masquerade.

The whole scene was an unutterable mixture of comedy and pathos. The wicked wolf that for half a day had paralysed London and set all the children in the town shivering in their shoes, was there in a sort of penitent mood, and was received and petted like a sort of vulpine prodigal son. Old Bilder examined him all over with most tender solicitude, and when he had finished with his penitent said:—

"There, I knew the poor old chap would get into some kind of trouble; didn't I say it all along? Here's his head all cut and full of broken glass. 'E's been a-gettin' over some bloomin' wall or other. It's a shyme that people are allowed to top their walls with broken bottles. This 'ere's what comes of it. Come along, Bersicker."

He took the wolf and locked him up in a cage, with a piece of meat that satisfied, in quantity at any rate, the elementary conditions of the fatted calf, and went off to report.

I came off, too, to report the only exclusive information that is given to-day regarding the strange escapade at the Zoo.

Dr. Seward's Diary.

17 September.— I was engaged after dinner in my study posting up my books, which, through press of other work and the many visits to Lucy, had fallen sadly into arrear. Suddenly the door was burst open, and in rushed my patient, with his face distorted with passion. I was thunderstruck, for such a thing as a patient getting of his own accord into the Superintendent's study is almost unknown. Without an instant's pause he made straight at me. He had a dinner-knife in his hand, and, as I saw he was dangerous, I tried to keep the table between us. He was too quick and too strong for me, however; for before I could get my balance he had struck at me and cut my left wrist rather severely. Before he could strike again, however, I got in my right and he was sprawling on his back on the floor. My wrist bled freely, and quite a little pool trickled on to the carpet. I saw that my friend was not intent on further effort, and occupied myself binding up my wrist, keeping a wary eye on the prostrate figure all the time. When the attendants rushed in, and we turned our attention to him, his employment positively sickened me. He was lying on his belly on the floor licking up, like a dog, the blood which had fallen from my wounded wrist. He was easily secured, and, to my surprise, went with the attendants quite placidly, simply repeating over and over again: "The blood is the life! The blood is the life!"

I cannot afford to lose blood just at present; I have lost too much of late for my physical good, and then the prolonged strain of Lucy's illness and its horrible phases is telling on me. I am over-excited and weary, and I need rest, rest, rest. Happily Van Helsing has not summoned me, so I need not forego my sleep; to-night I could not well do without it.

Telegram, Van Helsing, Antwerp, to Seward, Carfax.

(Sent to Carfax, Sussex, as no county given; delivered late by twenty-two hours.)

"17 September.— Do not fail to be at Hillingham to-night. If not watching all the time frequently, visit and see that flowers are as placed; very important; do not fail. Shall be with you as soon as possible after arrival."

Dr. Seward's Diary.

18 September.— Just off for train to London. The arrival of Van Helsing's telegram filled me with dismay. A whole night lost, and I know by bitter experience what may happen in a night. Of course it is possible that all may be well, but what may have happened? Surely there is some horrible doom hanging over us that every possible accident should thwart us in all we try to do. I shall take this cylinder with me, and then I can complete my entry on Lucy's phonograph.

Memorandum left by Lucy Westenra.

17 September. Night.— I write this and leave it to be seen, so that no one may by any chance get into trouble through me. This is an exact record of what took place to-night. I feel I am dying of weakness, and have barely strength to write, but it must be done if I die in the doing. I went to bed as usual, taking care that the flowers were placed as Dr. Van Helsing directed, and soon fell asleep.

I was waked by the flapping at the window, which had begun after that sleep-walking on the cliff at Whitby when Mina saved me, and which now I know so well. I was not afraid, but I did wish that Dr. Seward was in the next room— as Dr. Van Helsing said he would be— so that I might have called him. I tried to go to sleep, but could not. Then there came to me the old fear of sleep, and I determined to keep awake. Perversely sleep would try to come then when I did not want it; so, as I feared to be alone, I opened my door and called out: "Is there anybody there?" There was no answer. I was afraid to wake mother, and so closed my door again. Then outside in the shrubbery I heard a sort of howl like a dog's, but more fierce and deeper. I went to the window and looked out, but could see nothing, except a big bat, which had evidently been buffeting its wings against the window. So I went back to bed again, but determined not to go to sleep. Presently the door opened, and mother looked in; seeing by my moving that I was not asleep, came in, and sat by me. She said to me even more sweetly and softly than her wont:—

"I was uneasy about you, darling, and came in to see that you were all right."

I feared she might catch cold sitting there, and asked her to come in and sleep with me, so she came into bed, and lay down beside me; she did not take off her dressing gown, for she said she would only stay a while and then go back to her own bed. As she lay there in my arms, and I in hers, the flapping and buffeting came to the window again. She was startled and a little frightened, and cried out: "What is that?" I tried to pacify her, and at last succeeded, and she lay quiet; but I could hear her poor dear heart still beating terribly. After a while there was the low howl again out in the shrubbery, and shortly after there was a crash at the window, and a lot of broken glass was hurled on the floor. The window blind blew back with the wind that rushed in, and in the aperture of the broken panes there was the head of a great, gaunt grey wolf. Mother cried out in a fright, and struggled up into a sitting posture, and clutched wildly at anything that would help her. Amongst other things, she clutched the wreath of flowers that Dr. Van Helsing insisted on my wearing round my neck, and tore it away from me. For a second or two she sat up, pointing at the wolf, and there was a strange and horrible gurgling in her throat; then she fell over— as if struck with lightning, and her head hit my forehead and made me dizzy for a moment or two. The room and all round seemed to spin round. I kept my eyes fixed on the window, but the wolf drew his head back, and a whole myriad of little specks seemed to come blowing in through the broken window, and wheeling and circling round like the pillar of dust that travellers describe when there is a simoon in the desert. I tried to stir, but there was some spell upon me, and dear mother's poor body, which seemed to grow cold already— for her dear heart had ceased to beat— weighed me down; and I remembered no more for a while.

The time did not seem long, but very, very awful, till I recovered consciousness again. Somewhere near, a passing bell was tolling; the dogs all round the neighbourhood were howling; and in our shrubbery, seemingly just outside, a nightingale was singing. I was dazed and stupid with pain and terror and weakness, but the sound of the nightingale seemed like the voice of my dead mother come back to comfort me. The sounds seemed to have awakened the maids, too, for I could hear their bare feet pattering outside my door. I called to them, and they came in, and when they saw what had happened, and what it was that lay over me on the bed, they screamed out. The wind rushed in through the broken window, and the door slammed to. They lifted off the body of my dear mother, and laid her, covered up with a sheet, on the bed after I had got up. They were all so frightened and nervous that I directed them to go to the dining-room and have each a glass of wine. The door flew open for an instant and closed again. The maids shrieked, and then went in a body to the dining-room; and I laid what flowers I had on my dear mother's breast. When they were there I remembered what Dr. Van Helsing had told me, but I didn't like to remove them, and, besides, I would have some of the servants to sit up with me now. I was surprised that the maids did not come back. I called them, but got no answer, so I went to the dining-room to look for them. My heart sank when I saw what had happened. They all four lay helpless on the floor, breathing heavily. The decanter of sherry was on the table half full, but there was a queer, acrid smell about. I was suspicious, and examined the decanter. It smelt of laudanum, and looking on the sideboard, I found that the bottle which mother's doctor uses for her— oh! did use— was empty. What am I to do? what am I to do? I am back in the room with mother. I cannot leave her, and I am alone, save for the sleeping servants, whom some one has drugged. Alone with the dead! I dare not go out, for I can hear the low howl of the wolf through the broken window.

The air seems full of specks, floating and circling in the draught from the window, and the lights burn blue and dim. What am I to do? God shield me from harm this night! I shall hide this paper in my breast, where they shall find it when they come to lay me out. My dear mother gone! It is time that I go too. Good-bye, dear Arthur, if I should not survive this night. God keep you, dear, and God help me!

## CHAPTER XII
# DR. SEWARD'S DIARY

1 8 September.— I drove at once to Hillingham and arrived early. Keeping my cab at the gate, I went up the avenue alone. I knocked gently and rang as quietly as possible, for I feared to disturb Lucy or her mother, and hoped to only bring a servant to the door. After a while, finding no response, I knocked and rang again; still no answer. I cursed the laziness of the servants that they should lie abed at such an hour— for it was now ten o'clock— and so rang and knocked again, but more impatiently, but still without response. Hitherto I had blamed only the servants, but now a terrible fear began to assail me. Was this desolation but another link in the chain of doom which seemed drawing tight around us? Was it indeed a house of death to which I had come, too late? I knew that minutes, even seconds of delay, might mean hours of danger to Lucy, if she had had again one of those frightful relapses; and I went round the house to try if I could find by chance an entry anywhere.

I could find no means of ingress. Every window and door was fastened and locked, and I returned baffled to the porch. As I did so, I heard the rapid pit-pat of a swiftly driven horse's feet. They stopped at the gate, and a few seconds later I met Van Helsing running up the avenue. When he saw me, he gasped out:—

"Then it was you, and just arrived. How is she? Are we too late? Did you not get my telegram?"

I answered as quickly and coherently as I could that I had only got his telegram early in the morning, and had not lost a minute in coming here, and that I could not make any one in the house hear me. He paused and raised his hat as he said solemnly:—

"Then I fear we are too late. God's will be done!" With his usual recuperative energy, he went on: "Come. If there be no way open to get in, we must make one. Time is all in all to us now."

We went round to the back of the house, where there was a kitchen window. The Professor took a small surgical saw from his case, and handing it to me, pointed to the iron bars which guarded the window. I attacked them at once and had very soon cut through three of them. Then with a long, thin knife we pushed back the fastening of the sashes and opened the window. I helped the Professor in, and followed him. There was no one in the kitchen or in the servants' rooms, which were close at hand. We tried all the rooms as we went along, and in the dining-room, dimly lit by rays of light through the shutters, found four servant-women lying on the floor. There was no need to think them dead, for their stertorous breathing and the acrid smell of laudanum in the room left no doubt as to their condition. Van Helsing and I looked at each other, and as we moved away he said: "We can attend to them later." Then we ascended to Lucy's room. For an instant or two we paused at the door to listen, but there was no sound that we could hear. With white faces and trembling hands, we opened the door gently, and entered the room.

How shall I describe what we saw? On the bed lay two women, Lucy and her mother. The latter lay farthest in, and she was covered with a white sheet, the edge of which had been blown back by the draught through the broken window, showing the drawn, white face, with a look of terror fixed upon it. By her side lay Lucy, with face white and still more drawn. The flowers which had been round her neck we found upon her mother's bosom, and her throat was bare, showing the two little wounds which we had noticed before, but looking horribly white and mangled. Without a word the Professor bent over the bed, his head almost touching poor Lucy's breast; then he gave a quick turn of his head, as of one who listens, and leaping to his feet, he cried out to me:—

"It is not yet too late! Quick! quick! Bring the brandy!"

I flew downstairs and returned with it, taking care to smell and taste it, lest it, too, were drugged like the decanter of sherry which I found on the table. The maids were still breathing, but more restlessly, and I fancied that the narcotic was wearing off. I did not stay to make sure, but returned to Van Helsing. He rubbed the brandy, as on another occasion, on her lips and gums and on her wrists and the palms of her hands. He said to me:—

"I can do this, all that can be at the present. You go wake those maids. Flick them in the face with a wet towel, and flick them hard. Make them get heat and fire and a warm bath. This poor soul is nearly as cold as that beside her. She will need be heated before we can do anything more."

I went at once, and found little difficulty in waking three of the women. The fourth was only a young girl, and the drug had evidently affected her more strongly, so I lifted her on the sofa and let her sleep. The others were dazed at first, but as remembrance came back to them they cried and sobbed in a hysterical manner. I was stern with them, however, and would not let them talk. I told them that one life was bad enough to lose, and that if they delayed they would sacrifice Miss Lucy. So, sobbing and crying, they went about their way, half clad as they were, and prepared fire and water. Fortunately, the kitchen and boiler fires were still alive, and there was no lack of hot water. We got a bath and carried Lucy out as she was and placed her in it. Whilst we were busy chafing her limbs there was a knock at the hall door. One of the maids ran off, hurried on some more clothes, and opened it. Then she returned and whispered to us that there was a gentleman who had come with a message from Mr. Holmwood. I bade her simply tell him that he must wait, for we could see no one now. She went away with the message, and, engrossed with our work, I clean forgot all about him.

I never saw in all my experience the Professor work in such deadly earnest. I knew— as he knew— that it was a stand-up fight with death, and in a pause told him so. He answered me in a way that I did not understand, but with the sternest look that his face could wear:—

"If that were all, I would stop here where we are now, and let her fade away into peace, for I see no light in life over her horizon." He went on with his work with, if possible, renewed and more frenzied vigour.

Presently we both began to be conscious that the heat was beginning to be of some effect. Lucy's heart beat a trifle more audibly to the stethoscope, and her lungs had a perceptible movement. Van Helsing's face almost beamed, and as we lifted her from the bath and rolled her in a hot sheet to dry her he said to me:—

"The first gain is ours! Check to the King!"

We took Lucy into another room, which had by now been prepared, and laid her in bed and forced a few drops of brandy down her throat. I noticed that Van Helsing tied a soft silk handkerchief round her throat. She was still unconscious, and was quite as bad as, if not worse than, we had ever seen her.

Van Helsing called in one of the women, and told her to stay with her and not to take her eyes off her till we returned, and then beckoned me out of the room.

"We must consult as to what is to be done," he said as we descended the stairs. In the hall he opened the dining-room door, and we passed in, he closing the door carefully behind him. The shutters had been opened, but the blinds were already down, with that obedience to the etiquette of death which the British woman of the lower classes always rigidly observes. The room was, therefore, dimly dark. It was, however, light enough for our purposes. Van Helsing's sternness was somewhat relieved by a look of perplexity. He was evidently torturing his mind about something, so I waited for an instant, and he spoke:—

"What are we to do now? Where are we to turn for help? We must have another transfusion of blood, and that soon, or that poor girl's life won't be worth an hour's purchase. You are exhausted already; I am exhausted too. I fear to trust those women, even if they would have courage to submit. What are we to do for some one who will open his veins for her?"

"What's the matter with me, anyhow?"

The voice came from the sofa across the room, and its tones brought relief and joy to my heart, for they were those of Quincey Morris. Van Helsing started angrily at the first sound, but his face softened and a glad look came into his eyes as I cried out: "Quincey Morris!" and rushed towards him with outstretched hands.

"What brought you here?" I cried as our hands met.

"I guess Art is the cause."

He handed me a telegram:—

"Have not heard from Seward for three days, and am terribly anxious. Cannot leave. Father still in same condition. Send me word how Lucy is. Do not delay.— Holmwood."

"I think I came just in the nick of time. You know you have only to tell me what to do."

Van Helsing strode forward, and took his hand, looking him straight in the eyes as he said:—

"A brave man's blood is the best thing on this earth when a woman is in trouble. You're a man and no mistake. Well, the devil may work against us for all he's worth, but God sends us men when we want them."

Once again we went through that ghastly operation. I have not the heart to go through with the details. Lucy had got a terrible shock and it told on her more than before, for though plenty of blood went into her veins, her body did not respond to the treatment as well as on the other occasions. Her struggle back into life was something frightful to see and hear. However, the action of both heart and lungs improved, and Van Helsing made a subcutaneous injection of morphia, as before, and with good effect. Her faint became a profound slumber. The Professor watched whilst I went downstairs with Quincey Morris, and sent one of the maids to pay off one of the cabmen who were waiting. I left Quincey lying down after having a glass of wine, and told the cook to get ready a good breakfast. Then a thought struck me, and I went back to the room where Lucy now was. When I came softly in, I found Van Helsing with a sheet or two of note-paper in his hand. He had evidently read it, and was thinking it over as he sat with his hand to his brow. There was a look of grim satisfaction in his face, as of one who has had a doubt solved. He handed me the paper saying only: "It dropped from Lucy's breast when we carried her to the bath."

When I had read it, I stood looking at the Professor, and after a pause asked him: "In God's name, what does it all mean? Was she, or is she, mad; or what sort of horrible danger is it?" I was so bewildered that I did not know what to say more. Van Helsing put out his hand and took the paper, saying:—

"Do not trouble about it now. Forget it for the present. You shall know and understand it all in good time; but it will be later. And now what is it that you came to me to say?" This brought me back to fact, and I was all myself again.

"I came to speak about the certificate of death. If we do not act properly and wisely, there may be an inquest, and that paper would have to be produced. I am in hopes that we need have no inquest, for if we had it would surely kill poor Lucy, if nothing else did. I know, and you know, and the other doctor who attended her knows, that Mrs. Westenra had disease of the heart, and we can certify that she died of it. Let us fill up the certificate at once, and I shall take it myself to the registrar and go on to the undertaker."

"Good, oh my friend John! Well thought of! Truly Miss Lucy, if she be sad in the foes that beset her, is at least happy in the friends that love her. One, two, three, all open their veins for her, besides one old man. Ah yes, I know, friend John; I am not blind! I love you all the more for it! Now go."

In the hall I met Quincey Morris, with a telegram for Arthur telling him that Mrs. Westenra was dead; that Lucy also had been ill, but was now going on better; and that Van Helsing and I were with her. I told him where I was going, and he hurried me out, but as I was going said:—

"When you come back, Jack, may I have two words with you all to ourselves?" I nodded in reply and went out. I found no difficulty about the registration, and arranged with the local undertaker to come up in the evening to measure for the coffin and to make arrangements.

When I got back Quincey was waiting for me. I told him I would see him as soon as I knew about Lucy, and went up to her room. She was still sleeping, and the Professor seemingly had not moved from his seat at her side. From his putting his finger to his lips, I gathered that he expected her to wake before long and was afraid of forestalling nature. So I went down to Quincey and took him into the breakfast-room, where the blinds were not drawn down, and which was a little more cheerful, or rather less cheerless, than the other rooms. When we were alone, he said to me:—

"Jack Seward, I don't want to shove myself in anywhere where I've no right to be; but this is no ordinary case. You know I loved that girl and wanted to marry her; but, although that's all past and gone, I can't help feeling anxious about her all the same. What is it that's wrong with her? The Dutchman— and a fine old fellow he is; I can see that— said, that time you two came into the room, that you must have another transfusion of blood, and that both you and he were exhausted. Now I know well that you medical men speak in camera, and that a man must not expect to know what they consult about in private. But this is no common matter, and, whatever it is, I have done my part. Is not that so?"

"That's so," I said, and he went on:—

"I take it that both you and Van Helsing had done already what I did to-day. Is not that so?"

"That's so."

"And I guess Art was in it too. When I saw him four days ago down at his own place he looked queer. I have not seen anything pulled down so quick since I was on the Pampas and had a mare that I was fond of go to grass all in a night. One of those big bats that they call vampires had got at her in the night, and what with his gorge and the vein left open, there wasn't enough blood in her to let her stand up, and I had to put a bullet through her as she lay. Jack, if you may tell me without betraying confidence, Arthur was the first, is not that so?" As he spoke the poor fellow looked terribly anxious. He was in a torture of suspense regarding the woman he loved, and his utter ignorance of the terrible mystery which seemed to surround her intensified his pain. His very heart was bleeding, and it took all the manhood of him— and there was a royal lot of it, too— to keep him from breaking down. I paused before answering, for I felt that I must not betray anything which the Professor wished kept secret; but already he knew so much, and guessed so much, that there could be no reason for not answering, so I answered in the same phrase: "That's so."

"And how long has this been going on?"

"About ten days."

"Ten days! Then I guess, Jack Seward, that that poor pretty creature that we all love has had put into her veins within that time the blood of four strong men. Man alive, her whole body wouldn't hold it." Then, coming close to me, he spoke in a fierce half-whisper: "What took it out?"

I shook my head. "That," I said, "is the crux. Van Helsing is simply frantic about it, and I am at my wits' end. I can't even hazard a guess. There has been a series of little circumstances which have thrown out all our calculations as to Lucy being properly watched. But these shall not occur again. Here we stay until all be well— or ill." Quincey held out his hand. "Count me in," he said. "You and the Dutchman will tell me what to do, and I'll do it."

When she woke late in the afternoon, Lucy's first movement was to feel in her breast, and, to my surprise, produced the paper which Van Helsing had given me to read. The careful Professor had replaced it where it had come from, lest on waking she should be alarmed. Her eye then lit on Van Helsing and on me too, and gladdened. Then she looked around the room, and seeing where she was, shuddered; she gave a loud cry, and put her poor thin hands before her pale face. We both understood what that meant— that she had realised to the full her mother's death; so we tried what we could to comfort her. Doubtless sympathy eased her somewhat, but she was very low in thought and spirit, and wept silently and weakly for a long time. We told her that either or both of us would now remain with her all the time, and that seemed to comfort her. Towards dusk she fell into a doze. Here a very odd thing occurred. Whilst still asleep she took the paper from her breast and tore it in two. Van Helsing stepped over and took the pieces from her. All the same, however, she went on with the action of tearing, as though the material were still in her hands; finally she lifted her hands and opened them as though scattering the fragments. Van Helsing seemed surprised, and his brows gathered as if in thought, but he said nothing.

19 September.— All last night she slept fitfully, being always afraid to sleep, and something weaker when she woke from it. The Professor and I took it in turns to watch, and we never left her for a moment unattended. Quincey Morris said nothing about his intention, but I knew that all night long he patrolled round and round the house.
When the day came, its searching light showed the ravages in poor Lucy's strength. She was hardly able to turn her head, and the little nourishment which she could take seemed to do her no good. At times she slept, and both Van Helsing and I noticed the difference in her, between sleeping and waking. Whilst asleep she looked stronger, although more haggard, and her breathing was softer; her open mouth showed the pale gums drawn back from the teeth, which thus looked positively longer and sharper than usual; when she woke the softness of her eyes evidently changed the expression, for she looked her own self, although a dying one. In the afternoon she asked for Arthur, and we telegraphed for him. Quincey went off to meet him at the station.

When he arrived it was nearly six o'clock, and the sun was setting full and warm, and the red light streamed in through the window and gave more colour to the pale cheeks. When he saw her, Arthur was simply choking with emotion, and none of us could speak. In the hours that had passed, the fits of sleep, or the comatose condition that passed for it, had grown more frequent, so that the pauses when conversation was possible were shortened. Arthur's presence, however, seemed to act as a stimulant; she rallied a little, and spoke to him more brightly than she had done since we arrived. He too pulled himself together, and spoke as cheerily as he could, so that the best was made of everything. It was now nearly one o'clock, and he and Van Helsing are sitting with her. I am to relieve them in a quarter of an hour, and I am entering this on Lucy's phonograph. Until six o'clock they are to try to rest. I fear that to-morrow will end our watching, for the shock has been too great; the poor child cannot rally. God help us all.

Letter, Mina Harker to Lucy Westenra.

(Unopened by her.)

"17 September.

"My dearest Lucy,—

"It seems an age since I heard from you, or indeed since I wrote. You will pardon me, I know, for all my faults when you have read all my budget of news. Well, I got my husband back all right; when we arrived at Exeter there was a carriage waiting for us, and in it, though he had an attack of gout, Mr. Hawkins. He took us to his house, where there were rooms for us all nice and comfortable, and we dined together. After dinner Mr. Hawkins said:—

" 'My dears, I want to drink your health and prosperity; and may every blessing attend you both. I know you both from children, and have, with love and pride, seen you grow up. Now I want you to make your home here with me. I have left to me neither chick nor child; all are gone, and in my will I have left you everything.' I cried, Lucy dear, as Jonathan and the old man clasped hands. Our evening was a very, very happy one.

"So here we are, installed in this beautiful old house, and from both my bedroom and the drawing-room I can see the great elms of the cathedral close, with their great black stems standing out against the old yellow stone of the cathedral and I can hear the rooks overhead cawing and cawing and chattering and gossiping all day, after the manner of rooks— and humans. I am busy, I need not tell you, arranging things and housekeeping. Jonathan and Mr. Hawkins are busy all day; for, now that Jonathan is a partner, Mr. Hawkins wants to tell him all about the clients.

"How is your dear mother getting on? I wish I could run up to town for a day or two to see you, dear, but I dare not go yet, with so much on my shoulders; and Jonathan wants looking after still. He is beginning to put some flesh on his bones again, but he was terribly weakened by the long illness; even now he sometimes starts out of his sleep in a sudden way and awakes all trembling until I can coax him back to his usual placidity. However, thank God, these occasions grow less frequent as the days go on, and they will in time pass away altogether, I trust. And now I have told you my news, let me ask yours. When are you to be married, and where, and who is to perform the ceremony, and what are you to wear, and is it to be a public or a private wedding? Tell me all about it, dear; tell me all about everything, for there is nothing which interests you which will not be dear to me. Jonathan asks me to send his 'respectful duty,' but I do not think that is good enough from the junior partner of the important firm Hawkins & Harker; and so, as you love me, and he loves me, and I love you with all the moods and tenses of the verb, I send you simply his 'love' instead. Good-bye, my dearest Lucy, and all blessings on you.

"Yours,

"Mina Harker."

Report from Patrick Hennessey, M. D., M. R. C. S. L. K. Q. C. P. I., etc., etc., to John Seward, M. D.

"20 September.

"My dear Sir,—

"In accordance with your wishes, I enclose report of the conditions of everything left in my charge.... With regard to patient, Renfield, there is more to say. He has had another outbreak, which might have had a dreadful ending, but which, as it fortunately happened, was unattended with any unhappy results. This afternoon a carrier's cart with two men made a call at the empty house whose grounds abut on ours— the house to which, you will remember, the patient twice ran away. The men stopped at our gate to ask the porter their way, as they were strangers. I was myself looking out of the study window, having a smoke after dinner, and saw one of them come up to the house. As he passed the window of Renfield's room, the patient began to rate him from within, and called him all the foul names he could lay his tongue to. The man, who seemed a decent fellow enough, contented himself by telling him to "shut up for a foul-mouthed beggar," whereon our man accused him of robbing him and wanting to murder him and said that he would hinder him if he were to swing for it. I opened the window and signed to the man not to notice, so he contented himself after looking the place over and making up his mind as to what kind of a place he had got to by saying: 'Lor' bless yer, sir, I wouldn't mind what was said to me in a bloomin' madhouse. I pity ye and the guv'nor for havin' to live in the house with a wild beast like that.' Then he asked his way civilly enough, and I told him where the gate of the empty house was; he went away, followed by threats and curses and revilings from our man. I went down to see if I could make out any cause for his anger, since he is usually such a well-behaved man, and except his violent fits nothing of the kind had ever occurred. I found him, to my astonishment, quite composed and most genial in his manner. I tried to get him to talk of the incident, but he blandly asked me questions as to what I meant, and led me to believe that he was completely oblivious of the affair. It was, I am sorry to say, however, only another instance of his cunning, for within half an hour I heard of him again. This time he had broken out through the window of his room, and was running down the avenue. I called to the attendants to follow me, and ran after him, for I feared he was intent on some mischief. My fear was justified when I saw the same cart which had passed before coming down the road, having on it some great wooden boxes. The men were wiping their foreheads, and were flushed in the face, as if with violent exercise. Before I could get up to him the patient rushed at them, and pulling one of them off the cart, began to knock his head against the ground. If I had not seized him just at the moment I believe he would have killed the man there and then. The other fellow jumped down and struck him over the head with the butt-end of his heavy whip. It was a terrible blow; but he did not seem to mind it, but seized him also, and struggled with the three of us, pulling us to and fro as if we were kittens. You know I am no light weight, and the others were both burly men. At first he was silent in his fighting; but as we began to master him, and the attendants were putting a strait-waistcoat on him, he began to shout: 'I'll frustrate them! They shan't rob me! they shan't murder me by inches! I'll fight for my Lord and Master!' and all sorts of similar incoherent ravings. It was with very considerable difficulty that they got him back to the house and put him in the padded room. One of the attendants, Hardy, had a finger broken. However, I set it all right; and he is going on well.

"The two carriers were at first loud in their threats of actions for damages, and promised to rain all the penalties of the law on us. Their threats were, however, mingled with some sort of indirect apology for the defeat of the two of them by a feeble madman. They said that if it had not been for the way their strength had been spent in carrying and raising the heavy boxes to the cart they would have made short work of him. They gave as another reason for their defeat the extraordinary state of drouth to which they had been reduced by the dusty nature of their occupation and the reprehensible distance from the scene of their labours of any place of public entertainment. I quite understood their drift, and after a stiff glass of grog, or rather more of the same, and with each a sovereign in hand, they made light of the attack, and swore that they would encounter a worse madman any day for the pleasure of meeting so 'bloomin' good a bloke' as your correspondent. I took their names and addresses, in case they might be needed. They are as follows:— Jack Smollet, of Dudding's Rents, King George's Road, Great Walworth, and Thomas Snelling, Peter Farley's Row, Guide Court, Bethnal Green. They are both in the employment of Harris & Sons, Moving and Shipment Company, Orange Master's Yard, Soho.

"I shall report to you any matter of interest occurring here, and shall wire you at once if there is anything of importance.

"Believe me, dear Sir,

"Yours faithfully,

"Patrick Hennessey."

Letter, Mina Harker to Lucy Westenra.

(Unopened by her.)

"18 September.

"My dearest Lucy,—

"Such a sad blow has befallen us. Mr. Hawkins has died very suddenly. Some may not think it so sad for us, but we had both come to so love him that it really seems as though we had lost a father. I never knew either father or mother, so that the dear old man's death is a real blow to me. Jonathan is greatly distressed. It is not only that he feels sorrow, deep sorrow, for the dear, good man who has befriended him all his life, and now at the end has treated him like his own son and left him a fortune which to people of our modest bringing up is wealth beyond the dream of avarice, but Jonathan feels it on another account. He says the amount of responsibility which it puts upon him makes him nervous. He begins to doubt himself. I try to cheer him up, and my belief in him helps him to have a belief in himself. But it is here that the grave shock that he experienced tells upon him the most. Oh, it is too hard that a sweet, simple, noble, strong nature such as his— a nature which enabled him by our dear, good friend's aid to rise from clerk to master in a few years— should be so injured that the very essence of its strength is gone. Forgive me, dear, if I worry you with my troubles in the midst of your own happiness; but, Lucy dear, I must tell some one, for the strain of keeping up a brave and cheerful appearance to Jonathan tries me, and I have no one here that I can confide in. I dread coming up to London, as we must do the day after to-morrow; for poor Mr. Hawkins left in his will that he was to be buried in the grave with his father. As there are no relations at all, Jonathan will have to be chief mourner. I shall try to run over to see you, dearest, if only for a few minutes. Forgive me for troubling you. With all blessings,
"Your loving
"Mina Harker."
Dr. Seward's Diary.
20 September.— Only resolution and habit can let me make an entry to-night. I am too miserable, too low-spirited, too sick of the world and all in it, including life itself, that I would not care if I heard this moment the flapping of the wings of the angel of death. And he has been flapping those grim wings to some purpose of late— Lucy's mother and Arthur's father, and now.... Let me get on with my work.

I duly relieved Van Helsing in his watch over Lucy. We wanted Arthur to go to rest also, but he refused at first. It was only when I told him that we should want him to help us during the day, and that we must not all break down for want of rest, lest Lucy should suffer, that he agreed to go. Van Helsing was very kind to him. "Come, my child," he said; "come with me. You are sick and weak, and have had much sorrow and much mental pain, as well as that tax on your strength that we know of. You must not be alone; for to be alone is to be full of fears and alarms. Come to the drawing-room, where there is a big fire, and there are two sofas. You shall lie on one, and I on the other, and our sympathy will be comfort to each other, even though we do not speak, and even if we sleep." Arthur went off with him, casting back a longing look on Lucy's face, which lay in her pillow, almost whiter than the lawn. She lay quite still, and I looked round the room to see that all was as it should be. I could see that the Professor had carried out in this room, as in the other, his purpose of using the garlic; the whole of the window-sashes reeked with it, and round Lucy's neck, over the silk handkerchief which Van Helsing made her keep on, was a rough chaplet of the same odorous flowers. Lucy was breathing somewhat stertorously, and her face was at its worst, for the open mouth showed the pale gums. Her teeth, in the dim, uncertain light, seemed longer and sharper than they had been in the morning. In particular, by some trick of the light, the canine teeth looked longer and sharper than the rest. I sat down by her, and presently she moved uneasily. At the same moment there came a sort of dull flapping or buffeting at the window. I went over to it softly, and peeped out by the corner of the blind. There was a full moonlight, and I could see that the noise was made by a great bat, which wheeled round— doubtless attracted by the light, although so dim— and every now and again struck the window with its wings. When I came back to my seat, I found that Lucy had moved slightly, and had torn away the garlic flowers from her throat. I replaced them as well as I could, and sat watching her.

Presently she woke, and I gave her food, as Van Helsing had prescribed. She took but a little, and that languidly. There did not seem to be with her now the unconscious struggle for life and strength that had hitherto so marked her illness. It struck me as curious that the moment she became conscious she pressed the garlic flowers close to her. It was certainly odd that whenever she got into that lethargic state, with the stertorous breathing, she put the flowers from her; but that when she waked she clutched them close. There was no possibility of making any mistake about this, for in the long hours that followed, she had many spells of sleeping and waking and repeated both actions many times.

At six o'clock Van Helsing came to relieve me. Arthur had then fallen into a doze, and he mercifully let him sleep on. When he saw Lucy's face I could hear the sissing indraw of his breath, and he said to me in a sharp whisper: "Draw up the blind; I want light!" Then he bent down, and, with his face almost touching Lucy's, examined her carefully. He removed the flowers and lifted the silk handkerchief from her throat. As he did so he started back, and I could hear his ejaculation, "Mein Gott!" as it was smothered in his throat. I bent over and looked, too, and as I noticed some queer chill came over me.

The wounds on the throat had absolutely disappeared.

For fully five minutes Van Helsing stood looking at her, with his face at its sternest. Then he turned to me and said calmly:—

"She is dying. It will not be long now. It will be much difference, mark me, whether she dies conscious or in her sleep. Wake that poor boy, and let him come and see the last; he trusts us, and we have promised him."

I went to the dining-room and waked him. He was dazed for a moment, but when he saw the sunlight streaming in through the edges of the shutters he thought he was late, and expressed his fear. I assured him that Lucy was still asleep, but told him as gently as I could that both Van Helsing and I feared that the end was near. He covered his face with his hands, and slid down on his knees by the sofa, where he remained, perhaps a minute, with his head buried, praying, whilst his shoulders shook with grief. I took him by the hand and raised him up. "Come," I said, "my dear old fellow, summon all your fortitude: it will be best and easiest for her."

When we came into Lucy's room I could see that Van Helsing had, with his usual forethought, been putting matters straight and making everything look as pleasing as possible. He had even brushed Lucy's hair, so that it lay on the pillow in its usual sunny ripples. When we came into the room she opened her eyes, and seeing him, whispered softly:—

"Arthur! Oh, my love, I am so glad you have come!" He was stooping to kiss her, when Van Helsing motioned him back. "No," he whispered, "not yet! Hold her hand; it will comfort her more."

So Arthur took her hand and knelt beside her, and she looked her best, with all the soft lines matching the angelic beauty of her eyes. Then gradually her eyes closed, and she sank to sleep. For a little bit her breast heaved softly, and her breath came and went like a tired child's. And then insensibly there came the strange change which I had noticed in the night. Her breathing grew stertorous, the mouth opened, and the pale gums, drawn back, made the teeth look longer and sharper than ever. In a sort of sleep-waking, vague, unconscious way she opened her eyes, which were now dull and hard at once, and said in a soft, voluptuous voice, such as I had never heard from her lips:—

"Arthur! Oh, my love, I am so glad you have come! Kiss me!" Arthur bent eagerly over to kiss her; but at that instant Van Helsing, who, like me, had been startled by her voice, swooped upon him, and catching him by the neck with both hands, dragged him back with a fury of strength which I never thought he could have possessed, and actually hurled him almost across the room.

"Not for your life!" he said; "not for your living soul and hers!" And he stood between them like a lion at bay.

Arthur was so taken aback that he did not for a moment know what to do or say; and before any impulse of violence could seize him he realised the place and the occasion, and stood silent, waiting.

I kept my eyes fixed on Lucy, as did Van Helsing, and we saw a spasm as of rage flit like a shadow over her face; the sharp teeth champed together. Then her eyes closed, and she breathed heavily.

Very shortly after she opened her eyes in all their softness, and putting out her poor, pale, thin hand, took Van Helsing's great brown one; drawing it to her, she kissed it. "My true friend," she said, in a faint voice, but with untellable pathos, "My true friend, and his! Oh, guard him, and give me peace!"

"I swear it!" he said solemnly, kneeling beside her and holding up his hand, as one who registers an oath. Then he turned to Arthur, and said to him: "Come, my child, take her hand in yours, and kiss her on the forehead, and only once."

Their eyes met instead of their lips; and so they parted.

Lucy's eyes closed; and Van Helsing, who had been watching closely, took Arthur's arm, and drew him away.

And then Lucy's breathing became stertorous again, and all at once it ceased.

"It is all over," said Van Helsing. "She is dead!"

I took Arthur by the arm, and led him away to the drawing-room, where he sat down, and covered his face with his hands, sobbing in a way that nearly broke me down to see.

I went back to the room, and found Van Helsing looking at poor Lucy, and his face was sterner than ever. Some change had come over her body. Death had given back part of her beauty, for her brow and cheeks had recovered some of their flowing lines; even the lips had lost their deadly pallor. It was as if the blood, no longer needed for the working of the heart, had gone to make the harshness of death as little rude as might be.

"We thought her dying whilst she slept,
And sleeping when she died."

I stood beside Van Helsing, and said:—

"Ah, well, poor girl, there is peace for her at last. It is the end!"

He turned to me, and said with grave solemnity:—

"Not so; alas! not so. It is only the beginning!"

When I asked him what he meant, he only shook his head and answered:—

"We can do nothing as yet. Wait and see."

## CHAPTER XIII
# DR. SEWARD'S DIARY— continued.

THE funeral was arranged for the next succeeding day, so that Lucy and her mother might be buried together. I attended to all the ghastly formalities, and the urbane undertaker proved that his staff were afflicted— or blessed— with something of his own obsequious suavity. Even the woman who performed the last offices for the dead remarked to me, in a confidential, brother-professional way, when she had come out from the death-chamber:—

"She makes a very beautiful corpse, sir. It's quite a privilege to attend on her. It's not too much to say that she will do credit to our establishment!"

I noticed that Van Helsing never kept far away. This was possible from the disordered state of things in the household. There were no relatives at hand; and as Arthur had to be back the next day to attend at his father's funeral, we were unable to notify any one who should have been bidden. Under the circumstances, Van Helsing and I took it upon ourselves to examine papers, etc. He insisted upon looking over Lucy's papers himself. I asked him why, for I feared that he, being a foreigner, might not be quite aware of English legal requirements, and so might in ignorance make some unnecessary trouble. He answered me:—

"I know; I know. You forget that I am a lawyer as well as a doctor. But this is not altogether for the law. You knew that, when you avoided the coroner. I have more than him to avoid. There may be papers more— such as this."

As he spoke he took from his pocket-book the memorandum which had been in Lucy's breast, and which she had torn in her sleep.

"When you find anything of the solicitor who is for the late Mrs. Westenra, seal all her papers, and write him to-night. For me, I watch here in the room and in Miss Lucy's old room all night, and I myself search for what may be. It is not well that her very thoughts go into the hands of strangers."

I went on with my part of the work, and in another half hour had found the name and address of Mrs. Westenra's solicitor and had written to him. All the poor lady's papers were in order; explicit directions regarding the place of burial were given. I had hardly sealed the letter, when, to my surprise, Van Helsing walked into the room, saying:—

"Can I help you, friend John? I am free, and if I may, my service is to you."

"Have you got what you looked for?" I asked, to which he replied:—

"I did not look for any specific thing. I only hoped to find, and find I have, all that there was— only some letters and a few memoranda, and a diary new begun. But I have them here, and we shall for the present say nothing of them. I shall see that poor lad to-morrow evening, and, with his sanction, I shall use some."

When we had finished the work in hand, he said to me:—

"And now, friend John, I think we may to bed. We want sleep, both you and I, and rest to recuperate. To-morrow we shall have much to do, but for the to-night there is no need of us. Alas!"

Before turning in we went to look at poor Lucy. The undertaker had certainly done his work well, for the room was turned into a small chapelle ardente. There was a wilderness of beautiful white flowers, and death was made as little repulsive as might be. The end of the winding-sheet was laid over the face; when the Professor bent over and turned it gently back, we both started at the beauty before us, the tall wax candles showing a sufficient light to note it well. All Lucy's loveliness had come back to her in death, and the hours that had passed, instead of leaving traces of "decay's effacing fingers," had but restored the beauty of life, till positively I could not believe my eyes that I was looking at a corpse.

The Professor looked sternly grave. He had not loved her as I had, and there was no need for tears in his eyes. He said to me: "Remain till I return," and left the room. He came back with a handful of wild garlic from the box waiting in the hall, but which had not been opened, and placed the flowers amongst the others on and around the bed. Then he took from his neck, inside his collar, a little gold crucifix, and placed it over the mouth. He restored the sheet to its place, and we came away.

I was undressing in my own room, when, with a premonitory tap at the door, he entered, and at once began to speak:—

"To-morrow I want you to bring me, before night, a set of post-mortem knives."

"Must we make an autopsy?" I asked.

"Yes and no. I want to operate, but not as you think. Let me tell you now, but not a word to another. I want to cut off her head and take out her heart. Ah! you a surgeon, and so shocked! You, whom I have seen with no tremble of hand or heart, do operations of life and death that make the rest shudder. Oh, but I must not forget, my dear friend John, that you loved her; and I have not forgotten it, for it is I that shall operate, and you must only help. I would like to do it to-night, but for Arthur I must not; he will be free after his father's funeral to-morrow, and he will want to see her— to see it. Then, when she is coffined ready for the next day, you and I shall come when all sleep. We shall unscrew the coffin-lid, and shall do our operation: and then replace all, so that none know, save we alone."

"But why do it at all? The girl is dead. Why mutilate her poor body without need? And if there is no necessity for a post-mortem and nothing to gain by it— no good to her, to us, to science, to human knowledge— why do it? Without such it is monstrous."

For answer he put his hand on my shoulder, and said, with infinite tenderness:—

"Friend John, I pity your poor bleeding heart; and I love you the more because it does so bleed. If I could, I would take on myself the burden that you do bear. But there are things that you know not, but that you shall know, and bless me for knowing, though they are not pleasant things. John, my child, you have been my friend now many years, and yet did you ever know me to do any without good cause? I may err— I am but man; but I believe in all I do. Was it not for these causes that you send for me when the great trouble came? Yes! Were you not amazed, nay horrified, when I would not let Arthur kiss his love— though she was dying— and snatched him away by all my strength? Yes! And yet you saw how she thanked me, with her so beautiful dying eyes, her voice, too, so weak, and she kiss my rough old hand and bless me? Yes! And did you not hear me swear promise to her, that so she closed her eyes grateful? Yes!

"Well, I have good reason now for all I want to do. You have for many years trust me; you have believe me weeks past, when there be things so strange that you might have well doubt. Believe me yet a little, friend John. If you trust me not, then I must tell what I think; and that is not perhaps well. And if I work— as work I shall, no matter trust or no trust— without my friend trust in me, I work with heavy heart and feel, oh! so lonely when I want all help and courage that may be!" He paused a moment and went on solemnly: "Friend John, there are strange and terrible days before us. Let us not be two, but one, that so we work to a good end. Will you not have faith in me?"

I took his hand, and promised him. I held my door open as he went away, and watched him go into his room and close the door. As I stood without moving, I saw one of the maids pass silently along the passage— she had her back towards me, so did not see me— and go into the room where Lucy lay. The sight touched me. Devotion is so rare, and we are so grateful to those who show it unasked to those we love. Here was a poor girl putting aside the terrors which she naturally had of death to go watch alone by the bier of the mistress whom she loved, so that the poor clay might not be lonely till laid to eternal rest....

I must have slept long and soundly, for it was broad daylight when Van Helsing waked me by coming into my room. He came over to my bedside and said:—

"You need not trouble about the knives; we shall not do it."

"Why not?" I asked. For his solemnity of the night before had greatly impressed me.

"Because," he said sternly, "it is too late— or too early. See!" Here he held up the little golden crucifix. "This was stolen in the night."

"How, stolen," I asked in wonder, "since you have it now?"

"Because I get it back from the worthless wretch who stole it, from the woman who robbed the dead and the living. Her punishment will surely come, but not through me; she knew not altogether what she did and thus unknowing, she only stole. Now we must wait."

He went away on the word, leaving me with a new mystery to think of, a new puzzle to grapple with.

The forenoon was a dreary time, but at noon the solicitor came: Mr. Marquand, of Wholeman, Sons, Marquand & Lidderdale. He was very genial and very appreciative of what we had done, and took off our hands all cares as to details. During lunch he told us that Mrs. Westenra had for some time expected sudden death from her heart, and had put her affairs in absolute order; he informed us that, with the exception of a certain entailed property of Lucy's father's which now, in default of direct issue, went back to a distant branch of the family, the whole estate, real and personal, was left absolutely to Arthur Holmwood. When he had told us so much he went on:—

"Frankly we did our best to prevent such a testamentary disposition, and pointed out certain contingencies that might leave her daughter either penniless or not so free as she should be to act regarding a matrimonial alliance. Indeed, we pressed the matter so far that we almost came into collision, for she asked us if we were or were not prepared to carry out her wishes. Of course, we had then no alternative but to accept. We were right in principle, and ninety-nine times out of a hundred we should have proved, by the logic of events, the accuracy of our judgment. Frankly, however, I must admit that in this case any other form of disposition would have rendered impossible the carrying out of her wishes. For by her predeceasing her daughter the latter would have come into possession of the property, and, even had she only survived her mother by five minutes, her property would, in case there were no will— and a will was a practical impossibility in such a case— have been treated at her decease as under intestacy. In which case Lord Godalming, though so dear a friend, would have had no claim in the world; and the inheritors, being remote, would not be likely to abandon their just rights, for sentimental reasons regarding an entire stranger. I assure you, my dear sirs, I am rejoiced at the result, perfectly rejoiced."

He was a good fellow, but his rejoicing at the one little part— in which he was officially interested— of so great a tragedy, was an object-lesson in the limitations of sympathetic understanding.

He did not remain long, but said he would look in later in the day and see Lord Godalming. His coming, however, had been a certain comfort to us, since it assured us that we should not have to dread hostile criticism as to any of our acts. Arthur was expected at five o'clock, so a little before that time we visited the death-chamber. It was so in very truth, for now both mother and daughter lay in it. The undertaker, true to his craft, had made the best display he could of his goods, and there was a mortuary air about the place that lowered our spirits at once. Van Helsing ordered the former arrangement to be adhered to, explaining that, as Lord Godalming was coming very soon, it would be less harrowing to his feelings to see all that was left of his fiancée quite alone. The undertaker seemed shocked at his own stupidity and exerted himself to restore things to the condition in which we left them the night before, so that when Arthur came such shocks to his feelings as we could avoid were saved.

Poor fellow! He looked desperately sad and broken; even his stalwart manhood seemed to have shrunk somewhat under the strain of his much-tried emotions. He had, I knew, been very genuinely and devotedly attached to his father; and to lose him, and at such a time, was a bitter blow to him. With me he was warm as ever, and to Van Helsing he was sweetly courteous; but I could not help seeing that there was some constraint with him. The Professor noticed it, too, and motioned me to bring him upstairs. I did so, and left him at the door of the room, as I felt he would like to be quite alone with her, but he took my arm and led me in, saying huskily:—

"You loved her too, old fellow; she told me all about it, and there was no friend had a closer place in her heart than you. I don't know how to thank you for all you have done for her. I can't think yet...."

Here he suddenly broke down, and threw his arms round my shoulders and laid his head on my breast, crying:—

"Oh, Jack! Jack! What shall I do! The whole of life seems gone from me all at once, and there is nothing in the wide world for me to live for."

I comforted him as well as I could. In such cases men do not need much expression. A grip of the hand, the tightening of an arm over the shoulder, a sob in unison, are expressions of sympathy dear to a man's heart. I stood still and silent till his sobs died away, and then I said softly to him:—

"Come and look at her."

Together we moved over to the bed, and I lifted the lawn from her face. God! how beautiful she was. Every hour seemed to be enhancing her loveliness. It frightened and amazed me somewhat; and as for Arthur, he fell a-trembling, and finally was shaken with doubt as with an ague. At last, after a long pause, he said to me in a faint whisper:—

"Jack, is she really dead?"

I assured him sadly that it was so, and went on to suggest— for I felt that such a horrible doubt should not have life for a moment longer than I could help— that it often happened that after death faces became softened and even resolved into their youthful beauty; that this was especially so when death had been preceded by any acute or prolonged suffering. It seemed to quite do away with any doubt, and, after kneeling beside the couch for a while and looking at her lovingly and long, he turned aside. I told him that that must be good-bye, as the coffin had to be prepared; so he went back and took her dead hand in his and kissed it, and bent over and kissed her forehead. He came away, fondly looking back over his shoulder at her as he came.

I left him in the drawing-room, and told Van Helsing that he had said good-bye; so the latter went to the kitchen to tell the undertaker's men to proceed with the preparations and to screw up the coffin. When he came out of the room again I told him of Arthur's question, and he replied:—

"I am not surprised. Just now I doubted for a moment myself!"

We all dined together, and I could see that poor Art was trying to make the best of things. Van Helsing had been silent all dinner-time; but when we had lit our cigars he said—

"Lord— — "; but Arthur interrupted him:—

"No, no, not that, for God's sake! not yet at any rate. Forgive me, sir: I did not mean to speak offensively; it is only because my loss is so recent."

The Professor answered very sweetly:—

"I only used that name because I was in doubt. I must not call you 'Mr.,' and I have grown to love you— yes, my dear boy, to love you— as Arthur."

Arthur held out his hand, and took the old man's warmly.

"Call me what you will," he said. "I hope I may always have the title of a friend. And let me say that I am at a loss for words to thank you for your goodness to my poor dear." He paused a moment, and went on: "I know that she understood your goodness even better than I do; and if I was rude or in any way wanting at that time you acted so— you remember"— the Professor nodded— "you must forgive me."

He answered with a grave kindness:—

"I know it was hard for you to quite trust me then, for to trust such violence needs to understand; and I take it that you do not— that you cannot— trust me now, for you do not yet understand. And there may be more times when I shall want you to trust when you cannot— and may not— and must not yet understand. But the time will come when your trust shall be whole and complete in me, and when you shall understand as though the sunlight himself shone through. Then you shall bless me from first to last for your own sake, and for the sake of others and for her dear sake to whom I swore to protect."

"And, indeed, indeed, sir," said Arthur warmly, "I shall in all ways trust you. I know and believe you have a very noble heart, and you are Jack's friend, and you were hers. You shall do what you like."

The Professor cleared his throat a couple of times, as though about to speak, and finally said:—

"May I ask you something now?"

"Certainly."

"You know that Mrs. Westenra left you all her property?"

"No, poor dear; I never thought of it."

"And as it is all yours, you have a right to deal with it as you will. I want you to give me permission to read all Miss Lucy's papers and letters. Believe me, it is no idle curiosity. I have a motive of which, be sure, she would have approved. I have them all here. I took them before we knew that all was yours, so that no strange hand might touch them— no strange eye look through words into her soul. I shall keep them, if I may; even you may not see them yet, but I shall keep them safe. No word shall be lost; and in the good time I shall give them back to you. It's a hard thing I ask, but you will do it, will you not, for Lucy's sake?"

Arthur spoke out heartily, like his old self:—

"Dr. Van Helsing, you may do what you will. I feel that in saying this I am doing what my dear one would have approved. I shall not trouble you with questions till the time comes."

The old Professor stood up as he said solemnly:—

"And you are right. There will be pain for us all; but it will not be all pain, nor will this pain be the last. We and you too— you most of all, my dear boy— will have to pass through the bitter water before we reach the sweet. But we must be brave of heart and unselfish, and do our duty, and all will be well!"

I slept on a sofa in Arthur's room that night. Van Helsing did not go to bed at all. He went to and fro, as if patrolling the house, and was never out of sight of the room where Lucy lay in her coffin, strewn with the wild garlic flowers, which sent, through the odour of lily and rose, a heavy, overpowering smell into the night.

Mina Harker's Journal.

22 September.— In the train to Exeter. Jonathan sleeping.

It seems only yesterday that the last entry was made, and yet how much between then, in Whitby and all the world before me, Jonathan away and no news of him; and now, married to Jonathan, Jonathan a solicitor, a partner, rich, master of his business, Mr. Hawkins dead and buried, and Jonathan with another attack that may harm him. Some day he may ask me about it. Down it all goes. I am rusty in my shorthand— see what unexpected prosperity does for us— so it may be as well to freshen it up again with an exercise anyhow....

The service was very simple and very solemn. There were only ourselves and the servants there, one or two old friends of his from Exeter, his London agent, and a gentleman representing Sir John Paxton, the President of the Incorporated Law Society. Jonathan and I stood hand in hand, and we felt that our best and dearest friend was gone from us....

We came back to town quietly, taking a 'bus to Hyde Park Corner. Jonathan thought it would interest me to go into the Row for a while, so we sat down; but there were very few people there, and it was sad-looking and desolate to see so many empty chairs. It made us think of the empty chair at home; so we got up and walked down Piccadilly. Jonathan was holding me by the arm, the way he used to in old days before I went to school. I felt it very improper, for you can't go on for some years teaching etiquette and decorum to other girls without the pedantry of it biting into yourself a bit; but it was Jonathan, and he was my husband, and we didn't know anybody who saw us— and we didn't care if they did— so on we walked. I was looking at a very beautiful girl, in a big cart-wheel hat, sitting in a victoria outside Guiliano's, when I felt Jonathan clutch my arm so tight that he hurt me, and he said under his breath: "My God!" I am always anxious about Jonathan, for I fear that some nervous fit may upset him again; so I turned to him quickly, and asked him what it was that disturbed him.

He was very pale, and his eyes seemed bulging out as, half in terror and half in amazement, he gazed at a tall, thin man, with a beaky nose and black moustache and pointed beard, who was also observing the pretty girl. He was looking at her so hard that he did not see either of us, and so I had a good view of him. His face was not a good face; it was hard, and cruel, and sensual, and his big white teeth, that looked all the whiter because his lips were so red, were pointed like an animal's. Jonathan kept staring at him, till I was afraid he would notice. I feared he might take it ill, he looked so fierce and nasty. I asked Jonathan why he was disturbed, and he answered, evidently thinking that I knew as much about it as he did: "Do you see who it is?"

"No, dear," I said; "I don't know him; who is it?" His answer seemed to shock and thrill me, for it was said as if he did not know that it was to me, Mina, to whom he was speaking:—

"It is the man himself!"

The poor dear was evidently terrified at something— very greatly terrified; I do believe that if he had not had me to lean on and to support him he would have sunk down. He kept staring; a man came out of the shop with a small parcel, and gave it to the lady, who then drove off. The dark man kept his eyes fixed on her, and when the carriage moved up Piccadilly he followed in the same direction, and hailed a hansom. Jonathan kept looking after him, and said, as if to himself:—

"I believe it is the Count, but he has grown young. My God, if this be so! Oh, my God! my God! If I only knew! if I only knew!" He was distressing himself so much that I feared to keep his mind on the subject by asking him any questions, so I remained silent. I drew him away quietly, and he, holding my arm, came easily. We walked a little further, and then went in and sat for a while in the Green Park. It was a hot day for autumn, and there was a comfortable seat in a shady place. After a few minutes' staring at nothing, Jonathan's eyes closed, and he went quietly into a sleep, with his head on my shoulder. I thought it was the best thing for him, so did not disturb him. In about twenty minutes he woke up, and said to me quite cheerfully:—

"Why, Mina, have I been asleep! Oh, do forgive me for being so rude. Come, and we'll have a cup of tea somewhere." He had evidently forgotten all about the dark stranger, as in his illness he had forgotten all that this episode had reminded him of. I don't like this lapsing into forgetfulness; it may make or continue some injury to the brain. I must not ask him, for fear I shall do more harm than good; but I must somehow learn the facts of his journey abroad. The time is come, I fear, when I must open that parcel, and know what is written. Oh, Jonathan, you will, I know, forgive me if I do wrong, but it is for your own dear sake.

Later.— A sad home-coming in every way— the house empty of the dear soul who was so good to us; Jonathan still pale and dizzy under a slight relapse of his malady; and now a telegram from Van Helsing, whoever he may be:—
"You will be grieved to hear that Mrs. Westenra died five days ago, and that Lucy died the day before yesterday. They were both buried to-day."
Oh, what a wealth of sorrow in a few words! Poor Mrs. Westenra! poor Lucy! Gone, gone, never to return to us! And poor, poor Arthur, to have lost such sweetness out of his life! God help us all to bear our troubles.
Dr. Seward's Diary.

22 September.— It is all over. Arthur has gone back to Ring, and has taken Quincey Morris with him. What a fine fellow is Quincey! I believe in my heart of hearts that he suffered as much about Lucy's death as any of us; but he bore himself through it like a moral Viking. If America can go on breeding men like that, she will be a power in the world indeed. Van Helsing is lying down, having a rest preparatory to his journey. He goes over to Amsterdam to-night, but says he returns to-morrow night; that he only wants to make some arrangements which can only be made personally. He is to stop with me then, if he can; he says he has work to do in London which may take him some time. Poor old fellow! I fear that the strain of the past week has broken down even his iron strength. All the time of the burial he was, I could see, putting some terrible restraint on himself. When it was all over, we were standing beside Arthur, who, poor fellow, was speaking of his part in the operation where his blood had been transfused to his Lucy's veins; I could see Van Helsing's face grow white and purple by turns. Arthur was saying that he felt since then as if they two had been really married and that she was his wife in the sight of God. None of us said a word of the other operations, and none of us ever shall. Arthur and Quincey went away together to the station, and Van Helsing and I came on here. The moment we were alone in the carriage he gave way to a regular fit of hysterics. He has denied to me since that it was hysterics, and insisted that it was only his sense of humour asserting itself under very terrible conditions. He laughed till he cried, and I had to draw down the blinds lest any one should see us and misjudge; and then he cried, till he laughed again; and laughed and cried together, just as a woman does. I tried to be stern with him, as one is to a woman under the circumstances; but it had no effect. Men and women are so different in manifestations of nervous strength or weakness! Then when his face grew grave and stern again I asked him why his mirth, and why at such a time. His reply was in a way characteristic of him, for it was logical and forceful and mysterious. He said:—

"Ah, you don't comprehend, friend John. Do not think that I am not sad, though I laugh. See, I have cried even when the laugh did choke me. But no more think that I am all sorry when I cry, for the laugh he come just the same. Keep it always with you that laughter who knock at your door and say, 'May I come in?' is not the true laughter. No! he is a king, and he come when and how he like. He ask no person; he choose no time of suitability. He say, 'I am here.' Behold, in example I grieve my heart out for that so sweet young girl; I give my blood for her, though I am old and worn; I give my time, my skill, my sleep; I let my other sufferers want that so she may have all. And yet I can laugh at her very grave— laugh when the clay from the spade of the sexton drop upon her coffin and say 'Thud! thud!' to my heart, till it send back the blood from my cheek. My heart bleed for that poor boy— that dear boy, so of the age of mine own boy had I been so blessed that he live, and with his hair and eyes the same. There, you know now why I love him so. And yet when he say things that touch my husband-heart to the quick, and make my father-heart yearn to him as to no other man— not even to you, friend John, for we are more level in experiences than father and son— yet even at such moment King Laugh he come to me and shout and bellow in my ear, 'Here I am! here I am!' till the blood come dance back and bring some of the sunshine that he carry with him to my cheek. Oh, friend John, it is a strange world, a sad world, a world full of miseries, and woes, and troubles; and yet when King Laugh come he make them all dance to the tune he play. Bleeding hearts, and dry bones of the churchyard, and tears that burn as they fall— all dance together to the music that he make with that smileless mouth of him. And believe me, friend John, that he is good to come, and kind. Ah, we men and women are like ropes drawn tight with strain that pull us different ways. Then tears come; and, like the rain on the ropes, they brace us up, until perhaps the strain become too great, and we break. But King Laugh he come like the sunshine, and he ease off the strain again; and we bear to go on with our labour, what it may be."
I did not like to wound him by pretending not to see his idea; but, as I did not yet understand the cause of his laughter, I asked him. As he answered me his face grew stern, and he said in quite a different tone:—

"Oh, it was the grim irony of it all— this so lovely lady garlanded with flowers, that looked so fair as life, till one by one we wondered if she were truly dead; she laid in that so fine marble house in that lonely churchyard, where rest so many of her kin, laid there with the mother who loved her, and whom she loved; and that sacred bell going 'Toll! toll! toll!' so sad and slow; and those holy men, with the white garments of the angel, pretending to read books, and yet all the time their eyes never on the page; and all of us with the bowed head. And all for what? She is dead; so! Is it not?"

"Well, for the life of me, Professor," I said, "I can't see anything to laugh at in all that. Why, your explanation makes it a harder puzzle than before. But even if the burial service was comic, what about poor Art and his trouble? Why, his heart was simply breaking."

"Just so. Said he not that the transfusion of his blood to her veins had made her truly his bride?"

"Yes, and it was a sweet and comforting idea for him."

"Quite so. But there was a difficulty, friend John. If so that, then what about the others? Ho, ho! Then this so sweet maid is a polyandrist, and me, with my poor wife dead to me, but alive by Church's law, though no wits, all gone— even I, who am faithful husband to this now-no-wife, am bigamist."

"I don't see where the joke comes in there either!" I said; and I did not feel particularly pleased with him for saying such things. He laid his hand on my arm, and said:—

"Friend John, forgive me if I pain. I showed not my feeling to others when it would wound, but only to you, my old friend, whom I can trust. If you could have looked into my very heart then when I want to laugh; if you could have done so when the laugh arrived; if you could do so now, when King Laugh have pack up his crown, and all that is to him— for he go far, far away from me, and for a long, long time— maybe you would perhaps pity me the most of all."

I was touched by the tenderness of his tone, and asked why.

"Because I know!"

And now we are all scattered; and for many a long day loneliness will sit over our roofs with brooding wings. Lucy lies in the tomb of her kin, a lordly death-house in a lonely churchyard, away from teeming London; where the air is fresh, and the sun rises over Hampstead Hill, and where wild flowers grow of their own accord.

So I can finish this diary; and God only knows if I shall ever begin another. If I do, or if I even open this again, it will be to deal with different people and different themes; for here at the end, where the romance of my life is told, ere I go back to take up the thread of my life-work, I say sadly and without hope,

"FINIS."

"The Westminster Gazette," 25 September.

A HAMPSTEAD MYSTERY.

The neighbourhood of Hampstead is just at present exercised with a series of events which seem to run on lines parallel to those of what was known to the writers of headlines as "The Kensington Horror," or "The Stabbing Woman," or "The Woman in Black." During the past two or three days several cases have occurred of young children straying from home or neglecting to return from their playing on the Heath. In all these cases the children were too young to give any properly intelligible account of themselves, but the consensus of their excuses is that they had been with a "bloofer lady." It has always been late in the evening when they have been missed, and on two occasions the children have not been found until early in the following morning. It is generally supposed in the neighbourhood that, as the first child missed gave as his reason for being away that a "bloofer lady" had asked him to come for a walk, the others had picked up the phrase and used it as occasion served. This is the more natural as the favourite game of the little ones at present is luring each other away by wiles. A correspondent writes us that to see some of the tiny tots pretending to be the "bloofer lady" is supremely funny. Some of our caricaturists might, he says, take a lesson in the irony of grotesque by comparing the reality and the picture. It is only in accordance with general principles of human nature that the "bloofer lady" should be the popular rôle at these al fresco performances. Our correspondent naïvely says that even Ellen Terry could not be so winningly attractive as some of these grubby-faced little children pretend— and even imagine themselves— to be.

There is, however, possibly a serious side to the question, for some of the children, indeed all who have been missed at night, have been slightly torn or wounded in the throat. The wounds seem such as might be made by a rat or a small dog, and although of not much importance individually, would tend to show that whatever animal inflicts them has a system or method of its own. The police of the division have been instructed to keep a sharp look-out for straying children, especially when very young, in and around Hampstead Heath, and for any stray dog which may be about.

"The Westminster Gazette," 25 September.

Extra Special.

THE HAMPSTEAD HORROR.

ANOTHER CHILD INJURED.

The "Bloofer Lady."

We have just received intelligence that another child, missed last night, was only discovered late in the morning under a furze bush at the Shooter's Hill side of Hampstead Heath, which is, perhaps, less frequented than the other parts. It has the same tiny wound in the throat as has been noticed in other cases. It was terribly weak, and looked quite emaciated. It too, when partially restored, had the common story to tell of being lured away by the "bloofer lady."

## CHAPTER XIV
## MINA HARKER'S JOURNAL

**2**3 September.— Jonathan is better after a bad night. I am so glad that he has plenty of work to do, for that keeps his mind off the terrible things; and oh, I am rejoiced that he is not now weighed down with the responsibility of his new position. I knew he would be true to himself, and now how proud I am to see my Jonathan rising to the height of his advancement and keeping pace in all ways with the duties that come upon him. He will be away all day till late, for he said he could not lunch at home. My household work is done, so I shall take his foreign journal, and lock myself up in my room and read it....

24 September.— I hadn't the heart to write last night; that terrible record of Jonathan's upset me so. Poor dear! How he must have suffered, whether it be true or only imagination. I wonder if there is any truth in it at all. Did he get his brain fever, and then write all those terrible things, or had he some cause for it all? I suppose I shall never know, for I dare not open the subject to him.... And yet that man we saw yesterday! He seemed quite certain of him.... Poor fellow! I suppose it was the funeral upset him and sent his mind back on some train of thought.... He believes it all himself. I remember how on our wedding-day he said: "Unless some solemn duty come upon me to go back to the bitter hours, asleep or awake, mad or sane." There seems to be through it all some thread of continuity.... That fearful Count was coming to London.... If it should be, and he came to London, with his teeming millions.... There may be a solemn duty; and if it come we must not shrink from it.... I shall be prepared. I shall get my typewriter this very hour and begin transcribing. Then we shall be ready for other eyes if required. And if it be wanted; then, perhaps, if I am ready, poor Jonathan may not be upset, for I can speak for him and never let him be troubled or worried with it at all. If ever Jonathan quite gets over the nervousness he may want to tell me of it all, and I can ask him questions and find out things, and see how I may comfort him.

Letter, Van Helsing to Mrs. Harker.

"24 September.

(Confidence)

"Dear Madam,—

"I pray you to pardon my writing, in that I am so far friend as that I sent to you sad news of Miss Lucy Westenra's death. By the kindness of Lord Godalming, I am empowered to read her letters and papers, for I am deeply concerned about certain matters vitally important. In them I find some letters from you, which show how great friends you were and how you love her. Oh, Madam Mina, by that love, I implore you, help me. It is for others' good that I ask— to redress great wrong, and to lift much and terrible troubles— that may be more great than you can know. May it be that I see you? You can trust me. I am friend of Dr. John Seward and of Lord Godalming (that was Arthur of Miss Lucy). I must keep it private for the present from all. I should come to Exeter to see you at once if you tell me I am privilege to come, and where and when. I implore your pardon, madam. I have read your letters to poor Lucy, and know how good you are and how your husband suffer; so I pray you, if it may be, enlighten him not, lest it may harm. Again your pardon, and forgive me.

"Van Helsing."

Telegram, Mrs. Harker to Van Helsing.

"25 September.— Come to-day by quarter-past ten train if you can catch it. Can see you any time you call.

"Wilhelmina Harker."

MINA HARKER'S JOURNAL.

25 September.— I cannot help feeling terribly excited as the time draws near for the visit of Dr. Van Helsing, for somehow I expect that it will throw some light upon Jonathan's sad experience; and as he attended poor dear Lucy in her last illness, he can tell me all about her. That is the reason of his coming; it is concerning Lucy and her sleep-walking, and not about Jonathan. Then I shall never know the real truth now! How silly I am. That awful journal gets hold of my imagination and tinges everything with something of its own colour. Of course it is about Lucy. That habit came back to the poor dear, and that awful night on the cliff must have made her ill. I had almost forgotten in my own affairs how ill she was afterwards. She must have told him of her sleep-walking adventure on the cliff, and that I knew all about it; and now he wants me to tell him what she knows, so that he may understand. I hope I did right in not saying anything of it to Mrs. Westenra; I should never forgive myself if any act of mine, were it even a negative one, brought harm on poor dear Lucy. I hope, too, Dr. Van Helsing will not blame me; I have had so much trouble and anxiety of late that I feel I cannot bear more just at present.

I suppose a cry does us all good at times— clears the air as other rain does. Perhaps it was reading the journal yesterday that upset me, and then Jonathan went away this morning to stay away from me a whole day and night, the first time we have been parted since our marriage. I do hope the dear fellow will take care of himself, and that nothing will occur to upset him. It is two o'clock, and the doctor will be here soon now. I shall say nothing of Jonathan's journal unless he asks me. I am so glad I have type-written out my own journal, so that, in case he asks about Lucy, I can hand it to him; it will save much questioning.

Later.— He has come and gone. Oh, what a strange meeting, and how it all makes my head whirl round! I feel like one in a dream. Can it be all possible, or even a part of it? If I had not read Jonathan's journal first, I should never have accepted even a possibility. Poor, poor, dear Jonathan! How he must have suffered. Please the good God, all this may not upset him again. I shall try to save him from it; but it may be even a consolation and a help to him— terrible though it be and awful in its consequences— to know for certain that his eyes and ears and brain did not deceive him, and that it is all true. It may be that it is the doubt which haunts him; that when the doubt is removed, no matter which— waking or dreaming— may prove the truth, he will be more satisfied and better able to bear the shock. Dr. Van Helsing must be a good man as well as a clever one if he is Arthur's friend and Dr. Seward's, and if they brought him all the way from Holland to look after Lucy. I feel from having seen him that he is good and kind and of a noble nature. When he comes to-morrow I shall ask him about Jonathan; and then, please God, all this sorrow and anxiety may lead to a good end. I used to think I would like to practise interviewing; Jonathan's friend on "The Exeter News" told him that memory was everything in such work— that you must be able to put down exactly almost every word spoken, even if you had to refine some of it afterwards. Here was a rare interview; I shall try to record it verbatim. It was half-past two o'clock when the knock came. I took my courage à deux mains and waited. In a few minutes Mary opened the door, and announced "Dr. Van Helsing."

I rose and bowed, and he came towards me; a man of medium weight, strongly built, with his shoulders set back over a broad, deep chest and a neck well balanced on the trunk as the head is on the neck. The poise of the head strikes one at once as indicative of thought and power; the head is noble, well-sized, broad, and large behind the ears. The face, clean-shaven, shows a hard, square chin, a large, resolute, mobile mouth, a good-sized nose, rather straight, but with quick, sensitive nostrils, that seem to broaden as the big, bushy brows come down and the mouth tightens. The forehead is broad and fine, rising at first almost straight and then sloping back above two bumps or ridges wide apart; such a forehead that the reddish hair cannot possibly tumble over it, but falls naturally back and to the sides. Big, dark blue eyes are set widely apart, and are quick and tender or stern with the man's moods. He said to me:—

"Mrs. Harker, is it not?" I bowed assent.

"That was Miss Mina Murray?" Again I assented.

"It is Mina Murray that I came to see that was friend of that poor dear child Lucy Westenra. Madam Mina, it is on account of the dead I come."

"Sir," I said, "you could have no better claim on me than that you were a friend and helper of Lucy Westenra." And I held out my hand. He took it and said tenderly:—

"Oh, Madam Mina, I knew that the friend of that poor lily girl must be good, but I had yet to learn— — " He finished his speech with a courtly bow. I asked him what it was that he wanted to see me about, so he at once began:—

"I have read your letters to Miss Lucy. Forgive me, but I had to begin to inquire somewhere, and there was none to ask. I know that you were with her at Whitby. She sometimes kept a diary— you need not look surprised, Madam Mina; it was begun after you had left, and was in imitation of you— and in that diary she traces by inference certain things to a sleep-walking in which she puts down that you saved her. In great perplexity then I come to you, and ask you out of your so much kindness to tell me all of it that you can remember."

"I can tell you, I think, Dr. Van Helsing, all about it."

"Ah, then you have good memory for facts, for details? It is not always so with young ladies."

"No, doctor, but I wrote it all down at the time. I can show it to you if you like."

"Oh, Madam Mina, I will be grateful; you will do me much favour." I could not resist the temptation of mystifying him a bit— I suppose it is some of the taste of the original apple that remains still in our mouths— so I handed him the shorthand diary. He took it with a grateful bow, and said:—

"May I read it?"

"If you wish," I answered as demurely as I could. He opened it, and for an instant his face fell. Then he stood up and bowed.

"Oh, you so clever woman!" he said. "I knew long that Mr. Jonathan was a man of much thankfulness; but see, his wife have all the good things. And will you not so much honour me and so help me as to read it for me? Alas! I know not the shorthand." By this time my little joke was over, and I was almost ashamed; so I took the typewritten copy from my workbasket and handed it to him.

"Forgive me," I said: "I could not help it; but I had been thinking that it was of dear Lucy that you wished to ask, and so that you might not have time to wait— not on my account, but because I know your time must be precious— I have written it out on the typewriter for you."

He took it and his eyes glistened. "You are so good," he said. "And may I read it now? I may want to ask you some things when I have read."

"By all means," I said, "read it over whilst I order lunch; and then you can ask me questions whilst we eat." He bowed and settled himself in a chair with his back to the light, and became absorbed in the papers, whilst I went to see after lunch chiefly in order that he might not be disturbed. When I came back, I found him walking hurriedly up and down the room, his face all ablaze with excitement. He rushed up to me and took me by both hands.

"Oh, Madam Mina," he said, "how can I say what I owe to you? This paper is as sunshine. It opens the gate to me. I am daze, I am dazzle, with so much light, and yet clouds roll in behind the light every time. But that you do not, cannot, comprehend. Oh, but I am grateful to you, you so clever woman. Madam"— he said this very solemnly— "if ever Abraham Van Helsing can do anything for you or yours, I trust you will let me know. It will be pleasure and delight if I may serve you as a friend; as a friend, but all I have ever learned, all I can ever do, shall be for you and those you love. There are darknesses in life, and there are lights; you are one of the lights. You will have happy life and good life, and your husband will be blessed in you."

"But, doctor, you praise me too much, and— and you do not know me."

"Not know you— I, who am old, and who have studied all my life men and women; I, who have made my specialty the brain and all that belongs to him and all that follow from him! And I have read your diary that you have so goodly written for me, and which breathes out truth in every line. I, who have read your so sweet letter to poor Lucy of your marriage and your trust, not know you! Oh, Madam Mina, good women tell all their lives, and by day and by hour and by minute, such things that angels can read; and we men who wish to know have in us something of angels' eyes. Your husband is noble nature, and you are noble too, for you trust, and trust cannot be where there is mean nature. And your husband— tell me of him. Is he quite well? Is all that fever gone, and is he strong and hearty?" I saw here an opening to ask him about Jonathan, so I said:—

"He was almost recovered, but he has been greatly upset by Mr. Hawkins's death." He interrupted:—

"Oh, yes, I know, I know. I have read your last two letters." I went on:—

"I suppose this upset him, for when we were in town on Thursday last he had a sort of shock."

"A shock, and after brain fever so soon! That was not good. What kind of a shock was it?"

"He thought he saw some one who recalled something terrible, something which led to his brain fever." And here the whole thing seemed to overwhelm me in a rush. The pity for Jonathan, the horror which he experienced, the whole fearful mystery of his diary, and the fear that has been brooding over me ever since, all came in a tumult. I suppose I was hysterical, for I threw myself on my knees and held up my hands to him, and implored him to make my husband well again. He took my hands and raised me up, and made me sit on the sofa, and sat by me; he held my hand in his, and said to me with, oh, such infinite sweetness:—

"My life is a barren and lonely one, and so full of work that I have not had much time for friendships; but since I have been summoned to here by my friend John Seward I have known so many good people and seen such nobility that I feel more than ever— and it has grown with my advancing years— the loneliness of my life. Believe, me, then, that I come here full of respect for you, and you have given me hope— hope, not in what I am seeking of, but that there are good women still left to make life happy— good women, whose lives and whose truths may make good lesson for the children that are to be. I am glad, glad, that I may here be of some use to you; for if your husband suffer, he suffer within the range of my study and experience. I promise you that I will gladly do all for him that I can— all to make his life strong and manly, and your life a happy one. Now you must eat. You are overwrought and perhaps over-anxious. Husband Jonathan would not like to see you so pale; and what he like not where he love, is not to his good. Therefore for his sake you must eat and smile. You have told me all about Lucy, and so now we shall not speak of it, lest it distress. I shall stay in Exeter to-night, for I want to think much over what you have told me, and when I have thought I will ask you questions, if I may. And then, too, you will tell me of husband Jonathan's trouble so far as you can, but not yet. You must eat now; afterwards you shall tell me all."

After lunch, when we went back to the drawing-room, he said to me:—
"And now tell me all about him." When it came to speaking to this great learned man, I began to fear that he would think me a weak fool, and Jonathan a madman— that journal is all so strange— and I hesitated to go on. But he was so sweet and kind, and he had promised to help, and I trusted him, so I said:—

"Dr. Van Helsing, what I have to tell you is so queer that you must not laugh at me or at my husband. I have been since yesterday in a sort of fever of doubt; you must be kind to me, and not think me foolish that I have even half believed some very strange things." He reassured me by his manner as well as his words when he said:—

"Oh, my dear, if you only know how strange is the matter regarding which I am here, it is you who would laugh. I have learned not to think little of any one's belief, no matter how strange it be. I have tried to keep an open mind; and it is not the ordinary things of life that could close it, but the strange things, the extraordinary things, the things that make one doubt if they be mad or sane."

"Thank you, thank you, a thousand times! You have taken a weight off my mind. If you will let me, I shall give you a paper to read. It is long, but I have typewritten it out. It will tell you my trouble and Jonathan's. It is the copy of his journal when abroad, and all that happened. I dare not say anything of it; you will read for yourself and judge. And then when I see you, perhaps, you will be very kind and tell me what you think."

"I promise," he said as I gave him the papers; "I shall in the morning, so soon as I can, come to see you and your husband, if I may."

"Jonathan will be here at half-past eleven, and you must come to lunch with us and see him then; you could catch the quick 3:34 train, which will leave you at Paddington before eight." He was surprised at my knowledge of the trains off-hand, but he does not know that I have made up all the trains to and from Exeter, so that I may help Jonathan in case he is in a hurry.

So he took the papers with him and went away, and I sit here thinking— thinking I don't know what.

Letter (by hand), Van Helsing to Mrs. Harker.

"25 September, 6 o'clock.

"Dear Madam Mina,—

"I have read your husband's so wonderful diary. You may sleep without doubt. Strange and terrible as it is, it is true! I will pledge my life on it. It may be worse for others; but for him and you there is no dread. He is a noble fellow; and let me tell you from experience of men, that one who would do as he did in going down that wall and to that room— ay, and going a second time— is not one to be injured in permanence by a shock. His brain and his heart are all right; this I swear, before I have even seen him; so be at rest. I shall have much to ask him of other things. I am blessed that to-day I come to see you, for I have learn all at once so much that again I am dazzle— dazzle more than ever, and I must think.

"Yours the most faithful,

"Abraham Van Helsing."

Letter, Mrs. Harker to Van Helsing.

"25 September, 6:30 p. m.

"My dear Dr. Van Helsing,—

"A thousand thanks for your kind letter, which has taken a great weight off my mind. And yet, if it be true, what terrible things there are in the world, and what an awful thing if that man, that monster, be really in London! I fear to think. I have this moment, whilst writing, had a wire from Jonathan, saying that he leaves by the 6:25 to-night from Launceston and will be here at 10:18, so that I shall have no fear to-night. Will you, therefore, instead of lunching with us, please come to breakfast at eight o'clock, if this be not too early for you? You can get away, if you are in a hurry, by the 10:30 train, which will bring you to Paddington by 2:35. Do not answer this, as I shall take it that, if I do not hear, you will come to breakfast.

"Believe me,

"Your faithful and grateful friend,

"Mina Harker."

Jonathan Harker's Journal.

26 September.— I thought never to write in this diary again, but the time has come. When I got home last night Mina had supper ready, and when we had supped she told me of Van Helsing's visit, and of her having given him the two diaries copied out, and of how anxious she has been about me. She showed me in the doctor's letter that all I wrote down was true. It seems to have made a new man of me. It was the doubt as to the reality of the whole thing that knocked me over. I felt impotent, and in the dark, and distrustful. But, now that I know, I am not afraid, even of the Count. He has succeeded after all, then, in his design in getting to London, and it was he I saw. He has got younger, and how? Van Helsing is the man to unmask him and hunt him out, if he is anything like what Mina says. We sat late, and talked it all over. Mina is dressing, and I shall call at the hotel in a few minutes and bring him over....

He was, I think, surprised to see me. When I came into the room where he was, and introduced myself, he took me by the shoulder, and turned my face round to the light, and said, after a sharp scrutiny:—

"But Madam Mina told me you were ill, that you had had a shock." It was so funny to hear my wife called "Madam Mina" by this kindly, strong-faced old man. I smiled, and said:—

"I was ill, I have had a shock; but you have cured me already."

"And how?"

"By your letter to Mina last night. I was in doubt, and then everything took a hue of unreality, and I did not know what to trust, even the evidence of my own senses. Not knowing what to trust, I did not know what to do; and so had only to keep on working in what had hitherto been the groove of my life. The groove ceased to avail me, and I mistrusted myself. Doctor, you don't know what it is to doubt everything, even yourself. No, you don't; you couldn't with eyebrows like yours." He seemed pleased, and laughed as he said:—

"So! You are physiognomist. I learn more here with each hour. I am with so much pleasure coming to you to breakfast; and, oh, sir, you will pardon praise from an old man, but you are blessed in your wife." I would listen to him go on praising Mina for a day, so I simply nodded and stood silent.

"She is one of God's women, fashioned by His own hand to show us men and other women that there is a heaven where we can enter, and that its light can be here on earth. So true, so sweet, so noble, so little an egoist— and that, let me tell you, is much in this age, so sceptical and selfish. And you, sir— I have read all the letters to poor Miss Lucy, and some of them speak of you, so I know you since some days from the knowing of others; but I have seen your true self since last night. You will give me your hand, will you not? And let us be friends for all our lives."

We shook hands, and he was so earnest and so kind that it made me quite choky.

"And now," he said, "may I ask you for some more help? I have a great task to do, and at the beginning it is to know. You can help me here. Can you tell me what went before your going to Transylvania? Later on I may ask more help, and of a different kind; but at first this will do."

"Look here, sir," I said, "does what you have to do concern the Count?"

"It does," he said solemnly.

"Then I am with you heart and soul. As you go by the 10:30 train, you will not have time to read them; but I shall get the bundle of papers. You can take them with you and read them in the train."

After breakfast I saw him to the station. When we were parting he said:—

"Perhaps you will come to town if I send to you, and take Madam Mina too."

"We shall both come when you will," I said.

200

I had got him the morning papers and the London papers of the previous night, and while we were talking at the carriage window, waiting for the train to start, he was turning them over. His eyes suddenly seemed to catch something in one of them, "The Westminster Gazette"— I knew it by the colour— and he grew quite white. He read something intently, groaning to himself: "Mein Gott! Mein Gott! So soon! so soon!" I do not think he remembered me at the moment. Just then the whistle blew, and the train moved off. This recalled him to himself, and he leaned out of the window and waved his hand, calling out: "Love to Madam Mina; I shall write so soon as ever I can."

Dr. Seward's Diary.

26 September.— Truly there is no such thing as finality. Not a week since I said "Finis," and yet here I am starting fresh again, or rather going on with the same record. Until this afternoon I had no cause to think of what is done. Renfield had become, to all intents, as sane as he ever was. He was already well ahead with his fly business; and he had just started in the spider line also; so he had not been of any trouble to me. I had a letter from Arthur, written on Sunday, and from it I gather that he is bearing up wonderfully well. Quincey Morris is with him, and that is much of a help, for he himself is a bubbling well of good spirits. Quincey wrote me a line too, and from him I hear that Arthur is beginning to recover something of his old buoyancy; so as to them all my mind is at rest. As for myself, I was settling down to my work with the enthusiasm which I used to have for it, so that I might fairly have said that the wound which poor Lucy left on me was becoming cicatrised. Everything is, however, now reopened; and what is to be the end God only knows. I have an idea that Van Helsing thinks he knows, too, but he will only let out enough at a time to whet curiosity. He went to Exeter yesterday, and stayed there all night. To-day he came back, and almost bounded into the room at about half-past five o'clock, and thrust last night's "Westminster Gazette" into my hand.

"What do you think of that?" he asked as he stood back and folded his arms.

I looked over the paper, for I really did not know what he meant; but he took it from me and pointed out a paragraph about children being decoyed away at Hampstead. It did not convey much to me, until I reached a passage where it described small punctured wounds on their throats. An idea struck me, and I looked up. "Well?" he said.

"It is like poor Lucy's."

"And what do you make of it?"

"Simply that there is some cause in common. Whatever it was that injured her has injured them." I did not quite understand his answer:— "That is true indirectly, but not directly."

"How do you mean, Professor?" I asked. I was a little inclined to take his seriousness lightly— for, after all, four days of rest and freedom from burning, harrowing anxiety does help to restore one's spirits— but when I saw his face, it sobered me. Never, even in the midst of our despair about poor Lucy, had he looked more stern.

"Tell me!" I said. "I can hazard no opinion. I do not know what to think, and I have no data on which to found a conjecture."

"Do you mean to tell me, friend John, that you have no suspicion as to what poor Lucy died of; not after all the hints given, not only by events, but by me?"

"Of nervous prostration following on great loss or waste of blood."

"And how the blood lost or waste?" I shook my head. He stepped over and sat down beside me, and went on:—

"You are clever man, friend John; you reason well, and your wit is bold; but you are too prejudiced. You do not let your eyes see nor your ears hear, and that which is outside your daily life is not of account to you. Do you not think that there are things which you cannot understand, and yet which are; that some people see things that others cannot? But there are things old and new which must not be contemplate by men's eyes, because they know— or think they know— some things which other men have told them. Ah, it is the fault of our science that it wants to explain all; and if it explain not, then it says there is nothing to explain. But yet we see around us every day the growth of new beliefs, which think themselves new; and which are yet but the old, which pretend to be young— like the fine ladies at the opera. I suppose now you do not believe in corporeal transference. No? Nor in materialisation. No? Nor in astral bodies. No? Nor in the reading of thought. No? Nor in hypnotism— — "

"Yes," I said. "Charcot has proved that pretty well." He smiled as he went on: "Then you are satisfied as to it. Yes? And of course then you understand how it act, and can follow the mind of the great Charcot— alas that he is no more!— into the very soul of the patient that he influence. No? Then, friend John, am I to take it that you simply accept fact, and are satisfied to let from premise to conclusion be a blank? No? Then tell me— for I am student of the brain— how you accept the hypnotism and reject the thought reading. Let me tell you, my friend, that there are things done to-day in electrical science which would have been deemed unholy by the very men who discovered electricity— who would themselves not so long before have been burned as wizards. There are always mysteries in life. Why was it that Methuselah lived nine hundred years, and 'Old Parr' one hundred and sixty-nine, and yet that poor Lucy, with four men's blood in her poor veins, could not live even one day? For, had she live one more day, we could have save her. Do you know all the mystery of life and death? Do you know the altogether of comparative anatomy and can say wherefore the qualities of brutes are in some men, and not in others? Can you tell me why, when other spiders die small and soon, that one great spider lived for centuries in the tower of the old Spanish church and grew and grew, till, on descending, he could drink the oil of all the church lamps? Can you tell me why in the Pampas, ay and elsewhere, there are bats that come at night and open the veins of cattle and horses and suck dry their veins; how in some islands of the Western seas there are bats which hang on the trees all day, and those who have seen describe as like giant nuts or pods, and that when the sailors sleep on the deck, because that it is hot, flit down on them, and then— and then in the morning are found dead men, white as even Miss Lucy was?"

"Good God, Professor!" I said, starting up. "Do you mean to tell me that Lucy was bitten by such a bat; and that such a thing is here in London in the nineteenth century?" He waved his hand for silence, and went on:—

"Can you tell me why the tortoise lives more long than generations of men; why the elephant goes on and on till he have seen dynasties; and why the parrot never die only of bite of cat or dog or other complaint? Can you tell me why men believe in all ages and places that there are some few who live on always if they be permit; that there are men and women who cannot die? We all know— because science has vouched for the fact— that there have been toads shut up in rocks for thousands of years, shut in one so small hole that only hold him since the youth of the world. Can you tell me how the Indian fakir can make himself to die and have been buried, and his grave sealed and corn sowed on it, and the corn reaped and be cut and sown and reaped and cut again, and then men come and take away the unbroken seal and that there lie the Indian fakir, not dead, but that rise up and walk amongst them as before?" Here I interrupted him. I was getting bewildered; he so crowded on my mind his list of nature's eccentricities and possible impossibilities that my imagination was getting fired. I had a dim idea that he was teaching me some lesson, as long ago he used to do in his study at Amsterdam; but he used then to tell me the thing, so that I could have the object of thought in mind all the time. But now I was without this help, yet I wanted to follow him, so I said:—

"Professor, let me be your pet student again. Tell me the thesis, so that I may apply your knowledge as you go on. At present I am going in my mind from point to point as a mad man, and not a sane one, follows an idea. I feel like a novice lumbering through a bog in a mist, jumping from one tussock to another in the mere blind effort to move on without knowing where I am going."

"That is good image," he said. "Well, I shall tell you. My thesis is this: I want you to believe."

"To believe what?"

"To believe in things that you cannot. Let me illustrate. I heard once of an American who so defined faith: 'that faculty which enables us to believe things which we know to be untrue.' For one, I follow that man. He meant that we shall have an open mind, and not let a little bit of truth check the rush of a big truth, like a small rock does a railway truck. We get the small truth first. Good! We keep him, and we value him; but all the same we must not let him think himself all the truth in the universe."

"Then you want me not to let some previous conviction injure the receptivity of my mind with regard to some strange matter. Do I read your lesson aright?"

"Ah, you are my favourite pupil still. It is worth to teach you. Now that you are willing to understand, you have taken the first step to understand. You think then that those so small holes in the children's throats were made by the same that made the hole in Miss Lucy?"

"I suppose so." He stood up and said solemnly:—

"Then you are wrong. Oh, would it were so! but alas! no. It is worse, far, far worse."

"In God's name, Professor Van Helsing, what do you mean?" I cried.

He threw himself with a despairing gesture into a chair, and placed his elbows on the table, covering his face with his hands as he spoke:—

"They were made by Miss Lucy!"

## CHAPTER XV
## DR. SEWARD'S DIARY— continued.

FOR a while sheer anger mastered me; it was as if he had during her life struck Lucy on the face. I smote the table hard and rose up as I said to him:—

"Dr. Van Helsing, are you mad?" He raised his head and looked at me, and somehow the tenderness of his face calmed me at once. "Would I were!" he said. "Madness were easy to bear compared with truth like this. Oh, my friend, why, think you, did I go so far round, why take so long to tell you so simple a thing? Was it because I hate you and have hated you all my life? Was it because I wished to give you pain? Was it that I wanted, now so late, revenge for that time when you saved my life, and from a fearful death? Ah no!"

"Forgive me," said I. He went on:—

"My friend, it was because I wished to be gentle in the breaking to you, for I know you have loved that so sweet lady. But even yet I do not expect you to believe. It is so hard to accept at once any abstract truth, that we may doubt such to be possible when we have always believed the 'no' of it; it is more hard still to accept so sad a concrete truth, and of such a one as Miss Lucy. To-night I go to prove it. Dare you come with me?"

This staggered me. A man does not like to prove such a truth; Byron excepted from the category, jealousy.

"And prove the very truth he most abhorred."

He saw my hesitation, and spoke:—

"The logic is simple, no madman's logic this time, jumping from tussock to tussock in a misty bog. If it be not true, then proof will be relief; at worst it will not harm. If it be true! Ah, there is the dread; yet very dread should help my cause, for in it is some need of belief. Come, I tell you what I propose: first, that we go off now and see that child in the hospital. Dr. Vincent, of the North Hospital, where the papers say the child is, is friend of mine, and I think of yours since you were in class at Amsterdam. He will let two scientists see his case, if he will not let two friends. We shall tell him nothing, but only that we wish to learn. And then— — "

"And then?" He took a key from his pocket and held it up. "And then we spend the night, you and I, in the churchyard where Lucy lies. This is the key that lock the tomb. I had it from the coffin-man to give to Arthur." My heart sank within me, for I felt that there was some fearful ordeal before us. I could do nothing, however, so I plucked up what heart I could and said that we had better hasten, as the afternoon was passing....

We found the child awake. It had had a sleep and taken some food, and altogether was going on well. Dr. Vincent took the bandage from its throat, and showed us the punctures. There was no mistaking the similarity to those which had been on Lucy's throat. They were smaller, and the edges looked fresher; that was all. We asked Vincent to what he attributed them, and he replied that it must have been a bite of some animal, perhaps a rat; but, for his own part, he was inclined to think that it was one of the bats which are so numerous on the northern heights of London. "Out of so many harmless ones," he said, "there may be some wild specimen from the South of a more malignant species. Some sailor may have brought one home, and it managed to escape; or even from the Zoölogical Gardens a young one may have got loose, or one be bred there from a vampire. These things do occur, you know. Only ten days ago a wolf got out, and was, I believe, traced up in this direction. For a week after, the children were playing nothing but Red Riding Hood on the Heath and in every alley in the place until this 'bloofer lady' scare came along, since when it has been quite a gala-time with them. Even this poor little mite, when he woke up to-day, asked the nurse if he might go away. When she asked him why he wanted to go, he said he wanted to play with the 'bloofer lady.' "

"I hope," said Van Helsing, "that when you are sending the child home you will caution its parents to keep strict watch over it. These fancies to stray are most dangerous; and if the child were to remain out another night, it would probably be fatal. But in any case I suppose you will not let it away for some days?"

"Certainly not, not for a week at least; longer if the wound is not healed."

Our visit to the hospital took more time than we had reckoned on, and the sun had dipped before we came out. When Van Helsing saw how dark it was, he said:—

"There is no hurry. It is more late than I thought. Come, let us seek somewhere that we may eat, and then we shall go on our way."

We dined at "Jack Straw's Castle" along with a little crowd of bicyclists and others who were genially noisy. About ten o'clock we started from the inn. It was then very dark, and the scattered lamps made the darkness greater when we were once outside their individual radius. The Professor had evidently noted the road we were to go, for he went on unhesitatingly; but, as for me, I was in quite a mixup as to locality. As we went further, we met fewer and fewer people, till at last we were somewhat surprised when we met even the patrol of horse police going their usual suburban round. At last we reached the wall of the churchyard, which we climbed over. With some little difficulty— for it was very dark, and the whole place seemed so strange to us— we found the Westenra tomb. The Professor took the key, opened the creaky door, and standing back, politely, but quite unconsciously, motioned me to precede him. There was a delicious irony in the offer, in the courtliness of giving preference on such a ghastly occasion. My companion followed me quickly, and cautiously drew the door to, after carefully ascertaining that the lock was a falling, and not a spring, one. In the latter case we should have been in a bad plight. Then he fumbled in his bag, and taking out a matchbox and a piece of candle, proceeded to make a light. The tomb in the day-time, and when wreathed with fresh flowers, had looked grim and gruesome enough; but now, some days afterwards, when the flowers hung lank and dead, their whites turning to rust and their greens to browns; when the spider and the beetle had resumed their accustomed dominance; when time-discoloured stone, and dust-encrusted mortar, and rusty, dank iron, and tarnished brass, and clouded silver-plating gave back the feeble glimmer of a candle, the effect was more miserable and sordid than could have been imagined. It conveyed irresistibly the idea that life— animal life— was not the only thing which could pass away.

Van Helsing went about his work systematically. Holding his candle so that he could read the coffin plates, and so holding it that the sperm dropped in white patches which congealed as they touched the metal, he made assurance of Lucy's coffin. Another search in his bag, and he took out a turnscrew.

"What are you going to do?" I asked.

"To open the coffin. You shall yet be convinced." Straightway he began taking out the screws, and finally lifted off the lid, showing the casing of lead beneath. The sight was almost too much for me. It seemed to be as much an affront to the dead as it would have been to have stripped off her clothing in her sleep whilst living; I actually took hold of his hand to stop him. He only said: "You shall see," and again fumbling in his bag, took out a tiny fret-saw. Striking the turnscrew through the lead with a swift downward stab, which made me wince, he made a small hole, which was, however, big enough to admit the point of the saw. I had expected a rush of gas from the week-old corpse. We doctors, who have had to study our dangers, have to become accustomed to such things, and I drew back towards the door. But the Professor never stopped for a moment; he sawed down a couple of feet along one side of the lead coffin, and then across, and down the other side. Taking the edge of the loose flange, he bent it back towards the foot of the coffin, and holding up the candle into the aperture, motioned to me to look.

I drew near and looked. The coffin was empty.

It was certainly a surprise to me, and gave me a considerable shock, but Van Helsing was unmoved. He was now more sure than ever of his ground, and so emboldened to proceed in his task. "Are you satisfied now, friend John?" he asked.

I felt all the dogged argumentativeness of my nature awake within me as I answered him:—

"I am satisfied that Lucy's body is not in that coffin; but that only proves one thing."

"And what is that, friend John?"

"That it is not there."

"That is good logic," he said, "so far as it goes. But how do you— how can you— account for it not being there?"

"Perhaps a body-snatcher," I suggested. "Some of the undertaker's people may have stolen it." I felt that I was speaking folly, and yet it was the only real cause which I could suggest. The Professor sighed. "Ah well!" he said, "we must have more proof. Come with me."

He put on the coffin-lid again, gathered up all his things and placed them in the bag, blew out the light, and placed the candle also in the bag. We opened the door, and went out. Behind us he closed the door and locked it. He handed me the key, saying: "Will you keep it? You had better be assured." I laughed— it was not a very cheerful laugh, I am bound to say— as I motioned him to keep it. "A key is nothing," I said; "there may be duplicates; and anyhow it is not difficult to pick a lock of that kind." He said nothing, but put the key in his pocket. Then he told me to watch at one side of the churchyard whilst he would watch at the other. I took up my place behind a yew-tree, and I saw his dark figure move until the intervening headstones and trees hid it from my sight.

It was a lonely vigil. Just after I had taken my place I heard a distant clock strike twelve, and in time came one and two. I was chilled and unnerved, and angry with the Professor for taking me on such an errand and with myself for coming. I was too cold and too sleepy to be keenly observant, and not sleepy enough to betray my trust so altogether I had a dreary, miserable time.

Suddenly, as I turned round, I thought I saw something like a white streak, moving between two dark yew-trees at the side of the churchyard farthest from the tomb; at the same time a dark mass moved from the Professor's side of the ground, and hurriedly went towards it. Then I too moved; but I had to go round headstones and railed-off tombs, and I stumbled over graves. The sky was overcast, and somewhere far off an early cock crew. A little way off, beyond a line of scattered juniper-trees, which marked the pathway to the church, a white, dim figure flitted in the direction of the tomb. The tomb itself was hidden by trees, and I could not see where the figure disappeared. I heard the rustle of actual movement where I had first seen the white figure, and coming over, found the Professor holding in his arms a tiny child. When he saw me he held it out to me, and said:—

"Are you satisfied now?"

"No," I said, in a way that I felt was aggressive.

"Do you not see the child?"

"Yes, it is a child, but who brought it here? And is it wounded?" I asked.

"We shall see," said the Professor, and with one impulse we took our way out of the churchyard, he carrying the sleeping child.

When we had got some little distance away, we went into a clump of trees, and struck a match, and looked at the child's throat. It was without a scratch or scar of any kind.

"Was I right?" I asked triumphantly.

"We were just in time," said the Professor thankfully.

We had now to decide what we were to do with the child, and so consulted about it. If we were to take it to a police-station we should have to give some account of our movements during the night; at least, we should have had to make some statement as to how we had come to find the child. So finally we decided that we would take it to the Heath, and when we heard a policeman coming, would leave it where he could not fail to find it; we would then seek our way home as quickly as we could. All fell out well. At the edge of Hampstead Heath we heard a policeman's heavy tramp, and laying the child on the pathway, we waited and watched until he saw it as he flashed his lantern to and fro. We heard his exclamation of astonishment, and then we went away silently. By good chance we got a cab near the "Spaniards," and drove to town.

I cannot sleep, so I make this entry. But I must try to get a few hours' sleep, as Van Helsing is to call for me at noon. He insists that I shall go with him on another expedition.

27 September.— It was two o'clock before we found a suitable opportunity for our attempt. The funeral held at noon was all completed, and the last stragglers of the mourners had taken themselves lazily away, when, looking carefully from behind a clump of alder-trees, we saw the sexton lock the gate after him. We knew then that we were safe till morning did we desire it; but the Professor told me that we should not want more than an hour at most. Again I felt that horrid sense of the reality of things, in which any effort of imagination seemed out of place; and I realised distinctly the perils of the law which we were incurring in our unhallowed work. Besides, I felt it was all so useless. Outrageous as it was to open a leaden coffin, to see if a woman dead nearly a week were really dead, it now seemed the height of folly to open the tomb again, when we knew, from the evidence of our own eyesight, that the coffin was empty. I shrugged my shoulders, however, and rested silent, for Van Helsing had a way of going on his own road, no matter who remonstrated. He took the key, opened the vault, and again courteously motioned me to precede. The place was not so gruesome as last night, but oh, how unutterably mean-looking when the sunshine streamed in. Van Helsing walked over to Lucy's coffin, and I followed. He bent over and again forced back the leaden flange; and then a shock of surprise and dismay shot through me.

There lay Lucy, seemingly just as we had seen her the night before her funeral. She was, if possible, more radiantly beautiful than ever; and I could not believe that she was dead. The lips were red, nay redder than before; and on the cheeks was a delicate bloom.

"Is this a juggle?" I said to him.

"Are you convinced now?" said the Professor in response, and as he spoke he put over his hand, and in a way that made me shudder, pulled back the dead lips and showed the white teeth.

"See," he went on, "see, they are even sharper than before. With this and this"— and he touched one of the canine teeth and that below it— "the little children can be bitten. Are you of belief now, friend John?" Once more, argumentative hostility woke within me. I could not accept such an overwhelming idea as he suggested; so, with an attempt to argue of which I was even at the moment ashamed, I said:—

"She may have been placed here since last night."

"Indeed? That is so, and by whom?"

"I do not know. Some one has done it."

"And yet she has been dead one week. Most peoples in that time would not look so." I had no answer for this, so was silent. Van Helsing did not seem to notice my silence; at any rate, he showed neither chagrin nor triumph. He was looking intently at the face of the dead woman, raising the eyelids and looking at the eyes, and once more opening the lips and examining the teeth. Then he turned to me and said:—

"Here, there is one thing which is different from all recorded; here is some dual life that is not as the common. She was bitten by the vampire when she was in a trance, sleep-walking— oh, you start; you do not know that, friend John, but you shall know it all later— and in trance could he best come to take more blood. In trance she died, and in trance she is Un-Dead, too. So it is that she differ from all other. Usually when the Un-Dead sleep at home"— as he spoke he made a comprehensive sweep of his arm to designate what to a vampire was "home"— "their face show what they are, but this so sweet that was when she not Un-Dead she go back to the nothings of the common dead. There is no malign there, see, and so it make hard that I must kill her in her sleep." This turned my blood cold, and it began to dawn upon me that I was accepting Van Helsing's theories; but if she were really dead, what was there of terror in the idea of killing her? He looked up at me, and evidently saw the change in my face, for he said almost joyously:—

"Ah, you believe now?"

I answered: "Do not press me too hard all at once. I am willing to accept. How will you do this bloody work?"

"I shall cut off her head and fill her mouth with garlic, and I shall drive a stake through her body." It made me shudder to think of so mutilating the body of the woman whom I had loved. And yet the feeling was not so strong as I had expected. I was, in fact, beginning to shudder at the presence of this being, this Un-Dead, as Van Helsing called it, and to loathe it. Is it possible that love is all subjective, or all objective?

I waited a considerable time for Van Helsing to begin, but he stood as if wrapped in thought. Presently he closed the catch of his bag with a snap, and said:—

"I have been thinking, and have made up my mind as to what is best. If I did simply follow my inclining I would do now, at this moment, what is to be done; but there are other things to follow, and things that are thousand times more difficult in that them we do not know. This is simple. She have yet no life taken, though that is of time; and to act now would be to take danger from her for ever. But then we may have to want Arthur, and how shall we tell him of this? If you, who saw the wounds on Lucy's throat, and saw the wounds so similar on the child's at the hospital; if you, who saw the coffin empty last night and full to-day with a woman who have not change only to be more rose and more beautiful in a whole week, after she die— if you know of this and know of the white figure last night that brought the child to the churchyard, and yet of your own senses you did not believe, how, then, can I expect Arthur, who know none of those things, to believe? He doubted me when I took him from her kiss when she was dying. I know he has forgiven me because in some mistaken idea I have done things that prevent him say good-bye as he ought; and he may think that in some more mistaken idea this woman was buried alive; and that in most mistake of all we have killed her. He will then argue back that it is we, mistaken ones, that have killed her by our ideas; and so he will be much unhappy always. Yet he never can be sure; and that is the worst of all. And he will sometimes think that she he loved was buried alive, and that will paint his dreams with horrors of what she must have suffered; and again, he will think that we may be right, and that his so beloved was, after all, an Un-Dead. No! I told him once, and since then I learn much. Now, since I know it is all true, a hundred thousand times more do I know that he must pass through the bitter waters to reach the sweet. He, poor fellow, must have one hour that will make the very face of heaven grow black to him; then we can act for good all round and send him peace. My mind is made up. Let us go. You return home for to-night to your asylum, and see that all be well. As for me, I shall spend the night here in this churchyard in my own way. To-morrow night you will come to me to the Berkeley Hotel at ten of the clock. I shall send for Arthur to come too, and also that so fine young man of America that gave his blood. Later we shall all have work to do. I come with you so far as Piccadilly and there dine, for I must be back here before the sun set."

So we locked the tomb and came away, and got over the wall of the churchyard, which was not much of a task, and drove back to Piccadilly. Note left by Van Helsing in his portmanteau, Berkeley Hotel directed to John Seward, M. D.

(Not delivered.)

"27 September.

"Friend John,—

"I write this in case anything should happen. I go alone to watch in that churchyard. It pleases me that the Un-Dead, Miss Lucy, shall not leave to-night, that so on the morrow night she may be more eager. Therefore I shall fix some things she like not— garlic and a crucifix— and so seal up the door of the tomb. She is young as Un-Dead, and will heed. Moreover, these are only to prevent her coming out; they may not prevail on her wanting to get in; for then the Un-Dead is desperate, and must find the line of least resistance, whatsoever it may be. I shall be at hand all the night from sunset till after the sunrise, and if there be aught that may be learned I shall learn it. For Miss Lucy or from her, I have no fear; but that other to whom is there that she is Un-Dead, he have now the power to seek her tomb and find shelter. He is cunning, as I know from Mr. Jonathan and from the way that all along he have fooled us when he played with us for Miss Lucy's life, and we lost; and in many ways the Un-Dead are strong. He have always the strength in his hand of twenty men; even we four who gave our strength to Miss Lucy it also is all to him. Besides, he can summon his wolf and I know not what. So if it be that he come thither on this night he shall find me; but none other shall— until it be too late. But it may be that he will not attempt the place. There is no reason why he should; his hunting ground is more full of game than the churchyard where the Un-Dead woman sleep, and the one old man watch.

"Therefore I write this in case.... Take the papers that are with this, the diaries of Harker and the rest, and read them, and then find this great Un-Dead, and cut off his head and burn his heart or drive a stake through it, so that the world may rest from him.

"If it be so, farewell.

"Van Helsing."

Dr. Seward's Diary.

28 September.— It is wonderful what a good night's sleep will do for one. Yesterday I was almost willing to accept Van Helsing's monstrous ideas; but now they seem to start out lurid before me as outrages on common sense. I have no doubt that he believes it all. I wonder if his mind can have become in any way unhinged. Surely there must be some rational explanation of all these mysterious things. Is it possible that the Professor can have done it himself? He is so abnormally clever that if he went off his head he would carry out his intent with regard to some fixed idea in a wonderful way. I am loath to think it, and indeed it would be almost as great a marvel as the other to find that Van Helsing was mad; but anyhow I shall watch him carefully. I may get some light on the mystery.

29 September, morning..... Last night, at a little before ten o'clock, Arthur and Quincey came into Van Helsing's room; he told us all that he wanted us to do, but especially addressing himself to Arthur, as if all our wills were centred in his. He began by saying that he hoped we would all come with him too, "for," he said, "there is a grave duty to be done there. You were doubtless surprised at my letter?" This query was directly addressed to Lord Godalming.

"I was. It rather upset me for a bit. There has been so much trouble around my house of late that I could do without any more. I have been curious, too, as to what you mean. Quincey and I talked it over; but the more we talked, the more puzzled we got, till now I can say for myself that I'm about up a tree as to any meaning about anything."

"Me too," said Quincey Morris laconically.

"Oh," said the Professor, "then you are nearer the beginning, both of you, than friend John here, who has to go a long way back before he can even get so far as to begin."

It was evident that he recognised my return to my old doubting frame of mind without my saying a word. Then, turning to the other two, he said with intense gravity:—

"I want your permission to do what I think good this night. It is, I know, much to ask; and when you know what it is I propose to do you will know, and only then, how much. Therefore may I ask that you promise me in the dark, so that afterwards, though you may be angry with me for a time— I must not disguise from myself the possibility that such may be— you shall not blame yourselves for anything."

"That's frank anyhow," broke in Quincey. "I'll answer for the Professor. I don't quite see his drift, but I swear he's honest; and that's good enough for me."

"I thank you, sir," said Van Helsing proudly. "I have done myself the honour of counting you one trusting friend, and such endorsement is dear to me." He held out a hand, which Quincey took.

Then Arthur spoke out:—

"Dr. Van Helsing, I don't quite like to 'buy a pig in a poke,' as they say in Scotland, and if it be anything in which my honour as a gentleman or my faith as a Christian is concerned, I cannot make such a promise. If you can assure me that what you intend does not violate either of these two, then I give my consent at once; though for the life of me, I cannot understand what you are driving at."

"I accept your limitation," said Van Helsing, "and all I ask of you is that if you feel it necessary to condemn any act of mine, you will first consider it well and be satisfied that it does not violate your reservations."

"Agreed!" said Arthur; "that is only fair. And now that the pourparlers are over, may I ask what it is we are to do?"

"I want you to come with me, and to come in secret, to the churchyard at Kingstead."

Arthur's face fell as he said in an amazed sort of way:—

"Where poor Lucy is buried?" The Professor bowed. Arthur went on: "And when there?"

"To enter the tomb!" Arthur stood up.

"Professor, are you in earnest; or it is some monstrous joke? Pardon me, I see that you are in earnest." He sat down again, but I could see that he sat firmly and proudly, as one who is on his dignity. There was silence until he asked again:—

"And when in the tomb?"

"To open the coffin."

"This is too much!" he said, angrily rising again. "I am willing to be patient in all things that are reasonable; but in this— this desecration of the grave— of one who— — " He fairly choked with indignation. The Professor looked pityingly at him.

"If I could spare you one pang, my poor friend," he said, "God knows I would. But this night our feet must tread in thorny paths; or later, and for ever, the feet you love must walk in paths of flame!"

Arthur looked up with set white face and said:—

"Take care, sir, take care!"

"Would it not be well to hear what I have to say?" said Van Helsing. "And then you will at least know the limit of my purpose. Shall I go on?"

"That's fair enough," broke in Morris.

After a pause Van Helsing went on, evidently with an effort:—

"Miss Lucy is dead; is it not so? Yes! Then there can be no wrong to her. But if she be not dead— — "

Arthur jumped to his feet.

"Good God!" he cried. "What do you mean? Has there been any mistake; has she been buried alive?" He groaned in anguish that not even hope could soften.

"I did not say she was alive, my child; I did not think it. I go no further than to say that she might be Un-Dead."

"Un-Dead! Not alive! What do you mean? Is this all a nightmare, or what is it?"

"There are mysteries which men can only guess at, which age by age they may solve only in part. Believe me, we are now on the verge of one. But I have not done. May I cut off the head of dead Miss Lucy?"

"Heavens and earth, no!" cried Arthur in a storm of passion. "Not for the wide world will I consent to any mutilation of her dead body. Dr. Van Helsing, you try me too far. What have I done to you that you should torture me so? What did that poor, sweet girl do that you should want to cast such dishonour on her grave? Are you mad to speak such things, or am I mad to listen to them? Don't dare to think more of such a desecration; I shall not give my consent to anything you do. I have a duty to do in protecting her grave from outrage; and, by God, I shall do it!"

Van Helsing rose up from where he had all the time been seated, and said, gravely and sternly:—

"My Lord Godalming, I, too, have a duty to do, a duty to others, a duty to you, a duty to the dead; and, by God, I shall do it! All I ask you now is that you come with me, that you look and listen; and if when later I make the same request you do not be more eager for its fulfilment even than I am, then— then I shall do my duty, whatever it may seem to me. And then, to follow of your Lordship's wishes I shall hold myself at your disposal to render an account to you, when and where you will." His voice broke a little, and he went on with a voice full of pity:—

"But, I beseech you, do not go forth in anger with me. In a long life of acts which were often not pleasant to do, and which sometimes did wring my heart, I have never had so heavy a task as now. Believe me that if the time comes for you to change your mind towards me, one look from you will wipe away all this so sad hour, for I would do what a man can to save you from sorrow. Just think. For why should I give myself so much of labour and so much of sorrow? I have come here from my own land to do what I can of good; at the first to please my friend John, and then to help a sweet young lady, whom, too, I came to love. For her— I am ashamed to say so much, but I say it in kindness— I gave what you gave; the blood of my veins; I gave it, I, who was not, like you, her lover, but only her physician and her friend. I gave to her my nights and days— before death, after death; and if my death can do her good even now, when she is the dead Un-Dead, she shall have it freely." He said this with a very grave, sweet pride, and Arthur was much affected by it. He took the old man's hand and said in a broken voice:—

"Oh, it is hard to think of it, and I cannot understand; but at least I shall go with you and wait."

## CHAPTER XVI
## DR. SEWARD'S DIARY— continued

I T was just a quarter before twelve o'clock when we got into the churchyard over the low wall. The night was dark with occasional gleams of moonlight between the rents of the heavy clouds that scudded across the sky. We all kept somehow close together, with Van Helsing slightly in front as he led the way. When we had come close to the tomb I looked well at Arthur, for I feared that the proximity to a place laden with so sorrowful a memory would upset him; but he bore himself well. I took it that the very mystery of the proceeding was in some way a counteractant to his grief. The Professor unlocked the door, and seeing a natural hesitation amongst us for various reasons, solved the difficulty by entering first himself. The rest of us followed, and he closed the door. He then lit a dark lantern and pointed to the coffin. Arthur stepped forward hesitatingly; Van Helsing said to me:—

"You were with me here yesterday. Was the body of Miss Lucy in that coffin?"

"It was." The Professor turned to the rest saying:—

"You hear; and yet there is no one who does not believe with me." He took his screwdriver and again took off the lid of the coffin. Arthur looked on, very pale but silent; when the lid was removed he stepped forward. He evidently did not know that there was a leaden coffin, or, at any rate, had not thought of it. When he saw the rent in the lead, the blood rushed to his face for an instant, but as quickly fell away again, so that he remained of a ghastly whiteness; he was still silent. Van Helsing forced back the leaden flange, and we all looked in and recoiled.

The coffin was empty!

For several minutes no one spoke a word. The silence was broken by Quincey Morris:—

"Professor, I answered for you. Your word is all I want. I wouldn't ask such a thing ordinarily— I wouldn't so dishonour you as to imply a doubt; but this is a mystery that goes beyond any honour or dishonour. Is this your doing?"

"I swear to you by all that I hold sacred that I have not removed nor touched her. What happened was this: Two nights ago my friend Seward and I came here— with good purpose, believe me. I opened that coffin, which was then sealed up, and we found it, as now, empty. We then waited, and saw something white come through the trees. The next day we came here in day-time, and she lay there. Did she not, friend John?"

"Yes."

"That night we were just in time. One more so small child was missing, and we find it, thank God, unharmed amongst the graves. Yesterday I came here before sundown, for at sundown the Un-Dead can move. I waited here all the night till the sun rose, but I saw nothing. It was most probable that it was because I had laid over the clamps of those doors garlic, which the Un-Dead cannot bear, and other things which they shun. Last night there was no exodus, so to-night before the sundown I took away my garlic and other things. And so it is we find this coffin empty. But bear with me. So far there is much that is strange. Wait you with me outside, unseen and unheard, and things much stranger are yet to be. So"— here he shut the dark slide of his lantern— "now to the outside." He opened the door, and we filed out, he coming last and locking the door behind him.

Oh! but it seemed fresh and pure in the night air after the terror of that vault. How sweet it was to see the clouds race by, and the passing gleams of the moonlight between the scudding clouds crossing and passing— like the gladness and sorrow of a man's life; how sweet it was to breathe the fresh air, that had no taint of death and decay; how humanising to see the red lighting of the sky beyond the hill, and to hear far away the muffled roar that marks the life of a great city. Each in his own way was solemn and overcome. Arthur was silent, and was, I could see, striving to grasp the purpose and the inner meaning of the mystery. I was myself tolerably patient, and half inclined again to throw aside doubt and to accept Van Helsing's conclusions. Quincey Morris was phlegmatic in the way of a man who accepts all things, and accepts them in the spirit of cool bravery, with hazard of all he has to stake. Not being able to smoke, he cut himself a good-sized plug of tobacco and began to chew. As to Van Helsing, he was employed in a definite way. First he took from his bag a mass of what looked like thin, wafer-like biscuit, which was carefully rolled up in a white napkin; next he took out a double-handful of some whitish stuff, like dough or putty. He crumbled the wafer up fine and worked it into the mass between his hands. This he then took, and rolling it into thin strips, began to lay them into the crevices between the door and its setting in the tomb. I was somewhat puzzled at this, and being close, asked him what it was that he was doing. Arthur and Quincey drew near also, as they too were curious. He answered:—

"I am closing the tomb, so that the Un-Dead may not enter."

"And is that stuff you have put there going to do it?" asked Quincey. "Great Scott! Is this a game?"

"It is."

"What is that which you are using?" This time the question was by Arthur. Van Helsing reverently lifted his hat as he answered:—

"The Host. I brought it from Amsterdam. I have an Indulgence." It was an answer that appalled the most sceptical of us, and we felt individually that in the presence of such earnest purpose as the Professor's, a purpose which could thus use the to him most sacred of things, it was impossible to distrust. In respectful silence we took the places assigned to us close round the tomb, but hidden from the sight of any one approaching. I pitied the others, especially Arthur. I had myself been apprenticed by my former visits to this watching horror; and yet I, who had up to an hour ago repudiated the proofs, felt my heart sink within me. Never did tombs look so ghastly white; never did cypress, or yew, or juniper so seem the embodiment of funereal gloom; never did tree or grass wave or rustle so ominously; never did bough creak so mysteriously; and never did the far-away howling of dogs send such a woeful presage through the night.

There was a long spell of silence, a big, aching void, and then from the Professor a keen "S-s-s-s!" He pointed; and far down the avenue of yews we saw a white figure advance— a dim white figure, which held something dark at its breast. The figure stopped, and at the moment a ray of moonlight fell upon the masses of driving clouds and showed in startling prominence a dark-haired woman, dressed in the cerements of the grave. We could not see the face, for it was bent down over what we saw to be a fair-haired child. There was a pause and a sharp little cry, such as a child gives in sleep, or a dog as it lies before the fire and dreams. We were starting forward, but the Professor's warning hand, seen by us as he stood behind a yew-tree, kept us back; and then as we looked the white figure moved forwards again. It was now near enough for us to see clearly, and the moonlight still held. My own heart grew cold as ice, and I could hear the gasp of Arthur, as we recognised the features of Lucy Westenra. Lucy Westenra, but yet how changed. The sweetness was turned to adamantine, heartless cruelty, and the purity to voluptuous wantonness. Van Helsing stepped out, and, obedient to his gesture, we all advanced too; the four of us ranged in a line before the door of the tomb. Van Helsing raised his lantern and drew the slide; by the concentrated light that fell on Lucy's face we could see that the lips were crimson with fresh blood, and that the stream had trickled over her chin and stained the purity of her lawn death-robe.

We shuddered with horror. I could see by the tremulous light that even Van Helsing's iron nerve had failed. Arthur was next to me, and if I had not seized his arm and held him up, he would have fallen.

When Lucy— I call the thing that was before us Lucy because it bore her shape— saw us she drew back with an angry snarl, such as a cat gives when taken unawares; then her eyes ranged over us. Lucy's eyes in form and colour; but Lucy's eyes unclean and full of hell-fire, instead of the pure, gentle orbs we knew. At that moment the remnant of my love passed into hate and loathing; had she then to be killed, I could have done it with savage delight. As she looked, her eyes blazed with unholy light, and the face became wreathed with a voluptuous smile. Oh, God, how it made me shudder to see it! With a careless motion, she flung to the ground, callous as a devil, the child that up to now she had clutched strenuously to her breast, growling over it as a dog growls over a bone. The child gave a sharp cry, and lay there moaning. There was a cold-bloodedness in the act which wrung a groan from Arthur; when she advanced to him with outstretched arms and a wanton smile he fell back and hid his face in his hands.

She still advanced, however, and with a languorous, voluptuous grace, said:—

"Come to me, Arthur. Leave these others and come to me. My arms are hungry for you. Come, and we can rest together. Come, my husband, come!"

There was something diabolically sweet in her tones— something of the tingling of glass when struck— which rang through the brains even of us who heard the words addressed to another. As for Arthur, he seemed under a spell; moving his hands from his face, he opened wide his arms. She was leaping for them, when Van Helsing sprang forward and held between them his little golden crucifix. She recoiled from it, and, with a suddenly distorted face, full of rage, dashed past him as if to enter the tomb.

When within a foot or two of the door, however, she stopped, as if arrested by some irresistible force. Then she turned, and her face was shown in the clear burst of moonlight and by the lamp, which had now no quiver from Van Helsing's iron nerves. Never did I see such baffled malice on a face; and never, I trust, shall such ever be seen again by mortal eyes. The beautiful colour became livid, the eyes seemed to throw out sparks of hell-fire, the brows were wrinkled as though the folds of the flesh were the coils of Medusa's snakes, and the lovely, blood-stained mouth grew to an open square, as in the passion masks of the Greeks and Japanese. If ever a face meant death— if looks could kill— we saw it at that moment.

And so for full half a minute, which seemed an eternity, she remained between the lifted crucifix and the sacred closing of her means of entry. Van Helsing broke the silence by asking Arthur:—

"Answer me, oh my friend! Am I to proceed in my work?"

Arthur threw himself on his knees, and hid his face in his hands, as he answered:—

"Do as you will, friend; do as you will. There can be no horror like this ever any more;" and he groaned in spirit. Quincey and I simultaneously moved towards him, and took his arms. We could hear the click of the closing lantern as Van Helsing held it down; coming close to the tomb, he began to remove from the chinks some of the sacred emblem which he had placed there. We all looked on in horrified amazement as we saw, when he stood back, the woman, with a corporeal body as real at that moment as our own, pass in through the interstice where scarce a knife-blade could have gone. We all felt a glad sense of relief when we saw the Professor calmly restoring the strings of putty to the edges of the door.

When this was done, he lifted the child and said:

"Come now, my friends; we can do no more till to-morrow. There is a funeral at noon, so here we shall all come before long after that. The friends of the dead will all be gone by two, and when the sexton lock the gate we shall remain. Then there is more to do; but not like this of to-night. As for this little one, he is not much harm, and by to-morrow night he shall be well. We shall leave him where the police will find him, as on the other night; and then to home." Coming close to Arthur, he said:—

"My friend Arthur, you have had a sore trial; but after, when you look back, you will see how it was necessary. You are now in the bitter waters, my child. By this time to-morrow you will, please God, have passed them, and have drunk of the sweet waters; so do not mourn overmuch. Till then I shall not ask you to forgive me."

Arthur and Quincey came home with me, and we tried to cheer each other on the way. We had left the child in safety, and were tired; so we all slept with more or less reality of sleep.

29 September, night.— A little before twelve o'clock we three— Arthur, Quincey Morris, and myself— called for the Professor. It was odd to notice that by common consent we had all put on black clothes. Of course, Arthur wore black, for he was in deep mourning, but the rest of us wore it by instinct. We got to the churchyard by half-past one, and strolled about, keeping out of official observation, so that when the gravediggers had completed their task and the sexton under the belief that every one had gone, had locked the gate, we had the place all to ourselves. Van Helsing, instead of his little black bag, had with him a long leather one, something like a cricketing bag; it was manifestly of fair weight.

When we were alone and had heard the last of the footsteps die out up the road, we silently, and as if by ordered intention, followed the Professor to the tomb. He unlocked the door, and we entered, closing it behind us. Then he took from his bag the lantern, which he lit, and also two wax candles, which, when lighted, he stuck, by melting their own ends, on other coffins, so that they might give light sufficient to work by. When he again lifted the lid off Lucy's coffin we all looked— Arthur trembling like an aspen— and saw that the body lay there in all its death-beauty. But there was no love in my own heart, nothing but loathing for the foul Thing which had taken Lucy's shape without her soul. I could see even Arthur's face grow hard as he looked. Presently he said to Van Helsing:—

"Is this really Lucy's body, or only a demon in her shape?"

"It is her body, and yet not it. But wait a while, and you all see her as she was, and is."

She seemed like a nightmare of Lucy as she lay there; the pointed teeth, the bloodstained, voluptuous mouth— which it made one shudder to see— the whole carnal and unspiritual appearance, seeming like a devilish mockery of Lucy's sweet purity. Van Helsing, with his usual methodicalness, began taking the various contents from his bag and placing them ready for use. First he took out a soldering iron and some plumbing solder, and then a small oil-lamp, which gave out, when lit in a corner of the tomb, gas which burned at fierce heat with a blue flame; then his operating knives, which he placed to hand; and last a round wooden stake, some two and a half or three inches thick and about three feet long. One end of it was hardened by charring in the fire, and was sharpened to a fine point. With this stake came a heavy hammer, such as in households is used in the coal-cellar for breaking the lumps. To me, a doctor's preparations for work of any kind are stimulating and bracing, but the effect of these things on both Arthur and Quincey was to cause them a sort of consternation. They both, however, kept their courage, and remained silent and quiet.

When all was ready, Van Helsing said:—

"Before we do anything, let me tell you this; it is out of the lore and experience of the ancients and of all those who have studied the powers of the Un-Dead. When they become such, there comes with the change the curse of immortality; they cannot die, but must go on age after age adding new victims and multiplying the evils of the world; for all that die from the preying of the Un-Dead becomes themselves Un-Dead, and prey on their kind. And so the circle goes on ever widening, like as the ripples from a stone thrown in the water. Friend Arthur, if you had met that kiss which you know of before poor Lucy die; or again, last night when you open your arms to her, you would in time, when you had died, have become nosferatu, as they call it in Eastern Europe, and would all time make more of those Un-Deads that so have fill us with horror. The career of this so unhappy dear lady is but just begun. Those children whose blood she suck are not as yet so much the worse; but if she live on, Un-Dead, more and more they lose their blood and by her power over them they come to her; and so she draw their blood with that so wicked mouth. But if she die in truth, then all cease; the tiny wounds of the throats disappear, and they go back to their plays unknowing ever of what has been. But of the most blessed of all, when this now Un-Dead be made to rest as true dead, then the soul of the poor lady whom we love shall again be free. Instead of working wickedness by night and growing more debased in the assimilating of it by day, she shall take her place with the other Angels. So that, my friend, it will be a blessed hand for her that shall strike the blow that sets her free. To this I am willing; but is there none amongst us who has a better right? Will it be no joy to think of hereafter in the silence of the night when sleep is not: 'It was my hand that sent her to the stars; it was the hand of him that loved her best; the hand that of all she would herself have chosen, had it been to her to choose?' Tell me if there be such a one amongst us?"

We all looked at Arthur. He saw, too, what we all did, the infinite kindness which suggested that his should be the hand which would restore Lucy to us as a holy, and not an unholy, memory; he stepped forward and said bravely, though his hand trembled, and his face was as pale as snow:—

"My true friend, from the bottom of my broken heart I thank you. Tell me what I am to do, and I shall not falter!" Van Helsing laid a hand on his shoulder, and said:—

"Brave lad! A moment's courage, and it is done. This stake must be driven through her. It will be a fearful ordeal— be not deceived in that— but it will be only a short time, and you will then rejoice more than your pain was great; from this grim tomb you will emerge as though you tread on air. But you must not falter when once you have begun. Only think that we, your true friends, are round you, and that we pray for you all the time."

"Go on," said Arthur hoarsely. "Tell me what I am to do."

"Take this stake in your left hand, ready to place the point over the heart, and the hammer in your right. Then when we begin our prayer for the dead— I shall read him, I have here the book, and the others shall follow— strike in God's name, that so all may be well with the dead that we love and that the Un-Dead pass away."

Arthur took the stake and the hammer, and when once his mind was set on action his hands never trembled nor even quivered. Van Helsing opened his missal and began to read, and Quincey and I followed as well as we could. Arthur placed the point over the heart, and as I looked I could see its dint in the white flesh. Then he struck with all his might. The Thing in the coffin writhed; and a hideous, blood-curdling screech came from the opened red lips. The body shook and quivered and twisted in wild contortions; the sharp white teeth champed together till the lips were cut, and the mouth was smeared with a crimson foam. But Arthur never faltered. He looked like a figure of Thor as his untrembling arm rose and fell, driving deeper and deeper the mercy-bearing stake, whilst the blood from the pierced heart welled and spurted up around it. His face was set, and high duty seemed to shine through it; the sight of it gave us courage so that our voices seemed to ring through the little vault.

And then the writhing and quivering of the body became less, and the teeth seemed to champ, and the face to quiver. Finally it lay still. The terrible task was over.

The hammer fell from Arthur's hand. He reeled and would have fallen had we not caught him. The great drops of sweat sprang from his forehead, and his breath came in broken gasps. It had indeed been an awful strain on him; and had he not been forced to his task by more than human considerations he could never have gone through with it. For a few minutes we were so taken up with him that we did not look towards the coffin. When we did, however, a murmur of startled surprise ran from one to the other of us. We gazed so eagerly that Arthur rose, for he had been seated on the ground, and came and looked too; and then a glad, strange light broke over his face and dispelled altogether the gloom of horror that lay upon it.

There, in the coffin lay no longer the foul Thing that we had so dreaded and grown to hate that the work of her destruction was yielded as a privilege to the one best entitled to it, but Lucy as we had seen her in her life, with her face of unequalled sweetness and purity. True that there were there, as we had seen them in life, the traces of care and pain and waste; but these were all dear to us, for they marked her truth to what we knew. One and all we felt that the holy calm that lay like sunshine over the wasted face and form was only an earthly token and symbol of the calm that was to reign for ever.

Van Helsing came and laid his hand on Arthur's shoulder, and said to him:—

"And now, Arthur my friend, dear lad, am I not forgiven?"

The reaction of the terrible strain came as he took the old man's hand in his, and raising it to his lips, pressed it, and said:—

"Forgiven! God bless you that you have given my dear one her soul again, and me peace." He put his hands on the Professor's shoulder, and laying his head on his breast, cried for a while silently, whilst we stood unmoving. When he raised his head Van Helsing said to him:—

"And now, my child, you may kiss her. Kiss her dead lips if you will, as she would have you to, if for her to choose. For she is not a grinning devil now— not any more a foul Thing for all eternity. No longer she is the devil's Un-Dead. She is God's true dead, whose soul is with Him!"

Arthur bent and kissed her, and then we sent him and Quincey out of the tomb; the Professor and I sawed the top off the stake, leaving the point of it in the body. Then we cut off the head and filled the mouth with garlic. We soldered up the leaden coffin, screwed on the coffin-lid, and gathering up our belongings, came away. When the Professor locked the door he gave the key to Arthur.

Outside the air was sweet, the sun shone, and the birds sang, and it seemed as if all nature were tuned to a different pitch. There was gladness and mirth and peace everywhere, for we were at rest ourselves on one account, and we were glad, though it was with a tempered joy. Before we moved away Van Helsing said:—

"Now, my friends, one step of our work is done, one the most harrowing to ourselves. But there remains a greater task: to find out the author of all this our sorrow and to stamp him out. I have clues which we can follow; but it is a long task, and a difficult, and there is danger in it, and pain. Shall you not all help me? We have learned to believe, all of us— is it not so? And since so, do we not see our duty? Yes! And do we not promise to go on to the bitter end?"

Each in turn, we took his hand, and the promise was made. Then said the Professor as we moved off:—

"Two nights hence you shall meet with me and dine together at seven of the clock with friend John. I shall entreat two others, two that you know not as yet; and I shall be ready to all our work show and our plans unfold. Friend John, you come with me home, for I have much to consult about, and you can help me. To-night I leave for Amsterdam, but shall return to-morrow night. And then begins our great quest. But first I shall have much to say, so that you may know what is to do and to dread. Then our promise shall be made to each other anew; for there is a terrible task before us, and once our feet are on the ploughshare we must not draw back."

CHAPTER XVII

## DR. SEWARD'S DIARY— continued

WHEN we arrived at the Berkeley Hotel, Van Helsing found a telegram waiting for him:—

"Am coming up by train. Jonathan at Whitby. Important news.— Mina Harker."

The Professor was delighted. "Ah, that wonderful Madam Mina," he said, "pearl among women! She arrive, but I cannot stay. She must go to your house, friend John. You must meet her at the station. Telegraph her en route, so that she may be prepared."

When the wire was despatched he had a cup of tea; over it he told me of a diary kept by Jonathan Harker when abroad, and gave me a typewritten copy of it, as also of Mrs. Harker's diary at Whitby. "Take these," he said, "and study them well. When I have returned you will be master of all the facts, and we can then better enter on our inquisition. Keep them safe, for there is in them much of treasure. You will need all your faith, even you who have had such an experience as that of to-day. What is here told," he laid his hand heavily and gravely on the packet of papers as he spoke, "may be the beginning of the end to you and me and many another; or it may sound the knell of the Un-Dead who walk the earth. Read all, I pray you, with the open mind; and if you can add in any way to the story here told do so, for it is all-important. You have kept diary of all these so strange things; is it not so? Yes! Then we shall go through all these together when we meet." He then made ready for his departure, and shortly after drove off to Liverpool Street. I took my way to Paddington, where I arrived about fifteen minutes before the train came in.

The crowd melted away, after the bustling fashion common to arrival platforms; and I was beginning to feel uneasy, lest I might miss my guest, when a sweet-faced, dainty-looking girl stepped up to me, and, after a quick glance, said: "Dr. Seward, is it not?"

"And you are Mrs. Harker!" I answered at once; whereupon she held out her hand.

"I knew you from the description of poor dear Lucy; but— — " She stopped suddenly, and a quick blush overspread her face.

The blush that rose to my own cheeks somehow set us both at ease, for it was a tacit answer to her own. I got her luggage, which included a typewriter, and we took the Underground to Fenchurch Street, after I had sent a wire to my housekeeper to have a sitting-room and bedroom prepared at once for Mrs. Harker.

In due time we arrived. She knew, of course, that the place was a lunatic asylum, but I could see that she was unable to repress a shudder when we entered.

She told me that, if she might, she would come presently to my study, as she had much to say. So here I am finishing my entry in my phonograph diary whilst I await her. As yet I have not had the chance of looking at the papers which Van Helsing left with me, though they lie open before me. I must get her interested in something, so that I may have an opportunity of reading them. She does not know how precious time is, or what a task we have in hand. I must be careful not to frighten her. Here she is!

Mina Harker's Journal.

29 September.— After I had tidied myself, I went down to Dr. Seward's study. At the door I paused a moment, for I thought I heard him talking with some one. As, however, he had pressed me to be quick, I knocked at the door, and on his calling out, "Come in," I entered.

To my intense surprise, there was no one with him. He was quite alone, and on the table opposite him was what I knew at once from the description to be a phonograph. I had never seen one, and was much interested.

"I hope I did not keep you waiting," I said; "but I stayed at the door as I heard you talking, and thought there was some one with you."

"Oh," he replied with a smile, "I was only entering my diary."

"Your diary?" I asked him in surprise.

"Yes," he answered. "I keep it in this." As he spoke he laid his hand on the phonograph. I felt quite excited over it, and blurted out:—

"Why, this beats even shorthand! May I hear it say something?"

"Certainly," he replied with alacrity, and stood up to put it in train for speaking. Then he paused, and a troubled look overspread his face.

"The fact is," he began awkwardly, "I only keep my diary in it; and as it is entirely— almost entirely— about my cases, it may be awkward— that is, I mean— — " He stopped, and I tried to help him out of his embarrassment:—

"You helped to attend dear Lucy at the end. Let me hear how she died; for all that I know of her, I shall be very grateful. She was very, very dear to me."

To my surprise, he answered, with a horrorstruck look in his face:—
"Tell you of her death? Not for the wide world!"

"Why not?" I asked, for some grave, terrible feeling was coming over me. Again he paused, and I could see that he was trying to invent an excuse. At length he stammered out:—

"You see, I do not know how to pick out any particular part of the diary." Even while he was speaking an idea dawned upon him, and he said with unconscious simplicity, in a different voice, and with the naïveté of a child: "That's quite true, upon my honour. Honest Indian!" I could not but smile, at which he grimaced. "I gave myself away that time!" he said. "But do you know that, although I have kept the diary for months past, it never once struck me how I was going to find any particular part of it in case I wanted to look it up?" By this time my mind was made up that the diary of a doctor who attended Lucy might have something to add to the sum of our knowledge of that terrible Being, and I said boldly:—

"Then, Dr. Seward, you had better let me copy it out for you on my typewriter." He grew to a positively deathly pallor as he said:—

"No! no! no! For all the world, I wouldn't let you know that terrible story!"

Then it was terrible; my intuition was right! For a moment I thought, and as my eyes ranged the room, unconsciously looking for something or some opportunity to aid me, they lit on a great batch of typewriting on the table. His eyes caught the look in mine, and, without his thinking, followed their direction. As they saw the parcel he realised my meaning.

"You do not know me," I said. "When you have read those papers— my own diary and my husband's also, which I have typed— you will know me better. I have not faltered in giving every thought of my own heart in this cause; but, of course, you do not know me— yet; and I must not expect you to trust me so far."

He is certainly a man of noble nature; poor dear Lucy was right about him. He stood up and opened a large drawer, in which were arranged in order a number of hollow cylinders of metal covered with dark wax, and said:—

"You are quite right. I did not trust you because I did not know you. But I know you now; and let me say that I should have known you long ago. I know that Lucy told you of me; she told me of you too. May I make the only atonement in my power? Take the cylinders and hear them— the first half-dozen of them are personal to me, and they will not horrify you; then you will know me better. Dinner will by then be ready. In the meantime I shall read over some of these documents, and shall be better able to understand certain things." He carried the phonograph himself up to my sitting-room and adjusted it for me. Now I shall learn something pleasant, I am sure; for it will tell me the other side of a true love episode of which I know one side already....

Dr. Seward's Diary.

29 September.— I was so absorbed in that wonderful diary of Jonathan Harker and that other of his wife that I let the time run on without thinking. Mrs. Harker was not down when the maid came to announce dinner, so I said: "She is possibly tired; let dinner wait an hour," and I went on with my work. I had just finished Mrs. Harker's diary, when she came in. She looked sweetly pretty, but very sad, and her eyes were flushed with crying. This somehow moved me much. Of late I have had cause for tears, God knows! but the relief of them was denied me; and now the sight of those sweet eyes, brightened with recent tears, went straight to my heart. So I said as gently as I could:—

"I greatly fear I have distressed you."

"Oh, no, not distressed me," she replied, "but I have been more touched than I can say by your grief. That is a wonderful machine, but it is cruelly true. It told me, in its very tones, the anguish of your heart. It was like a soul crying out to Almighty God. No one must hear them spoken ever again! See, I have tried to be useful. I have copied out the words on my typewriter, and none other need now hear your heart beat, as I did."

"No one need ever know, shall ever know," I said in a low voice. She laid her hand on mine and said very gravely:—

"Ah, but they must!"

"Must! But why?" I asked.

"Because it is a part of the terrible story, a part of poor dear Lucy's death and all that led to it; because in the struggle which we have before us to rid the earth of this terrible monster we must have all the knowledge and all the help which we can get. I think that the cylinders which you gave me contained more than you intended me to know; but I can see that there are in your record many lights to this dark mystery. You will let me help, will you not? I know all up to a certain point; and I see already, though your diary only took me to 7 September, how poor Lucy was beset, and how her terrible doom was being wrought out. Jonathan and I have been working day and night since Professor Van Helsing saw us. He is gone to Whitby to get more information, and he will be here to-morrow to help us. We need have no secrets amongst us; working together and with absolute trust, we can surely be stronger than if some of us were in the dark." She looked at me so appealingly, and at the same time manifested such courage and resolution in her bearing, that I gave in at once to her wishes. "You shall," I said, "do as you like in the matter. God forgive me if I do wrong! There are terrible things yet to learn of; but if you have so far travelled on the road to poor Lucy's death, you will not be content, I know, to remain in the dark. Nay, the end— the very end— may give you a gleam of peace. Come, there is dinner. We must keep one another strong for what is before us; we have a cruel and dreadful task. When you have eaten you shall learn the rest, and I shall answer any questions you ask— if there be anything which you do not understand, though it was apparent to us who were present."

Mina Harker's Journal.

29 September.— After dinner I came with Dr. Seward to his study. He brought back the phonograph from my room, and I took my typewriter. He placed me in a comfortable chair, and arranged the phonograph so that I could touch it without getting up, and showed me how to stop it in case I should want to pause. Then he very thoughtfully took a chair, with his back to me, so that I might be as free as possible, and began to read. I put the forked metal to my ears and listened.

When the terrible story of Lucy's death, and— and all that followed, was done, I lay back in my chair powerless. Fortunately I am not of a fainting disposition. When Dr. Seward saw me he jumped up with a horrified exclamation, and hurriedly taking a case-bottle from a cupboard, gave me some brandy, which in a few minutes somewhat restored me. My brain was all in a whirl, and only that there came through all the multitude of horrors, the holy ray of light that my dear, dear Lucy was at last at peace, I do not think I could have borne it without making a scene. It is all so wild, and mysterious, and strange that if I had not known Jonathan's experience in Transylvania I could not have believed. As it was, I didn't know what to believe, and so got out of my difficulty by attending to something else. I took the cover off my typewriter, and said to Dr. Seward:—

"Let me write this all out now. We must be ready for Dr. Van Helsing when he comes. I have sent a telegram to Jonathan to come on here when he arrives in London from Whitby. In this matter dates are everything, and I think that if we get all our material ready, and have every item put in chronological order, we shall have done much. You tell me that Lord Godalming and Mr. Morris are coming too. Let us be able to tell him when they come." He accordingly set the phonograph at a slow pace, and I began to typewrite from the beginning of the seventh cylinder. I used manifold, and so took three copies of the diary, just as I had done with all the rest. It was late when I got through, but Dr. Seward went about his work of going his round of the patients; when he had finished he came back and sat near me, reading, so that I did not feel too lonely whilst I worked. How good and thoughtful he is; the world seems full of good men— even if there are monsters in it. Before I left him I remembered what Jonathan put in his diary of the Professor's perturbation at reading something in an evening paper at the station at Exeter; so, seeing that Dr. Seward keeps his newspapers, I borrowed the files of "The Westminster Gazette" and "The Pall Mall Gazette," and took them to my room. I remember how much "The Dailygraph" and "The Whitby Gazette," of which I had made cuttings, helped us to understand the terrible events at Whitby when Count Dracula landed, so I shall look through the evening papers since then, and perhaps I shall get some new light. I am not sleepy, and the work will help to keep me quiet.

Dr. Seward's Diary.

30 September.— Mr. Harker arrived at nine o'clock. He had got his wife's wire just before starting. He is uncommonly clever, if one can judge from his face, and full of energy. If this journal be true— and judging by one's own wonderful experiences, it must be— he is also a man of great nerve. That going down to the vault a second time was a remarkable piece of daring. After reading his account of it I was prepared to meet a good specimen of manhood, but hardly the quiet, business-like gentleman who came here to-day.

Later.— After lunch Harker and his wife went back to their own room, and as I passed a while ago I heard the click of the typewriter. They are hard at it. Mrs. Harker says that they are knitting together in chronological order every scrap of evidence they have. Harker has got the letters between the consignee of the boxes at Whitby and the carriers in London who took charge of them. He is now reading his wife's typescript of my diary. I wonder what they make out of it. Here it is....

Strange that it never struck me that the very next house might be the Count's hiding-place! Goodness knows that we had enough clues from the conduct of the patient Renfield! The bundle of letters relating to the purchase of the house were with the typescript. Oh, if we had only had them earlier we might have saved poor Lucy! Stop; that way madness lies! Harker has gone back, and is again collating his material. He says that by dinner-time they will be able to show a whole connected narrative. He thinks that in the meantime I should see Renfield, as hitherto he has been a sort of index to the coming and going of the Count. I hardly see this yet, but when I get at the dates I suppose I shall. What a good thing that Mrs. Harker put my cylinders into type! We never could have found the dates otherwise....

I found Renfield sitting placidly in his room with his hands folded, smiling benignly. At the moment he seemed as sane as any one I ever saw. I sat down and talked with him on a lot of subjects, all of which he treated naturally. He then, of his own accord, spoke of going home, a subject he has never mentioned to my knowledge during his sojourn here. In fact, he spoke quite confidently of getting his discharge at once. I believe that, had I not had the chat with Harker and read the letters and the dates of his outbursts, I should have been prepared to sign for him after a brief time of observation. As it is, I am darkly suspicious. All those outbreaks were in some way linked with the proximity of the Count. What then does this absolute content mean? Can it be that his instinct is satisfied as to the vampire's ultimate triumph? Stay; he is himself zoöphagous, and in his wild ravings outside the chapel door of the deserted house he always spoke of "master." This all seems confirmation of our idea. However, after a while I came away; my friend is just a little too sane at present to make it safe to probe him too deep with questions. He might begin to think, and then— ! So I came away. I mistrust these quiet moods of his; so I have given the attendant a hint to look closely after him, and to have a strait-waistcoat ready in case of need.
Jonathan Harker's Journal.

29 September, in train to London.— When I received Mr. Billington's courteous message that he would give me any information in his power I thought it best to go down to Whitby and make, on the spot, such inquiries as I wanted. It was now my object to trace that horrid cargo of the Count's to its place in London. Later, we may be able to deal with it. Billington junior, a nice lad, met me at the station, and brought me to his father's house, where they had decided that I must stay the night. They are hospitable, with true Yorkshire hospitality: give a guest everything, and leave him free to do as he likes. They all knew that I was busy, and that my stay was short, and Mr. Billington had ready in his office all the papers concerning the consignment of boxes. It gave me almost a turn to see again one of the letters which I had seen on the Count's table before I knew of his diabolical plans. Everything had been carefully thought out, and done systematically and with precision. He seemed to have been prepared for every obstacle which might be placed by accident in the way of his intentions being carried out. To use an Americanism, he had "taken no chances," and the absolute accuracy with which his instructions were fulfilled, was simply the logical result of his care. I saw the invoice, and took note of it: "Fifty cases of common earth, to be used for experimental purposes." Also the copy of letter to Carter Paterson, and their reply; of both of these I got copies. This was all the information Mr. Billington could give me, so I went down to the port and saw the coastguards, the Customs officers and the harbour-master. They had all something to say of the strange entry of the ship, which is already taking its place in local tradition; but no one could add to the simple description "Fifty cases of common earth." I then saw the station-master, who kindly put me in communication with the men who had actually received the boxes. Their tally was exact with the list, and they had nothing to add except that the boxes were "main and mortal heavy," and that shifting them was dry work. One of them added that it was hard lines that there wasn't any gentleman "such-like as yourself, squire," to show some sort of appreciation of their efforts in a liquid form; another put in a rider that the thirst then generated was such that even the time which had elapsed had not completely allayed it. Needless to add, I took care before leaving to lift, for ever and adequately, this source of reproach.

30 September.— The station-master was good enough to give me a line to his old companion the station-master at King's Cross, so that when I arrived there in the morning I was able to ask him about the arrival of the boxes. He, too, put me at once in communication with the proper officials, and I saw that their tally was correct with the original invoice. The opportunities of acquiring an abnormal thirst had been here limited; a noble use of them had, however, been made, and again I was compelled to deal with the result in an ex post facto manner.

From thence I went on to Carter Paterson's central office, where I met with the utmost courtesy. They looked up the transaction in their day-book and letter-book, and at once telephoned to their King's Cross office for more details. By good fortune, the men who did the teaming were waiting for work, and the official at once sent them over, sending also by one of them the way-bill and all the papers connected with the delivery of the boxes at Carfax. Here again I found the tally agreeing exactly; the carriers' men were able to supplement the paucity of the written words with a few details. These were, I shortly found, connected almost solely with the dusty nature of the job, and of the consequent thirst engendered in the operators. On my affording an opportunity, through the medium of the currency of the realm, of the allaying, at a later period, this beneficial evil, one of the men remarked:—

"That 'ere 'ouse, guv'nor, is the rummiest I ever was in. Blyme! but it ain't been touched sence a hundred years. There was dust that thick in the place that you might have slep' on it without 'urtin' of yer bones; an' the place was that neglected that yer might 'ave smelled ole Jerusalem in it. But the ole chapel— that took the cike, that did! Me and my mate, we thort we wouldn't never git out quick enough. Lor', I wouldn't take less nor a quid a moment to stay there arter dark."

Having been in the house, I could well believe him; but if he knew what I know, he would, I think, have raised his terms.

Of one thing I am now satisfied: that all the boxes which arrived at Whitby from Varna in the Demeter were safely deposited in the old chapel at Carfax. There should be fifty of them there, unless any have since been removed— as from Dr. Seward's diary I fear.

I shall try to see the carter who took away the boxes from Carfax when Renfield attacked them. By following up this clue we may learn a good deal.

Later.— Mina and I have worked all day, and we have put all the papers into order.

Mina Harker's Journal

30 September.— I am so glad that I hardly know how to contain myself. It is, I suppose, the reaction from the haunting fear which I have had: that this terrible affair and the reopening of his old wound might act detrimentally on Jonathan. I saw him leave for Whitby with as brave a face as I could, but I was sick with apprehension. The effort has, however, done him good. He was never so resolute, never so strong, never so full of volcanic energy, as at present. It is just as that dear, good Professor Van Helsing said: he is true grit, and he improves under strain that would kill a weaker nature. He came back full of life and hope and determination; we have got everything in order for to-night. I feel myself quite wild with excitement. I suppose one ought to pity any thing so hunted as is the Count. That is just it: this Thing is not human— not even beast. To read Dr. Seward's account of poor Lucy's death, and what followed, is enough to dry up the springs of pity in one's heart.

Later.— Lord Godalming and Mr. Morris arrived earlier than we expected. Dr. Seward was out on business, and had taken Jonathan with him, so I had to see them. It was to me a painful meeting, for it brought back all poor dear Lucy's hopes of only a few months ago. Of course they had heard Lucy speak of me, and it seemed that Dr. Van Helsing, too, has been quite "blowing my trumpet," as Mr. Morris expressed it. Poor fellows, neither of them is aware that I know all about the proposals they made to Lucy. They did not quite know what to say or do, as they were ignorant of the amount of my knowledge; so they had to keep on neutral subjects. However, I thought the matter over, and came to the conclusion that the best thing I could do would be to post them in affairs right up to date. I knew from Dr. Seward's diary that they had been at Lucy's death— her real death— and that I need not fear to betray any secret before the time. So I told them, as well as I could, that I had read all the papers and diaries, and that my husband and I, having typewritten them, had just finished putting them in order. I gave them each a copy to read in the library. When Lord Godalming got his and turned it over— it does make a pretty good pile— he said:—

"Did you write all this, Mrs. Harker?"

I nodded, and he went on:—

"I don't quite see the drift of it; but you people are all so good and kind, and have been working so earnestly and so energetically, that all I can do is to accept your ideas blindfold and try to help you. I have had one lesson already in accepting facts that should make a man humble to the last hour of his life. Besides, I know you loved my poor Lucy— "
Here he turned away and covered his face with his hands. I could hear the tears in his voice. Mr. Morris, with instinctive delicacy, just laid a hand for a moment on his shoulder, and then walked quietly out of the room. I suppose there is something in woman's nature that makes a man free to break down before her and express his feelings on the tender or emotional side without feeling it derogatory to his manhood; for when Lord Godalming found himself alone with me he sat down on the sofa and gave way utterly and openly. I sat down beside him and took his hand. I hope he didn't think it forward of me, and that if he ever thinks of it afterwards he never will have such a thought. There I wrong him; I know he never will— he is too true a gentleman. I said to him, for I could see that his heart was breaking:—
"I loved dear Lucy, and I know what she was to you, and what you were to her. She and I were like sisters; and now she is gone, will you not let me be like a sister to you in your trouble? I know what sorrows you have had, though I cannot measure the depth of them. If sympathy and pity can help in your affliction, won't you let me be of some little service— for Lucy's sake?"
In an instant the poor dear fellow was overwhelmed with grief. It seemed to me that all that he had of late been suffering in silence found a vent at once. He grew quite hysterical, and raising his open hands, beat his palms together in a perfect agony of grief. He stood up and then sat down again, and the tears rained down his cheeks. I felt an infinite pity for him, and opened my arms unthinkingly. With a sob he laid his head on my shoulder and cried like a wearied child, whilst he shook with emotion.
We women have something of the mother in us that makes us rise above smaller matters when the mother-spirit is invoked; I felt this big sorrowing man's head resting on me, as though it were that of the baby that some day may lie on my bosom, and I stroked his hair as though he were my own child. I never thought at the time how strange it all was.

After a little bit his sobs ceased, and he raised himself with an apology, though he made no disguise of his emotion. He told me that for days and nights past— weary days and sleepless nights— he had been unable to speak with any one, as a man must speak in his time of sorrow. There was no woman whose sympathy could be given to him, or with whom, owing to the terrible circumstance with which his sorrow was surrounded, he could speak freely. "I know now how I suffered," he said, as he dried his eyes, "but I do not know even yet— and none other can ever know— how much your sweet sympathy has been to me to-day. I shall know better in time; and believe me that, though I am not ungrateful now, my gratitude will grow with my understanding. You will let me be like a brother, will you not, for all our lives— for dear Lucy's sake?"

"For dear Lucy's sake," I said as we clasped hands. "Ay, and for your own sake," he added, "for if a man's esteem and gratitude are ever worth the winning, you have won mine to-day. If ever the future should bring to you a time when you need a man's help, believe me, you will not call in vain. God grant that no such time may ever come to you to break the sunshine of your life; but if it should ever come, promise me that you will let me know." He was so earnest, and his sorrow was so fresh, that I felt it would comfort him, so I said:—

"I promise."

As I came along the corridor I saw Mr. Morris looking out of a window. He turned as he heard my footsteps. "How is Art?" he said. Then noticing my red eyes, he went on: "Ah, I see you have been comforting him. Poor old fellow! he needs it. No one but a woman can help a man when he is in trouble of the heart; and he had no one to comfort him." He bore his own trouble so bravely that my heart bled for him. I saw the manuscript in his hand, and I knew that when he read it he would realise how much I knew; so I said to him:—

"I wish I could comfort all who suffer from the heart. Will you let me be your friend, and will you come to me for comfort if you need it? You will know, later on, why I speak." He saw that I was in earnest, and stooping, took my hand, and raising it to his lips, kissed it. It seemed but poor comfort to so brave and unselfish a soul, and impulsively I bent over and kissed him. The tears rose in his eyes, and there was a momentary choking in his throat; he said quite calmly:—

"Little girl, you will never regret that true-hearted kindness, so long as ever you live!" Then he went into the study to his friend.

"Little girl!"— the very words he had used to Lucy, and oh, but he proved himself a friend!

## CHAPTER XVIII
# DR. SEWARD'S DIARY

3 0 September.— I got home at five o'clock, and found that Godalming and Morris had not only arrived, but had already studied the transcript of the various diaries and letters which Harker and his wonderful wife had made and arranged. Harker had not yet returned from his visit to the carriers' men, of whom Dr. Hennessey had written to me. Mrs. Harker gave us a cup of tea, and I can honestly say that, for the first time since I have lived in it, this old house seemed like home. When we had finished, Mrs. Harker said:—

"Dr. Seward, may I ask a favour? I want to see your patient, Mr. Renfield. Do let me see him. What you have said of him in your diary interests me so much!" She looked so appealing and so pretty that I could not refuse her, and there was no possible reason why I should; so I took her with me. When I went into the room, I told the man that a lady would like to see him; to which he simply answered: "Why?"

"She is going through the house, and wants to see every one in it," I answered. "Oh, very well," he said; "let her come in, by all means; but just wait a minute till I tidy up the place." His method of tidying was peculiar: he simply swallowed all the flies and spiders in the boxes before I could stop him. It was quite evident that he feared, or was jealous of, some interference. When he had got through his disgusting task, he said cheerfully: "Let the lady come in," and sat down on the edge of his bed with his head down, but with his eyelids raised so that he could see her as she entered. For a moment I thought that he might have some homicidal intent; I remembered how quiet he had been just before he attacked me in my own study, and I took care to stand where I could seize him at once if he attempted to make a spring at her. She came into the room with an easy gracefulness which would at once command the respect of any lunatic— for easiness is one of the qualities mad people most respect. She walked over to him, smiling pleasantly, and held out her hand.

"Good-evening, Mr. Renfield," said she. "You see, I know you, for Dr. Seward has told me of you." He made no immediate reply, but eyed her all over intently with a set frown on his face. This look gave way to one of wonder, which merged in doubt; then, to my intense astonishment, he said:—

"You're not the girl the doctor wanted to marry, are you? You can't be, you know, for she's dead." Mrs. Harker smiled sweetly as she replied:—

"Oh no! I have a husband of my own, to whom I was married before I ever saw Dr. Seward, or he me. I am Mrs. Harker."

"Then what are you doing here?"

"My husband and I are staying on a visit with Dr. Seward."

"Then don't stay."

"But why not?" I thought that this style of conversation might not be pleasant to Mrs. Harker, any more than it was to me, so I joined in:—

"How did you know I wanted to marry any one?" His reply was simply contemptuous, given in a pause in which he turned his eyes from Mrs. Harker to me, instantly turning them back again:—

"What an asinine question!"

"I don't see that at all, Mr. Renfield," said Mrs. Harker, at once championing me. He replied to her with as much courtesy and respect as he had shown contempt to me:—

"You will, of course, understand, Mrs. Harker, that when a man is so loved and honoured as our host is, everything regarding him is of interest in our little community. Dr. Seward is loved not only by his household and his friends, but even by his patients, who, being some of them hardly in mental equilibrium, are apt to distort causes and effects. Since I myself have been an inmate of a lunatic asylum, I cannot but notice that the sophistic tendencies of some of its inmates lean towards the errors of non causa and ignoratio elenchi." I positively opened my eyes at this new development. Here was my own pet lunatic— the most pronounced of his type that I had ever met with— talking elemental philosophy, and with the manner of a polished gentleman. I wonder if it was Mrs. Harker's presence which had touched some chord in his memory. If this new phase was spontaneous, or in any way due to her unconscious influence, she must have some rare gift or power.

We continued to talk for some time; and, seeing that he was seemingly quite reasonable, she ventured, looking at me questioningly as she began, to lead him to his favourite topic. I was again astonished, for he addressed himself to the question with the impartiality of the completest sanity; he even took himself as an example when he mentioned certain things.

"Why, I myself am an instance of a man who had a strange belief. Indeed, it was no wonder that my friends were alarmed, and insisted on my being put under control. I used to fancy that life was a positive and perpetual entity, and that by consuming a multitude of live things, no matter how low in the scale of creation, one might indefinitely prolong life. At times I held the belief so strongly that I actually tried to take human life. The doctor here will bear me out that on one occasion I tried to kill him for the purpose of strengthening my vital powers by the assimilation with my own body of his life through the medium of his blood— relying, of course, upon the Scriptural phrase, 'For the blood is the life.' Though, indeed, the vendor of a certain nostrum has vulgarised the truism to the very point of contempt. Isn't that true, doctor?" I nodded assent, for I was so amazed that I hardly knew what to either think or say; it was hard to imagine that I had seen him eat up his spiders and flies not five minutes before. Looking at my watch, I saw that I should go to the station to meet Van Helsing, so I told Mrs. Harker that it was time to leave. She came at once, after saying pleasantly to Mr. Renfield: "Good-bye, and I hope I may see you often, under auspices pleasanter to yourself," to which, to my astonishment, he replied:—

"Good-bye, my dear. I pray God I may never see your sweet face again. May He bless and keep you!"

When I went to the station to meet Van Helsing I left the boys behind me. Poor Art seemed more cheerful than he has been since Lucy first took ill, and Quincey is more like his own bright self than he has been for many a long day.

Van Helsing stepped from the carriage with the eager nimbleness of a boy. He saw me at once, and rushed up to me, saying:—

"Ah, friend John, how goes all? Well? So! I have been busy, for I come here to stay if need be. All affairs are settled with me, and I have much to tell. Madam Mina is with you? Yes. And her so fine husband? And Arthur and my friend Quincey, they are with you, too? Good!"

As I drove to the house I told him of what had passed, and of how my own diary had come to be of some use through Mrs. Harker's suggestion; at which the Professor interrupted me:—

"Ah, that wonderful Madam Mina! She has man's brain— a brain that a man should have were he much gifted— and a woman's heart. The good God fashioned her for a purpose, believe me, when He made that so good combination. Friend John, up to now fortune has made that woman of help to us; after to-night she must not have to do with this so terrible affair. It is not good that she run a risk so great. We men are determined— nay, are we not pledged?— to destroy this monster; but it is no part for a woman. Even if she be not harmed, her heart may fail her in so much and so many horrors; and hereafter she may suffer— both in waking, from her nerves, and in sleep, from her dreams. And, besides, she is young woman and not so long married; there may be other things to think of some time, if not now. You tell me she has wrote all, then she must consult with us; but to-morrow she say good-bye to this work, and we go alone." I agreed heartily with him, and then I told him what we had found in his absence: that the house which Dracula had bought was the very next one to my own. He was amazed, and a great concern seemed to come on him. "Oh that we had known it before!" he said, "for then we might have reached him in time to save poor Lucy. However, 'the milk that is spilt cries not out afterwards,' as you say. We shall not think of that, but go on our way to the end." Then he fell into a silence that lasted till we entered my own gateway. Before we went to prepare for dinner he said to Mrs. Harker:—

"I am told, Madam Mina, by my friend John that you and your husband have put up in exact order all things that have been, up to this moment."

"Not up to this moment, Professor," she said impulsively, "but up to this morning."

"But why not up to now? We have seen hitherto how good light all the little things have made. We have told our secrets, and yet no one who has told is the worse for it."

Mrs. Harker began to blush, and taking a paper from her pockets, she said:—

"Dr. Van Helsing, will you read this, and tell me if it must go in. It is my record of to-day. I too have seen the need of putting down at present everything, however trivial; but there is little in this except what is personal. Must it go in?" The Professor read it over gravely, and handed it back, saying:—

"It need not go in if you do not wish it; but I pray that it may. It can but make your husband love you the more, and all us, your friends, more honour you— as well as more esteem and love." She took it back with another blush and a bright smile.

And so now, up to this very hour, all the records we have are complete and in order. The Professor took away one copy to study after dinner, and before our meeting, which is fixed for nine o'clock. The rest of us have already read everything; so when we meet in the study we shall all be informed as to facts, and can arrange our plan of battle with this terrible and mysterious enemy.

Mina Harker's Journal.

30 September.— When we met in Dr. Seward's study two hours after dinner, which had been at six o'clock, we unconsciously formed a sort of board or committee. Professor Van Helsing took the head of the table, to which Dr. Seward motioned him as he came into the room. He made me sit next to him on his right, and asked me to act as secretary; Jonathan sat next to me. Opposite us were Lord Godalming, Dr. Seward, and Mr. Morris— Lord Godalming being next the Professor, and Dr. Seward in the centre. The Professor said:—

"I may, I suppose, take it that we are all acquainted with the facts that are in these papers." We all expressed assent, and he went on:—

"Then it were, I think good that I tell you something of the kind of enemy with which we have to deal. I shall then make known to you something of the history of this man, which has been ascertained for me. So we then can discuss how we shall act, and can take our measure according.

"There are such beings as vampires; some of us have evidence that they exist. Even had we not the proof of our own unhappy experience, the teachings and the records of the past give proof enough for sane peoples. I admit that at the first I was sceptic. Were it not that through long years I have train myself to keep an open mind, I could not have believe until such time as that fact thunder on my ear. 'See! see! I prove; I prove.' Alas! Had I known at the first what now I know— nay, had I even guess at him— one so precious life had been spared to many of us who did love her. But that is gone; and we must so work, that other poor souls perish not, whilst we can save. The nosferatu do not die like the bee when he sting once. He is only stronger; and being stronger, have yet more power to work evil. This vampire which is amongst us is of himself so strong in person as twenty men; he is of cunning more than mortal, for his cunning be the growth of ages; he have still the aids of necromancy, which is, as his etymology imply, the divination by the dead, and all the dead that he can come nigh to are for him at command; he is brute, and more than brute; he is devil in callous, and the heart of him is not; he can, within limitations, appear at will when, and where, and in any of the forms that are to him; he can, within his range, direct the elements; the storm, the fog, the thunder; he can command all the meaner things: the rat, and the owl, and the bat— the moth, and the fox, and the wolf; he can grow and become small; and he can at times vanish and come unknown. How then are we to begin our strike to destroy him? How shall we find his where; and having found it, how can we destroy? My friends, this is much; it is a terrible task that we undertake, and there may be consequence to make the brave shudder. For if we fail in this our fight he must surely win; and then where end we? Life is nothings; I heed him not. But to fail here, is not mere life or death. It is that we become as him; that we henceforward become foul things of the night like him— without heart or conscience, preying on the bodies and the souls of those we love best. To us for ever are the gates of heaven shut; for who shall open them to us again? We go on for all time abhorred by all; a blot on the face of God's sunshine; an arrow in the side of Him who died for man. But we are face to face with duty; and in such case must we shrink? For me, I say, no; but then I am old, and life, with his sunshine, his fair places, his song of birds, his music and his love, lie far behind. You others are young. Some have seen sorrow; but there are fair days yet in store. What say you?"

Whilst he was speaking, Jonathan had taken my hand. I feared, oh so much, that the appalling nature of our danger was overcoming him when I saw his hand stretch out; but it was life to me to feel its touch— so strong, so self-reliant, so resolute. A brave man's hand can speak for itself; it does not even need a woman's love to hear its music.

When the Professor had done speaking my husband looked in my eyes, and I in his; there was no need for speaking between us.

"I answer for Mina and myself," he said.

"Count me in, Professor," said Mr. Quincey Morris, laconically as usual.

"I am with you," said Lord Godalming, "for Lucy's sake, if for no other reason."

Dr. Seward simply nodded. The Professor stood up and, after laying his golden crucifix on the table, held out his hand on either side. I took his right hand, and Lord Godalming his left; Jonathan held my right with his left and stretched across to Mr. Morris. So as we all took hands our solemn compact was made. I felt my heart icy cold, but it did not even occur to me to draw back. We resumed our places, and Dr. Van Helsing went on with a sort of cheerfulness which showed that the serious work had begun. It was to be taken as gravely, and in as businesslike a way, as any other transaction of life:—

"Well, you know what we have to contend against; but we, too, are not without strength. We have on our side power of combination— a power denied to the vampire kind; we have sources of science; we are free to act and think; and the hours of the day and the night are ours equally. In fact, so far as our powers extend, they are unfettered, and we are free to use them. We have self-devotion in a cause, and an end to achieve which is not a selfish one. These things are much.

"Now let us see how far the general powers arrayed against us are restrict, and how the individual cannot. In fine, let us consider the limitations of the vampire in general, and of this one in particular.

"All we have to go upon are traditions and superstitions. These do not at the first appear much, when the matter is one of life and death— nay of more than either life or death. Yet must we be satisfied; in the first place because we have to be— no other means is at our control— and secondly, because, after all, these things— tradition and superstition— are everything. Does not the belief in vampires rest for others— though not, alas! for us— on them? A year ago which of us would have received such a possibility, in the midst of our scientific, sceptical, matter-of-fact nineteenth century? We even scouted a belief that we saw justified under our very eyes. Take it, then, that the vampire, and the belief in his limitations and his cure, rest for the moment on the same base. For, let me tell you, he is known everywhere that men have been. In old Greece, in old Rome; he flourish in Germany all over, in France, in India, even in the Chernosese; and in China, so far from us in all ways, there even is he, and the peoples fear him at this day. He have follow the wake of the berserker Icelander, the devil-begotten Hun, the Slav, the Saxon, the Magyar. So far, then, we have all we may act upon; and let me tell you that very much of the beliefs are justified by what we have seen in our own so unhappy experience. The vampire live on, and cannot die by mere passing of the time; he can flourish when that he can fatten on the blood of the living. Even more, we have seen amongst us that he can even grow younger; that his vital faculties grow strenuous, and seem as though they refresh themselves when his special pabulum is plenty. But he cannot flourish without this diet; he eat not as others. Even friend Jonathan, who lived with him for weeks, did never see him to eat, never! He throws no shadow; he make in the mirror no reflect, as again Jonathan observe. He has the strength of many of his hand— witness again Jonathan when he shut the door against the wolfs, and when he help him from the diligence too. He can transform himself to wolf, as we gather from the ship arrival in Whitby, when he tear open the dog; he can be as bat, as Madam Mina saw him on the window at Whitby, and as friend John saw him fly from this so near house, and as my friend Quincey saw him at the window of Miss Lucy. He can come in mist which he create— that noble ship's captain proved him of this; but, from what we know, the distance he can make this mist is limited, and it can only be round himself. He come on moonlight rays as elemental dust— as again Jonathan saw those sisters in the castle of Dracula. He become so small— we ourselves saw Miss Lucy, ere she was at peace, slip through a hairbreadth space at the tomb door. He can, when once he find his way, come out from anything or into anything, no matter how close it be bound or even fused up with fire— solder you call it. He can see in the dark— no small power this, in a world which is one half shut from the light. Ah, but hear me through. He can do all these things, yet he is not free. Nay; he is even more prisoner than the slave of the galley, than the madman in his cell. He cannot go where he lists; he who is not of nature has yet to obey some of nature's laws— why we know not. He may not enter anywhere at the first, unless there be some one of the household who bid him to come; though afterwards he can come as he please. His power ceases, as does that of all evil things, at the coming of the day. Only at certain times can he have limited freedom. If he be not at the place whither he is bound, he can only change himself at noon or at exact sunrise or sunset. These things are we told, and in this record of ours we have proof by inference. Thus, whereas he can do as he will within his limit, when he have his earth-home, his coffin-home, his hell-home, the place unhallowed, as we saw when he went to the grave of the suicide at Whitby; still at other time he can only change when the time come. It is said, too, that he can only pass running water at the slack or the flood of the tide. Then there are things which so afflict him that he has no power, as the garlic that we know of; and as for things sacred, as this symbol, my crucifix, that was amongst us even now when we resolve, to them he is nothing, but in their presence he take his place far off and silent with respect. There are others, too, which I shall tell you of, lest in our seeking we may need them. The branch of wild rose on his coffin keep him that he move not from it; a sacred bullet fired into the coffin kill him so that he be true dead; and as for the stake through him, we know already of its peace; or the cut-off head that giveth rest. We have seen it with our eyes.

"Thus when we find the habitation of this man-that-was, we can confine him to his coffin and destroy him, if we obey what we know. But he is clever. I have asked my friend Arminius, of Buda-Pesth University, to make his record; and, from all the means that are, he tell me of what he has been. He must, indeed, have been that Voivode Dracula who won his name against the Turk, over the great river on the very frontier of Turkey-land. If it be so, then was he no common man; for in that time, and for centuries after, he was spoken of as the cleverest and the most cunning, as well as the bravest of the sons of the 'land beyond the forest.' That mighty brain and that iron resolution went with him to his grave, and are even now arrayed against us. The Draculas were, says Arminius, a great and noble race, though now and again were scions who were held by their coevals to have had dealings with the Evil One. They learned his secrets in the Scholomance, amongst the mountains over Lake Hermanstadt, where the devil claims the tenth scholar as his due. In the records are such words as 'stregoica'— witch, 'ordog,' and 'pokol'— Satan and hell; and in one manuscript this very Dracula is spoken of as 'wampyr,' which we all understand too well. There have been from the loins of this very one great men and good women, and their graves make sacred the earth where alone this foulness can dwell. For it is not the least of its terrors that this evil thing is rooted deep in all good; in soil barren of holy memories it cannot rest."

Whilst they were talking Mr. Morris was looking steadily at the window, and he now got up quietly, and went out of the room. There was a little pause, and then the Professor went on:—

"And now we must settle what we do. We have here much data, and we must proceed to lay out our campaign. We know from the inquiry of Jonathan that from the castle to Whitby came fifty boxes of earth, all of which were delivered at Carfax; we also know that at least some of these boxes have been removed. It seems to me, that our first step should be to ascertain whether all the rest remain in the house beyond that wall where we look to-day; or whether any more have been removed. If the latter, we must trace— — "

Here we were interrupted in a very startling way. Outside the house came the sound of a pistol-shot; the glass of the window was shattered with a bullet, which, ricochetting from the top of the embrasure, struck the far wall of the room. I am afraid I am at heart a coward, for I shrieked out. The men all jumped to their feet; Lord Godalming flew over to the window and threw up the sash. As he did so we heard Mr. Morris's voice without:—

"Sorry! I fear I have alarmed you. I shall come in and tell you about it."
A minute later he came in and said:—

"It was an idiotic thing of me to do, and I ask your pardon, Mrs. Harker, most sincerely; I fear I must have frightened you terribly. But the fact is that whilst the Professor was talking there came a big bat and sat on the window-sill. I have got such a horror of the damned brutes from recent events that I cannot stand them, and I went out to have a shot, as I have been doing of late of evenings, whenever I have seen one. You used to laugh at me for it then, Art."

"Did you hit it?" asked Dr. Van Helsing.

"I don't know; I fancy not, for it flew away into the wood." Without saying any more he took his seat, and the Professor began to resume his statement:—

"We must trace each of these boxes; and when we are ready, we must either capture or kill this monster in his lair; or we must, so to speak, sterilise the earth, so that no more he can seek safety in it. Thus in the end we may find him in his form of man between the hours of noon and sunset, and so engage with him when he is at his most weak.

"And now for you, Madam Mina, this night is the end until all be well. You are too precious to us to have such risk. When we part to-night, you no more must question. We shall tell you all in good time. We are men and are able to bear; but you must be our star and our hope, and we shall act all the more free that you are not in the danger, such as we are."

All the men, even Jonathan, seemed relieved; but it did not seem to me good that they should brave danger and, perhaps, lessen their safety— strength being the best safety— through care of me; but their minds were made up, and, though it was a bitter pill for me to swallow, I could say nothing, save to accept their chivalrous care of me.

Mr. Morris resumed the discussion:—

"As there is no time to lose, I vote we have a look at his house right now. Time is everything with him; and swift action on our part may save another victim."

I own that my heart began to fail me when the time for action came so close, but I did not say anything, for I had a greater fear that if I appeared as a drag or a hindrance to their work, they might even leave me out of their counsels altogether. They have now gone off to Carfax, with means to get into the house.

Manlike, they had told me to go to bed and sleep; as if a woman can sleep when those she loves are in danger! I shall lie down and pretend to sleep, lest Jonathan have added anxiety about me when he returns.

Dr. Seward's Diary.

1 October, 4 a. m.— Just as we were about to leave the house, an urgent message was brought to me from Renfield to know if I would see him at once, as he had something of the utmost importance to say to me. I told the messenger to say that I would attend to his wishes in the morning; I was busy just at the moment. The attendant added:—

"He seems very importunate, sir. I have never seen him so eager. I don't know but what, if you don't see him soon, he will have one of his violent fits." I knew the man would not have said this without some cause, so I said: "All right; I'll go now"; and I asked the others to wait a few minutes for me, as I had to go and see my "patient."

"Take me with you, friend John," said the Professor. "His case in your diary interest me much, and it had bearing, too, now and again on our case. I should much like to see him, and especial when his mind is disturbed."

"May I come also?" asked Lord Godalming.

"Me too?" said Quincey Morris. "May I come?" said Harker. I nodded, and we all went down the passage together.

We found him in a state of considerable excitement, but far more rational in his speech and manner than I had ever seen him. There was an unusual understanding of himself, which was unlike anything I had ever met with in a lunatic; and he took it for granted that his reasons would prevail with others entirely sane. We all four went into the room, but none of the others at first said anything. His request was that I would at once release him from the asylum and send him home. This he backed up with arguments regarding his complete recovery, and adduced his own existing sanity. "I appeal to your friends," he said, "they will, perhaps, not mind sitting in judgment on my case. By the way, you have not introduced me." I was so much astonished, that the oddness of introducing a madman in an asylum did not strike me at the moment; and, besides, there was a certain dignity in the man's manner, so much of the habit of equality, that I at once made the introduction: "Lord Godalming; Professor Van Helsing; Mr. Quincey Morris, of Texas; Mr. Renfield." He shook hands with each of them, saying in turn:—

"Lord Godalming, I had the honour of seconding your father at the Windham; I grieve to know, by your holding the title, that he is no more. He was a man loved and honoured by all who knew him; and in his youth was, I have heard, the inventor of a burnt rum punch, much patronised on Derby night. Mr. Morris, you should be proud of your great state. Its reception into the Union was a precedent which may have far-reaching effects hereafter, when the Pole and the Tropics may hold alliance to the Stars and Stripes. The power of Treaty may yet prove a vast engine of enlargement, when the Monroe doctrine takes its true place as a political fable. What shall any man say of his pleasure at meeting Van Helsing? Sir, I make no apology for dropping all forms of conventional prefix. When an individual has revolutionised therapeutics by his discovery of the continuous evolution of brain-matter, conventional forms are unfitting, since they would seem to limit him to one of a class. You, gentlemen, who by nationality, by heredity, or by the possession of natural gifts, are fitted to hold your respective places in the moving world, I take to witness that I am as sane as at least the majority of men who are in full possession of their liberties. And I am sure that you, Dr. Seward, humanitarian and medico-jurist as well as scientist, will deem it a moral duty to deal with me as one to be considered as under exceptional circumstances." He made this last appeal with a courtly air of conviction which was not without its own charm.

I think we were all staggered. For my own part, I was under the conviction, despite my knowledge of the man's character and history, that his reason had been restored; and I felt under a strong impulse to tell him that I was satisfied as to his sanity, and would see about the necessary formalities for his release in the morning. I thought it better to wait, however, before making so grave a statement, for of old I knew the sudden changes to which this particular patient was liable. So I contented myself with making a general statement that he appeared to be improving very rapidly; that I would have a longer chat with him in the morning, and would then see what I could do in the direction of meeting his wishes. This did not at all satisfy him, for he said quickly:—

"But I fear, Dr. Seward, that you hardly apprehend my wish. I desire to go at once— here— now— this very hour— this very moment, if I may. Time presses, and in our implied agreement with the old scytheman it is of the essence of the contract. I am sure it is only necessary to put before so admirable a practitioner as Dr. Seward so simple, yet so momentous a wish, to ensure its fulfilment." He looked at me keenly, and seeing the negative in my face, turned to the others, and scrutinised them closely. Not meeting any sufficient response, he went on:—

"Is it possible that I have erred in my supposition?"

"You have," I said frankly, but at the same time, as I felt, brutally. There was a considerable pause, and then he said slowly:—

"Then I suppose I must only shift my ground of request. Let me ask for this concession— boon, privilege, what you will. I am content to implore in such a case, not on personal grounds, but for the sake of others. I am not at liberty to give you the whole of my reasons; but you may, I assure you, take it from me that they are good ones, sound and unselfish, and spring from the highest sense of duty. Could you look, sir, into my heart, you would approve to the full the sentiments which animate me. Nay, more, you would count me amongst the best and truest of your friends." Again he looked at us all keenly. I had a growing conviction that this sudden change of his entire intellectual method was but yet another form or phase of his madness, and so determined to let him go on a little longer, knowing from experience that he would, like all lunatics, give himself away in the end. Van Helsing was gazing at him with a look of utmost intensity, his bushy eyebrows almost meeting with the fixed concentration of his look. He said to Renfield in a tone which did not surprise me at the time, but only when I thought of it afterwards— for it was as of one addressing an equal:—

"Can you not tell frankly your real reason for wishing to be free to-night? I will undertake that if you will satisfy even me— a stranger, without prejudice, and with the habit of keeping an open mind— Dr. Seward will give you, at his own risk and on his own responsibility, the privilege you seek." He shook his head sadly, and with a look of poignant regret on his face. The Professor went on:—

"Come, sir, bethink yourself. You claim the privilege of reason in the highest degree, since you seek to impress us with your complete reasonableness. You do this, whose sanity we have reason to doubt, since you are not yet released from medical treatment for this very defect. If you will not help us in our effort to choose the wisest course, how can we perform the duty which you yourself put upon us? Be wise, and help us; and if we can we shall aid you to achieve your wish." He still shook his head as he said:—

"Dr. Van Helsing, I have nothing to say. Your argument is complete, and if I were free to speak I should not hesitate a moment; but I am not my own master in the matter. I can only ask you to trust me. If I am refused, the responsibility does not rest with me." I thought it was now time to end the scene, which was becoming too comically grave, so I went towards the door, simply saying:—

"Come, my friends, we have work to do. Good-night."

As, however, I got near the door, a new change came over the patient. He moved towards me so quickly that for the moment I feared that he was about to make another homicidal attack. My fears, however, were groundless, for he held up his two hands imploringly, and made his petition in a moving manner. As he saw that the very excess of his emotion was militating against him, by restoring us more to our old relations, he became still more demonstrative. I glanced at Van Helsing, and saw my conviction reflected in his eyes; so I became a little more fixed in my manner, if not more stern, and motioned to him that his efforts were unavailing. I had previously seen something of the same constantly growing excitement in him when he had to make some request of which at the time he had thought much, such, for instance, as when he wanted a cat; and I was prepared to see the collapse into the same sullen acquiescence on this occasion. My expectation was not realised, for, when he found that his appeal would not be successful, he got into quite a frantic condition. He threw himself on his knees, and held up his hands, wringing them in plaintive supplication, and poured forth a torrent of entreaty, with the tears rolling down his cheeks, and his whole face and form expressive of the deepest emotion:—

"Let me entreat you, Dr. Seward, oh, let me implore you, to let me out of this house at once. Send me away how you will and where you will; send keepers with me with whips and chains; let them take me in a strait-waistcoat, manacled and leg-ironed, even to a gaol; but let me go out of this. You don't know what you do by keeping me here. I am speaking from the depths of my heart— of my very soul. You don't know whom you wrong, or how; and I may not tell. Woe is me! I may not tell. By all you hold sacred— by all you hold dear— by your love that is lost— by your hope that lives— for the sake of the Almighty, take me out of this and save my soul from guilt! Can't you hear me, man? Can't you understand? Will you never learn? Don't you know that I am sane and earnest now; that I am no lunatic in a mad fit, but a sane man fighting for his soul? Oh, hear me! hear me! Let me go! let me go! let me go!"

I thought that the longer this went on the wilder he would get, and so would bring on a fit; so I took him by the hand and raised him up.

"Come," I said sternly, "no more of this; we have had quite enough already. Get to your bed and try to behave more discreetly."

He suddenly stopped and looked at me intently for several moments. Then, without a word, he rose and moving over, sat down on the side of the bed. The collapse had come, as on former occasion, just as I had expected.

When I was leaving the room, last of our party, he said to me in a quiet, well-bred voice:—

"You will, I trust, Dr. Seward, do me the justice to bear in mind, later on, that I did what I could to convince you to-night."

## CHAPTER XIX
## JONATHAN HARKER'S JOURNAL

1 October, 5 a. m.— I went with the party to the search with an easy mind, for I think I never saw Mina so absolutely strong and well. I am so glad that she consented to hold back and let us men do the work. Somehow, it was a dread to me that she was in this fearful business at all; but now that her work is done, and that it is due to her energy and brains and foresight that the whole story is put together in such a way that every point tells, she may well feel that her part is finished, and that she can henceforth leave the rest to us. We were, I think, all a little upset by the scene with Mr. Renfield. When we came away from his room we were silent till we got back to the study. Then Mr. Morris said to Dr. Seward:—

"Say, Jack, if that man wasn't attempting a bluff, he is about the sanest lunatic I ever saw. I'm not sure, but I believe that he had some serious purpose, and if he had, it was pretty rough on him not to get a chance." Lord Godalming and I were silent, but Dr. Van Helsing added:—

"Friend John, you know more of lunatics than I do, and I'm glad of it, for I fear that if it had been to me to decide I would before that last hysterical outburst have given him free. But we live and learn, and in our present task we must take no chance, as my friend Quincey would say. All is best as they are." Dr. Seward seemed to answer them both in a dreamy kind of way:—

"I don't know but that I agree with you. If that man had been an ordinary lunatic I would have taken my chance of trusting him; but he seems so mixed up with the Count in an indexy kind of way that I am afraid of doing anything wrong by helping his fads. I can't forget how he prayed with almost equal fervour for a cat, and then tried to tear my throat out with his teeth. Besides, he called the Count 'lord and master,' and he may want to get out to help him in some diabolical way. That horrid thing has the wolves and the rats and his own kind to help him, so I suppose he isn't above trying to use a respectable lunatic. He certainly did seem earnest, though. I only hope we have done what is best. These things, in conjunction with the wild work we have in hand, help to unnerve a man." The Professor stepped over, and laying his hand on his shoulder, said in his grave, kindly way:—

"Friend John, have no fear. We are trying to do our duty in a very sad and terrible case; we can only do as we deem best. What else have we to hope for, except the pity of the good God?" Lord Godalming had slipped away for a few minutes, but now he returned. He held up a little silver whistle, as he remarked:—

"That old place may be full of rats, and if so, I've got an antidote on call." Having passed the wall, we took our way to the house, taking care to keep in the shadows of the trees on the lawn when the moonlight shone out. When we got to the porch the Professor opened his bag and took out a lot of things, which he laid on the step, sorting them into four little groups, evidently one for each. Then he spoke:—

"My friends, we are going into a terrible danger, and we need arms of many kinds. Our enemy is not merely spiritual. Remember that he has the strength of twenty men, and that, though our necks or our windpipes are of the common kind— and therefore breakable or crushable— his are not amenable to mere strength. A stronger man, or a body of men more strong in all than him, can at certain times hold him; but they cannot hurt him as we can be hurt by him. We must, therefore, guard ourselves from his touch. Keep this near your heart"— as he spoke he lifted a little silver crucifix and held it out to me, I being nearest to him— "put these flowers round your neck"— here he handed to me a wreath of withered garlic blossoms— "for other enemies more mundane, this revolver and this knife; and for aid in all, these so small electric lamps, which you can fasten to your breast; and for all, and above all at the last, this, which we must not desecrate needless." This was a portion of Sacred Wafer, which he put in an envelope and handed to me. Each of the others was similarly equipped. "Now," he said, "friend John, where are the skeleton keys? If so that we can open the door, we need not break house by the window, as before at Miss Lucy's."

Dr. Seward tried one or two skeleton keys, his mechanical dexterity as a surgeon standing him in good stead. Presently he got one to suit; after a little play back and forward the bolt yielded, and, with a rusty clang, shot back. We pressed on the door, the rusty hinges creaked, and it slowly opened. It was startlingly like the image conveyed to me in Dr. Seward's diary of the opening of Miss Westenra's tomb; I fancy that the same idea seemed to strike the others, for with one accord they shrank back. The Professor was the first to move forward, and stepped into the open door.

"In manus tuas, Domine!" he said, crossing himself as he passed over the threshold. We closed the door behind us, lest when we should have lit our lamps we should possibly attract attention from the road. The Professor carefully tried the lock, lest we might not be able to open it from within should we be in a hurry making our exit. Then we all lit our lamps and proceeded on our search.

The light from the tiny lamps fell in all sorts of odd forms, as the rays crossed each other, or the opacity of our bodies threw great shadows. I could not for my life get away from the feeling that there was some one else amongst us. I suppose it was the recollection, so powerfully brought home to me by the grim surroundings, of that terrible experience in Transylvania. I think the feeling was common to us all, for I noticed that the others kept looking over their shoulders at every sound and every new shadow, just as I felt myself doing.

The whole place was thick with dust. The floor was seemingly inches deep, except where there were recent footsteps, in which on holding down my lamp I could see marks of hobnails where the dust was cracked. The walls were fluffy and heavy with dust, and in the corners were masses of spider's webs, whereon the dust had gathered till they looked like old tattered rags as the weight had torn them partly down. On a table in the hall was a great bunch of keys, with a time-yellowed label on each. They had been used several times, for on the table were several similar rents in the blanket of dust, similar to that exposed when the Professor lifted them. He turned to me and said:—

"You know this place, Jonathan. You have copied maps of it, and you know it at least more than we do. Which is the way to the chapel?" I had an idea of its direction, though on my former visit I had not been able to get admission to it; so I led the way, and after a few wrong turnings found myself opposite a low, arched oaken door, ribbed with iron bands. "This is the spot," said the Professor as he turned his lamp on a small map of the house, copied from the file of my original correspondence regarding the purchase. With a little trouble we found the key on the bunch and opened the door. We were prepared for some unpleasantness, for as we were opening the door a faint, malodorous air seemed to exhale through the gaps, but none of us ever expected such an odour as we encountered. None of the others had met the Count at all at close quarters, and when I had seen him he was either in the fasting stage of his existence in his rooms or, when he was gloated with fresh blood, in a ruined building open to the air; but here the place was small and close, and the long disuse had made the air stagnant and foul. There was an earthy smell, as of some dry miasma, which came through the fouler air. But as to the odour itself, how shall I describe it? It was not alone that it was composed of all the ills of mortality and with the pungent, acrid smell of blood, but it seemed as though corruption had become itself corrupt. Faugh! it sickens me to think of it. Every breath exhaled by that monster seemed to have clung to the place and intensified its loathsomeness.

Under ordinary circumstances such a stench would have brought our enterprise to an end; but this was no ordinary case, and the high and terrible purpose in which we were involved gave us a strength which rose above merely physical considerations. After the involuntary shrinking consequent on the first nauseous whiff, we one and all set about our work as though that loathsome place were a garden of roses. We made an accurate examination of the place, the Professor saying as we began:—

"The first thing is to see how many of the boxes are left; we must then examine every hole and corner and cranny and see if we cannot get some clue as to what has become of the rest." A glance was sufficient to show how many remained, for the great earth chests were bulky, and there was no mistaking them.

There were only twenty-nine left out of the fifty! Once I got a fright, for, seeing Lord Godalming suddenly turn and look out of the vaulted door into the dark passage beyond, I looked too, and for an instant my heart stood still. Somewhere, looking out from the shadow, I seemed to see the high lights of the Count's evil face, the ridge of the nose, the red eyes, the red lips, the awful pallor. It was only for a moment, for, as Lord Godalming said, "I thought I saw a face, but it was only the shadows," and resumed his inquiry, I turned my lamp in the direction, and stepped into the passage. There was no sign of any one; and as there were no corners, no doors, no aperture of any kind, but only the solid walls of the passage, there could be no hiding-place even for him. I took it that fear had helped imagination, and said nothing.

A few minutes later I saw Morris step suddenly back from a corner, which he was examining. We all followed his movements with our eyes, for undoubtedly some nervousness was growing on us, and we saw a whole mass of phosphorescence, which twinkled like stars. We all instinctively drew back. The whole place was becoming alive with rats. For a moment or two we stood appalled, all save Lord Godalming, who was seemingly prepared for such an emergency. Rushing over to the great iron-bound oaken door, which Dr. Seward had described from the outside, and which I had seen myself, he turned the key in the lock, drew the huge bolts, and swung the door open. Then, taking his little silver whistle from his pocket, he blew a low, shrill call. It was answered from behind Dr. Seward's house by the yelping of dogs, and after about a minute three terriers came dashing round the corner of the house. Unconsciously we had all moved towards the door, and as we moved I noticed that the dust had been much disturbed: the boxes which had been taken out had been brought this way. But even in the minute that had elapsed the number of the rats had vastly increased. They seemed to swarm over the place all at once, till the lamplight, shining on their moving dark bodies and glittering, baleful eyes, made the place look like a bank of earth set with fireflies. The dogs dashed on, but at the threshold suddenly stopped and snarled, and then, simultaneously lifting their noses, began to howl in most lugubrious fashion. The rats were multiplying in thousands, and we moved out.

Lord Godalming lifted one of the dogs, and carrying him in, placed him on the floor. The instant his feet touched the ground he seemed to recover his courage, and rushed at his natural enemies. They fled before him so fast that before he had shaken the life out of a score, the other dogs, who had by now been lifted in the same manner, had but small prey ere the whole mass had vanished.

With their going it seemed as if some evil presence had departed, for the dogs frisked about and barked merrily as they made sudden darts at their prostrate foes, and turned them over and over and tossed them in the air with vicious shakes. We all seemed to find our spirits rise. Whether it was the purifying of the deadly atmosphere by the opening of the chapel door, or the relief which we experienced by finding ourselves in the open I know not; but most certainly the shadow of dread seemed to slip from us like a robe, and the occasion of our coming lost something of its grim significance, though we did not slacken a whit in our resolution. We closed the outer door and barred and locked it, and bringing the dogs with us, began our search of the house. We found nothing throughout except dust in extraordinary proportions, and all untouched save for my own footsteps when I had made my first visit. Never once did the dogs exhibit any symptom of uneasiness, and even when we returned to the chapel they frisked about as though they had been rabbit-hunting in a summer wood.

The morning was quickening in the east when we emerged from the front. Dr. Van Helsing had taken the key of the hall-door from the bunch, and locked the door in orthodox fashion, putting the key into his pocket when he had done.

"So far," he said, "our night has been eminently successful. No harm has come to us such as I feared might be and yet we have ascertained how many boxes are missing. More than all do I rejoice that this, our first— and perhaps our most difficult and dangerous— step has been accomplished without the bringing thereinto our most sweet Madam Mina or troubling her waking or sleeping thoughts with sights and sounds and smells of horror which she might never forget. One lesson, too, we have learned, if it be allowable to argue a particulari: that the brute beasts which are to the Count's command are yet themselves not amenable to his spiritual power; for look, these rats that would come to his call, just as from his castle top he summon the wolves to your going and to that poor mother's cry, though they come to him, they run pell-mell from the so little dogs of my friend Arthur. We have other matters before us, other dangers, other fears; and that monster— he has not used his power over the brute world for the only or the last time to-night. So be it that he has gone elsewhere. Good! It has given us opportunity to cry 'check' in some ways in this chess game, which we play for the stake of human souls. And now let us go home. The dawn is close at hand, and we have reason to be content with our first night's work. It may be ordained that we have many nights and days to follow, if full of peril; but we must go on, and from no danger shall we shrink."

The house was silent when we got back, save for some poor creature who was screaming away in one of the distant wards, and a low, moaning sound from Renfield's room. The poor wretch was doubtless torturing himself, after the manner of the insane, with needless thoughts of pain.

I came tiptoe into our own room, and found Mina asleep, breathing so softly that I had to put my ear down to hear it. She looks paler than usual. I hope the meeting to-night has not upset her. I am truly thankful that she is to be left out of our future work, and even of our deliberations. It is too great a strain for a woman to bear. I did not think so at first, but I know better now. Therefore I am glad that it is settled. There may be things which would frighten her to hear; and yet to conceal them from her might be worse than to tell her if once she suspected that there was any concealment. Henceforth our work is to be a sealed book to her, till at least such time as we can tell her that all is finished, and the earth free from a monster of the nether world. I daresay it will be difficult to begin to keep silence after such confidence as ours; but I must be resolute, and to-morrow I shall keep dark over to-night's doings, and shall refuse to speak of anything that has happened. I rest on the sofa, so as not to disturb her.

1 October, later.— I suppose it was natural that we should have all overslept ourselves, for the day was a busy one, and the night had no rest at all. Even Mina must have felt its exhaustion, for though I slept till the sun was high, I was awake before her, and had to call two or three times before she awoke. Indeed, she was so sound asleep that for a few seconds she did not recognize me, but looked at me with a sort of blank terror, as one looks who has been waked out of a bad dream. She complained a little of being tired, and I let her rest till later in the day. We now know of twenty-one boxes having been removed, and if it be that several were taken in any of these removals we may be able to trace them all. Such will, of course, immensely simplify our labour, and the sooner the matter is attended to the better. I shall look up Thomas Snelling to-day.

Dr. Seward's Diary.

1 October.— It was towards noon when I was awakened by the Professor walking into my room. He was more jolly and cheerful than usual, and it is quite evident that last night's work has helped to take some of the brooding weight off his mind. After going over the adventure of the night he suddenly said:—

"Your patient interests me much. May it be that with you I visit him this morning? Or if that you are too occupy, I can go alone if it may be. It is a new experience to me to find a lunatic who talk philosophy, and reason so sound." I had some work to do which pressed, so I told him that if he would go alone I would be glad, as then I should not have to keep him waiting; so I called an attendant and gave him the necessary instructions. Before the Professor left the room I cautioned him against getting any false impression from my patient. "But," he answered, "I want him to talk of himself and of his delusion as to consuming live things. He said to Madam Mina, as I see in your diary of yesterday, that he had once had such a belief. Why do you smile, friend John?"

"Excuse me," I said, "but the answer is here." I laid my hand on the type-written matter. "When our sane and learned lunatic made that very statement of how he used to consume life, his mouth was actually nauseous with the flies and spiders which he had eaten just before Mrs. Harker entered the room." Van Helsing smiled in turn. "Good!" he said. "Your memory is true, friend John. I should have remembered. And yet it is this very obliquity of thought and memory which makes mental disease such a fascinating study. Perhaps I may gain more knowledge out of the folly of this madman than I shall from the teaching of the most wise. Who knows?" I went on with my work, and before long was through that in hand. It seemed that the time had been very short indeed, but there was Van Helsing back in the study. "Do I interrupt?" he asked politely as he stood at the door.

"Not at all," I answered. "Come in. My work is finished, and I am free. I can go with you now, if you like.

"It is needless; I have seen him!"

"Well?"

"I fear that he does not appraise me at much. Our interview was short. When I entered his room he was sitting on a stool in the centre, with his elbows on his knees, and his face was the picture of sullen discontent. I spoke to him as cheerfully as I could, and with such a measure of respect as I could assume. He made no reply whatever. "Don't you know me?" I asked. His answer was not reassuring: "I know you well enough; you are the old fool Van Helsing. I wish you would take yourself and your idiotic brain theories somewhere else. Damn all thick-headed Dutchmen!" Not a word more would he say, but sat in his implacable sullenness as indifferent to me as though I had not been in the room at all. Thus departed for this time my chance of much learning from this so clever lunatic; so I shall go, if I may, and cheer myself with a few happy words with that sweet soul Madam Mina. Friend John, it does rejoice me unspeakable that she is no more to be pained, no more to be worried with our terrible things. Though we shall much miss her help, it is better so."

"I agree with you with all my heart," I answered earnestly, for I did not want him to weaken in this matter. "Mrs. Harker is better out of it. Things are quite bad enough for us, all men of the world, and who have been in many tight places in our time; but it is no place for a woman, and if she had remained in touch with the affair, it would in time infallibly have wrecked her."

So Van Helsing has gone to confer with Mrs. Harker and Harker; Quincey and Art are all out following up the clues as to the earth-boxes. I shall finish my round of work and we shall meet to-night.

Mina Harker's Journal.

1 October.— It is strange to me to be kept in the dark as I am to-day; after Jonathan's full confidence for so many years, to see him manifestly avoid certain matters, and those the most vital of all. This morning I slept late after the fatigues of yesterday, and though Jonathan was late too, he was the earlier. He spoke to me before he went out, never more sweetly or tenderly, but he never mentioned a word of what had happened in the visit to the Count's house. And yet he must have known how terribly anxious I was. Poor dear fellow! I suppose it must have distressed him even more than it did me. They all agreed that it was best that I should not be drawn further into this awful work, and I acquiesced. But to think that he keeps anything from me! And now I am crying like a silly fool, when I know it comes from my husband's great love and from the good, good wishes of those other strong men.

That has done me good. Well, some day Jonathan will tell me all; and lest it should ever be that he should think for a moment that I kept anything from him, I still keep my journal as usual. Then if he has feared of my trust I shall show it to him, with every thought of my heart put down for his dear eyes to read. I feel strangely sad and low-spirited to-day. I suppose it is the reaction from the terrible excitement.

Last night I went to bed when the men had gone, simply because they told me to. I didn't feel sleepy, and I did feel full of devouring anxiety. I kept thinking over everything that has been ever since Jonathan came to see me in London, and it all seems like a horrible tragedy, with fate pressing on relentlessly to some destined end. Everything that one does seems, no matter how right it may be, to bring on the very thing which is most to be deplored. If I hadn't gone to Whitby, perhaps poor dear Lucy would be with us now. She hadn't taken to visiting the churchyard till I came, and if she hadn't come there in the day-time with me she wouldn't have walked there in her sleep; and if she hadn't gone there at night and asleep, that monster couldn't have destroyed her as he did. Oh, why did I ever go to Whitby? There now, crying again! I wonder what has come over me to-day. I must hide it from Jonathan, for if he knew that I had been crying twice in one morning— I, who never cried on my own account, and whom he has never caused to shed a tear— the dear fellow would fret his heart out. I shall put a bold face on, and if I do feel weepy, he shall never see it. I suppose it is one of the lessons that we poor women have to learn....

I can't quite remember how I fell asleep last night. I remember hearing the sudden barking of the dogs and a lot of queer sounds, like praying on a very tumultuous scale, from Mr. Renfield's room, which is somewhere under this. And then there was silence over everything, silence so profound that it startled me, and I got up and looked out of the window. All was dark and silent, the black shadows thrown by the moonlight seeming full of a silent mystery of their own. Not a thing seemed to be stirring, but all to be grim and fixed as death or fate; so that a thin streak of white mist, that crept with almost imperceptible slowness across the grass towards the house, seemed to have a sentience and a vitality of its own. I think that the digression of my thoughts must have done me good, for when I got back to bed I found a lethargy creeping over me. I lay a while, but could not quite sleep, so I got out and looked out of the window again. The mist was spreading, and was now close up to the house, so that I could see it lying thick against the wall, as though it were stealing up to the windows. The poor man was more loud than ever, and though I could not distinguish a word he said, I could in some way recognise in his tones some passionate entreaty on his part. Then there was the sound of a struggle, and I knew that the attendants were dealing with him. I was so frightened that I crept into bed, and pulled the clothes over my head, putting my fingers in my ears. I was not then a bit sleepy, at least so I thought; but I must have fallen asleep, for, except dreams, I do not remember anything until the morning, when Jonathan woke me. I think that it took me an effort and a little time to realise where I was, and that it was Jonathan who was bending over me. My dream was very peculiar, and was almost typical of the way that waking thoughts become merged in, or continued in, dreams.

I thought that I was asleep, and waiting for Jonathan to come back. I was very anxious about him, and I was powerless to act; my feet, and my hands, and my brain were weighted, so that nothing could proceed at the usual pace. And so I slept uneasily and thought. Then it began to dawn upon me that the air was heavy, and dank, and cold. I put back the clothes from my face, and found, to my surprise, that all was dim around. The gaslight which I had left lit for Jonathan, but turned down, came only like a tiny red spark through the fog, which had evidently grown thicker and poured into the room. Then it occurred to me that I had shut the window before I had come to bed. I would have got out to make certain on the point, but some leaden lethargy seemed to chain my limbs and even my will. I lay still and endured; that was all. I closed my eyes, but could still see through my eyelids. (It is wonderful what tricks our dreams play us, and how conveniently we can imagine.) The mist grew thicker and thicker and I could see now how it came in, for I could see it like smoke— or with the white energy of boiling water— pouring in, not through the window, but through the joinings of the door. It got thicker and thicker, till it seemed as if it became concentrated into a sort of pillar of cloud in the room, through the top of which I could see the light of the gas shining like a red eye. Things began to whirl through my brain just as the cloudy column was now whirling in the room, and through it all came the scriptural words "a pillar of cloud by day and of fire by night." Was it indeed some such spiritual guidance that was coming to me in my sleep? But the pillar was composed of both the day and the night-guiding, for the fire was in the red eye, which at the thought got a new fascination for me; till, as I looked, the fire divided, and seemed to shine on me through the fog like two red eyes, such as Lucy told me of in her momentary mental wandering when, on the cliff, the dying sunlight struck the windows of St. Mary's Church. Suddenly the horror burst upon me that it was thus that Jonathan had seen those awful women growing into reality through the whirling mist in the moonlight, and in my dream I must have fainted, for all became black darkness. The last conscious effort which imagination made was to show me a livid white face bending over me out of the mist. I must be careful of such dreams, for they would unseat one's reason if there were too much of them. I would get Dr. Van Helsing or Dr. Seward to prescribe something for me which would make me sleep, only that I fear to alarm them. Such a dream at the present time would become woven into their fears for me. To-night I shall strive hard to sleep naturally. If I do not, I shall to-morrow night get them to give me a dose of chloral; that cannot hurt me for once, and it will give me a good night's sleep. Last night tired me more than if I had not slept at all.

2 October 10 p. m.— Last night I slept, but did not dream. I must have slept soundly, for I was not waked by Jonathan coming to bed; but the sleep has not refreshed me, for to-day I feel terribly weak and spiritless. I spent all yesterday trying to read, or lying down dozing. In the afternoon Mr. Renfield asked if he might see me. Poor man, he was very gentle, and when I came away he kissed my hand and bade God bless me. Some way it affected me much; I am crying when I think of him. This is a new weakness, of which I must be careful. Jonathan would be miserable if he knew I had been crying. He and the others were out till dinner-time, and they all came in tired. I did what I could to brighten them up, and I suppose that the effort did me good, for I forgot how tired I was. After dinner they sent me to bed, and all went off to smoke together, as they said, but I knew that they wanted to tell each other of what had occurred to each during the day; I could see from Jonathan's manner that he had something important to communicate. I was not so sleepy as I should have been; so before they went I asked Dr. Seward to give me a little opiate of some kind, as I had not slept well the night before. He very kindly made me up a sleeping draught, which he gave to me, telling me that it would do me no harm, as it was very mild.... I have taken it, and am waiting for sleep, which still keeps aloof. I hope I have not done wrong, for as sleep begins to flirt with me, a new fear comes: that I may have been foolish in thus depriving myself of the power of waking. I might want it. Here comes sleep. Good-night.

## CHAPTER XX
## JONATHAN HARKER'S JOURNAL

1 October, evening.— I found Thomas Snelling in his house at Bethnal Green, but unhappily he was not in a condition to remember anything. The very prospect of beer which my expected coming had opened to him had proved too much, and he had begun too early on his expected debauch. I learned, however, from his wife, who seemed a decent, poor soul, that he was only the assistant to Smollet, who of the two mates was the responsible person. So off I drove to Walworth, and found Mr. Joseph Smollet at home and in his shirtsleeves, taking a late tea out of a saucer. He is a decent, intelligent fellow, distinctly a good, reliable type of workman, and with a headpiece of his own. He remembered all about the incident of the boxes, and from a wonderful dog's-eared notebook, which he produced from some mysterious receptacle about the seat of his trousers, and which had hieroglyphical entries in thick, half-obliterated pencil, he gave me the destinations of the boxes. There were, he said, six in the cartload which he took from Carfax and left at 197, Chicksand Street, Mile End New Town, and another six which he deposited at Jamaica Lane, Bermondsey. If then the Count meant to scatter these ghastly refuges of his over London, these places were chosen as the first of delivery, so that later he might distribute more fully. The systematic manner in which this was done made me think that he could not mean to confine himself to two sides of London. He was now fixed on the far east of the northern shore, on the east of the southern shore, and on the south. The north and west were surely never meant to be left out of his diabolical scheme— let alone the City itself and the very heart of fashionable London in the south-west and west. I went back to Smollet, and asked him if he could tell us if any other boxes had been taken from Carfax.

He replied:—

"Well, guv'nor, you've treated me wery 'an'some"— I had given him half a sovereign— "an' I'll tell yer all I know. I heard a man by the name of Bloxam say four nights ago in the 'Are an' 'Ounds, in Pincher's Alley, as 'ow he an' his mate 'ad 'ad a rare dusty job in a old 'ouse at Purfect. There ain't a-many such jobs as this 'ere, an' I'm thinkin' that maybe Sam Bloxam could tell ye summut." I asked if he could tell me where to find him. I told him that if he could get me the address it would be worth another half-sovereign to him. So he gulped down the rest of his tea and stood up, saying that he was going to begin the search then and there. At the door he stopped, and said:—

"Look 'ere, guv'nor, there ain't no sense in me a-keepin' you 'ere. I may find Sam soon, or I mayn't; but anyhow he ain't like to be in a way to tell ye much to-night. Sam is a rare one when he starts on the booze. If you can give me a envelope with a stamp on it, and put yer address on it, I'll find out where Sam is to be found and post it ye to-night. But ye'd better be up arter 'im soon in the mornin', or maybe ye won't ketch 'im; for Sam gets off main early, never mind the booze the night afore."

This was all practical, so one of the children went off with a penny to buy an envelope and a sheet of paper, and to keep the change. When she came back, I addressed the envelope and stamped it, and when Smollet had again faithfully promised to post the address when found, I took my way to home. We're on the track anyhow. I am tired to-night, and want sleep. Mina is fast asleep, and looks a little too pale; her eyes look as though she had been crying. Poor dear, I've no doubt it frets her to be kept in the dark, and it may make her doubly anxious about me and the others. But it is best as it is. It is better to be disappointed and worried in such a way now than to have her nerve broken. The doctors were quite right to insist on her being kept out of this dreadful business. I must be firm, for on me this particular burden of silence must rest. I shall not ever enter on the subject with her under any circumstances. Indeed, it may not be a hard task, after all, for she herself has become reticent on the subject, and has not spoken of the Count or his doings ever since we told her of our decision.

2 October, evening.— A long and trying and exciting day. By the first post I got my directed envelope with a dirty scrap of paper enclosed, on which was written with a carpenter's pencil in a sprawling hand:—
"Sam Bloxam, Korkrans, 4, Poters Cort, Bartel Street, Walworth. Arsk for the depite."

I got the letter in bed, and rose without waking Mina. She looked heavy and sleepy and pale, and far from well. I determined not to wake her, but that, when I should return from this new search, I would arrange for her going back to Exeter. I think she would be happier in our own home, with her daily tasks to interest her, than in being here amongst us and in ignorance. I only saw Dr. Seward for a moment, and told him where I was off to, promising to come back and tell the rest so soon as I should have found out anything. I drove to Walworth and found, with some difficulty, Potter's Court. Mr. Smollet's spelling misled me, as I asked for Poter's Court instead of Potter's Court. However, when I had found the court, I had no difficulty in discovering Corcoran's lodging-house. When I asked the man who came to the door for the "depite," he shook his head, and said: "I dunno 'im. There ain't no such a person 'ere; I never 'eard of 'im in all my bloomin' days. Don't believe there ain't nobody of that kind livin' ere or anywheres." I took out Smollet's letter, and as I read it it seemed to me that the lesson of the spelling of the name of the court might guide me. "What are you?" I asked.

"I'm the depity," he answered. I saw at once that I was on the right track; phonetic spelling had again misled me. A half-crown tip put the deputy's knowledge at my disposal, and I learned that Mr. Bloxam, who had slept off the remains of his beer on the previous night at Corcoran's, had left for his work at Poplar at five o'clock that morning. He could not tell me where the place of work was situated, but he had a vague idea that it was some kind of a "new-fangled ware'us"; and with this slender clue I had to start for Poplar. It was twelve o'clock before I got any satisfactory hint of such a building, and this I got at a coffee-shop, where some workmen were having their dinner. One of these suggested that there was being erected at Cross Angel Street a new "cold storage" building; and as this suited the condition of a "new-fangled ware'us," I at once drove to it. An interview with a surly gatekeeper and a surlier foreman, both of whom were appeased with the coin of the realm, put me on the track of Bloxam; he was sent for on my suggesting that I was willing to pay his day's wages to his foreman for the privilege of asking him a few questions on a private matter. He was a smart enough fellow, though rough of speech and bearing. When I had promised to pay for his information and given him an earnest, he told me that he had made two journeys between Carfax and a house in Piccadilly, and had taken from this house to the latter nine great boxes— "main heavy ones"— with a horse and cart hired by him for this purpose. I asked him if he could tell me the number of the house in Piccadilly, to which he replied:—

"Well, guv'nor, I forgits the number, but it was only a few doors from a big white church or somethink of the kind, not long built. It was a dusty old 'ouse, too, though nothin' to the dustiness of the 'ouse we tooked the bloomin' boxes from."

"How did you get into the houses if they were both empty?"

"There was the old party what engaged me a-waitin' in the 'ouse at Purfleet. He 'elped me to lift the boxes and put them in the dray. Curse me, but he was the strongest chap I ever struck, an' him a old feller, with a white moustache, one that thin you would think he couldn't throw a shadder."

How this phrase thrilled through me!

"Why, 'e took up 'is end o' the boxes like they was pounds of tea, and me a-puffin' an' a-blowin' afore I could up-end mine anyhow— an' I'm no chicken, neither."

"How did you get into the house in Piccadilly?" I asked.

"He was there too. He must 'a' started off and got there afore me, for when I rung of the bell he kem an' opened the door 'isself an' 'elped me to carry the boxes into the 'all."

"The whole nine?" I asked.

"Yus; there was five in the first load an' four in the second. It was main dry work, an' I don't so well remember 'ow I got 'ome." I interrupted him:—

"Were the boxes left in the hall?"

"Yus; it was a big 'all, an' there was nothin' else in it." I made one more attempt to further matters:—

"You didn't have any key?"

"Never used no key nor nothink. The old gent, he opened the door 'isself an' shut it again when I druv off. I don't remember the last time— but that was the beer."

"And you can't remember the number of the house?"

"No, sir. But ye needn't have no difficulty about that. It's a 'igh 'un with a stone front with a bow on it, an' 'igh steps up to the door. I know them steps, 'avin' 'ad to carry the boxes up with three loafers what come round to earn a copper. The old gent give them shillin's, an' they seein' they got so much, they wanted more; but 'e took one of them by the shoulder and was like to throw 'im down the steps, till the lot of them went away cussin'." I thought that with this description I could find the house, so, having paid my friend for his information, I started off for Piccadilly. I had gained a new painful experience; the Count could, it was evident, handle the earth-boxes himself. If so, time was precious; for, now that he had achieved a certain amount of distribution, he could, by choosing his own time, complete the task unobserved. At Piccadilly Circus I discharged my cab, and walked westward; beyond the Junior Constitutional I came across the house described, and was satisfied that this was the next of the lairs arranged by Dracula. The house looked as though it had been long untenanted. The windows were encrusted with dust, and the shutters were up. All the framework was black with time, and from the iron the paint had mostly scaled away. It was evident that up to lately there had been a large notice-board in front of the balcony; it had, however, been roughly torn away, the uprights which had supported it still remaining. Behind the rails of the balcony I saw there were some loose boards, whose raw edges looked white. I would have given a good deal to have been able to see the notice-board intact, as it would, perhaps, have given some clue to the ownership of the house. I remembered my experience of the investigation and purchase of Carfax, and I could not but feel that if I could find the former owner there might be some means discovered of gaining access to the house.

There was at present nothing to be learned from the Piccadilly side, and nothing could be done; so I went round to the back to see if anything could be gathered from this quarter. The mews were active, the Piccadilly houses being mostly in occupation. I asked one or two of the grooms and helpers whom I saw around if they could tell me anything about the empty house. One of them said that he heard it had lately been taken, but he couldn't say from whom. He told me, however, that up to very lately there had been a notice-board of "For Sale" up, and that perhaps Mitchell, Sons, & Candy, the house agents, could tell me something, as he thought he remembered seeing the name of that firm on the board. I did not wish to seem too eager, or to let my informant know or guess too much, so, thanking him in the usual manner, I strolled away. It was now growing dusk, and the autumn night was closing in, so I did not lose any time. Having learned the address of Mitchell, Sons, & Candy from a directory at the Berkeley, I was soon at their office in Sackville Street.

The gentleman who saw me was particularly suave in manner, but uncommunicative in equal proportion. Having once told me that the Piccadilly house— which throughout our interview he called a "mansion"— was sold, he considered my business as concluded. When I asked who had purchased it, he opened his eyes a thought wider, and paused a few seconds before replying:—

"It is sold, sir."

"Pardon me," I said, with equal politeness, "but I have a special reason for wishing to know who purchased it."

Again he paused longer, and raised his eyebrows still more. "It is sold, sir," was again his laconic reply.

"Surely," I said, "you do not mind letting me know so much."

"But I do mind," he answered. "The affairs of their clients are absolutely safe in the hands of Mitchell, Sons, & Candy." This was manifestly a prig of the first water, and there was no use arguing with him. I thought I had best meet him on his own ground, so I said:—

"Your clients, sir, are happy in having so resolute a guardian of their confidence. I am myself a professional man." Here I handed him my card. "In this instance I am not prompted by curiosity; I act on the part of Lord Godalming, who wishes to know something of the property which was, he understood, lately for sale." These words put a different complexion on affairs. He said:—

"I would like to oblige you if I could, Mr. Harker, and especially would I like to oblige his lordship. We once carried out a small matter of renting some chambers for him when he was the Honourable Arthur Holmwood. If you will let me have his lordship's address I will consult the House on the subject, and will, in any case, communicate with his lordship by to-night's post. It will be a pleasure if we can so far deviate from our rules as to give the required information to his lordship."

I wanted to secure a friend, and not to make an enemy, so I thanked him, gave the address at Dr. Seward's and came away. It was now dark, and I was tired and hungry. I got a cup of tea at the Aërated Bread Company and came down to Purfleet by the next train.

I found all the others at home. Mina was looking tired and pale, but she made a gallant effort to be bright and cheerful, it wrung my heart to think that I had had to keep anything from her and so caused her inquietude. Thank God, this will be the last night of her looking on at our conferences, and feeling the sting of our not showing our confidence. It took all my courage to hold to the wise resolution of keeping her out of our grim task. She seems somehow more reconciled; or else the very subject seems to have become repugnant to her, for when any accidental allusion is made she actually shudders. I am glad we made our resolution in time, as with such a feeling as this, our growing knowledge would be torture to her.

I could not tell the others of the day's discovery till we were alone; so after dinner— followed by a little music to save appearances even amongst ourselves— I took Mina to her room and left her to go to bed. The dear girl was more affectionate with me than ever, and clung to me as though she would detain me; but there was much to be talked of and I came away. Thank God, the ceasing of telling things has made no difference between us.

When I came down again I found the others all gathered round the fire in the study. In the train I had written my diary so far, and simply read it off to them as the best means of letting them get abreast of my own information; when I had finished Van Helsing said:—

"This has been a great day's work, friend Jonathan. Doubtless we are on the track of the missing boxes. If we find them all in that house, then our work is near the end. But if there be some missing, we must search until we find them. Then shall we make our final coup, and hunt the wretch to his real death." We all sat silent awhile and all at once Mr. Morris spoke:—

"Say! how are we going to get into that house?"

"We got into the other," answered Lord Godalming quickly.

"But, Art, this is different. We broke house at Carfax, but we had night and a walled park to protect us. It will be a mighty different thing to commit burglary in Piccadilly, either by day or night. I confess I don't see how we are going to get in unless that agency duck can find us a key of some sort; perhaps we shall know when you get his letter in the morning." Lord Godalming's brows contracted, and he stood up and walked about the room. By-and-by he stopped and said, turning from one to another of us:—

"Quincey's head is level. This burglary business is getting serious; we got off once all right; but we have now a rare job on hand— unless we can find the Count's key basket."

As nothing could well be done before morning, and as it would be at least advisable to wait till Lord Godalming should hear from Mitchell's, we decided not to take any active step before breakfast time. For a good while we sat and smoked, discussing the matter in its various lights and bearings; I took the opportunity of bringing this diary right up to the moment. I am very sleepy and shall go to bed....

Just a line. Mina sleeps soundly and her breathing is regular. Her forehead is puckered up into little wrinkles, as though she thinks even in her sleep. She is still too pale, but does not look so haggard as she did this morning. To-morrow will, I hope, mend all this; she will be herself at home in Exeter. Oh, but I am sleepy!

Dr. Seward's Diary.

1 October.— I am puzzled afresh about Renfield. His moods change so rapidly that I find it difficult to keep touch of them, and as they always mean something more than his own well-being, they form a more than interesting study. This morning, when I went to see him after his repulse of Van Helsing, his manner was that of a man commanding destiny. He was, in fact, commanding destiny— subjectively. He did not really care for any of the things of mere earth; he was in the clouds and looked down on all the weaknesses and wants of us poor mortals. I thought I would improve the occasion and learn something, so I asked him:—

"What about the flies these times?" He smiled on me in quite a superior sort of way— such a smile as would have become the face of Malvolio— as he answered me:—

"The fly, my dear sir, has one striking feature; its wings are typical of the aërial powers of the psychic faculties. The ancients did well when they typified the soul as a butterfly!"

I thought I would push his analogy to its utmost logically, so I said quickly:—

"Oh, it is a soul you are after now, is it?" His madness foiled his reason, and a puzzled look spread over his face as, shaking his head with a decision which I had but seldom seen in him, he said:—

"Oh, no, oh no! I want no souls. Life is all I want." Here he brightened up; "I am pretty indifferent about it at present. Life is all right; I have all I want. You must get a new patient, doctor, if you wish to study zoöphagy!"

This puzzled me a little, so I drew him on:—

"Then you command life; you are a god, I suppose?" He smiled with an ineffably benign superiority.

"Oh no! Far be it from me to arrogate to myself the attributes of the Deity. I am not even concerned in His especially spiritual doings. If I may state my intellectual position I am, so far as concerns things purely terrestrial, somewhat in the position which Enoch occupied spiritually!" This was a poser to me. I could not at the moment recall Enoch's appositeness; so I had to ask a simple question, though I felt that by so doing I was lowering myself in the eyes of the lunatic:—

"And why with Enoch?"

"Because he walked with God." I could not see the analogy, but did not like to admit it; so I harked back to what he had denied:—

"So you don't care about life and you don't want souls. Why not?" I put my question quickly and somewhat sternly, on purpose to disconcert him. The effort succeeded; for an instant he unconsciously relapsed into his old servile manner, bent low before me, and actually fawned upon me as he replied:—

"I don't want any souls, indeed, indeed! I don't. I couldn't use them if I had them; they would be no manner of use to me. I couldn't eat them or— — " He suddenly stopped and the old cunning look spread over his face, like a wind-sweep on the surface of the water. "And doctor, as to life, what is it after all? When you've got all you require, and you know that you will never want, that is all. I have friends— good friends— like you, Dr. Seward"; this was said with a leer of inexpressible cunning. "I know that I shall never lack the means of life!"

I think that through the cloudiness of his insanity he saw some antagonism in me, for he at once fell back on the last refuge of such as he— a dogged silence. After a short time I saw that for the present it was useless to speak to him. He was sulky, and so I came away.

Later in the day he sent for me. Ordinarily I would not have come without special reason, but just at present I am so interested in him that I would gladly make an effort. Besides, I am glad to have anything to help to pass the time. Harker is out, following up clues; and so are Lord Godalming and Quincey. Van Helsing sits in my study poring over the record prepared by the Harkers; he seems to think that by accurate knowledge of all details he will light upon some clue. He does not wish to be disturbed in the work, without cause. I would have taken him with me to see the patient, only I thought that after his last repulse he might not care to go again. There was also another reason: Renfield might not speak so freely before a third person as when he and I were alone.

I found him sitting out in the middle of the floor on his stool, a pose which is generally indicative of some mental energy on his part. When I came in, he said at once, as though the question had been waiting on his lips:—

"What about souls?" It was evident then that my surmise had been correct. Unconscious cerebration was doing its work, even with the lunatic. I determined to have the matter out. "What about them yourself?" I asked. He did not reply for a moment but looked all round him, and up and down, as though he expected to find some inspiration for an answer.

"I don't want any souls!" he said in a feeble, apologetic way. The matter seemed preying on his mind, and so I determined to use it— to "be cruel only to be kind." So I said:—

"You like life, and you want life?"

"Oh yes! but that is all right; you needn't worry about that!"

"But," I asked, "how are we to get the life without getting the soul also?" This seemed to puzzle him, so I followed it up:—

"A nice time you'll have some time when you're flying out there, with the souls of thousands of flies and spiders and birds and cats buzzing and twittering and miauing all round you. You've got their lives, you know, and you must put up with their souls!" Something seemed to affect his imagination, for he put his fingers to his ears and shut his eyes, screwing them up tightly just as a small boy does when his face is being soaped. There was something pathetic in it that touched me; it also gave me a lesson, for it seemed that before me was a child— only a child, though the features were worn, and the stubble on the jaws was white. It was evident that he was undergoing some process of mental disturbance, and, knowing how his past moods had interpreted things seemingly foreign to himself, I thought I would enter into his mind as well as I could and go with him. The first step was to restore confidence, so I asked him, speaking pretty loud so that he would hear me through his closed ears:—

"Would you like some sugar to get your flies round again?" He seemed to wake up all at once, and shook his head. With a laugh he replied:—

"Not much! flies are poor things, after all!" After a pause he added, "But I don't want their souls buzzing round me, all the same."

"Or spiders?" I went on.

"Blow spiders! What's the use of spiders? There isn't anything in them to eat or"— he stopped suddenly, as though reminded of a forbidden topic.

"So, so!" I thought to myself, "this is the second time he has suddenly stopped at the word 'drink'; what does it mean?" Renfield seemed himself aware of having made a lapse, for he hurried on, as though to distract my attention from it:—

"I don't take any stock at all in such matters. 'Rats and mice and such small deer,' as Shakespeare has it, 'chicken-feed of the larder' they might be called. I'm past all that sort of nonsense. You might as well ask a man to eat molecules with a pair of chop-sticks, as to try to interest me about the lesser carnivora, when I know of what is before me."

"I see," I said. "You want big things that you can make your teeth meet in? How would you like to breakfast on elephant?"

"What ridiculous nonsense you are talking!" He was getting too wide awake, so I thought I would press him hard. "I wonder," I said reflectively, "what an elephant's soul is like!"

The effect I desired was obtained, for he at once fell from his high-horse and became a child again.

"I don't want an elephant's soul, or any soul at all!" he said. For a few moments he sat despondently. Suddenly he jumped to his feet, with his eyes blazing and all the signs of intense cerebral excitement. "To hell with you and your souls!" he shouted. "Why do you plague me about souls? Haven't I got enough to worry, and pain, and distract me already, without thinking of souls!" He looked so hostile that I thought he was in for another homicidal fit, so I blew my whistle. The instant, however, that I did so he became calm, and said apologetically:—

"Forgive me, Doctor; I forgot myself. You do not need any help. I am so worried in my mind that I am apt to be irritable. If you only knew the problem I have to face, and that I am working out, you would pity, and tolerate, and pardon me. Pray do not put me in a strait-waistcoat. I want to think and I cannot think freely when my body is confined. I am sure you will understand!" He had evidently self-control; so when the attendants came I told them not to mind, and they withdrew. Renfield watched them go; when the door was closed he said, with considerable dignity and sweetness:—

"Dr. Seward, you have been very considerate towards me. Believe me that I am very, very grateful to you!" I thought it well to leave him in this mood, and so I came away. There is certainly something to ponder over in this man's state. Several points seem to make what the American interviewer calls "a story," if one could only get them in proper order. Here they are:—

Will not mention "drinking."

Fears the thought of being burdened with the "soul" of anything.

Has no dread of wanting "life" in the future.

Despises the meaner forms of life altogether, though he dreads being haunted by their souls.

Logically all these things point one way! he has assurance of some kind that he will acquire some higher life. He dreads the consequence— the burden of a soul. Then it is a human life he looks to!

And the assurance— ?

Merciful God! the Count has been to him, and there is some new scheme of terror afoot!

Later.— I went after my round to Van Helsing and told him my suspicion. He grew very grave; and, after thinking the matter over for a while asked me to take him to Renfield. I did so. As we came to the door we heard the lunatic within singing gaily, as he used to do in the time which now seems so long ago. When we entered we saw with amazement that he had spread out his sugar as of old; the flies, lethargic with the autumn, were beginning to buzz into the room. We tried to make him talk of the subject of our previous conversation, but he would not attend. He went on with his singing, just as though we had not been present. He had got a scrap of paper and was folding it into a note-book. We had to come away as ignorant as we went in.

His is a curious case indeed; we must watch him to-night.

Letter, Mitchell, Sons and Candy to Lord Godalming.

"1 October.

"My Lord,

"We are at all times only too happy to meet your wishes. We beg, with regard to the desire of your Lordship, expressed by Mr. Harker on your behalf, to supply the following information concerning the sale and purchase of No. 347, Piccadilly. The original vendors are the executors of the late Mr. Archibald Winter-Suffield. The purchaser is a foreign nobleman, Count de Ville, who effected the purchase himself paying the purchase money in notes 'over the counter,' if your Lordship will pardon us using so vulgar an expression. Beyond this we know nothing whatever of him.

"We are, my Lord,

"Your Lordship's humble servants,

"Mitchell, Sons & Candy."

Dr. Seward's Diary.

2 October.— I placed a man in the corridor last night, and told him to make an accurate note of any sound he might hear from Renfield's room, and gave him instructions that if there should be anything strange he was to call me. After dinner, when we had all gathered round the fire in the study— Mrs. Harker having gone to bed— we discussed the attempts and discoveries of the day. Harker was the only one who had any result, and we are in great hopes that his clue may be an important one.

Before going to bed I went round to the patient's room and looked in through the observation trap. He was sleeping soundly, and his heart rose and fell with regular respiration.

This morning the man on duty reported to me that a little after midnight he was restless and kept saying his prayers somewhat loudly. I asked him if that was all; he replied that it was all he heard. There was something about his manner so suspicious that I asked him point blank if he had been asleep. He denied sleep, but admitted to having "dozed" for a while. It is too bad that men cannot be trusted unless they are watched.

To-day Harker is out following up his clue, and Art and Quincey are looking after horses. Godalming thinks that it will be well to have horses always in readiness, for when we get the information which we seek there will be no time to lose. We must sterilise all the imported earth between sunrise and sunset; we shall thus catch the Count at his weakest, and without a refuge to fly to. Van Helsing is off to the British Museum looking up some authorities on ancient medicine. The old physicians took account of things which their followers do not accept, and the Professor is searching for witch and demon cures which may be useful to us later.

I sometimes think we must be all mad and that we shall wake to sanity in strait-waistcoats.

Later.— We have met again. We seem at last to be on the track, and our work of to-morrow may be the beginning of the end. I wonder if Renfield's quiet has anything to do with this. His moods have so followed the doings of the Count, that the coming destruction of the monster may be carried to him in some subtle way. If we could only get some hint as to what passed in his mind, between the time of my argument with him to-day and his resumption of fly-catching, it might afford us a valuable clue. He is now seemingly quiet for a spell.... Is he?— — That wild yell seemed to come from his room....

The attendant came bursting into my room and told me that Renfield had somehow met with some accident. He had heard him yell; and when he went to him found him lying on his face on the floor, all covered with blood. I must go at once....

## CHAPTER XXI
# DR. SEWARD'S DIARY

3 October.— Let me put down with exactness all that happened, as well as I can remember it, since last I made an entry. Not a detail that I can recall must be forgotten; in all calmness I must proceed.

When I came to Renfield's room I found him lying on the floor on his left side in a glittering pool of blood. When I went to move him, it became at once apparent that he had received some terrible injuries; there seemed none of that unity of purpose between the parts of the body which marks even lethargic sanity. As the face was exposed I could see that it was horribly bruised, as though it had been beaten against the floor— indeed it was from the face wounds that the pool of blood originated. The attendant who was kneeling beside the body said to me as we turned him over:—

"I think, sir, his back is broken. See, both his right arm and leg and the whole side of his face are paralysed." How such a thing could have happened puzzled the attendant beyond measure. He seemed quite bewildered, and his brows were gathered in as he said:—

"I can't understand the two things. He could mark his face like that by beating his own head on the floor. I saw a young woman do it once at the Eversfield Asylum before anyone could lay hands on her. And I suppose he might have broke his neck by falling out of bed, if he got in an awkward kink. But for the life of me I can't imagine how the two things occurred. If his back was broke, he couldn't beat his head; and if his face was like that before the fall out of bed, there would be marks of it." I said to him:—

"Go to Dr. Van Helsing, and ask him to kindly come here at once. I want him without an instant's delay." The man ran off, and within a few minutes the Professor, in his dressing gown and slippers, appeared. When he saw Renfield on the ground, he looked keenly at him a moment, and then turned to me. I think he recognised my thought in my eyes, for he said very quietly, manifestly for the ears of the attendant:—

"Ah, a sad accident! He will need very careful watching, and much attention. I shall stay with you myself; but I shall first dress myself. If you will remain I shall in a few minutes join you."

The patient was now breathing stertorously and it was easy to see that he had suffered some terrible injury. Van Helsing returned with extraordinary celerity, bearing with him a surgical case. He had evidently been thinking and had his mind made up; for, almost before he looked at the patient, he whispered to me:—

"Send the attendant away. We must be alone with him when he becomes conscious, after the operation." So I said:—

"I think that will do now, Simmons. We have done all that we can at present. You had better go your round, and Dr. Van Helsing will operate. Let me know instantly if there be anything unusual anywhere."

The man withdrew, and we went into a strict examination of the patient. The wounds of the face was superficial; the real injury was a depressed fracture of the skull, extending right up through the motor area. The Professor thought a moment and said:—

"We must reduce the pressure and get back to normal conditions, as far as can be; the rapidity of the suffusion shows the terrible nature of his injury. The whole motor area seems affected. The suffusion of the brain will increase quickly, so we must trephine at once or it may be too late." As he was speaking there was a soft tapping at the door. I went over and opened it and found in the corridor without, Arthur and Quincey in pajamas and slippers: the former spoke:—

"I heard your man call up Dr. Van Helsing and tell him of an accident. So I woke Quincey or rather called for him as he was not asleep. Things are moving too quickly and too strangely for sound sleep for any of us these times. I've been thinking that to-morrow night will not see things as they have been. We'll have to look back— and forward a little more than we have done. May we come in?" I nodded, and held the door open till they had entered; then I closed it again. When Quincey saw the attitude and state of the patient, and noted the horrible pool on the floor, he said softly:—

"My God! what has happened to him? Poor, poor devil!" I told him briefly, and added that we expected he would recover consciousness after the operation— for a short time, at all events. He went at once and sat down on the edge of the bed, with Godalming beside him; we all watched in patience.

"We shall wait," said Van Helsing, "just long enough to fix the best spot for trephining, so that we may most quickly and perfectly remove the blood clot; for it is evident that the hæmorrhage is increasing."

The minutes during which we waited passed with fearful slowness. I had a horrible sinking in my heart, and from Van Helsing's face I gathered that he felt some fear or apprehension as to what was to come. I dreaded the words that Renfield might speak. I was positively afraid to think; but the conviction of what was coming was on me, as I have read of men who have heard the death-watch. The poor man's breathing came in uncertain gasps. Each instant he seemed as though he would open his eyes and speak; but then would follow a prolonged stertorous breath, and he would relapse into a more fixed insensibility. Inured as I was to sick beds and death, this suspense grew, and grew upon me. I could almost hear the beating of my own heart; and the blood surging through my temples sounded like blows from a hammer. The silence finally became agonising. I looked at my companions, one after another, and saw from their flushed faces and damp brows that they were enduring equal torture. There was a nervous suspense over us all, as though overhead some dread bell would peal out powerfully when we should least expect it.

At last there came a time when it was evident that the patient was sinking fast; he might die at any moment. I looked up at the Professor and caught his eyes fixed on mine. His face was sternly set as he spoke:—

"There is no time to lose. His words may be worth many lives; I have been thinking so, as I stood here. It may be there is a soul at stake! We shall operate just above the ear."

Without another word he made the operation. For a few moments the breathing continued to be stertorous. Then there came a breath so prolonged that it seemed as though it would tear open his chest. Suddenly his eyes opened, and became fixed in a wild, helpless stare. This was continued for a few moments; then it softened into a glad surprise, and from the lips came a sigh of relief. He moved convulsively, and as he did so, said:—

"I'll be quiet, Doctor. Tell them to take off the strait-waistcoat. I have had a terrible dream, and it has left me so weak that I cannot move. What's wrong with my face? it feels all swollen, and it smarts dreadfully." He tried to turn his head; but even with the effort his eyes seemed to grow glassy again so I gently put it back. Then Van Helsing said in a quiet grave tone:—

"Tell us your dream, Mr. Renfield." As he heard the voice his face brightened, through its mutilation, and he said:—

"That is Dr. Van Helsing. How good it is of you to be here. Give me some water, my lips are dry; and I shall try to tell you. I dreamed"— he stopped and seemed fainting, I called quietly to Quincey— "The brandy— it is in my study— quick!" He flew and returned with a glass, the decanter of brandy and a carafe of water. We moistened the parched lips, and the patient quickly revived. It seemed, however, that his poor injured brain had been working in the interval, for, when he was quite conscious, he looked at me piercingly with an agonised confusion which I shall never forget, and said:—

"I must not deceive myself; it was no dream, but all a grim reality." Then his eyes roved round the room; as they caught sight of the two figures sitting patiently on the edge of the bed he went on:—

"If I were not sure already, I would know from them." For an instant his eyes closed— not with pain or sleep but voluntarily, as though he were bringing all his faculties to bear; when he opened them he said, hurriedly, and with more energy than he had yet displayed:—

"Quick, Doctor, quick. I am dying! I feel that I have but a few minutes; and then I must go back to death— or worse! Wet my lips with brandy again. I have something that I must say before I die; or before my poor crushed brain dies anyhow. Thank you! It was that night after you left me, when I implored you to let me go away. I couldn't speak then, for I felt my tongue was tied; but I was as sane then, except in that way, as I am now. I was in an agony of despair for a long time after you left me; it seemed hours. Then there came a sudden peace to me. My brain seemed to become cool again, and I realised where I was. I heard the dogs bark behind our house, but not where He was!" As he spoke, Van Helsing's eyes never blinked, but his hand came out and met mine and gripped it hard. He did not, however, betray himself; he nodded slightly and said: "Go on," in a low voice. Renfield proceeded:—

"He came up to the window in the mist, as I had seen him often before; but he was solid then— not a ghost, and his eyes were fierce like a man's when angry. He was laughing with his red mouth; the sharp white teeth glinted in the moonlight when he turned to look back over the belt of trees, to where the dogs were barking. I wouldn't ask him to come in at first, though I knew he wanted to— just as he had wanted all along. Then he began promising me things— not in words but by doing them." He was interrupted by a word from the Professor:—

"How?"

"By making them happen; just as he used to send in the flies when the sun was shining. Great big fat ones with steel and sapphire on their wings; and big moths, in the night, with skull and cross-bones on their backs." Van Helsing nodded to him as he whispered to me unconsciously:—

"The Acherontia Aitetropos of the Sphinges— what you call the 'Death's-head Moth'?" The patient went on without stopping.

"Then he began to whisper: 'Rats, rats, rats! Hundreds, thousands, millions of them, and every one a life; and dogs to eat them, and cats too. All lives! all red blood, with years of life in it; and not merely buzzing flies!' I laughed at him, for I wanted to see what he could do. Then the dogs howled, away beyond the dark trees in His house. He beckoned me to the window. I got up and looked out, and He raised his hands, and seemed to call out without using any words. A dark mass spread over the grass, coming on like the shape of a flame of fire; and then He moved the mist to the right and left, and I could see that there were thousands of rats with their eyes blazing red— like His, only smaller. He held up his hand, and they all stopped; and I thought he seemed to be saying: 'All these lives will I give you, ay, and many more and greater, through countless ages, if you will fall down and worship me!' And then a red cloud, like the colour of blood, seemed to close over my eyes; and before I knew what I was doing, I found myself opening the sash and saying to Him: 'Come in, Lord and Master!' The rats were all gone, but He slid into the room through the sash, though it was only open an inch wide— just as the Moon herself has often come in through the tiniest crack and has stood before me in all her size and splendour."

His voice was weaker, so I moistened his lips with the brandy again, and he continued; but it seemed as though his memory had gone on working in the interval for his story was further advanced. I was about to call him back to the point, but Van Helsing whispered to me: "Let him go on. Do not interrupt him; he cannot go back, and maybe could not proceed at all if once he lost the thread of his thought." He proceeded:—

"All day I waited to hear from him, but he did not send me anything, not even a blow-fly, and when the moon got up I was pretty angry with him. When he slid in through the window, though it was shut, and did not even knock, I got mad with him. He sneered at me, and his white face looked out of the mist with his red eyes gleaming, and he went on as though he owned the whole place, and I was no one. He didn't even smell the same as he went by me. I couldn't hold him. I thought that, somehow, Mrs. Harker had come into the room."

The two men sitting on the bed stood up and came over, standing behind him so that he could not see them, but where they could hear better. They were both silent, but the Professor started and quivered; his face, however, grew grimmer and sterner still. Renfield went on without noticing:—

"When Mrs. Harker came in to see me this afternoon she wasn't the same; it was like tea after the teapot had been watered." Here we all moved, but no one said a word; he went on:—

"I didn't know that she was here till she spoke; and she didn't look the same. I don't care for the pale people; I like them with lots of blood in them, and hers had all seemed to have run out. I didn't think of it at the time; but when she went away I began to think, and it made me mad to know that He had been taking the life out of her." I could feel that the rest quivered, as I did, but we remained otherwise still. "So when He came to-night I was ready for Him. I saw the mist stealing in, and I grabbed it tight. I had heard that madmen have unnatural strength; and as I knew I was a madman— at times anyhow— I resolved to use my power. Ay, and He felt it too, for He had to come out of the mist to struggle with me. I held tight; and I thought I was going to win, for I didn't mean Him to take any more of her life, till I saw His eyes. They burned into me, and my strength became like water. He slipped through it, and when I tried to cling to Him, He raised me up and flung me down. There was a red cloud before me, and a noise like thunder, and the mist seemed to steal away under the door." His voice was becoming fainter and his breath more stertorous. Van Helsing stood up instinctively.

"We know the worst now," he said. "He is here, and we know his purpose. It may not be too late. Let us be armed— the same as we were the other night, but lose no time; there is not an instant to spare." There was no need to put our fear, nay our conviction, into words— we shared them in common. We all hurried and took from our rooms the same things that we had when we entered the Count's house. The Professor had his ready, and as we met in the corridor he pointed to them significantly as he said:—

"They never leave me; and they shall not till this unhappy business is over. Be wise also, my friends. It is no common enemy that we deal with. Alas! alas! that that dear Madam Mina should suffer!" He stopped; his voice was breaking, and I do not know if rage or terror predominated in my own heart.

Outside the Harkers' door we paused. Art and Quincey held back, and the latter said:—

"Should we disturb her?"

"We must," said Van Helsing grimly. "If the door be locked, I shall break it in."

"May it not frighten her terribly? It is unusual to break into a lady's room!"

Van Helsing said solemnly, "You are always right; but this is life and death. All chambers are alike to the doctor; and even were they not they are all as one to me to-night. Friend John, when I turn the handle, if the door does not open, do you put your shoulder down and shove; and you too, my friends. Now!"

He turned the handle as he spoke, but the door did not yield. We threw ourselves against it; with a crash it burst open, and we almost fell headlong into the room. The Professor did actually fall, and I saw across him as he gathered himself up from hands and knees. What I saw appalled me. I felt my hair rise like bristles on the back of my neck, and my heart seemed to stand still.

The moonlight was so bright that through the thick yellow blind the room was light enough to see. On the bed beside the window lay Jonathan Harker, his face flushed and breathing heavily as though in a stupor. Kneeling on the near edge of the bed facing outwards was the white-clad figure of his wife. By her side stood a tall, thin man, clad in black. His face was turned from us, but the instant we saw we all recognised the Count— in every way, even to the scar on his forehead. With his left hand he held both Mrs. Harker's hands, keeping them away with her arms at full tension; his right hand gripped her by the back of the neck, forcing her face down on his bosom. Her white nightdress was smeared with blood, and a thin stream trickled down the man's bare breast which was shown by his torn-open dress. The attitude of the two had a terrible resemblance to a child forcing a kitten's nose into a saucer of milk to compel it to drink. As we burst into the room, the Count turned his face, and the hellish look that I had heard described seemed to leap into it. His eyes flamed red with devilish passion; the great nostrils of the white aquiline nose opened wide and quivered at the edge; and the white sharp teeth, behind the full lips of the blood-dripping mouth, champed together like those of a wild beast. With a wrench, which threw his victim back upon the bed as though hurled from a height, he turned and sprang at us. But by this time the Professor had gained his feet, and was holding towards him the envelope which contained the Sacred Wafer. The Count suddenly stopped, just as poor Lucy had done outside the tomb, and cowered back. Further and further back he cowered, as we, lifting our crucifixes, advanced. The moonlight suddenly failed, as a great black cloud sailed across the sky; and when the gaslight sprang up under Quincey's match, we saw nothing but a faint vapour. This, as we looked, trailed under the door, which with the recoil from its bursting open, had swung back to its old position. Van Helsing, Art, and I moved forward to Mrs. Harker, who by this time had drawn her breath and with it had given a scream so wild, so ear-piercing, so despairing that it seems to me now that it will ring in my ears till my dying day. For a few seconds she lay in her helpless attitude and disarray. Her face was ghastly, with a pallor which was accentuated by the blood which smeared her lips and cheeks and chin; from her throat trickled a thin stream of blood; her eyes were mad with terror. Then she put before her face her poor crushed hands, which bore on their whiteness the red mark of the Count's terrible grip, and from behind them came a low desolate wail which made the terrible scream seem only the quick expression of an endless grief. Van Helsing stepped forward and drew the coverlet gently over her body, whilst Art, after looking at her face for an instant despairingly, ran out of the room. Van Helsing whispered to me:—

"Jonathan is in a stupor such as we know the Vampire can produce. We can do nothing with poor Madam Mina for a few moments till she recovers herself; I must wake him!" He dipped the end of a towel in cold water and with it began to flick him on the face, his wife all the while holding her face between her hands and sobbing in a way that was heart-breaking to hear. I raised the blind, and looked out of the window. There was much moonshine; and as I looked I could see Quincey Morris run across the lawn and hide himself in the shadow of a great yew-tree. It puzzled me to think why he was doing this; but at the instant I heard Harker's quick exclamation as he woke to partial consciousness, and turned to the bed. On his face, as there might well be, was a look of wild amazement. He seemed dazed for a few seconds, and then full consciousness seemed to burst upon him all at once, and he started up. His wife was aroused by the quick movement, and turned to him with her arms stretched out, as though to embrace him; instantly, however, she drew them in again, and putting her elbows together, held her hands before her face, and shuddered till the bed beneath her shook.

"In God's name what does this mean?" Harker cried out. "Dr. Seward, Dr. Van Helsing, what is it? What has happened? What is wrong? Mina, dear, what is it? What does that blood mean? My God, my God! has it come to this!" and, raising himself to his knees, he beat his hands wildly together. "Good God help us! help her! oh, help her!" With a quick movement he jumped from bed, and began to pull on his clothes,— all the man in him awake at the need for instant exertion. "What has happened? Tell me all about it!" he cried without pausing. "Dr. Van Helsing, you love Mina, I know. Oh, do something to save her. It cannot have gone too far yet. Guard her while I look for him!" His wife, through her terror and horror and distress, saw some sure danger to him: instantly forgetting her own grief, she seized hold of him and cried out:—

"No! no! Jonathan, you must not leave me. I have suffered enough to-night, God knows, without the dread of his harming you. You must stay with me. Stay with these friends who will watch over you!" Her expression became frantic as she spoke; and, he yielding to her, she pulled him down sitting on the bed side, and clung to him fiercely.

Van Helsing and I tried to calm them both. The Professor held up his little golden crucifix, and said with wonderful calmness:—

"Do not fear, my dear. We are here; and whilst this is close to you no foul thing can approach. You are safe for to-night; and we must be calm and take counsel together." She shuddered and was silent, holding down her head on her husband's breast. When she raised it, his white night-robe was stained with blood where her lips had touched, and where the thin open wound in her neck had sent forth drops. The instant she saw it she drew back, with a low wail, and whispered, amidst choking sobs:—

"Unclean, unclean! I must touch him or kiss him no more. Oh, that it should be that it is I who am now his worst enemy, and whom he may have most cause to fear." To this he spoke out resolutely:—

"Nonsense, Mina. It is a shame to me to hear such a word. I would not hear it of you; and I shall not hear it from you. May God judge me by my deserts, and punish me with more bitter suffering than even this hour, if by any act or will of mine anything ever come between us!" He put out his arms and folded her to his breast; and for a while she lay there sobbing. He looked at us over her bowed head, with eyes that blinked damply above his quivering nostrils; his mouth was set as steel. After a while her sobs became less frequent and more faint, and then he said to me, speaking with a studied calmness which I felt tried his nervous power to the utmost:—

"And now, Dr. Seward, tell me all about it. Too well I know the broad fact; tell me all that has been." I told him exactly what had happened, and he listened with seeming impassiveness; but his nostrils twitched and his eyes blazed as I told how the ruthless hands of the Count had held his wife in that terrible and horrid position, with her mouth to the open wound in his breast. It interested me, even at that moment, to see, that, whilst the face of white set passion worked convulsively over the bowed head, the hands tenderly and lovingly stroked the ruffled hair. Just as I had finished, Quincey and Godalming knocked at the door. They entered in obedience to our summons. Van Helsing looked at me questioningly. I understood him to mean if we were to take advantage of their coming to divert if possible the thoughts of the unhappy husband and wife from each other and from themselves; so on nodding acquiescence to him he asked them what they had seen or done. To which Lord Godalming answered:—

"I could not see him anywhere in the passage, or in any of our rooms. I looked in the study but, though he had been there, he had gone. He had, however— — " He stopped suddenly, looking at the poor drooping figure on the bed. Van Helsing said gravely:—

"Go on, friend Arthur. We want here no more concealments. Our hope now is in knowing all. Tell freely!" So Art went on:—

"He had been there, and though it could only have been for a few seconds, he made rare hay of the place. All the manuscript had been burned, and the blue flames were flickering amongst the white ashes; the cylinders of your phonograph too were thrown on the fire, and the wax had helped the flames." Here I interrupted. "Thank God there is the other copy in the safe!" His face lit for a moment, but fell again as he went on: "I ran downstairs then, but could see no sign of him. I looked into Renfield's room; but there was no trace there except— — !" Again he paused. "Go on," said Harker hoarsely; so he bowed his head and moistening his lips with his tongue, added: "except that the poor fellow is dead." Mrs. Harker raised her head, looking from one to the other of us she said solemnly:—

"God's will be done!" I could not but feel that Art was keeping back something; but, as I took it that it was with a purpose, I said nothing. Van Helsing turned to Morris and asked:—

"And you, friend Quincey, have you any to tell?"

"A little," he answered. "It may be much eventually, but at present I can't say. I thought it well to know if possible where the Count would go when he left the house. I did not see him; but I saw a bat rise from Renfield's window, and flap westward. I expected to see him in some shape go back to Carfax; but he evidently sought some other lair. He will not be back to-night; for the sky is reddening in the east, and the dawn is close. We must work to-morrow!"

He said the latter words through his shut teeth. For a space of perhaps a couple of minutes there was silence, and I could fancy that I could hear the sound of our hearts beating; then Van Helsing said, placing his hand very tenderly on Mrs. Harker's head:—

"And now, Madam Mina— poor, dear, dear Madam Mina— tell us exactly what happened. God knows that I do not want that you be pained; but it is need that we know all. For now more than ever has all work to be done quick and sharp, and in deadly earnest. The day is close to us that must end all, if it may be so; and now is the chance that we may live and learn."

The poor, dear lady shivered, and I could see the tension of her nerves as she clasped her husband closer to her and bent her head lower and lower still on his breast. Then she raised her head proudly, and held out one hand to Van Helsing who took it in his, and, after stooping and kissing it reverently, held it fast. The other hand was locked in that of her husband, who held his other arm thrown round her protectingly. After a pause in which she was evidently ordering her thoughts, she began:—

"I took the sleeping draught which you had so kindly given me, but for a long time it did not act. I seemed to become more wakeful, and myriads of horrible fancies began to crowd in upon my mind— all of them connected with death, and vampires; with blood, and pain, and trouble." Her husband involuntarily groaned as she turned to him and said lovingly: "Do not fret, dear. You must be brave and strong, and help me through the horrible task. If you only knew what an effort it is to me to tell of this fearful thing at all, you would understand how much I need your help. Well, I saw I must try to help the medicine to its work with my will, if it was to do me any good, so I resolutely set myself to sleep. Sure enough sleep must soon have come to me, for I remember no more. Jonathan coming in had not waked me, for he lay by my side when next I remember. There was in the room the same thin white mist that I had before noticed. But I forget now if you know of this; you will find it in my diary which I shall show you later. I felt the same vague terror which had come to me before and the same sense of some presence. I turned to wake Jonathan, but found that he slept so soundly that it seemed as if it was he who had taken the sleeping draught, and not I. I tried, but I could not wake him. This caused me a great fear, and I looked around terrified. Then indeed, my heart sank within me: beside the bed, as if he had stepped out of the mist— or rather as if the mist had turned into his figure, for it had entirely disappeared— stood a tall, thin man, all in black. I knew him at once from the description of the others. The waxen face; the high aquiline nose, on which the light fell in a thin white line; the parted red lips, with the sharp white teeth showing between; and the red eyes that I had seemed to see in the sunset on the windows of St. Mary's Church at Whitby. I knew, too, the red scar on his forehead where Jonathan had struck him. For an instant my heart stood still, and I would have screamed out, only that I was paralysed. In the pause he spoke in a sort of keen, cutting whisper, pointing as he spoke to Jonathan:—

" 'Silence! If you make a sound I shall take him and dash his brains out before your very eyes.' I was appalled and was too bewildered to do or say anything. With a mocking smile, he placed one hand upon my shoulder and, holding me tight, bared my throat with the other, saying as he did so, 'First, a little refreshment to reward my exertions. You may as well be quiet; it is not the first time, or the second, that your veins have appeased my thirst!' I was bewildered, and, strangely enough, I did not want to hinder him. I suppose it is a part of the horrible curse that such is, when his touch is on his victim. And oh, my God, my God, pity me! He placed his reeking lips upon my throat!" Her husband groaned again. She clasped his hand harder, and looked at him pityingly, as if he were the injured one, and went on:—
"I felt my strength fading away, and I was in a half swoon. How long this horrible thing lasted I know not; but it seemed that a long time must have passed before he took his foul, awful, sneering mouth away. I saw it drip with the fresh blood!" The remembrance seemed for a while to overpower her, and she drooped and would have sunk down but for her husband's sustaining arm. With a great effort she recovered herself and went on:—

"Then he spoke to me mockingly, 'And so you, like the others, would play your brains against mine. You would help these men to hunt me and frustrate me in my designs! You know now, and they know in part already, and will know in full before long, what it is to cross my path. They should have kept their energies for use closer to home. Whilst they played wits against me— against me who commanded nations, and intrigued for them, and fought for them, hundreds of years before they were born— I was countermining them. And you, their best beloved one, are now to me, flesh of my flesh; blood of my blood; kin of my kin; my bountiful wine-press for a while; and shall be later on my companion and my helper. You shall be avenged in turn; for not one of them but shall minister to your needs. But as yet you are to be punished for what you have done. You have aided in thwarting me; now you shall come to my call. When my brain says "Come!" to you, you shall cross land or sea to do my bidding; and to that end this!' With that he pulled open his shirt, and with his long sharp nails opened a vein in his breast. When the blood began to spurt out, he took my hands in one of his, holding them tight, and with the other seized my neck and pressed my mouth to the wound, so that I must either suffocate or swallow some of the— — Oh my God! my God! what have I done? What have I done to deserve such a fate, I who have tried to walk in meekness and righteousness all my days. God pity me! Look down on a poor soul in worse than mortal peril; and in mercy pity those to whom she is dear!" Then she began to rub her lips as though to cleanse them from pollution.

As she was telling her terrible story, the eastern sky began to quicken, and everything became more and more clear. Harker was still and quiet; but over his face, as the awful narrative went on, came a grey look which deepened and deepened in the morning light, till when the first red streak of the coming dawn shot up, the flesh stood darkly out against the whitening hair.

We have arranged that one of us is to stay within call of the unhappy pair till we can meet together and arrange about taking action.

Of this I am sure: the sun rises to-day on no more miserable house in all the great round of its daily course.

## CHAPTER XXII
## JONATHAN HARKER'S JOURNAL

**3** October.— As I must do something or go mad, I write this diary. It is now six o'clock, and we are to meet in the study in half an hour and take something to eat; for Dr. Van Helsing and Dr. Seward are agreed that if we do not eat we cannot work our best. Our best will be, God knows, required to-day. I must keep writing at every chance, for I dare not stop to think. All, big and little, must go down; perhaps at the end the little things may teach us most. The teaching, big or little, could not have landed Mina or me anywhere worse than we are to-day. However, we must trust and hope. Poor Mina told me just now, with the tears running down her dear cheeks, that it is in trouble and trial that our faith is tested— that we must keep on trusting; and that God will aid us up to the end. The end! oh my God! what end?... To work! To work!

When Dr. Van Helsing and Dr. Seward had come back from seeing poor Renfield, we went gravely into what was to be done. First, Dr. Seward told us that when he and Dr. Van Helsing had gone down to the room below they had found Renfield lying on the floor, all in a heap. His face was all bruised and crushed in, and the bones of the neck were broken. Dr. Seward asked the attendant who was on duty in the passage if he had heard anything. He said that he had been sitting down— he confessed to half dozing— when he heard loud voices in the room, and then Renfield had called out loudly several times, "God! God! God!" after that there was a sound of falling, and when he entered the room he found him lying on the floor, face down, just as the doctors had seen him. Van Helsing asked if he had heard "voices" or "a voice," and he said he could not say; that at first it had seemed to him as if there were two, but as there was no one in the room it could have been only one. He could swear to it, if required, that the word "God" was spoken by the patient. Dr. Seward said to us, when we were alone, that he did not wish to go into the matter; the question of an inquest had to be considered, and it would never do to put forward the truth, as no one would believe it. As it was, he thought that on the attendant's evidence he could give a certificate of death by misadventure in falling from bed. In case the coroner should demand it, there would be a formal inquest, necessarily to the same result.

When the question began to be discussed as to what should be our next step, the very first thing we decided was that Mina should be in full confidence; that nothing of any sort— no matter how painful— should be kept from her. She herself agreed as to its wisdom, and it was pitiful to see her so brave and yet so sorrowful, and in such a depth of despair. "There must be no concealment," she said, "Alas! we have had too much already. And besides there is nothing in all the world that can give me more pain than I have already endured— than I suffer now! Whatever may happen, it must be of new hope or of new courage to me!" Van Helsing was looking at her fixedly as she spoke, and said, suddenly but quietly:—

"But dear Madam Mina, are you not afraid; not for yourself, but for others from yourself, after what has happened?" Her face grew set in its lines, but her eyes shone with the devotion of a martyr as she answered:—

"Ah no! for my mind is made up!"

"To what?" he asked gently, whilst we were all very still; for each in our own way we had a sort of vague idea of what she meant. Her answer came with direct simplicity, as though she were simply stating a fact:—

"Because if I find in myself— and I shall watch keenly for it— a sign of harm to any that I love, I shall die!"

"You would not kill yourself?" he asked, hoarsely.

"I would; if there were no friend who loved me, who would save me such a pain, and so desperate an effort!" She looked at him meaningly as she spoke. He was sitting down; but now he rose and came close to her and put his hand on her head as he said solemnly:

"My child, there is such an one if it were for your good. For myself I could hold it in my account with God to find such an euthanasia for you, even at this moment if it were best. Nay, were it safe! But my child— — " For a moment he seemed choked, and a great sob rose in his throat; he gulped it down and went on:—

"There are here some who would stand between you and death. You must not die. You must not die by any hand; but least of all by your own. Until the other, who has fouled your sweet life, is true dead you must not die; for if he is still with the quick Un-Dead, your death would make you even as he is. No, you must live! You must struggle and strive to live, though death would seem a boon unspeakable. You must fight Death himself, though he come to you in pain or in joy; by the day, or the night; in safety or in peril! On your living soul I charge you that you do not die— nay, nor think of death— till this great evil be past." The poor dear grew white as death, and shock and shivered, as I have seen a quicksand shake and shiver at the incoming of the tide. We were all silent; we could do nothing. At length she grew more calm and turning to him said, sweetly, but oh! so sorrowfully, as she held out her hand:— "I promise you, my dear friend, that if God will let me live, I shall strive to do so; till, if it may be in His good time, this horror may have passed away from me." She was so good and brave that we all felt that our hearts were strengthened to work and endure for her, and we began to discuss what we were to do. I told her that she was to have all the papers in the safe, and all the papers or diaries and phonographs we might hereafter use; and was to keep the record as she had done before. She was pleased with the prospect of anything to do— if "pleased" could be used in connection with so grim an interest.

As usual Van Helsing had thought ahead of everyone else, and was prepared with an exact ordering of our work.

"It is perhaps well," he said, "that at our meeting after our visit to Carfax we decided not to do anything with the earth-boxes that lay there. Had we done so, the Count must have guessed our purpose, and would doubtless have taken measures in advance to frustrate such an effort with regard to the others; but now he does not know our intentions. Nay, more, in all probability, he does not know that such a power exists to us as can sterilise his lairs, so that he cannot use them as of old. We are now so much further advanced in our knowledge as to their disposition that, when we have examined the house in Piccadilly, we may track the very last of them. To-day, then, is ours; and in it rests our hope. The sun that rose on our sorrow this morning guards us in its course. Until it sets to-night, that monster must retain whatever form he now has. He is confined within the limitations of his earthly envelope. He cannot melt into thin air nor disappear through cracks or chinks or crannies. If he go through a doorway, he must open the door like a mortal. And so we have this day to hunt out all his lairs and sterilise them. So we shall, if we have not yet catch him and destroy him, drive him to bay in some place where the catching and the destroying shall be, in time, sure." Here I started up for I could not contain myself at the thought that the minutes and seconds so preciously laden with Mina's life and happiness were flying from us, since whilst we talked action was impossible. But Van Helsing held up his hand warningly. "Nay, friend Jonathan," he said, "in this, the quickest way home is the longest way, so your proverb say. We shall all act and act with desperate quick, when the time has come. But think, in all probable the key of the situation is in that house in Piccadilly. The Count may have many houses which he has bought. Of them he will have deeds of purchase, keys and other things. He will have paper that he write on; he will have his book of cheques. There are many belongings that he must have somewhere; why not in this place so central, so quiet, where he come and go by the front or the back at all hour, when in the very vast of the traffic there is none to notice. We shall go there and search that house; and when we learn what it holds, then we do what our friend Arthur call, in his phrases of hunt 'stop the earths' and so we run down our old fox— so? is it not?"

"Then let us come at once," I cried, "we are wasting the precious, precious time!" The Professor did not move, but simply said:—

"And how are we to get into that house in Piccadilly?"

"Any way!" I cried. "We shall break in if need be."

"And your police; where will they be, and what will they say?"

I was staggered; but I knew that if he wished to delay he had a good reason for it. So I said, as quietly as I could:—

"Don't wait more than need be; you know, I am sure, what torture I am in."

"Ah, my child, that I do; and indeed there is no wish of me to add to your anguish. But just think, what can we do, until all the world be at movement. Then will come our time. I have thought and thought, and it seems to me that the simplest way is the best of all. Now we wish to get into the house, but we have no key; is it not so?" I nodded.

"Now suppose that you were, in truth, the owner of that house, and could not still get in; and think there was to you no conscience of the housebreaker, what would you do?"

"I should get a respectable locksmith, and set him to work to pick the lock for me."

"And your police, they would interfere, would they not?"

"Oh, no! not if they knew the man was properly employed."

"Then," he looked at me as keenly as he spoke, "all that is in doubt is the conscience of the employer, and the belief of your policemen as to whether or no that employer has a good conscience or a bad one. Your police must indeed be zealous men and clever— oh, so clever!— in reading the heart, that they trouble themselves in such matter. No, no, my friend Jonathan, you go take the lock off a hundred empty house in this your London, or of any city in the world; and if you do it as such things are rightly done, and at the time such things are rightly done, no one will interfere. I have read of a gentleman who owned a so fine house in London, and when he went for months of summer to Switzerland and lock up his house, some burglar came and broke window at back and got in. Then he went and made open the shutters in front and walk out and in through the door, before the very eyes of the police. Then he have an auction in that house, and advertise it, and put up big notice; and when the day come he sell off by a great auctioneer all the goods of that other man who own them. Then he go to a builder, and he sell him that house, making an agreement that he pull it down and take all away within a certain time. And your police and other authority help him all they can. And when that owner come back from his holiday in Switzerland he find only an empty hole where his house had been. This was all done en règle; and in our work we shall be en règle too. We shall not go so early that the policemen who have then little to think of, shall deem it strange; but we shall go after ten o'clock, when there are many about, and such things would be done were we indeed owners of the house."

I could not but see how right he was and the terrible despair of Mina's face became relaxed a thought; there was hope in such good counsel. Van Helsing went on:—

"When once within that house we may find more clues; at any rate some of us can remain there whilst the rest find the other places where there be more earth-boxes— at Bermondsey and Mile End."

Lord Godalming stood up. "I can be of some use here," he said. "I shall wire to my people to have horses and carriages where they will be most convenient."

"Look here, old fellow," said Morris, "it is a capital idea to have all ready in case we want to go horsebacking; but don't you think that one of your snappy carriages with its heraldic adornments in a byway of Walworth or Mile End would attract too much attention for our purposes? It seems to me that we ought to take cabs when we go south or east; and even leave them somewhere near the neighbourhood we are going to."

"Friend Quincey is right!" said the Professor. "His head is what you call in plane with the horizon. It is a difficult thing that we go to do, and we do not want no peoples to watch us if so it may."

Mina took a growing interest in everything and I was rejoiced to see that the exigency of affairs was helping her to forget for a time the terrible experience of the night. She was very, very pale— almost ghastly, and so thin that her lips were drawn away, showing her teeth in somewhat of prominence. I did not mention this last, lest it should give her needless pain; but it made my blood run cold in my veins to think of what had occurred with poor Lucy when the Count had sucked her blood. As yet there was no sign of the teeth growing sharper; but the time as yet was short, and there was time for fear.

When we came to the discussion of the sequence of our efforts and of the disposition of our forces, there were new sources of doubt. It was finally agreed that before starting for Piccadilly we should destroy the Count's lair close at hand. In case he should find it out too soon, we should thus be still ahead of him in our work of destruction; and his presence in his purely material shape, and at his weakest, might give us some new clue.

As to the disposal of forces, it was suggested by the Professor that, after our visit to Carfax, we should all enter the house in Piccadilly; that the two doctors and I should remain there, whilst Lord Godalming and Quincey found the lairs at Walworth and Mile End and destroyed them. It was possible, if not likely, the Professor urged, that the Count might appear in Piccadilly during the day, and that if so we might be able to cope with him then and there. At any rate, we might be able to follow him in force. To this plan I strenuously objected, and so far as my going was concerned, for I said that I intended to stay and protect Mina, I thought that my mind was made up on the subject; but Mina would not listen to my objection. She said that there might be some law matter in which I could be useful; that amongst the Count's papers might be some clue which I could understand out of my experience in Transylvania; and that, as it was, all the strength we could muster was required to cope with the Count's extraordinary power. I had to give in, for Mina's resolution was fixed; she said that it was the last hope for her that we should all work together. "As for me," she said, "I have no fear. Things have been as bad as they can be; and whatever may happen must have in it some element of hope or comfort. Go, my husband! God can, if He wishes it, guard me as well alone as with any one present." So I started up crying out: "Then in God's name let us come at once, for we are losing time. The Count may come to Piccadilly earlier than we think."

"Not so!" said Van Helsing, holding up his hand.

"But why?" I asked.

"Do you forget," he said, with actually a smile, "that last night he banqueted heavily, and will sleep late?"

Did I forget! shall I ever— can I ever! Can any of us ever forget that terrible scene! Mina struggled hard to keep her brave countenance; but the pain overmastered her and she put her hands before her face, and shuddered whilst she moaned. Van Helsing had not intended to recall her frightful experience. He had simply lost sight of her and her part in the affair in his intellectual effort. When it struck him what he said, he was horrified at his thoughtlessness and tried to comfort her. "Oh, Madam Mina," he said, "dear, dear Madam Mina, alas! that I of all who so reverence you should have said anything so forgetful. These stupid old lips of mine and this stupid old head do not deserve so; but you will forget it, will you not?" He bent low beside her as he spoke; she took his hand, and looking at him through her tears, said hoarsely:—

"No, I shall not forget, for it is well that I remember; and with it I have so much in memory of you that is sweet, that I take it all together. Now, you must all be going soon. Breakfast is ready, and we must all eat that we may be strong."

Breakfast was a strange meal to us all. We tried to be cheerful and encourage each other, and Mina was the brightest and most cheerful of us. When it was over, Van Helsing stood up and said:—

"Now, my dear friends, we go forth to our terrible enterprise. Are we all armed, as we were on that night when first we visited our enemy's lair; armed against ghostly as well as carnal attack?" We all assured him. "Then it is well. Now, Madam Mina, you are in any case quite safe here until the sunset; and before then we shall return— if— — We shall return! But before we go let me see you armed against personal attack. I have myself, since you came down, prepared your chamber by the placing of things of which we know, so that He may not enter. Now let me guard yourself. On your forehead I touch this piece of Sacred Wafer in the name of the Father, the Son, and— — "

There was a fearful scream which almost froze our hearts to hear. As he had placed the Wafer on Mina's forehead, it had seared it— had burned into the flesh as though it had been a piece of white-hot metal. My poor darling's brain had told her the significance of the fact as quickly as her nerves received the pain of it; and the two so overwhelmed her that her overwrought nature had its voice in that dreadful scream. But the words to her thought came quickly; the echo of the scream had not ceased to ring on the air when there came the reaction, and she sank on her knees on the floor in an agony of abasement. Pulling her beautiful hair over her face, as the leper of old his mantle, she wailed out:—

"Unclean! Unclean! Even the Almighty shuns my polluted flesh! I must bear this mark of shame upon my forehead until the Judgment Day."

They all paused. I had thrown myself beside her in an agony of helpless grief, and putting my arms around held her tight. For a few minutes our sorrowful hearts beat together, whilst the friends around us turned away their eyes that ran tears silently. Then Van Helsing turned and said gravely; so gravely that I could not help feeling that he was in some way inspired, and was stating things outside himself:—

"It may be that you may have to bear that mark till God himself see fit, as He most surely shall, on the Judgment Day, to redress all wrongs of the earth and of His children that He has placed thereon. And oh, Madam Mina, my dear, my dear, may we who love you be there to see, when that red scar, the sign of God's knowledge of what has been, shall pass away, and leave your forehead as pure as the heart we know. For so surely as we live, that scar shall pass away when God sees right to lift the burden that is hard upon us. Till then we bear our Cross, as His Son did in obedience to His Will. It may be that we are chosen instruments of His good pleasure, and that we ascend to His bidding as that other through stripes and shame; through tears and blood; through doubts and fears, and all that makes the difference between God and man."

There was hope in his words, and comfort; and they made for resignation. Mina and I both felt so, and simultaneously we each took one of the old man's hands and bent over and kissed it. Then without a word we all knelt down together, and, all holding hands, swore to be true to each other. We men pledged ourselves to raise the veil of sorrow from the head of her whom, each in his own way, we loved; and we prayed for help and guidance in the terrible task which lay before us.

It was then time to start. So I said farewell to Mina, a parting which neither of us shall forget to our dying day; and we set out.

To one thing I have made up my mind: if we find out that Mina must be a vampire in the end, then she shall not go into that unknown and terrible land alone. I suppose it is thus that in old times one vampire meant many; just as their hideous bodies could only rest in sacred earth, so the holiest love was the recruiting sergeant for their ghastly ranks.

We entered Carfax without trouble and found all things the same as on the first occasion. It was hard to believe that amongst so prosaic surroundings of neglect and dust and decay there was any ground for such fear as already we knew. Had not our minds been made up, and had there not been terrible memories to spur us on, we could hardly have proceeded with our task. We found no papers, or any sign of use in the house; and in the old chapel the great boxes looked just as we had seen them last. Dr. Van Helsing said to us solemnly as we stood before them:—

"And now, my friends, we have a duty here to do. We must sterilise this earth, so sacred of holy memories, that he has brought from a far distant land for such fell use. He has chosen this earth because it has been holy. Thus we defeat him with his own weapon, for we make it more holy still. It was sanctified to such use of man, now we sanctify it to God." As he spoke he took from his bag a screwdriver and a wrench, and very soon the top of one of the cases was thrown open. The earth smelled musty and close; but we did not somehow seem to mind, for our attention was concentrated on the Professor. Taking from his box a piece of the Sacred Wafer he laid it reverently on the earth, and then shutting down the lid began to screw it home, we aiding him as he worked.

One by one we treated in the same way each of the great boxes, and left them as we had found them to all appearance; but in each was a portion of the Host.

When we closed the door behind us, the Professor said solemnly:—

"So much is already done. If it may be that with all the others we can be so successful, then the sunset of this evening may shine on Madam Mina's forehead all white as ivory and with no stain!"

As we passed across the lawn on our way to the station to catch our train we could see the front of the asylum. I looked eagerly, and in the window of my own room saw Mina. I waved my hand to her, and nodded to tell that our work there was successfully accomplished. She nodded in reply to show that she understood. The last I saw, she was waving her hand in farewell. It was with a heavy heart that we sought the station and just caught the train, which was steaming in as we reached the platform.

I have written this in the train.


Piccadilly, 12:30 o'clock.— Just before we reached Fenchurch Street Lord Godalming said to me:—

"Quincey and I will find a locksmith. You had better not come with us in case there should be any difficulty; for under the circumstances it wouldn't seem so bad for us to break into an empty house. But you are a solicitor and the Incorporated Law Society might tell you that you should have known better." I demurred as to my not sharing any danger even of odium, but he went on: "Besides, it will attract less attention if there are not too many of us. My title will make it all right with the locksmith, and with any policeman that may come along. You had better go with Jack and the Professor and stay in the Green Park, somewhere in sight of the house; and when you see the door opened and the smith has gone away, do you all come across. We shall be on the lookout for you, and shall let you in."

"The advice is good!" said Van Helsing, so we said no more. Godalming and Morris hurried off in a cab, we following in another. At the corner of Arlington Street our contingent got out and strolled into the Green Park. My heart beat as I saw the house on which so much of our hope was centred, looming up grim and silent in its deserted condition amongst its more lively and spruce-looking neighbours. We sat down on a bench within good view, and began to smoke cigars so as to attract as little attention as possible. The minutes seemed to pass with leaden feet as we waited for the coming of the others.

At length we saw a four-wheeler drive up. Out of it, in leisurely fashion, got Lord Godalming and Morris; and down from the box descended a thick-set working man with his rush-woven basket of tools. Morris paid the cabman, who touched his hat and drove away. Together the two ascended the steps, and Lord Godalming pointed out what he wanted done. The workman took off his coat leisurely and hung it on one of the spikes of the rail, saying something to a policeman who just then sauntered along. The policeman nodded acquiescence, and the man kneeling down placed his bag beside him. After searching through it, he took out a selection of tools which he produced to lay beside him in orderly fashion. Then he stood up, looked into the keyhole, blew into it, and turning to his employers, made some remark. Lord Godalming smiled, and the man lifted a good-sized bunch of keys; selecting one of them, he began to probe the lock, as if feeling his way with it. After fumbling about for a bit he tried a second, and then a third. All at once the door opened under a slight push from him, and he and the two others entered the hall. We sat still; my own cigar burnt furiously, but Van Helsing's went cold altogether. We waited patiently as we saw the workman come out and bring in his bag. Then he held the door partly open, steadying it with his knees, whilst he fitted a key to the lock. This he finally handed to Lord Godalming, who took out his purse and gave him something. The man touched his hat, took his bag, put on his coat and departed; not a soul took the slightest notice of the whole transaction.

When the man had fairly gone, we three crossed the street and knocked at the door. It was immediately opened by Quincey Morris, beside whom stood Lord Godalming lighting a cigar.

"The place smells so vilely," said the latter as we came in. It did indeed smell vilely— like the old chapel at Carfax— and with our previous experience it was plain to us that the Count had been using the place pretty freely. We moved to explore the house, all keeping together in case of attack; for we knew we had a strong and wily enemy to deal with, and as yet we did not know whether the Count might not be in the house. In the dining-room, which lay at the back of the hall, we found eight boxes of earth. Eight boxes only out of the nine, which we sought! Our work was not over, and would never be until we should have found the missing box. First we opened the shutters of the window which looked out across a narrow stone-flagged yard at the blank face of a stable, pointed to look like the front of a miniature house. There were no windows in it, so we were not afraid of being over-looked. We did not lose any time in examining the chests. With the tools which we had brought with us we opened them, one by one, and treated them as we had treated those others in the old chapel. It was evident to us that the Count was not at present in the house, and we proceeded to search for any of his effects.

After a cursory glance at the rest of the rooms, from basement to attic, we came to the conclusion that the dining-room contained any effects which might belong to the Count; and so we proceeded to minutely examine them. They lay in a sort of orderly disorder on the great dining-room table. There were title deeds of the Piccadilly house in a great bundle; deeds of the purchase of the houses at Mile End and Bermondsey; note-paper, envelopes, and pens and ink. All were covered up in thin wrapping paper to keep them from the dust. There were also a clothes brush, a brush and comb, and a jug and basin— the latter containing dirty water which was reddened as if with blood. Last of all was a little heap of keys of all sorts and sizes, probably those belonging to the other houses. When we had examined this last find, Lord Godalming and Quincey Morris taking accurate notes of the various addresses of the houses in the East and the South, took with them the keys in a great bunch, and set out to destroy the boxes in these places. The rest of us are, with what patience we can, waiting their return— or the coming of the Count.

## CHAPTER XXIII
## DR. SEWARD'S DIARY

3 October.— The time seemed terrible long whilst we were waiting for the coming of Godalming and Quincey Morris. The Professor tried to keep our minds active by using them all the time. I could see his beneficent purpose, by the side glances which he threw from time to time at Harker. The poor fellow is overwhelmed in a misery that is appalling to see. Last night he was a frank, happy-looking man, with strong, youthful face, full of energy, and with dark brown hair. To-day he is a drawn, haggard old man, whose white hair matches well with the hollow burning eyes and grief-written lines of his face. His energy is still intact; in fact, he is like a living flame. This may yet be his salvation, for, if all go well, it will tide him over the despairing period; he will then, in a kind of way, wake again to the realities of life. Poor fellow, I thought my own trouble was bad enough, but his— — ! The Professor knows this well enough, and is doing his best to keep his mind active. What he has been saying was, under the circumstances, of absorbing interest. So well as I can remember, here it is:—

"I have studied, over and over again since they came into my hands, all the papers relating to this monster; and the more I have studied, the greater seems the necessity to utterly stamp him out. All through there are signs of his advance; not only of his power, but of his knowledge of it. As I learned from the researches of my friend Arminus of Buda-Pesth, he was in life a most wonderful man. Soldier, statesman, and alchemist— which latter was the highest development of the science-knowledge of his time. He had a mighty brain, a learning beyond compare, and a heart that knew no fear and no remorse. He dared even to attend the Scholomance, and there was no branch of knowledge of his time that he did not essay. Well, in him the brain powers survived the physical death; though it would seem that memory was not all complete. In some faculties of mind he has been, and is, only a child; but he is growing, and some things that were childish at the first are now of man's stature. He is experimenting, and doing it well; and if it had not been that we have crossed his path he would be yet— he may be yet if we fail— the father or furtherer of a new order of beings, whose road must lead through Death, not Life."

Harker groaned and said, "And this is all arrayed against my darling! But how is he experimenting? The knowledge may help us to defeat him!"

"He has all along, since his coming, been trying his power, slowly but surely; that big child-brain of his is working. Well for us, it is, as yet, a child-brain; for had he dared, at the first, to attempt certain things he would long ago have been beyond our power. However, he means to succeed, and a man who has centuries before him can afford to wait and to go slow. Festina lente may well be his motto."

"I fail to understand," said Harker wearily. "Oh, do be more plain to me! Perhaps grief and trouble are dulling my brain."

The Professor laid his hand tenderly on his shoulder as he spoke:—

"Ah, my child, I will be plain. Do you not see how, of late, this monster has been creeping into knowledge experimentally. How he has been making use of the zoöphagous patient to effect his entry into friend John's home; for your Vampire, though in all afterwards he can come when and how he will, must at the first make entry only when asked thereto by an inmate. But these are not his most important experiments. Do we not see how at the first all these so great boxes were moved by others. He knew not then but that must be so. But all the time that so great child-brain of his was growing, and he began to consider whether he might not himself move the box. So he began to help; and then, when he found that this be all-right, he try to move them all alone. And so he progress, and he scatter these graves of him; and none but he know where they are hidden. He may have intend to bury them deep in the ground. So that he only use them in the night, or at such time as he can change his form, they do him equal well; and none may know these are his hiding-place! But, my child, do not despair; this knowledge come to him just too late! Already all of his lairs but one be sterilise as for him; and before the sunset this shall be so. Then he have no place where he can move and hide. I delayed this morning that so we might be sure. Is there not more at stake for us than for him? Then why we not be even more careful than him? By my clock it is one hour and already, if all be well, friend Arthur and Quincey are on their way to us. To-day is our day, and we must go sure, if slow, and lose no chance. See! there are five of us when those absent ones return."

Whilst he was speaking we were startled by a knock at the hall door, the double postman's knock of the telegraph boy. We all moved out to the hall with one impulse, and Van Helsing, holding up his hand to us to keep silence, stepped to the door and opened it. The boy handed in a despatch. The Professor closed the door again, and, after looking at the direction, opened it and read aloud.

"Look out for D. He has just now, 12:45, come from Carfax hurriedly and hastened towards the South. He seems to be going the round and may want to see you: Mina."

There was a pause, broken by Jonathan Harker's voice:—

"Now, God be thanked, we shall soon meet!" Van Helsing turned to him quickly and said:—

"God will act in His own way and time. Do not fear, and do not rejoice as yet; for what we wish for at the moment may be our undoings."

"I care for nothing now," he answered hotly, "except to wipe out this brute from the face of creation. I would sell my soul to do it!"

"Oh, hush, hush, my child!" said Van Helsing. "God does not purchase souls in this wise; and the Devil, though he may purchase, does not keep faith. But God is merciful and just, and knows your pain and your devotion to that dear Madam Mina. Think you, how her pain would be doubled, did she but hear your wild words. Do not fear any of us, we are all devoted to this cause, and to-day shall see the end. The time is coming for action; to-day this Vampire is limit to the powers of man, and till sunset he may not change. It will take him time to arrive here— see, it is twenty minutes past one— and there are yet some times before he can hither come, be he never so quick. What we must hope for is that my Lord Arthur and Quincey arrive first."

About half an hour after we had received Mrs. Harker's telegram, there came a quiet, resolute knock at the hall door. It was just an ordinary knock, such as is given hourly by thousands of gentlemen, but it made the Professor's heart and mine beat loudly. We looked at each other, and together moved out into the hall; we each held ready to use our various armaments— the spiritual in the left hand, the mortal in the right. Van Helsing pulled back the latch, and, holding the door half open, stood back, having both hands ready for action. The gladness of our hearts must have shown upon our faces when on the step, close to the door, we saw Lord Godalming and Quincey Morris. They came quickly in and closed the door behind them, the former saying, as they moved along the hall:—

"It is all right. We found both places; six boxes in each and we destroyed them all!"

"Destroyed?" asked the Professor.

"For him!" We were silent for a minute, and then Quincey said:—

"There's nothing to do but to wait here. If, however, he doesn't turn up by five o'clock, we must start off; for it won't do to leave Mrs. Harker alone after sunset."

"He will be here before long now," said Van Helsing, who had been consulting his pocket-book. "Nota bene, in Madam's telegram he went south from Carfax, that means he went to cross the river, and he could only do so at slack of tide, which should be something before one o'clock. That he went south has a meaning for us. He is as yet only suspicious; and he went from Carfax first to the place where he would suspect interference least. You must have been at Bermondsey only a short time before him. That he is not here already shows that he went to Mile End next. This took him some time; for he would then have to be carried over the river in some way. Believe me, my friends, we shall not have long to wait now. We should have ready some plan of attack, so that we may throw away no chance. Hush, there is no time now. Have all your arms! Be ready!" He held up a warning hand as he spoke, for we all could hear a key softly inserted in the lock of the hall door.

I could not but admire, even at such a moment, the way in which a dominant spirit asserted itself. In all our hunting parties and adventures in different parts of the world, Quincey Morris had always been the one to arrange the plan of action, and Arthur and I had been accustomed to obey him implicitly. Now, the old habit seemed to be renewed instinctively. With a swift glance around the room, he at once laid out our plan of attack, and, without speaking a word, with a gesture, placed us each in position. Van Helsing, Harker, and I were just behind the door, so that when it was opened the Professor could guard it whilst we two stepped between the incomer and the door. Godalming behind and Quincey in front stood just out of sight ready to move in front of the window. We waited in a suspense that made the seconds pass with nightmare slowness. The slow, careful steps came along the hall; the Count was evidently prepared for some surprise—at least he feared it.

Suddenly with a single bound he leaped into the room, winning a way past us before any of us could raise a hand to stay him. There was something so panther-like in the movement— something so unhuman, that it seemed to sober us all from the shock of his coming. The first to act was Harker, who, with a quick movement, threw himself before the door leading into the room in the front of the house. As the Count saw us, a horrible sort of snarl passed over his face, showing the eye-teeth long and pointed; but the evil smile as quickly passed into a cold stare of lion-like disdain. His expression again changed as, with a single impulse, we all advanced upon him. It was a pity that we had not some better organised plan of attack, for even at the moment I wondered what we were to do. I did not myself know whether our lethal weapons would avail us anything. Harker evidently meant to try the matter, for he had ready his great Kukri knife and made a fierce and sudden cut at him. The blow was a powerful one; only the diabolical quickness of the Count's leap back saved him. A second less and the trenchant blade had shorne through his heart. As it was, the point just cut the cloth of his coat, making a wide gap whence a bundle of bank-notes and a stream of gold fell out. The expression of the Count's face was so hellish, that for a moment I feared for Harker, though I saw him throw the terrible knife aloft again for another stroke. Instinctively I moved forward with a protective impulse, holding the Crucifix and Wafer in my left hand. I felt a mighty power fly along my arm; and it was without surprise that I saw the monster cower back before a similar movement made spontaneously by each one of us. It would be impossible to describe the expression of hate and baffled malignity— of anger and hellish rage— which came over the Count's face. His waxen hue became greenish-yellow by the contrast of his burning eyes, and the red scar on the forehead showed on the pallid skin like a palpitating wound. The next instant, with a sinuous dive he swept under Harker's arm, ere his blow could fall, and, grasping a handful of the money from the floor, dashed across the room, threw himself at the window. Amid the crash and glitter of the falling glass, he tumbled into the flagged area below. Through the sound of the shivering glass I could hear the "ting" of the gold, as some of the sovereigns fell on the flagging.

We ran over and saw him spring unhurt from the ground. He, rushing up the steps, crossed the flagged yard, and pushed open the stable door. There he turned and spoke to us:—

"You think to baffle me, you— with your pale faces all in a row, like sheep in a butcher's. You shall be sorry yet, each one of you! You think you have left me without a place to rest; but I have more. My revenge is just begun! I spread it over centuries, and time is on my side. Your girls that you all love are mine already; and through them you and others shall yet be mine— my creatures, to do my bidding and to be my jackals when I want to feed. Bah!" With a contemptuous sneer, he passed quickly through the door, and we heard the rusty bolt creak as he fastened it behind him. A door beyond opened and shut. The first of us to speak was the Professor, as, realising the difficulty of following him through the stable, we moved toward the hall.

"We have learnt something— much! Notwithstanding his brave words, he fears us; he fear time, he fear want! For if not, why he hurry so? His very tone betray him, or my ears deceive. Why take that money? You follow quick. You are hunters of wild beast, and understand it so. For me, I make sure that nothing here may be of use to him, if so that he return." As he spoke he put the money remaining into his pocket; took the title-deeds in the bundle as Harker had left them, and swept the remaining things into the open fireplace, where he set fire to them with a match.

Godalming and Morris had rushed out into the yard, and Harker had lowered himself from the window to follow the Count. He had, however, bolted the stable door; and by the time they had forced it open there was no sign of him. Van Helsing and I tried to make inquiry at the back of the house; but the mews was deserted and no one had seen him depart.

It was now late in the afternoon, and sunset was not far off. We had to recognise that our game was up; with heavy hearts we agreed with the Professor when he said:—

"Let us go back to Madam Mina— poor, poor dear Madam Mina. All we can do just now is done; and we can there, at least, protect her. But we need not despair. There is but one more earth-box, and we must try to find it; when that is done all may yet be well." I could see that he spoke as bravely as he could to comfort Harker. The poor fellow was quite broken down; now and again he gave a low groan which he could not suppress— he was thinking of his wife.

With sad hearts we came back to my house, where we found Mrs. Harker waiting us, with an appearance of cheerfulness which did honour to her bravery and unselfishness. When she saw our faces, her own became as pale as death: for a second or two her eyes were closed as if she were in secret prayer; and then she said cheerfully:—

"I can never thank you all enough. Oh, my poor darling!" As she spoke, she took her husband's grey head in her hands and kissed it— "Lay your poor head here and rest it. All will yet be well, dear! God will protect us if He so will it in His good intent." The poor fellow groaned. There was no place for words in his sublime misery.

We had a sort of perfunctory supper together, and I think it cheered us all up somewhat. It was, perhaps, the mere animal heat of food to hungry people— for none of us had eaten anything since breakfast— or the sense of companionship may have helped us; but anyhow we were all less miserable, and saw the morrow as not altogether without hope. True to our promise, we told Mrs. Harker everything which had passed; and although she grew snowy white at times when danger had seemed to threaten her husband, and red at others when his devotion to her was manifested, she listened bravely and with calmness. When we came to the part where Harker had rushed at the Count so recklessly, she clung to her husband's arm, and held it tight as though her clinging could protect him from any harm that might come. She said nothing, however, till the narration was all done, and matters had been brought right up to the present time. Then without letting go her husband's hand she stood up amongst us and spoke. Oh, that I could give any idea of the scene; of that sweet, sweet, good, good woman in all the radiant beauty of her youth and animation, with the red scar on her forehead, of which she was conscious, and which we saw with grinding of our teeth— remembering whence and how it came; her loving kindness against our grim hate; her tender faith against all our fears and doubting; and we, knowing that so far as symbols went, she with all her goodness and purity and faith, was outcast from God.

"Jonathan," she said, and the word sounded like music on her lips it was so full of love and tenderness, "Jonathan dear, and you all my true, true friends, I want you to bear something in mind through all this dreadful time. I know that you must fight— that you must destroy even as you destroyed the false Lucy so that the true Lucy might live hereafter; but it is not a work of hate. That poor soul who has wrought all this misery is the saddest case of all. Just think what will be his joy when he, too, is destroyed in his worser part that his better part may have spiritual immortality. You must be pitiful to him, too, though it may not hold your hands from his destruction."

As she spoke I could see her husband's face darken and draw together, as though the passion in him were shrivelling his being to its core. Instinctively the clasp on his wife's hand grew closer, till his knuckles looked white. She did not flinch from the pain which I knew she must have suffered, but looked at him with eyes that were more appealing than ever. As she stopped speaking he leaped to his feet, almost tearing his hand from hers as he spoke:—

"May God give him into my hand just for long enough to destroy that earthly life of him which we are aiming at. If beyond it I could send his soul for ever and ever to burning hell I would do it!"

"Oh, hush! oh, hush! in the name of the good God. Don't say such things, Jonathan, my husband; or you will crush me with fear and horror. Just think, my dear— I have been thinking all this long, long day of it— that ... perhaps ... some day ... I, too, may need such pity; and that some other like you— and with equal cause for anger— may deny it to me! Oh, my husband! my husband, indeed I would have spared you such a thought had there been another way; but I pray that God may not have treasured your wild words, except as the heart-broken wail of a very loving and sorely stricken man. Oh, God, let these poor white hairs go in evidence of what he has suffered, who all his life has done no wrong, and on whom so many sorrows have come."

We men were all in tears now. There was no resisting them, and we wept openly. She wept, too, to see that her sweeter counsels had prevailed. Her husband flung himself on his knees beside her, and putting his arms round her, hid his face in the folds of her dress. Van Helsing beckoned to us and we stole out of the room, leaving the two loving hearts alone with their God.

Before they retired the Professor fixed up the room against any coming of the Vampire, and assured Mrs. Harker that she might rest in peace. She tried to school herself to the belief, and, manifestly for her husband's sake, tried to seem content. It was a brave struggle; and was, I think and believe, not without its reward. Van Helsing had placed at hand a bell which either of them was to sound in case of any emergency. When they had retired, Quincey, Godalming, and I arranged that we should sit up, dividing the night between us, and watch over the safety of the poor stricken lady. The first watch falls to Quincey, so the rest of us shall be off to bed as soon as we can. Godalming has already turned in, for his is the second watch. Now that my work is done I, too, shall go to bed.

Jonathan Harker's Journal.

3-4 October, close to midnight.— I thought yesterday would never end. There was over me a yearning for sleep, in some sort of blind belief that to wake would be to find things changed, and that any change must now be for the better. Before we parted, we discussed what our next step was to be, but we could arrive at no result. All we knew was that one earth-box remained, and that the Count alone knew where it was. If he chooses to lie hidden, he may baffle us for years; and in the meantime!— the thought is too horrible, I dare not think of it even now. This I know: that if ever there was a woman who was all perfection, that one is my poor wronged darling. I love her a thousand times more for her sweet pity of last night, a pity that made my own hate of the monster seem despicable. Surely God will not permit the world to be the poorer by the loss of such a creature. This is hope to me. We are all drifting reefwards now, and faith is our only anchor. Thank God! Mina is sleeping, and sleeping without dreams. I fear what her dreams might be like, with such terrible memories to ground them in. She has not been so calm, within my seeing, since the sunset. Then, for a while, there came over her face a repose which was like spring after the blasts of March. I thought at the time that it was the softness of the red sunset on her face, but somehow now I think it has a deeper meaning. I am not sleepy myself, though I am weary— weary to death. However, I must try to sleep; for there is to-morrow to think of, and there is no rest for me until....

Later.— I must have fallen asleep, for I was awaked by Mina, who was sitting up in bed, with a startled look on her face. I could see easily, for we did not leave the room in darkness; she had placed a warning hand over my mouth, and now she whispered in my ear:—
"Hush! there is someone in the corridor!" I got up softly, and crossing the room, gently opened the door.
Just outside, stretched on a mattress, lay Mr. Morris, wide awake. He raised a warning hand for silence as he whispered to me:—
"Hush! go back to bed; it is all right. One of us will be here all night. We don't mean to take any chances!"
His look and gesture forbade discussion, so I came back and told Mina. She sighed and positively a shadow of a smile stole over her poor, pale face as she put her arms round me and said softly:—
"Oh, thank God for good brave men!" With a sigh she sank back again to sleep. I write this now as I am not sleepy, though I must try again.

4 October, morning.— Once again during the night I was wakened by Mina. This time we had all had a good sleep, for the grey of the coming dawn was making the windows into sharp oblongs, and the gas flame was like a speck rather than a disc of light. She said to me hurriedly:—
"Go, call the Professor. I want to see him at once."
"Why?" I asked.
"I have an idea. I suppose it must have come in the night, and matured without my knowing it. He must hypnotise me before the dawn, and then I shall be able to speak. Go quick, dearest; the time is getting close." I went to the door. Dr. Seward was resting on the mattress, and, seeing me, he sprang to his feet.
"Is anything wrong?" he asked, in alarm.
"No," I replied; "but Mina wants to see Dr. Van Helsing at once."
"I will go," he said, and hurried into the Professor's room.
In two or three minutes later Van Helsing was in the room in his dressing-gown, and Mr. Morris and Lord Godalming were with Dr. Seward at the door asking questions. When the Professor saw Mina smile— a positive smile ousted the anxiety of his face; he rubbed his hands as he said:—
"Oh, my dear Madam Mina, this is indeed a change. See! friend Jonathan, we have got our dear Madam Mina, as of old, back to us to-day!" Then turning to her, he said, cheerfully: "And what am I do for you? For at this hour you do not want me for nothings."
"I want you to hypnotise me!" she said. "Do it before the dawn, for I feel that then I can speak, and speak freely. Be quick, for the time is short!" Without a word he motioned her to sit up in bed.
Looking fixedly at her, he commenced to make passes in front of her, from over the top of her head downward, with each hand in turn. Mina gazed at him fixedly for a few minutes, during which my own heart beat like a trip hammer, for I felt that some crisis was at hand. Gradually her eyes closed, and she sat, stock still; only by the gentle heaving of her bosom could one know that she was alive. The Professor made a few more passes and then stopped, and I could see that his forehead was covered with great beads of perspiration. Mina opened her eyes; but she did not seem the same woman. There was a far-away look in her eyes, and her voice had a sad dreaminess which was new to me. Raising his hand to impose silence, the Professor motioned to me to bring the others in. They came on tip-toe, closing the door behind them, and stood at the foot of the bed, looking on. Mina appeared not to see them. The stillness was broken by Van Helsing's voice speaking in a low level tone which would not break the current of her thoughts:—

"Where are you?" The answer came in a neutral way:—

"I do not know. Sleep has no place it can call its own." For several minutes there was silence. Mina sat rigid, and the Professor stood staring at her fixedly; the rest of us hardly dared to breathe. The room was growing lighter; without taking his eyes from Mina's face, Dr. Van Helsing motioned me to pull up the blind. I did so, and the day seemed just upon us. A red streak shot up, and a rosy light seemed to diffuse itself through the room. On the instant the Professor spoke again:—

"Where are you now?" The answer came dreamily, but with intention; it were as though she were interpreting something. I have heard her use the same tone when reading her shorthand notes.

"I do not know. It is all strange to me!"

"What do you see?"

"I can see nothing; it is all dark."

"What do you hear?" I could detect the strain in the Professor's patient voice.

"The lapping of water. It is gurgling by, and little waves leap. I can hear them on the outside."

"Then you are on a ship?" We all looked at each other, trying to glean something each from the other. We were afraid to think. The answer came quick:—

"Oh, yes!"

"What else do you hear?"

"The sound of men stamping overhead as they run about. There is the creaking of a chain, and the loud tinkle as the check of the capstan falls into the rachet."

"What are you doing?"

"I am still— oh, so still. It is like death!" The voice faded away into a deep breath as of one sleeping, and the open eyes closed again.

By this time the sun had risen, and we were all in the full light of day. Dr. Van Helsing placed his hands on Mina's shoulders, and laid her head down softly on her pillow. She lay like a sleeping child for a few moments, and then, with a long sigh, awoke and stared in wonder to see us all around her. "Have I been talking in my sleep?" was all she said. She seemed, however, to know the situation without telling, though she was eager to know what she had told. The Professor repeated the conversation, and she said:—

"Then there is not a moment to lose: it may not be yet too late!" Mr. Morris and Lord Godalming started for the door but the Professor's calm voice called them back:—

"Stay, my friends. That ship, wherever it was, was weighing anchor whilst she spoke. There are many ships weighing anchor at the moment in your so great Port of London. Which of them is it that you seek? God be thanked that we have once again a clue, though whither it may lead us we know not. We have been blind somewhat; blind after the manner of men, since when we can look back we see what we might have seen looking forward if we had been able to see what we might have seen! Alas, but that sentence is a puddle; is it not? We can know now what was in the Count's mind, when he seize that money, though Jonathan's so fierce knife put him in the danger that even he dread. He meant escape. Hear me, ESCAPE! He saw that with but one earth-box left, and a pack of men following like dogs after a fox, this London was no place for him. He have take his last earth-box on board a ship, and he leave the land. He think to escape, but no! we follow him. Tally Ho! as friend Arthur would say when he put on his red frock! Our old fox is wily; oh! so wily, and we must follow with wile. I, too, am wily and I think his mind in a little while. In meantime we may rest and in peace, for there are waters between us which he do not want to pass, and which he could not if he would— unless the ship were to touch the land, and then only at full or slack tide. See, and the sun is just rose, and all day to sunset is to us. Let us take bath, and dress, and have breakfast which we all need, and which we can eat comfortably since he be not in the same land with us." Mina looked at him appealingly as she asked:—

"But why need we seek him further, when he is gone away from us?"
He took her hand and patted it as he replied:—
"Ask me nothings as yet. When we have breakfast, then I answer all questions." He would say no more, and we separated to dress.
After breakfast Mina repeated her question. He looked at her gravely for a minute and then said sorrowfully:—
"Because my dear, dear Madam Mina, now more than ever must we find him even if we have to follow him to the jaws of Hell!" She grew paler as she asked faintly:—
"Why?"
"Because," he answered solemnly, "he can live for centuries, and you are but mortal woman. Time is now to be dreaded— since once he put that mark upon your throat."
I was just in time to catch her as she fell forward in a faint.

## CHAPTER XXIV
# DR. SEWARD'S PHONOGRAPH DIARY, SPOKEN BY VAN HELSING

THIS to Jonathan Harker.

You are to stay with your dear Madam Mina. We shall go to make our search— if I can call it so, for it is not search but knowing, and we seek confirmation only. But do you stay and take care of her to-day. This is your best and most holiest office. This day nothing can find him here. Let me tell you that so you will know what we four know already, for I have tell them. He, our enemy, have gone away; he have gone back to his Castle in Transylvania. I know it so well, as if a great hand of fire wrote it on the wall. He have prepare for this in some way, and that last earth-box was ready to ship somewheres. For this he took the money; for this he hurry at the last, lest we catch him before the sun go down. It was his last hope, save that he might hide in the tomb that he think poor Miss Lucy, being as he thought like him, keep open to him. But there was not of time. When that fail he make straight for his last resource— his last earth-work I might say did I wish double entente. He is clever, oh, so clever! he know that his game here was finish; and so he decide he go back home. He find ship going by the route he came, and he go in it. We go off now to find what ship, and whither bound; when we have discover that, we come back and tell you all. Then we will comfort you and poor dear Madam Mina with new hope. For it will be hope when you think it over: that all is not lost. This very creature that we pursue, he take hundreds of years to get so far as London; and yet in one day, when we know of the disposal of him we drive him out. He is finite, though he is powerful to do much harm and suffers not as we do. But we are strong, each in our purpose; and we are all more strong together. Take heart afresh, dear husband of Madam Mina. This battle is but begun, and in the end we shall win— so sure as that God sits on high to watch over His children. Therefore be of much comfort till we return.

Van Helsing.

Jonathan Harker's Journal.

4 October.— When I read to Mina, Van Helsing's message in the phonograph, the poor girl brightened up considerably. Already the certainty that the Count is out of the country has given her comfort; and comfort is strength to her. For my own part, now that his horrible danger is not face to face with us, it seems almost impossible to believe in it. Even my own terrible experiences in Castle Dracula seem like a long-forgotten dream. Here in the crisp autumn air in the bright sunlight— —

Alas! how can I disbelieve! In the midst of my thought my eye fell on the red scar on my poor darling's white forehead. Whilst that lasts, there can be no disbelief. And afterwards the very memory of it will keep faith crystal clear. Mina and I fear to be idle, so we have been over all the diaries again and again. Somehow, although the reality seems greater each time, the pain and the fear seem less. There is something of a guiding purpose manifest throughout, which is comforting. Mina says that perhaps we are the instruments of ultimate good. It may be! I shall try to think as she does. We have never spoken to each other yet of the future. It is better to wait till we see the Professor and the others after their investigations.

The day is running by more quickly than I ever thought a day could run for me again. It is now three o'clock.

Mina Harker's Journal.

5 October, 5 p. m.— Our meeting for report. Present: Professor Van Helsing, Lord Godalming, Dr. Seward, Mr. Quincey Morris, Jonathan Harker, Mina Harker.

Dr. Van Helsing described what steps were taken during the day to discover on what boat and whither bound Count Dracula made his escape:—

"As I knew that he wanted to get back to Transylvania, I felt sure that he must go by the Danube mouth; or by somewhere in the Black Sea, since by that way he come. It was a dreary blank that was before us. Omne ignotum pro magnifico; and so with heavy hearts we start to find what ships leave for the Black Sea last night. He was in sailing ship, since Madam Mina tell of sails being set. These not so important as to go in your list of the shipping in the Times, and so we go, by suggestion of Lord Godalming, to your Lloyd's, where are note of all ships that sail, however so small. There we find that only one Black-Sea-bound ship go out with the tide. She is the Czarina Catherine, and she sail from Doolittle's Wharf for Varna, and thence on to other parts and up the Danube. 'Soh!' said I, 'this is the ship whereon is the Count.' So off we go to Doolittle's Wharf, and there we find a man in an office of wood so small that the man look bigger than the office. From him we inquire of the goings of the Czarina Catherine. He swear much, and he red face and loud of voice, but he good fellow all the same; and when Quincey give him something from his pocket which crackle as he roll it up, and put it in a so small bag which he have hid deep in his clothing, he still better fellow and humble servant to us. He come with us, and ask many men who are rough and hot; these be better fellows too when they have been no more thirsty. They say much of blood and bloom, and of others which I comprehend not, though I guess what they mean; but nevertheless they tell us all things which we want to know.

"They make known to us among them, how last afternoon at about five o'clock comes a man so hurry. A tall man, thin and pale, with high nose and teeth so white, and eyes that seem to be burning. That he be all in black, except that he have a hat of straw which suit not him or the time. That he scatter his money in making quick inquiry as to what ship sails for the Black Sea and for where. Some took him to the office and then to the ship, where he will not go aboard but halt at shore end of gang-plank, and ask that the captain come to him. The captain come, when told that he will be pay well; and though he swear much at the first he agree to term. Then the thin man go and some one tell him where horse and cart can be hired. He go there and soon he come again, himself driving cart on which a great box; this he himself lift down, though it take several to put it on truck for the ship. He give much talk to captain as to how and where his box is to be place; but the captain like it not and swear at him in many tongues, and tell him that if he like he can come and see where it shall be. But he say 'no'; that he come not yet, for that he have much to do. Whereupon the captain tell him that he had better be quick— with blood— for that his ship will leave the place— of blood— before the turn of the tide— with blood. Then the thin man smile and say that of course he must go when he think fit; but he will be surprise if he go quite so soon. The captain swear again, polyglot, and the thin man make him bow, and thank him, and say that he will so far intrude on his kindness as to come aboard before the sailing. Final the captain, more red than ever, and in more tongues tell him that he doesn't want no Frenchmen— with bloom upon them and also with blood— in his ship— with blood on her also. And so, after asking where there might be close at hand a ship where he might purchase ship forms, he departed.

"No one knew where he went 'or bloomin' well cared,' as they said, for they had something else to think of— well with blood again; for it soon became apparent to all that the Czarina Catherine would not sail as was expected. A thin mist began to creep up from the river, and it grew, and grew; till soon a dense fog enveloped the ship and all around her. The captain swore polyglot— very polyglot— polyglot with bloom and blood; but he could do nothing. The water rose and rose; and he began to fear that he would lose the tide altogether. He was in no friendly mood, when just at full tide, the thin man came up the gang-plank again and asked to see where his box had been stowed. Then the captain replied that he wished that he and his box— old and with much bloom and blood— were in hell. But the thin man did not be offend, and went down with the mate and saw where it was place, and came up and stood awhile on deck in fog. He must have come off by himself, for none notice him. Indeed they thought not of him; for soon the fog begin to melt away, and all was clear again. My friends of the thirst and the language that was of bloom and blood laughed, as they told how the captain's swears exceeded even his usual polyglot, and was more than ever full of picturesque, when on questioning other mariners who were on movement up and down on the river that hour, he found that few of them had seen any of fog at all, except where it lay round the wharf. However, the ship went out on the ebb tide; and was doubtless by morning far down the river mouth. She was by then, when they told us, well out to sea.

"And so, my dear Madam Mina, it is that we have to rest for a time, for our enemy is on the sea, with the fog at his command, on his way to the Danube mouth. To sail a ship takes time, go she never so quick; and when we start we go on land more quick, and we meet him there. Our best hope is to come on him when in the box between sunrise and sunset; for then he can make no struggle, and we may deal with him as we should. There are days for us, in which we can make ready our plan. We know all about where he go; for we have seen the owner of the ship, who have shown us invoices and all papers that can be. The box we seek is to be landed in Varna, and to be given to an agent, one Ristics who will there present his credentials; and so our merchant friend will have done his part. When he ask if there be any wrong, for that so, he can telegraph and have inquiry made at Varna, we say 'no'; for what is to be done is not for police or of the customs. It must be done by us alone and in our own way."

When Dr. Van Helsing had done speaking, I asked him if he were certain that the Count had remained on board the ship. He replied: "We have the best proof of that: your own evidence, when in the hypnotic trance this morning." I asked him again if it were really necessary that they should pursue the Count, for oh! I dread Jonathan leaving me, and I know that he would surely go if the others went. He answered in growing passion, at first quietly. As he went on, however, he grew more angry and more forceful, till in the end we could not but see wherein was at least some of that personal dominance which made him so long a master amongst men:—

"Yes, it is necessary— necessary— necessary! For your sake in the first, and then for the sake of humanity. This monster has done much harm already, in the narrow scope where he find himself, and in the short time when as yet he was only as a body groping his so small measure in darkness and not knowing. All this have I told these others; you, my dear Madam Mina, will learn it in the phonograph of my friend John, or in that of your husband. I have told them how the measure of leaving his own barren land— barren of peoples— and coming to a new land where life of man teems till they are like the multitude of standing corn, was the work of centuries. Were another of the Un-Dead, like him, to try to do what he has done, perhaps not all the centuries of the world that have been, or that will be, could aid him. With this one, all the forces of nature that are occult and deep and strong must have worked together in some wondrous way. The very place, where he have been alive, Un-Dead for all these centuries, is full of strangeness of the geologic and chemical world. There are deep caverns and fissures that reach none know whither. There have been volcanoes, some of whose openings still send out waters of strange properties, and gases that kill or make to vivify. Doubtless, there is something magnetic or electric in some of these combinations of occult forces which work for physical life in strange way; and in himself were from the first some great qualities. In a hard and warlike time he was celebrate that he have more iron nerve, more subtle brain, more braver heart, than any man. In him some vital principle have in strange way found their utmost; and as his body keep strong and grow and thrive, so his brain grow too. All this without that diabolic aid which is surely to him; for it have to yield to the powers that come from, and are, symbolic of good. And now this is what he is to us. He have infect you— oh, forgive me, my dear, that I must say such; but it is for good of you that I speak. He infect you in such wise, that even if he do no more, you have only to live— to live in your own old, sweet way; and so in time, death, which is of man's common lot and with God's sanction, shall make you like to him. This must not be! We have sworn together that it must not. Thus are we ministers of God's own wish: that the world, and men for whom His Son die, will not be given over to monsters, whose very existence would defame Him. He have allowed us to redeem one soul already, and we go out as the old knights of the Cross to redeem more. Like them we shall travel towards the sunrise; and like them, if we fall, we fall in good cause." He paused and I said:—

"But will not the Count take his rebuff wisely? Since he has been driven from England, will he not avoid it, as a tiger does the village from which he has been hunted?"

"Aha!" he said, "your simile of the tiger good, for me, and I shall adopt him. Your man-eater, as they of India call the tiger who has once tasted blood of the human, care no more for the other prey, but prowl unceasing till he get him. This that we hunt from our village is a tiger, too, a man-eater, and he never cease to prowl. Nay, in himself he is not one to retire and stay afar. In his life, his living life, he go over the Turkey frontier and attack his enemy on his own ground; he be beaten back, but did he stay? No! He come again, and again, and again. Look at his persistence and endurance. With the child-brain that was to him he have long since conceive the idea of coming to a great city. What does he do? He find out the place of all the world most of promise for him. Then he deliberately set himself down to prepare for the task. He find in patience just how is his strength, and what are his powers. He study new tongues. He learn new social life; new environment of old ways, the politic, the law, the finance, the science, the habit of a new land and a new people who have come to be since he was. His glimpse that he have had, whet his appetite only and enkeen his desire. Nay, it help him to grow as to his brain; for it all prove to him how right he was at the first in his surmises. He have done this alone; all alone! from a ruin tomb in a forgotten land. What more may he not do when the greater world of thought is open to him. He that can smile at death, as we know him; who can flourish in the midst of diseases that kill off whole peoples. Oh, if such an one was to come from God, and not the Devil, what a force for good might he not be in this old world of ours. But we are pledged to set the world free. Our toil must be in silence, and our efforts all in secret; for in this enlightened age, when men believe not even what they see, the doubting of wise men would be his greatest strength. It would be at once his sheath and his armour, and his weapons to destroy us, his enemies, who are willing to peril even our own souls for the safety of one we love— for the good of mankind, and for the honour and glory of God."

After a general discussion it was determined that for to-night nothing be definitely settled; that we should all sleep on the facts, and try to think out the proper conclusions. To-morrow, at breakfast, we are to meet again, and, after making our conclusions known to one another, we shall decide on some definite cause of action.

. . . . . . . . . . . . . . . . . . . . . . . . . . . . . . . .

I feel a wonderful peace and rest to-night. It is as if some haunting presence were removed from me. Perhaps ...

My surmise was not finished, could not be; for I caught sight in the mirror of the red mark upon my forehead; and I knew that I was still unclean.

Dr. Seward's Diary.

5 October.— We all rose early, and I think that sleep did much for each and all of us. When we met at early breakfast there was more general cheerfulness than any of us had ever expected to experience again.

It is really wonderful how much resilience there is in human nature. Let any obstructing cause, no matter what, be removed in any way— even by death— and we fly back to first principles of hope and enjoyment. More than once as we sat around the table, my eyes opened in wonder whether the whole of the past days had not been a dream. It was only when I caught sight of the red blotch on Mrs. Harker's forehead that I was brought back to reality. Even now, when I am gravely revolving the matter, it is almost impossible to realise that the cause of all our trouble is still existent. Even Mrs. Harker seems to lose sight of her trouble for whole spells; it is only now and again, when something recalls it to her mind, that she thinks of her terrible scar. We are to meet here in my study in half an hour and decide on our course of action. I see only one immediate difficulty, I know it by instinct rather than reason: we shall all have to speak frankly; and yet I fear that in some mysterious way poor Mrs. Harker's tongue is tied. I know that she forms conclusions of her own, and from all that has been I can guess how brilliant and how true they must be; but she will not, or cannot, give them utterance. I have mentioned this to Van Helsing, and he and I are to talk it over when we are alone. I suppose it is some of that horrid poison which has got into her veins beginning to work. The Count had his own purposes when he gave her what Van Helsing called "the Vampire's baptism of blood." Well, there may be a poison that distils itself out of good things; in an age when the existence of ptomaines is a mystery we should not wonder at anything! One thing I know: that if my instinct be true regarding poor Mrs. Harker's silences, then there is a terrible difficulty— an unknown danger— in the work before us. The same power that compels her silence may compel her speech. I dare not think further; for so I should in my thoughts dishonour a noble woman!

Van Helsing is coming to my study a little before the others. I shall try to open the subject with him.

Later.— When the Professor came in, we talked over the state of things. I could see that he had something on his mind which he wanted to say, but felt some hesitancy about broaching the subject. After beating about the bush a little, he said suddenly:—

"Friend John, there is something that you and I must talk of alone, just at the first at any rate. Later, we may have to take the others into our confidence"; then he stopped, so I waited; he went on:—

"Madam Mina, our poor, dear Madam Mina is changing." A cold shiver ran through me to find my worst fears thus endorsed. Van Helsing continued:—

"With the sad experience of Miss Lucy, we must this time be warned before things go too far. Our task is now in reality more difficult than ever, and this new trouble makes every hour of the direst importance. I can see the characteristics of the vampire coming in her face. It is now but very, very slight; but it is to be seen if we have eyes to notice without to prejudge. Her teeth are some sharper, and at times her eyes are more hard. But these are not all, there is to her the silence now often; as so it was with Miss Lucy. She did not speak, even when she wrote that which she wished to be known later. Now my fear is this. If it be that she can, by our hypnotic trance, tell what the Count see and hear, is it not more true that he who have hypnotise her first, and who have drink of her very blood and make her drink of his, should, if he will, compel her mind to disclose to him that which she know?" I nodded acquiescence; he went on:—

"Then, what we must do is to prevent this; we must keep her ignorant of our intent, and so she cannot tell what she know not. This is a painful task! Oh, so painful that it heart-break me to think of; but it must be. When to-day we meet, I must tell her that for reason which we will not to speak she must not more be of our council, but be simply guarded by us." He wiped his forehead, which had broken out in profuse perspiration at the thought of the pain which he might have to inflict upon the poor soul already so tortured. I knew that it would be some sort of comfort to him if I told him that I also had come to the same conclusion; for at any rate it would take away the pain of doubt. I told him, and the effect was as I expected.

It is now close to the time of our general gathering. Van Helsing has gone away to prepare for the meeting, and his painful part of it. I really believe his purpose is to be able to pray alone.

Later.— At the very outset of our meeting a great personal relief was experienced by both Van Helsing and myself. Mrs. Harker had sent a message by her husband to say that she would not join us at present, as she thought it better that we should be free to discuss our movements without her presence to embarrass us. The Professor and I looked at each other for an instant, and somehow we both seemed relieved. For my own part, I thought that if Mrs. Harker realised the danger herself, it was much pain as well as much danger averted. Under the circumstances we agreed, by a questioning look and answer, with finger on lip, to preserve silence in our suspicions, until we should have been able to confer alone again. We went at once into our Plan of Campaign. Van Helsing roughly put the facts before us first:—

"The Czarina Catherine left the Thames yesterday morning. It will take her at the quickest speed she has ever made at least three weeks to reach Varna; but we can travel overland to the same place in three days. Now, if we allow for two days less for the ship's voyage, owing to such weather influences as we know that the Count can bring to bear; and if we allow a whole day and night for any delays which may occur to us, then we have a margin of nearly two weeks. Thus, in order to be quite safe, we must leave here on 17th at latest. Then we shall at any rate be in Varna a day before the ship arrives, and able to make such preparations as may be necessary. Of course we shall all go armed— armed against evil things, spiritual as well as physical." Here Quincey Morris added:—

"I understand that the Count comes from a wolf country, and it may be that he shall get there before us. I propose that we add Winchesters to our armament. I have a kind of belief in a Winchester when there is any trouble of that sort around. Do you remember, Art, when we had the pack after us at Tobolsk? What wouldn't we have given then for a repeater apiece!"

"Good!" said Van Helsing, "Winchesters it shall be. Quincey's head is level at all times, but most so when there is to hunt, metaphor be more dishonour to science than wolves be of danger to man. In the meantime we can do nothing here; and as I think that Varna is not familiar to any of us, why not go there more soon? It is as long to wait here as there. To-night and to-morrow we can get ready, and then, if all be well, we four can set out on our journey."

"We four?" said Harker interrogatively, looking from one to another of us.

"Of course!" answered the Professor quickly, "you must remain to take care of your so sweet wife!" Harker was silent for awhile and then said in a hollow voice:—

"Let us talk of that part of it in the morning. I want to consult with Mina." I thought that now was the time for Van Helsing to warn him not to disclose our plans to her; but he took no notice. I looked at him significantly and coughed. For answer he put his finger on his lips and turned away.

Jonathan Harker's Journal.

5 October, afternoon.— For some time after our meeting this morning I could not think. The new phases of things leave my mind in a state of wonder which allows no room for active thought. Mina's determination not to take any part in the discussion set me thinking; and as I could not argue the matter with her, I could only guess. I am as far as ever from a solution now. The way the others received it, too, puzzled me; the last time we talked of the subject we agreed that there was to be no more concealment of anything amongst us. Mina is sleeping now, calmly and sweetly like a little child. Her lips are curved and her face beams with happiness. Thank God, there are such moments still for her.

Later.— How strange it all is. I sat watching Mina's happy sleep, and came as near to being happy myself as I suppose I shall ever be. As the evening drew on, and the earth took its shadows from the sun sinking lower, the silence of the room grew more and more solemn to me. All at once Mina opened her eyes, and looking at me tenderly, said:—

"Jonathan, I want you to promise me something on your word of honour. A promise made to me, but made holily in God's hearing, and not to be broken though I should go down on my knees and implore you with bitter tears. Quick, you must make it to me at once."

"Mina," I said, "a promise like that, I cannot make at once. I may have no right to make it."

"But, dear one," she said, with such spiritual intensity that her eyes were like pole stars, "it is I who wish it; and it is not for myself. You can ask Dr. Van Helsing if I am not right; if he disagrees you may do as you will. Nay, more, if you all agree, later, you are absolved from the promise."

"I promise!" I said, and for a moment she looked supremely happy; though to me all happiness for her was denied by the red scar on her forehead. She said:—

"Promise me that you will not tell me anything of the plans formed for the campaign against the Count. Not by word, or inference, or implication; not at any time whilst this remains to me!" and she solemnly pointed to the scar. I saw that she was in earnest, and said solemnly:—

"I promise!" and as I said it I felt that from that instant a door had been shut between us.

Later, midnight.— Mina has been bright and cheerful all the evening. So much so that all the rest seemed to take courage, as if infected somewhat with her gaiety; as a result even I myself felt as if the pall of gloom which weighs us down were somewhat lifted. We all retired early. Mina is now sleeping like a little child; it is a wonderful thing that her faculty of sleep remains to her in the midst of her terrible trouble. Thank God for it, for then at least she can forget her care. Perhaps her example may affect me as her gaiety did to-night. I shall try it. Oh! for a dreamless sleep.

6 October, morning.— Another surprise. Mina woke me early, about the same time as yesterday, and asked me to bring Dr. Van Helsing. I thought that it was another occasion for hypnotism, and without question went for the Professor. He had evidently expected some such call, for I found him dressed in his room. His door was ajar, so that he could hear the opening of the door of our room. He came at once; as he passed into the room, he asked Mina if the others might come, too.

"No," she said quite simply, "it will not be necessary. You can tell them just as well. I must go with you on your journey."

Dr. Van Helsing was as startled as I was. After a moment's pause he asked:—

"But why?"

"You must take me with you. I am safer with you, and you shall be safer, too."

"But why, dear Madam Mina? You know that your safety is our solemnest duty. We go into danger, to which you are, or may be, more liable than any of us from— from circumstances— things that have been." He paused, embarrassed.

As she replied, she raised her finger and pointed to her forehead:—

"I know. That is why I must go. I can tell you now, whilst the sun is coming up; I may not be able again. I know that when the Count wills me I must go. I know that if he tells me to come in secret, I must come by wile; by any device to hoodwink— even Jonathan." God saw the look that she turned on me as she spoke, and if there be indeed a Recording Angel that look is noted to her everlasting honour. I could only clasp her hand. I could not speak; my emotion was too great for even the relief of tears. She went on:—

"You men are brave and strong. You are strong in your numbers, for you can defy that which would break down the human endurance of one who had to guard alone. Besides, I may be of service, since you can hypnotise me and so learn that which even I myself do not know." Dr. Van Helsing said very gravely:—

"Madam Mina, you are, as always, most wise. You shall with us come; and together we shall do that which we go forth to achieve." When he had spoken, Mina's long spell of silence made me look at her. She had fallen back on her pillow asleep; she did not even wake when I had pulled up the blind and let in the sunlight which flooded the room. Van Helsing motioned to me to come with him quietly. We went to his room, and within a minute Lord Godalming, Dr. Seward, and Mr. Morris were with us also. He told them what Mina had said, and went on:—

"In the morning we shall leave for Varna. We have now to deal with a new factor: Madam Mina. Oh, but her soul is true. It is to her an agony to tell us so much as she has done; but it is most right, and we are warned in time. There must be no chance lost, and in Varna we must be ready to act the instant when that ship arrives."

"What shall we do exactly?" asked Mr. Morris laconically. The Professor paused before replying:—

"We shall at the first board that ship; then, when we have identified the box, we shall place a branch of the wild rose on it. This we shall fasten, for when it is there none can emerge; so at least says the superstition. And to superstition must we trust at the first; it was man's faith in the early, and it have its root in faith still. Then, when we get the opportunity that we seek, when none are near to see, we shall open the box, and— and all will be well."

"I shall not wait for any opportunity," said Morris. "When I see the box I shall open it and destroy the monster, though there were a thousand men looking on, and if I am to be wiped out for it the next moment!" I grasped his hand instinctively and found it as firm as a piece of steel. I think he understood my look; I hope he did.

"Good boy," said Dr. Van Helsing. "Brave boy. Quincey is all man. God bless him for it. My child, believe me none of us shall lag behind or pause from any fear. I do but say what we may do— what we must do. But, indeed, indeed we cannot say what we shall do. There are so many things which may happen, and their ways and their ends are so various that until the moment we may not say. We shall all be armed, in all ways; and when the time for the end has come, our effort shall not be lack. Now let us to-day put all our affairs in order. Let all things which touch on others dear to us, and who on us depend, be complete; for none of us can tell what, or when, or how, the end may be. As for me, my own affairs are regulate; and as I have nothing else to do, I shall go make arrangements for the travel. I shall have all tickets and so forth for our journey."

There was nothing further to be said, and we parted. I shall now settle up all my affairs of earth, and be ready for whatever may come....

Later.— It is all done; my will is made, and all complete. Mina if she survive is my sole heir. If it should not be so, then the others who have been so good to us shall have remainder.

It is now drawing towards the sunset; Mina's uneasiness calls my attention to it. I am sure that there is something on her mind which the time of exact sunset will reveal. These occasions are becoming harrowing times for us all, for each sunrise and sunset opens up some new danger— some new pain, which, however, may in God's will be means to a good end. I write all these things in the diary since my darling must not hear them now; but if it may be that she can see them again, they shall be ready.

She is calling to me.

## CHAPTER XXV
# DR. SEWARD'S DIARY

1 1 October, Evening.— Jonathan Harker has asked me to note this, as he says he is hardly equal to the task, and he wants an exact record kept.

I think that none of us were surprised when we were asked to see Mrs. Harker a little before the time of sunset. We have of late come to understand that sunrise and sunset are to her times of peculiar freedom; when her old self can be manifest without any controlling force subduing or restraining her, or inciting her to action. This mood or condition begins some half hour or more before actual sunrise or sunset, and lasts till either the sun is high, or whilst the clouds are still aglow with the rays streaming above the horizon. At first there is a sort of negative condition, as if some tie were loosened, and then the absolute freedom quickly follows; when, however, the freedom ceases the change-back or relapse comes quickly, preceded only by a spell of warning silence.

To-night, when we met, she was somewhat constrained, and bore all the signs of an internal struggle. I put it down myself to her making a violent effort at the earliest instant she could do so. A very few minutes, however, gave her complete control of herself; then, motioning her husband to sit beside her on the sofa where she was half reclining, she made the rest of us bring chairs up close. Taking her husband's hand in hers began:—

"We are all here together in freedom, for perhaps the last time! I know, dear; I know that you will always be with me to the end." This was to her husband whose hand had, as we could see, tightened upon hers. "In the morning we go out upon our task, and God alone knows what may be in store for any of us. You are going to be so good to me as to take me with you. I know that all that brave earnest men can do for a poor weak woman, whose soul perhaps is lost— no, no, not yet, but is at any rate at stake— you will do. But you must remember that I am not as you are. There is a poison in my blood, in my soul, which may destroy me; which must destroy me, unless some relief comes to us. Oh, my friends, you know as well as I do, that my soul is at stake; and though I know there is one way out for me, you must not and I must not take it!" She looked appealingly to us all in turn, beginning and ending with her husband.

"What is that way?" asked Van Helsing in a hoarse voice. "What is that way, which we must not— may not— take?"

"That I may die now, either by my own hand or that of another, before the greater evil is entirely wrought. I know, and you know, that were I once dead you could and would set free my immortal spirit, even as you did my poor Lucy's. Were death, or the fear of death, the only thing that stood in the way I would not shrink to die here, now, amidst the friends who love me. But death is not all. I cannot believe that to die in such a case, when there is hope before us and a bitter task to be done, is God's will. Therefore, I, on my part, give up here the certainty of eternal rest, and go out into the dark where may be the blackest things that the world or the nether world holds!" We were all silent, for we knew instinctively that this was only a prelude. The faces of the others were set and Harker's grew ashen grey; perhaps he guessed better than any of us what was coming. She continued:—

"This is what I can give into the hotch-pot." I could not but note the quaint legal phrase which she used in such a place, and with all seriousness. "What will each of you give? Your lives I know," she went on quickly, "that is easy for brave men. Your lives are God's, and you can give them back to Him; but what will you give to me?" She looked again questioningly, but this time avoided her husband's face. Quincey seemed to understand; he nodded, and her face lit up. "Then I shall tell you plainly what I want, for there must be no doubtful matter in this connection between us now. You must promise me, one and all— even you, my beloved husband— that, should the time come, you will kill me."

"What is that time?" The voice was Quincey's, but it was low and strained.

"When you shall be convinced that I am so changed that it is better that I die than I may live. When I am thus dead in the flesh, then you will, without a moment's delay, drive a stake through me and cut off my head; or do whatever else may be wanting to give me rest!"

Quincey was the first to rise after the pause. He knelt down before her and taking her hand in his said solemnly:—

"I'm only a rough fellow, who hasn't, perhaps, lived as a man should to win such a distinction, but I swear to you by all that I hold sacred and dear that, should the time ever come, I shall not flinch from the duty that you have set us. And I promise you, too, that I shall make all certain, for if I am only doubtful I shall take it that the time has come!"

"My true friend!" was all she could say amid her fast-falling tears, as, bending over, she kissed his hand.

"I swear the same, my dear Madam Mina!" said Van Helsing.

"And I!" said Lord Godalming, each of them in turn kneeling to her to take the oath. I followed, myself. Then her husband turned to her wan-eyed and with a greenish pallor which subdued the snowy whiteness of his hair, and asked:—

"And must I, too, make such a promise, oh, my wife?"

"You too, my dearest," she said, with infinite yearning of pity in her voice and eyes. "You must not shrink. You are nearest and dearest and all the world to me; our souls are knit into one, for all life and all time. Think, dear, that there have been times when brave men have killed their wives and their womenkind, to keep them from falling into the hands of the enemy. Their hands did not falter any the more because those that they loved implored them to slay them. It is men's duty towards those whom they love, in such times of sore trial! And oh, my dear, if it is to be that I must meet death at any hand, let it be at the hand of him that loves me best. Dr. Van Helsing, I have not forgotten your mercy in poor Lucy's case to him who loved"— she stopped with a flying blush, and changed her phrase— "to him who had best right to give her peace. If that time shall come again, I look to you to make it a happy memory of my husband's life that it was his loving hand which set me free from the awful thrall upon me."

"Again I swear!" came the Professor's resonant voice. Mrs. Harker smiled, positively smiled, as with a sigh of relief she leaned back and said:—

"And now one word of warning, a warning which you must never forget: this time, if it ever come, may come quickly and unexpectedly, and in such case you must lose no time in using your opportunity. At such a time I myself might be— nay! if the time ever comes, shall be— leagued with your enemy against you."

"One more request;" she became very solemn as she said this, "it is not vital and necessary like the other, but I want you to do one thing for me, if you will." We all acquiesced, but no one spoke; there was no need to speak:—

"I want you to read the Burial Service." She was interrupted by a deep groan from her husband; taking his hand in hers, she held it over her heart, and continued: "You must read it over me some day. Whatever may be the issue of all this fearful state of things, it will be a sweet thought to all or some of us. You, my dearest, will I hope read it, for then it will be in your voice in my memory for ever— come what may!"

"But oh, my dear one," he pleaded, "death is afar off from you."

"Nay," she said, holding up a warning hand. "I am deeper in death at this moment than if the weight of an earthly grave lay heavy upon me!"

"Oh, my wife, must I read it?" he said, before he began.

"It would comfort me, my husband!" was all she said; and he began to read when she had got the book ready.

"How can I— how could any one— tell of that strange scene, its solemnity, its gloom, its sadness, its horror; and, withal, its sweetness. Even a sceptic, who can see nothing but a travesty of bitter truth in anything holy or emotional, would have been melted to the heart had he seen that little group of loving and devoted friends kneeling round that stricken and sorrowing lady; or heard the tender passion of her husband's voice, as in tones so broken with emotion that often he had to pause, he read the simple and beautiful service from the Burial of the Dead. I— I cannot go on— words— and— v-voice— f-fail m-me!"

She was right in her instinct. Strange as it all was, bizarre as it may hereafter seem even to us who felt its potent influence at the time, it comforted us much; and the silence, which showed Mrs. Harker's coming relapse from her freedom of soul, did not seem so full of despair to any of us as we had dreaded.

Jonathan Harker's Journal.

15 October, Varna.— We left Charing Cross on the morning of the 12th, got to Paris the same night, and took the places secured for us in the Orient Express. We travelled night and day, arriving here at about five o'clock. Lord Godalming went to the Consulate to see if any telegram had arrived for him, whilst the rest of us came on to this hotel— "the Odessus." The journey may have had incidents; I was, however, too eager to get on, to care for them. Until the Czarina Catherine comes into port there will be no interest for me in anything in the wide world. Thank God! Mina is well, and looks to be getting stronger; her colour is coming back. She sleeps a great deal; throughout the journey she slept nearly all the time. Before sunrise and sunset, however, she is very wakeful and alert; and it has become a habit for Van Helsing to hypnotise her at such times. At first, some effort was needed, and he had to make many passes; but now, she seems to yield at once, as if by habit, and scarcely any action is needed. He seems to have power at these particular moments to simply will, and her thoughts obey him. He always asks her what she can see and hear. She answers to the first:—

"Nothing; all is dark." And to the second:—

"I can hear the waves lapping against the ship, and the water rushing by. Canvas and cordage strain and masts and yards creak. The wind is high— I can hear it in the shrouds, and the bow throws back the foam." It is evident that the Czarina Catherine is still at sea, hastening on her way to Varna. Lord Godalming has just returned. He had four telegrams, one each day since we started, and all to the same effect: that the Czarina Catherine had not been reported to Lloyd's from anywhere. He had arranged before leaving London that his agent should send him every day a telegram saying if the ship had been reported. He was to have a message even if she were not reported, so that he might be sure that there was a watch being kept at the other end of the wire.

We had dinner and went to bed early. To-morrow we are to see the Vice-Consul, and to arrange, if we can, about getting on board the ship as soon as she arrives. Van Helsing says that our chance will be to get on the boat between sunrise and sunset. The Count, even if he takes the form of a bat, cannot cross the running water of his own volition, and so cannot leave the ship. As he dare not change to man's form without suspicion— which he evidently wishes to avoid— he must remain in the box. If, then, we can come on board after sunrise, he is at our mercy; for we can open the box and make sure of him, as we did of poor Lucy, before he wakes. What mercy he shall get from us will not count for much. We think that we shall not have much trouble with officials or the seamen. Thank God! this is the country where bribery can do anything, and we are well supplied with money. We have only to make sure that the ship cannot come into port between sunset and sunrise without our being warned, and we shall be safe. Judge Moneybag will settle this case, I think!

16 October.— Mina's report still the same: lapping waves and rushing water, darkness and favouring winds. We are evidently in good time, and when we hear of the Czarina Catherine we shall be ready. As she must pass the Dardanelles we are sure to have some report.

. . . . . . . . . . . . . . . . . . . . . . . . . . . . . . . . .

17 October.— Everything is pretty well fixed now, I think, to welcome the Count on his return from his tour. Godalming told the shippers that he fancied that the box sent aboard might contain something stolen from a friend of his, and got a half consent that he might open it at his own risk. The owner gave him a paper telling the Captain to give him every facility in doing whatever he chose on board the ship, and also a similar authorisation to his agent at Varna. We have seen the agent, who was much impressed with Godalming's kindly manner to him, and we are all satisfied that whatever he can do to aid our wishes will be done. We have already arranged what to do in case we get the box open. If the Count is there, Van Helsing and Seward will cut off his head at once and drive a stake through his heart. Morris and Godalming and I shall prevent interference, even if we have to use the arms which we shall have ready. The Professor says that if we can so treat the Count's body, it will soon after fall into dust. In such case there would be no evidence against us, in case any suspicion of murder were aroused. But even if it were not, we should stand or fall by our act, and perhaps some day this very script may be evidence to come between some of us and a rope. For myself, I should take the chance only too thankfully if it were to come. We mean to leave no stone unturned to carry out our intent. We have arranged with certain officials that the instant the Czarina Catherine is seen, we are to be informed by a special messenger.

24 October.— A whole week of waiting. Daily telegrams to Godalming, but only the same story: "Not yet reported." Mina's morning and evening hypnotic answer is unvaried: lapping waves, rushing water, and creaking masts.
Telegram, October 24th.
Rufus Smith, Lloyd's, London, to Lord Godalming, care of H. B. M. Vice-Consul, Varna.
"Czarina Catherine reported this morning from Dardanelles."
Dr. Seward's Diary.

25 October.— How I miss my phonograph! To write diary with a pen is irksome to me; but Van Helsing says I must. We were all wild with excitement yesterday when Godalming got his telegram from Lloyd's. I know now what men feel in battle when the call to action is heard. Mrs. Harker, alone of our party, did not show any signs of emotion. After all, it is not strange that she did not; for we took special care not to let her know anything about it, and we all tried not to show any excitement when we were in her presence. In old days she would, I am sure, have noticed, no matter how we might have tried to conceal it; but in this way she is greatly changed during the past three weeks. The lethargy grows upon her, and though she seems strong and well, and is getting back some of her colour, Van Helsing and I are not satisfied. We talk of her often; we have not, however, said a word to the others. It would break poor Harker's heart— certainly his nerve— if he knew that we had even a suspicion on the subject. Van Helsing examines, he tells me, her teeth very carefully, whilst she is in the hypnotic condition, for he says that so long as they do not begin to sharpen there is no active danger of a change in her. If this change should come, it would be necessary to take steps!... We both know what those steps would have to be, though we do not mention our thoughts to each other. We should neither of us shrink from the task— awful though it be to contemplate. "Euthanasia" is an excellent and a comforting word! I am grateful to whoever invented it.

It is only about 24 hours' sail from the Dardanelles to here, at the rate the Czarina Catherine has come from London. She should therefore arrive some time in the morning; but as she cannot possibly get in before then, we are all about to retire early. We shall get up at one o'clock, so as to be ready.

25 October, Noon.— No news yet of the ship's arrival. Mrs. Harker's hypnotic report this morning was the same as usual, so it is possible that we may get news at any moment. We men are all in a fever of excitement, except Harker, who is calm; his hands are cold as ice, and an hour ago I found him whetting the edge of the great Ghoorka knife which he now always carries with him. It will be a bad lookout for the Count if the edge of that "Kukri" ever touches his throat, driven by that stern, ice-cold hand!

Van Helsing and I were a little alarmed about Mrs. Harker to-day. About noon she got into a sort of lethargy which we did not like; although we kept silence to the others, we were neither of us happy about it. She had been restless all the morning, so that we were at first glad to know that she was sleeping. When, however, her husband mentioned casually that she was sleeping so soundly that he could not wake her, we went to her room to see for ourselves. She was breathing naturally and looked so well and peaceful that we agreed that the sleep was better for her than anything else. Poor girl, she has so much to forget that it is no wonder that sleep, if it brings oblivion to her, does her good.

Later.— Our opinion was justified, for when after a refreshing sleep of some hours she woke up, she seemed brighter and better than she had been for days. At sunset she made the usual hypnotic report. Wherever he may be in the Black Sea, the Count is hurrying to his destination. To his doom, I trust!

26 October.— Another day and no tidings of the Czarina Catherine. She ought to be here by now. That she is still journeying somewhere is apparent, for Mrs. Harker's hypnotic report at sunrise was still the same. It is possible that the vessel may be lying by, at times, for fog; some of the steamers which came in last evening reported patches of fog both to north and south of the port. We must continue our watching, as the ship may now be signalled any moment.

27 October, Noon.— Most strange; no news yet of the ship we wait for. Mrs. Harker reported last night and this morning as usual: "lapping waves and rushing water," though she added that "the waves were very faint." The telegrams from London have been the same: "no further report." Van Helsing is terribly anxious, and told me just now that he fears the Count is escaping us. He added significantly:—
"I did not like that lethargy of Madam Mina's. Souls and memories can do strange things during trance." I was about to ask him more, but Harker just then came in, and he held up a warning hand. We must try to-night at sunset to make her speak more fully when in her hypnotic state.

28 October.— Telegram. Rufus Smith, London, to Lord Godalming, care H. B. M. Vice Consul, Varna.
"Czarina Catherine reported entering Galatz at one o'clock to-day."

Dr. Seward's Diary.

28 October.— When the telegram came announcing the arrival in Galatz I do not think it was such a shock to any of us as might have been expected. True, we did not know whence, or how, or when, the bolt would come; but I think we all expected that something strange would happen. The delay of arrival at Varna made us individually satisfied that things would not be just as we had expected; we only waited to learn where the change would occur. None the less, however, was it a surprise. I suppose that nature works on such a hopeful basis that we believe against ourselves that things will be as they ought to be, not as we should know that they will be. Transcendentalism is a beacon to the angels, even if it be a will-o'-the-wisp to man. It was an odd experience and we all took it differently. Van Helsing raised his hand over his head for a moment, as though in remonstrance with the Almighty; but he said not a word, and in a few seconds stood up with his face sternly set. Lord Godalming grew very pale, and sat breathing heavily. I was myself half stunned and looked in wonder at one after another. Quincey Morris tightened his belt with that quick movement which I knew so well; in our old wandering days it meant "action." Mrs. Harker grew ghastly white, so that the scar on her forehead seemed to burn, but she folded her hands meekly and looked up in prayer. Harker smiled— actually smiled— the dark, bitter smile of one who is without hope; but at the same time his action belied his words, for his hands instinctively sought the hilt of the great Kukri knife and rested there. "When does the next train start for Galatz?" said Van Helsing to us generally.

"At 6:30 to-morrow morning!" We all started, for the answer came from Mrs. Harker.

"How on earth do you know?" said Art.

"You forget— or perhaps you do not know, though Jonathan does and so does Dr. Van Helsing— that I am the train fiend. At home in Exeter I always used to make up the time-tables, so as to be helpful to my husband. I found it so useful sometimes, that I always make a study of the time-tables now. I knew that if anything were to take us to Castle Dracula we should go by Galatz, or at any rate through Bucharest, so I learned the times very carefully. Unhappily there are not many to learn, as the only train to-morrow leaves as I say."

"Wonderful woman!" murmured the Professor.

"Can't we get a special?" asked Lord Godalming. Van Helsing shook his head: "I fear not. This land is very different from yours or mine; even if we did have a special, it would probably not arrive as soon as our regular train. Moreover, we have something to prepare. We must think. Now let us organize. You, friend Arthur, go to the train and get the tickets and arrange that all be ready for us to go in the morning. Do you, friend Jonathan, go to the agent of the ship and get from him letters to the agent in Galatz, with authority to make search the ship just as it was here. Morris Quincey, you see the Vice-Consul, and get his aid with his fellow in Galatz and all he can do to make our way smooth, so that no times be lost when over the Danube. John will stay with Madam Mina and me, and we shall consult. For so if time be long you may be delayed; and it will not matter when the sun set, since I am here with Madam to make report."

"And I," said Mrs. Harker brightly, and more like her old self than she had been for many a long day, "shall try to be of use in all ways, and shall think and write for you as I used to do. Something is shifting from me in some strange way, and I feel freer than I have been of late!" The three younger men looked happier at the moment as they seemed to realise the significance of her words; but Van Helsing and I, turning to each other, met each a grave and troubled glance. We said nothing at the time, however.

When the three men had gone out to their tasks Van Helsing asked Mrs. Harker to look up the copy of the diaries and find him the part of Harker's journal at the Castle. She went away to get it; when the door was shut upon her he said to me:—

"We mean the same! speak out!"

"There is some change. It is a hope that makes me sick, for it may deceive us."

"Quite so. Do you know why I asked her to get the manuscript?"

"No!" said I, "unless it was to get an opportunity of seeing me alone."

"You are in part right, friend John, but only in part. I want to tell you something. And oh, my friend, I am taking a great— a terrible— risk; but I believe it is right. In the moment when Madam Mina said those words that arrest both our understanding, an inspiration came to me. In the trance of three days ago the Count sent her his spirit to read her mind; or more like he took her to see him in his earth-box in the ship with water rushing, just as it go free at rise and set of sun. He learn then that we are here; for she have more to tell in her open life with eyes to see and ears to hear than he, shut, as he is, in his coffin-box. Now he make his most effort to escape us. At present he want her not.

"He is sure with his so great knowledge that she will come at his call; but he cut her off— take her, as he can do, out of his own power, that so she come not to him. Ah! there I have hope that our man-brains that have been of man so long and that have not lost the grace of God, will come higher than his child-brain that lie in his tomb for centuries, that grow not yet to our stature, and that do only work selfish and therefore small. Here comes Madam Mina; not a word to her of her trance! She know it not; and it would overwhelm her and make despair just when we want all her hope, all her courage; when most we want all her great brain which is trained like man's brain, but is of sweet woman and have a special power which the Count give her, and which he may not take away altogether— though he think not so. Hush! let me speak, and you shall learn. Oh, John, my friend, we are in awful straits. I fear, as I never feared before. We can only trust the good God. Silence! here she comes!"

I thought that the Professor was going to break down and have hysterics, just as he had when Lucy died, but with a great effort he controlled himself and was at perfect nervous poise when Mrs. Harker tripped into the room, bright and happy-looking and, in the doing of work, seemingly forgetful of her misery. As she came in, she handed a number of sheets of typewriting to Van Helsing. He looked over them gravely, his face brightening up as he read. Then holding the pages between his finger and thumb he said:—

"Friend John, to you with so much of experience already— and you, too, dear Madam Mina, that are young— here is a lesson: do not fear ever to think. A half-thought has been buzzing often in my brain, but I fear to let him loose his wings. Here now, with more knowledge, I go back to where that half-thought come from and I find that he be no half-thought at all; that be a whole thought, though so young that he is not yet strong to use his little wings. Nay, like the "Ugly Duck" of my friend Hans Andersen, he be no duck-thought at all, but a big swan-thought that sail nobly on big wings, when the time come for him to try them. See I read here what Jonathan have written:—

"That other of his race who, in a later age, again and again, brought his forces over The Great River into Turkey Land; who, when he was beaten back, came again, and again, and again, though he had to come alone from the bloody field where his troops were being slaughtered, since he knew that he alone could ultimately triumph."

"What does this tell us? Not much? no! The Count's child-thought see nothing; therefore he speak so free. Your man-thought see nothing; my man-thought see nothing, till just now. No! But there comes another word from some one who speak without thought because she, too, know not what it mean— what it might mean. Just as there are elements which rest, yet when in nature's course they move on their way and they touch— then pouf! and there comes a flash of light, heaven wide, that blind and kill and destroy some; but that show up all earth below for leagues and leagues. Is it not so? Well, I shall explain. To begin, have you ever study the philosophy of crime? 'Yes' and 'No.' You, John, yes; for it is a study of insanity. You, no, Madam Mina; for crime touch you not— not but once. Still, your mind works true, and argues not a particulari ad universale. There is this peculiarity in criminals. It is so constant, in all countries and at all times, that even police, who know not much from philosophy, come to know it empirically, that it is. That is to be empiric. The criminal always work at one crime— that is the true criminal who seems predestinate to crime, and who will of none other. This criminal has not full man-brain. He is clever and cunning and resourceful; but he be not of man-stature as to brain. He be of child-brain in much. Now this criminal of ours is predestinate to crime also; he, too, have child-brain, and it is of the child to do what he have done. The little bird, the little fish, the little animal learn not by principle, but empirically; and when he learn to do, then there is to him the ground to start from to do more. 'Dos pou sto,' said Archimedes. 'Give me a fulcrum, and I shall move the world!' To do once, is the fulcrum whereby child-brain become man-brain; and until he have the purpose to do more, he continue to do the same again every time, just as he have done before! Oh, my dear, I see that your eyes are opened, and that to you the lightning flash show all the leagues," for Mrs. Harker began to clap her hands and her eyes sparkled. He went on:—

"Now you shall speak. Tell us two dry men of science what you see with those so bright eyes." He took her hand and held it whilst she spoke. His finger and thumb closed on her pulse, as I thought instinctively and unconsciously, as she spoke:—

"The Count is a criminal and of criminal type. Nordau and Lombroso would so classify him, and quâ criminal he is of imperfectly formed mind. Thus, in a difficulty he has to seek resource in habit. His past is a clue, and the one page of it that we know— and that from his own lips— tells that once before, when in what Mr. Morris would call a 'tight place,' he went back to his own country from the land he had tried to invade, and thence, without losing purpose, prepared himself for a new effort. He came again better equipped for his work; and won. So he came to London to invade a new land. He was beaten, and when all hope of success was lost, and his existence in danger, he fled back over the sea to his home; just as formerly he had fled back over the Danube from Turkey Land."

"Good, good! oh, you so clever lady!" said Van Helsing, enthusiastically, as he stooped and kissed her hand. A moment later he said to me, as calmly as though we had been having a sick-room consultation:—

"Seventy-two only; and in all this excitement. I have hope." Turning to her again, he said with keen expectation:—

"But go on. Go on! there is more to tell if you will. Be not afraid; John and I know. I do in any case, and shall tell you if you are right. Speak, without fear!"

"I will try to; but you will forgive me if I seem egotistical."

"Nay! fear not, you must be egotist, for it is of you that we think."

"Then, as he is criminal he is selfish; and as his intellect is small and his action is based on selfishness, he confines himself to one purpose. That purpose is remorseless. As he fled back over the Danube, leaving his forces to be cut to pieces, so now he is intent on being safe, careless of all. So his own selfishness frees my soul somewhat from the terrible power which he acquired over me on that dreadful night. I felt it! Oh, I felt it! Thank God, for His great mercy! My soul is freer than it has been since that awful hour; and all that haunts me is a fear lest in some trance or dream he may have used my knowledge for his ends." The Professor stood up:—

"He has so used your mind; and by it he has left us here in Varna, whilst the ship that carried him rushed through enveloping fog up to Galatz, where, doubtless, he had made preparation for escaping from us. But his child-mind only saw so far; and it may be that, as ever is in God's Providence, the very thing that the evil-doer most reckoned on for his selfish good, turns out to be his chiefest harm. The hunter is taken in his own snare, as the great Psalmist says. For now that he think he is free from every trace of us all, and that he has escaped us with so many hours to him, then his selfish child-brain will whisper him to sleep. He think, too, that as he cut himself off from knowing your mind, there can be no knowledge of him to you; there is where he fail! That terrible baptism of blood which he give you makes you free to go to him in spirit, as you have as yet done in your times of freedom, when the sun rise and set. At such times you go by my volition and not by his; and this power to good of you and others, as you have won from your suffering at his hands. This is now all the more precious that he know it not, and to guard himself have even cut himself off from his knowledge of our where. We, however, are not selfish, and we believe that God is with us through all this blackness, and these many dark hours. We shall follow him; and we shall not flinch; even if we peril ourselves that we become like him. Friend John, this has been a great hour; and it have done much to advance us on our way. You must be scribe and write him all down, so that when the others return from their work you can give it to them; then they shall know as we do."

And so I have written it whilst we wait their return, and Mrs. Harker has written with her typewriter all since she brought the MS. to us.

## CHAPTER XXVI
# DR. SEWARD'S DIARY

2

9 October.— This is written in the train from Varna to Galatz. Last night we all assembled a little before the time of sunset. Each of us had done his work as well as he could; so far as thought, and endeavour, and opportunity go, we are prepared for the whole of our journey, and for our work when we get to Galatz. When the usual time came round Mrs. Harker prepared herself for her hypnotic effort; and after a longer and more serious effort on the part of Van Helsing than has been usually necessary, she sank into the trance. Usually she speaks on a hint; but this time the Professor had to ask her questions, and to ask them pretty resolutely, before we could learn anything; at last her answer came:—

"I can see nothing; we are still; there are no waves lapping, but only a steady swirl of water softly running against the hawser. I can hear men's voices calling, near and far, and the roll and creak of oars in the rowlocks. A gun is fired somewhere; the echo of it seems far away. There is tramping of feet overhead, and ropes and chains are dragged along. What is this? There is a gleam of light; I can feel the air blowing upon me."

Here she stopped. She had risen, as if impulsively, from where she lay on the sofa, and raised both her hands, palms upwards, as if lifting a weight. Van Helsing and I looked at each other with understanding. Quincey raised his eyebrows slightly and looked at her intently, whilst Harker's hand instinctively closed round the hilt of his Kukri. There was a long pause. We all knew that the time when she could speak was passing; but we felt that it was useless to say anything. Suddenly she sat up, and, as she opened her eyes, said sweetly:—

"Would none of you like a cup of tea? You must all be so tired!" We could only make her happy, and so acquiesced. She bustled off to get tea; when she had gone Van Helsing said:—

"You see, my friends. He is close to land: he has left his earth-chest. But he has yet to get on shore. In the night he may lie hidden somewhere; but if he be not carried on shore, or if the ship do not touch it, he cannot achieve the land. In such case he can, if it be in the night, change his form and can jump or fly on shore, as he did at Whitby. But if the day come before he get on shore, then, unless he be carried he cannot escape. And if he be carried, then the customs men may discover what the box contain. Thus, in fine, if he escape not on shore to-night, or before dawn, there will be the whole day lost to him. We may then arrive in time; for if he escape not at night we shall come on him in daytime, boxed up and at our mercy; for he dare not be his true self, awake and visible, lest he be discovered."

There was no more to be said, so we waited in patience until the dawn; at which time we might learn more from Mrs. Harker.

Early this morning we listened, with breathless anxiety, for her response in her trance. The hypnotic stage was even longer in coming than before; and when it came the time remaining until full sunrise was so short that we began to despair. Van Helsing seemed to throw his whole soul into the effort; at last, in obedience to his will she made reply:—

"All is dark. I hear lapping water, level with me, and some creaking as of wood on wood." She paused, and the red sun shot up. We must wait till to-night.

And so it is that we are travelling towards Galatz in an agony of expectation. We are due to arrive between two and three in the morning; but already, at Bucharest, we are three hours late, so we cannot possibly get in till well after sun-up. Thus we shall have two more hypnotic messages from Mrs. Harker; either or both may possibly throw more light on what is happening.

Later.— Sunset has come and gone. Fortunately it came at a time when there was no distraction; for had it occurred whilst we were at a station, we might not have secured the necessary calm and isolation. Mrs. Harker yielded to the hypnotic influence even less readily than this morning. I am in fear that her power of reading the Count's sensations may die away, just when we want it most. It seems to me that her imagination is beginning to work. Whilst she has been in the trance hitherto she has confined herself to the simplest of facts. If this goes on it may ultimately mislead us. If I thought that the Count's power over her would die away equally with her power of knowledge it would be a happy thought; but I am afraid that it may not be so. When she did speak, her words were enigmatical:—

"Something is going out; I can feel it pass me like a cold wind. I can hear, far off, confused sounds— as of men talking in strange tongues, fierce-falling water, and the howling of wolves." She stopped and a shudder ran through her, increasing in intensity for a few seconds, till, at the end, she shook as though in a palsy. She said no more, even in answer to the Professor's imperative questioning. When she woke from the trance, she was cold, and exhausted, and languid; but her mind was all alert. She could not remember anything, but asked what she had said; when she was told, she pondered over it deeply for a long time and in silence.

30 October, 7 a. m.— We are near Galatz now, and I may not have time to write later. Sunrise this morning was anxiously looked for by us all. Knowing of the increasing difficulty of procuring the hypnotic trance, Van Helsing began his passes earlier than usual. They produced no effect, however, until the regular time, when she yielded with a still greater difficulty, only a minute before the sun rose. The Professor lost no time in his questioning; her answer came with equal quickness:—

"All is dark. I hear water swirling by, level with my ears, and the creaking of wood on wood. Cattle low far off. There is another sound, a queer one like— — " She stopped and grew white, and whiter still.

"Go on; go on! Speak, I command you!" said Van Helsing in an agonised voice. At the same time there was despair in his eyes, for the risen sun was reddening even Mrs. Harker's pale face. She opened her eyes, and we all started as she said, sweetly and seemingly with the utmost unconcern:—

"Oh, Professor, why ask me to do what you know I can't? I don't remember anything." Then, seeing the look of amazement on our faces, she said, turning from one to the other with a troubled look:—

"What have I said? What have I done? I know nothing, only that I was lying here, half asleep, and heard you say go on! speak, I command you!' It seemed so funny to hear you order me about, as if I were a bad child!"

"Oh, Madam Mina," he said, sadly, "it is proof, if proof be needed, of how I love and honour you, when a word for your good, spoken more earnest than ever, can seem so strange because it is to order her whom I am proud to obey!"

The whistles are sounding; we are nearing Galatz. We are on fire with anxiety and eagerness.

Mina Harker's Journal.

30 October.— Mr. Morris took me to the hotel where our rooms had been ordered by telegraph, he being the one who could best be spared, since he does not speak any foreign language. The forces were distributed much as they had been at Varna, except that Lord Godalming went to the Vice-Consul, as his rank might serve as an immediate guarantee of some sort to the official, we being in extreme hurry. Jonathan and the two doctors went to the shipping agent to learn particulars of the arrival of the Czarina Catherine.

Later.— Lord Godalming has returned. The Consul is away, and the Vice-Consul sick; so the routine work has been attended to by a clerk. He was very obliging, and offered to do anything in his power.

Jonathan Harker's Journal.

30 October.— At nine o'clock Dr. Van Helsing, Dr. Seward, and I called on Messrs. Mackenzie & Steinkoff, the agents of the London firm of Hapgood. They had received a wire from London, in answer to Lord Godalming's telegraphed request, asking us to show them any civility in their power. They were more than kind and courteous, and took us at once on board the Czarina Catherine, which lay at anchor out in the river harbour. There we saw the Captain, Donelson by name, who told us of his voyage. He said that in all his life he had never had so favourable a run.

"Man!" he said, "but it made us afeard, for we expeckit that we should have to pay for it wi' some rare piece o' ill luck, so as to keep up the average. It's no canny to run frae London to the Black Sea wi' a wind ahint ye, as though the Deil himself were blawin' on yer sail for his ain purpose. An' a' the time we could no speer a thing. Gin we were nigh a ship, or a port, or a headland, a fog fell on us and travelled wi' us, till when after it had lifted and we looked out, the deil a thing could we see. We ran by Gibraltar wi'oot bein' able to signal; an' till we came to the Dardanelles and had to wait to get our permit to pass, we never were within hail o' aught. At first I inclined to slack off sail and beat about till the fog was lifted; but whiles, I thocht that if the Deil was minded to get us into the Black Sea quick, he was like to do it whether we would or no. If we had a quick voyage it would be no to our miscredit wi' the owners, or no hurt to our traffic; an' the Old Mon who had served his ain purpose wad be decently grateful to us for no hinderin' him." This mixture of simplicity and cunning, of superstition and commercial reasoning, aroused Van Helsing, who said:—

"Mine friend, that Devil is more clever than he is thought by some; and he know when he meet his match!" The skipper was not displeased with the compliment, and went on:—

"When we got past the Bosphorus the men began to grumble; some o' them, the Roumanians, came and asked me to heave overboard a big box which had been put on board by a queer lookin' old man just before we had started frae London. I had seen them speer at the fellow, and put out their twa fingers when they saw him, to guard against the evil eye. Man! but the supersteetion of foreigners is pairfectly rideeculous! I sent them aboot their business pretty quick; but as just after a fog closed in on us I felt a wee bit as they did anent something, though I wouldn't say it was agin the big box. Well, on we went, and as the fog didn't let up for five days I joost let the wind carry us; for if the Deil wanted to get somewheres— well, he would fetch it up a'reet. An' if he didn't, well, we'd keep a sharp lookout anyhow. Sure eneuch, we had a fair way and deep water all the time; and two days ago, when the mornin' sun came through the fog, we found ourselves just in the river opposite Galatz. The Roumanians were wild, and wanted me right or wrong to take out the box and fling it in the river. I had to argy wi' them aboot it wi' a handspike; an' when the last o' them rose off the deck wi' his head in his hand, I had convinced them that, evil eye or no evil eye, the property and the trust of my owners were better in my hands than in the river Danube. They had, mind ye, taken the box on the deck ready to fling in, and as it was marked Galatz via Varna, I thocht I'd let it lie till we discharged in the port an' get rid o't althegither. We didn't do much clearin' that day, an' had to remain the nicht at anchor; but in the mornin', braw an' airly, an hour before sun-up, a man came aboard wi' an order, written to him from England, to receive a box marked for one Count Dracula. Sure eneuch the matter was one ready to his hand. He had his papers a' reet, an' glad I was to be rid o' the dam' thing, for I was beginnin' masel' to feel uneasy at it. If the Deil did have any luggage aboord the ship, I'm thinkin' it was nane ither than that same!"

"What was the name of the man who took it?" asked Dr. Van Helsing with restrained eagerness.

"I'll be tellin' ye quick!" he answered, and, stepping down to his cabin, produced a receipt signed "Immanuel Hildesheim." Burgen-strasse 16 was the address. We found out that this was all the Captain knew; so with thanks we came away.

We found Hildesheim in his office, a Hebrew of rather the Adelphi Theatre type, with a nose like a sheep, and a fez. His arguments were pointed with specie— we doing the punctuation— and with a little bargaining he told us what he knew. This turned out to be simple but important. He had received a letter from Mr. de Ville of London, telling him to receive, if possible before sunrise so as to avoid customs, a box which would arrive at Galatz in the Czarina Catherine. This he was to give in charge to a certain Petrof Skinsky, who dealt with the Slovaks who traded down the river to the port. He had been paid for his work by an English bank note, which had been duly cashed for gold at the Danube International Bank. When Skinsky had come to him, he had taken him to the ship and handed over the box, so as to save porterage. That was all he knew.

We then sought for Skinsky, but were unable to find him. One of his neighbours, who did not seem to bear him any affection, said that he had gone away two days before, no one knew whither. This was corroborated by his landlord, who had received by messenger the key of the house together with the rent due, in English money. This had been between ten and eleven o'clock last night. We were at a standstill again.

Whilst we were talking one came running and breathlessly gasped out that the body of Skinsky had been found inside the wall of the churchyard of St. Peter, and that the throat had been torn open as if by some wild animal. Those we had been speaking with ran off to see the horror, the women crying out "This is the work of a Slovak!" We hurried away lest we should have been in some way drawn into the affair, and so detained.

As we came home we could arrive at no definite conclusion. We were all convinced that the box was on its way, by water, to somewhere; but where that might be we would have to discover. With heavy hearts we came home to the hotel to Mina.

When we met together, the first thing was to consult as to taking Mina again into our confidence. Things are getting desperate, and it is at least a chance, though a hazardous one. As a preliminary step, I was released from my promise to her.

Mina Harker's Journal.

30 October, evening.— They were so tired and worn out and dispirited that there was nothing to be done till they had some rest; so I asked them all to lie down for half an hour whilst I should enter everything up to the moment. I feel so grateful to the man who invented the "Traveller's" typewriter, and to Mr. Morris for getting this one for me. I should have felt quite astray doing the work if I had to write with a pen....

It is all done; poor dear, dear Jonathan, what he must have suffered, what must he be suffering now. He lies on the sofa hardly seeming to breathe, and his whole body appears in collapse. His brows are knit; his face is drawn with pain. Poor fellow, maybe he is thinking, and I can see his face all wrinkled up with the concentration of his thoughts. Oh! if I could only help at all.... I shall do what I can.

I have asked Dr. Van Helsing, and he has got me all the papers that I have not yet seen.... Whilst they are resting, I shall go over all carefully, and perhaps I may arrive at some conclusion. I shall try to follow the Professor's example, and think without prejudice on the facts before me....

I do believe that under God's providence I have made a discovery. I shall get the maps and look over them....

I am more than ever sure that I am right. My new conclusion is ready, so I shall get our party together and read it. They can judge it; it is well to be accurate, and every minute is precious.

Mina Harker's Memorandum.

(Entered in her Journal.)

Ground of inquiry.— Count Dracula's problem is to get back to his own place.

(a) He must be brought back by some one. This is evident; for had he power to move himself as he wished he could go either as man, or wolf, or bat, or in some other way. He evidently fears discovery or interference, in the state of helplessness in which he must be— confined as he is between dawn and sunset in his wooden box.

(b) How is he to be taken?— Here a process of exclusions may help us. By road, by rail, by water?

1. By Road.— There are endless difficulties, especially in leaving the city.

(x) There are people; and people are curious, and investigate. A hint, a surmise, a doubt as to what might be in the box, would destroy him.

(y) There are, or there may be, customs and octroi officers to pass.

(z) His pursuers might follow. This is his highest fear; and in order to prevent his being betrayed he has repelled, so far as he can, even his victim— me!

2. By Rail.— There is no one in charge of the box. It would have to take its chance of being delayed; and delay would be fatal, with enemies on the track. True, he might escape at night; but what would he be, if left in a strange place with no refuge that he could fly to? This is not what he intends; and he does not mean to risk it.

3. By Water.— Here is the safest way, in one respect, but with most danger in another. On the water he is powerless except at night; even then he can only summon fog and storm and snow and his wolves. But were he wrecked, the living water would engulf him, helpless; and he would indeed be lost. He could have the vessel drive to land; but if it were unfriendly land, wherein he was not free to move, his position would still be desperate.

We know from the record that he was on the water; so what we have to do is to ascertain what water.

The first thing is to realise exactly what he has done as yet; we may, then, get a light on what his later task is to be.

Firstly.— We must differentiate between what he did in London as part of his general plan of action, when he was pressed for moments and had to arrange as best he could.

Secondly we must see, as well as we can surmise it from the facts we know of, what he has done here.

As to the first, he evidently intended to arrive at Galatz, and sent invoice to Varna to deceive us lest we should ascertain his means of exit from England; his immediate and sole purpose then was to escape. The proof of this, is the letter of instructions sent to Immanuel Hildesheim to clear and take away the box before sunrise. There is also the instruction to Petrof Skinsky. These we must only guess at; but there must have been some letter or message, since Skinsky came to Hildesheim.

That, so far, his plans were successful we know. The Czarina Catherine made a phenomenally quick journey— so much so that Captain Donelson's suspicions were aroused; but his superstition united with his canniness played the Count's game for him, and he ran with his favouring wind through fogs and all till he brought up blindfold at Galatz. That the Count's arrangements were well made, has been proved. Hildesheim cleared the box, took it off, and gave it to Skinsky. Skinsky took it— and here we lose the trail. We only know that the box is somewhere on the water, moving along. The customs and the octroi, if there be any, have been avoided.

Now we come to what the Count must have done after his arrival— on land, at Galatz.

The box was given to Skinsky before sunrise. At sunrise the Count could appear in his own form. Here, we ask why Skinsky was chosen at all to aid in the work? In my husband's diary, Skinsky is mentioned as dealing with the Slovaks who trade down the river to the port; and the man's remark, that the murder was the work of a Slovak, showed the general feeling against his class. The Count wanted isolation.

My surmise is, this: that in London the Count decided to get back to his castle by water, as the most safe and secret way. He was brought from the castle by Szgany, and probably they delivered their cargo to Slovaks who took the boxes to Varna, for there they were shipped for London. Thus the Count had knowledge of the persons who could arrange this service. When the box was on land, before sunrise or after sunset, he came out from his box, met Skinsky and instructed him what to do as to arranging the carriage of the box up some river. When this was done, and he knew that all was in train, he blotted out his traces, as he thought, by murdering his agent.

I have examined the map and find that the river most suitable for the Slovaks to have ascended is either the Pruth or the Sereth. I read in the typescript that in my trance I heard cows low and water swirling level with my ears and the creaking of wood. The Count in his box, then, was on a river in an open boat— propelled probably either by oars or poles, for the banks are near and it is working against stream. There would be no such sound if floating down stream.

Of course it may not be either the Sereth or the Pruth, but we may possibly investigate further. Now of these two, the Pruth is the more easily navigated, but the Sereth is, at Fundu, joined by the Bistritza which runs up round the Borgo Pass. The loop it makes is manifestly as close to Dracula's castle as can be got by water.

Mina Harker's Journal— continued.

When I had done reading, Jonathan took me in his arms and kissed me. The others kept shaking me by both hands, and Dr. Van Helsing said:—

"Our dear Madam Mina is once more our teacher. Her eyes have been where we were blinded. Now we are on the track once again, and this time we may succeed. Our enemy is at his most helpless; and if we can come on him by day, on the water, our task will be over. He has a start, but he is powerless to hasten, as he may not leave his box lest those who carry him may suspect; for them to suspect would be to prompt them to throw him in the stream where he perish. This he knows, and will not. Now men, to our Council of War; for, here and now, we must plan what each and all shall do."

"I shall get a steam launch and follow him," said Lord Godalming.

"And I, horses to follow on the bank lest by chance he land," said Mr. Morris.

"Good!" said the Professor, "both good. But neither must go alone. There must be force to overcome force if need be; the Slovak is strong and rough, and he carries rude arms." All the men smiled, for amongst them they carried a small arsenal. Said Mr. Morris:—

"I have brought some Winchesters; they are pretty handy in a crowd, and there may be wolves. The Count, if you remember, took some other precautions; he made some requisitions on others that Mrs. Harker could not quite hear or understand. We must be ready at all points." Dr. Seward said:—

"I think I had better go with Quincey. We have been accustomed to hunt together, and we two, well armed, will be a match for whatever may come along. You must not be alone, Art. It may be necessary to fight the Slovaks, and a chance thrust— for I don't suppose these fellows carry guns— would undo all our plans. There must be no chances, this time; we shall not rest until the Count's head and body have been separated, and we are sure that he cannot re-incarnate." He looked at Jonathan as he spoke, and Jonathan looked at me. I could see that the poor dear was torn about in his mind. Of course he wanted to be with me; but then the boat service would, most likely, be the one which would destroy the … the … the … Vampire. (Why did I hesitate to write the word?) He was silent awhile, and during his silence Dr. Van Helsing spoke:—

"Friend Jonathan, this is to you for twice reasons. First, because you are young and brave and can fight, and all energies may be needed at the last; and again that it is your right to destroy him— that— which has wrought such woe to you and yours. Be not afraid for Madam Mina; she will be my care, if I may. I am old. My legs are not so quick to run as once; and I am not used to ride so long or to pursue as need be, or to fight with lethal weapons. But I can be of other service; I can fight in other way. And I can die, if need be, as well as younger men. Now let me say that what I would is this: while you, my Lord Godalming and friend Jonathan go in your so swift little steamboat up the river, and whilst John and Quincey guard the bank where perchance he might be landed, I will take Madam Mina right into the heart of the enemy's country. Whilst the old fox is tied in his box, floating on the running stream whence he cannot escape to land— where he dares not raise the lid of his coffin-box lest his Slovak carriers should in fear leave him to perish— we shall go in the track where Jonathan went,— from Bistritz over the Borgo, and find our way to the Castle of Dracula. Here, Madam Mina's hypnotic power will surely help, and we shall find our way— all dark and unknown otherwise— after the first sunrise when we are near that fateful place. There is much to be done, and other places to be made sanctify, so that that nest of vipers be obliterated." Here Jonathan interrupted him hotly:—

"Do you mean to say, Professor Van Helsing, that you would bring Mina, in her sad case and tainted as she is with that devil's illness, right into the jaws of his death-trap? Not for the world! Not for Heaven or Hell!" He became almost speechless for a minute, and then went on:—

"Do you know what the place is? Have you seen that awful den of hellish infamy— with the very moonlight alive with grisly shapes, and every speck of dust that whirls in the wind a devouring monster in embryo? Have you felt the Vampire's lips upon your throat?" Here he turned to me, and as his eyes lit on my forehead he threw up his arms with a cry: "Oh, my God, what have we done to have this terror upon us!" and he sank down on the sofa in a collapse of misery. The Professor's voice, as he spoke in clear, sweet tones, which seemed to vibrate in the air, calmed us all:—

"Oh, my friend, it is because I would save Madam Mina from that awful place that I would go. God forbid that I should take her into that place. There is work— wild work— to be done there, that her eyes may not see. We men here, all save Jonathan, have seen with their own eyes what is to be done before that place can be purify. Remember that we are in terrible straits. If the Count escape us this time— and he is strong and subtle and cunning— he may choose to sleep him for a century, and then in time our dear one"— he took my hand— "would come to him to keep him company, and would be as those others that you, Jonathan, saw. You have told us of their gloating lips; you heard their ribald laugh as they clutched the moving bag that the Count threw to them. You shudder; and well may it be. Forgive me that I make you so much pain, but it is necessary. My friend, is it not a dire need for the which I am giving, possibly my life? If it were that any one went into that place to stay, it is I who would have to go to keep them company." "Do as you will," said Jonathan, with a sob that shook him all over, "we are in the hands of God!"

Later.— Oh, it did me good to see the way that these brave men worked. How can women help loving men when they are so earnest, and so true, and so brave! And, too, it made me think of the wonderful power of money! What can it not do when it is properly applied; and what might it do when basely used. I felt so thankful that Lord Godalming is rich, and that both he and Mr. Morris, who also has plenty of money, are willing to spend it so freely. For if they did not, our little expedition could not start, either so promptly or so well equipped, as it will within another hour. It is not three hours since it was arranged what part each of us was to do; and now Lord Godalming and Jonathan have a lovely steam launch, with steam up ready to start at a moment's notice. Dr. Seward and Mr. Morris have half a dozen good horses, well appointed. We have all the maps and appliances of various kinds that can be had. Professor Van Helsing and I are to leave by the 11:40 train to-night for Veresti, where we are to get a carriage to drive to the Borgo Pass. We are bringing a good deal of ready money, as we are to buy a carriage and horses. We shall drive ourselves, for we have no one whom we can trust in the matter. The Professor knows something of a great many languages, so we shall get on all right. We have all got arms, even for me a large-bore revolver; Jonathan would not be happy unless I was armed like the rest. Alas! I cannot carry one arm that the rest do; the scar on my forehead forbids that. Dear Dr. Van Helsing comforts me by telling me that I am fully armed as there may be wolves; the weather is getting colder every hour, and there are snow-flurries which come and go as warnings.

Later.— It took all my courage to say good-bye to my darling. We may never meet again. Courage, Mina! the Professor is looking at you keenly; his look is a warning. There must be no tears now— unless it may be that God will let them fall in gladness.
Jonathan Harker's Journal.

October 30. Night.— I am writing this in the light from the furnace door of the steam launch: Lord Godalming is firing up. He is an experienced hand at the work, as he has had for years a launch of his own on the Thames, and another on the Norfolk Broads. Regarding our plans, we finally decided that Mina's guess was correct, and that if any waterway was chosen for the Count's escape back to his Castle, the Sereth and then the Bistritza at its junction, would be the one. We took it, that somewhere about the 47th degree, north latitude, would be the place chosen for the crossing the country between the river and the Carpathians. We have no fear in running at good speed up the river at night; there is plenty of water, and the banks are wide enough apart to make steaming, even in the dark, easy enough. Lord Godalming tells me to sleep for a while, as it is enough for the present for one to be on watch. But I cannot sleep— how can I with the terrible danger hanging over my darling, and her going out into that awful place.... My only comfort is that we are in the hands of God. Only for that faith it would be easier to die than to live, and so be quit of all the trouble. Mr. Morris and Dr. Seward were off on their long ride before we started; they are to keep up the right bank, far enough off to get on higher lands where they can see a good stretch of river and avoid the following of its curves. They have, for the first stages, two men to ride and lead their spare horses— four in all, so as not to excite curiosity. When they dismiss the men, which shall be shortly, they shall themselves look after the horses. It may be necessary for us to join forces; if so they can mount our whole party. One of the saddles has a movable horn, and can be easily adapted for Mina, if required.

It is a wild adventure we are on. Here, as we are rushing along through the darkness, with the cold from the river seeming to rise up and strike us; with all the mysterious voices of the night around us, it all comes home. We seem to be drifting into unknown places and unknown ways; into a whole world of dark and dreadful things. Godalming is shutting the furnace door....

31 October.— Still hurrying along. The day has come, and Godalming is sleeping. I am on watch. The morning is bitterly cold; the furnace heat is grateful, though we have heavy fur coats. As yet we have passed only a few open boats, but none of them had on board any box or package of anything like the size of the one we seek. The men were scared every time we turned our electric lamp on them, and fell on their knees and prayed.

1 November, evening.— No news all day; we have found nothing of the kind we seek. We have now passed into the Bistritza; and if we are wrong in our surmise our chance is gone. We have over-hauled every boat, big and little. Early this morning, one crew took us for a Government boat, and treated us accordingly. We saw in this a way of smoothing matters, so at Fundu, where the Bistritza runs into the Sereth, we got a Roumanian flag which we now fly conspicuously. With every boat which we have over-hauled since then this trick has succeeded; we have had every deference shown to us, and not once any objection to whatever we chose to ask or do. Some of the Slovaks tell us that a big boat passed them, going at more than usual speed as she had a double crew on board. This was before they came to Fundu, so they could not tell us whether the boat turned into the Bistritza or continued on up the Sereth. At Fundu we could not hear of any such boat, so she must have passed there in the night. I am feeling very sleepy; the cold is perhaps beginning to tell upon me, and nature must have rest some time. Godalming insists that he shall keep the first watch. God bless him for all his goodness to poor dear Mina and me.

2 November, morning.— It is broad daylight. That good fellow would not wake me. He says it would have been a sin to, for I slept peacefully and was forgetting my trouble. It seems brutally selfish to me to have slept so long, and let him watch all night; but he was quite right. I am a new man this morning; and, as I sit here and watch him sleeping, I can do all that is necessary both as to minding the engine, steering, and keeping watch. I can feel that my strength and energy are coming back to me. I wonder where Mina is now, and Van Helsing. They should have got to Veresti about noon on Wednesday. It would take them some time to get the carriage and horses; so if they had started and travelled hard, they would be about now at the Borgo Pass. God guide and help them! I am afraid to think what may happen. If we could only go faster! but we cannot; the engines are throbbing and doing their utmost. I wonder how Dr. Seward and Mr. Morris are getting on. There seem to be endless streams running down the mountains into this river, but as none of them are very large— at present, at all events, though they are terrible doubtless in winter and when the snow melts— the horsemen may not have met much obstruction. I hope that before we get to Strasba we may see them; for if by that time we have not overtaken the Count, it may be necessary to take counsel together what to do next.

Dr. Seward's Diary.

2 November.— Three days on the road. No news, and no time to write it if there had been, for every moment is precious. We have had only the rest needful for the horses; but we are both bearing it wonderfully. Those adventurous days of ours are turning up useful. We must push on; we shall never feel happy till we get the launch in sight again.

3 November.— We heard at Fundu that the launch had gone up the Bistritza. I wish it wasn't so cold. There are signs of snow coming; and if it falls heavy it will stop us. In such case we must get a sledge and go on, Russian fashion.

4 November.— To-day we heard of the launch having been detained by an accident when trying to force a way up the rapids. The Slovak boats get up all right, by aid of a rope and steering with knowledge. Some went up only a few hours before. Godalming is an amateur fitter himself, and evidently it was he who put the launch in trim again. Finally, they got up the rapids all right, with local help, and are off on the chase afresh. I fear that the boat is not any better for the accident; the peasantry tell us that after she got upon smooth water again, she kept stopping every now and again so long as she was in sight. We must push on harder than ever; our help may be wanted soon.

Mina Harker's Journal.

31 October.— Arrived at Veresti at noon. The Professor tells me that this morning at dawn he could hardly hypnotise me at all, and that all I could say was: "dark and quiet." He is off now buying a carriage and horses. He says that he will later on try to buy additional horses, so that we may be able to change them on the way. We have something more than 70 miles before us. The country is lovely, and most interesting; if only we were under different conditions, how delightful it would be to see it all. If Jonathan and I were driving through it alone what a pleasure it would be. To stop and see people, and learn something of their life, and to fill our minds and memories with all the colour and picturesqueness of the whole wild, beautiful country and the quaint people! But, alas!—

Later.— Dr. Van Helsing has returned. He has got the carriage and horses; we are to have some dinner, and to start in an hour. The landlady is putting us up a huge basket of provisions; it seems enough for a company of soldiers. The Professor encourages her, and whispers to me that it may be a week before we can get any good food again. He has been shopping too, and has sent home such a wonderful lot of fur coats and wraps, and all sorts of warm things. There will not be any chance of our being cold.

. . . . . . . . . . . . . . . . . . . . . . . . . . . . . . .

We shall soon be off. I am afraid to think what may happen to us. We are truly in the hands of God. He alone knows what may be, and I pray Him, with all the strength of my sad and humble soul, that He will watch over my beloved husband; that whatever may happen, Jonathan may know that I loved him and honoured him more than I can say, and that my latest and truest thought will be always for him.

## CHAPTER XXVII
## MINA HARKER'S JOURNAL

1 November.— All day long we have travelled, and at a good speed. The horses seem to know that they are being kindly treated, for they go willingly their full stage at best speed. We have now had so many changes and find the same thing so constantly that we are encouraged to think that the journey will be an easy one. Dr. Van Helsing is laconic; he tells the farmers that he is hurrying to Bistritz, and pays them well to make the exchange of horses. We get hot soup, or coffee, or tea; and off we go. It is a lovely country; full of beauties of all imaginable kinds, and the people are brave, and strong, and simple, and seem full of nice qualities. They are very, very superstitious. In the first house where we stopped, when the woman who served us saw the scar on my forehead, she crossed herself and put out two fingers towards me, to keep off the evil eye. I believe they went to the trouble of putting an extra amount of garlic into our food; and I can't abide garlic. Ever since then I have taken care not to take off my hat or veil, and so have escaped their suspicions. We are travelling fast, and as we have no driver with us to carry tales, we go ahead of scandal; but I daresay that fear of the evil eye will follow hard behind us all the way. The Professor seems tireless; all day he would not take any rest, though he made me sleep for a long spell. At sunset time he hypnotised me, and he says that I answered as usual "darkness, lapping water and creaking wood"; so our enemy is still on the river. I am afraid to think of Jonathan, but somehow I have now no fear for him, or for myself. I write this whilst we wait in a farmhouse for the horses to be got ready. Dr. Van Helsing is sleeping, Poor dear, he looks very tired and old and grey, but his mouth is set as firmly as a conqueror's; even in his sleep he is instinct with resolution. When we have well started I must make him rest whilst I drive. I shall tell him that we have days before us, and we must not break down when most of all his strength will be needed.... All is ready; we are off shortly.

2 November, morning.— I was successful, and we took turns driving all night; now the day is on us, bright though cold. There is a strange heaviness in the air— I say heaviness for want of a better word; I mean that it oppresses us both. It is very cold, and only our warm furs keep us comfortable. At dawn Van Helsing hypnotised me; he says I answered "darkness, creaking wood and roaring water," so the river is changing as they ascend. I do hope that my darling will not run any chance of danger— more than need be; but we are in God's hands.

2 November, night.— All day long driving. The country gets wilder as we go, and the great spurs of the Carpathians, which at Veresti seemed so far from us and so low on the horizon, now seem to gather round us and tower in front. We both seem in good spirits; I think we make an effort each to cheer the other; in the doing so we cheer ourselves. Dr. Van Helsing says that by morning we shall reach the Borgo Pass. The houses are very few here now, and the Professor says that the last horse we got will have to go on with us, as we may not be able to change. He got two in addition to the two we changed, so that now we have a rude four-in-hand. The dear horses are patient and good, and they give us no trouble. We are not worried with other travellers, and so even I can drive. We shall get to the Pass in daylight; we do not want to arrive before. So we take it easy, and have each a long rest in turn. Oh, what will to-morrow bring to us? We go to seek the place where my poor darling suffered so much. God grant that we may be guided aright, and that He will deign to watch over my husband and those dear to us both, and who are in such deadly peril. As for me, I am not worthy in His sight. Alas! I am unclean to His eyes, and shall be until He may deign to let me stand forth in His sight as one of those who have not incurred His wrath.
Memorandum by Abraham Van Helsing.

4 November.— This to my old and true friend John Seward, M.D., of Purfleet, London, in case I may not see him. It may explain. It is morning, and I write by a fire which all the night I have kept alive— Madam Mina aiding me. It is cold, cold; so cold that the grey heavy sky is full of snow, which when it falls will settle for all winter as the ground is hardening to receive it. It seems to have affected Madam Mina; she has been so heavy of head all day that she was not like herself. She sleeps, and sleeps, and sleeps! She who is usual so alert, have done literally nothing all the day; she even have lost her appetite. She make no entry into her little diary, she who write so faithful at every pause. Something whisper to me that all is not well. However, to-night she is more vif. Her long sleep all day have refresh and restore her, for now she is all sweet and bright as ever. At sunset I try to hypnotise her, but alas! with no effect; the power has grown less and less with each day, and to-night it fail me altogether. Well, God's will be done— whatever it may be, and whithersoever it may lead!

Now to the historical, for as Madam Mina write not in her stenography, I must, in my cumbrous old fashion, that so each day of us may not go unrecorded.

We got to the Borgo Pass just after sunrise yesterday morning. When I saw the signs of the dawn I got ready for the hypnotism. We stopped our carriage, and got down so that there might be no disturbance. I made a couch with furs, and Madam Mina, lying down, yield herself as usual, but more slow and more short time than ever, to the hypnotic sleep. As before, came the answer: "darkness and the swirling of water." Then she woke, bright and radiant and we go on our way and soon reach the Pass. At this time and place, she become all on fire with zeal; some new guiding power be in her manifested, for she point to a road and say:—

"This is the way."

"How know you it?" I ask.

"Of course I know it," she answer, and with a pause, add: "Have not my Jonathan travelled it and wrote of his travel?"

At first I think somewhat strange, but soon I see that there be only one such by-road. It is used but little, and very different from the coach road from the Bukovina to Bistritz, which is more wide and hard, and more of use.

So we came down this road; when we meet other ways— not always were we sure that they were roads at all, for they be neglect and light snow have fallen— the horses know and they only. I give rein to them, and they go on so patient. By-and-by we find all the things which Jonathan have note in that wonderful diary of him. Then we go on for long, long hours and hours. At the first, I tell Madam Mina to sleep; she try, and she succeed. She sleep all the time; till at the last, I feel myself to suspicious grow, and attempt to wake her. But she sleep on, and I may not wake her though I try. I do not wish to try too hard lest I harm her; for I know that she have suffer much, and sleep at times be all-in-all to her. I think I drowse myself, for all of sudden I feel guilt, as though I have done something; I find myself bolt up, with the reins in my hand, and the good horses go along jog, jog, just as ever. I look down and find Madam Mina still sleep. It is now not far off sunset time, and over the snow the light of the sun flow in big yellow flood, so that we throw great long shadow on where the mountain rise so steep. For we are going up, and up; and all is oh! so wild and rocky, as though it were the end of the world.

Then I arouse Madam Mina. This time she wake with not much trouble, and then I try to put her to hypnotic sleep. But she sleep not, being as though I were not. Still I try and try, till all at once I find her and myself in dark; so I look round, and find that the sun have gone down. Madam Mina laugh, and I turn and look at her. She is now quite awake, and look so well as I never saw her since that night at Carfax when we first enter the Count's house. I am amaze, and not at ease then; but she is so bright and tender and thoughtful for me that I forget all fear. I light a fire, for we have brought supply of wood with us, and she prepare food while I undo the horses and set them, tethered in shelter, to feed. Then when I return to the fire she have my supper ready. I go to help her; but she smile, and tell me that she have eat already— that she was so hungry that she would not wait. I like it not, and I have grave doubts; but I fear to affright her, and so I am silent of it. She help me and I eat alone; and then we wrap in fur and lie beside the fire, and I tell her to sleep while I watch. But presently I forget all of watching; and when I sudden remember that I watch, I find her lying quiet, but awake, and looking at me with so bright eyes. Once, twice more the same occur, and I get much sleep till before morning. When I wake I try to hypnotise her; but alas! though she shut her eyes obedient, she may not sleep. The sun rise up, and up, and up; and then sleep come to her too late, but so heavy that she will not wake. I have to lift her up, and place her sleeping in the carriage when I have harnessed the horses and made all ready. Madam still sleep, and she look in her sleep more healthy and more redder than before. And I like it not. And I am afraid, afraid, afraid!— I am afraid of all things— even to think but I must go on my way. The stake we play for is life and death, or more than these, and we must not flinch.

5 November, morning.— Let me be accurate in everything, for though you and I have seen some strange things together, you may at the first think that I, Van Helsing, am mad— that the many horrors and the so long strain on nerves has at the last turn my brain.

All yesterday we travel, ever getting closer to the mountains, and moving into a more and more wild and desert land. There are great, frowning precipices and much falling water, and Nature seem to have held sometime her carnival. Madam Mina still sleep and sleep; and though I did have hunger and appeased it, I could not waken her— even for food. I began to fear that the fatal spell of the place was upon her, tainted as she is with that Vampire baptism. "Well," said I to myself, "if it be that she sleep all the day, it shall also be that I do not sleep at night." As we travel on the rough road, for a road of an ancient and imperfect kind there was, I held down my head and slept. Again I waked with a sense of guilt and of time passed, and found Madam Mina still sleeping, and the sun low down. But all was indeed changed; the frowning mountains seemed further away, and we were near the top of a steep-rising hill, on summit of which was such a castle as Jonathan tell of in his diary. At once I exulted and feared; for now, for good or ill, the end was near.

I woke Madam Mina, and again tried to hypnotise her; but alas! unavailing till too late. Then, ere the great dark came upon us— for even after down-sun the heavens reflected the gone sun on the snow, and all was for a time in a great twilight— I took out the horses and fed them in what shelter I could. Then I make a fire; and near it I make Madam Mina, now awake and more charming than ever, sit comfortable amid her rugs. I got ready food: but she would not eat, simply saying that she had not hunger. I did not press her, knowing her unavailingness. But I myself eat, for I must needs now be strong for all. Then, with the fear on me of what might be, I drew a ring so big for her comfort, round where Madam Mina sat; and over the ring I passed some of the wafer, and I broke it fine so that all was well guarded. She sat still all the time— so still as one dead; and she grew whiter and ever whiter till the snow was not more pale; and no word she said. But when I drew near, she clung to me, and I could know that the poor soul shook her from head to feet with a tremor that was pain to feel. I said to her presently, when she had grown more quiet:—

"Will you not come over to the fire?" for I wished to make a test of what she could. She rose obedient, but when she have made a step she stopped, and stood as one stricken.

"Why not go on?" I asked. She shook her head, and, coming back, sat down in her place. Then, looking at me with open eyes, as of one waked from sleep, she said simply:—

"I cannot!" and remained silent. I rejoiced, for I knew that what she could not, none of those that we dreaded could. Though there might be danger to her body, yet her soul was safe!

Presently the horses began to scream, and tore at their tethers till I came to them and quieted them. When they did feel my hands on them, they whinnied low as in joy, and licked at my hands and were quiet for a time. Many times through the night did I come to them, till it arrive to the cold hour when all nature is at lowest; and every time my coming was with quiet of them. In the cold hour the fire began to die, and I was about stepping forth to replenish it, for now the snow came in flying sweeps and with it a chill mist. Even in the dark there was a light of some kind, as there ever is over snow; and it seemed as though the snow-flurries and the wreaths of mist took shape as of women with trailing garments. All was in dead, grim silence only that the horses whinnied and cowered, as if in terror of the worst. I began to fear— horrible fears; but then came to me the sense of safety in that ring wherein I stood. I began, too, to think that my imaginings were of the night, and the gloom, and the unrest that I have gone through, and all the terrible anxiety. It was as though my memories of all Jonathan's horrid experience were befooling me; for the snow flakes and the mist began to wheel and circle round, till I could get as though a shadowy glimpse of those women that would have kissed him. And then the horses cowered lower and lower, and moaned in terror as men do in pain. Even the madness of fright was not to them, so that they could break away. I feared for my dear Madam Mina when these weird figures drew near and circled round. I looked at her, but she sat calm, and smiled at me; when I would have stepped to the fire to replenish it, she caught me and held me back, and whispered, like a voice that one hears in a dream, so low it was:—

"No! No! Do not go without. Here you are safe!" I turned to her, and looking in her eyes, said:—

"But you? It is for you that I fear!" whereat she laughed— a laugh, low and unreal, and said:—

"Fear for me! Why fear for me? None safer in all the world from them than I am," and as I wondered at the meaning of her words, a puff of wind made the flame leap up, and I see the red scar on her forehead. Then, alas! I knew. Did I not, I would soon have learned, for the wheeling figures of mist and snow came closer, but keeping ever without the Holy circle. Then they began to materialise till— if God have not take away my reason, for I saw it through my eyes— there were before me in actual flesh the same three women that Jonathan saw in the room, when they would have kissed his throat. I knew the swaying round forms, the bright hard eyes, the white teeth, the ruddy colour, the voluptuous lips. They smiled ever at poor dear Madam Mina; and as their laugh came through the silence of the night, they twined their arms and pointed to her, and said in those so sweet tingling tones that Jonathan said were of the intolerable sweetness of the water-glasses:—

"Come, sister. Come to us. Come! Come!" In fear I turned to my poor Madam Mina, and my heart with gladness leapt like flame; for oh! the terror in her sweet eyes, the repulsion, the horror, told a story to my heart that was all of hope. God be thanked she was not, yet, of them. I seized some of the firewood which was by me, and holding out some of the Wafer, advanced on them towards the fire. They drew back before me, and laughed their low horrid laugh. I fed the fire, and feared them not; for I knew that we were safe within our protections. They could not approach, me, whilst so armed, nor Madam Mina whilst she remained within the ring, which she could not leave no more than they could enter. The horses had ceased to moan, and lay still on the ground; the snow fell on them softly, and they grew whiter. I knew that there was for the poor beasts no more of terror.

And so we remained till the red of the dawn to fall through the snow-gloom. I was desolate and afraid, and full of woe and terror; but when that beautiful sun began to climb the horizon life was to me again. At the first coming of the dawn the horrid figures melted in the whirling mist and snow; the wreaths of transparent gloom moved away towards the castle, and were lost.

Instinctively, with the dawn coming, I turned to Madam Mina, intending to hypnotise her; but she lay in a deep and sudden sleep, from which I could not wake her. I tried to hypnotise through her sleep, but she made no response, none at all; and the day broke. I fear yet to stir. I have made my fire and have seen the horses, they are all dead. To-day I have much to do here, and I keep waiting till the sun is up high; for there may be places where I must go, where that sunlight, though snow and mist obscure it, will be to me a safety.

I will strengthen me with breakfast, and then I will to my terrible work. Madam Mina still sleeps; and, God be thanked! she is calm in her sleep....

Jonathan Harker's Journal.

4 November, evening.— The accident to the launch has been a terrible thing for us. Only for it we should have overtaken the boat long ago; and by now my dear Mina would have been free. I fear to think of her, off on the wolds near that horrid place. We have got horses, and we follow on the track. I note this whilst Godalming is getting ready. We have our arms. The Szgany must look out if they mean fight. Oh, if only Morris and Seward were with us. We must only hope! If I write no more Good-bye, Mina! God bless and keep you.

Dr. Seward's Diary.

5 November.— With the dawn we saw the body of Szgany before us dashing away from the river with their leiter-wagon. They surrounded it in a cluster, and hurried along as though beset. The snow is falling lightly and there is a strange excitement in the air. It may be our own feelings, but the depression is strange. Far off I hear the howling of wolves; the snow brings them down from the mountains, and there are dangers to all of us, and from all sides. The horses are nearly ready, and we are soon off. We ride to death of some one. God alone knows who, or where, or what, or when, or how it may be....

Dr. Van Helsing's Memorandum.

5 November, afternoon.— I am at least sane. Thank God for that mercy at all events, though the proving it has been dreadful. When I left Madam Mina sleeping within the Holy circle, I took my way to the castle. The blacksmith hammer which I took in the carriage from Veresti was useful; though the doors were all open I broke them off the rusty hinges, lest some ill-intent or ill-chance should close them, so that being entered I might not get out. Jonathan's bitter experience served me here. By memory of his diary I found my way to the old chapel, for I knew that here my work lay. The air was oppressive; it seemed as if there was some sulphurous fume, which at times made me dizzy. Either there was a roaring in my ears or I heard afar off the howl of wolves. Then I bethought me of my dear Madam Mina, and I was in terrible plight. The dilemma had me between his horns.

Her, I had not dare to take into this place, but left safe from the Vampire in that Holy circle; and yet even there would be the wolf! I resolve me that my work lay here, and that as to the wolves we must submit, if it were God's will. At any rate it was only death and freedom beyond. So did I choose for her. Had it but been for myself the choice had been easy, the maw of the wolf were better to rest in than the grave of the Vampire! So I make my choice to go on with my work.

I knew that there were at least three graves to find— graves that are inhabit; so I search, and search, and I find one of them. She lay in her Vampire sleep, so full of life and voluptuous beauty that I shudder as though I have come to do murder. Ah, I doubt not that in old time, when such things were, many a man who set forth to do such a task as mine, found at the last his heart fail him, and then his nerve. So he delay, and delay, and delay, till the mere beauty and the fascination of the wanton Un-Dead have hypnotise him; and he remain on and on, till sunset come, and the Vampire sleep be over. Then the beautiful eyes of the fair woman open and look love, and the voluptuous mouth present to a kiss— and man is weak. And there remain one more victim in the Vampire fold; one more to swell the grim and grisly ranks of the Un-Dead!...

There is some fascination, surely, when I am moved by the mere presence of such an one, even lying as she lay in a tomb fretted with age and heavy with the dust of centuries, though there be that horrid odour such as the lairs of the Count have had. Yes, I was moved— I, Van Helsing, with all my purpose and with my motive for hate— I was moved to a yearning for delay which seemed to paralyse my faculties and to clog my very soul. It may have been that the need of natural sleep, and the strange oppression of the air were beginning to overcome me. Certain it was that I was lapsing into sleep, the open-eyed sleep of one who yields to a sweet fascination, when there came through the snow-stilled air a long, low wail, so full of woe and pity that it woke me like the sound of a clarion. For it was the voice of my dear Madam Mina that I heard.

Then I braced myself again to my horrid task, and found by wrenching away tomb-tops one other of the sisters, the other dark one. I dared not pause to look on her as I had on her sister, lest once more I should begin to be enthrall; but I go on searching until, presently, I find in a high great tomb as if made to one much beloved that other fair sister which, like Jonathan I had seen to gather herself out of the atoms of the mist. She was so fair to look on, so radiantly beautiful, so exquisitely voluptuous, that the very instinct of man in me, which calls some of my sex to love and to protect one of hers, made my head whirl with new emotion. But God be thanked, that soul-wail of my dear Madam Mina had not died out of my ears; and, before the spell could be wrought further upon me, I had nerved myself to my wild work. By this time I had searched all the tombs in the chapel, so far as I could tell; and as there had been only three of these Un-Dead phantoms around us in the night, I took it that there were no more of active Un-Dead existent. There was one great tomb more lordly than all the rest; huge it was, and nobly proportioned. On it was but one word

DRACULA.

This then was the Un-Dead home of the King-Vampire, to whom so many more were due. Its emptiness spoke eloquent to make certain what I knew. Before I began to restore these women to their dead selves through my awful work, I laid in Dracula's tomb some of the Wafer, and so banished him from it, Un-Dead, for ever.

Then began my terrible task, and I dreaded it. Had it been but one, it had been easy, comparative. But three! To begin twice more after I had been through a deed of horror; for if it was terrible with the sweet Miss Lucy, what would it not be with these strange ones who had survived through centuries, and who had been strengthened by the passing of the years; who would, if they could, have fought for their foul lives....

Oh, my friend John, but it was butcher work; had I not been nerved by thoughts of other dead, and of the living over whom hung such a pall of fear, I could not have gone on. I tremble and tremble even yet, though till all was over, God be thanked, my nerve did stand. Had I not seen the repose in the first place, and the gladness that stole over it just ere the final dissolution came, as realisation that the soul had been won, I could not have gone further with my butchery. I could not have endured the horrid screeching as the stake drove home; the plunging of writhing form, and lips of bloody foam. I should have fled in terror and left my work undone. But it is over! And the poor souls, I can pity them now and weep, as I think of them placid each in her full sleep of death for a short moment ere fading. For, friend John, hardly had my knife severed the head of each, before the whole body began to melt away and crumble in to its native dust, as though the death that should have come centuries agone had at last assert himself and say at once and loud "I am here!"

Before I left the castle I so fixed its entrances that never more can the Count enter there Un-Dead.

When I stepped into the circle where Madam Mina slept, she woke from her sleep, and, seeing, me, cried out in pain that I had endured too much.

"Come!" she said, "come away from this awful place! Let us go to meet my husband who is, I know, coming towards us." She was looking thin and pale and weak; but her eyes were pure and glowed with fervour. I was glad to see her paleness and her illness, for my mind was full of the fresh horror of that ruddy vampire sleep.

And so with trust and hope, and yet full of fear, we go eastward to meet our friends— and him— whom Madam Mina tell me that she know are coming to meet us.

Mina Harker's Journal.

6 November.— It was late in the afternoon when the Professor and I took our way towards the east whence I knew Jonathan was coming. We did not go fast, though the way was steeply downhill, for we had to take heavy rugs and wraps with us; we dared not face the possibility of being left without warmth in the cold and the snow. We had to take some of our provisions, too, for we were in a perfect desolation, and, so far as we could see through the snowfall, there was not even the sign of habitation. When we had gone about a mile, I was tired with the heavy walking and sat down to rest. Then we looked back and saw where the clear line of Dracula's castle cut the sky; for we were so deep under the hill whereon it was set that the angle of perspective of the Carpathian mountains was far below it. We saw it in all its grandeur, perched a thousand feet on the summit of a sheer precipice, and with seemingly a great gap between it and the steep of the adjacent mountain on any side. There was something wild and uncanny about the place. We could hear the distant howling of wolves. They were far off, but the sound, even though coming muffled through the deadening snowfall, was full of terror. I knew from the way Dr. Van Helsing was searching about that he was trying to seek some strategic point, where we would be less exposed in case of attack. The rough roadway still led downwards; we could trace it through the drifted snow.

In a little while the Professor signalled to me, so I got up and joined him. He had found a wonderful spot, a sort of natural hollow in a rock, with an entrance like a doorway between two boulders. He took me by the hand and drew me in: "See!" he said, "here you will be in shelter; and if the wolves do come I can meet them one by one." He brought in our furs, and made a snug nest for me, and got out some provisions and forced them upon me. But I could not eat; to even try to do so was repulsive to me, and, much as I would have liked to please him, I could not bring myself to the attempt. He looked very sad, but did not reproach me. Taking his field-glasses from the case, he stood on the top of the rock, and began to search the horizon. Suddenly he called out:—

"Look! Madam Mina, look! look!" I sprang up and stood beside him on the rock; he handed me his glasses and pointed. The snow was now falling more heavily, and swirled about fiercely, for a high wind was beginning to blow. However, there were times when there were pauses between the snow flurries and I could see a long way round. From the height where we were it was possible to see a great distance; and far off, beyond the white waste of snow, I could see the river lying like a black ribbon in kinks and curls as it wound its way. Straight in front of us and not far off— in fact, so near that I wondered we had not noticed before— came a group of mounted men hurrying along. In the midst of them was a cart, a long leiter-wagon which swept from side to side, like a dog's tail wagging, with each stern inequality of the road. Outlined against the snow as they were, I could see from the men's clothes that they were peasants or gypsies of some kind.

On the cart was a great square chest. My heart leaped as I saw it, for I felt that the end was coming. The evening was now drawing close, and well I knew that at sunset the Thing, which was till then imprisoned there, would take new freedom and could in any of many forms elude all pursuit. In fear I turned to the Professor; to my consternation, however, he was not there. An instant later, I saw him below me. Round the rock he had drawn a circle, such as we had found shelter in last night. When he had completed it he stood beside me again, saying:—

"At least you shall be safe here from him!" He took the glasses from me, and at the next lull of the snow swept the whole space below us. "See," he said, "they come quickly; they are flogging the horses, and galloping as hard as they can." He paused and went on in a hollow voice:—

"They are racing for the sunset. We may be too late. God's will be done!" Down came another blinding rush of driving snow, and the whole landscape was blotted out. It soon passed, however, and once more his glasses were fixed on the plain. Then came a sudden cry:—

"Look! Look! Look! See, two horsemen follow fast, coming up from the south. It must be Quincey and John. Take the glass. Look before the snow blots it all out!" I took it and looked. The two men might be Dr. Seward and Mr. Morris. I knew at all events that neither of them was Jonathan. At the same time I knew that Jonathan was not far off; looking around I saw on the north side of the coming party two other men, riding at break-neck speed. One of them I knew was Jonathan, and the other I took, of course, to be Lord Godalming. They, too, were pursuing the party with the cart. When I told the Professor he shouted in glee like a schoolboy, and, after looking intently till a snow fall made sight impossible, he laid his Winchester rifle ready for use against the boulder at the opening of our shelter. "They are all converging," he said. "When the time comes we shall have gypsies on all sides." I got out my revolver ready to hand, for whilst we were speaking the howling of wolves came louder and closer. When the snow storm abated a moment we looked again. It was strange to see the snow falling in such heavy flakes close to us, and beyond, the sun shining more and more brightly as it sank down towards the far mountain tops. Sweeping the glass all around us I could see here and there dots moving singly and in twos and threes and larger numbers— the wolves were gathering for their prey.

Every instant seemed an age whilst we waited. The wind came now in fierce bursts, and the snow was driven with fury as it swept upon us in circling eddies. At times we could not see an arm's length before us; but at others, as the hollow-sounding wind swept by us, it seemed to clear the air-space around us so that we could see afar off. We had of late been so accustomed to watch for sunrise and sunset, that we knew with fair accuracy when it would be; and we knew that before long the sun would set. It was hard to believe that by our watches it was less than an hour that we waited in that rocky shelter before the various bodies began to converge close upon us. The wind came now with fiercer and more bitter sweeps, and more steadily from the north. It seemingly had driven the snow clouds from us, for, with only occasional bursts, the snow fell. We could distinguish clearly the individuals of each party, the pursued and the pursuers. Strangely enough those pursued did not seem to realise, or at least to care, that they were pursued; they seemed, however, to hasten with redoubled speed as the sun dropped lower and lower on the mountain tops.

Closer and closer they drew. The Professor and I crouched down behind our rock, and held our weapons ready; I could see that he was determined that they should not pass. One and all were quite unaware of our presence.

All at once two voices shouted out to: "Halt!" One was my Jonathan's, raised in a high key of passion; the other Mr. Morris' strong resolute tone of quiet command. The gypsies may not have known the language, but there was no mistaking the tone, in whatever tongue the words were spoken. Instinctively they reined in, and at the instant Lord Godalming and Jonathan dashed up at one side and Dr. Seward and Mr. Morris on the other. The leader of the gypsies, a splendid-looking fellow who sat his horse like a centaur, waved them back, and in a fierce voice gave to his companions some word to proceed. They lashed the horses which sprang forward; but the four men raised their Winchester rifles, and in an unmistakable way commanded them to stop. At the same moment Dr. Van Helsing and I rose behind the rock and pointed our weapons at them. Seeing that they were surrounded the men tightened their reins and drew up. The leader turned to them and gave a word at which every man of the gypsy party drew what weapon he carried, knife or pistol, and held himself in readiness to attack. Issue was joined in an instant.

The leader, with a quick movement of his rein, threw his horse out in front, and pointing first to the sun— now close down on the hill tops— and then to the castle, said something which I did not understand. For answer, all four men of our party threw themselves from their horses and dashed towards the cart. I should have felt terrible fear at seeing Jonathan in such danger, but that the ardour of battle must have been upon me as well as the rest of them; I felt no fear, but only a wild, surging desire to do something. Seeing the quick movement of our parties, the leader of the gypsies gave a command; his men instantly formed round the cart in a sort of undisciplined endeavour, each one shouldering and pushing the other in his eagerness to carry out the order.

In the midst of this I could see that Jonathan on one side of the ring of men, and Quincey on the other, were forcing a way to the cart; it was evident that they were bent on finishing their task before the sun should set. Nothing seemed to stop or even to hinder them. Neither the levelled weapons nor the flashing knives of the gypsies in front, nor the howling of the wolves behind, appeared to even attract their attention. Jonathan's impetuosity, and the manifest singleness of his purpose, seemed to overawe those in front of him; instinctively they cowered, aside and let him pass. In an instant he had jumped upon the cart, and, with a strength which seemed incredible, raised the great box, and flung it over the wheel to the ground. In the meantime, Mr. Morris had had to use force to pass through his side of the ring of Szgany. All the time I had been breathlessly watching Jonathan I had, with the tail of my eye, seen him pressing desperately forward, and had seen the knives of the gypsies flash as he won a way through them, and they cut at him. He had parried with his great bowie knife, and at first I thought that he too had come through in safety; but as he sprang beside Jonathan, who had by now jumped from the cart, I could see that with his left hand he was clutching at his side, and that the blood was spurting through his fingers. He did not delay notwithstanding this, for as Jonathan, with desperate energy, attacked one end of the chest, attempting to prize off the lid with his great Kukri knife, he attacked the other frantically with his bowie. Under the efforts of both men the lid began to yield; the nails drew with a quick screeching sound, and the top of the box was thrown back.

By this time the gypsies, seeing themselves covered by the Winchesters, and at the mercy of Lord Godalming and Dr. Seward, had given in and made no resistance. The sun was almost down on the mountain tops, and the shadows of the whole group fell long upon the snow. I saw the Count lying within the box upon the earth, some of which the rude falling from the cart had scattered over him. He was deathly pale, just like a waxen image, and the red eyes glared with the horrible vindictive look which I knew too well.

As I looked, the eyes saw the sinking sun, and the look of hate in them turned to triumph.

But, on the instant, came the sweep and flash of Jonathan's great knife. I shrieked as I saw it shear through the throat; whilst at the same moment Mr. Morris's bowie knife plunged into the heart.

It was like a miracle; but before our very eyes, and almost in the drawing of a breath, the whole body crumble into dust and passed from our sight.

I shall be glad as long as I live that even in that moment of final dissolution, there was in the face a look of peace, such as I never could have imagined might have rested there.

The Castle of Dracula now stood out against the red sky, and every stone of its broken battlements was articulated against the light of the setting sun.

The gypsies, taking us as in some way the cause of the extraordinary disappearance of the dead man, turned, without a word, and rode away as if for their lives. Those who were unmounted jumped upon the leiter-wagon and shouted to the horsemen not to desert them. The wolves, which had withdrawn to a safe distance, followed in their wake, leaving us alone.

Mr. Morris, who had sunk to the ground, leaned on his elbow, holding his hand pressed to his side; the blood still gushed through his fingers. I flew to him, for the Holy circle did not now keep me back; so did the two doctors. Jonathan knelt behind him and the wounded man laid back his head on his shoulder. With a sigh he took, with a feeble effort, my hand in that of his own which was unstained. He must have seen the anguish of my heart in my face, for he smiled at me and said:—

"I am only too happy to have been of any service! Oh, God!" he cried suddenly, struggling up to a sitting posture and pointing to me, "It was worth for this to die! Look! look!"

The sun was now right down upon the mountain top, and the red gleams fell upon my face, so that it was bathed in rosy light. With one impulse the men sank on their knees and a deep and earnest "Amen" broke from all as their eyes followed the pointing of his finger. The dying man spoke:—

"Now God be thanked that all has not been in vain! See! the snow is not more stainless than her forehead! The curse has passed away!"

And, to our bitter grief, with a smile and in silence, he died, a gallant gentleman.

NOTE

Seven years ago we all went through the flames; and the happiness of some of us since then is, we think, well worth the pain we endured. It is an added joy to Mina and to me that our boy's birthday is the same day as that on which Quincey Morris died. His mother holds, I know, the secret belief that some of our brave friend's spirit has passed into him. His bundle of names links all our little band of men together; but we call him Quincey.

In the summer of this year we made a journey to Transylvania, and went over the old ground which was, and is, to us so full of vivid and terrible memories. It was almost impossible to believe that the things which we had seen with our own eyes and heard with our own ears were living truths. Every trace of all that had been was blotted out. The castle stood as before, reared high above a waste of desolation.

When we got home we were talking of the old time— which we could all look back on without despair, for Godalming and Seward are both happily married. I took the papers from the safe where they had been ever since our return so long ago. We were struck with the fact, that in all the mass of material of which the record is composed, there is hardly one authentic document; nothing but a mass of typewriting, except the later note-books of Mina and Seward and myself, and Van Helsing's memorandum. We could hardly ask any one, even did we wish to, to accept these as proofs of so wild a story. Van Helsing summed it all up as he said, with our boy on his knee:—

"We want no proofs; we ask none to believe us! This boy will some day know what a brave and gallant woman his mother is. Already he knows her sweetness and loving care; later on he will understand how some men so loved her, that they did dare much for her sake."

Jonathan Harker.

THE END

# How to Experience the Augmented Reality Book Cover

*Dracula QR code*

- **Open the camera** on your Smartphone and ensure you have **Internet connectivity.**
- Ensure the **volume is turned** up on your Smartphone.
- **Scan the QR code** above (or on the back cover or spine) by placing your camera over the QR image.
- **Click the new link** that appears on your Smartphone.
- A welcome page will appear, click **LAUNCH.**
- If you are asked for access to your camera and motion and orientation click **ALLOW.**
- Wait as the augmented reality cover loads.
- Close this book and hold the Smartphone screen above this cover to bring it to life.
- **Enjoy** the Augmented Reality experience.

If you have any questions or need support visit:

**www.augmentedclassics.com**

Collect all 5 titles in this Classic Horror series and experience each cover coming to life through Augmented Reality!

Available from Amazon on Kindle, Hardback or Paperback.

Frankenstein
Mary Shelley

Dracula
Bram Stoker

The Picture of Dorian Gray
Oscar Wilde

Jekyll and Hyde
Robert Louis Stevenson

Phantom of the Opera
Gaston Leroux

Keep up to date with the latest titles, offers and other Augmented Reality genres by visiting:

www.augmentedclassics.com

Instagram: @augmentedclassics

Printed in Great Britain
by Amazon

AN ONGOING PROJECT to encourage people in Moray to
women connected with the area has grown up arou
*Women of Moray.* Schools, organisations and individuals across Moray are
beginning to find out their own stories of women's history. These stories will
be told through conferences, exhibitions, drama events, booklets and on the
website www.womenofmoray.org.uk. All royalties from the sale of this book
go to Moray Women's Aid.

# Women of Moray

*Editors*
Susan Bennett, Mary Byatt, Jenny Main, Anne Oliver, Janet Trythall
*With contributions by the editors and*
Richard Bennett, Janet Carolan, Lorna Glendinning, Sheila McColl,
William (Bill) Smith and Eleanor Thom.

**Luath** Press Limited
EDINBURGH
www.luath.co.uk

The Women of Moray project is being part-financed by the Scottish Government and the European Community Moray Leader 2007–2013 programme; sponsorship has also been received from the Gordon and Ena Baxter Foundation.

First published 2012

ISBN: 978 1 908373 16 8

Printed and bound by Charlesworth Press, Wakefield

Typeset in 10.5 point Sabon

Map © Jim Lewis

To all the women of Moray – past, present and future

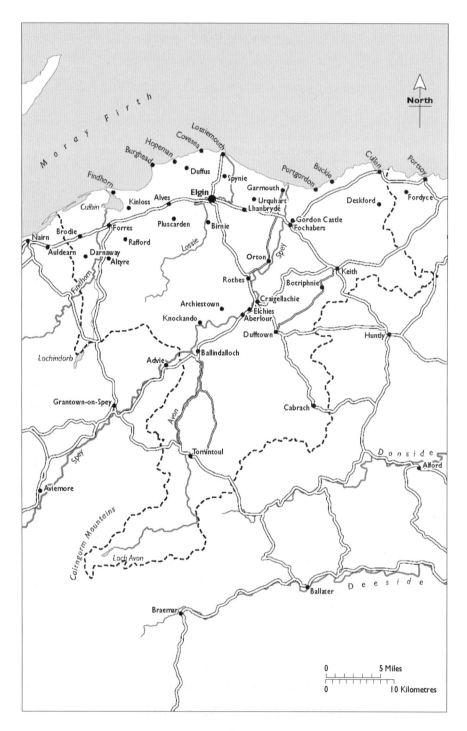

North

Moray Firth

Lossiemouth
Covesea
Hopeman
Burghead
Findhorn
Duffus
Spynie
Portgordon
Buckie
Cullen
Portsoy
Elgin
Garmouth
Deskford
Fordyce
Alves
Urquhart
Kinloss
Lhanbryde
Culbin
Pluscarden
Birnie
Gordon Castle
Fochabers
Forres
Brodie
Nairn
Rafford
Auldearn
Darnaway
Altyre
Lossie
Orton
Spey
Keith
Rothes
Botriphnie
Craigellachie
Archiestown
Elchies
Knockando
Aberlour
Findhorn
Dufftown
Huntly
Lochindorb
Advie
Ballindalloch
Grantown-on-Spey
Avon
Cabrach
Spey
Tomintoul
Donside
Alford
Aviemore
Cairngorm Mountains
Loch Avon
Ballater
Deeside
Braemar

0        5 Miles
0        10 Kilometres

6

# Contents

Map of Modern Moray ........................................... 6

Acknowledgements ............................................. 11

Introduction ...................................................... 13

Editors' Note ................................................... 17

CHAPTER 1    MEDIEVAL WOMEN ........................ 19

Gruoch (Lady Macbeth) (mid 11th century) ........... 22

Euphemia of Duffus (1210–post 1263) ................. 25

Agnes Randolph (d c.1368) .............................. 26

Elizabeth Dunbar (1425–1495) .......................... 28

Janet Kennedy (1480–1547) .............................. 30

Agnes (Annas) Keith (1540–1588) ...................... 33

CHAPTER 2    POWER AND PERSECUTION ................ 38

Isobel Gowdie (mid 17th century) ....................... 43

Mary Ker (1640–1708) .................................... 46

CHAPTER 3    WOMEN OF THE ENLIGHTENMENT ........ 50

Mary Sleigh (1704–1760) ................................. 52

Jane Maxwell (1749–1812) ............................... 58

CHAPTER 4    FOLLOWING THE DRUM .................... 64

Marjory Anderson (d 1790) .............................. 67

Isabel Mackenzie (1731–post 1780) .................... 69

Margaret Dawson (1770–1829) .......................... 71

Barbara Simpkin (1913–1995) ........................... 74

CHAPTER 5    ESCAPING POVERTY ....................... 78

Annie Ramsay (1843–1910) .............................. 82

Margaret Stephen (c.1847–1924) ........................ 87

Helen Leslie Mackenzie (1859–1945) .................. 92

Helen Rose (1857–1922)                                    96

Ella Munro (1873–1945)                                    99

CHAPTER 6    EDUCATION AND POLITICS: FINDING A VOICE       105

Lavinia Malcolm (c.1847–1920)                             109

Isabella Mitchell (1851–1931)                             114

Alice Ker (1853–1943)                                     115

Ethel Bedford Fenwick (1858–1947)                         119

Nora Mackay (1872–1952)                                   124

Nannie Katharin Wells (1875–1945)                         128

Johanna Forbes (1879–1957)                                131

Griselda Dow (1891–1936)                                  137

Beatrice Sellar (1898–1985)                               141

Isobel (Sybil) Duncan (1910–1986)                         145

CHAPTER 7    TWO WORLD WARS                                147

Amelia Culbard (1860–1942)

and Christina Culbard (1869–1947)                         151

Isabella (Gugu) Grant (1875–1921)                         153

Annabella Ralph (1884–1962)                               158

Tibby Gordon (1885–1970)                                  160

Clara Main (1886–1975)                                    165

Olga Byatt (1891–1943)                                    169

Helen Cattanach (1920–1994)                               176

CHAPTER 8    ACROSS THE WORLD                              179

Georgiana McCrae (1804–1890)                              180

Penuel Hossack (1821–1921)

and Helen Findlay (1829–1879)                             186

Eka Gordon Cumming (1837–1924)                            190

Margaret Chrystie (1860–1941)

and Jean Chrystie (1874–1957)                             196

Elsie Watson (1870–1945) 198

Isabella Kerr (1875–1932) 202

Margaret Hasluck (1885–1948) 206

Sylvia Benton (1887–1985) 212

Anne Hardie (1888–1974) 217

Elma Napier (1892–1973) 220

CHAPTER 9    RUNNING A BUSINESS 225

Elizabeth Cumming (1827–1894) 226

Ethel Baxter (1883–1963) 229

Isobel Brown (1900–1985) 233

CHAPTER 10    BREAKING INTO SCIENCE 238

Eliza Gordon Cumming (c.1799–1842) 240

Grace Milne (1832–1899) 245

Anna Buchan (1897–1964) 249

Isabella Gordon (1901–1988) 253

Mary McCallum Webster (1906–1985) 259

Lesley Souter (1917–1981) 263

CHAPTER 11    THE CREATIVE LIFE 267

Sophia Dunbar (1814–1909) 269

Mary Seton Watts (1849–1939) 274

Mary Symon (1863–1938) 278

Emma Black (c.1870–1945) 284

Isabel Cameron (1873–1957) 286

Dorothy Brown (1886–1964) 288

Margaret Winefride Simpson (1893–1972) 291

Kim Murray (1902–1985) 292

Elizabeth Macpherson (1906–1998) 294

John Aubrey (1909–1985) 297

Veronica Bruce (1911–2000) 301

Jessie Kesson (1916–1994)     303

CHAPTER 12   SPORTING SUCCESS     310

Margaret (Meg) Farquhar (1910–1988)     313

CHAPTER 13   TRADITION AND MEMORY     316

Christina Munro (dates unknown)     318

Jean Carr (or Kerr) (c.1770–1830)     320

Lucky Jonson (mid 19th century)     321

Jeannie Shaw (mid 19th century)     322

Janet Levack (1842–1927)     323

Jessie Pozzi (1856–1943)     325

Christina Macdonald (Joyful) (c.1857–1927)     327

Betsy Whyte (1879–1971)     327

Joanne McCulloch (c.1890–1960)     330

Ida McPherson (1910–1998)     331

APPENDICES

'The Glen's Muster Roll' by Mary Symon     337

Three Stories by Janet Levack     341

Lossiemouth Fisher Wedding Guests     342

Books Useful for General Background     343

Notes on Contributors     345

Chapter Notes and Main Sources     347

Index of Women's Names     371

Index of Places in North-East Scotland     377

# Acknowledgements

The editors have many people to thank: Richard Bennett for the initial idea, for his contributions, and for continuing support; Janet Carolan, Lorna Glendinning, the late Sheila McColl, William (Bill) Smith and Eleanor Thom for writing articles about the women of whom we had little knowledge; all the relatives of the women featured, who gave so freely of their information and photographs and whom we were so pleased to meet or contact; Dr Alison Lumsden of the University of Aberdeen, who read our script and gave advice and encouragement; the Moray Society, Heather Townsend, Museum Assistant and volunteers at Elgin Museum; Alistair Campbell, Libraries and Museums manager, Moray Council, for support; Professor Lynn Abrams, Rose Pipes, Dr Karly Kehoe and other members of Women's History Scotland, for support; Councillor Pearl Paul and the Rothes group who supported the Women of Moray Project; and Graeme Wilson and Sharon Slater, forever obliging, at the Local Heritage Centre for Moray.

Thanks also to all the libraries, museums and other organisations where staff were helpful with our research: Phil Astley, Ruaraidh Wishart, Carol Innes and staff at Aberdeen City and Aberdeenshire Archives; Aberdeen University Library; Neil Curtis of Marischal Museum of the University of Aberdeen; Sir John Boardman and Dr Donna Kurtz of the Ashmolean Museum, Oxford; Buckie Heritage Centre; Charlie Finlayson and Mhairi Ross of Brodie Castle; Cardhu Distillery; Brian Stanley at the Centre for the Study of World Christianity, University of Edinburgh; Christie's, Scotland; Liz Trevethick and staff of Falconer Museum, Forres; Fochabers Heritage Centre; Ann Sinclair and other islanders of the George Waterston Memorial Centre, Fair Isle; Kate Perry at Girton College, Cambridge; Eleanor Rowe archivist at Moray Council; the Trustees of the National Library of Scotland, Sally Harrower, Alison Metcalfe and staff at the National Library of Scotland; Chantal Knowles at National Museums Scotland; Ian Riches at the National Trust for Scotland; John Hatton, Juliet McConnell and the staff of the Natural History Museum, London; *The Northern Scot* for allowing us to use photographs from its Christmas Numbers; Debby Cramer and the Presbyterian Ladies' College, Sydney; Fiona Bourne, queen's nurse archivist, Royal College of Nursing, Edinburgh; Steven Kerr, assistant librarian, Royal College of Surgeons, Edinburgh; School of Oriental and African Studies, London; Lis Smith of the University of St Andrews; the State Library of Victoria, Australia; the Vintage Motor Cycle Club; Catherine Hilary at the Watts Gallery, Compton; the

Women's Library, London, with special thanks to the staff who took care of one of the team who became ill when visiting the library. We are also grateful to Gavin MacDougall and Kirsten Graham at Luath Press and to our editor, Jennie Renton. Working with them has been a pleasure.

Conversations with many people have shaped this book and we thank them all, especially: Doreen Aldridge; the late Daphne Agar; Gordon Baxter; Irene Beanland; Eleanor Bodger; Dr Sandy Buchan; Hugh, Robin and David Byatt; Dr John Caldwell; Diana Chadwick; Joanne Collie; Dr Rod Ewins; Peter Dawson; Vicky Dawson; Sheila Dick; the late Alexander Dunbar; Sir Archibald Dunbar; Professor Sir James Dunbar-Nasmith; Margaret Elphinstone; Elizabeth Fitzgibbon; Ann Gollan; Jane Gordon-Cumming; Kay Griffin; Penny Hartley; Patricia Honychurch; Professor Theo Hoppen; Rona Hossack; General Sir Alistair and Lady Irwin; Jim Inglis; Andrew Johnson; the late Ian Keillar; Marcelle Kennedy; Iona Kielhorn; Sandy MacAdam; the late Dr John Macdonald; the late Dr John McConachie; Ronald J Macgregor; Samuel McKibben and other members of the Apostolic Church; Jean McLatchey; Dr Catherine Macleod; Bobby Macpherson; David McWilliam; David Marshall; the twentieth and twenty-first Earls of Moray; Professor Isobel Murray; Lorna Murray; Margaret Murray; John Mustard; William Mustard; Michael and Josette Napier; Professor Richard Oram; Polly Patullo; Peter Rennie; Hugh Roberston; Carol and Ian Robertson; Kris Sangster; Jennifer Shaw; the late Ian Shepherd; Alexandra Shepherd; Karolyn Shindler; Stella Sievwright; Alexander Simpkin; Michael Simpkin; William and Sara Sleigh; Sheila Stewart; Jean Stocks; Elizabeth Sutherland; Ian Suttie; Dr Mike A Taylor; Barbara Templeton; Farquhar Thompson; Mary Thorogood; Phyllis Titt; Clair Tombe; Marjorie Whytock; Derek Wood; Margaret Woodward; Bridget Whyte; Jane Yeadon; and Lesley Young.

The wealth of images in this book has been made possible by financial support from the Gordon and Ena Baxter Foundation, while the scope of its outreach has been enhanced by funding from Leader.

Every effort has been made to ascertain and acknowledge copyright of the images used in *Women of Moray*.

# Introduction

The women who have been involved in writing and editing this book were born mostly during, or just after, the Second World War. We were raised at a time when, in comparison with our mothers, many more opportunities – in education, employment, travel – were open to us, whatever our background. The twentieth century was a time of growing emancipation for women: the vote was achieved; improved education and the introduction of antibiotics reduced infant mortality; contraception took away the draining effect of repeated pregnancies, and, by the 1960s, the British economy was thriving. People were full of optimism for the future, and young women were making exciting choices about their lives. The passage of time has brought us to different places than those envisaged in our youth, but we recognise our good fortune and find satisfaction in retirement – a time that offers new interests and further opportunities.

In uncovering the stories of women's lives, we have seen misfortune, prejudice and abuse; we have seen opportunities grasped and challenges met; above all we have seen the changing attitudes to women over the centuries. History has tended to tell stories of battles and wars, and of the achievements of great men; it was usually the men who wrote the records. Few women, other than the rich, left records from earlier times. The women we have chosen reflect, in some ways, women's situations, not only in the North-East of Scotland, but across the world.

Moray is both highland and lowland. Its modern borders stretch from the middle of the Cairngorm massif in the south to the Laigh of Moray, a fertile area that borders the Moray Firth, in the north. Westwards it takes in the lower reaches of the Findhorn and the remote Dava Moor; eastwards it encompasses much of the old Banffshire; it looks both west to Inverness and east to Aberdeen. In medieval times the Province of Moray was much larger. It was a place where kings and queens came to feast in the castles and to hunt in the great deer forests. The main town of Moray is Elgin. A royal burgh from the twelfth century, Elgin was originally prosperous because of the grain grown in the Laigh, the animals hunted for their hides in the upland forests, and the salmon caught in the rivers Spey, Findhorn and Lossie. Today the barley grown in the Laigh provides the grain for the many distilleries that give Moray its tagline 'Malt Whisky Country'.

We wanted to find out stories about the women who had lived in Moray from early to modern times. It is about eighty years since Robert Douglas wrote *The Sons of Moray* and it is long past time for a complementary 'Daughters of Moray'.[1] Not all our women were born in Moray, but they did connect with Moray in some way for some time in their lives.

Finding the women was easy. We started with our own lists which grew rapidly as others learnt about the project. Somebody's friend's late husband's grandmother was added to the list; a chance meeting on a train in England introduced us to Elsie Watson; someone else had great photographs; surprisingly, some of our own relatives were relevant. Libindx has been invaluable in leading us to obituaries and other information. This database, developed over many years by the Local Heritage Centre, is now online and always a first port of call for Moray researchers. Eventually we had more than enough candidates and trying to fit everyone in became a problem. There were latecomers too: Annie Maude Sellar, granddaughter of the infamous Patrick Sellar, caused excitement. She became Vice-Principal of Lady Margaret Hall, Oxford. But her brush with Moray was only for a year or two.[2] Inevitably, some women had to go; doubtless, there are many others whom we never happened upon.

If finding the women was relatively easy, going a little deeper into their histories was not. There were new subjects to learn about: the history of China, of Albania, of Dominica, of Fair Isle; the battle of Copenhagen, the Women's Hospital Service, the feuing of Tomintoul, the Women's Rural Institute, amongst others. Sometimes the research involved travel to archives and locations – Dominica even being visited by one of the team. Women's history is rarely recorded and some research went nowhere. Who was Mona Milne, an aero engine designer? A brief biography in the *Banffshire Advertiser* is the only reference we could find.[3]

Distinguishing between the work of wife and husband has also been a problem: Georgiana MacCrae travelled with her husband to Australia, but made her mark in the 1850s and 1860s when they were separated. She had been much inhibited by her husband. On the other hand, Margaret Hasluck, herself a scholar, made her first trip to the Balkans with her husband and benefited from his scholarship. Later as a widow she pursued her own researches. Elma Napier, a member of the intrepid Gordon Cumming family, was in Dominica because of her second husband's health. Isabella Kerr, called by God, travelled with her husband to India. Couples such as Johanna and Forbes Tocher, and Helen and Leslie MacKenzie worked together as a team, each bringing different strengths to the partnership – the wives often disregarded in newspaper reports and official records.

There is much helpful oral history about the more recent women, given by friends and acquaintances, but such reminiscences are often about the later years of a woman's life. Sylvia Benton is remembered in Moray as

Miss Benton, an old woman of spirit; similarly, in Botriphnie, Johanna Forbes was Mrs Tocher, the minister's wife, a good woman, an old woman. Probably few of the people who met these women in their old age knew much about their earlier adventures.

The chapters of the book are loosely chronological. A glance at the themes chosen may suggest imbalance; there are ten women in *Education and Politics* (Chapter Six), but only one in *Sporting Success* (Chapter Twelve). But that is how it was. The time around the turn of the nineteenth century was particularly productive of women with interesting stories; sportswomen of note were few and far between. Similarly, there is disproportionate comment on Australia, and nothing of the American west, although there are bound to be stories that we missed. Some of those women that we missed or did not have room for will, we hope, appear in the legacy of the project that has grown up around the book.

The women whose lives we have recorded here do not fit into a seamless story of emancipation; there is no such story because the history of women's rights is complex and open to many interpretations. But the lives of the women we have chosen do tell, in some ways, of a woman's place in the world they inhabited, of how the world changed through the centuries and, in many cases, of how they helped to change it.

And if, after the Second World War, women's lives became easier, with washing machines and 'the pill', they did not get simpler. The sixties were not a straight road to equality of opportunity just because women were better educated and could aspire to having a marriage, children and a career. It was though, a fairer society, the one that we inherited. And working on this book has made us appreciate that. To remember the past and how we arrived in the twenty-first century has been a rewarding and sometimes salutary experience.

# Editors' Note

Because the shape of Moray has changed so often, we have used the modern boundaries (see map on p6). Modern Moray includes much of the old Banffshire.

Not all of the women selected were born in Moray, but all have spent part of their lives in Moray. All died before or during 2000. We have done our best to represent the women selected fairly and correctly. Any unintentional misrepresentation is much regretted.

Please visit the website www.womenofmoray.org.uk to find out about the Women of Moray Project that accompanies this book and promotes women's history in Moray.

Libindx is the Moray Heritage Centre reference system (online). Each entry contains references such as publications, obituaries and newspaper articles and is thus important for further sources. Abbreviations are usually explained in the text. *DNB* refers to the *Oxford Dictionary of National Biography*.

Individual authors' initials are given at the end of each entry, as follows:

RB  Richard Bennett
SB  Susan Bennett
MB  Mary Byatt
JC  Janet Carolan
LG  Lorna Glendinning
SM  Sheila McColl
JM  Jenny Main
AO  Anne Oliver
WS  William (Bill) Smith
ET  Eleanor Thom
JT  Janet Trythall

Sadly Sheila McColl died just before this book went to press. It was Sheila who brought Meg Farquhar to our notice. Her article marks her love of Moray and its history.

'Notes and Main Sources' are to be found at the end of the book on pages 347–70.

# CHAPTER ONE
# Medieval Women

*I once thought with others that learning was quite useless to the female sex. [Sir*
*Thomas] More has quite changed that opinion. Nothing so completely preserves*
*the modesty or so sensibly employs the thoughts of young girls as learning.*
Erasmus 1527[1]

ON 17 JUNE 1390, Alexander Stewart, the Wolf of Badenoch, emerged
from Lochindorb Castle with his 'Wyld Wyked Heilandmen' to burn the
burgh of Elgin and, the glory of the kingdom, Elgin Cathedral. Behind
those terrible acts of destruction lay the Wolf's feelings for a woman. Eight
years earlier, Alexander Stewart had married Euphemia of Ross, thereby
increasing his territory and gaining the earldom of Ross. But his heart lay
with Mariota and it was Mariota, mother of his children, who had lived
with him in his remote castle of Lochindorb on the western fringe of
Moray. In November 1389, however, Alexander had been forced to agree
to return to his wife Euphemia and to treat her well. This settlement was
ordered by the bishops of Ross and of Moray. The Bishop of Moray,
Alexander Bur, and Alexander Stewart had long been at odds; their dispute
centred on the bishop's refusal to accept the superior jurisdiction of
Alexander Stewart. The humiliating settlement regarding Euphemia was
an important factor in Alexander's decision to burn the cathedral. Despite
the settlement of 1389, three years later Euphemia petitioned the pope for
a separation from Alexander. The separation was granted in light of the
'wars, plundering, arson, murders' that were a result of their union. What
of Mariota? Almost nothing is known of Mariota, sometimes known as
Mairead daughter of Eachann, but her name continues to inspire stories of
romance and mystery.[2]

Similarly, little is known of any women who lived in Moray before the
Reformation of 1560. Most of the records that remain are of noblewomen
whose lives are sketched in marriage contracts, divorces and legal disputes,
interwoven with reports of the intrigues and violence of their fathers,
brothers, husbands and sons. Occasionally their deeds, like Agnes
Randolph's defence of Dunbar Castle, are recorded independently.

Lochindorb Castle 2003 (Mary Byatt)

These noblewomen came from the great castles of medieval Moray – from Duffus, where an impressive motte and bailey castle arose from the flat marshy fringes of Loch Spynie, and where another Euphemia would come as a bride bringing wealth from Ross; from Lochindorb, ancient seat of the earls of Moray until gifted to Alexander Stewart in 1371; and from Ternway, or Darnaway, Castle, probably built by the earls of Moray to replace the loss of Lochindorb. The medieval castle of Darnaway is gone, although the magnificent oak roof of the great hall remains encased in an early nineteenth century shell. Gone too is the royal forest of Darnaway where kings and queens went hunting.

The earldom of Moray is an important part of the medieval story. Thomas Randolph, the first earl, was granted the earldom by Robert the Bruce. The territory was large, stretching from lands on the west coast to the Spey, and south through Badenoch to Perthshire. The earldom, its area reducing in size over time, passed through different families: the Randolphs, the Dunbars, the Douglases and various Stewart lines.

The education of girls was a matter of chance. James IV's education act of 1496 related only to the first sons of the landed gentry. The great Renaissance philosopher Erasmus, quoted at the head of this chapter, was initially opposed to the education of women. Signatures on marriage contracts and other legal documents tell that some women were literate in the fifteenth century. By the middle of the sixteenth century, Agnes Keith was able to keep up a regular correspondence with her family and employees.

There was not much in the way of a childhood for girls of high rank; by twelve they might well be married. The church condoned early marriage because it was a way of avoiding the sin of fornication.[3] Despite the church's attitude, illegitimacy was common among the aristocracy. The legitimate line of succession, however, was of enormous importance. This need for legitimate claims to property explains the profusion of marriage contracts. Notaries were in high demand. The bride's father paid a tocher, or dowry, to the husband's family, and the bride might receive life rents of lands and property in return.

Girls did have some rights: marriage arrangements made before they were twelve could be dissolved, and when the girls reached a marriageable age they were consulted about their prospective husbands; they did not have to accept a man they did not like.[4] It was the general practice for sons to inherit titles and property, but if there were no sons, the daughters could inherit. However, married women had no legal property rights and their husbands took the titles and land that their wives had inherited, as is evident in the cases of Agnes Randolph and Elizabeth Dunbar. In practice, noblewomen were often quick to defend the rights of their children. Janet Kennedy, Elizabeth Dunbar and Agnes Keith were well known in the courts.

Marriage among the aristocracy in medieval times was about making deals and acquiring land. If the couple were related, dispensation from the pope was often necessary before the marriage could take place, but for those with power gaining the dispensation was just a formality. The importance of the land and its inheritance was crucial; love might or might not have been a factor. Agnes Keith's apparent love match was remarked upon as unusual. Divorce was possible in medieval times, although not recognised by the church. Amongst royalty and the aristocracy the notion of marriage as a business transaction continued into the twentieth century.

One only has to visit Elgin Cathedral to understand the authority of the church. The building itself speaks of wealth and power. Not even the king was immune from the control of the church. James IV did penance all his life for his involvement in his father's death, wearing an iron belt and going on long pilgrimages. The tension between church and monarch is played out in Janet Kennedy's life. When Janet donated money for a priest to pray for Archibald Douglas, it might have been that she was thinking partly of herself and trying to lessen her own time in purgatory as well as his. The church, though unable to control the sexual urges of its flock, remained an ever present influence on custom and practice.

Our perception of women from these early days will inevitably be unbalanced because the records of women of lower rank are generally missing, and single women are practically invisible. There is mention, by James IV's treasurer, of the 'madinnis that dansit at Elgun' (1504) and the 'wemen that sang to the king' (1506).[5] Of the lives of the maidens that danced and the women that sang we know nothing. We do have a snapshot of Cristen Varden who in June 1542 called Margarat Froster a common whore and thief; Margarat then retaliated by attacking Cristen, and the two ended up before the burgh court of Elgin:

The assise deliuerit that Margarat Froster wrangit in the striking of
Cristen Varden with ane pan vpon the heid and draving the said
Cristenis hair to greit quantate out of hir heid.[6]

Such squabbles amongst women are common in the burgh court records
which are about all that remain to inform us of the everyday life of the
women of Moray towards the end of the medieval period.

Inevitably, it is the noblewomen that appear in this chapter, and it is
their marriages and liaisons that give us some insight into their lives.
Marriage for women of high rank was a highly desirable legal arrangement
that enhanced the status of the woman and her family and accumulated
lands and income for the next generation. For some, happiness might have
ensued.

The noblewomen selected here may have been important players in the
unfolding history of Scotland, but their stories reside in that place where
history meets myth and where imagination sets the scene.

# Gruoch (Lady Macbeth)

*Gruoch, or Grwok, born early eleventh century; married 1) Gillacomgain;*
*2) Macbeth 1033; died post 1056.*

Gruoch was the first queen of Scotland to be named in historical records.
Centuries after her death she was misrepresented as the scheming and
manipulative Lady Macbeth of Shakespeare's tragedy.

Of royal descent, Gruoch was recorded as being the daughter of Bohde,
or Boite, who was a son of Kenneth II, although some sources discount
Boite and claim that her father was Kenneth II. With such a distance in time
and with difficulties of translation between Gaelic and Latin writers, and
later accounts of those times woven through with legends it is not surprising
that there is some confusion. Whatever the facts, she is generally
acknowledged to be of direct royal lineage and from the Cenél Gabrain
line. Her brother and her father, (and/or her grandfather, depending on
which version of her parentage is accepted) were slain during the struggle
for the throne of Scots.

The two main rivals in the north during this struggle were the houses of
the Cenél Loairn and the Cenél Gabrain. Gruoch grew up in the tumultuous
times when Malcolm II, of the Gabrain, secured his throne by exterminating
all other claimants. Because Gruoch was a direct descendant of the royal
family, her children would continue the royal line, and consequently a

22

politically suitable marriage was required for her.

As a girl Gruoch was married to one of the many aspiring warlords of the time, so uniting two rival families. The marriage produced a son, Lulach. In the political struggle for supremacy, her husband, Gillacomgain of the Cenél Loairn, slaughtered his own relative Findaleach, mormaer (overlord) of Moray and father of Macbeth. In 1032 Gillacomgain was burnt to death in revenge for this killing, but it is not clear who was responsible for his murder. Gruoch was then a widow, but did not remain one for long. Her royal blood and her connections made her a valuable pawn in the very complex game of kings.

Gruoch married Macbeth, rightful mormaer of Moray, her late husband's cousin and, perhaps, his murderer. Although Macbeth already had a valid claim to the kingship, his marriage to Gruoch, a direct descendant of the royal line, helped add to his status and strengthen his claim to the throne. In contrast to the turmoil of her earlier years, Gruoch's second marriage lasted for twenty-four years and appears to have been a successful one. Some clans such as MacQuarries, MacKinnons and MacMillans, claim their descent from Macbeth and Gruoch. However, these unsubstantiated claims emerged many centuries later and any verifiable facts are lost in the mists of time.

As a powerful mormaer, Macbeth would have travelled throughout his domain with Gruoch, staying in the various hilltop forts within the area. One of these residences could have been the hill fort on top of Cluny Hill at Forres. The supposed connection with Cawdor has no historical basis.

In 1040, aged twenty-seven, King Duncan died at Bothgowan (Pitgaveny), near Elgin, after initiating a battle with his cousin Macbeth. Macbeth then became king of Alba and, as a descendant of the MacAlpin dynasty, proved to be the last of the great Celtic kings. His lands were under constant threat from Norse, Orcadian and English invaders, but with Gruoch as his queen, he kept them safe, despite the violent upheavals of the era, and created the first relatively peaceful governance over the country during a reign renowned for prosperity and stability. Gruoch was more than just the king's consort; she was definitely acknowledged as a queen and the couple are described as 'Rex et Regina Scottorum'. The St Andrews register records that, as king and queen, they supported the Columban, or Culdee, church with 'gifts of Kirkness, Portmoak and Bogie to the Culdees of Lochleven'. This act may well have been partly political in order to gain church support, but there is no evidence that Queen Gruoch was anything like the scheming monster of Shakespeare's play.

Kings in those times were answerable to the populace and credited with the ability to affect harvest and famine. The prosperity of a good king would be reflected in the well-being of his subjects as people protected from the ravages of war would have time and opportunity to nurture good harvests and successfully raise stock. A Latin poem composed within a generation of his death praises Macbeth's rule and states that – *fertile tempus erat* – in his time there was great plenty. Another record of his reign appears in the prophecy of St Berchan which says of Macbeth:

> after the slaughter of the foreigners,
> The liberal king will possess Scotland.
> The strong one was fair, yellow haired and tall.
> Very pleasant was that handsome youth to me.
> Brimful of food was Scotland, east and west,
> During the reign of the ruddy, brave king.

King Macbeth was killed in 1057 by his rival for the throne of Alba, the heir of the Cenél Gabrain line, Malcolm Canmore. Macbeth's chosen successor from the bloodline of the Cenél Loairn was Gruoch's son Lulach, from her first marriage. Within a few months Lulach too was eliminated by Malcolm – the line of the Cenél Loairn was thus effectively destroyed.

After the death of her husband and her son, Queen Gruoch disappeared from history while chroniclers concentrated on recording the ensuing power struggle in the land. There followed a deliberate campaign by the conquering Canmore dynasty to blacken the name of Macbeth and his queen. This was a propaganda technique to suppress any chance of revolt or support for any possible heirs of the Macbeth dynasty. Facts were manipulated and invented throughout the centuries until the sixteenth century writer Holinshed gave a final twist to the reputation of Queen Gruoch in his interpretation of Hector Boece's history and created the wicked Lady Macbeth.

William Shakespeare, using Holinshed's version of history, composed his great political play warning of the dangers of kingly corruption and tyranny. King James VI and I, who reigned during Shakespeare's later years, was a descendant of the House of Canmore and needed to boost his own credibility. King James did not get on with his own wife, Anne of Denmark, and the creation of a wicked queen, the monstrous Lady Macbeth, suited his prejudices. In life Macbeth and Gruoch were victims of the ambitious Malcolm Canmore but in Shakespeare's play, written to flatter the king, facts gave way to fiction, and their reputations were destroyed for generations.

In an age of constant warfare and feuding, rulers who did not meet the needs of their people were swiftly deposed. Despite having to quell the uprisings common in a violent age, Macbeth retained respect, support and loyalty within his kingdom for seventeen years and was confident enough of this support to leave Moray while he went on a pilgrimage to Rome.

King Macbeth was interred on Iona by his people in the traditional burial place of the Scots kings. Gruoch's fate is not recorded because with the change of dynasty she had lost her power and status. Perhaps she was slain by members of the new order, but we can hope that, since she was no longer of childbearing age and thus presented no threat to Malcolm Canmore, she was able to spend her final years in safety, sheltered by those who revered the woman who had been their queen. (JM)

# Euphemia of Duffus

*Euphemia Mactaggart, born Applecross, Wester Ross, c.1210; married Walter of Duffus, 1224; died post 1263.*

Euphemia of Duffus must be one of the earliest female residents of Moray, excepting Gruoch, to be recorded by name. By her marriage, she brought together the families of a knight of Celtic origin and of one of the foreigners granted land in Moray by David I.

Her father was Farquhar, or Ferchard, Mactaggart, second Earl of Ross and lay abbot of Applecross, where she was born. There were four surviving children – a younger sister, Christina, and two brothers, William and Malcolm. When King William the Lion died in 1214, Farquhar fought for the new king, Alexander II, and was knighted and awarded lands in Easter Ross at Delny and founded an abbey at Fearn.

In 1224 Euphemia was married to Walter de Moravia, great-grandson of Freskin the Fleming. David I had annexed the lands of Moray in 1143 after an episode of insurgency, and the foreigner Freskin, who already had lands in Linlithgow, was given Duffus. It was Freskin who probably built the first motte and bailey castle at Duffus. David I stayed there when he was in Moray founding the monastery at nearby Kinloss in about 1150. The stone castle, the landmark ruin of today, was not built until the fourteenth century.

Euphemia's brother-in-law was Andrew de Moravia, formerly parson of Duffus, who succeeded Bishop Brice de Douglas as bishop of Moray. The church of Holy Trinity juxta Elgin was consecrated as the cathedral in 1224, so it can be imagined that the development of the cathedral would have been a significant event in Euphemia's married life. She had one surviving son, Freskin II. He married Joanna, heiress of Strathnaver in 1248 and they had two daughters. Euphemia's husband, Walter, died in

Duffus Castle 2003 (Susan Bennett)

1262/3 and was buried 'with his father the blessed Hugo... in the church of Duffus near the altar of the blessed Kathrine.' Freskin II died in 1269 and 'is buried in the chapel of S. Laurence of the parochial church of Duffus.' There is no record of the death of Euphemia.

An undated charter may relate to her father's arrangement for her dowry of lands at Clyne in Easter Ross. In a charter signed and sealed by Euphemia herself in 1263, she granted these lands to the diocese of Moray for the maintenance of chaplains in the cathedral church of Elgin. Though we know little of her life, Euphemia's impact on Moray was important, because her land, and the income it brought, was used to develop the power and influence of Elgin Cathedral. (JT)

# Agnes Randolph (Black Agnes)

*Agnes Randolph, born pre 1320; married Patrick Dunbar, eight Earl of Dunbar and second Earl of March, c1320; died 1369.*

Agnes Randolph or Dunbar is famous for holding Dunbar Castle against the English. Through her, and her sister, the earldom of Moray passed to the Dunbar family.

Black Agnes, so called because of her swarthy complexion, was the daughter of Thomas Randolph, the first Earl of Moray, and Isabel Stewart, daughter of Sir John Stewart of Bunkle.

Nothing is known of Agnes's early life. She was the eldest of four siblings: she had one sister and two brothers. It is likely that she spent some of her childhood at Lochindorb and, maybe, at a royal hunting lodge at Darnaway.

By 1324 Agnes was married to Patrick Dunbar, eighth Earl of Dunbar and second Earl of March. A dispensation from the pope was required because Agnes and Patrick were cousins. Patrick initially supported both Edward II and Edward III of England in the Wars of Independence and was made governor of Berwick Castle. He was allowed to refortify his castle of Dunbar, about thirty miles to the north of Berwick, which was of crucial strategic importance to the English. At this point, Patrick changed his allegiance. The English, under the Earl of Salisbury, besieged Dunbar Castle in 1338 in an attempt to regain it. Since Patrick was absent from home at the time of the siege, Agnes commanded the defence of the castle herself. When the English threatened to execute her brother John, Earl of Moray, whom they held a prisoner, it is said that Agnes retorted that, if that were to happen, she would become Countess of Moray. The castle was not taken. Black Agnes won the day. The five-month siege was much reported and Agnes's role became a legend. Robert Lindsay of Pitscottie, writing of her over two centuries later, commented that she was 'of greater spirit than it became a woman to be'. Walter Scott, in his *Tales of Grandfather*, had her ladies dusting the battlements to goad the English. He quotes a ballad, said to have told of her exploits:

> She kept a stir in tower and trench,
> That brawling boisterous Scottish wench;
> Came I early, came I late,
> I found Agnes at the gate.

Agnes was following in the tradition of her father, fighting for the independence of Scotland. Her husband is reported to have changed his allegiance more than once.

When Agnes's brother John died fighting the English in 1346, Agnes and her sister, Isabella, inherited his lands. Patrick and Agnes took the title

Dunbar Castle 2011 (Susan Bennett)

of Earl and Countess of Moray although the earldom was technically vacant and had reverted to the Crown when John died. Patrick and Agnes had no children, but Isabella, who married another Patrick Dunbar, nephew of Agnes's husband, had two sons, the younger of whom, John, became Earl of Moray in 1372 by royal charter. Thus the title stayed in the family. John, Agnes's nephew, became known as the first Dunbar Earl of Moray. (SB)

# Elizabeth Dunbar

*Elizabeth Dunbar, born c.1425; married 1) Archibald Douglas, c.1442; 2) Lord George Gordon, 1455; 3) Sir John Colquhoun of Luss, c.1463; died c.1494.*

It was in the early 1450s that Richard Holland, precentor of Elgin Cathedral, dedicated his poem, 'The Buke of the Howlat', to Elizabeth Dunbar, Countess of Moray – 'Thus for ane dow of Dunbar drew I this dyte'.

Elizabeth and Janet, her older sister, were the only legitimate children of James Dunbar, the fourth Dunbar Earl of Moray, and his wife, Margaret Seton. James's illegitimate son, also James, founded the Dunbar of Westfield line; a line which is still extant in Moray.

James Dunbar, the fourth earl, died when Elizabeth was about five years old. Janet and Elizabeth must have received some sort of education because they were able to sign legal documents in their own hand. The two girls probably spent some of their early life at the seat of the Earl of Moray at Darnaway. It was Elizabeth, the younger daughter, who inherited her father's estates. Sometime before 26 April 1442, she married Archibald Douglas, third son of James, seventh Earl of Douglas. The couple became known as the Earl and Countess of Moray. They had at least two children, James and Janet. Richard Holland acted as Archibald's secretary.

> In mirthfull moneth of May,
> In myddis Murraye,
> Thus on a tyme by Ternway
> Happinnit Holland.
> [written in May, in Moray, in Darnaway, by Holland]

Thus ends the poem 'The Buke of the Howlat', written at a time when the Douglases were at the height of their power. The poem, of 1,001 lines in an ornate and complex style, is about an owl that complains to the pope of his ugly appearance. The owl is given feathers, by other birds, with which to adorn himself, but, growing arrogant, the feathers are taken away as a punishment. The poem is, in part, an elaborate tribute to the Douglases:

> O Douglas, O Douglas
> Tender and trewe...
> To James, lord Dowglas thay the gre gaif.
> To ga with the kingis hart tharwith he nocht growit
> [James Douglas was given the foremost place and did not
> shrink from going with the king's heart]

In contrast to the tribute, the owl's downfall is also a reminder about the pitfalls of high office.

The heart referred to in the poem is that of Robert the Bruce, taken by James Douglas, 'The Good Sir James' (c.1286–1330) to the crusades – an act of unprecedented chivalry. James did not reach the Holy Land, but was killed in Spain fighting the Moors. The Douglas clan made good use of James's daring deeds to promote themselves; they adopted the heart as their emblem. They became the most powerful family in Scotland and as James II grew up he came to resent that power.

The power of the Douglases, however, was coming to an end. In 1455, James II met the Douglases in battle at Arkinholm, near Langholm, and Elizabeth's husband was killed.

On 20 May, nineteen days after she became a widow, Elizabeth signed a marriage contract with George Gordon, Master of Huntly (c.1440–1501). The contract, signed in Forres on 20 May 1455, stated that 'he [Huntly] sall not constrenzie the said lady to carnal copulation but of her free will'. Because they were cousins, and there were many rules about marrying relatives, the pope had to be approached 'in gudely haste' for dispensation. There was to be no harm to James, Elizabeth's son. Huntly would not get the earldom of Moray automatically. 'Richard Holande, Chantour of Murrave is one of the many signatories. Elizabeth signed the document 'Elyzabeth Contas of Murray with my hand'. The surviving document is a notarial copy. The marriage, however, did not last and by 1459 Elizabeth was divorced.

Elizabeth's third marriage, in about 1463, was to Sir John Colquhoun of Luss, Sheriff of Dumbarton and Comptroller of the Royal Household. Moving west to Luss, by Loch Lomond, Elizabeth and John had a son, also John. In 1479, Sir John Colquhoun was killed by a cannonball at one of the many sieges of Dunbar Castle. Elizabeth spent much of her widowhood fighting for her inheritance.

Roof-truss of Darnaway medieval hall showing hunting scene ( © Crown Copyright RCAHMS)

Elizabeth's life shows us that dispensation from the pope was always an option for those with power, and that divorce was possible despite the teaching of the church. Her marriage contract demonstrates that noblewomen had certain rights that protected their status and inheritance.

At the distance of over 500 years, it is not possible to get an idea of Elizabeth Dunbar as a person. She may have danced in the great hall of Darnaway; she may have hunted in the extensive deer forests. What does remain of her is a copy of her marriage contract to Huntly, and an impressive medieval poem dedicated to 'The Dow of Dunbar', which places Elizabeth at the heart of chivalric medieval Scotland. (SB and RB)

# Janet Kennedy

*Janet Kennedy, birth unknown; various marriages of doubtful legality from c.1492; died post November 1543.*

Janet Kennedy from the south-west of Scotland became the king's mistress and bore three of his children. She spent a brief but important period of her life at Darnaway.

Flaming Janet, as she has been called, was the daughter of John, second Lord Kennedy and his second wife, Elizabeth Gordon. Elizabeth was daughter of the Earl of Huntly (Alexander Seton, died 1470 – the children took the name of Gordon). Janet's childhood is not recorded, but it is known that she had four older brothers and three sisters, one older and two younger.

In 1491 a dispensation was granted by the pope for Janet's marriage to a relative, Alexander Gordon, son of John Gordon of Lochinvar. There is no actual record of the marriage, but a daughter, Janet, was born in 1496. A year later Janet Kennedy was the mistress of Archibald Douglas, fifth Earl of Angus, and a man of some importance in the court of James IV. Both Janet and Archibald seem to have been already married to other people. To show his 'affectione et amore' Archibald gave Janet the baronies of Bothwell and Crawford Lindsay, and Janet became known as Lady

Bothwell. These lands were formally transferred to her in 1498 by a charter witnessed by the Abbot of Crossraguel and members of Janet's family.

Another year on, the Earl of Angus was out of favour in the court, and Janet had become the king's mistress. James IV was a bachelor with three illegitimate children. He was twenty-six; Janet was probably some years younger. But James needed legitimate heirs, and so negotiations soon began for his marriage to Margaret Tudor, daughter of Henry VII of England. At ten years old Margaret was considered too young for marriage. She was also related to James, and so a dispensation from the pope was needed. This dispensation was granted in 1500. Meanwhile James and Janet enjoyed court life in Stirling. Ishbel Barnes (2007) gives an account of the lively happenings:

> Entertainment was provided by Peter and Francis de Lucca, two Italian 'spelairs' who seem to have been some sort of dancers, and by a whole group of minstrels, luters, trumpeters, harpers, pipers and drummers, as well as Jame Widderspune, 'fithelar and teller of tales'. The names suggest a group speaking many languages, Gaelic, French, Dutch and Italian as well as Scots... and finally Master William Dunbar [the poet].

In March 1501 Janet gave birth to the king's son at Stirling Castle. To Janet, the king not only gave lavish gifts of velvet, silk and gold cloth for her and the baby, but also the castle of Darnaway. This gift came with a condition: Darnaway was Janet's as long as she was faithful to the king. Her son, James, was to have the earldom of Moray, and the castle would be his in due course. The roof of Darnaway was repaired and furnishings were ordered to make it ready for Janet and her retainers. Janet did not stay long at Darnaway; sometimes she went to Bothwell Castle, sometimes she was at Stirling. It was at Stirling that, in 1502, she had her second child by the king,

Great Hall of Darnaway roof 1965
(© Crown Copyright RCAHMS)

this time a daughter (who was to die shortly after her first birthday).

By now Margaret Tudor was approaching thirteen and a suitable age for marriage. The royal wedding ceremony took place at Holyrood on 8 August 1503. At about the same time Janet Kennedy moved out of Stirling Castle and went north to Darnaway. She was again pregnant with the king's child. A daughter was born at Darnaway, and Janet remained there until the child was about five months old. Janet then spent her time between Darnaway and Bothwell and was visited by the king in both places. But by 1505 she was married to Sir John Ramsay of Trarinzean and so forfeited Darnaway Castle. Since Janet was apparently still married to Alexander Gordon, this was not a marriage that could be recognised by the church, but the king must have liked the arrangement because Sir John Ramsay was part of his court. As Sir John's wife, Janet Kennedy could also attend the court. There were tournaments with brightly coloured silk pavilions and jousting knights, and other celebrations organised by Sir John. The marriage, however, was not to last; by 1508 Sir John was married to Isobel Levingston.

Janet Kennedy then moved to Edinburgh where she lived in the Cowgate beside her brother Sir David Kennedy. She lived in this fashionable part of Edinburgh for at least twenty years.

On 9 September 1513, King James IV, nine earls, fourteen lords of parliament and maybe as many as 8,000 other Scots lay dead on the field of Flodden. Scotland had lost the 'flowers of the forest'; Janet had lost her king, her brother David, and many others of her circle. Fortunately her son, the Earl of Moray, was away in Italy being educated by Erasmus, as befitted the son of a Renaissance king.

The new king, James V, was not yet two and there was much jostling for power between the various nobles and the king's mother. With James IV dead, Janet lost her protector. For much of her life she had been litigious, acquiring land and looking after her children's interests, and while she was the king's mistress the courts found in her favour. Later, Janet did not have such an easy time in the courts. She managed, however, to retain some of her lands to pass on to her son. This son, James Stewart, Earl of Moray and half brother to the James V, was soon to become one of the most important men in the court. The earl was to support the king throughout his life and when James V died in 1542, it was Moray who organised his funeral. Moray, however, was also nearing the end of his life and he died in 1544 with no legitimate children to inherit the earldom. Janet's death, sometime after 1543, is, like her birth, unrecorded.

Was she married once only, or was she divorced? Long after her various partners were dead, on 16 May 1531, Janet Kennedy paid for a priest, in the collegiate church of St Mary in the Fields in Edinburgh, to pray for the soul of Archibald, Earl of Angus 'olim mariti' – once her husband. This was the man Janet chose to remember as her husband; this was the man whom she hoped the church would consider her husband.

Such a colourful woman: glimpses of her life tell of scarlet hats, hanks of gold and coloured threads for embroidery, a silver gilt salt cellar and a black horse given by the king. Janet Kennedy had connections with Moray for only a few years but as mother of the Earl of Moray, she is part of Moray's story. (SB)

## Agnes (Annas) Keith

*Agnes Keith, born c.1540; married 1) Lord James Stewart, 8 February 1562;*
*2) Sir Colin Campbell, Earl of Argyll, 1572; died 16 July 1588.*

Agnes Keith, Countess of Moray, managed the Moray estates after the murder of her husband, Regent Moray. When her second husband, the Earl of Argyll, died she managed the Argyll estates as well.

Lady Agnes Keith was born in 1540 at Dunnottar Castle to William Keith, fourth Earl Marischal, and to Margaret Keith of Inverugie. She was one of nine daughters and three sons and lived a privileged life in a wealthy family. She married when she was aged twenty-two and unlike most marriages of the time, hers was said to be a love match. Her first husband was Lord James Stewart, son of James V and his mistress Margaret Erskine. Lord James had been contracted at the age of nineteen to marry the orphaned Christina Stewart of Buchan, aged three. He accepted the earldom of Buchan but on meeting Agnes Keith fell in love with her and married her instead of waiting for Christina to come of age.

Lord James Stewart had converted to the protestant faith around 1555. In spite of this he was responsible for persuading his Catholic half sister, Mary, to return to Scotland and to take up the Scottish throne in 1562. Mary then drew up the marriage contract for Lord James and Agnes Keith and they were married within a few weeks in St Giles, Edinburgh. John Knox preached during the service. Mary gave a banquet at Holyrood in honour of the newly weds. She and Agnes were good friends. John Knox disapproved and warned Lord James to stick to his protestant principles or 'it will be said that your wife hath changed your nature'. Mary secretly created Lord James 'the Earl of Moray'.

Portraits of Agnes Keith and her husband James, Earl of Moray, commendator of St Andrews, were painted by Hans Eworth in London.

Both are shown clothed in fashionable black garments with gold trim. Agnes's face is long and oval, her eyes dark and wide set and her mouth small and neat. Her hair, mainly hidden under a French hood, is auburn.

For a while there was friendship and harmony between the queen and the Morays, but when in 1565 Mary married her first cousin, Lord Darnley, Moray disapproved and led an armed revolt. His skirmishes became known as the 'Chaseabout Raid' and resulted in temporary exile to England where he sought support of Elizabeth I. Agnes was left to look after her husband's affairs in his absence. Moray wrote to her from England:

> I pray you be blythe and praise God for all that he sends, for it is He only that gives and takes and it is He only that may restore again.

Agnes, living in their house St Andrews Priory, received three sacks containing 3,000 gold coins from Queen Elizabeth. Mary Queen of Scots intercepted Agnes's receipt for the coins and sent a letter of protest to Elizabeth.

Moray did not return to Mary's favour until after the murder in March 1566 of Riccio, her private secretary. The murder was arranged by none other than Darnley, who had become insanely jealous of him. Darnley himself was murdered in February 1567 and Moray withdrew from Edinburgh under the pretext of visiting Agnes who he said had just had a miscarriage. In fact he went to England via France, leaving Agnes once more to look after his affairs.

When a short time later Mary married Bothwell, the uprising of the Scottish nobles was no 'chaseabout'. Mary was taken prisoner and held on an island in Loch Leven. Mary abdicated and, much to her fury, the Earl of Moray was named regent for her small son James VI. The resentment must have extended to Agnes who was now lady regent.

The position of lady regent required fine clothing. Agnes ordered a gown bordered with lizard skin and another of figured velvet trimmed with sables. A later inventory of her possessions made in 1575 describes a coffer of clothes kept at Dunnottar Castle. It included seven regal 'long-tailed' gowns (i.e. with trains), one of cloth of gold and others in crimson, purple and black velvet. Also in the coffer were elaborate skirts of satin and figured velvet, trimmed with silver and gold, some slashed to show brightly coloured petticoats beneath. And there were fashionable detached sleeves, slashed and trimmed.

Agnes's position as lady regent was cut short after only three years by the assassination of her husband when riding through Linlithgow on 23 January 1570; the first recorded assassination by firearm. It was said that

Elizabeth wept but Mary rejoiced. Moray's funeral in St Giles, was conducted by John Knox. It was just eight years after his marriage to Agnes there. He was interred in a vault beneath St Anthony's aisle. A month later, Agnes commissioned two masons, Murdoch Walker and John Ryotell, to build him a handsome stone tomb bearing an inscribed brass plate. Agnes was by then seven months pregnant and retired to Dunnottar where her third daughter, Margaret, was born.

Moray's will, dated 2 April 1567, appointed Agnes as principal executor 'provided she remains widow undeflowered'. She was

Portrait of Agnes Keith by Hans Eworth, mid-sixteenth century

also made guardian of their eldest daughter Elizabeth, now Countess of Moray in her own right. Agnes was left with the task of repaying Moray's debts. These had presumably accumulated during his time as regent. She made an inventory of her own jewels and used them as surety against loans to pay off the debts. William Duncan of Dundee lent 600 merks for which she gave as surety 'the belt chain which my lord himself gave me' and another gold belt and 'an enamelled garnishing of gold'. The parson of Duffus lent 200 merks against surety of an enamelled gold neck chain. James Keith lent 500 merks and received in surety 'my principal tablet set with diamonds'. Her gowns were impounded by her creditors. During this time she looked after her dead husband's estates, lived at Darnaway and became known in Moray as an 'overswoman', capable of sorting out disputes between neighbouring landowners, notably between Cawdor and Kilravock.

Agnes was only a widow for a couple of years. In January 1572 she married the childless Sir Colin Campbell, heir to the fifth Earl of Argyll. It was a marriage of her choice; widows were free to marry whom they pleased, and it is unlikely that strong-minded Agnes would have married against her will. She had probably known Colin Campbell for many years as his brother, Archibald, the ailing Earl of Argyll, had been a friend of her late husband. The fifth Earl of Argyll, died the following year and Agnes became Countess of Argyll and Moray. She now spent less time at

Darnaway and remained with her new husband in his houses at Dunoon, Stirling and rented lodgings in Edinburgh. Her husband, now the sixth Earl of Argyll, acted as chancellor of Scotland, but Agnes was considered to be the dominant partner, Argyll being 'overmuch led by his wife'.

In 1573 Agnes Keith became involved in a dispute with Regent Morton about her children's property. She instructed the English ambassador to seek the support of Queen Elizabeth. Mary tried to disinherit Agnes's daughter Elizabeth, Countess of Moray, saying that the earldom should revert to the Crown. This never took place.

Meanwhile Mary, now captive in England, demanded return of the jewels she had left behind in Scotland. They had fallen into Regent Moray's hands and he had sold the famous pearls to Queen Elizabeth. Agnes denied having any of the rest, but is thought to have retained certain jewels which Moray had been paid as part of his expenses as regent. Being mindful of the need for personal security in those troubled times, she wrote to Queen Elizabeth with a request for Mary that

> the Queen of Scotland should at all times hereafter accept her [Agnes] and her children into her favour and be to them in all times coming their protector, so that they could peacefully enjoy their inheritance, untroubled by legal action.

People still thought that one day Queen Mary would return to the throne of Scotland.

Agnes continued to run the Moray estates for her young daughter, Elizabeth, until Elizabeth married James Stewart in 1580 and he became Earl of Moray. She employed two chamberlains, one for Moray and the other presumably for Argyll. Alexander Stewart, Darnaway chamberlain, was constantly hectored by letter and on one occasion replied:

> Your Ladyship sees the small mote in my eye and oversees [overlooks] the great animal in other men's eyes.

Much of Agnes's correspondence remains at Darnaway and illustrates her power of personality. Elizabeth addressed her mother in letters as 'My most special lady and mother, my Lady Countess of Argyll and Moray'. She was generally held in the greatest respect, and her siblings and other surviving daughter addressed her as 'Madame' and signed off as 'Your Ladyship's most loving and humble sister' and 'Your Ladyship's most humble and obedient daughter at command'. Only her brother William, master of Marischal, showed any tenderness, addressing her as 'Dearest and best beloved sister'.

Three years after their marriage, Agnes provided Colin Campbell with an heir. Their first child, Archibald, was born in 1575, followed later by Colin and Agnes. They were but small children when their father died on 10 September 1584. Agnes was still looking after the Moray estates and now took on Argyll too for her young son, Archibald, the seventh Earl of Argyll. Agnes herself survived another four years and died in Edinburgh on 16 July 1588 aged only forty-eight, leaving an estate worth £11,314:6:8, with £1,968:6:8 owed in debts. She was buried in St Giles, Edinburgh, beside her first husband, the Regent Moray.

Early nineteenth century restoration of St Giles Cathedral destroyed many old tombs including the handsome stone monument Agnes had had erected for her first husband. In 1850, descendants of the Earl of Moray requested that the vault be opened to see if his remains could be located. There was no sign of his coffin, but of three lead coffins stacked inside, the lowest contained the embalmed body of an auburn-haired, middle-aged lady, almost certainly that of Agnes Keith. It was carefully replaced and a plaque put on the wall above recording her burial there. (MB)

CHAPTER TWO

# Power and Persecution

*Where is the blythnes that hes been*
*Baith in burgh and landwart seen*
*Amang lordis and ladeis sheen;*
*Dansing, singing, game and play?*
*But weill I wait nocht what they mean:*
*All merriness is worn away.*
Sir Richard Maitland (1496–1586)

ON 16 OCTOBER 1665, Janet and Isobell Ragge, Margaret Feld, Agnes Mitchell and Isobell Naughtie were all summoned before the Urquhart Kirk Session for 'superstitious repairing to the chapel well at Speyside'. The five women confessed to their sin and were 'therfor rebuked and ordained to publict repentance a day in sackcloth'.[1] Five and a half centuries later, Marywell, beside the Spey near Dipple, continues to be a site for Catholic pilgrimage.

The Reformation came to Scotland by act of parliament in 1560, when, overnight, Scotland became a protestant nation. In practice the change from Catholicism to the protestant faith was more gradual and the pace of change varied in different parts of the country. It was quite a challenge for the newly formed church to supply and train ministers to cover the whole of Scotland. The new ministers (and sometimes they were the old ministers with a new message) were themselves challenged because there was no guarantee that the populace would follow their teachings. Richard Maitland's poem, at the beginning of the chapter, encapsulates the regret of a people who had lost 'all merriness'. For 200 years following the Reformation, disputes and wars concerning matters of faith continued. Religion was interwoven with the politics and the personal and dynastic intrigues of the nation. The tension between Mary Queen of Scots and John Knox – between Catholicism and the protestant faith – has been played out through the centuries and down to the present day.

In Elgin, the Kirk Session minutes begin in 1584.[2] The reformed church worked hard at its task:

Elgin Cathedral – the Chanonrie Kirk, 1722

[21 April 1586] Compeirit Effame Peddar being summonit for fornica-
tioun with Johne Clark confessit the samyn is ordainit to mak hir repentance publiclie on Sonday nixt bair fuittit and bare leggitt and giff evir
scho sall be found in the lyke failye in tyme cuming to be banischit
durying hir lyftyme of this towne.

Some evidence suggests that the Elgin Kirk Session struggled to keep
control. An entry in January 1597 records an act against laughing –
'schamefull and insolent lauching within the kirk the tyme of the preiching'.
Christmas was a particularly difficult time for the session. On 26 December
1599, twenty-five women were detected singing in the Chanonrie kirk
(Elgin Cathedral). The following January, a new act was declared:

[4 January 1600] that all sic personis as beis found dansing, guysing
and singing carrellis through the toune or in the Chanonrie kirk and
wther publict places the tyme callit the halie dayis, sic as beis doaris
thairof sall be committit to the joiggis and stand thairin thrie houris and
thair heades clippit or scheavin for that offence... and this same act to
strik on Marion Andersone for guysing through the toun in menis
claythis and to be put in the joiggis.

39

The joiggis, or jougs, was an iron collar, attached to the kirk or to the market cross, and locked around the neck of the offender. The problems of the kirk did not go away; a hundred years after the Reformation the kirk session was still trying to assert its authority in day to day matters:

> [11 February 1649] Ordained the ruling elders of the Colledge and ane officer to visit the Chanrie kirkyard everie Lords day that there be no abuse there and bring the report to the Sessioun...

Dissent was evident in all ranks of society. In Lhanbryde, just to the east of Elgin, the presbytery minutes note the rebellion of the goodwife of Cokstoune:[3]

> [24 December 1640] Gilbert Ross, minister of Elgin is appointed to go to the goodman of Cokstoune and his wyfe Marie Gourdon that she may quyte her obstinacie in poperie, repair to the kirk and hear the word and partake of the Sacrament.

> [29 April 1641] the goodwyfe of Cokstoune has promised to come to church...

> [27 January 1642] As for Marie Gourdon, goodwife of Cokstoune, the minister has good hopes of her conversion. For the present she is sick unto death, so no process to be used against her.

> [27 July 1643] The goodwife of Cokstoune to be processed if she be not a constant hearer of the word and use conferences, reading and other good meanes whilk may most conduce for her conversione from poperie and superstitione.

> [10 August 1643] She declares herself to be a Protestant and of the reformed religione and promises to be a constant hearer of the word.

> [2 November 1643] The goodwyfe of Cokstoune to be excommunicated if she do not constantlie heare the word.

And so it went on, through seven years of prevarication, until her death in 1647.

Ladie Grant was similarly in trouble with the presbytery of Aberlour in 1656, when it was reported that 'even on the Sabbath day at night there is playing at the cards', and 'the children are bred in popperie'.[4]

Mary Ker, a covenanter, was at the opposite end of the religious spectrum to the goodwife and Ladie Grant. The covenanters adhered to the Solemn League and Covenant of 1643 and did not recognise the monarch as head of the kirk, or the bishops as part of its hierarchy. Lady Mary's father-in-law, Alexander Brodie of Brodie (1617–1679) was one of a party who vandalised Elgin Cathedral in 1640. He kept a diary from 1652 until his death in 1680; his son James (Mary's husband) continued the diary for five years until the trial of the covenanters and the death of Charles II. From these diaries we can chart Lady Mary's attempts to remain true to the principles of the covenant. In 1662 Charles II reinstated the bishops, patronage was re-introduced, and the covenanters became the subject of persecution.

This continuing atmosphere of censure is the background to the witch hunts. There had been witches around for centuries in Scotland and across Europe; some were healers, some traded on superstition, some were just eccentrics. Between the first act against witchcraft of 1563, and the Act of Repeal in 1736, there were in Scotland roughly 3,000–4,000 cases of witchcraft with maybe over 1,000 executions. Eighty-five per cent of the witches were women. There were definite peak periods of persecution mostly between 1590 and 1662, after which witch hunting tailed off.[5] Janet Horne of Dornoch is said to be the last woman executed for witchcraft in Scotland (in either 1722 or 1727).[6]

Whilst at local level the accusations against witches were usually about neighbours' quarrels and superstition, the witch hunts arose because of an intellectual movement led by the elite: the lairds, like Brodie of Lethen and the kirk sessions (supposedly democratic, but in practice often consisting of the lairds and town councillors). James VI also joined the debate, writing *Daemonologie* (1597) – a dialogue about witchcraft. This intellectual persecution was driven by religion: witches were considered to be in contract with the devil. Confessions of sexual intercourse with the devil were guaranteed to excite righteousness on the part of the persecutors (though this was hardly an intellectual response). The confessions of many witches obtained under physical torture and sleep deprivation helped to develop, over many years, a culture and mythology that women like Isobel Gowdie could draw upon to influence their behaviour and their confessions.

The practice of identifying a witch was particularly unpleasant. A witch's mark had to be found by a person known as a pricker. The mark was a place where an inserted needle would not hurt. The marks were said to indicate the places where the devil had held the witch. To find such a place the supposed witch had to remove her clothes and be pricked all over. The process had to be watched by others. James Patterson, who was a known pricker around Inverness and Elgin, was said to rub 'the whole body with his palms' before inserting the pin up to the hilt. For this he was paid.[7] The case of Christian Caldwell illustrates the strange culture and hysteria that surrounded witch hunts. On 5 March 1662, disguised as John Dicksone, burgess of Forfar, Christian Caldwell entered into a contract with the shire of Moray to spend a year identifying witches and pricking them to find their marks. His (her) salary was six shillings a day plus six pounds for each person found guilty; a commission that could only encourage corruption. On 30 August 1662 in Edinburgh, this same Christian Caldwell was charged with false accusations, torture, and with causing the death of innocent people in Moray. One of the ways she identified witches was by looking to see if their eyes were cloudy, which suggests that anyone with cataracts was immediately suspect. At an unknown date she was charged that she 'tock on the habit of a man'. Her fate is unknown.[8]

In Elgin, the Order Pot, a pool just outside the eastern boundaries of the town, was said to have been used to test witches; if the accused sank she was deemed innocent (but might well drown), if she floated she was considered guilty and burned at the stake. The pool has since been filled in. When Barbara Innes and Mary Collie were put on trial in Elgin in 1662 and found guilty they were taken to the West Port of the town where they were strangled and then burnt.[9] In Forres, witches were said to be squashed into a barrel into which metal spikes were driven before being rolled down the Cluny Hill. The barrel was burned where it stopped. A stone called the Witches' Stone remains at the foot of the hill. Alexander Brodie of Brodie, father-in-law of Mary Ker, wrote in his diary on 4 May 1663:

> In the efternoon, Isobel Elder and Isabel Simson wer burnt at Forres: died obstinat; and the Lord seims to shut the dor, so that wickedness should not be discouerd nor expeld out of the land. Oh! Let the Lord glorifi himself, bring down this kingdom of Sathan, and deliuer us.[10]

Driven by bigots and fuelled by the fear of dissent, religious persecutions and witch hunts may be seen as an attempt to control the masses. Women, more vulnerable than men, were the easier target.

# Isobel Gowdie

*Isobel Gowdie, mid 17th century; married John Gilbert.*

Isobel Gowdie achieved fame – and infamy – through her graphic, extensive and allegedly unprovoked confessions of witchcraft in April and May of 1662. Nothing is known of a trial, a sentence, or of her life after these confessions.

> As I was goeing betuix the townes of Drumdewin and Headis, I met with THE DEVILL, and ther covenanted, in a manner, with him; and I promesied to meit him, in the night time, in the Kirk of Aulderne, quilk I did.

So begins the first of the four confessions that she made in the presence of Harry Forbes minister of Auldearn, William Dallas of Cantray, sheriff-depute of Nairn, Thomas Dunbar of Grange, Alexander Brodie, Yr, of Leathen and half a dozen other men from the district who were witnesses. The date was 13 April 1662. Isobel detailed her first meeting with the devil and her subsequent covenant with him.

Over the next six weeks she confessed three more times; minister Harry Forbes and a varying group of men were present to hear what she had to say at each tribunal.

Following her graphic description of her meeting with the devil in the Kirk of Auldearn, she goes on:

> I denied my baptisme... he was at the Readeris dask, and a blak book in his hand. Margaret Brodie in Auldearne, held me up to the Divell to be baptised by him; and he marked me on the showlder and suked out my blood at that mark...

She later confesses to 'carnall cowpulation' with the devil on a number of occasions:

> he was a meikle blak roch man verie cold and I faund his nature as cold within me as spring well water.

She went on to describe a coven in the Nairn kirkyard where an 'unchristened child' was removed from its grave in order to make a potion which would ensure crop failure for landowner Breadley. 'It was pairted between two covens... Ther ar threetein persons in my Coven', she added.

43

Isobel Gowdie's second confession, on the afternoon of 3 May was embellished with diabolic rhymes and tales of herself and coven members being transformed into hares, cats or other animals in order to carry out their devilish deeds; the third, on 15 May, tells tales of visiting the fairies and dining with them under the Downie Hill, on the edge of Culbin, site of an Iron Age fort. The king was 'weill favoured and broad faced' and the queen 'brawlie clothed in whyt linens'. The 'boyes' who made the elf-arrows, that the coven used to murder their victims, were small, 'hollow and bossis baked' and they spoke 'gowstie lyk'.

Isobel and her companions paid a nocturnal visit to the 'Earle of Murreyes hous' at Darnaway. They entered through the windows, feasted on food and drink and after uttering: 'Horse and hattack in the devil's name', a well known oath, then flew off on 'little horses', or corn straws.

Each confession lists the names of other people allegedly involved in the coven, including Janet Breadheid, who made a detailed confession to a similarly constituted group of men in Inshoch Castle on 14 April 1662, the day after Isobel's first confession. Janet's confession corresponds in substance and in significant detail to those of Isobel.

Isobel's confessions are peppered with the names of places on the Nairnshire/Moray borders where her coven 'practised' the black arts. At East Kinloss they 'yoaked an plewghe of paddokis' (yoked a plough of frogs) and went up and down, praying to the 'divell' that thistles and briars might grow there. They killed men at Struthers, Conicavel, Tarras and Burgie. Sometimes the clerk of the proceedings cuts short the detail of Isobel's confession or resorts to an 'etc', perhaps on grounds of decency. At one point, Robert Pitcairn, in an aside to his transcription in *Criminal Trials in Scotland* (1833), complains:

> It is a thousand pities that the learned Examinators have so piously declined indulging the world with the detailed descriptions of these illustrious personages. Under the singularly descriptive powers of Issobel Gowdie, much might have been learned of Fairyland and its Mythology.

Whether Isobel's confessions were the result of psychotic illness, during which she suffered hallucinations and delusions, or whether she had come to the notice of the church for practising witchcraft is unknown. It could be that she did indeed confess through remorse or hope of leniency. She declares, to her great 'greiff and sham', that she has been a practising witch for fifteen years; that Harry Forbes, her chief inquisitor, and John Hay of Park, landlord of the fermtoun of Lochloy, were principal targets of her

Interpretation of seventeenth century Culbin (Kris Sangster)

malevolent magic; and that what troubled her conscience most was the killing of several persons.

Isobel Gowdie's confessions are remarkable for a number of reasons: for their length; for their attention to detail and their graphic narrative style; for their coverage of the world of faerie; and for their vivid accounts of the processes of malevolent magic. It is believed that the first recorded use of the word 'coven', as being applied to witches, is found in her confessions.

The assertion that these confessions were 'voluntary' must be viewed with scepticism. In 1662 Scotland was in the grip of the most intensive and hysterical witch hunt since the previous century; hundreds were accused; perhaps 120 were executed. Isobel was almost certainly imprisoned during the six weeks that covered her confessions; if not tortured, she was almost certainly subject to sleep deprivation. Her interrogation was conducted by men who, in some instances, had felt themselves to be victims of witchcraft; questioning was hostile and was designed to elicit particular responses; there was an assumption of guilt.

From the distance of 350 years it is too easy to dismiss these confessions as the ramblings of a deranged woman. What we know of Isobel Gowdie is extremely limited: she was the wife of a poor tenant farmer, or cottar, on the fermtoun of Lochloy, on the edge of Culbin, scraping a subsistence at a time of desperate hardship in the North-East of Scotland – a time of extremes of climate, of ruined harvests, of people dying of starvation in the streets of Elgin. It was too, a time of extreme religious and political unrest, of fighting and persecution. People looked for someone to blame. In the highlands they were accustomed to ascribe misfortune to the fairies; in the lowlands they tended to blame witches. Isobel's fate is unknown, nor do we know what became of the forty or so individuals she implicated. There is no record of a trial or of a sentence. No burial record has been found.

However, her remarkable confessions make Isobel Gowdie the most celebrated single subject in the academic study of European witchcraft, demonology and 'faerie' matters. An extensive entry appears in the *Oxford Dictionary of National Biography*. She has also excited the imagination of writers of fiction in works such as *The Devil's Mistress* (1915) by JW Brodie-Innes and Graham Masterton's fantasy *Night Plague* (1994). Musicians have been attracted to her story; *The Ballad of Isobel Gowdie* is included in Creeping Myrtle's album *Devils in the Details* (2003). Scottish composer James MacMillan composed *The Confession of Isobel Gowdie*, which was premiered in the Royal Albert Hall in 1990. In his composer's notes MacMillan says he was initially drawn by the dramatic potential of this 'insane and terrible story'. He adds that he tried to produce a work which offers her the mercy and humanity which was denied her at the end of her life. 'This work is the requiem that Isobel Gowdie never had', he concludes. (RB and AO)

# Mary Ker

*Mary Ker, born 28 March 1640; married James Brodie, 28 July 1659; died Brodie, March 1708.*

Born at the time of religious troubles in Scotland and reaching adulthood at the time of the Restoration of 1660, Mary Ker was brought to trial for her convenanting views.

Mary Ker was the daughter of Ann, Countess of Lothian in her own right, and William Ker, first Earl of Ancrum and, by right of marriage, the third Earl of Lothian. Ann and William had three sons and seven daughters. William was an ardent covenanter. The Brodies were also of the covenanting tradition, embracing the protestant faith and shunning a church hierarchy of bishops and monarch. Mary married James Brodie, son of Alexander, fifteenth Brodie of Brodie. Alexander, Mary's father-in-law, wrote in his diary:

> My son was married with Lady Mary Ker; and on the 31st July, 1659, she did subscribe her covenant to and with God, and became his and gave up herself to him.

Lady Mary was apparently irritated by her father-in-law, complaining that he meddled in her affairs. She and her husband may have moved out of Brodie Castle to live elsewhere on the estate.

At the time of the marriage Cromwell's Commonwealth was in decline and on 14 May 1660 the Restoration of Charles II was proclaimed in Edinburgh amidst great celebrations. With the formal reintroduction of episcopacy in 1662, covenanters and some ministers went underground, gathering at conventicles – illegal meetings in big houses or hidden parts of the country. Around Brodie they met in places such as Lethen House and Inshoch Castle. Although a staunch presbyterian and constantly torn between following his principles and avoiding trouble, Alexander strived to keep a low profile. He worried about Lady Mary and the baptisms of her many daughters:

> [14 October 1673] This morning my daughter-in-law was delivered (efter sor labour) of another daughter... I am perceaud that my daughter-in-law had noe mind, as she said to me, to be hastie in baptizing the child; which makes me apprehend that she inclins not to hav her baptized by any of the conform ministers.

Mary relented and the child was baptised on 29 October 1673 by Colin Falconer, the conforming minister of Forres who later became a bishop.

When Mary's husband James took over Alexander's diary in 1680 he frequently commented on his concerns about Mary. By then forty years old, her health was poor and her religious habits continued to court danger. This period of history is known as the 'Killing Times' because of the violent persecution of the covenanters. James Brodie showed caution in the practice of his religion, but Mary was less judicious. James recorded:

> [10 September 1684] Lord Tweddal... spoke anent my wiffe's not hearing [going to church], and told me the danger of it... I knew not what to doe anent her.

> [29 September 1684] My wiffe was persuaded this day to goe to Church.

In 1685 the situation came to a head and commissioners were appointed to prosecute those who attended conventicles in and around Moray. The commissioners and soldiers arriving in Elgin for the trial in January 1685 organised the erection of new gallows. Amongst those called by the commissioners were Mary and James. James, alarmed by the gallows, suffered from a troubled conscience:

[1 February 1685] I continued in this toun [Elgin] many dais. My wiffe came to toun and appeird before the Lords. I was cald to ansvear my libel. I disound frequenting conventicls without my own hous. This is to decline fynns and punishment. Is there ani guilt in this befor God?

Mary gave her evidence on 3 February:

Lady Mary Ker, Lady Brodie, being examined upon the libel, declares she abstained from the Church until September last, and that Alexander Dunbar was a servant in their family, and has prayed and read the Scriptures there, when the laird of Brodie has been from home.

James was fined £24,000 scots (£2,000 sterling), enough to cripple the family financially; many of his neighbours were similarly fined. Alexander Dunbar, the preacher, suffered a worse punishment – he was sent to the Bass Rock, an island prison noted for its appalling treatment of covenanters. On 15 April 1690, after the revolution, James Brodie petitioned the parliament of Scotland, and of William and Mary, for the return of his fine. One of his arguments was that he should not have been made liable for his wife's crime of withdrawing from the church. The money, however, was not forthcoming and the Brodie family remained financially impoverished.

Mary and James had nine daughters, all of whom married men of Moray or nearby. Emelia married her cousin George Brodie of Asliesk and it was he who inherited the Brodie title when James died.

With the reign of William and Mary, presbyterianism became the established religion of Scotland; thus was born the Church of Scotland. The peace was uneasy; there was famine, the disaster of the Darien adventure in the Caribbean, and the massacre of Glencoe. In the closing years of the seventeenth century, debate about a union of the parliaments took hold of the nation and came to fruition in 1707. As Mary and James

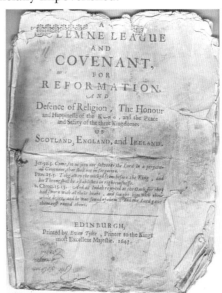

Rothes Solemn League and Covenant 1643
(Elgin Museum)

Brodie reached the end of their lives in 1708 a new chapter was beginning in the history of Scotland. Religious persecution did not come to an end, but the pendulum swung in favour of presbyterianism as Episcopalians and Catholics became associated with the Jacobite risings of the eighteenth century.

Some references to the personal life of Mary Ker remain in the diaries: her continuing poor health, her visits to Edinburgh, to the 'Castle Bogg' (Gordon Castle) and Innes House, but the lasting sense is of a woman caught in the turbulence of sectarian dispute who stood by her religious convictions as best she could. She died a few days before her husband, and they were buried together. (SB)

CHAPTER THREE

# Women of the Enlightenment

*If you happen to have any learning, keep it a profound secret especially from the men, who generally look with a jealous and malignant eye on a woman of great pairts and cultivated understanding.*

John Gregory's advice to his daughters, *1774*[1]

JOHN GREGORY WAS BORN in Aberdeen and was professor of medicine there and in Edinburgh. His bestseller, *A Father's Legacy to his Daughters,* was published a year after his death in 1775. The book sold 6,000 copies in its first two years and was reprinted many times.[2] The above quotation illustrates the duality of men's thinking on female education at the time. Women could and should be educated and independent, but intellectual thought should be concealed, and the 'natural softness and sensibility' of women should always be evident. A quarter of a century later, Jane Austen's novels reflect the same duality.

The Scottish Enlightenment was an eighteenth century intellectual movement that flourished in the congeniality found in clubs, taverns, and gatherings in urban societies in Scotland, principally in Edinburgh, Glasgow and Aberdeen. Following the Union of the Crowns in 1603 and the Union of the Parliaments in 1707, English culture had increasing influence in Scotland. However, the establishment of a distinct Scottish culture in education, law and religion, counteracted to some extent, the prevailing influence of London-based ideas and fashions of thought. The very fact that all the politicians moved to London in 1707 created a vacuum which was filled by giants of the Enlightenment like David Hume, Lord Kames, James Hutton, Adam Smith, Adam Ferguson and Hugh Blair, and there were many more – botanists, lawyers, chemists, poets and artists. Alongside the intellectual culture, the Scottish vernacular literary tradition flourished in the work of Allan Ramsay, Robert Fergusson and Robert Burns.

There were women who contributed to Enlightenment thinking, but it is difficult to know to what degree. Elizabeth Dawson from Yorkshire, who married the Edinburgh advocate Archibald Fletcher, was known for

Gordon Castle from Lachlan Shaw's *The History of the Province of Moray* (1827)

her social circle, largely a group of whig ladies who were focused on the intellectual aspects of the age. Lord Jeffrey referred to Mrs Fletcher as one of those 'women who plague me with rational conversation'.[3] Mrs Fletcher's group included Mary Brunton, the evangelical novelist, the Miller sisters, daughters of Dr John Miller, professor of Civil Law at the university of Glasgow between 1761 and 1790, and the Cullen sisters, daughters of William Cullen (1710–1790), professor of medicine in Glasgow and then Edinburgh. This group of women was interested in literature, women's education and reform. Also interested in literature and education, but not in reform, were Mrs Fletcher's Tory friends. They included Elizabeth Hamilton, novelist and educationalist, Joanna Baillie, poet and playwright, and Anne Grant of Laggan, poet and author, born in Glasgow, who married the minister of Laggan and was widowed in 1801. Thereafter, she moved south, settling in Edinburgh in 1810.

Whilst philosophical debate in the clubs and lecture halls of the cities drove the Scottish Enlightenment, developments and improvements in industrial and agricultural practice, underpinned by scientific enquiry, were vital to the movement. Men like Archibald Grant of Monymusk (1696–1778), founder of Archiestown, and James Ogilvy (c.1714–1770), sixth Earl of Findlater and third Earl of Seafield, altered the landscape of the North-East lowlands. Moray began to change from a landscape of small, poor farms, runrig and extensive boggy moorland to expansive planned villages, large fields, hedges and plantations.

Among those who contributed to the development and improvement of social conditions, and the advancement of agriculture and intellectual thought in the eighteenth and early nineteenth century were two Moray women.

Mary Sleigh was the great beauty of her day, sung about in a popular ballad of the time (and further mentioned in RL Stevenson's *Catriona*). As the wife of Alexander Brodie of Brodie, she made important improvements around that estate.

Jane Maxwell, in the second half of the eighteenth century, was also involved with improvements, around Gordon Castle. Whilst some historians refer to the Duke of Gordon's development of Kingussie, it was Duchess Jane who instigated and oversaw the project. However, Jane Maxwell's greatest contribution to the Enlightenment was probably her consummate skill at providing a setting where both men and women could meet for discussion and feel at ease in debate.

These two ladies of Brodie and Gordon Castle were renowned beauties in their youth and desirable as wives for the great Moray landowners; their brains, strong personalities and organisational skills were a bonus to the area. Having travelled much and spent time in London, their horizons were extensive, but their passion for their estates is evident from the time and energy expended in the north. Both these women benefited from their husbands' money and helped to spend it; improvements were a drain on estate resources and did not always repay the investment. Mary Sleigh and Jane Maxwell lived in a world of luxury that was supported by the hard, grinding, unceasing work of their servants, but in their lives they made statements about the capabilities of women that are remembered today.

# Mary Sleigh

*Mary Sleigh, born 1704; married Alexander Brodie of Brodie, 3 September 1724; died 21 March 1760.*

A well known Edinburgh beauty, Mary Sleigh married the laird of Brodie. Her work on the Brodie estate makes her a pioneer of the age of improvement.

Mary's mother, Isabella Corbet, married Samuel Sleigh from Leeds and Derbyshire, a major in the regiment later called the 16th Foot. In 1714 the regiment returned from abroad and was sent to Leith and later Stirling. Its mission was to contain the Jacobite rebels.

Mary was celebrated in Edinburgh by a popular ballad. In copying the ballad, Robert Chambers, in *Traditions of Edinburgh*, notes that the name Lee is a misprint for Sleigh (pronounced Slee). The ballad tells of Mally Lee walking down the Canongate, turning heads as she went and dancing with a prince at Holyrood Palace:

> And ilka bab her pong pong gi'ed, ilk lad thought that's to me;
> But fient a ane was in the thought of bonnie Mally Lee
>
> And we're a' gaun east and wast, we're a' gone agee,
> We're a' gone east and wast, courtin' Mally Lee

The pong pong was a jewel fixed to a wire with a long pin. It was worn at the front of the head and bobbed about as the wearer moved.

> Frae Seton's Land, a Countess fair look'd owre a window hie,
> And pined to see the genty shape of bonnie Mally Lee

Seton's Land, at the lower end of the Canongate, was the residence of the Earl of Seton (on the site of Whitefoord House, presently sheltered housing for ex-servicemen). A final verse is thought to have been added later:

> A Prince cam' out frae mang them a', with garter at his knee,
> And danced a stately rigadoon, wi' bonnie Mally Lee.

The suggestion is that Bonnie Prince Charlie was the prince – a romantic notion that was hardly in accord with the politics of Mary Sleigh.

Alexander Brodie, seven years older than Mary, was the successful suitor – nineteenth Brodie of Brodie and MP for Elginshire. The couple were married in 1724 and the event was celebrated in verses by the poet Allan Ramsay, who noted Mary's intelligence as well as her beauty:

> Her beauty might for ever warm,
> Altho' her soul were less divine;
> The brightness of her mind could charm,
> Did less her graceful beauties shine:
> But both united, with full force inspire
> The warmest wish, and the most lasting fire.

A copy of the twenty-one-page marriage contract is to be found in the

53

On the back of the frame of this small picture is written:'Mary Sleigh spouse to Alexr Brodie of Brodie Lord Lyon. Done by Mr Jas Ferguson the famous Mally Lee'. (Brodie Castle and the National Trust for Scotland)

Brodie archives. Samuel Sleigh was to give 'One thousand pounds Sterling money in the name of Tocher' – to be returned if Mary were to die within one year and a day without children. In return Mary was to receive life rent of the lands around Brodie. She was not allowed to cut the wood on these lands. Should she die, any daughters would be provided for, including their education. The contract was witnessed by Sir Walter Pringle of Newhall and Sir Robert Gordon of Gordonstoun.

Alexander Brodie (grandson of Mary Ker) and his new wife were Hanoverians. Alexander's work with Lord Islay under Walpole's government earned him the honour of Lord Lyon King of Arms in 1727. At the time of Culloden, Alexander provided information to the government on the Jacobite troops in the area, and Cumberland's men camped in what was later called the 'Forty-five Wood' on the Brodie estate. Alexander was a great friend of Duncan Forbes of Culloden, although some political dispute caused a coolness between them for a while. A letter from Mary's Mother, Isabella Sleigh, to Duncan Forbes, suggests that Forbes was an important neighbour for Mary:

[From Brodie, 29 September 1735] I wish to God those unhappy differences between you and Brodie had never had a being, and next to that, that there may soon be an end to them. Tis now a great many years since I told your Lop. [Lordship] of what consequence your friendship was to my daughter and me and though I know you do us the honour to value us, yet we should be still much happier if you and the Lyon were as you have been.

Forbes, lord advocate, and eventually president of the Court of Session, had succeeded to the family estates of Culloden the previous year.

Brodie House, as it was called when the newly married couple arrived, and its surroundings, were in stark contrast to Edinburgh for the fashion conscious Mary. Not one to settle for less, she took upon herself the task of improving the estate. Alexander, being an MP, was often in London and apparently happy to leave her in charge. It is unusual for a woman to be noted in the statistical accounts of Scotland but the first *Statistical Account*, published more than thirty years after Mary Sleigh's death, gives us a good history of her achievements:

> for the first judicious and spirited exertion on a larger scale, in planting and improving an estate, this parish and county has been much indebted to the example of a Lady, of most respectable memory, Mary Sleigh.

A footnote gives further information:

> The men she employed in levelling, trenching, draining and raising fences; and trained the women to industry by establishing a school for spinning, and for dispensing premiums. She raised quantities of flax, encouraged her tenants to cultivate it, and built them a mill, for bruising and scutching it. She enclosed and subdivided an extensive mains substantially; trained up hedges with uncommon care, and, further, sheltered the enclosures, with belts planted with great varieties of trees. Her gardens, orchards and nurseries surpassed everything but Dunkeld and Blair benorth Tay.

An estate map, surveyed by George Brown of Elgin, and dated to 1770, ten years after Mary Sleigh's death, is said to show improvements carried out in the 1730s. The map is full of interesting pieces of information: the miln or mill, the turnip park (quite near to the house), the washing house – referred to in a bill of 1739, the fruit orchard, and the fir plantations (Scots pine was called fir at the time). Puzzling notes on the map around Kintessack give a hint of the disputes that arose from enclosure:

> Ground called Cloddy Moss was inclosed and drained some years ago by the leat Dunbar of Grang hill but was defased by the tennants of Dyke at the desire of the Lord Lyon.

and

> Moss ground was inclosed by Dalvey and Brock down by Brodie

Possibly these disputes were about access to peat or turf cutting. Peat was scarce, and coal only affordable to the wealthy.

55

Oil painting, thought to be of Mary Sleigh (Brodie Castle and the National Trust for Scotland)

Lady Brodie and Alexander had eight children, only two of whom are usually mentioned: Emilia born in 1730, and Alexander born in 1741. James Brodie, in *Brodie Country* (1999), states that she lost two sons in the same year as she lost her husband (1754); others probably died in infancy. Lachlan Shaw's *History of Moray* (new edition, 1882) relates a legend stating that Brodie House was cursed by a witch who foretold that heirs would never be born there. Mary apparently refused to accept such an idea, but is said to have regretted her decision as her children died one after the other. Only Emilia outlived her. Emilia married Captain John Macleod of Dunvegan and gave birth to an heir to Dunvegan, at Brodie, on 4 March 1754, five days before her father's death. It was Emilia that Dr Johnson met and thought well of on his travels in the Western Isles. Alexander, Mary's son, was only twelve when his father died. He inherited over £18,000 of debts, some probably caused by his parents' enthusiasm for improvement. The bundle of debts at Brodie Castle includes such notes as 'John Falconer £7- 3- Sterling as price of an half hogshead of Malega wine' and '£7 due to Isabela Harper for wages'; also £127 due to Lady Brodie for a bill she paid herself.

Lady Brodie spent her widowhood trying to reduce her son's debts. In January 1755 she wrote from London to her husband's cousin, James Brodie of Spynie, about her business concerns. She reported that she was in London for three reasons: to settle her son at school in Hackney, to get help from the government, and to get money at low interest to pay the debts. She was unable to 'touch a penny' of her own. The help Lady Brodie required from the government seems to refer to a petition presented to the House of Lords regarding an election dispute in Forres. The Brodies had long held power in the Forres Town Council, but following the Lord Lyon's death, the liability for debts was left in the hands of the minority party. At a complex action in the Court of Session the minority party won their case. Lady Brodie sought the support of the Duke of Argyll who won the appeal in the House of Lords – she had friends in high places.

The last years of Mary Brodie's life contained little joy. Her remaining son, Alexander, died in 1759. The son of James Brodie of Spynie inherited the estate and he and his wife Margaret Duff continued with the improvements. Mary died the following year. The coffin plate in Dyke Church bears an inscrutable reference:

Mary Sleigh, only child of Major Sam Sleigh and of Isabella Corbet, his wife. This truly worthy lady died universally regretted 21st March 1760, in the 56th year of her age, the widow of Alex. Brodie of Brodie, Esq., Lord Lyon, by whom she had eight children, three most promising sons and five daughters, all which she survived, except one most unspeakably afflicted daughter, Emilia, the wife of John Macleod of Macleod Esq.

The sunshine and promise of Mary Sleigh's early life was never fulfilled. With the early deaths of almost all of her children, her personal life harboured much sorrow. The legacy of her improvements can still be seen in the layout of the grounds at Brodie. The eighteenth century was a time when the great estate owners in Scotland were beginning to develop the vistas and landscapes around the house and move the walled gardens to a distance from the residence. The pond and walk to the west of the castle and maybe the walled garden to the east retain some of the features first established by Mary. The trees she planted, however, are gone. The National Trust expert from Inverewe recorded only one yew tree as being old enough to have been around at the same time as Mary Sleigh. At 300 years old, it must have been planted before Mary came to Brodie. The landscape in Moray, however, was changed by her commitment, not just around Brodie, but also in neighbouring properties. The first *Statistical Account* mentions that the Earl of Moray is following her example and has begun to experiment with tree planting. There is evidence from Cosmo Innes in a lecture given to the Elgin and Morayshire Scientific Association in 1860, that Mary Sleigh gave fifty beech trees to Kilravock, and that she was a breeder of horses.

Despite the debts accumulated by the estate in her lifetime, she left investments for others to reap. An advertisement in the *Edinburgh Advertiser* of 26 July 1798 offered a hundred acres of fifty-year-old firs (Scots pine) for sale at Brodie, and in 1806 another offered a hundred acres of sixty-year-old firs – almost certainly planted under Mary Sleigh's instruction. (SB)

# Jane Maxwell

*Jane Maxwell, born Edinburgh, c.1749; married Alexander Gordon, fourth Duke of Gordon, 23 October 1767; died London, 11 April 1812.*

As Duchess of Gordon, Jane Maxwell was a flamboyant society hostess in London, Edinburgh, Moray and Strathspey. Her gatherings encouraged political and intellectual debate. She was involved in agricultural improvements around Fochabers and Kingussie.

Said to be a wild tomboy in her youth, Jane was brought up in Hyndford's Close, at the bottom of the High Street in Edinburgh. Magdalene Blair, her mother, had married and later separated from Jane's father, Sir William Maxwell of Monreith. Stories tell of Jane and her sister riding pigs through the Old Town and creating havoc. Her father encouraged her to be respectful of people of all stations in life; he also believed that women should be able to contribute to the intellectual life of the day.

Jane's marriage in 1767 to Alexander, the fourth Duke of Gordon, one of the biggest landowners in Scotland, took her into the very centre of Scottish society. She made the most of her position.

In Edinburgh the duke and duchess lived in the fashionable George Square and were neighbours of Henry Dundas. In London, the duke rented a house on Pall Mall and, through Dundas, the duchess became good friends with Pitt the Younger. She took as active a part in the politics of the day as was possible for a woman, sometimes attending debates in the House of Commons. Dundas, solicitor general and lord advocate for Scotland, and home secretary in Pitt's government, was an important player in world politics, and also a master at controlling the patronage system in Scotland. He created an oligarchy that earned him the nickname of 'King Harry the Ninth'. It has been suggested that the duchess and he were lovers. They were certainly close, and Jane was never slow to use her influence with Dundas. Edinburgh, in the latter part of the eighteenth century was at the height of its golden age. Henry Dundas was not exactly a man of the Enlightenment, but the duchess had many acquaintances who were. Henry Home, Lord Kames, was a particular friend and his many interests included agricultural improvement. Gordon Castle, the ducal seat, just to the east of the Spey, became a focus for improvement in 1776. The old village of Fochabers, said by Pennant in 1769 to be 'a wretched town', was rather too close to the castle for the liking of the duke and duchess. John Baxter, architect, was hired to design a new village to be located at a respectable distance from the castle. The villagers were not impressed, but money eventually enticed them to move. Bellie Kirk in the square at Fochabers is said by McKean (1987) to lend a touch of 'European sophistication' to the village. The castle itself was extended by Baxter and the grounds beautified by Thomas White, a landscape architect from Nottingham. The parks were planted with fine trees and populated with fallow deer.

James Beattie, Professor of Moral Philosophy at Marischal College, Aberdeen, was a frequent visitor to the castle. Beattie, a peripheral figure in the Enlightenment and opponent of David Hume's sceptical views, was associated, like Kames, with the 'common sense' philoso

Jane Maxwell, Duchess of Gordon, with her son George – later the fifth Duke of Gordon (Scottish National Portrait Gallery; Scran)

phy. Beattie spent five weeks at Gordon Castle in 1780. The duchess became his patroness and a good support in his somewhat troubled life. The two took pleasure in each other's company. It was while the Beatties were staying at Gordon Castle that Elizabeth Rose of Kilravock visited and recorded the scene: there was conversation and music, Scotch songs, and an inspection of the duchess's farm; there was no hard drinking. Writing to Beattie in 1783, the duchess gives another view of her life at Gordon Castle:

> I like to walk amongst the rustling leaves and plan future forests, upon 'the breezy hill that skirts the down'... The surrounding mountains, indeed the plains are white with snow, but we have no company and are very happy. I and my girls work, and Mr Hoy reads aloud. I wish you were of the party.

Letters from Jane to Sir William Forbes of Pitsligo also tell of her great love for the scenery and culture of Scotland. An undated letter from Gordon Castle reports:

> We are just returned from Banf – much delighted with every moment we spent there – I never saw so many people Gay and pleased & willing to please. I hope sometime not far hence you will dedicate a few weeks

'Burns in Edinburgh – 1787', painting by Charles Martin Hardie showing the Duchess of Gordon entertaining in her Edinburgh house. (Trustees of Burns Monument and Burns Cottage; Scran)

to these social parties, good dinners, singing, dancing, & perfect sobriety in <u>General</u> as for the sports of the field my Susan & the Gay Sons of the chace talked of it with rapture the weather at both Inverness & Banff was uncommonly fine for the gloomy month of Nov$^r$. The Rocks Woods and torrents of Invernessshire in great glory.

The story of Burns' brief visit to Gordon Castle in 1787 is well recorded and the poem he wrote on returning home was a sort of apology for his hurried departure. Not one of his most memorable poems, it ends:

> Where waters flow and wild woods wave
> By bonny Castle Gordon

In the 1790s the government was desperate for more troops to fight Napoleon, and a repeal of the restrictions on highland customs following Culloden became necessary if highlanders were to be readily recruited. The highland regiments had been exempted from the ban on highland dress, but in London there was a horror of tartan and all things highland. Duchess Jane, inspired by her son George, the Marquis of Huntly, who had raised an independent company for the Black Watch, ordered silk tartan and determined to change the outlook of the capital. In no time, tartan became the height of fashion, even the Duchess of Cumberland succumbing to its charms. The cartoonists had a field day. Following this success a special tartan was designed for the Gordon Highlanders, the design based on the Black Watch tartan with a yellow stripe added. One of the legends associated with the duchess is that of the recruiting of the Gordon Highlanders with a guinea between the teeth given to recruits with a kiss. Certainly she and her daughters worked hard recruiting soldiers for the Marquis, whilst the duke provided the money (usually more than a guinea) that guaranteed success.

The duke and duchess had five daughters and two sons together, but the duke, by mistresses, had many more children who were acknowledged and provided for. The duchess generally accepted these children. George, born in 1766 and son of the duke by Bathia Largue, was brought up with Jane's own children and referred to as 'the duke's George' as opposed to her own George. In the late 1780s the duke began a relationship with Jean Christie, a servant girl in Gordon Castle.

Jean Christie bore five of the duke's children. Some years after Jane Maxwell's death in 1812, the duke married Jean. Although she was not universally accepted by society, the duke insisted on calling Jean Christie 'my duchess'. When she died in 1824, he erected an elaborate memorial to her in Bellie Kirkyard. The mausoleum stands as a canopy supported by twelve pillars.

In 1793 the duke and Jane Maxwell separated and Jane went to live at a farmhouse at Kinrara, near Aviemore. There with the help of a French chef, a footman and other servants, she lived a life of relative simplicity. Her youngest daughter, as yet unmarried, stayed with her and the rest of the family were often around. Later the duchess had a grander house built nearby. As Elizabeth Grant recalls in her memoirs, the entertaining did not stop.

The duchess was interested in the economy of her new surroundings and was instrumental in the laying out of Kingussie in 1799, of which her husband was proprietor. The village included a lintmill, and the duchess, with her many connections, was involved in establishing the new linen industry. On 4 April 1804 the *Aberdeen Journal* announced:

An Agricultural Society has been established at Strathspey under the auspices of the Duchess of Gordon. It is to be named the Strathspey Farming Society. Her Grace has named the following Gentlemen to be Managers.

Among the gentlemen named were: The Hon. Archibald Fraser of Lovat,

Sir James Grant of Grant, Bart. and Lieutenant Colonel George Gordon of Invertromy (the son of the duke and Bathia Largue). The duchess apparently needed more than just the social round.

But the social round was still causing comment. On 23 June 1803 a letter from George Skene in London to Lord Fife at Duff House giving him the London gossip runs:

> Her Grace of Gordon has made very free with your Lordships house, which I am afraid will bear the marks and ravages of her frequent balls. An immense crowd were dancing at Fife House until six o'clock this morning, about which hour the ladies departed half stupid with fatigue and dissipation, and their naked arms dangling out of their carriage windows. The rattling of the carriages all night, together with singing, swearing and squabbling of drunken coachmen, prevented any sleeping in the neighbourhood... [and as a post script] The principal supper table used last night at the Duchess of Gordon's was forty-two feet long and eight feet wide; down the centre was a plateau of flowers and framework.

In contrast to the opulence of her entertaining, a year later the duchess was writing to Francis Farquharson of Haughton (who acted as go-between for the duke and duchess) complaining of her lack of money, about the duke's extravagance, and of bills unpaid at Kinrara. But lack of money did not stop the habits of a lifetime – in Edinburgh, the season of 1808 was said to be especially lively because the Duchess of Gordon was in town. Her health, however, was suffering and her looks were going. She had been a great beauty in her youth, but the fashion for thick white make-up which caked and peeled was not kind to ageing women. The death of her younger son in 1808 hurt badly.

When she died in a London hotel in 1812, people could view her body for a shilling a time. In death, as in life, Jane Maxwell created a stir. Her body was then brought north to Kinrara where she was buried. Her memorial stone gives details of her children and the prestigious marriages of her daughters. The cartoonists had often made fun of Duchess Jane's ambitions for her daughters, but she remained proud of her family and of her matchmaking.

To some, Jane Maxwell was too Scottish, too straightforward and too rumbustious – even coarse; others found her kind, refreshing and exciting. Jane's notoriety followed her throughout her life and ensured that she would not be forgotten. Along with the verifiable records are the legends. Was there a lover that she thought had died, but returned after she was married? Did she give a kiss and a guinea in exchange for a new recruit? Did she tell the Marquis of Cornwallis, who was to marry her daughter Louisa but was concerned about madness in the Gordon family, that 'there was not a drop of Gordon blood' in Louisa, or were these just stories that adhered to her along the way?

If her duke was a disappointment to her, Jane loved the glory she gained as duchess and revelled in the society of the golden age of Enlightenment.
(SB)

CHAPTER FOUR

# Following the Drum

*Ye'll busk and bundle braw, bonny Betsy, and go,*
*Ye'll busk and bundle braw and go along wi' me,*
*Ye'll busk and bundle braw, and go along wi' me,*
*And I'll take ye to the wars that's in High Germanie.*

*I'll hire a horse Betsy, I'll cause ye to ride,*
*And I will be your footboy to run by your side;*
*And we'll all drink in Elgin, as we gang by,*
*And dance upon the bonny braes o' Norawa'.*

North-East ballad[1]

IN BRUSSELS, CHARLOTTE, Duchess of Richmond (daughter of Jane Maxwell), planned her ball for 15 June 1815. An English garrison was stationed in Brussels at that time to establish some sort of order in the chaos
that had followed the downfall of Napoleon in April 1814, and the town
had become a fashionable stopping place for those travelling on the grand
tour. However, in February 1815, Napoleon escaped from Elba, and Brussels suddenly became a town of strategic importance. By late afternoon on
the day of the ball, the people of Brussels could hear gunfire to the south.
The ball started at about ten o'clock in the evening, and the 200 or so
guests were offered the best in entertainment. The Gordon Highlanders
danced reels, and the waltz, still frowned on by the Duke of Richmond,
was, as usual, the most popular of all the dances. The company had just
risen from the supper table when a note was passed to the Duke of Wellington telling of a Prussian defeat. Almost immediately the admirals, the
commanders, the lieutenant-generals, the major-generals, the aides-de-
camps (including two of the duchess's sons) and all military guests left the
ball to prepare for the forthcoming action. The duchess might have been
disappointed at the sudden and early end to the evening, but she need not
have worried that the gathering would be forgotten or thought of as a
failure. The Duchess of Richmond's ball became one of the most famous
balls in history and a focal point in Thackeray's *Vanity Fair* – the 'Waterloo

Ball'. Three days later some of her guests lay dead on the battlefield just ten miles away.[2]

The camp followers of the regular troops were not concerned with ball dresses and waltzes. Their duty was to look after their men the best they could – cooking, washing clothes, looking after children and providing sexual comfort. These women were a mixed blessing to the higher ranks, but the army tolerated them because, in the days before a nursing service, women were especially useful after battle in caring for the wounded. Some of the women were reputed to have loose morals and coarse ways;

French print of a highland soldier and his family
(© National Museums Scotland)

it was after all a very rough way of life to choose. Others, Marjory Anderson and Margaret Dawson among them, may have been enticed by the romance of the soldier in his uniform and the apparent glory of going to war. Life as a soldier's wife promised an escape from boredom and predictability. Apart from the obvious danger of war, the reality was hard graft and there were the hazards of moving across unknown country. Before the battle of Culloden, when Cumberland's army crossed the Spey near Fochabers, one dragoon and four women were drowned.[3] Abroad, there was the possibility of being left a widow in a foreign land with knowledge of neither language nor customs, and with no money. Both Marjory Anderson and Margaret Dawson had the added complication of babies to care for. Isabel MacKenzie went initially as a single girl looking for adventure and she found it.

The first formal highland regiment, the Black Watch, was instituted in 1740.[4] This regiment was intended to police the highlands, but with war in Europe, the regiment was called to London and then to France. When the Duke of Cumberland was defeated at the battle of Fontenoy in 1745, during the war of Austrian Succession, the Black Watch was needed to cover the retreat, and their aggressive defence earned them much praise; the legend of the 'fighting Scot' was established. However, the fact that the regiment was in France instead of policing the highlands left Scotland open to the Jacobite rising of 1745. It was sometime about 1745 that Marjory Anderson and her newborn son, Andrew, were caught up in the continental wars. After Culloden the idea of raising more Scottish regiments was considered too dangerous to entertain, but, by 1756, events in America called for military action and the Black Watch (including John and Isabel MacKenzie) joined Cumberland in the war against the French and the Indians in Canada. Later, in 1794, Margaret Dawson followed the Gordon Highlanders in the Napoleonic wars. There was usually a war somewhere that needed Scottish soldiers, and there were always women willing to follow.

It was events in the Crimea that occasioned Ida, sister of Eka Gordon Cumming, to follow her husband to war. In Dublin, on 20 May 1854, she was cheered aboard ship as she accompanied her husband William Cresswell of the 11th Hussars. A catalogue of disasters followed. The ship was filthy, and the camp in Varna was ill-organised and full of sickness. Unaware that her husband had died of cholera on the morning of the battle of Alma, Ida, nursing soldiers on board ship, was also overcome by illness. The tales of horror continued: troops taken on board accompanied by 110 horses (where there was room for sixty); enduring two days of storm, and watching seventy-five dead horses lowered overboard; drifting when tow ropes were broken; and the dreadful news of defeat at Alma. Eventually Ida made her way to Sevastopol, and into the heat of the action to verify the rumours of her husband's death.[5]

In the aftermath of the Crimean War, and the role performed in that war by Florence Nightingale, there was a realisation that women should have a formal position as nurses working in field hospitals near the battlefield. By the time of the Boer War (1899–1902) camp followers were no more, and the foundation of the Army Nursing Service made women part of the official apparatus of warfare. During the First World War some women were able to work as doctors, though not initially as part of the British Army. The nurses' and doctors' roles during two world wars are dealt with in Chapter Seven.

Following the Second World War, married quarters were especially important for the military who were stationed abroad. In places like Hong Kong and Germany where large numbers of military personnel were employed in peacetime, such quarters enabled families to stay together. While some wives found camp life claustrophobic and took living accommodation outside, good married quarters and facilities like the NAAFI, the mess and the swimming pool could help make camp life tolerable for families. Barbara Simpkin, who had herself given up a good career to follow her husband, worked for improvements to the lot of wives and families who followed their men abroad – from posting to posting, from school to school.

# Marjory Anderson

*Marjory Gilzean, born Lossiemouth, date unknown; married Andrew Anderson*
*1745; died Lossiemouth 1790.*

Marjory Gilzean or Gillon, sometimes called Margaret, has a place in history as the mother of Major-General Anderson, founder of the Elgin Institution, now known simply as 'Anderson's', and still very much in use as a residential home.

Any account of Marjory Anderson's life relies heavily on the research by John Taylor, keeper of Elgin Cathedral, who interviewed those who had known her, and on Bailie Robert Jeans, proprietor of the *Elgin and Morayshire Courier*, who in 1851 published these results.

It is told that Marjory's parents lived in comfortable circumstances in Drainie Parish (now the Lossiemouth area) and that the young girl, an only child, was handsome, amiable and of great promise. Against advice, she married Andrew Anderson, from Lhanbryde, who in 1745 enlisted in a Hanoverian regiment that was quartered in Elgin; together they went overseas.

In 1745 the Black Watch Regiment followed the Duke of Cumberland to France, but no information remains about Marjory's travels or adventures. Marjory returned to Moray in 1748, penniless, her mind completely shattered, with a babe in arms and without the father. Her parents may have died meanwhile or disowned her. Marjory settled in the ruins of Elgin Cathedral – home was the roofed chamber, the sacristy, and the young Andrew's crib, the piscina.

As the boy grew up, Marjory and her son were supported by the benevolence of local people. Andrew's natural brightness was recognised and he attended the Old Grammar and Sang schools as a pauper pupil, in return for menial duties. He was apprenticed as a staymaker to an uncle in Lhan-

Piscina in Elgin Cathedral (Susan Bennett)

Anderson's Institution (Elgin Museum)

bryde, which suggests some contact with his father's family, but they quar-
relled and he ran away to London. It is said that, in the 1760s, as a tailor's
apprentice, he was asked to deliver a uniform to a Scots soldier about to
sail for India to join the Honourable East India Company – and Andrew
sailed too. He rose through the ranks and after fifty years' service, retired
as a major-general. The story of his successful career is told in *A History of
General Anderson 1745–1824*.

One missing part of the story is the relationship between man and
mother. Andrew left Marjory living on the margins, and yet there is no
indication of subsequent contact. He is supposed to have visited Elgin in
1811 and searched in vain, not surprisingly, for his mother's grave in the
cathedral grounds. He was certainly in Elgin in 1823, presiding as life
governor at the first annual meeting of the Elgin Education Society. This
society ran a charity school for some years prior to the opening of the Elgin
Institution. Andrew Anderson died in 1824 in London. In his Trust
Deposition, dated 1815, the residue of his estate (£70,000) was left to
found 'The Elgin Institution, for The Support of Old Age and the Education
of Youth', the elegant sandstone building in the eastern approaches to the
town, designed by Archibald Simpson. He also bequeathed an annuity of
£200 to Miss Jean Gilzean, believed to be the daughter of the benefactor
who had paid for Marjory's funeral. It was left to the trustees of the major-

general to erect Marjory's headstone on her grave near the entrance to Kinneddar graveyard (Ki419), sometime after 1851.

Marjory, in her son's absence, seems to have maintained her independence, travelling through the county and occupying herself in spinning lint or linen yarn, always carrying her wheel, and a wooden stoup for any contribution of victuals from friends. She is said to have become the owner of a black hen making it her daily companion. For a time she stayed in Ballindalloch, but tormented by a 'fatuous female', she returned to Elgin, where home, until it was destroyed, was a shed near the Little Cross. She soon went back to the cathedral: 'I'm no feart of the dead - they're very quiet neighbours; it's the living, if they would but let me be.'

The implication is that Marjory had some form of mental illness as a consequence of her hardships as an army follower. She is described as being of prepossessing appearance, with beautiful fair hair, and of middle size, and a harmless and inoffensive creature. She always wore a short blue cloak, tightly fastened round the neck, and attended church regularly.

She left the cathedral in 1788 to live for a short time in the house of Alexander Stronach, near Ladyhill, Elgin. In her last years, Marjory was taken in by a Mrs Macleod and her husband, in Stotfield, Lossiemouth. The wife had been servant to a family Marjory had known. Marjory continued her way of life with the spinning wheel. A farmer looking for seaweed was surprised by a 'birr-birring' coming from a cave at Craighead - that is, where Covesea Skerries Lighthouse would be first lit in 1846. Marjory had been benighted, and restarted her spinning at daybreak.

One evening during the harvest of 1790, she took to her death bed, and in the absence of any available minister or elder, Mrs Macleod read to her from the scriptures. Coincidentally, a gentleman with the name Gilzean happened to be in Lossie, and paid for the coffin and gave a sum of money to aid the respectability of the funeral. (JT)

# Isabel Mackenzie

*Isabel (unknown surname), born 1731; married John Mackenzie c.1775; died post 1780.*

Isabel travelled with the troops as a camp follower for many years. Later she became a successful and legendary innkeeper.

'Gay, lively polite, and insinuating', declared a smitten traveller on meeting the innkeeper at Tomintoul for the first time. The visitor was no callow youth but a man of the cloth, the Rev. James Hall, who described his meeting with Mrs Mackenzie in his *Travels in Scotland* (1807). Isabel was by this time over seventy years old and still, it would appear, with much of the vibrancy and allure of her youth.

Number 1 The Square, Tomintoul
(Anne Oliver)

Little is known of Isabel's early life; her parents are not recorded. She was born in 1731 and by the age of fourteen was a shepherdess in a nearby parish. In 1745 she met up with a platoon of soldiers and took up their offer to go with them to Flanders where, according to the Rev. John Grant, who knew her in later life, she spent her time 'caressing and being caressed', working her way through the regiment and finally attaching herself to a high ranking officer with noble blood.

Isabel eventually returned to Scotland, but rural life was not for her; she found herself a husband, John Mackenzie. At the outbreak of the Seven Years War in 1756, Isabel persuaded John to enlist in the Royal Highlanders, and the two sailed across the Atlantic to follow the regiment through all its campaigns. They returned to Scotland in 1763 having spent time in England, Ireland, Germany, France and America.

Despite the hardships and deprivation of war Isabel and John seem to have returned with cash in their pockets. Isabel's astute business sense came to the fore in 1766 when they were among the first feuers in the new town of Grantown. They kept an inn there for a number of years before moving to Campdalemore near Tomintoul in 1774. It may have been a speculative move; the inn had been in a run-down state for years. Isabel tried many ways to improve matters to no avail. Her cousin Lt John Grant of Rippachy complained to James Ross at Gordon Castle about the lack of fodder for his horses. He added that Isabel was very disappointed that she had not acquired any land since moving to the country. It was a blow to a woman who 'would wish to supply and accommodate travellers in a gentile and easy way'.

Isabel was not defeated, however. When, in 1775, the Duke of Gordon's surveyor and factor stayed at the inn while drawing up plans for the new town of Tomintoul, John and Isabel took the opportunity to make the first steps towards acquiring feus in the new town. A couple of years later they were laying down their conditions which included a demand that an order should be given to 'stop the huts of Tomintoul from selling ale or whiskie as I will becom to pay all duties and that they do not'.

The demands paid off and in December 1779 Mrs Mackenzie was in possession of nine lots of land, and three free feus in one corner of the Square.

Mrs Mackenzie was soon established at the new inn; her clientele included the Duke of Gordon and his friends as well as local crofters. Travellers like Rev. James Hall went out of their way to visit there and according to Mr Hall they were not disappointed. Two pages of his journal are taken up with an account of her life; according to the gossip he heard there, Isabel bore at least twenty-three children.

The minister was not the first to express his admiration for the inn keeper; the Rev. John Grant provides a detailed biography of her life in *The Statistical Account of Scotland* (1791–99). He described her as at the head of the inhabitants of Tomintoul in 'personal respect and fortune'. Despite a hairy mole on her face and ruddy complexion, Rev. Grant observed that she had retained the 'apparent freshness and vigour of youth'. He obviously felt she was as important to the village as its antiquities, churches and agriculture.

Isabel Mackenzie had a zest for life, an adventurous spirit, an astute business head and a beauty which was outshone by her love for and interest in the people around her and those she met on her way through life. (AO)

# Margaret Dawson

*Margaret Miller or Mallat, born Elgin, 27 October 1770; married Thomas*
*Dawson, 23 December 1793; died Elgin, 1829.*

Margaret Dawson was pregnant when she followed her husband to war. She returned a widow with a baby in her arms.

Margaret met Thomas Dawson in 1792. He was indentured to tailor James Asher of Quarrywood but absconded from the apprenticeship in 1793, eleven months before it was completed. His father was left to pay a three guinea fine. Though Margaret and Thomas had married on 23 December that year, another romantic alliance may have been the cause of his decision. Rumours were rife that Bonnie Jean, the fourth Duchess of Gordon, Jane Maxwell, was travelling the countryside on horseback with a guinea between her teeth, offering a kiss to bright youths ready to fight Napoleon. Margaret and Thomas would have been aware of the stories. For a restless young man the lure of a distinctive highland dress uniform and the chance to serve his country would have been irresistible.

Thomas exchanged his scissors for a musket and gave up his life of cutting and sewing to join the newly formed 92nd Regiment of Foot (later the Gordon Highlanders). Thomas enlisted at Inverness on 25 March 1794 when he was twenty years old. By July the 92nd had sailed for Gibraltar. It was not unusual for wives to 'follow the drum' but there was a stringent selection process and the first record of Margaret joining the ranks was during the second Battle of Copenhagen in September 1807. Wives were selected by ballot providing they were of good character, robust and less than six months pregnant. The selection took place at the docks on the eve or even the very day of embarkation. Not to be chosen meant despair, loneliness – Margaret was already many miles from home – and a real prospect of destitution as there was no financial allowance for soldiers' families in the early 1800s.

As a camp follower Margaret faced a difficult time as she was expected to look after her husband, provide food and laundry for the officers and men, and tend those injured on the battlefield. For these duties she received half-rations and was allowed to live in the barracks with Thomas and all the other men. However, because the regiment regarded the women as a bit of a nuisance with their loud and undisciplined behaviour, they had to march at the rear with the supplies – a practice which was the origin of the derogatory term 'baggage' for a certain type of woman.

The 92nd wives were generally of good character but there was a noted occasion while Margaret was in Denmark when one wife was punished for procuring copious quantities of alcohol. The resulting drunkenness amongst the men and their women came to the attention of the commanding officer who also had cause to deal with another wife on the same occasion. It was reported in records of the day that this woman had behaved in a manner 'too disgraceful to spell out'. It was only through the good conduct of her husband that she was not 'drummed through the regimental quarters'. It must have taken a great deal of love, determination and courage for Margaret to stand by her man, especially as she was four months pregnant at the time. She lost the heel from one of her shoes whilst marching along and was forced to continue without it, which left her with a permanent weakness in her leg. She also found a little bell which she kept as a souvenir.

The battle went well for the British who encircled Copenhagen. During several nights of bombardment they killed more than 2,000 civilians before the Danish army surrendered. Casualties were light on the British side, with forty-two killed. Just four of those were from the 92nd. Margaret's husband Thomas was one of the wounded. A captured Danish vessel, the *Neptunos,* was used as a hospital ship but it was wrecked before Margaret could go aboard with her injured husband. They were taken on to the

*Olive Branch* and into yet more disaster; it was a stormy night and the ship was reputedly manned by a drunken crew. It ran aground near Camp Vere on the Dutch coast. On 1 November Margaret and Thomas were rescued and taken to the Langeldelft Hospital in Middelburg, a city on the island of Walcheren, Zeeland, in Holland. They were well treated, but to add to their distress Thomas's pay was reduced to eightpence ha'penny while he was in hospital. Camp Vere was a regular disembarkation port for the British army and there was a place of worship known as the 'English Church'. This was fortunate for Margaret and Thomas as church members helped look after them.

The army appeared to lose interest in their injured or captured soldiers and their wives. The low-lying area had an annual epidemic of swamp fever, and this is what finally finished off the wounded Thomas. He died on 1 December 1807, aged thirty-five, and was buried in the English Churchyard. Margaret was able to stay at Langeldelft as by this time she was heavily pregnant as well as grief-stricken, homeless and penniless. There was a small birthing room attached to the hospital. Her fatherless son, Thomas, was born two months later on 1 February 1808. He was baptised on 21 February in the church where his father was buried and he and Margaret were sent to Fort Loevestein on 10 March. This was a prisoner of war camp for Russian, Spanish and British soldiers.

It is not known what happened to Margaret and young Thomas in the aftermath of their release, or how she got herself and her baby across the English Channel and north back to Elgin. Her husband had earned battle prize money over the years but according to the records it was 'unclaimed'; £3 8s 2d twice over for the Battle of Copenhagen might have made quite a difference to Margaret. She did manage to find her way home and worked at Johnston's of Newmill, Elgin for a number of years.

Alexander Johnston, founded the company in 1797 with linen, flax, tobacco and oatmeal being the main line of business. By 1808 carding engines had been installed and teasels bought, indicating that wool and weaving had become important and profitable. In 1810 broad and narrow loom shuttles were in place and the workforce was growing. Alexander Johnston and his son James were kind to Margaret and took an interest in Thomas, giving him a position there as soon as he was old enough. By 1829 Alexander had built a double row of houses in Collie Street for his workers. They were of varying sizes to accommodate the different needs of his employees. None had rooms big enough to house a loom, possibly to prevent his employees from taking in work. However, the street soon became known as 'Shuttle Ra'. Thomas and his wife moved into 7 and remained there all their days, working at the mill and raising a family including sons named Thomas Alexander and James Johnston in recognition of the mill-owners' support of the family.

Thomas died at home in 1867. Though he was content to remain in Elgin for the rest of his life following his dramatic birth in Zeeland, his son Thomas inherited his grandparents' adventurous spirit and he emigrated to New Zealand where he died in 1914.

Family papers indicate that Margaret died in 1829 and was buried at Birnie Kirkyard with her Miller family, but there is no record of her death or any sign of her tombstone there. Ordinary women have long been shadowy supporters of their parents, husbands and children and Margaret was no exception. She experienced battle on alien soil, bereavement, birth, shipwreck and incarceration before finally getting herself and her infant back to Elgin, and thence to obscurity. (AO)

# Barbara Simpkin

*Barbara Grant Johnson, born London, 8 July 1913; married Richard Simpkin,*
*2 April 1941; died Elgin, 27 December 1995.*

Barbara Simpkin, officer's wife, gave up her career and ambitions to devote herself to the army. She was a founder member of Amnesty International.

Barbara was grand-daughter of James 'The Major' Grant of Glen Grant Distillery, Rothes. Her mother, Hilda, left her first husband and daughter Rose for Noel Johnson whom she married in 1912. Barbara was born a year later. The Major disinherited Hilda and Barbara. By 1919 they were living in the north of England; here they converted to the Catholic faith. At the age of nineteen Barbara began writing articles on the nature of faith for the *Catholic Gazette*.

Hilda died in 1935. Barbara was secretary of the Westminster Legion of Mary Annual Pilgrimage to Walsingham where she became a friend of Frank Duff. He was the founder of a worldwide organisation of lay people who devote themselves to voluntary pastoral work. She was also an active member of the Catholic Evidence Guild. Following stringent training on public speaking and crowd interaction Barbara regularly stood on a soap box at Speakers' Corner proclaiming her faith.

With war approaching, Barbara joined the Civil Defence Corps in London. She was one of the first women ambulance drivers. She learned Russian at the Cambridge Summer School Russian Group, set up to support the priests of the Russian Mission.

In October 1940 Richard Simpkin, a nineteen-year-old Cambridge student, awaiting call-up, volunteered at the Dolphin Square ambulance station where Barbara was stationed. Richard and Barbara were married in Westminster Cathedral on 2 April 1941. Barbara was twenty-seven years old. Two months later Richard embarked with the Royal Tank Regiment for North Africa. He was wounded at the end of 1941 and awarded the Military Cross in 1942. It was four years before Barbara saw her husband again. She enrolled at the Colwyn Bay Wireless School which trained naval ratings. Barbara was one of a few women who learned Morse code and achieved City and Guilds in Technical Electricity.

Barbara Simpkin, 1940s (Michael Simpkin)

Employed by the BBC as a woman operator in engineering, Barbara was promoted to technical engineer class 1 in 1943 and to maintenance engineer in May 1944; probably the first woman to achieve this position. With her highly developed technical skills and command of Russian and French she was delighted to be transferred to Bush House, the home of the World Service in January 1945.

Richard had been posted missing in 1942 and confirmed as a POW in Italy later that year. He returned to his bride in April 1945. As was to become the pattern of her life throughout their marriage, Barbara resigned her job. 'Any attempt to serve two masters would be courting catastrophe', she remarked.

Their first child, Michael was born in February 1946. The family moved frequently for the next quarter of a century. With each posting Barbara made a home and found voluntary work. She played her part as an officer's wife diligently, counselling soldiers and their wives as well as the young officers. Their second child, Veronica was born in 1948. The first of many nannies arrived the following day. Barbara again busied herself with voluntary work. She was secretary of the Alverstoke Conservative Association and wrote articles including 'Politics the modern home help' where she averred:

> It is we women who have run a home on whatever the Government leaves in our man's pay packet... Knowing what is going on in politics

and seeing that we have a say in them should be as important and routine a job as spring-cleaning or stocking the store cupboard.

Barbara went to Germany for the first time in 1953 soon after their youngest child, Alexander was born. Richard was promoted to major and eight-year-old Michael, was sent home to boarding school. Barbara immersed herself in regimental life and local charities. They returned to the UK in 1957 and Veronica went off to boarding school.

Richard was posted to Hong Kong in 1959. Barbara threw herself into wives' club duties; her sense of fun culminated in an encounter with the riot squad one night when rickshaws had been commandeered for midnight racing. She was involved with the pastoral care of the soldiers and their wives and played an active part easing the life of refugees who were living in appalling conditions. At the end of 1961 she was diagnosed with tuberculosis, probably contracted from the refugees. She spent six months in a British sanatorium.

Though Barbara was minus a lung she returned to her life of voluntary work. She became a founder member of Appeal for Amnesty 1961, the forerunner of Amnesty International. She was one of the earliest volunteers in the office at Mitre Court, London. Her work there was cut short by Richard's promotion to Lieutenant Colonel of 1 Royal Tank Regiment and posting back to Germany in 1963. Once more Barbara was fully involved in the care of the families. This time she determined to abolish the outmoded wives' club, of which she was president.

When they left Hohne in 1965 the regimental colonel included Barbara in his formal thanks, saying she had lifted the spirits of the regiment. Richard, by now a colonel, was director of studies (Weapons and Vehicles) at the Royal Military College of Science (RMCS) at Shrivenham.

When she was fifty-four years old and had been married to the army for nearly a quarter of a century Barbara began to travel alone, visiting Israel and Jordan in 1967. She resumed her support for the Prisoners' Aid Society and in 1970 started to work for Shelter, the charity for the homeless where she led the Fatherless Families Department. A year later Richard retired from the army; Barbara left Shelter. The director, Rev. Francis Park, said:

> The fact that you have done so much in such an unobtrusive way is all the more reason that I should express in a more formal way my appreciation of all you have done.

Richard set up the European Language Service on retirement and Barbara was installed as company secretary. She was also doing an Open

University Arts degree and graduated in 1974.

In 1978 Barbara returned to her Moray roots, settling in Elgin at Over Deanshaugh with Richard. She was now able to concentrate on her Catholic faith. She became involved in St Sylvester's Catholic Church in Elgin and Pluscarden Abbey. She professed as a Benedictine Oblate in 1983.

Richard died at home in November 1986. Barbara's lifelong ambition to visit Russia was fulfilled after her husband's death; because of his military connections she had never been able to go.

On her return she devoted herself to the ministry of the sick and the dying; she was 'worth five curates', parish priest Canon Robert Macdonald maintained. The newly formed Rite of Christian Initiation for Adults inquiry programme (RCIA) had recently started and Barbara was able to use her talents honed at Speakers' Corner sixty years earlier to speak imaginatively and with passion about the beliefs of the church.

Her health was failing and she moved to a small flat in Hawthorn Court. On Christmas Day 1995 she left a note on her door saying that she was well, but tired and wanted to sleep. A close friend visited her on Boxing Day and felt her time was very short. She died on 27 December and was buried with Richard at Pluscarden Abbey.

In 2002, seven years after her death, Ogilvie Institute, Aberdeen, the educational arm of the Catholic Diocese of Aberdeen and the Highlands and Islands, held her work in sufficient regard to publish a book. *In Search of God, a Resource for Parish RCIA Programmes*, by Barbara Simpkin, was put together from her writings during the eighties and nineties. It contains twenty-eight articles; it remains a useful reference book and Barbara is still held in high esteem within the diocese.

While other women of her intellect were forging careers Barbara Simpkin followed the drum so diligently that her prospects, beliefs and desires were subsumed by the demands of the army. (AO)

## CHAPTER FIVE

# Escaping Poverty:

# The Beginnings of a Social Service

*300 of [Elgin's] necessitous poor are to be presented on New Year's Day with 1lb of sugar, 1oz of tea, a 2lb fine loaf and a biscuit.* Forres Gazette, 1863[1]

FOR CENTURIES THERE had been some small provision for the poor of Scotland, and various benefactors had made generous contributions to alleviate suffering for the people of Moray. In Elgin, Dr Gray's Hospital (1819), Anderson's Institution (1833), and the Morayshire Union Poorhouse (1865) had looked after the destitute in some way. Although it was all very well for people to benefit from soup kitchens, parochial relief or from the donations of philanthropic benefactors, what was really needed was a means of escaping poverty. Society itself had to change.

For the working classes, secure employment could lift the family above the breadline. The Elgin Ladies Benevolent Society had understood this when it was founded, following the great Moray floods of 1829, to provide employment for women made destitute by the floods. At the beginning of the nineteenth century, domestic service, either in the fields or in the house, was the most obvious choice for employment for working-class girls before marriage. Sewing skills were also useful. As the century progressed, teaching and nursing jobs became accessible. Teaching became possible because of the pupil-teacher system which was formally adopted in 1846. In return for the 'teaching' the pupil-teacher got, for five years, free education and eventually a small wage. Many of the pupil-teachers passed the entrance qualifications for teacher training colleges and gained bursaries to pay for fees and board. There was some criticism that the system was exploitative of pupil-teachers and provided inferior education for the children, but, at a time of severe teacher shortage, it served the needs of the country and provided a pathway out of poverty.

Nursing was, likewise, accessible because (by the late nineteenth century) training took place on the job with board and, after an initial period, a small wage. Because teaching and nursing also appealed to

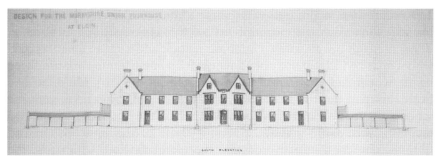

Original design for the Morayshire Union Poorhouse 1863 (Elgin Museum)

middle-class girls, these jobs were a means of moving up the social scale. Not only did Margaret Stephen's salary contribute to the family income, success in her teaching career gave her a respected position in Elgin society.

A job, then, could keep the lower classes off the pauper list, provided that their health was good. If a girl married she might need to give up a job, but there would be a husband's wage to help set up the home, even if it was just one room. Children usually followed, at about one to two year intervals. It was hard in limited accommodation, with maybe elderly parents to care for as well. There was the constant fear of losing children to one of the epidemics of the nineteenth century – measles, diphtheria, smallpox, whooping cough, or scarlet fever.

With *Oliver Twist* (1837–39) Charles Dickens had brought the evils of poverty to popular attention, and in the 1840s Friedrich Engels had made a study of the deprivation of the working classes in Manchester and Salford and Henry Mayhew had recorded dreadful poverty in London. Further north, in the 1860s, Dr Henry Littlejohn, the first Medical Officer of Health in Scotland, described the squalor that was common in cities and towns across the land. The condition of the closes of Elgin where Margaret Stephen and Ella Munro were raised were well described by Littlejohn in 1867:

> In close connection with each midden and pigstye there was a privy, which, as a general rule, admitting of remarkably few exceptions, was kept in a disgusting state, and gave little evidence of cleanly habits among the poor.[3]

The squalor was seen by the expanding middle classes as a threat to the health of the whole population because of the danger of epidemics such as cholera, typhus and typhoid. Poor health was also damaging to the economy. These reports on the sanitary state of the nation, important in awakening the social conscience of Scotland, were milestones on the way to a social service.

Another mark of progress was the 1872 Education Act (Scotland) when the state took away the responsibility for the schools from the churches. The state schools were known as board schools and each area had its own school board which carried out administration in the framework produced by the Scotch (later Scottish) Education Department (SED). Children aged five to thirteen had to attend school. A regime of inspections kept the schools up to standard. The practicalities of the act took a while to establish, with some schools, especially those of the Episcopalian and Catholic churches, initially resisting the reorganisation. Ultimately, the 1872 act enabled the evolution of free elementary education, followed by access to free higher education, for all children in Scotland.

In Edinburgh, such women as Christian Guthrie Wright[4] and the Stevenson sisters, Flora and Louisa[5], were active on many fronts: serving on the new school boards, fighting for women's access to higher education, campaigning for properly trained nurses to care for the sick poor, and fighting for women's suffrage, to name a good few. The campaigns were not so much about 'doing good' and supporting the poor, but more about changing society itself. These women wanted a say in how the country was run. One of their first successes was the founding of the Edinburgh School of Cookery which opened in November 1875. The opening was attended with great excitement and interest and it was not long before the school was organising lectures throughout the country. Such a lecture was held in Elgin in January 1877 – probably attended by twenty-nine-year-old Margaret Stephen who had been back in Elgin for about a year.[6] Glasgow too had opened a cookery school. It had been hoped that these schools would be important factors in training working-class women and teachers, but the courses had more success with middle-class women, and it was to be some years before most of the school boards accepted the need for domestic training (other than sewing and knitting) in their schools. In Elgin, Miss Stephen's cookery classes, although apparently instigated entirely by herself, reflected national aspirations. She was fortunate because the Elgin School Board were supportive of her mission. Miss Stephen courted controversy in her campaign to introduce cooking to the school curriculum and was well ahead of her time, but she was not the only teacher of cookery in Moray in the 1880s. In Cullen, cookery was suggested as a curriculum subject by Her Majesty's Inspectors (HMI) as early as 1876, and, by 1877, girls were visiting ladies in the town to see demonstrations. However, it is not clear if 'practical cookery' allowed the girls to do the cooking, as in Elgin, or just to watch a demonstration. By 1892 the school log book stated that 'cooking is now being taught almost daily', but in 1894, HMI commented that 'the discontinuance of cookery seems a retrograde step'. There was no more cooking until 1907 when sixteen boys and twenty girls were enrolled for the new cookery class. Flora Stevenson had suggested in the 1870s that boys should be taught cooking, but such an idea was dismissed by the male members of the Edinburgh School Board without a second thought.[7] The teaching of cookery to boys in Cullen is likely to have related to the fishing industry and the need for a cook on the fishing boats.

Following the success of the Edinburgh School of Cookery, Christian Guthrie Wright and Louisa Stevenson turned their attention to the queen's nurses. Queen Victoria's Jubilee Institute for Nurses (QVJIN) originated in 1887 when 'the women of England' raised money for a jubilee present for Victoria. After the gift of jewellery was commissioned £70,000 pounds remained, and the queen chose to use the money to support a district nursing scheme. The Misses Wright and Stevenson were active members of the Scottish branch of the Institute, raising impressive amounts of money and organising training.[8] Originally the service was for the sick poor only and small fees were accepted from patients when possible. In Buckie the QVJIN was established in 1892.[9] The Nursing Association, of which Helen Rose was secretary in Elgin, became affiliated with the QVJIN in 1911. queen's nurses were important all across Scotland, but nowhere as much as in the highlands and islands, where doctors were few and far between. It was in Shetland that Ella Munro served as a queen's nurse for eighteen years.

A social service was slowly taking shape. The old age pension was introduced in 1908, and a national insurance bill was introduced by Lloyd George in 1911. With the introduction of the old age pension, the poorhouse lost some of its menace.

Helen MacKenzie was amongst those who highlighted the need for such a social service and contributed to its development. Margaret Stephen and Helen Rose were instrumental in leading the way in a local sense: Miss Stephen with her innovative shaping of the Girls' School curriculum and Helen Rose with her vision of connecting pre-school childcare and medical welfare. Ella Munro, who struggled with poverty all her life, was, as a queen's nurse, one of the foot soldiers of the Highlands and Islands Medical Service – a service that the MacKenzies helped to establish, a forerunner of the National Health Service of 1948.

The lives of these women shared similar concerns. What is certain is that they all saw education as a key factor in their attempt to improve the social conditions of the world that surrounded them.

Annie Ramsay, farm outworker, also understood the importance of education. An outworker's life entailed long hours of backbreaking work: hoeing turnips, helping with thrashing corn, lifting potatoes, spreading muck and maybe milking the cows. Apart from working with the horses, which was strictly a male province, an outworker was expected to do any of the jobs that men carried out. For this work a woman could expect board and lodging and, in 1860, a wage of about five pounds per annum – about half that of a male agricultural labourer.[10] James Ramsay Macdonald, Annie Ramsay's son, became the first Labour prime minister of Britain. Both Annie Ramsay and Ella Munro ended their lives in relative com-

Annie Ramsay (Iona Kielhorn)

fort, partly because their children had made their way up the social ladder and had thus escaped the poverty of their early lives.

Joyful was one of the many women who did not escape poverty. Her story illustrates how declining health could be dominated by fear of the poorhouse. By 1925 the Morayshire Union Poorhouse had changed its name to Craigmoray, and in 1932 the words 'pauper' and 'poorhouse' were no longer officially used, but the people of Moray still referred to it as 'the poorhouse' and continued to do so until it was demolished in 1976. The threat of poverty remained very real for those who had to survive on the old age pension alone.

## Annie Ramsay

*Anne Ramsay, born Elgin, 4 August 1843; died Lossiemouth, 11 February 1910.*

Annie Ramsay, farm servant in Moray, and mother of James Ramsay Macdonald, the first Labour prime minister of Great Britain, supported and encouraged her son in self improvement.

Annie Ramsay was the daughter of Isabella Allan or Ramsay and William Ramsay, baker in Elgin. She was the second of four children: a boy and three girls. Isabella, or Bella, Annie's mother, brought up her children in Lossiemouth by herself, earning some money by sewing. The circumstances of Bella's separation from her husband are unknown, but there is little doubt that it resulted in hardship for the family. After the separation, Bella reverted to her Allan surname.

In 1866 Annie Ramsay was placed at Claydales farm, near Alves, as an outworker. When she became pregnant by one of the farm labourers, John Macdonald, she was in no way unusual; the illegitimacy figures were higher in the North-East than anywhere else in Scotland. Annie returned to her mother in the fishertown of Lossiemouth, where her son, named James Macdonald Ramsay on the birth certificate, was born on 12 October 1866.

Two months later, on 14 December 1866, John Macdonald and Anne Ramsay came before the Free Kirk Session of Alves 'of their

Bella Allan (Iona Kielhorn)

own accord' to report the birth of their son and to confess their 'sins' so that they could be 'absolved from Church censure and be restored to Church privileges'. This may suggest that the two planned to marry, but John Macdonald returned to his job as foreman at Sweethillock Farm, also near Alves, and Annie returned to Lossiemouth. Nothing more is heard of John Macdonald in Annie's story.

In Lossiemouth Annie earned money by sewing, working in the fishing community, and by getting seasonal farm work. She never needed to apply for poor relief. Her son long remembered her bleeding hands at the time of harvest. Annie's mother, Bella, who died in 1893 at the age of eighty-two, supported her daughter, doted on her grandson, and filled the house with stories. Both women were skilled in needlework and made exquisite lace.

Annie was known for her strong radical views. She was remembered arguing violently with the local fishermen and when, during the Boer War, Ladysmith was relieved, it is said that she hung black mourning crepe on her door. In response, the locals burnt her effigy on the celebration bonfire.

Annie's son, James, did well at school, benefiting from the traditional but sympathetic teaching of John Macdonald (no relation), the dominie at Drainie School, a couple of miles to the west of Lossiemouth. On leaving

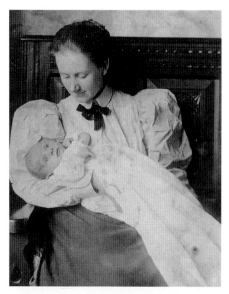

Margaret MacDonald with Alister, her firstborn
(Iona Kielhorn)

school James took work at a local farm, but after a few months he was fortunate enough to attain the coveted position of pupil-teacher at his old school. By the age of eighteen James Macdonald had a good education that included a grounding in the classics, but that, above all, led to an understanding of 'the delight of knowledge'. In 1884 he left Lossiemouth for England to pursue his education and to develop his political interests. In London he did not initially find an escape from poverty, and the oatmeal sent by Annie helped eke out a threadbare existence. He took menial jobs and completed his education by going to evening classes and studying in libraries. In 1891 he joined Keir Hardie's Independent Labour Party.

In 1896 James, now called Ramsay, married Margaret Gladstone, a woman active in the Woman's Labour League and the Woman's Industrial Council, who was interested in women's suffrage and many social issues, including the welfare of young children and babies. Margaret came from a middle class intellectual background and had a small private income.

Margaret got on well with her mother-in-law, Annie Ramsay, and they exchanged letters:

[From Annie, 13 July 1896] My dear gural you spake of Milking cowes i have milked cowes and mad butter and all that work but for the last 29 years doing little but sowing in My dear little home now My dear i will not forgoet to pray to god for you as i doun for him in the past that god may be with you both and that you may be happy

[from Annie, The Cottage, 27 September 1897]
Just a fue lines to sea if som of them will find you i saw Mr McDonald Drany asking for you on Saterday they are all well Davie West got his plase all burned on Saterday night I have not hard nothing more about it but that he had lost all his things
[David West was a local artist]

Two of the MacDonald's six children were born in Lossiemouth and Annie sometimes looked after her grandchildren when Ramsay and Margaret were travelling abroad. In 1909 Ramsay built a house – 'The Hillocks' – for his mother to live in, and where his children could stay when he and Margaret were away. He had wished to build it on Prospect Terrace, looking out across the east beach, but was told that 'Red bastards don't build up here'.

On 17 September 1909 the MacDonalds went to India for six weeks. They left the younger children with Annie who wrote with general news:

[September 1909, 'The Hillocks'] We are geting on very well I have got my blanks dray [blankets dry] and I felt very tired yesterday but my bilor [boiler] is redy fir to do the close you left David is geting on well I think the Doctir will be here today… Tell Alister how I miss him and theyt Joan was singin and saying two on two this morning how she woke up I do not now she is all right and walk som steps yesterday alone.

On 24 December 1909 Annie's photograph was taken at a Lossiemouth fisher wedding. It may be that the picture was taken sometime prior to the actual wedding, since no one appears to be dressed in their best attire.

Family and friends taken before the wedding of Joseph Stewart (Dovie) and Maggie Anne Stewart, 24 December 1909. Annie Ramsay is fourth from right, middle row. Other names listed in Appendix 3 (Iona Kielhorn)

Ishbel Macdonald flies (as a passenger) to London from Seaham Harbour 1931, after Ramsay won the seat with a majority of 5,951 (Iona Kielhorn).

Annie's health, however, was declining and she was not to enjoy her new home for long. In January 1910 she was ill and, directly following the general election, Ramsay came up to see her. On 28 January he wrote that Annie was suffering from delusions. Meanwhile David, Ramsay's son in London, had caught diphtheria. He died on 3 February. A week later, on 11 February, Annie too was dead. She is buried in Old Spynie Kirkyard. By the time of her death Ramsay was a leading member of the Independent Labour Party and destined for higher position. Annie had seen her son attain some success in his life, and this success had saved her from worrying about how she would manage in her old age.

A year after the deaths of David and Annie, Margaret died of blood poisoning. Devastated , Ramsay looked to his eldest daughter for support and it was she who, at the age of twenty, acted as hostess at Number 10 when he became prime minister in 1924. In this role Ishbel travelled to America, Canada and the Continent taking on her mother's position with charm and efficiency. After her father died in 1937 Ishbel married a farmer and ran a pub in Buckinghamshire. On being widowed she returned to Lossiemouth and married widower James Peterkin. Widowed once more, she fostered three sons and was active in the community. Many will remember her involvement in bowling, hillwalking and community ventures. She died at 'The Hillocks' in 1982. Ishbel and her siblings never had to suffer the poverty that their father knew. They lived the life of the middle classes; a world away from the life of Annie Ramsay.

Ramsay Macdonald always acknowledged that it was his mother, Annie Ramsay, and his grandmother, Bella Allan, who had encouraged him to aspire to be something other than a farm labourer or a fisherman. On entering Number 10 Downing Street for the first time as Prime Minister, he wrote in his diary, 'Ah, were she [Margaret] here to help me. Why are they both dead – my mother and she?' (SB)

This photograph of 'The Hillocks' was produced as a postcard. Ramsay MacDonald wears the cap (Iona Kielhorn)

# Margaret Stephen

*Margaret Stephen, born Elgin, 19 December 1847; died Elgin, 16 April 1924.*

Whilst well aware of the importance of academic achievement, Margaret Stephen believed that domestic training could help to alleviate the poverty of Victorian and Edwardian Elgin. As headmistress of Elgin Girls' School, she was able to put her beliefs into practice.

Margaret was the daughter of Catherine Macdonald and Alexander Stephen, shoemaker. The family lived in Lady Lane, Elgin, in 1861 and until the 1880s. It was a small family for the times, there apparently being only three children, all of whom survived into adulthood. Margaret was the eldest, William became an accountant, and Anne later kept house for the family. Margaret Stephen did well at the Elgin Girls' School and was appointed pupil-teacher when about thirteen years old. This enabled her to study for the examination to Moray House – the Free Church Training College in Edinburgh.

Success at college resulted in a post as headmistress of the Tyne Dock British School, a large new school on Tyneside, built to provide education for the children of the 'working poor'. This was followed by a period as headmistress of Lilliesleaf Public School, a small country school near Selkirk. In 1876 Miss Stephen was appointed headmistress of her old school, the Elgin Girls' School. This school, initially a charity school called The Elgin Infant School and charging a penny a week, had catered for the children of Elgin since the 1830s. In 1872 the school became one of the board schools and as such was presided over by the Elgin School Board and was subject to visits by Her Majesty's Inspectors (HMI). The Elgin Girls' School log book survives with an account of the progress of the school through to its closure in 1904. On arrival, Miss Stephen found a school that was well run but short of accommodation. Her pupils, both girls and boys, numbered 319 at the end of 1876. She had one probationer as assistant teacher and eight pupil-teachers. HMI reported in 1879:

> This school under the management of Miss Stephen is taught with great skill and earnestness and the results as might be expected are exceedingly good.

The school was situated in Academy Street, on the corner with Moray Street. The accommodation was poor and overcrowded, with plaster falling off the walls. Attendance fluctuated; there were epidemics of scarlet fever, measles, whooping cough, influenza and diphtheria to keep pupils at home – the school was closed for a month in April 1901 because of a measles epidemic. Girls often had to stay at home to help mother with the younger children or with the spring cleaning; boys sometimes played truant. Floods and snow also kept the children at home. A recurring problem arose from the academy boys 'ill using the children on their way to school'. That there was poverty is shown by the entry:

> [5 February 1897] The soup kitchen is now open and from thirty to forty children get a warm dinner every day. Two pupil-teachers accompany the pupils to the Town Hall [at that time in Moray Street].

The greatest difference from today's schools was the system of teaching. With over 300 pupils and only one assistant, the school was dependent on its eight pupil-teachers. Their quality depended on the training that they were given by the head teacher.

Miss Stephen did well for her pupils, teaching them a wide variety of subjects including French, stocks and shares, and the study of poems such

Margaret Stephen (Aberdeen City and Aberdeenshire Archives)

as Milton's *Paradise Lost* and Scott's *Lady of the Lake*. She prepared them for examinations to gain free admittance to Elgin Academy, for the Civil Service examinations, for Aberdeen University local examinations, and to win bursaries to teacher training colleges. Mr Crowe, a singing master, came regularly, and drawing lessons were also given. There was playground drill for the infants and in 1895 the 'senior classes have their practice in Musical Drill with Indian Clubs in the morning at 9.30'. There were physiography lessons (relating to physical geography) at the Victoria School of Science and Art in 1892; the pupil-teachers also went there for chemistry two evenings a week. When, in 1897, Miss Allardyce joined the staff and took over the teaching of French, German was added to the curriculum. Less than a year later these language students were good enough to take Lady Literate in Arts (LLA) classes at Elgin Academy. Religious education was not neglected.

That Margaret Stephen was a teacher of some stature was formally recognised when she was made a Fellow of the Educational Institute of Scotland (FEIS) in 1890. This honour was and continues to be a degree. The EIS is the only trade union that is able to confer degrees.

The abiding theme of the school log book is Miss Stephen's interest in domestic science. On 8 June 1888, she reported 'Instead of our usual French lesson this week, I gave the two advanced classes a lesson in Practical Cookery 'a cup of Arrowroot'. The girls were greatly interested'. The HMI report that year noted:

> A course of practical cookery has begun under the direction of Miss Stephen who recently took a high class degree in Glasgow School of Cookery. I had the pleasure of witnessing one complete lesson... I rejoice at the commencement of this course.

Miss Stephen soon had her pupils doing the cooking, bringing in their own ingredients and taking the results home: curried rabbit and rice, calves foot jelly, apple dumplings and other cheap healthy meals. By 1900 girls were also coming from the East and West End schools to get cookery lessons. There were evening classes too, paid for by the town council and taught by Miss Stephen. Furthermore, Miss Stephen was entitled to grant diplomas to trainee domestic science teachers in the area.

Into this seemingly innocuous scenario came politics. Some parents objected to cookery lessons; cooking should be taught at home. This debate about teaching domestic subjects was nothing new – such arguments had been heard throughout the century. It was particularly relevant following 1892 when girls were first admitted to universities, for which they needed Latin. At the West End School the pupils could do Latin and commercial subjects instead of domestic subjects. Though some parents objected to the cookery classes they were apparently the vocal few. After some organisational change to school arrangements in 1899 HMI reported:

> The ready manner in which the [Girls'] School filled up after the rearrangement by which parents were left free to choose their school shows their approbation of it.

The School Board was supportive of the cookery lessons, but it did nothing to improve facilities in the light of repeated criticism from HMI about the

Miss Stephen with her teachers and pupils of the day continuation class in the Technical School, Elgin, 1912.
Josephine Forsyth of Claydales farm is shown on the right of the second back row (William Mustard)

deplorable state of the school buildings. In 1902 Miss JG Crawford of the Edinburgh Cookery School was appointed sole HMI of domestic science in Scotland. Her report of 1903 highlights the problems at the Girls' School and the incredible lack of facilities:

> There is only one small gas stove between two classes of 36 girls, and no sink accommodation... I would strongly recommend the erection of new premises to serve as a Centre for all pupils in these schools.

And that is more or less what happened. The Girls' School was closed in 1904. After a refit, it was officially reopened in March 1905 as the Elgin Girls' Technical School, for girls only, with Margaret Stephen as the head teacher. Pupils attended from the nearby board schools, the evening classes continued and day continuation classes were introduced whereby girls who had left school could attend for domestic training. But the technical school did not have an easy start – parents continued to object to the teaching of domestic subjects in school and as the controversy rumbled on *The Educational News* (14 October 1905) reported that seventeen girls had been exempted from the Technical School classes so they could study a commercial course with Latin and mathematics.

Miss Stephen's opinions on the importance of domestic subjects in a girl's education can be summarised by the following 1905 extracts from her article in the *Educational News* (the journal of the Educational Institute of Scotland):

> household management, as laid down in the Education Code, would not be looked upon as so much time subtracted from other branches of the school curriculum, but as an aid to intellectual success.

and

> If every Scottish girl could receive an education such as I have sketched, I venture to say that the tone of the homes of our country would be vastly improved. The poison of intemperance would have its antidote in the well-prepared meal and the intelligently regulated home. There would be less need to provide feeding committees to provide bread to the starving and clothes to the naked.

On the occasion of Miss Stephen's retirement in 1913, *The Northern Scot* reported on the success of the Technical School, to which pupils came from all over Moray:

> A feature of the day continuation classes is the financial success which has attended them, large grants being earned for the School Board.

A colleague spoke of her:

> She has done her work well. Over the wide world, almost from China to Peru, in the homeland and the islands of the sea, wherever the wandering northern Scot has found a home, there are children, grown to be men and women, fathers and mothers, who will join us in our tribute now. Few have better claim to the leisure of the long afternoon.

We all know those teachers who are remembered affectionately for generations to come, until the pupils themselves are gone. With Margaret, the family died out, for none had married. Her brother William, who had also been interested in education, died in 1922. Her sister Anne, the housekeeper for the family, died the year before Margaret, who died in April 1924 – the family stone is found in Elgin Cathedral.

Margaret Stephen, brought up in the closes of Elgin, was well aware of poverty and hardship about the town. Her commitment to domestic science was part of her wish to better the lives of her pupils and their families. (SB)

# Helen Leslie MacKenzie

*Helen Carruthers Spence, born Dufftown, 13 April 1859; married William Leslie MacKenzie, 12 February 1892; died Edinburgh, 25 September 1945.*

Helen MacKenzie was instrumental in the design of many of the emerging social services of the early nineteenth century.

The daughter of Mary Scott Macdonell and William Spence, tailor, Helen Spence was the eldest of eight children. Three of her brothers died in infancy. Helen's father did well in business, employing five men and three boys by 1881, and serving as provost of Dufftown for a while. Helen attended the Female School in Dufftown and, aged about thirteen, became a pupil-teacher. After attending class VII of the Church of Scotland Training College in Aberdeen, Helen started teaching in Cairney (Cairnie) Primary School in December 1881.

Cairney, between Keith and Huntly, was very much a country school. The school log book gives a picture of a school run with difficulty by the head teacher, James Wilson MA, with Helen as assistant and two monitors. The main problem was low attendance because many of the children were needed on the land for such jobs as hoeing turnips, herding cattle and taking in the harvest. Bad weather and sickness (scarlet fever, diphtheria, and whooping cough) added to the problems. The 1883 report of Her Majesty's Inspectors (HMI) was not very flattering, but it did note that the Latin 'was creditable'.

In March 1884 Helen returned to Aberdeen where she became head teacher of the North Lodge Industrial School for about a year, followed by a year at the Middle School. Industrial schools were established to keep poor children off the street and prepare them for employment. By February 1887 Helen was infant mistress at the Skene Street School in Aberdeen. The school logbook gives an interesting entry in December of that year, noting that Miss Spence was in charge of 103 infants (under six years) with help from a pupil-teacher – two other classes in the infant school were also overseen by her. Despite the obvious overcrowding and the fact that the teachers, Helen included, were often ill, HMI reported in 1891:

> The Infant Department is conducted with Miss Spence's wonted tact, judgement and skill. The children are in excellent order and the Discipline, while gentle and sympathetic, is also firm. The subjects are in a very sound state of advancement and numerous interesting occupations have been added to increase the attractions of child life in school. Sewing and singing are very good.

Leaving the school in good heart, Helen embarked on a new stage of her life when she left teaching and married Dr William Leslie MacKenzie in 1892. Her teaching days had provided her with experience relating to both rural and urban poverty. The marriage was the forging of an important professional relationship.

William Leslie MacKenzie, known as Leslie, a grieve's son from Shandwick, Ross-shire, and like Helen a pupil-teacher, had taken an arts degree at Aberdeen, followed by a medical degree. Courteous, humorous, and impressive, Leslie MacKenzie's mission was to bring about a reform of the health services.

The couple moved to Edinburgh when Leslie was appointed medical officer for Leith in 1894. There were no children of the marriage. The MacKenzies stayed in Edinburgh for the rest of their lives, their interest in childcare and social welfare, and their liberal principles, interweaving through their various projects, often working together, sometimes following their own inclinations.

The Royal Commission into Physical Training (Scotland), 1902, was set up in an attempt to understand why soldiers fighting in the Boer War were in such poor physical condition. The expectation was that physical training would improve the soldiers' health. Leslie MacKenzie and Matthew Hay, however, held a different point of view and reported to the commission that large numbers of children in Aberdeen and Edinburgh had poor health that no amount of physical exercise could eradicate. Together, Leslie and Helen MacKenzie studied the health of school children from different schools in Edinburgh. Whilst Helen organised the project and wrote up the results, Leslie measured and weighed the children. This study showed that the children from poorer areas were smaller and lighter than children from wealthy areas. Nutrition and poor housing, it was realised, were the main factors to take into account when considering the health of the nation. A major concern related to the high rate of infant mortality. Helen was keen to point out that cooking and domestic skills should be added to the school curriculum, so that children could be properly fed, when she gave evidence to the Interdepartmental Committee on Physical Deterioration in 1904. Finally in 1908, twenty years after Miss Stephen had instituted cooking in the Elgin Girls' School, the Education (Scotland) Act required school boards to provide education for girls in domestic matters including cooking, to organise medical inspections of all schoolchildren, and to provide meal services for poor children. Dr Leslie MacKenzie was appointed as the first medical inspector of schools in Scotland.

The MacKenzies were also much involved in the setting up of the

Helen MacKenzie is on the right, with her husband Leslie behind. This photograph was taken in Keith 1916 when the National Union of Women Workers helped to stage a travelling exhibition on maternity and child welfare. The exhibition was also shown in Elgin, Dufftown and Aberlour. The National Union of Women Workers evolved into the National Council of Women of Great Britain, a pressure group working on women's issues (*The Northern Scot*)

Highlands and Islands Medical Service (HIMS), established in 1913. queen's nurses were crucial to this scheme, particularly as they had been specifically trained to treat the sick poor in their own homes. Progress, however, was upset by the First World War.

Sometime before the war Helen MacKenzie became a member of the Council of the Edinburgh School of Cookery and Domestic Economy. A new diploma course in social work was initiated during the war and Helen was one of the lecturers. She also took a particular interest in the conditions of women factory workers and with training welfare supervisors of the workers.

A great variety of social causes took up Helen's time, including the National Union of Women Workers, the Women's Emancipation Union, the Mental Welfare Association and the Royal Institution for Deaf and Dumb children. As a friend of Elsie Inglis, Helen helped to improve maternity services in Edinburgh. She was also a member of the Edinburgh School Board. She and her husband were still very much interested in the development of the HIMS. After the war Leslie MacKenzie was knighted, and Helen was generally known as Lady Leslie MacKenzie.

News of the HIMS had travelled far. In 1924 Helen and Leslie MacKenzie had a visit from a Mary Breckinridge of America. Appalled by the high death rate of American women in labour, Mary Breckinridge travelled round Scotland researching conditions in the highlands, and looking at the role of queen's nurses. A year later the first meeting was held of what was to become the Frontier Nursing Service in Kentucky. Relying on horses for transport, the service was modelled on that of the highlands with a touch of the Canadian Mounted Police. The service was a great success, more or less ending maternal deaths in the region. In 1928 it opened its first hospital at Thousandsticks Mountain in Hyden. The MacKenzies, who could not ride, went on a rather alarming journey on buckboard (an open cart) to open the new hospital. Later Helen MacKenzie gave lantern lectures about the brave nurses of Kentucky riding over mountain ranges to attend to their patients. Helen received her own honour when she was awarded CBE in 1933 for 'public services in the interests of women and children in Scotland'.

Following the Electoral Reform Bill of 1918, when some women of over thirty years were allowed to vote, The National Women Citizens' Association was established to educate women voters in their new role in society. Local groups had been active since 1913. In March 1931, Lady Leslie MacKenzie, by then the president of the Scottish Council of Women Citizens' Association, was the principal speaker at the newly established Arbroath branch, encouraging women to enter into Scottish politics.

Sir Leslie MacKenzie died in 1935 and Helen had to adjust to a new way of life. She and her husband had made such a good team, and together had engineered many social changes that had benefited Scotland and further afield. Sir Leslie was buried in Mortlach churchyard, Dufftown, in the Spence family plot, where Helen would later join him.

Helen MacKenzie lived for ten years after her husband died. She continued to work for social reform and on educational matters and this was further recognised when she received an LLD from Edinburgh University in 1937. She was chairman of the Edinburgh School of Domestic Science (formerly the Edinburgh School of Cookery) from 1943–45. She died in September 1945 and the *Dufftown News* commented:

> Lady MacKenzie, a pillar of the Women's Citizens Association, was always more concerned to stress the duties and new opportunities of her sex than to assert their rights and privileges. Her speeches at public meetings were marked by directness and candour, and spiced with a characteristic humour that gripped attention. (SB)

# Helen Rose

*Helen Rose, born 29 August 1856; died Maida Place, Elgin, 30 May 1922.*

Known for her benevolent works, the nursery Helen founded in 1922 was named in her honour and is still known as the Helen Rose Nursery School.

Helen Rose came from generations of well-known Moray folk and was the seventh of eight daughters born to Elizabeth Adam and William Rose, farmer of Sheriffston, near Lhanbryde. Helen was a keen church member and, while five of her sisters married well, she concerned herself with church welfare issues and benevolent work. In 1892 she became secretary to the Ladies Benevolent Society, a position she held for thirty years.

The Ladies Benevolent Society had been founded in 1829, the year of the great Moray floods – the 'Muckle Spate'. Cumbersomely named 'The Elgin Ladies Society for Promoting Industry among the most Necessitous of the Poor' with Lady Dunbar as patroness, the initial aim of the society was to prevent begging. As recorded in 1835, it was set up to:

> purchase materials for spinning, knitting and sewing which are then given to these females to be wrought up and for which they receive the ordinary rate of wages. The manufactured articles are then sold and may be used to purchase more materials... Beyond the incidental expenses, the annual loss upon the manufactured articles is a mere trifle.

A conscientious and hard-working secretary, Miss Rose was a familiar figure in Elgin households, and it was reported that 'nothing made a greater appeal to her than the care of the sick and poor, and anything she could do was done without a grudge'.

In 1895 a need was perceived for another type of welfare organisation and The Elgin and District Nursing Association and Child Welfare came into existence, with Helen Rose as joint secretary. By 1898 she had become the sole secretary, and, while continuing with her other welfare work, devoted the rest of her life to expanding the work of the association. Under her guidance this became one of the leading beneficent organisations in the

Helen Rose

city. Her colleagues admired her efficiency and quiet attention to detail, describing her as tender-hearted and generous, with a strong and gracious personality and 'a gift for inspiring confidence and hearty cooperation'.

Home of the Rose family – Sheriffston and its croquet lawn (Jennifer Shaw)

Helen Rose had a vision of a scheme connecting child welfare and medical care for children of school age. Along with other pioneering members of the association, she was instrumental in establishing a children's nursery to improve the health, education and welfare of young children. By 1922 her persistence resulted in the opening of a Day Nursery School in temporary accommodation at the West End Mission Hall, under the charge of a Miss Bowyer.

Although it supplied a much felt want in the district, the nursery was not universally appreciated. Some of the local clergymen thought it was unnecessary and accused the association of 'coddling' the working classes. Far from 'coddling', the nursery school acted as a link between infancy and school-age children, providing much needed welfare benefits and education. The work of the Nursing Association, combined with the care and social education given in the nursery, undoubtedly improved the health and welfare of mothers as well as children and succeeded in lowering the rates of infant mortality in the district.

Because many children of the poor were expected to help with work at home, some parents were initially hostile towards this new scheme. However, seeing the combination of discipline, education and fun that the children could enjoy within a safe and cheerful environment, they soon gave their support to the nursery, one sceptic eventually volunteering to do the laundry.

In the nursery every child helped with chores within their capacity such as washing up or keeping an eye on the new arrivals and the younger children. Long before the birth of the Welfare State or the National Health Service, the children who attended were all given health checks and, if necessary, spectacles, while the mothers received advice on hygiene and health issues. The children were taught to brush their teeth and wash their faces and hands before being cheerfully inspected for cleanliness.

Just as importantly, they were taught to play. Play was an alternative to the slavery of domestic chores and housework which was the lot of many children from impoverished homes. At mid-day they were given a nourishing drink of cocoa – which soon gave rise to the nickname 'The

Cocoa School'. Understandably it soon grew in popularity and in its first year between thirty and forty children were attending every day. In the Nursing Association's 1922 half-yearly report it is recorded that:

> there is pleasing outside testimony that the school had already considerably increased the general intelligence, good manners and physical cleanliness of the children attending it.

Helen Rose continued to guide the work of the Nursing Association right up until her death, in May 1922, at her home in Maida Place. She had been suffering from oesophageal cancer and its complications for two years but had continued her work undaunted. After her death Mr WC Young, presiding at the meeting of the Elgin District Nursing Association in 1922, paid his tribute to a woman of kindness and sympathy whom he had known ever since she was a schoolgirl and who had been the heart and soul of both the Benevolent Society and the Elgin District Nursing Association:

> She lived practically for the purpose of increasing the welfare and happiness and of mitigating the sorrows of the poor.

Two months after her death, the Elgin District Nursing Association and Child Welfare Organisation decided a permanent tribute was required. The Cocoa School was officially named the Helen Rose Nursery to perpetuate the memory of the woman who worked so hard towards its creation and who had left such an important legacy to her community.

The West End Mission Hall had been secured for use as the temporary

Elgin Nursery Choir 1924 (*The Northern Scot*)

nursery in 1922. Seeing the need for adequate playgrounds, the colourful and eccentric Moray benefactor Colonel Boyd Anderson donated a wooden hall set in extensive grounds in Northfield Terrace for use by the nursery, and this was opened by his mother in an official ceremony in 1929. Miss Rose would have been delighted to see her dream fulfilled.

Helen Rose came from a comfortable background, but she was not blind to the desperate circumstances of others in her community. Before the benefits of the welfare state, deprivation, disease and poverty blighted many lives. She worked tirelessly for improvement in the lives of the Elgin poor and, despite having no children of her own, she did her best to ensure the health of future generations. Today there is health care, social welfare, a choice of play groups, registered child minders and pre-school nurseries for young children, and the Rose Nursery School, still thriving, has relocated to Deanshaugh Terrace, Elgin. However, it was the vision of Helen Rose, and the fondly remembered Cocoa School, that began the climb out of poverty, ignorance and disease for many Elgin children. (JM)

# Ella Munro

*Helen Isabella McKenzie, born Elgin, 20 August 1873; married George Munro, 11 May 1898; died Edinburgh, 16 November 1946.*

Born into the direst poverty in Elgin, it was the training as a queen's nurse that enabled Ella Munro to struggle through misfortune and become a respected member of the community. Her nursing took her to Foula and Fair Isle.

The poorhouse cast a permanent shadow over the MacKenzie family. Ella's grandmother, mother and an aunt were registered as paupers. Ella and her sister, Jean, had no known father. Their mother, Isabella MacKenzie, was continually in need of poor relief because of bad health. Because she refused to go to the poorhouse, Isabella was discharged from the poor register and the small amount of money she received was withdrawn. It was policy to encourage unmarried mothers to go to the poorhouse, where their 'sexual urges' could be controlled, rather than to give them 'outdoor relief'.

To break away from all this misery, and maybe because she had been involved in nursing her mother, Ella decided to train as a nurse. It has not been possible to determine exactly when or where Ella obtained her qualifications. It is known that she worked as a nurse before 1906, and that she was a queen's nurse by 1920.

Ella's first child was born in 1896 and registered as Walter Munro, son of George Munro. In 1898 Ella, again pregnant, married George Munro in Forres. On her marriage certificate, Ella gave her grandparents' names as her parents. Illegitimacy was common enough, but maybe Ella was sensitive about her origins. It was also common for a child to be born before the parents were able to marry, lack of money being one reason. Because George was a distillery clerk, there must have been the hope that the future was bright for the growing family.

Ella Munro (Stella Seivwright)

Surely, there was some joy in the year after marriage, looking after Walter and baby George, with regular money coming into the household. Dark days were to follow. A little girl, Catherine, was born about July 1899 and in September of that year baby George and then Catherine died in the same week. Both scarlet fever and diphtheria were about Elgin in 1899. Another baby, Donald, was born in 1900. He lived for three months. Two more girls, Edith and Ellie, were born in 1902 and 1904. Then, about 1904, George, Ella's husband, was afflicted by polio and paralysed in the lower limbs. The Free Gardeners' Friendly Society provided five shillings (25p) a week and Ella was able to earn a little money nursing, but it must have been difficult with the girls so young. The family struggled on for some time, but in August 1906 George applied for poor relief and was granted six shillings a week. A request for an increase in October of the same year was refused, but a suit was provided for Walter in 1907.

There was some good news: in October 1908 the poor register noted that 'the pauper is a beneficiary to the extent of £100 from the estate of the late John Munro'. John Munro was a wealthy grocer and a whisky broker in Elgin. His name is still familiar to many local people, as in the now demolished Munro Baths and Munro Home (originally his home at The Knoll in Bishopmill). In his will, John Munro, who was not a relative of George, left money to charities and to his employees. Amongst the beneficiaries was his former clerk George Munro. Payments amounting to £11/2/- were claimed back by the parochial board in 1909 from the trustees of John Munro's estate 'for repayment of advances made to George Munro'. To understand how much the remaining £88 18s represented for George and Ella Munro, one only needs to look at their rent. At this time they were staying in rooms at 8 South College Street (later the site of the Red Shoes), and were paying £8 5s rent per year. No amount of money, however, could save George whose body was slowly weakening. He died in March 1909, when Ella was five months pregnant with her seventh child. Jean (later called Muriel) was born in the July. What was left of the £100 presumably saw Ella through the next few years – there was no recourse to the poor relief. The money provided for the growing family and removed some of the stress that accompanies poverty. The family were no longer classified as paupers.

Just as the First World War broke out in August 1914, misfortune struck again when Ella suffered an abscess on the lung and was unable to work. Once again the family was obliged to seek poor relief. Walter was working as a clerk and the family was living at 20 West High Street, Bishopmill. Ella was granted nine shillings (45p) a week for herself and her three girls, reducing to seven shillings and sixpence a week in November. Relief was discontinued in June 1915; she had been ill for nearly a year. Her lungs continued to bother her for the rest of her life. In Fair Isle they remember Nurse Munro as 'bronchial – you could always hear her breathing'.

A family photograph taken about the time of the First World War appears to show Ella wearing her nurse's uniform, dressed up by a fox fur. The people of Fair Isle thought that her one uniform was her only outfit. After she recovered from the abscess, Ella worked as a private nurse, but little is known of this period of her life. It is said by a friend of the family that Ella could not get a job at Dr Gray's Hospital because she did not get on with the matron.

In 1920, at the age of forty-seven, Ella Munro made a momentous decision. A vacancy for a queen's nurse in the Highlands and Islands Medical Service (HIMS) was available on the island of Foula in the Shetlands. Ella's life had hardened her to difficult decisions; she chose to go and nurse on one of the most remote islands in the

Left to right, Jean (Muriel), Edith, Ella, Walter, Ellie, and the dog, Mac (Stella Seivwright)

Shirva, Fair Isle (George Waterston Memorial Centre, Fair Isle)

British Isles. The older children stayed with Aunt Anna in Elgin and Muriel went with her mother and attended Foula Primary School. After eighteen months, Ella was transferred to Fair Isle, half way between the Shetlands and the Orkney Isles, and almost as remote as Foula. Muriel attended secondary school in Lerwick.

Poverty was never far away, but in Fair Isle everyone was in much the same situation and so there was a close-knit community. The people of Fair Isle were and are crofters; the women famous for their knitting, the men fishing when it was worthwhile. The island is small, only three and a half miles by one and a half miles, but the coastline, much of it sheer cliffs, is said to be forty miles long. About ninety people lived on the island in the 1920s and 30s, apart from the lighthouse families – there are two lighthouses. The summer days on Fair Isle are long, with the sun hardly setting; the short days make the winter dark and difficult. Fair Isle was good for Ella and Muriel, so much so that Ella asked if she could stay on when her year's service was finished. Ella had her own house at Shirva provided by the HIMS, about half a mile from the South Lighthouse. In the summer holidays the children helped with the fishing and the crofting, but there was always time to run wild. Muriel made good friends and remembered Fair Isle as a special place.

With no doctor and little communication with the outside world, Nurse

Lighthouse wedding on Fair Isle. Nurse Munro stands behind three little girls. The one on the left is Ella Stout, named after Ella Munro (George Waterston Memorial Centre, Fair Isle)

Munro had to be resourceful. There were babies to deliver, teeth to pull and epidemics to deal with. The distances were short, but the three miles to the North Lighthouse against a gale force wind could seem like a dozen miles, and, nearing the lighthouse, every step was hazardous, with cliffs falling away to the east. In Foula Ella had been told to lie flat and hold on to the heather when the weather was at its worst and she found this was good advice. On one occasion she had to go out in a small boat in a storm to attend to a fisherman. She remembered too, being driven pillion on a motor bike, at frightening speed, by a frantic father. She even had to deliver a cow. Much of her work with the children was preventative. Nurse Munro visited the school to talk about hygiene, and good nutrition. Every so often the children were walked down to the South Light store where there was a weighing machine to check their progress.

There was more personal sadness to suffer. Walter, who was teaching in Stronsay in the Orkneys, died of appendicitis in 1927.

Life became more settled through the thirties. Ella had people to stay at Shirva – it is thought that they were paying guests to help with the finances. George Waterston was one of her guests. He had come to the island for the birdwatching and it was his enthusiasm that would bring the bird observatory to Fair Isle in 1948. Ella's girls were doing well as teachers. After school Muriel attended Dunfermline College in Fife and trained as a gym teacher. She was the only one of Ella's children to marry. With the children grown up, money worries diminished.

In 1938 Ella Munro was sixty-five and ready for retirement. Her years of service in the Shetlands were recognised when she received the MBE in the king's birthday honours. Newspapers wanted to know about Ella and her time in the Shetlands. *The Scotsman* reported on some of her experiences and commented on her good humour.

Ella retired to Edinburgh and stayed with Edith and Ellie in Corstorphine. With the Second World War looming, she was soon helping in the rest centres and organising trainloads of evacuees. There were grandchildren too, the chil-

Edith, Ella, and Ellie when Ella received her MBE
(Stella Seivwright)

dren of Muriel. Ella died of an asthmatic attack in 1946.

Ella Munro was never well off – a nurse's wage was poor and there was no welfare state to give extra support. Whilst teachers' wages were not good, and equal pay for women teachers was not established until as late as 1962, the sharing of the house in Corstorphine made Edith and Ellie financially independent, and they were able to offer Ella a home so that she could live comfortably in her old age.

Ella once said that 'you need a good courage to live in the Isles'. She might have said that about all of her life. She conquered poverty, partly because society itself was changing, but mainly by her own wits, and by hard work. (SB)

## CHAPTER SIX
# Education and Politics: Finding a Voice

*It is in the faith that all injustices are wrong that I would appeal to every person who cares for justice, right, and fairness, to put aside this great injustice as between men and women, and allow women to develop not only socially but politically, as citizens, in the way that you develop – to give them a fair field and no favour.* Dr Elizabeth Garrett Anderson, Aberdeen Music Hall, 3 April 1871[1]

THE 'RIOT OF SURGEON'S HALL', Edinburgh, against women aspiring to be doctors, took place on 18 November 1870. When Sophia Jex Blake and four other women arrived to sit their anatomy examinations they were met by a large crowd of jeering male students, milling around the gates, shouting obscenities, and throwing mud. The jeering continued throughout the examination and at one point a sheep was pushed into the room. The Royal Medical Society of Edinburgh refused to condemn the riot.[2]

Two years after the riot, Alice Ker from Deskford, near Cullen, joined Sophia Jex Blake's group of trainee doctors. Although not able to qualify in Scotland at that time, Alice returned to Edinburgh over a decade later and set up her own general practice. The Dow sisters of Elgin, four of whom became doctors in the early twentieth century had an easier path to qualification, as did Beatrice Sellar from Aberlour who studied at the same time as Griselda Dow. If Alice Ker was a trailblazer in the fight for the right of women to qualify as doctors, the Dows and Dr Sellar were important in keeping the route open, so that women doctors became recognised as making a positive contribution to the medical profession. Prejudice forced the early women doctors to work in the field of women's medicine. Some worked as GPs, dealing mainly with women and children. The First World War gave women doctors the opportunity to widen their experience, but only after they had taken the initiative and set up their own hospitals in France and Serbia.

Whilst the doctors were fighting for their rights, Ethel Bedford Fenwick from Spynie, was engaged in 'the battle of the nurses' trying to get recognition for properly trained registered nurses. Her battle was with the traditional view of Florence Nightingale that nursing was a vocation that needed commitment and not certificates. Ethel Bedford Fenwick did not achieve her goal until 1919.

From the 1860s the Scottish universities began to offer lectures to women on various academic subjects. There was no prospect of gaining a degree, but St Andrews University offered a qualification with the title of Lady Literate in Arts (LLA) as a correspondence course. Elsie Watson, Nannie Katharin Wells, Isabel Kerr and Mary Symon took this qualification, and some of Margaret Stephen's pupils attended LLA classes at Elgin Academy. In 1892 Scottish Universities were allowed formally to admit women students to degree courses and Aberdeen was the first university to admit women to all faculties. Johanna Forbes from Cullen, an early classics graduate of Aberdeen, was the first woman faculty member in that university, but her appointment was only on a temporary basis. Just as female doctors had been restricted to working in women's medicine, so female teachers could only gain promotion in girls' schools. Before her marriage, Johanna Forbes had reached the peak of her career as principal teacher of classics at Hutcheson's Girls' School in Glasgow.

Whilst Alice Ker, Ethel Bedford Fenwick and Johanna Forbes were leading the way in their fields of study, Lavinia Malcolm, born in Forres in 1847, and Nannie Katharin Wells, educated in Fochabers, followed a more conventional path supporting their husbands in their careers, as teacher and solicitor respectively. Mrs Malcolm, however, was to become the first woman councillor in Scotland and subsequently the first lady provost; Mrs Wells, an early Scottish Nationalist, became a journalist and author. The career of Isabella Mitchell, librarian in Elgin from 1892 and not a pioneer in a national sense, demonstrates the slow march of women moving into increasingly responsible areas of employment.

As the nineteenth century progressed the voices of those supporting women's suffrage became louder. John Stuart Mill had put forward an amendment to the 1867 Reform Act (in England), calling for women's suffrage. It was the defeat of this amendment that resulted in the formation of the National Society for Women's Suffrage; an Edinburgh group was founded in the same year. By 1882 women ratepayers could vote in municipal elections in Scotland, but Gladstone's anti-suffrage position held back the progress towards women's parliamentary suffrage. Many of the suffrage groups joined together in the National Union of Women's Suffrage Societies (NUWSS). Despairing of any progress, in 1903 Emmeline and Christabel Pankhurst founded the Women's Social and Political Union (WSPU), a group comprising of militants who were prepared to commit violent acts and go to prison to bring publicity to the campaign. Members of the WSPU were known as suffragettes. The suffragists of the NUWSS, such as Lavinia Malcolm, Nannie Katharin Wells and Ethel Bedford Fenwick, thought that violence had a negative effect on their campaign. For them, acts such as the arson attack on the Ashley Road School in Aberdeen, could only be deplored.[3] A suffragette's ultimate commitment to the cause was demonstrated on 4 June 1913 when Emily Wilding Davison threw herself in front of the king's horse at the Derby. She died five days later without regaining consciousness. The campaign by the militants attracted even more attention when

'Skating on Thin ice' from *Alma Mater*, Aberdeen University magazine, 1896; a jibe at the presence of women students

some of the imprisoned women resorted to hunger strike. The forced feeding that was inflicted on these women was particularly horrific because their respiratory systems and rectums were often damaged by the tubes that were inserted into their bodies.

The first case of forcible feeding in Scotland took place on 21 February 1914 at Calton Jail, Edinburgh. On 26 February the medieval church of Whitekirk near North Berwick was destroyed by fire as an act of reprisal. Only the walls remained of the church and the damage was estimated as £8,000–£10,000.[4] There was outrage on all sides of the debate with no prospect of reconciliation.

Reports in the local newspapers indicate that women's suffrage was a subject for discussion in Moray from at least 1871. In that year some inhabitants of Forres agreed to petition for women's suffrage as a result of the visit of Miss Taylour of the Galloway Women's Suffrage group.[5] In 1873 Miss Jessie Craigen of London came to Forres.[6] As the campaign grew, speakers from the south became more frequent: Miss Jessie Munro and Helen Fraser of the NUWSS came to Forres in March 1909;[7] Miss Jamieson of the Scottish Universities Women's Suffrage Union came to Buckie in August 1910;[8] Miss Frances Parker and Miss Kate Macrae of the Scottish University Women's Social Union came to Buckie in April 1910,[9] where they were heckled by young fisher lads; 'Miss Alice Crompton MA and Miss Edith Bisset MA' of the NUWSS were in Banff, Macduff and Cullen in January 1912;[10] and Emmeline Pankhurst of the WSPU came to Forres in September 1911.[11] These women often achieved their objectives of raising a petition to support women's suffrage, but usually it was achieved because men – councillors – supported the motion. There is little evidence of local women being active, although lack of evidence does not mean it did not happen. Helen Fraser, who was in Elgin in June 1909, was reported to be returning in September to complete the formation of a NUWSS.[12]

The only known militant activity in Moray took place on the golf course at Lossiemouth when the Prime Minister, Herbert Asquith, was attacked by two suffragettes. An eye-witness account in *The Elgin Courant and Courier* for 29 August 1913 described the event:

> The two young dames we had passed were attacking Mr Asquith, each having hold of one arm and thus rendering him absolutely powerless. The caddies – only mites they were – stood by bewildered and amazed... I exclaimed 'You vicious brute!' Mr Asquith's hat had been knocked off, and his daughter was endeavouring as best she could to protect her father.

The women at first refused to give their names but later gave them as Winnie Wallace of Dundee and Flora Ellen Smith of Edinburgh. It was widely considered that these were false names. On being given bail the two women attended Duffus Church on the Sunday, where, after the service they called Mr Asquith a hypocrite. The affair never came to court because the Prime Minister would have had to attend. It was all rather feeble, but it had the desired effect and caused a great stir at the time. In fact, golf courses were a favourite target for suffragettes. They gave easy access to a number of famous politicians, and security was difficult to monitor. Furthermore, as the incident in Lossiemouth demonstrated, a small action gave maximum publicity.

At the end of June 1914 Archduke Franz Ferdinand of Austria was assassinated in Sarajevo by a Serb. On 4 August Britain declared war against Germany and the women who had fought so hard for suffrage put their cause aside and devoted their energies to a different war. Both the Women's Hospital Corps, active in France and London, and the Scottish Women's Hospital, active in France and Serbia, were suffrage organisations.

The field of local politics was pioneered by Lavinia Malcolm, in Dollar, in 1907. Moray would not see its first woman town councillor until 1931, but like Mrs Malcolm, Nora Mackay was well appreciated by both the electorate and her colleagues. Another thirty years would pass before Sybil Duncan, in 1961, became Elgin's first lady provost.

In February 1918 some women of thirty years were given the vote; in November of that year women were able to stand for parliament. It was 1928 before the franchise was given on equal terms to all men and women over the age of twenty-one.

Women in many other countries were similarly involved with fighting for their rights. The idea for a 'Women's Day' across the world was first mooted in Denmark in 1910. Held at the end of February (Julian Calender) or in early March (Gregorian Calender) it was honoured for the first time in 1911. The eighth of March was soon established as International Women's Day and its celebration slowly spread across the globe.

# Lavinia Malcolm

*Lavinia Laing, born Forres, 1847/8; married Richard Malcolm, Edinburgh, 27 December 1883; died Dollar, 2 November 1920.*

In Dollar Lavinia Malcolm won fame as the first woman town councillor in Scotland and then as the first woman provost.

Lavinia's maternal grandfather, John Kynoch, was a prosperous leather merchant, founder of the Forres Water Company and a director of Forres Gas Company. He was provost of Forres for nine years from 1848, which led the *Forres Gazette* to suggest that his granddaughter Lavinia's success in public life was perhaps due to hereditary aptitude.

Lavinia's mother was Janet Kynoch, the provost's eldest daughter. Lavinia's father, Alexander Laing, was variously described as an ironmonger, plumber or tinsmith and was manager of Forres Gas Works. In 1851 three-year-old Lavinia was living in Gas Works House, Forres, with her parents, her younger brother Theodore, her two older sisters, Margaret and Mary, and three servants.

Alexander Laing ceased to be manager of the Gas Works around 1858 and by 1861 he, his wife Janet, and Margaret, eighteen, Abigail, nine, Grace, seven and John, four, were living at Hempriggs, Alves, near Forres. Alexander was by now described as a farmer. Three of his older children were lodging with family or friends and attending school in Forres: on the night of the 1861 census Lavinia was thirteen and staying with her uncle Alex Kynoch. Mary, fifteen, was with her Kynoch grandparents and Theodore, eleven, was lodging with a family named Ross. Education was obviously important to the Laing family.

It was later said of Lavinia that her early work was in teaching and training the young but there is no record of her having been a school teacher. She and two of her sisters, Mary and Abigail, worked as governesses. In 1871 Abigail was employed by Captain McKenzie of Mountgerald, near Dingwall, in a very grand household with five children, aged one to eleven, and nine indoor servants. Lavinia worked for an even grander household:

Lavinia Malcolm, Provost of Dollar, in 1913
(Dollar Museum)

in 1871 she was governess to Charles, six, Reginald, five, and Florence, three, the children of Viscount Marsham, son of the Earl of Romney, in Norfolk.

In 1868 Lavinia's uncle, William Kynoch, died and his widow moved from Forres to Dollar, so that her six children could take advantage of the excellent and cheap education available at Dollar Academy. Her daughter Minnie Kynoch was one of the first women to go to St Andrews University and become a Lady Literate in Arts (LLA). Lavinia must have visited her Kynoch cousins in Dollar, where she met her future husband Richard 'Dickie' Malcolm, a teacher at the academy. She was particularly close to her cousin Minnie, who was a witness at Lavinia and Dickie's wedding in 1883. Lavinia was at this time thirty-six and Dickie was forty-one. She now had a husband and numerous schoolboy boarders to look after and showed no interest in political or municipal activity. This was certainly the case when on, 14 May 1887, Dick Gibson Malcolm was born.

Dick was a lively, intelligent boy. In the minutes of Dollar Burns Club there are several references to him winning prizes for recitation and a programme for a concert in February 1895 shows that Master Dick Malcolm (age seven) was to recite 'To a Louse'. That year the family spent their summer holiday in Findhorn, where Lavinia owned Briar Cottage. Shortly after they returned to Dollar, on 9 September, Dick died of pneumonia, an illness that nowadays would usually respond quickly to antibiotics. He was eight years old.

The death of their son led both Lavinia and Dickie to take up multiple activities outside their home. Richard Malcolm was already a town councillor and in 1896 he accepted the office of provost of Dollar.

In 1895 the Alloa and District Women's Liberal Society had been set up. Lavinia joined in 1896 and was quick to make her mark. She was soon in demand to give votes of thanks and to introduce speakers. By 1898 she was on the committee and by 1903 was a vice-president. She was by this time speaking on topics such as 'Current Politics' and 'The Franchise for Women'. Her position on votes for women was that women should have the franchise on the same terms as men, but she did not support militant action. In later years she chaired meetings of the Dollar branch of the National Union of Suffrage Societies.

In 1904 a new Liberal Club was to be opened in Alloa by Sir Henry Campbell-Bannerman. The Liberal ladies decided to present a bust of Gladstone. Although she was only a vice-president the honour of making the presentation was entrusted to Lavinia. Her speech was printed in full with the other speeches (all by men) in a special edition of the *Alloa Advertiser* and she became a minor local celebrity.

The Qualification of Women (County and Town Councils) Act, which became law on 28 August 1907, allowed women to be elected as town and county councillors. The first election in which they could stand would be in November. The Clackmannan and Kinross Women's Liberal Association (CKWLA) received a resolution from their Scottish Executive, which was read out and recorded at their committee meeting on 27 September 1907:

> The Executive calls the attention of Women's Liberal Associations to the fact that women ratepayers are now by Act of Parliament eligible for election to Town and County Councils as well as to Parish Councils and would urge that suitable candidates be asked to stand at the coming election.

The minutes of the committee meeting continue:

> The Committee agreed most heartily that in these councils there is a wide sphere of usefulness for Women Councillors but meanwhile could think of no woman who would be willing to enter these open doors.

Lavinia was absent from the committee meeting, although as chairman at the next meeting she signed the minute. She was at this time a Dollar ratepayer, having sold Briar Cottage in Findhorn and bought property in Dollar. This entitled her to vote in municipal elections – and from 1907 to stand in town council elections. She was also a vice-president of the CKWLA and was highly regarded locally as a public speaker. It seems extraordinary that the CKWLA committee did not consider her as a suitable candidate. Luckily Dollar men were more perceptive: Dr John Strachan and Michael Cochrane nominated her. On 6 November 1907, Mrs Malcolm was elected to Dollar Town Council and also to the Parish Council. Five women were candidates in the 1907 Scottish municipal elections but only Lavinia

Malcolm was successful. It was two years before another woman (Mrs Barlow in Callander) was elected to a Scottish town council.

Scotland's first woman town councillor was lauded in the Scottish press and congratulations flowed in. In July 1908 when she and her husband were on holiday in Forres they attended the opening of the new Castle Bridge. Provost Lawrence publicly invited them up to the platform. At the luncheon afterwards, asking Lavinia to reply to the toast to 'The Ladies', Mr John Smith of Inverallan said: 'I think it is the first time in the history of the world that a lady councillor will reply for the ladies.' Lavinia replied that she was deeply honoured at being asked to reply to the toast. She had led the way into the town council and she sincerely hoped many ladies would follow in her path. She might tell Forres ladies that she had always received the greatest kindness and politeness from the members of the council, and the provost said there had been no rows since she came amongst them.

On the town council, she was on many committees, including public health, water, sanitary and lighting. She particularly enjoyed working with children and old people. As a member of the parish council, Lavinia was made convener of the visiting committee, and lost no time in setting up a casual sick ward for the poor. In 1909 she was elected to the Dollar School Board and for many years was a very active member.

In 1910 she and Mrs Barlow represented their councils at the Convention of Royal Burghs of Scotland, the first two women to attend. In 1912 Lavinia was appointed by the convention as a representative to the National Association for the Prevention of Infant Mortality in Caxton Hall, Westminster, where she was the only lady councillor present. Seeing the splendid robes and chains of office worn at the convention made Lavinia think that Dollar also needed some regalia and in January 1913 she presented a gold chain to be worn by the provost of Dollar – at that time Provost Green. She cannot have suspected that she might soon wear it herself.

Later that year a disagreement arose between the town council and some ratepayers. Provost Green and both bailies refused to stand in the November election unless allegations of irregularity were withdrawn. The withdrawal was not made and this left Mrs Malcolm as the senior member of the new council. There appeared to be no legal reason why a woman, although she could not be a bailie, should not lead the council. So Councillor McDiarmid proposed that Mrs Malcolm, who was 'wise in counsel, able in administration and wholehearted in the performance of all duties relegated to her', should be appointed provost of Dollar.

As there were no other nominations she thus became, at the age of sixty-six, the first lady provost in Scotland, a post which she filled with 'zest and flair' through the difficult years of the First World War until 1919. She also became famous throughout the United Kingdom. *The Young Woman* wrote of her: 'Mrs Malcolm keenly enjoys her work, partly because of her enthusiasm and vivacious personality, and partly owing to her strong sense of humour, which has enlightened many a dull and dreary debate, and enlivened the prosaic details of town lighting and sanitation.'

When Lavinia became provost in 1913 she said she considered 'The want of readiness of women to come forward to take part in the privileges of local government work as a hindrance to the franchise being given to women'. When Lavinia retired in 1919 she said:

> There is no scarcity of ladies in Dollar fitted to take an active interest in Municipal work and I would take it as a great compliment if at least one was returned at the forthcoming election.

Two Dollar women did stand but both were defeated.

What was she like? Intelligent, articulate, hard-working, morally upright, sympathetic but definitely not sentimental, very good at organising and with loads of energy. She was much loved by generations of boys who boarded with the Malcolms – they wrote to Lavinia and Dickie from all over the world in later years, expressing their gratitude. A colleague on the Town Council said Lavinia was:

> A lady of high culture and refined taste. Her conduct in the chair has always been distinguished by dignity and courtesy. In public speech she is never long-winded, but always brief.

In 1920 Lavinia was made a justice of the peace: her name appeared in the first list of appointments to the commissioners of the peace in Scotland following upon the Sex Disqualification (Removal) Act. The women who were selected had all rendered themselves conspicuous by distinguished public service. Shortly after receiving this honour, Lavinia died, on 2 November 1920, aged seventy-three. Among the tributes paid to her was the following: 'Dollar will never look on her like again. She should never be forgotten.' However, Dollar did mostly forget her until 1988, when the new Dollar Museum revived her memory. Malcolm Court is now named after her and in 2004 Lavinia was included in the *DNB*. (JC)

# Isabella Mitchell

*Isabella Mitchell, born New Spynie, 13 November 1851; died Aberdeen,*
*10 November 1931.*

Miss Mitchell was the first librarian at Elgin Public Library.

Little is known of Bella's early life. Her father was postmaster at Quarrywood, just to the west of Elgin, and she had five siblings. She took over as postmistress on her father's retirement. He was working as a cobbler when he died in 1891, just months before her appointment as librarian. Bella's mother had died in 1884; three of her siblings died in their thirties. Her sister Helen died in Elgin Lunatic Asylum in 1881. A year earlier Bella's father wrote to her when she was in Rome. He said that he had not seen Helen but she was 'getting a little brighter – I hope she may continue...'

The new Elgin Free Library opened on 14 May 1892 in a side room of the Elgin Town Hall on Moray Street. Miss Mitchell was appointed librarian in late 1891 much to the delight of Peter Grant of the Morayshire Union Poor House who wrote to her to tell her the good news:

> Dear Bella
> *Victory*
> Appointed librarian by majority of meeting only two against us, the Sheriff and Provost Laird, Proposed by Grigor Allan, seconded by Ramsay...The Days our ain!! Hurrah! Hurrah! Hurrah!!!

She remained in post for thirty-four years. The library moved to Grant Lodge in 1903; Miss Mitchell held an arts and crafts exhibition during that first year. It was well patronised and included the Duchess of Fife and Princess Alexis Dolgouoski among its supporters. She also opened an art gallery and later a museum within the library. At that time she presided over a staff of fourteen. When the library opened in 1892 it held 3366 volumes; by

Library staff outside Grant Lodge 1903, Miss Mitchell seated in the centre (Elgin Museum)

Miss Mitchell's retirement in 1925 that number had increased to 8674; there were nearly 200 books in the reference section and double that in the local collection.

Throughout her adult life Bella wrote articles for the *Christian Women's Education Union* and the *Reading Guild*.

A special meeting of the Elgin Public Committee was held in December 1925 so that a eulogy could be read to mark her retirement at the age of seventy-four. Ill health prompted Bella to move to Aberdeen in her later years to be nearer her family. She died in Aberdeen Royal Infirmary on 10 November 1931, a few days short of her eightieth birthday. (AO)

# Alice Ker

*Alice Jane Shannan Stewart Ker, born Deskford, 2 December 1853; married Edward Stewart Ker, December 1888; died London, 20 March 1943.*

Alice Ker was the thirteenth woman on the British Medical Register. She continued with her career whilst she and her husband raised a family. As a suffragette she took a hammer to the windows of Harrods department store.

Alice was the eldest of nine children. Her mother, Margaret Miller Stevenson, was a member of a large family most of whom were intellectual liberals. Among Margaret's sisters were Flora and Louisa, active in a variety of campaigns that related to women's issues in Edinburgh. Alice and her sisters were brought up to consider themselves equal to their brothers and similarly able to take their place in society. Alice's father, William, was the Free Church minister at Deskford, a small Banffshire village now in Moray and not far from Cullen. Since her father was the minister, it is likely that Alice attended the Free Church school in Deskford, although there are no records to confirm this. Of her higher education nothing is as yet known until 1872 when she was in Edinburgh studying anatomy and physiology and staying at 13 Randolph Crescent with her Aunts Flora and Louisa. Alice joined the group led by Sophia Jex Blake, fighting for a woman's right to take a degree. The battle in Edinburgh was not successful and the group took off to London to see if they would fare better there. Ultimately these women had to train in Berne, Switzerland, and in Ireland.

Alice Ker went to Ireland in 1876, becoming a Licentiate of King and Queen's College of Physicians, Ireland. Following a year in Berne, Dr Ker was appointed house surgeon to the children's hospital in Birmingham

where she worked for about seven years. After a spell as a GP in Leeds, she returned to
Edinburgh and was able to sit the conjoint
examination at the Edinburgh Royal College
of Surgeons in 1886. Her battle for British
qualifications was now complete; she was
thirty-two. Two years later, with a newly established practice in Edinburgh, Alice married a distant cousin Edward Stewart Ker, and
went to live in Birkenhead where Edward was
a shipping merchant. Just before her marriage, she returned to Deskford to give a lecture in the Free Assembly Hall on 'How to
make children healthy and happy'.

The couple had three children: Stewart,
born 1889, who died at the age of sixteen
months, Margaret, born 1892, and Mary,

Alice Ker during an interview with
the BBC, 1942

born 1896. Edward was seen pushing the pram; he took his share of the
childrearing, enjoying the family until his death in 1907. Unusually, Alice
did not give up her career when she married. She continued as a general
practitioner working from the family home and was appointed honorary
medical officer for both the Wirral Hospital for Sick Children and the
Birkenhead Lying-In Hospital. She also lectured to the Manchester School
of Domestic Economy and wrote three books relating to the classes she
taught: *Motherhood* (1891), *Girlhood* (1893) and *Womanhood* (1893).
Dedicated to Dr Ker's mother, *Motherhood* was especially successful, running to a second edition. The book covers a wide range of women's medical and social issues. Nowadays it seems a mix of common sense and out-
dated notions. Girls should be prepared for menstruation and marriage by
being acquainted with the facts (this was the mother's role – no help is
given to the mother on how to achieve this); during pregnancy a women
should wear loose clothing and remain active. However, there was 'emphatic condemnation' of birth control, an insistence on ten days lying
down (no sitting up in bed) after childbirth, and disapproval of 'so-called
"Sanitary Towels"'.

Alice led a busy life, but there always seemed time to add other interests:
the RSPCC, the anti-vivisection movement, the Anglican Church, local
politics, and the Birkenhead Women's Suffrage Society. She was always
ready to let fellow suffrage workers stay at her house if they were giving
talks locally. Marie Stopes stayed with her in 1904 and Alice maintained
contact with her for many years. Maybe by this time Alice had changed her

opinion on birth control. After Edward's death Alice became more involved in woman's campaigns. Gradually she became disillusioned by the National Union of Women's Suffrage Societies (NUWSS) and, considering that the vote would never be won without more militant action, she joined the Women's Social and Political Union (WSPU), headed by Emmeline Pankhurst. This new commitment involved selling the newspaper *Votes for Women* at the railway stations, chalking up meeting information on the pavements and attending demonstrations in London. In 1911 the WSPU organised a census boycott, arguing that if the women were not entitled to a vote they were not part of society and need not be recorded. The easiest way to avoid giving details was to be absent from the home on the night in question and gather in one designated building where details were refused. Alice Ker offered her home, Skene House, at 6 James Street, as one of these safe houses. The women attending the so called 'census parties' were referred to as 'Lady Dodgers' by the local press. Alice wrote in her diary:

[Sunday 2 April] Census evaders here all night, 57 of them. Tea soon after midnight.

[3 April] Lay on floor of Mary's room for abt an hour till 2.30, all other rooms and floors being occupied. A meal abt 3.30.

By this time, Alice's daughters, Margaret and Mary, were becoming interested in the WSPU. When Cecily Hamilton, actress and playwright, wrote a *Pageant of Great Women* which was performed throughout the country, Alice and Margaret took part in the local production playing St Theresa and Flora McDonald respectively. Margaret would later go to prison for the cause.

Following the Liberals' close fought victory in 1910, a cross party committee was formed to frame a women's suffrage bill – known as the Conciliation Bill. The militant suffrage groups, WSPU and Women's Freedom League (WFL) declared a truce and stopped all militant action. But in November 1911 the Conciliation Bill was thrown out causing a fearful anger amongst the WSPU. Alice was now in no doubt that she would join wholeheartedly with the militants to draw attention to the women's plight; her girls were almost adult and she was prepared to go to prison if necessary. In late February 1912 she took the train down to London and was arrested a few days later for smashing the windows of Harrods. Encouraged by her daughters, Alice refused bail and spent three months in Holloway.

Her letters to her girls written from Holloway are largely about practical matters, such as making sure that the rent is paid and asking for some sewing materials. Her daughters' letters were a great support to her. Alice's replies showed how much she appreciated them:

[5 March 1912] Goodbye dears, God bless you. Truth is great, and it will prevail. Always your loving mother, Alice J Stewart Ker.

[8 March 1912] They are splendid letters, exactly the right thing – starch me up again completely if I am feeling limp... It is the greatest help to me to know how brave and bright you both are.

Alice confirmed her position as a suffragette at this time, and her attitude to the suffragists (referred to as the 'Nationals') hardened:

[16 March 1912] When I come out I am going to let the Nationals know what I think of them as well as the men. One sees clearly in this atmosphere, and, it makes even more difference, one has nothing left to be afraid of in speaking one's mind. Why should they not only not support us, the advance guard, as the rear guard should, but even fire into us from behind. No, I am associating with heroines here, and I don't feel inclined to suffer cowards so gladly as I have hitherto done.

[21 March 1912] Did you see that Mrs Fawcett was writing to Mr Asquith offering postponement of the Conciliation Bill? Such an unpolitical thing to do!

[23 March 1912] The more I think about the National Union, the more amazed I am. No other political party repudiates its extreme wing. The Labour Party did not dissociate itself from the rioters at Tonypandy, they just watched the case carefully to see if they were fairly dealt with and nobody ever thought of making the moderate people responsible for the disorderly ones. That is why we say that they are so unpolitical, and that is why we are all here. If all the Suffrage Societies had held firm, not necessarily approving, but not so elaborately firing into us from behind, the Government must have given way.

Dr Ker was fortunate that she was able to continue her general practice after her spell in jail. Margaret was also imprisoned for suffragette activities, but, after some string pulling by her mother, was able to continue her studies. The First World War brought an amnesty to the suffrage movement and Alice helped on the home front by giving first aid lessons for the Women's War Service Bureau. In 1916 the family moved to London where Alice worked with school clinics and infant welfare centres. Margaret and Mary both became teachers and Alice sometimes lived with one or other of them. In London too, she developed her interest in theosophy – a spiritual philosophy that has similarities with buddhism and other eastern religions, but is not in itself a religion.

Alice Ker's long and eventful life ended in March 1943 at the age of eighty-nine. (SB)

# Ethel Bedford Fenwick

*Ethel Gordon Manson, born Spynie, Moray, 26 January 1857; married Dr Bedford Fenwick 1887; died London, 13 March 1947.*

Nurse and suffragist, Ethel Bedford Fenwick battled the authorities for thirty years to ensure that nursing had recognised standards of training, with its own professional governing body and list of registered trained nurses.

She was born 26 January 1857 in Spynie House near Elgin, Moray. Her father, David Davidson Manson, had qualified as a doctor in Edinburgh but, on inheriting his brother's farm at Spynie, gave up his practice to concentrate on farming. He made a good job of his new career, winning a gold medal for land improvement before his untimely death from heart failure, at the aged of forty-six. Ethel was then just nine months old.

Three years later Ethel's mother, Henrietta, remarried, took her children to their new home, Thoroton Hall in Nottinghamshire. Henrietta was an imposing woman and a formidable character while her new husband, member of parliament George Storer, was a small but kindly man who was known in the family as 'the widow's mite'. During her formative years Ethel developed an interest in antiques, books and politics as well as the talents of organisation and supervision which were to prove so vital to her career. Aware of the efforts being made by many of the great Victorian reformers of the day, she gained an insight into the social changes that were so badly needed.

By the time she was twenty Ethel was determined to embark on a career in nursing. Training for nurses was in its infancy and Ethel was too young to be accepted by any of the general hospitals so she began her career as a paying probationer, firstly at the Children's Hospital, Nottingham, and then at the Manchester Royal Infirmary. Conditions were demanding and out of fifty nurses engaged in Manchester in 1880 only fifteen succeeded – two died and many failed because of ill health. Luckily Ethel had a strong constitu-

Ethel Bedford Fenwick in her finery (© St Bartholomew's Hospital Archives).

tion and her considerable talents were recognised. She was offered a post as ward sister in the Whitechapel Hospital, London. There she gained a reputation for excellence and efficiency and there she met her future husband. By the age of twenty-four she had been appointed to the prestigious post of matron at one of the great hospitals in the country – St Bartholomew's Hospital, London. During her time at St Bartholomew's she worked alongside the leading surgeons and physicians of the time in an era when great progress was being made in areas of anaesthesia, immunisation, refrigeration, radiation and steam sterilisation techniques.

Apart from being the youngest matron known, her appointment was resented because she was considered far too attractive! She soon made her mark, to be remembered in later years as 'one who swept through the Hospital like a whirlwind'. She constantly pestered the governors of the hospital for improvements in conditions and diet, implemented a strict standard uniform for the nurses and improved their working hours. She spent several hours a day visiting every ward to ensure high levels of cleanliness and efficiency were being maintained. Determined to staff the hospital with trained nurses, she managed to weed out most of the untrained ward sisters and, as long as they met her high standards, began to recruit girls from all backgrounds to train under her new regime.

When Ethel took up her post as matron, nursing was still considered a vocation, an almost religious calling, and as a consequence many patients suffered from well-intentioned but dangerously ignorant care. In 1889 Florence Nightingale wrote to a friend:

When very many years ago I planned a future, my one idea was not organising a hospital but organising a Religion.

Ethel Manson had very different ideas. She was determined to set universal standards for nurses – eliminating the incompetent romantics by creating a respected body of dedicated but well trained and registered professionals.

When she was thirty she married a brilliant young doctor who eventually became the royal gynaecologist. As was the custom on marriage, Ethel Manson was obliged to give up her career. However, as Mrs Bedford Fenwick, her battle to create a nationally recognised register for nurses was just beginning. She understood that efficient patient care and professional status for nurses could only be attained through completion of a three-year training course. This course must be followed by the regulation and registration of every successful

Ethel Manson during her early nursing years (© St Bartholomew's Hospital Archives).

nurse. The British Medical Association supported this registration scheme. However, many nurses, including Florence Nightingale, believed nursing should be purely vocational and fiercely opposed professionalisation. A woman's right to vote was causing great controversy and there was antagonism towards the new politicised female attitudes. Although Queen Victoria did not approve of the strident demands of the women's movement, Ethel had some strong supporters among other younger members of the royal family, particularly Princess Helena, Queen Victoria's third daughter.

The birth of her son did not deter Ethel from her campaign. She became honorary secretary of the first organisation of nurses, the British Nurses Association, which was soon to gain the prefix 'Royal'. Aware of the power of publicity, she wrote many articles for the *Nursing Record*, taking it over with her husband in 1893 and becoming the honorary editor.

The complex campaign for registration went on for thirty fraught years, during which time Ethel became involved with the International Council of Women as well as organising an International Nursing Congress held in London and a major nursing exhibition and conference. She was invited to superintend the nursing exhibition at the 1893 World's Fair in Chicago and while in America she was treated as an honoured guest, meeting like-minded suffragists and leading nurse educationalists.

Writing in the *Nursing Record* in a column called 'Women', reporting suffragist meetings, women's unionist affairs, and news of feminine organisations, she constantly urged her nurses to be involved in politics:

> they should be conversant more especially with all matters affecting the interests of Nurses and women... If, as we ardently hope, the present year should foreshadow the enfranchisement of women, this advance would give... an enormous impetus to the cause of nursing.

At the outbreak of the 1897 Graeco-Turkish War Ethel was appointed secretary of the National Fund for Crete and she went out personally to help organise the hospitals, continuing to send regular dispatches back to the *Nursing Record*.

With support of her husband, Ethel had no financial worries to constrain her campaigning. Forever conscious of the finer things in life and of the importance of appearance, she was reported attending a prestigious function in 1890:

> wearing a most artistic dress of apple green satin draped with black net, exquisitely embroidered with white lilies and green jewelled leaves and a long black velvet train; she wore only one jewel, a beautiful diamond and emerald heart, and the Order of St John of Jerusalem.

In 1900 she was elected President of the International Council of Nurses and in 1904 was President of the National Council of Trained Nurses, continuing to battle on for her ideals. In her editorial of 21 September 1901 she wrote in the *Nursing Record*:

> The era of the 'ministering angel' and the silly sentimentality inseparable from that aspect of the work, and which did so much harm, has, we hope, as completely passed as the days and degradation forever associated with Sairey Gamp. The era of the trained nurse as a woman desirous to do the best professional work in her power has dawned.

But her battle was far from over. The Edwardian age was politically turbulent and from 1906 onwards seven suffrage bills were defeated. Ethel Bedford Fenwick was an ardent supporter of women's suffrage and was the nursing representative on the committee of the National Union of Women's Suffrage. Writing in the *British Journal of Nursing*, she did her utmost to make nurses aware of the issues involved. She urged nurses to join the June 1908 Suffrage Sunday procession. This was a momentous event, with over 15,000 women from all over the country taking part. Ethel issued marching orders and directives, telling the nurses where to obtain ribbons and scarves in the suffrage colours of white, green and purple. Those incapable of marching could follow in a brake at tenpence a seat. The nurses were all in outdoor uniform and, led by Ethel, marched under a banner of rose satin emblazoned in gold with the name of Florence Nightingale and the emblem of a lighthouse.

Ethel Manson as matron with her ward sisters,
St Bartholomew's Hospital
(© St Bartholomew's Hospital Archives)

Ethel continued with her writing and in 1910 she was elected President of the Society of Women Journalists. In this capacity she represented the society at the coronation of George V in 1911.

At the outbreak of war in 1914 the suffragettes diverted their energies into war work. A suffragist but not a suffragette, by this time Ethel had separated amicably from her husband and threw herself wholeheartedly into the fray, working for the British Committee of the French Red Cross and travelling to France on several occasions. For her efforts she was awarded the Medaille de la Reconnaissance Française Cedilla. She was also on the Executive Committee of the Territorial Nursing Service for the City & County of London as well as a member of the ladies committee of the Order of St John of Jerusalem. The government departments still regarded nursing as relatively unskilled philanthropic work so Ethel's registration crusade continued. War was the catalyst in launching the College of Nursing in 1916.

In 1918 women over thirty were allowed to vote – doing so for the first time in the general election in December. By then the College of Nursing had 8,000 members and, after the frustration of several amendments and delays, the Registration of Nurses Bill became law in December 1919. At last nursing was officially recognised as a profession, governed by its own council and with a minimum of three years of training before examination and registration for nurses. Ethel Bedford Fenwick was the first name to be entered on the new list of registered nurses.

Ethel continued to express her views and remained heavily involved in the nursing scene, writing and editing the *British Journal of Nursing* for nearly fifty-three years. Described as a restless genius, she continued to travel, meeting the Italian head of state, Mussolini, in Italy as well as having an audience with the pope.

Outspoken and opinionated, she never ceased her involvement in nursing politics. Considering how long and hard her fight for her profession had been, the inflexibility of her later years is understandable. Age did not weary her – feisty as ever she was known to have wielded an umbrella in anger at a policeman when in her eighties! She had seen the birth of nursing as a profession and saw the beginnings of the National Health Service. She was still active and working when a fractured femur was her downfall. She never fully recovered from the injury and died in her ninetieth year, having improved the world of nursing immeasurably. (JM)

# Nora Mackay

*Nora Margaret Mackay, born Elgin, 1872; died Elgin, 19 March 1952.*

Nora Mackay was a campaigner for women's rights and the first woman elected on to Elgin Town Council.

'The first lady candidate in Elgin is certain to poll very heavily. She is a most versatile lady…' so said *The Elgin Courant* in its thumbnail sketch of Elgin Town Council candidates in 1931. Nora Mackay was returned top of the poll in the November elections. She was appointed a bailie two years later. By 1937 she chaired many committees and was regarded with affection by councillors and Elgin folk. The following ode appeared in *The Northern Scot* Christmas Number that year.

> Time flits along with sure and silent tread,
> While customs old and stale are surely shed
> The weaker sex, by man so long oppressed,
> With fuller share of life have now been blessed.
> So thus we see in this our native town
> A woman wearing bailie's hat and gown,
> And though those civic fathers long departed
> At such a sight in horror would have started
> Don't blame them, they knew not what passed them by
> When in their midst they had no 'real Mackay'.

Nora Mackay was born into a Moray family well known for devotion to duty and public works. Her father, grandfather and great-grandfather had all made their mark on the area. The Mackay family home was at The Tower on Elgin High Street. From such a vantage point Nora must have grown up with her sisters and brother well aware of her privileged position as well as a sense of 'right' and a campaigning instinct.

Her father, James William Norris Mackay, was a house surgeon at Dr Gray's Hospital, Elgin and medical officer for Elgin Lunacy Board. Her great-grandfather, George Mackay, Church of Scotland minister for Rafford, was one of more than 400 ministers who caused a sensation at the 1843 General Assembly in Edinburgh by walking out en masse. They were protesting against patronage and were supporting the right of congregations to elect their own ministers. This Disruption led to the formation of the Free Church of Scotland. Nora's grandfather David followed his

Nora Mackay (*The Northern Scot*)

father into the manse at Rafford. She and her family worshipped at the United Free Church in Moray Street, Elgin, which had been built in 1851 as a result of the Disruption. Nora's father James was an elder there for many years.

Little is known of Nora's early life. Her brother was thirteen by the time she was born and went on to become a surgeon in the 1st Elginshire Rifle Volunteers. He also worked in Vienna. He married Edith Culbard in 1889. Helen Mackay married solicitor Arthur Orr in 1894; his father Robert was bailie on Elgin Town Council. Perhaps these career and travel choices influenced the young Nora to carve out an interesting life for herself. She travelled widely; Australia, New Zealand and Canada were all visited as well as Ceylon and several European countries. She spent some time in Finland, the first major European country to extend to women the right to vote and stand for election in 1906. Women in the new world countries fared better; New Zealand women achieved the vote in 1893 and Australia in 1902. Canada was a little later in 1916.

In 1904 a new cookery school was planned; Elgin Girls' Technical School was opened in 1905, with Margaret Stephen as its headmistress. It gave the girls a broader and more relevant education. Nora took an active interest in this establishment.

At home Nora joined the Elgin Women Citizens' Association and was secretary for many years. Eventually part of a national group born out of years of campaigning for women's suffrage the first meetings were held in 1913. The aim was to stimulate women's interest in social and political issues and prepare them for active citizenship.

She was also vice-president of the local branch of the Young Women's

Christian Association (YWCA) an organisation which became very popular in the 1890s. The aims of the YWCA echoed Nora's interests. Monthly classes devoted to Bible study, education and domestic accomplishments were held and hostels set up to provide safe places for women to stay. Her other interests included the Elgin and District Nursing Association of which she was joint secretary. She was also county commissioner for the Wolf Cubs.

When war came in 1914 Nora was forty-two years old and the various secretarial and organisational skills she had developed through her voluntary work meant that she was well equipped for the 'important administration work' she took up at the Bellahouston Red Cross Hospital in Glasgow.

After the war Nora continued her campaigning and good works throughout the 1920s and by 1931, when she was fifty-nine, an age where many are looking to retirement, she was ready to tackle the masculine might of Elgin Town Council. In November that year she became the first woman to seek election. The electorate declared their support in the voting booth and she topped the poll. Within two years she was elected a bailie and remained a popular figure on the town council. She attended her first meeting on 6 November when Robert Hamilton, net manufacturer, was lord provost. She was appointed town council representative on the Moray

and Nairn County Council, Elgin City Band and Dr Gray's Hospital visitor. By January 1932 she was on the School Management Committee and Elgin Nursing Association Committee.

Throughout her life she was a devout member of the South Church and following the 1935 Act of Assembly, when women became eligible, she was the first woman in Moray to be ordained as a deaconess, on 26 April 1936.

As a representative on the Moray and Nairn County Council, she served on the education, public health and public assistance committees. During the Second World War she helped set up the British Restaurant in the former

Nora Mackay (*The Northern Scot*)

Moss Street Church. This had been unused for worship since the United Free Church united with the established Church of Scotland in 1929. The British Restaurant was the brainchild of the Prime Minister, Winston Churchill. The aim was to provide good food for the people at reasonable prices and without the need for coupons. Strict rules applied to the cooking and serving of the food and there were often long queues. They were a boon for people who had few coupons left at the end of the week. Nora was also a prime mover in setting up Elgin Sunday Night Entertainment (ESNE). Concerts were held for the troops every week throughout the war.

In 1946 Bailie Mackay had fifteen years' service under her belt and was approaching her seventy-fifth birthday. *The Courant* in its pen portraits of candidates standing for the November election, reported that she was:

> probably one of the most widely travelled members of the community... the oldest member of the Town Council and has stood on all its committees... she was vice-chairman of Elgin Food Control committee and she has done valuable work in connection with War Savings.

There were fourteen candidates and for the first time Nora was not the lone woman. Sybil Duncan had returned to Elgin a few months earlier. Sybil would spend twenty-nine years in office and eventually became the town council's only woman provost.

Nora Mackay lived in Grant Street, Elgin, for many years. Initially she took lodgings at the Mayne Road end of the street and eventually she bought number eight. She lived there with her Lossiemouth born housekeeper and her cat until she died at home in March 1952. One of her former neighbours remembers her fondly. Marcelle Kennedy was a young girl when Miss Mackay died but she remembers a kind lady who gave her gifts at Christmas and was a good neighbour. Her mother Anne Kennedy and Nora Mackay always helped each other out with plant-watering, cat-sitting and other neighbourly acts.

Though she was in ill-health towards the end of her life, the Elgin Soroptimist Club made her an honorary member in recognition of her public work, and especially for her support of women and women's issues. The original Soroptimists group was founded in California in 1921 and is still actively campaigning for 'the best for women' throughout the world. The Elgin branch, which was formed in 1950, folded some years ago.

Nora Mackay was an untiring campaigner and supporter of the underdog all her life. She led the way for women in Moray and beyond to take active roles in their communities. Twelve years after her death, on 7 October 1964 ex Lord Provost Harrison received the Freedom of the City of Elgin. It was a day of celebration and speeches. Mr Harrison charted his public life in Elgin; one of his memories was of Bailie Mackay 'who did so much to bring Anderson's out of the shadow of the Poor House and laboured so lovingly for our Girls' Technical School'. (AO)

# Nannie Katharin Wells

*Annie Katherine Smith, born Fordyce, 1875; married Bernard Norman Wells, 10 April 1901; died 15 March 1963, Oxford.*

Nannie Katharin Wells was well known as a novelist, poet, journalist and political activist.

She was born, one of six children, in 1875 in Fordyce, Banffshire, where her father, William Smith, was rector of Fordyce Academy until he was appointed rector of Milne's Institution, Fochabers, in 1880, a post he held until 1901. Her mother, Jane Garrow, was a farmer's daughter from Kinloss.

Annie Smith was educated at Milne's Institution. She later studied at Aberdeen University and, like many of her contemporaries, disqualified by her sex from graduating, took a Lady Literate in Arts (LLA) from St Andrews University. In 1901, she married, in Bellie Parish Church, Bernard Norman Wells, a solicitor from Ipswich, and moved to England.

In 1910 the family (there were now two sons) was settled in Barnard Castle in County Durham. Nannie, as she was now known, led the active life of the wife of a local solicitor. She was a committee member of the District Nursing Association, of the Dispensary for the Sick Poor, and – interestingly, given her later commitment to Scottish independence – of the Women's Unionist Association. In 1911 she was elected president of the local branch of the NUWSS, the moderate wing of the suffragist movement. The same year she chaired a meeting addressed by the distinguished Scottish suffragist Helen Fraser, who later described Nannie Wells as 'an outstanding advocate for women's suffrage – the equal of any opponent, male or female, in a debate on the issue'. Nannie Wells was committed to winning the fight on constitutional and educational lines. She was outspoken in her criticism of the tactics of the militant WSPU as 'unpatriotic, stupid and dangerous'.

During the First World War, Nannie Wells worked in the Foreign Office. She then moved with her family to Oxford before she returned to Scotland and threw herself wholeheartedly and with remarkable energy into the – in those days overlapping – worlds of politics and the arts. By 1929, she was secretary depute of the newly formed Scottish National

Party. She retained her commitment to
women's issues with the Edinburgh
Women Citizens' Association. The
EWCA, concerned initially with issues relating to suffrage, covered a wide range
of subjects of concern to women as citizens: pure milk supply, hygiene, women
police, the protection of children, laws
affecting women, housing, maternity
service and employment. Also working
for the EWCA in the 1930s was Lady
Helen Leslie MacKenzie.

A key figure in the Scottish Literary
Renaissance of the 1920s and 1930s,
Hugh MacDiarmid was also active in
the Nationalist movement. He and

Nannie Katharin Wells

Nannie Wells became close friends. One of the hubs of Edinburgh literary/
political society was Dinnieduff, the home in Corstorphine of the Angus
poet, Helen B Cruickshank, who tells in her *Octobiography* (1976) of the
endless arguments between MacDiarmid and Nannie Wells and of her
mother's response to one such: 'Ye baith speak far owre muckle. I'm seeck
o ye baith.' Others who were prominent in the circle at that time and with
whom Nannie Wells came into contact were Leslie Mitchell (Lewis Grassic
Gibbon), Neil Gunn, Eric Linklater, F Marian McNeill, Marion Angus,
Catherine and Donald Carswell and Edwin Muir. It is clear from
Cruickshank's autobiography and from other sources that Nannie Wells
was a well loved and influential figure in that circle.

We get a glimpse of how Nannie Wells perceived herself and her
achievements in the entry she submitted for the first Scottish *Who's Who*,
published under the title *Scottish Biographies* in 1938:

> Nannie Katharin Wells. Cullerne House, Findhorn. *b.* Morayshire. *ed*
> Berlin; Paris; Aberdeen: Fochabers. *m* 1901; 3 sons. Served in FO during
> Great War; Secretary, Edinburgh Women's Citizen's Association: Secre-
> tary Depute to the Scottish National Party since 1929. Author of 'Di-
> verse Roads' (novel); 'Wolfe of Badenoch' (biography, with Hugh Mc-
> Diarmid); 'Margaret Logg' (play). *Recreation*: managing rheumaticky
> minds with modern electric shock equipment.

Her novel, *Diverse Roads*, was published in 1932. In the love story of
Airlie Ogilvy, the daughter of a highland manse, and Stephen Temperley, a

well-connected young Englishman, who becomes an Anglican clergyman in the industrial midlands of England at the time of the general strike, she deals, sensitively and unsentimentally, with issues of religion, social class and national identity. Her epigraph to *Diverse Roads*, George Herbert's 'Love your neighbour – yet pull not down your hedge', may suggest something of her views on cross-border relations, but it is in her journalism that she directly addresses the condition of Scotland question. It is here that she pursues her aim of energising 'rheumaticky minds with modern electric shock equipment'.

In essays in the *Scots Magazine*, *The Free Man* and the Nationalist *Scots Independent* she made analyses of the position of women in the New Scotland:

> the Scotswoman has always been encouraged, both by Scots law and by custom, to 'individuate' herself, to take responsibility, to hold her own views, and make her beliefs felt.

She made the case for the economic independence of Scotland and she was one of the first to speak out strongly against Fascism:

> Democracy is hardly on its trial any more; it has been condemned and dismissed in too many countries... A time of heartsearching, of courageous decision, of endurance, of determined resistance to these false ideals awaits all Free Men. Maybe it is for them that our Scotland has lain fallow all these years so that, within us, Leadership and Liberty may again be reconciled as they have been more than once in our history as a Nation.

The Second World War changed things for Nannie Wells. She lost a son, Alan Moray Wells, in the London blitz. By this time, her husband long dead, she settled back in Oxford but retained her passionate commitment to and identification with Scotland. She averred that it was only after reaching the age of seventy that her mind and spirit became free, and that life in all its fullness was revealed to her. She became a Catholic in 1946, her interest in politics intensified and she took to writing verse.

She published two volumes of poetry: *Twentieth Century Mother and other Poems* (1952) and *The Golden Eagle* (1958). The Nationalist strain is still strong. In 'A prayer' she writes:

> God, give us the grace to hate
> our unemancipated state,

and to wipe from Scotland's face
her intellectual disgrace.

The state of the nation is rotten; a better future is possible. The poem concludes:

The things for which we ought to die
are plainly written on the sky:
God, now to us the vision give
To know for what we ought to live.

Her hymn to the potency of her homeland, 'Scotland My Lover', reaches a near-erotic climax:

Clear northern skies lit childhood's innocence
The day's darg over, dew under my feet, bare
On the cool grass, stars blaze and hover.
O still make love with me, far from the decadence
Of this dire century, of love's despair,
Scotland, my Jewel, my Lover.

In 1962, at the age of eighty-seven she published *George Gordon, Lord Byron: A Scottish Genius* with a Foreword written by Hugh MacDiarmid.

In her obituary in *The Scotsman*, F Marian McNeill described Nannie Wells as a 'perfervid Scot' who 'retained her enthusiasms and youthful vitality until very near the end'. She died in Oxford and was buried, beside her family, in Kinloss Abbey. Helen B Cruickshank and Marian McNeill sent red carnations to her grave. (RB)

# Johanna Forbes

*Johanna Forbes, born Cullen, 27 April 1879; married Forbes Tocher,*
*8 August 1917; died Cullen, 12 October 1957.*

The first woman academic at Aberdeen University, Johanna Forbes became principal teacher of classics at the prestigious, independent Hutcheson's Girls' School in Glasgow. At the age of thirty-eight she married the charismatic missionary Forbes Tocher and spent the years between the wars in central China.

Johanna was born in 1879 in Reidhaven Street, Cullen, where her grandfather, Thomas Forbes was a blacksmith, as was his son John, Johanna's father. Johanna's mother was Margaret Maggach, a crofter's daughter from Keith. By 1891 Margaret and John had moved to Anvil Cottage on Blantyre Street, a house with nine rooms with windows. Johanna had at least two brothers, Gordon and Thomas, and three sisters, Agnes, Jeannie and Elsie. Thomas became an optician in Elgin, and Elsie, like Johanna, attended Fordyce Academy and became a teacher.

In her middle age Johanna wrote 'Fordyce bred *men* in our day'; the italics are hers. In her article for the book *Fordyce Academy* (1936), she reported 'the joy and satisfaction of really laying hold of Latin and having regular living teaching in Maths'. Mr Emslie (headmaster) and Miss Bain (assistant) 'gave the school the best of their youth, and poured out all their rich gifts fresh for us. They gave us of their life-blood'.

Forbes Tocher from Whitehills, Johanna's future husband and six years her junior, remembered:

My first morning at Fordyce, Johanna Forbes crossing from the Academy House to the 'quines'' gate, with the biggest book under her arm that I had ever seen – Liddell and Scott [a Greek lexicon].

Fordyce is a small village just outside Moray. Pupils went to Fordyce Academy from all over the North-East because of its academic reputation. This reputation rested on the many endowments given to the school from the seventeenth century onwards that helped to finance children at school and on through Aberdeen University. The academic regime was rigorous, and remembered by all who wrote in the Fordyce Academy book of 1936. Some doubted its sense. Every boy had to take English (with history), mathematics, French, Latin, and Greek; the girls took the same except that they might take German instead of Greek. There was no science, no art, no physical recreation and very little music. Homework would take all evening and extra classes were given on Saturdays.

Some pupils went as boarders, but Johanna walked the three miles from Cullen and later remembered with pleasure 'the Birkenbog Woods and the fresh larches on the Towie Braes'. Johanna was an achiever; she was dux in 1898 and 1899 and won the gold medal from the school board for five honours in the leaving certificate. She was remembered by many of her fellow pupils, being large both in height and in personality.

Women were not admitted to the university in Aberdeen until 1892. Johanna, graduating with a first class degree in classics in 1903, was one of its early women graduates. A Miss Forbes, likely to be Johanna, was active in the Woman's Debating Society at the university, becoming

Johanna, at Fordyce Academy 1898, seen third from the right on the second front row

president in 1902. In 1903 Johanna Forbes was the first woman to take an academic position at the university, working, for four years as assistant to Professor Ramsay and, as a Latin assistant, lecturing to mixed classes, apparently with success. Her salary at this time was £60 per annum. Because academic posts were only available to women on a temporary basis at this time, school teaching was Johanna's choice as a career. She is listed as a teacher in the higher grade school at Cullen, then as teacher of classics at Falkirk High School and further as principal teacher of classics at Hutcheson's Girl's School in Glasgow.

Meanwhile Forbes Tocher had gone to China to work as a missionary in the Church of Scotland Mission at Ichang, or Yichang, (pronounced E-chang) on the Yangtze River. Ichang is about 1,000 miles from Shanghai, almost in the centre of China. It lies in an important strategic position being at the end of the big steamers' run from Shanghai and beneath the gorges that now contribute to the Three Gorges Dam; a junction between eastern and western China. Ichang was one of the treaty towns and it opened for foreign trade in 1877. The Church of Scotland Mission, with its schools and hospital, thrived, but was always vulnerable. Uprisings, rebellions, pirates, disease and the language problem made China the most hazardous of the missionary fields. The First World War, however, put a temporary end to Forbes Tocher's work in China. He was granted leave to fight in France where he was 'pushing the Bosche hard', eventually becoming an officer in the Royal Field Artillery. When he got leave he returned to the North-East and met old friends.

Johanna and Forbes were married in August 1917. Forbes went back to France and Johanna went to London, where in October 1918 she was training at Hackney College to be an officer in the newly established Women's Royal Air Force. Forbes survived at the front without 'a scratch' and was awarded the military cross. A year later on 27 November 1919 Johanna and Forbes were on the RMS *Metagama* on the way to Ichang, via St John, Canada.

Snapshots survive of their life in Ichang. Two daughters were born, one of whom died. In 1926 the Mission Council Minutes mentioned the voluntary work of Mrs Tocher:

> It was agreed that the Mission Council put on record its warm appreciation of the excellent work Mrs Tocher has done in St Andrew's School during the last five years. Her knowledge of the Chinese language has been such as to enable her to do regular teaching, and she has always taken a keen interest in the spiritual and material wellbeing of the boys, and has earned their deep gratitude.

Johanna also edited *The Ichang Tidings*, a mission newsletter. At Christmas time Johanna and Agnes, the surviving daughter, often came home to Cullen to stay with the family at Anvil Cottage, and Forbes would join them when he could. In the summer Johanna and Agnes might go to Kuling, a station further up in the hills where a bungalow was available for people from the mission. When the Tochers were back in Scotland they reconnected with their roots. Always they were trying to raise money for the foreign missions.

In 1927 the situation in Ichang was very tense. Forbes was involved in a local incident regarding the capture of a Captain Lalor of the Butterfield and Swire ship the *Siangtan*. Because of his bravery and diplomacy, which led to the release of Lalor, Forbes was awarded the CBE. Deteriorating circumstances resulted in all foreigners being evacuated to Shanghai. Johanna and Agnes came home until things settled down. In August Johanna was writing to the secretary of the Foreign Mission Committee:

> Yang Sen (the Szechuan General who passes up and down through Ichang as his fortunes wax and wane) had looted the foreign property in his passage up... It was no blow to us. We have expected it for some time and happily Mr Tocher and I are like-minded. We are not set on material possessions. Some things do matter but we have counted the cost, and we will go back as soon as ever we are allowed.

By October of that year Forbes reported that he could return to Ichang, but the ladies could not. Everyone, Chinese and British, had suffered and lost their belongings but the Chinese left in charge of the mission had managed to save most of the buildings. The Tochers did not agree with the principle of claiming compensation from the Chinese government.

The couple were back in Scotland in 1933, when Forbes was addressing the General Assembly, but by 1934 they had returned to Ichang and Johanna was spending her forenoons in the boys' school and a good part of her evenings preparing work for the boys. In China, the Communists under Mao, the Nationalists under Chang Kai-shek and the Japanese were all fighting for power. In 1937 the Japanese launched an all out invasion and by early summer 1939 refugees were pouring through Ichang on their way west. Johanna wrote an account of her journey from Ichang to Japanese-occupied Chefoo, north of Shanghai, where her daughter was at boarding school and about to take the Oxford exams. Forbes was to join them later, when the exams were finished. Like the other refugees, Johanna couldn't take the usual route eastwards down the Yangtze to Shanghai because the Japanese were moving up the river. She had to go west, 400 miles to Chongking, fly south for 800 miles to Kunming, then take the train to Hanoi and Haiphong where she got a ship passing Hong Kong and going north to Shanghai; a further 800 miles by sea to Chefoo completed the journey. As she left Ichang it was being shelled by the Japanese. Johanna wrote of her journey in the *Aberdeen University Review* of summer 1943:

Staff and leaving class of St Andrew's School, Ichang, January 1938. Mrs Tocher is seated on the front row and her husband is third from the right also seated (Trustees of the National Library of Scotland and the Church of Scotland)

We sailed before dawn to make sure of reaching a proper anchorage before nightfall, for no craft may sail through these waters in the dark and live – so powerful is the current; and so manifold the dangers of whirlpools and rapids. Five miles above Ichang the river turns at right angles west into the Ichang Gorge – dead stop for the Japanese armies: cheers for the dragon that guards the Yangtze! Above the Ichang Gorge we pass through a succession of other gorges, each one more wonderful than the last. The Wu-shan (Witch-Mountain) Gorge, the Ox-liver and Horse-lung Gorges (from the colours of the rocks), the Wind-box Gorge, and so on for two days. The sail through the gorges is a wonderful and thrilling experience. The mountains tower on either hand, broken by alluring glens and forbidding chasms. The scenery is always changing and the colour and light and shade are beautiful beyond words. The navigation demands the full attention of the man on the bridge, with his Chinese pilot by his side. No foreign captain sails these waters without his Chinese pilot.

When the family finally boarded the *Empress of China* on 4 September 1939 on their way home, via Vancouver, for furlough, they heard of the outbreak of war in Europe. Johanna, then aged sixty, would not see China again.

Forbes returned to China to work with destitute Britons in Shanghai. He was interned in the Lunghwa Civilian Assembly Centre by the Japanese. JG Ballard, who wrote about his own experiences in his best-seller *Empire of the Sun,* (London 1984), was interned in the same camp. At home Agnes joined the Women's Royal Naval Service (WRNS). After the war Forbes returned to Ichang and attempted to rescue the mission. Nine tenths of Ichang had been destroyed and the population had been reduced from 150,000 to about 5,000.

In 1947 Forbes, now also over sixty, was appointed minister at Botriphnie near Keith. The Ichang Mission struggled on for a while but the communists were taking over China and the mission's days were numbered. The Tochers spent ten years at Botriphnie before retiring to Cullen where Johanna died aged seventy-eight. Forbes remarried some years later, a mutual friend, Helen Wilson, who had worked with them both at Ichang and with whom he had been interned. At Forbes Tocher's funeral oration it was said of Johanna:

The devotion and enthusiasm for his work was shared by his late wife, a kindred spirit who sprang from the same generation of one of the 'Golden Ages' of Fordyce Academy. Together they built the Church of

Scotland Mission at Ichang until 'Ichang' and 'Tocher' were virtually synonyms.

Whilst the concept of missions to other cultures may be questioned, the presence of missionaries in China did contribute to the progress of both medicine and education; especially girls' education. When the mission was founded in Ichang infanticide was common for female babies, foot binding was an extremely painful means of restricting women physically, and the education of girls was unknown. By the 1930s a Chinese woman, Dr Margaret Wei Chen, was head of the Buchanan Memorial Hospital in Ichang.

There has recently been much debate regarding the myths and realities of Scottish education. Johanna was a bright girl, encouraged at home and able to access an elitist school locally; whether she was a 'lass o' pairts', if such a lass exists, is debatable. She was certainly one of those people who enjoyed excitement and loved a challenge. In her life there were plenty of both. (SB)

# Griselda Dow and her Sisters

*Griselda Annie Dow, born Elgin, 8 June 1891; married Robert Gregor, 26 September 1927; died Aberdeen, 18 June 1936.*

Griselda Dow and three of her sisters became doctors; the fifth sister became a teacher.

Griselda's mother, Marjorie Macpherson from Kingussie, had been teaching at Dallas school when Peter Dow, a Knockando man from Cardockhead, came to Dallas as the headmaster in 1886. Marjorie and Peter were married in 1888 and John, the eldest child, was born in 1889. A year later the family moved to Elgin, when Peter was appointed headmaster of the West End School. There were nine children in all.

Griselda Annie, known as Grisel, the second child, was born on 8 June 1891. After an elemen-

Back row from the left David (Eddie), John, Dorothy, Grisel, Elizabeth (Betty); seated Marjorie and Peter with baby Peter and little Marjorie (Mam); Donald in the front. Taken about 1905, Margaret was not yet born (Marjorie Whytock)

tary education at her father's school, she went on to Elgin Academy. Her last year at secondary school was spent at Fordyce Academy. Since the headmaster, Alexander Emslie, had just moved to Keith Grammar School, the regime at Fordyce, under George Simpson, was not quite so severe as in Johanna Forbes' day, but the academic excellence could not be questioned. Grisel's brother, John, had been dux under Emslie the year before, and her sister Elizabeth May (Betty, born 1894) would follow her, spending two years at Fordyce. Grisel had rather grand lodgings at the castle during her stay in Fordyce.

Grisel at graduation (Marjorie Whytock)

At Aberdeen University Grisel initially studied Greek and mathematics, but she took a shine to science and moved to Marischal College in her second year. In 1914 she graduated both MA and BSc. Because the zoology assistant had gone away to the First World War, Grisel was asked to take his post, which she did for two years, followed by a year as head of science at Elgin Academy.

Meanwhile John was already a doctor, Betty had gained her MA in Aberdeen in 1916 and had started on a medical degree course, and Dorothy Janet (born 1899) was about to start the same course. Grisel decided to join her siblings in medicine and entered the course at the same time as Dorothy.

Mary Esslemont, who later made her name in medicine in Aberdeen, was Grisel's great friend. Their studies had followed similar patterns: both doing arts, science and medical degrees. It was not all study for the two

Mary Esslemont (left) and Grisel in the laboratory at Marischal College (Marjorie Whytock)

bright girls; there was time to get involved in student organisations. Mary Esslemont, in the face of much male opposition, became the first woman president of the Students' Representative Council. Grisel became the first president of the Women's Union, which opened at 52 Skene Terrace around 1920. A plaque at the entrance commemorates Grisel's presidency. *Alma Mater*, 10 March 1921, commented:

> Those of us who have the privilege of knowing Miss Dow intimately all
> agree that the more one knows of her, the more one finds to admire, and
> that as a real friend, through all the ups and downs of life, she is without
> equal.

Dr Grisel's first job was in Manchester at the Victoria Memorial Jewish
Hospital. She stayed there for two years and then went to Dublin to study
midwifery at the Rotunda Hospital. By 1924 she had returned to the north
of England and was working in Chesterfield as assistant MOH. Betty was
not far away in Nottingham. Dorothy was also in Nottingham for a while.

Robert Gregor, from Cullen, had been at Fordyce Academy and
Aberdeen University at the same time as Grisel. Robert and Grisel were
married in the Scots Kirk in Colombo, Ceylon in September 1927. Robert
was working as superintendent at a tea and rubber estate, Opata,
Kahawatte, near Ratnapura. Grisel and Robert had two children: Marjorie
born in 1928 and Robert born in 1930. Young Robert contracted polio
and needed a lot of care. Although Grisel had a licence to work overseas,
she never practiced in Ceylon. She did, however, do some work amongst
the locals in a voluntary manner.

The family were back at home in the North-East in 1936 for six months'
leave. Grisel stayed on a little longer to settle Marjorie at Albyn School in
Aberdeen, and to undergo an operation. Tragically, she died on the

Baby's day at Chesterfield (Marjorie Whytock)

operating table. She was forty-five, Marjorie was eight, and Robert six. Grisel was buried in Knockando beside the family graves.

Marjorie spent some years at Albyn, often holidaying at Blelock, a house near Logie Coldstone that the school used for children who could not go home for holidays. It was to Blelock that Marjorie was evacuated in the war. She enjoyed her time there but was removed to school at Queenswood, Hatfield, in the south of England and from then on Auntie Betty and her husband, John Cox, took care of the children when the children's father, Robert, was in Ceylon, and it was they who provided a home for Marjorie when her father re-married. Robert, the father, eventually found a place for young Robert, at Gordonstoun, in Moray. When the Rev. Mair of Spynie heard of the arrangements he remarked 'You're no sending him to that German school?' But the school, which had been founded in 1934 by Kurt Hahn, suited Robert. Hahn was compassionate about the boy's disability and Robert did well there, but died at the age of twenty.

Grisel's sister Dorothy died in 1949. A few years later her younger sister, Marjorie Johanna Macpherson (born 1902), who worked as a maternity and welfare officer in Yorkshire, married Dorothy's widower, Alexander Cooper. The youngest sister, Margaret Mary MacLaren (born 1907), taught at Mackie Academy, Stonehaven, and Nairn Academy before marrying the Rev. Francis Fraser, Church of Scotland minister at Nairn. In 1949 they moved to Monifieth. After her husband's death, Margaret taught at Monifieth Primary School, and then at Harris Academy, Dundee. She died in 1989.

Marjorie, Grisel's daughter, remembers her holidays in Moray with her grandmother, also Marjorie, at Cardockhead in Mayne Road, Elgin. She reflects that her grandmother might have been a frustrated woman because of all the children she had to bear and care for, but that it was her drive that made sure all her children had the education 'to go anywhere'.

Neither Grisel nor her sisters married young. Only two of the sisters had children. It was the delay in marrying that gave them the opportunity to use their education, because in the years between the wars, educated women might have a career but, generally, they could not have children and a career. Grisel married at the age of thirty-six, and so had the opportunity to develop a career whilst single. Grisel and her doctor sisters helped to establish women doctors as an accepted and positive part of society. (SB)

# Beatrice Sellar

*Beatrice Mary Sellar, born Aberlour, 3 July 1898; died Aberlour, 2 April 1985.*

Beatrice Sellar gave up her musical ambitions to become the first woman GP in Aberlour.

Dr Thomas Sellar built the family home, Dunleigh, Queen's Road, Aberlour, in 1882 as a medical practitioner's house which included the surgery. Following his marriage to Magdelene Kynoch of Keith in 1889 the house was soon filled with the music and laughter of four lively children. Beatrice was the youngest child. She planned a future revolving round her piano and cello. She obtained the Licentiate of the Royal Academy of Music in 1916 and a year later was training in London to be a piano teacher.

Her life was turned upside down when a letter from her mother called her back to Aberlour to help her elderly father in his practice; by this time he was sixty-one years old and his wife Magdelene was looking to the future. Beatrice's brothers were making their own ways in life; Thomas had enlisted in the Gordon Highlanders and William was moving to West Africa as a rubber planter. Beatrice's sister Magdelene was destined to marry their father's assistant, Dr John Caldwell; Beatrice was the apparent solution.

She returned immediately to the family home and put her heart and mind into training as a family doctor. She had special tuition in Latin and the sciences before gaining entry to Aberdeen University. Beatrice graduated in April 1922 at the same ceremony as Griselda Dow. The following year she obtained the Diploma of Public Health from Cambridge University. When she retired in 1961 she said that she had no regrets about giving up her music career: 'Parents were often the best judges of what children should do' she commented.

Although she did not find it

Dr Beatrice Sellar (Dr John Caldwell)

easy to establish herself in the village, where people still saw her as the doctor's quine, Dr Bea, as she became known, assisted her father in the practice. After his retiral, she was assistant to her brother-in-law, Dr John Stewart Caldwell, who had also joined the practice. As she established herself in the community as a kind and competent GP, the suspicion of many patients confronted by a woman doctor, soon evaporated.

All the doctors stayed at the family home Dunleigh, Gaelic for fort of the physician. Though the house was well equipped there was no waiting room. The practice was rural and scattered; very few people were able to attend the surgery so the doctors visited their patients at home. These patients had presented Dr Thomas with a car in 1909 but Dr Bea usually walked. Speyside was rugged and the roads were poorly maintained; snow ploughs and tractors were not available to unblock winter roads and a way through the snow had to be cut by hand. Dr Bea found many of the homes she visited damp and cold.

Dr John Caldwell (junior), Magdelene's son, recalls many stories about his aunt Dr Bea and her time in the practice. To contact the doctor in an emergency a friend or family member would go to Dunleigh. One patient ran to the doctor's house in the middle of the night because her mother was ill; she threw pebbles at the window to rouse Dr Bea. There were few phones in the district; Beatrice's father had set up a system whereby if a doctor was needed a red flag was erected and then the message was passed to the postmaster who would telephone the practice.

On one visit to a remote croft when the burn was in spate Dr Bea threw her medical bag over, along with a gift for the patient from Mr Archibald Grant the local laird. She then waded across. The gift turned out to be a bottle of whisky which arrived at the bedside still intact, much to the relief of all concerned.

On a particularly bleak and wintry day she was visiting a sick woman who needed to be moved to hospital urgently. The men solved the problem of transport by using a barn door as a sledge. Having tucked the patient in, they then insisted that Dr Bea got in beside her for the journey across the fields to the roadside.

Although the practice car was reserved for the senior, male, doctors, Dr Bea eventually acquired a Baby BSA motorcycle. This was a great help to her but the gear she had to wear was a nuisance. The goggles, leather helmet and long boots were fine for a jaunt round the countryside but cumbersome in a cottage and tiring to walk in. Eventually the problem was solved when she crashed the bike into a stone dyke. She was then promoted to a car but found it an unreliable mode of transport as, in her opinion: 'it could be a perfect nuisance and a timewaster.' The engine boiled in the summer and froze in the winter, springs kept breaking on the rutted roads and on two occasions a front wheel rolled off in front of her stationary car.

Dr Bea took over the practice in 1935 following the early retirement and death of her brother-in-law Dr John Stewart Caldwell. She was well versed in looking after all her patients' various needs, from educating the family on good bed hygiene and nourishing food and drink to prescribing pills and potions for the local chemist to dispense. There was complete doctor-patient trust and the medicine was dutifully administered without the patient knowing what it was in it. Dr Bea's talents in obstetrics were well known. Patients and doctors alike maintained that she provided as good a service as a maternity unit. Her aim was always to have a healthy mother and baby and a clean and dry bed. Husbands would be despatched to find rubber sheets, large bowls and endless boiling water; this had the double result of keeping them occupied and out of the way and keeping the delivery bed clean and tidy.

In a difficult birth before ready access to safe caesarean section Dr Bea induced the mother with chloroform anaesthesia, which had first been used in 1847 by Sir James Simpson in Edinburgh. The district nurse administered judicious drops of chloroform onto a linen mask over the face and nose, a seemingly hit and miss procedure. Dr Bea was at the business end performing some pretty scary procedures to deliver the baby safely. If the baby's head was stuck in the pelvis she turned the child and delivered it by pulling the legs down producing a breech birth.

Dr Bea once delivered a baby in a traveller's tent and returned two days later to find the child being bathed in the burn. She was horrified, but was told by the mother that if the baby couldn't cope with it he would be no use to them.

Dr John Caldwell (junior), Dr Bea's nephew, joined the practice in 1949. He recalls attending a six-month obstetric course and returning full of new ideas and practices. When he enthusiastically demonstrated the use of obstetric forceps to his aunt, she retorted that they were as much use as teaspoons.

Dr Bea and the other doctors were well aware of the social needs of their patients and always kept a set of baby clothes for new arrivals. Bea's sister Magdalene would produce nourishing food for the elderly as required. Her favourite remedy was green jelly laced with whisky. Each Christmas Magdalene would make up parcels of goodies and a balloon for Dr Bea to take to all the sick children in the area.

Despite a busy professional life, on call twenty-four hours a day, Dr Sellar was very active in the community. She was a guider in the Aberlour troop and founder member and chairperson of the Senior Citizens Club.

Her piano playing was much in demand at local concerts. She regularly attended Aberlour Parish Church where her father was an elder for sixty-two years. When he died in 1950 at the age of ninety-three she gifted a stained glass window in his memory.

Dr Bea retired in 1961 after thirty-eight years devoted service to her patients. She refused the opportunity to continue on a part-time basis and immersed herself in community life. She held annual first aid classes in several local schools, gave talks on local history and provided active support to the Aberlour Flower Show. She loved gardening and won many prizes, especially for cordon grown sweet peas. In the garden at Dunleigh her legacy is a vibrant border of agapanthus and nerines as well as a scattering of liliums and other bulbs.

Travelling round the countryside in all weathers throughout her professional life gave Dr Bea a taste for walking and she regularly went over the Mannoch from Archiestown to Elgin as well as tackling the Lairig Ghru in the Cairngorms. The walking pleasure was enhanced for herself and companions through her expert knowledge of wild flowers. She kept several albums of pressed flowers from her local area, from Cambridge and from the Alps.

Dr Bea always made time for angling and loved to fish the Spey and the Avon; she particularly enjoyed fishing for brown trout when the burns were in spate. She found worms in the garden for bait. Her nephew, and later his children, enjoyed joining her in this pursuit.

Dr Beatrice Sellar died in 1985, nearly a quarter of a century after she retired; her obituarist noted:

> She was simply Dr Bea, not only a doctor but guide, counsellor and friend... she was the very heart of this village.

Dr Bea's retiral speech, 1961, showing audience appreciation (*The Northern Scot*)

She had given up her chosen career in music without a second thought, returned from the bright lights of London to study hard to enable her to enter the medical profession, an unusual occupation in such a rural area, but she overcame the suspicion of some of her patients and was happy to stay as assistant to her male colleagues for many years before becoming head of practice. Her hard work earned her the respect of all she met. She served her patients well and they loved her for it. (AO)

# Isobel (Sybil) Duncan

*Isobel Ann Duncan, born Elgin, 1910; died Elgin, 7 March 1986.*

Sybil Duncan was the only woman to be elected provost of Elgin Town Council. She worked in the slum areas of Edinburgh, Glasgow and London before being called home to manage the family business. She was a councillor for twenty-nine years.

Sybil, as she was always known, was the daughter of Elgin coal and potato merchant John Duncan and his wife Annabella Rose; she had one sibling, her brother James. She was born in the family home Rose Cottage, Academy Street, and attended Elgin Academy. Sybil gained a degree in social science from Edinburgh University – it was an unusual choice for a woman in the 1930s. In the Depression she worked at a slum resettlement centre in the east end of London. She was a social worker in several deprived inner city areas including Glasgow, Birmingham and Liverpool.

In 1945 Sybil was appointed head of Edinburgh's largest community centre. Her mother died in October that year and early in the New Year she returned to the family home to look after her father and the family business; she was thirty-seven years old. Her father died two years later. Sybil ran the coal and potato business in South Street for many years.

A few months after her return to Elgin Sybil stood for election to Elgin Town Council She was elected in November and remained on the council until reorganisation of local government in the mid-1970s. She was a diligent councillor with an almost perfect attendance at council meetings and the many sub-committees she sat on. Sybil was elevated to dean of guild in 1952 and bailie a little later. Despite her political acumen and social work credentials the *Glasgow Herald's* photograph caption said: 'Councillor Bailie Sybil Duncan, manager of a coal business and President of the Townswomen's Guild, admiring the latest fashions in a shop window in 1954.'

In 1961 *The Northern Scot* newspaper proclaimed: 'History was made last night'. On 6 May 1961 Miss IA Duncan had been unanimously appointed lord provost of Elgin Town Council, the first, and as it turned out, the only woman to hold that appointment. She was in post for three years.

During the 1960s Lord Provost Duncan presided over a number of projects to rejuvenate Elgin. The Civic Design Project of 1962 led to the beautifying of South Street. Road signs were hung on buildings, planters arranged outside the High Church and a civic ceremony held when the Duchess of Northumberland officially opened the new look street. She was keen to erect street signs which included

Bailie Sybil Duncan in Elgin in 1954
(Herald and Times; Scran.)

the original names on them. Sybil was also interested in the Moray Music Festival which was going from strength to strength. Dr Beeching's planned railway cuts were a cause for concern. Sybil Duncan's working life experience perhaps influenced her interest in social welfare in Elgin. She was actively involved in the former Munro Old People's Home in Bishopmill; she helped form the Elgin Venture Club for people with disabilities.

In May 1964, Lord Provost Duncan unexpectedly stood down from her position and returned to the back benches. There were no accolades or explanations in the town council minutes. Sybil remained on the town council for another ten years, working diligently behind the scenes. She died in March 1986 at the age of seventy-six.

Isobel Ann Duncan was a private person with a strong sense of duty. She worked hard to improve the lot of inner city slum-dwellers and obeyed the call to return to the family home when needed by her father and brother. She belonged to many organisations in Elgin and was a dedicated councillor. Though she later disappeared from public view, Lord Provost Duncan's part in Elgin's civic achievements are acknowledged in Bishopmill; Duncan Drive opposite Elgin Academy was so named in recognition of her public life and achievements. (AO)

CHAPTER SEVEN

# Two World Wars

*It's the one red rose,*
*The soldier knows;*
*It's the work of the Master's hand.*
*In the war's great curse*
*Stood the Red Cross Nurse,*
*She's the rose in No-Man's-Land!*

First World War song[1]

THE WOMEN WHO FOUGHT for the franchise without success went their various ways in August 1914 when war was declared. The women mentioned in the previous chapter all contributed differently to the war effort and a glance through the *Morayshire Roll of Honour* gives a further idea of the range of work undertaken by women.

Nurses were in high demand. Army and navy nursing services of the late nineteenth century had, by 1902, evolved into Queen Alexandra's Imperial Military Nursing Service (QAIMNS) and Queen Alexandra's Royal Naval Nursing Service (QARNNS) staffed by paid, trained nurses. Annabella Ralph from Rothes, who rose to the position of matron-in-chief of QARNNS, served in both the First World War and the Second World War. By coincidence, Helen Cattanach, born a generation later in Knockando, but only a few miles from Rothes, also became matron-in-chief – of Queen Alexandra's Royal Army Nursing Corps (QARANC), the successor to QAIMNS. Volunteer nurses belonged to the Volunteer Aid Detachment (VAD). The VADs – Red Cross Nurses – were unpaid, usually untrained, and frequently looked down on by the regular nursing staff; any social standing no longer held weight. The Wharton Duff sisters, Ella and Isabel, from Orton House, were active in the Lhanbryde Red Cross detachment in 1914 of which Helen Black of Sherriffston was VAD commandant. By December 1915 the Wharton Duff sisters were in Dartford and it was there that they joined QAIMNS; Ella served in London and Alexandria, and Isabel served at home. Isabella Grant (Gugu) from Elchies worked as a VAD nurse in England, Scotland and Russia. There were many different organisations working across Europe; Ethel Dunbar from Alves, for example, worked with the American Quakers in eastern Europe.[2]

Women doctors found it more difficult to offer their services because the Royal Army Medical Corps (RAMC) would not enlist women. But the women who had fought so hard to train as doctors, and had been campaigning in the suffrage movement, were not going to accept defeat easily and by September 1914, a privately funded surgical hospital, The Women's Hospital Corps, staffed entirely by women, was offered to the French Red Cross and gladly accepted. Olga Campbell, at that time unconnected with Moray, enrolled as an orderly in this hospital which was so successful that the RAMC gave it recognition in November 1914.

In Edinburgh, Elsie Inglis, similarly frustrated by the attitude of the RAMC, set up the Scottish Women's Hospital Service (SWH). Initially a suffragist organisation, the SWH eventually numbered over 1,000 women who came from Canada, Australia and New Zealand as well as Great Britain. France and Serbia were happy to accept the SWH. Tibby Gordon, from Garmouth, was caught up in a terrifying adventure in Serbia.

Often whole families were involved in the war effort, the brothers fighting, the sisters doing whatever came their way. Four of the Dunbar sisters of Newton House, near Alves, are listed in the *Morayshire Roll of Honour*: Catharina served in Nice and Grenoble hospitals; Ethel served in France and Salonica; Lilias was a driver in the YMCA; and Marjorie was 'Lady Manager' of a munitions works. There were two Dunbar brothers, one of whom was killed in action. Of the many Culbard sisters, Amelia became a VAD commandant, and Christina became a somewhat controversial administrator in the SWH in Salonica and Corsica. The Morrison sisters from Elgin both worked in censorship: Elspet, a teacher of modern languages in Motherwell, worked in the London censor's office from 1916; while Gertrude, only a student and newly turned eighteen when she joined a few months after Elspet, eventually went to France with the American Expeditionary Force. Of the three Hardie sisters from Pluscarden who were active in the First World War, only Mary, who was in France with the SWH, is listed in the *Morayshire Roll of Honour*. Anne worked in the War Office in London and received an MBE for her contribution; and Margaret, whose married name was Hasluck, worked for British intelligence in Athens and London in the First World War and advised the government on Albanian matters during the Second World War – briefing the underground agents before they entered Albania. Two Hardie brothers also served. Edith Wellwood, from Lossiemouth, had four brothers fighting in the war, two of whom were killed in action. Edith joined the Scottish Church Huts in Bologne. These huts, or canteens, both at home and abroad, provided such comforts as tea and buns, and moral support for the troops. They also sold cigarettes and useful small items such as postage stamps.

As the war continued, Moray's importance in farming and forestry became crucial to the nation's survival. By 1917 the country was facing starvation. At this point the Women's Land Army was formed. The forests too, needed extra 'manpower'. Jeannie Kelman, born in Boharm, and Mary Wilson, born

Lhanbryde Red Cross Detachment 1914, outside Sheriffston. Helen Black centre, second row (from front); Isabel Wharton Duff left, third row; Ella Wharton Duff centre, back row (*The Northern Scot*)

in Rafford, joined the Forestry Corps – a specialist part of the Land Army.

After the First World War there was nursing, teaching, domestic service and office and shop work to go back to, but many of the women who had found new niches during the war were expected to return to the domestic scene or the social round. With men returning home to Britain needing employment, and a weak economy, women had little prospects for interesting careers outside the medical and teaching professions. Ethel Dunbar, who had nursed in a military hospital in France during the war, moved on to work with refugees after the war, struggling with illness caught in the dreadful conditions of the Bialystok prison camp in Poland.[3] Olga Campbell was fortunate in finding an unusual and satisfying career with a shipping line in the 1920s. Edith Wellwood married a minister which, in effect gave her an unpaid career in the church, albeit subservient.[4] Isabel Wharton Duff[5] and Helen Black[6] became involved in community work on a voluntary basis. Isabel represented Moray in the Nursing Association, and on the Scottish Council of Queen Victoria's Jubilee Institute for Nurses. Helen, a founder of the WRI in Moray, and member of the board of governors of Anderson's Institution, Elgin, was also a district commissioner for Morayshire girl guides and a justice of the peace. Both Isabel and Helen served on the Moray and Nairn Education Committee. For most women, however, there was a return to monotony set against a background of the Depression of the 1920s. The Women's Royal Naval Service (WRNS) that had been established in 1917 was disbanded as was the Women's Auxiliary Air Force (WAAF) that Joanna Forbes had joined.

When the Second World War loomed, women found themselves needed again. Lesley Souter, who was instrumental in the development of flying bombs, proved her skills in the private sector. While women would not be allowed to go into combat, three military organisations were quickly established: the WRNS and the WAAF were re-formed and the Auxiliary

Territorial Service (ATS) was founded. The first of April 1939 saw the opening of RAF Kinloss, with RAF Lossiemouth following a month later. Approximately 2,000 WAAFs were stationed in Moray during the Second World War.[7] Initially those arriving at Kinloss were quartered in Kinloss House, a rather grand Victorian holiday house that had been commandeered by the government. The Land Army was reformed in June 1939. One hundred and eleven women are recorded as working in the Land Army in Moray in November 1943.[8] This would have included the lumberjills working in the timber corps. Lumberjill camps included those at Advie, on Speyside, and Edinkillie, near the Dava moor. Conditions were basic, the work was hard, the heavy horses had to be looked after and the weather could be foul.[9] As the trees were felled, so the landscape of Moray changed.

Aware of the problems that would arrive with air raids, the government set up the Women's Voluntary Service (WVS) to help with Air Raid Precautions (ARP). The WVS, apart from some paid staff at headquarters, was run entirely by volunteers. Initially organised largely by upper middle class women, it gradually drew volunteers from all ranks of society and prided itself on its lack of hierarchy. It made a huge contribution to the war effort and although there is little record of its activities in Moray. Mildred Gordon-Duff of Hopeman Lodge, Hopeman was involved in some way. Later in 1966 the WVS became the WRVS of today. Air raids were unusual in Moray, but there were evacuees to organise and forces personnel to support. Olga Campbell, by then Lady Byatt, and Nora Mackay had just the right experience to take on these tasks; both of them had served in the First World War and had honed their organisational skills in the years of peace.

Meanwhile, on the other side of the world, a Lossiemouth girl, Clara Gordon or Main, who had emigrated to America, was caught up in high drama in the South Pacific and interned by the Japanese. Also interned was Thérèse Levack, daughter-in-law of Mrs Levack of Rock House. Thérèse her husband, Robert Levack, and their daughter were living in Paris when it fell in 1940. Interned in the dungeons of Dijon Castle and later in Vittel Vosges, they had little knowledge of the progress of the war because, being civilians, they were unprotected by the Geneva Convention. An occasional Red Cross food parcel helped to assuage their desperate hunger.[10] Even after liberation the food parcels were badly needed. Later Thérèse lived at Boulah Bembah in Lossiemouth. Robert's sister, Ethel, had been a VAD nurse in the First World War, serving in Moray and France.

Post Second World War Britain took years to recover, but in time prospects brightened and opportunities opened up. Two world wars had changed women's perception of their roles in life. Some had died, many had lost fathers, brothers, sweethearts or friends, and had endured untold horrors. But they had glimpsed a future that would give women a fairer position in society; a future that would be inherited by the next generation.

# Amelia Culbard

*Amelia Jane Chisholm Culbard, born Elgin, 26 August 1860; died Elgin,
21 April 1942.*

# Christina Culbard

*Christina Margaret Culbard, born Elgin, 19 February 1869; died Elgin,
24 March 1947.*

Brought up in a comfortable, well-respected family, Amelia and Christina Culbard were middle-aged spinsters by the start of the First World War. Both joined the Red Cross Society in Elgin. Amelia became a VAD commandant and was awarded an MBE for her efforts. Christina joined the Scottish Women's Hospital (SWH) as an administrator and served with them in the front line. She resigned from the SWH and the Red Cross in 1917. Both women returned to the family home where they remained for the rest of their lives.

North Lodge, Elgin was the home of William Culbard, son of tannery owner James. William developed the business and was a prominent public figure who rose to be lieutenant colonel in the Elginshire Volunteers and lord provost of Elgin by 1880. He married Johanna Ross in 1859 and they soon produced a family of at least six daughters and a son. The children would have grown up aware of the necessity of doing their civic duty. Amelia was the firstborn. Her sister Edith, who arrived on Amelia's fifth birthday, married solicitor Robert Mackay, brother of the first female town councillor, Nora Mackay. Christina was last but one of the children.

Amelia, who proclaimed her occupation as gardener, joined the Red Cross Society in Elgin in 1912. She was fifty-four years old when the war started and spent her VAD service in Moray. She was on the Red Cross committee in Elgin from 1915 and spent time working at the War Dressings Depot in the town.

By the end of 1915 Miss Culbard was officer in command, or commandant, of a convalescent home for Belgian officers in Spey Bay. The Spey Bay Hotel had been requisitioned in October that year and Amelia was responsible for both staff and patients. At the end of the war she remained on the council of the Moray branch of the Red Cross. For her services she was awarded an MBE. Amelia died at Oldmills on 21 April 1942.

As Amelia began her work in Spey Bay Christina enrolled in the Red Cross Society as a VAD. She immediately began service with Elsie Inglis' SWH unit. She was attached to the Salonika Commission and travelled to Salonika with around seventy other women, including Dr Mary Blair, who was head of the unit. They arrived there at the end of October 1915 expecting to be deployed around the area. They found that there was little to do and nowhere to go. Serbia was in enemy hands and the SWH there was evacuated. Dr Blair set up a reception centre for Macedonian refugees. The entire unit used their skills to look after the destitute families. It is likely that Christina's organisational talents came to the fore in finding temporary accommodation and food for the starving people. Meanwhile the SWH's Edinburgh committee was pondering the problem of too many people in one small area. It was agreed that Dr Blair's unit would go to Corsica.

Christina arrived with the unit on Christmas morning. The Serbian Relief Fund welcomed the women but there were clashes about where the new hospital should be sited. Miss Culbard and Dr Blair, now the hospital's chief medical officer, were concerned that the CMO of the island appeared to assume he was in overall charge of the SWH as well as the Relief Fund. They disregarded his plans and set up the hospital at The Villa Miot, Ajaccio, which was sited in a beautiful position on the coast. Miss Culbard was appointed administrator, in overall charge of the nurses. The equipment ordered from Britain suffered many delays; Christina set to with relish: 'in a sort of beg and borrow picnic style... the hospital is wonderful,' she wrote to committee member Mrs Lawrie in February 1916.

Dr Blair moved to another unit fairly quickly which caused Christina to wonder if there should be a change of administrator as well. Dr Blair's successor was Dr Mary Phillips, who was in close alliance with the Serbian Relief Fund. Christina made no secret of the fact that she disapproved of this and gathered her own cohort around her and proceeded to 'make life hell' for Dr Phillips. It appears that there was a power struggle between the two women over who was the head of the hospital.

According to reports to the Edinburgh committee of the SWH, Dr Phillips was thinking of resigning from the SWH altogether; her assistant Dr Jackson wrote to the committee saying that her first few weeks there had been a nightmare and many of the best nurses had left. 'Miss Culbard', she added, 'seemed focused largely on picnics and playing cards for money'. Both women wrote regularly to members of the Edinburgh committee with their grievances; in the spring of 1917 a delegation from Edinburgh visited Corsica to assess the situation. It concluded that Miss Culbard's allegations were without foundation and that she had 'overstepped her powers'.

Christina left Corsica immediately and was discharged from the Red Cross Society on 24 April 1917. She returned to the family, who by this time was living at Oldmills. Christina received the King of Serbia's St Sava's medal for service to his country and served her own town of Elgin as a justice of the peace. She died at Oldmills on 24 March 1947, just after her seventy-eighth birthday, and is buried in the family plot in Elgin Cathedral.

Amelia and Christina Culbard's organisational skills ensured that they both held responsible positions as VADs. Elder sister Amelia spent many years working for the Red Cross Society while her younger sibling's more volatile nature meant that her war service was short lived. Despite their ages they both answered the call to serve their country and earned medals for good service. (AO)

# Isabella (Gugu) Grant

*Isabella Leonora Mary Emily Grant, born Natal, South Africa, 10 February 1875; died Durban, South Africa, 8 February 1921.*

Isabella (Gugu) Grant witnessed the Russian Revolution while serving as a VAD in 1917. She was her family's archivist, saving first-hand accounts of the Indian Mutiny, life and death in the First World War and rural life in nineteenth century Moray.

Isabella's father, Henry Alexander Grant, left Scotland to make his fortune prospecting for gold in Natal. When he was forty-six years old in 1873 he married local girl Mary Jane Jackson who was twenty. Four years later he unexpectedly inherited Wester Elchies estate on Speyside. He became the fifth laird and returned home with his family; Isabella, always known as Gugu, (Zulu for 'dear one'), was two years old. Her father's reign was short-lived as he died in 1886 when Gugu was only ten years old, and the eldest of seven children. The new laird, James, was eight. Gugu spent her adolescence supporting her mother with the youngsters and assisting in the role of lady of the manor.

Her life was rocked once more by a succession of events, starting with the death of her youngest sister, Violet, aged nine, in 1890. Her position in the family was weakened three years later when her mother remarried and then her brother James, the young laird took a bride on his twenty-first birthday in April 1897.

There was little space for a maiden aunt at the centre of this new family group. She contracted an unnamed illness during the ensuing years and

Wester Elchies, now demolished

retreated to Forres, lodging with two spinsters, the Misses Allan. It was here that she convalesced, working on her family tree and writing to cousins and older relatives about their lives and connections. She left a note in her writing box explaining that all the papers should be kept for future generations of the family. Among the papers she kept many anguished letters from her cousin Charles who had just got engaged when his fiancée was murdered during Indian Mutiny of 1857:

> If you didn't hear it earlier this mail will convey the events of the horrible massacre at Delhi... I wish I could add news of my poor dear Annie and her father for my heart sickens when I think of the uncertainty of their fate.

Gugu joined the Red Cross in Forres in 1913, 'an enthusiastic and efficient detachment' according to *The Northern Scot*. In December that year she became a VAD nurse and worked in hospitals around Britain before being posted to the Anglo–Russian Hospital in Petrograd (now St Petersburg) in 1916. She was forty-two years old, and as for many women of her generation and class it must have been quite an adjustment. She had been trained in basic first aid and nursing and honed her skills at various British auxiliary hospitals where soldiers with more minor injuries were patients. Nursing was somewhat bloodier in Russia.

The Anglo–Russian hospital was set up in 1916 by Lady Muriel Paget and Lady Sybil Grey. Patrons included Queen Alexandra and the Archbishop of Canterbury as well as the lord provost of Aberdeen Sir David Stewart. Through these illustrious connections the Russian Royal family were also keenly involved and assisted by offering various palaces as a base for the hospital. It was set up in the former Sergei Palace, the residence of the Grand Duke Dmitri on Nevsky Prospekt. It was a grand building and work was done to install baths and plumbing. The parquet floors were covered with linoleum and the damask walls boarded up. Only the chandeliers were visible. The hospital was officially opened on 1 February 1916. After all the pomp the real work began. Field hospitals were set up at the Front and a field ambulance was soon established. Many of the original staff went to the Front and Gugu arrived as a replacement in July, having travelled with other staff through dangerous seas to Archangel.

From there they boarded a train for the 1,000-mile journey to Petrograd.

Throughout Gugu's time there she wrote to her younger brothers who were at the front. Their replies were added to her archives. Her young brother Pat served in the 3rd Canadian Pioneers. He

Dimitri Palace, a red cross over the entrance, 1916/17

was injured in the Somme and invalided home for a while. He wrote to her from his hospital bed in Warwick:

> it is nothing but a piece of shrapnel in shoulder... personally I don't think I need to have stayed in bed at all with the amount of shelling I have been through I think it is a marvel I got off so easily... Miss Morris came to see me Thanks for arranging with her to send me out things

Her closest brother Sealy (Henry) wrote regularly. At Christmas 1916 he wished her a happy Christmas and added:

> I know it is a farce & that you have as much hope of enjoying yourself as I have but no matter. We have been having a quiet time for some weeks – though in many respects I prefer the line to resting... You are lucky not to get any news of the war. After all the result is what will count, & setbacks, how ever appalling they may seem will make no difference to the finale.

Gugu received a special Christmas gift in 1916, a book of pictures. She kept it in her archive box along with a note with it which said:

> Given to Isabella Grant (whilst working in the Anglo Russian Hospital in the Dimitri Palace Petrograd) at Christmas time 1916 – from the Czarina.

She had a number of Russian mementos. Along with her Russian identity card there was a letter from an RB Findlay written on 21 July 1916, just before she left for Russia:

> I shall be delighted to vouch for you – I suppose the authorities will write to me if they think it necessary in your case. I wish you all good luck in your work of mercy.

When Gugu received her final letter from Sealy, he was already dead, killed in an incident with a Lewis gun on 27 February 1917. He was becoming increasingly angry with the futility of war and by February was predicting his imminent demise. He also said he thought that she would have returned from Russia while she still had the chance. He added:

> I don't suppose they will put you too close to the line… after all a dead nurse is as much use as a dead horse. Hope you won't have too tough a time all the same… I hope when your time is up you will give nursing a rest. It can't be very pleasant and you have earned a good rest after two years.

While she was worrying about her brothers, another drama was unfolding on her doorstep. She and the rest of the hospital staff were having a grandstand view of the uprising which led to the abdication of the tsar. By the end of the year they witnessed dramatic changes to the Russian way of life with the advent of the Bolshevik rule.

The harsh winter and lack of food as well as the war were taking their toll on the people. Russian women chose International Women's Day (23 February on the Julian Calendar) to launch their protests for 'bread and peace'. This was followed by several strikes and demonstrations staged by the workers. On the afternoon of 26 February, the nurses had been watching people queuing for bread in the freezing cold; they were unsurprised when they heard rumours of bread riots. Mill hands and munitions workers had reached the end of their tether and gathered along Nevsky Prospekt and the surrounding streets. Cossacks were on hand to quell them, but though shots were fired they were undeterred and threw snow and stones at the troops. Soldiers had been sent to guard the hospital but Lady Sybil thought it wise to make up Red Cross flags out of sheets and Father Christmas suits and string them over the balcony.

Though nervous of the threatening mobs who wanted to search the building they tended the casualties as they appeared. The nurses were escorted to their sleeping quarters across the street during a lull in the fighting but there was to be no slumber for several days; the streets were alive with gunshot, screams and shouting. The police headquarters next to the nurses' home was sacked and many of the police were murdered. But there was a great air of excitement; within days the tsar had abdicated.

In the months that followed the field hospitals were having an active time but work at the Anglo-Russian Hospital was slowing down. Gugu was posted to Rosherville Military Hospital, Gravesend in July 1917. Her war service ended at Berrington Military Hospital, Shrewsbury in 1919 when her record shows that her work and character was 'very good'.

Following the death of Sealy, Gugu's archive came to an abrupt end. The end of the war must have been a difficult time for her. Her useful work was finished; her elder brother was ensconced in her family home with his own family; her younger siblings were dead or scattered around the world. She decided to go to Durban, South Africa where she was born. She had relatives to meet and there was a need for nurses. She worked at Seatland, Natal, until she was taken ill. Her Aunt Addison, one of her family-tree correspondents was with her when she died at Berea Nursing Home a month after her forty-fifth birthday. The death certificate does not record the cause of death.

Gugu's legacy is her fabric-covered writing box which contained the letters, documents and heirlooms of five generations of her family from 1780 to 1920. She had included carefully written notes recording information for future generations. Her great-grandfather Robert was a young farmer's son when he emigrated to Nova Scotia and made his fortune. He returned in triumph and bought the Wester Elchies estate becoming the first laird. His son Charles inherited in 1803 and founded the village of Charlestown of Aberlour. Charles's brother James became third laird when he was in India with the Honourable East India Company and he wrote many letters home which provide an insight into life in India as well as estate life for the gentry and the tenants. James's nephew Charles Thomason was intimately involved in the Indian Mutiny. Thomason's new fiancée was murdered in the Red Fort, Delhi, and he wrote heartrending letters to his aunts.

The final document is a letter from Gugu's solicitor to her sister-in-law in September 1922:

> I received two medals from the War Office addressed to Miss Grant, being the British War and the Victory medal which fell to her in view of her services with the Red Cross... I am not sure what should be done with them. I'm sure Miss Grant's executors could keep them, but for whom?

Gugu died far from home after a life of service to her relatives and to her adopted country. Like many women of her generation she had proved useful in family and national emergencies; with family grown and scattered and the war over there was little left. Her early death meant that she was unable to forge another niche for herself.

The Grant family died out in the 1950s; Gugu's box and its contents are stored in Elgin Museum, a useful and valued resource for historians. (AO)

# Annabella Ralph

*Annabella Ralph, born Rothes, 13 July 1884; died Aberdeen, 28 June 1962.*

Bella Ralph served in both world wars. She retired as matron-in-chief of the Queen Alexandra's Royal Naval Nursing Service.

Bella, as she was known, was the eldest child of Jessie and Alexander Ralph. She was born at the family home in Old Street, Rothes. Bella's father took work where he could get it, from railway carter to coppersmith's labourer. The family grew rapidly; Bella had a least six siblings. They moved from Rothes to Alves, Duffus and Hopeman before returning to Rothes. They eventually settled at Easter Elchies Gardens, Craigellachie.

In 1906 she applied to the Royal Infirmary, Aberdeen, to train as a nurse. This seems a bold move for a girl who had had a disrupted education as the family were continually on the move. Annabella Ralph was accepted and spent three years at Woolmanhill, qualifying in 1909. She took a position as a private nurse at the Royal Northern Nursing Home in Aberdeen a year later. She did not receive official recognition of her achievements until 1923 when she was added to the Nurses Register as RGN 2953; a member of a small band of fully qualified nurses.

Annabella Ralph (Royal College of Nursing)

The contribution made by British nurses during the Boer War was recognised with the formation of the Queen Alexandra's Imperial Military Nursing Service in 1902. By the outbreak of the First World War in 1914, 297 trained nurses had enrolled; Nurse Ralph was one of those; she enlisted on the first day of war, 4 August. She must have acquitted herself well at the interview. It was an exclusive service with all applicants required to be well educated, to have trained at War Office approved hospitals and be of impeccable social standing. Recruiting problems led to some relaxation of the rules but the insistence on the women being 'well bred' was strongly ad-

hered to. It was felt they needed
this social status to enable them to
give orders to orderlies and sergeants.

Nurse Ralph served in most of
the home naval hospitals and
many hospital ships. She was posted to Malta in 1915. The island
was known as the 'Nurse of the

British Military Hospital, Hong Kong

Mediterranean' because so many sick and wounded troops were sent there.
Annabella was head sister on the *St Margaret of Scotland* for two years.
This hospital ship was unusual in that all the staff including doctors, nurses and orderlies were Scottish. A flag day throughout Scotland raised
£22,000 to equip her. These ships were painted in distinctive colours with
red crosses prominently displayed to avoid attack. Despite this they were
vulnerable. Hospital ships were mined or torpedoed fairly often; three
were sunk in November 1916.

Annabella was posted to Hong Kong in 1917 where she was
superintendent sister at the 200-bed military hospital in Bowen Road. By
1932 she was serving at RNH Haslar in Portsmouth. She was one of only
seven superintending sisters in post at the time. These women reviewed the
senior nurse's work and pay structure which resulted in improved salaries
and conditions.

Miss Annabella Ralph's name appeared in the New Year's Honours list
for the first time in 1935. As the *British Journal of Nursing* noted: 'The list
of honours filled ten columns in *The Times*, and here and there the name
of a woman appears'. Bella was decorated with the Royal Red Cross,
Second Class, entitling her to use ARRC after her name.

At the start of the Second World War, Bella was at the pinnacle of her
career. She had returned to Malta as matron in 1936 and four years later
she was promoted to matron-in-chief, head of the QARNNS, the highest
rank possible at the time. In September that year, on the first anniversary
of the start of the war, King George VI held an investiture. Twenty-six years
after she joined the service Bella was presented with the Royal Red Cross,
RRC, for her dedication to nursing. This decoration was instigated by
Queen Victoria in 1883 in order to recognise heroism in women 'providing
for the nursing of sick and wounded soldiers and sailors'. Though bearing
the same name, it is not associated with the Red Cross Society. It was
considered the equivalent of the Victoria Cross. She was awarded the Bar
to the Royal Red Cross after her retirement in 1946 at the age of sixty-two.
She was also awarded the CBE. Annabella Ralph retired as matron-in-chief

in 1942 but continued working at The Royal Navy Auxilliary Hospital Kilmacolm in Renfrewshire, finally returning to Rothes at the end of the war.

Following her retirement, Bella attended annual luncheons at the London United Nursing Services Club where she and other retired matrons-in-chief were entertained by the current incumbents. She died aged seventy-seven at her brother William's home, Cullen House Gardens, where he was head gardener. Bella was buried with her parents Jessie and Alex in Rothes Cemetery.

From inauspicious beginnings, Annabella Ralph made her mark on the world through hard work, dedication and service throughout two world wars. She enlisted on the first day of the First World War and served continuously until the end of the Second World War. (AO)

# Tibby Gordon

*Mary Isabella Gordon, born County Cavan, Ireland, 22 July 1885; married John Leggat Anderson; died Elgin, 15 November 1970.*

Tibby Gordon joined the Scottish Women's Hospital during the First World War. After only a few months in Serbia she got caught up in the great retreat of winter 1915: a trek of 500 miles across the mountains of Montenegro and Albania.

Tibby Gordon's parents came from Moray and Banffshire: her mother, Margaret Duncan from the farm of Begrow, Duffus, and her father John from Glasterim farm, near Portgordon. Tibby, or Isabella (but never Mary), was born in Ireland because her father was working as land agent for an Irish landowner. The family returned to Moray and took the farm of Silverhills, on the Gordonstoun Estate, and then, in 1896 the farm of Connagedale, in Garmouth. Tibby, her older brother William, and younger sisters, Alice and Jean, would have attended the local Garmouth School and some went to Milne's Instituiton in Fochabers. Tibby trained as a nurse, possibly in Edinburgh, and was working at 'Dr Brewis' Home' there when the First World War began.

Famously told by the Royal Army Medical Corps to 'go home and sit still', Elsie Inglis had responded to this instruction by setting up the Scottish Women's Hospital (SWH) and offering its services to the Allies. By December 1914 the 1st SWH unit had been established at Royaumont Abbey, near Paris, and another unit was on its way to Serbia.

Tibby joined the 2nd Unit SWH in Edinburgh in June 1915. By the time

she arrived in Serbia the SWH had made progress, establishing some order and routine in
various buildings in the town of Kraguievatz.
Hundreds of wounded Serbs and Austrian
prisoners needed attention and there were very
few facilities available. The fact that there were
no trained Serbian nurses explains some of the
chaos that was found when the SWH first arrived. To add to the problems, typhus fever,
spread by lice, was sweeping the country from
the north. The disease thrived when people
were undernourished. A regime of whitewash
and disinfectant was instantly established.
Eventually a line of hospitals extended to the
north of Kraguievatz helping to arrest the
spread of infectious diseases into the main
body of Serbia. Surgical cases were mostly
dealt with in Kraguievatz. Soon after her arrival in Serbia, Sister Gordon was working

Tibby Gordon, August 1932 at
Glasterim (Hugh Robertson).

further north at Lazaravatz, about twenty-five miles south of Belgrade,
where Dr Holloway had taken over the Serbian hospital. The hospital was
spread throughout the village – 200 beds in eight different houses. Sometimes there were many more than 600 patients. One day a hundred wounded men came all at once, followed by fifty the next day. Generally, however, there was a lull in the fighting; 1915 was called 'the long peaceful
summer'. By September rumours were circulating about the Bulgarians
joining with the Germans and Austrians. In October, with the country encircled, the Serbian Army prepared to retreat.

When Tibby Gordon returned to Moray she gave an account of her
experiences of the retreat to a reporter of *The Elgin Courant* – it was
printed on Hogmanay 1915 – which gives an invaluable record of the journey. Tibby was in Lazaravatz when the SWH received orders to leave on 19
October 1915. They, along with their equipment and many refugees, got
the last train south; the railway line was destroyed shortly after they left.
At Krushavatz they managed to find one room to house the twenty-two
people in their party. They stayed there for seventeen days helping in the
Serbian hospital; 300 to 500 soldiers arrived each day and they were kept
busy dressing wounds.

On 5 November orders came to evacuate. Dr Inglis, Dr Holloway and
a number of other women decided to stay in Eastern Europe, but most of
the SWH joined the retreat: a moving mass of people streaming through the

town. To begin with, the SWH women had a donkey each and the use of a bullock cart, but most of their possessions were jettisoned on the journey. There were twenty-two women in Tibby's group. They covered twelve miles the first day and camped in the open by the roadside. The next day:

The Serbian Retreat, from a drawing by William Smith

> The road was in a frightful state with mud, through which we had to wade at times almost up to the knees, and we were held up in most places by a continuous stream of traffic both of refugees and of the retreating Serbian Army. We camped at night by the roadside again; rain came on, and it was dismal. Those who were lucky to have umbrellas used them, but the others had to cover themselves as well as possible with their blankets, which by morning were drenched with rain.

The party started off with a selection of food: bully beef, sardines, syrup, condensed milk, tea, coffee, sugar and bread, but soon they were reduced to half a loaf of black bread a day, with sometimes a little milk given by the local people. Often they had to sleep out; once a 'filthy hut' kept the worst of the weather away.

Moving south across the Plain of Kossovo, they came to Prisren. William Smith who was transport officer for the SWH in Serbia, and was travelling with the women, reported that there they found a great congregation of different groups of people: French, Russian and British medical missions and diplomats. They discovered that the route through Albania to the Allies' base at Salonica was blocked by Bulgarians and the only way of escape was over the Montenegrin Alps and westwards to the Adriatic coast. But first they had to get to Ipek where the mountains began:

> From Prisrin we went to Jackovitza, a distance of thirty-six miles, leaving in the morning about six o'clock and reaching Jackovitza at 12.30 the next morning. Our legs were tired and aching on the way, and our feet were blistered, but we trudged on. Some of us hummed tunes most of the way, including 'It's a long way to Tipperary', which helped cheer us up.

Another two days took them to Ipek where there was food and time to recuperate. For three nights they slept in the barracks; during the day they organised themselves for the journey over the Alps. A pony was shared between three and food was carried in a tuck bag. The snow began on the third day of the trek over the mountains. It snowed all day and the narrow track became treacherous when the frost set in. There was no comfort at night:

> We reached a place that night where there was neither food nor shelter, and spent the night round a campfire in the open, singing the whole time. When morning came we set off after having a cup of hot tea and a piece of bread.

The next day the pony carrying Tibby's blankets fell over one of the precipices that they encountered along the way. The worst night was when Tibby and two other SWH women who had gone on ahead got bogged down in snowdrifts up to the waist:

> At the very top of the mountain we came on a small hut. Half of the roof was off, and we saw there was a good fire, so we thought it would be a good place at which to put up. Here we met an old Serbian woman, refugee, with two donkeys and a Montenegrin man with a horse. We
took off our boots which were frozen to our feet, icicles being on our stockings. At 9pm a severe blizzard came on, our fire went out, the snow came down and we could see nothing around us. We had no food with us and had had nothing since morning. We could neither go on nor back to our party. The old woman was starving but she was very good to us. She gave us a bag, into which the three of us got and lay very close to each other to keep warm. The Montenegrin was our pillow, and he did not object for he was starving. Here we lay till morning. I don't know how we lived through that night.

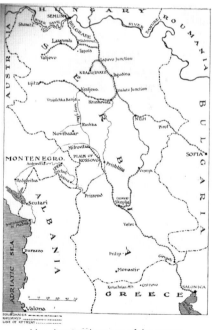

Map showing the route of the retreat

Though it was the worst night of the journey, there was more hardship to come, with streams to wade (resulting in water frozen in their boots) and a 7,000-ft mountain to climb. All of the women suffered frostbite to some degree. Some days there was no food. At Leverika there was some relief; motor buses took them to Podgoritza where they stayed for two days and had a good meal in the Hotel Balkan. There were more hitches, but eventually they got a boat across Lake Skadarsko, to Scutari (now Shkodra) where there was food. They stayed for three days there and were comfortable enough, but for the occasional bombs which fell on the town. Two days' hard walking took them to port San Gohan O Medua on the Adriatic. It too, was war torn: Austrian submarines had sunk several ships in the harbour three days previously. Tibby and her colleagues waited there five days, desperately short of food. Finding bacon washed up on the shore from the wrecks, they fried it with black bread.

From there it was relatively easy: an Italian boat took the SWH women to Brindisi in Italy, thence they went by train to Turin, and further to Paris where they were able to wash properly for the first time since the beginning of the retreat. Tibby was reduced to wearing slippers by this point. On arrival in London, a reporter wrote, 'Never has London seen such a worn out, travel-stained, ragged company of professional women.' By Christmas Eve, Tibby Gordon was back with her family in Garmouth. It had been quite a year.

There was a price to pay for the adventure. Not only had there been the frostbite and starvation, Tibby had also contracted malaria in Serbia; a serious disease that returns from time to time. At home in Garmouth she had time to rest and recover, but also to worry about her brother, William, who joined as a Gunner in 1917 and was wounded in France. Christina Culbard's story throws some light on the SWH activities following the retreat from Serbia.

Once recovered, Tibby worked as matron of the Forres Fever Hospital and soon afterwards returned to the capital where she worked at Edinburgh Royal Infirmary. In Edinburgh she met John, or Jock, Anderson who worked for the jewellers, Hamilton and Inches. They were married, possibly in the early 1920s. The couple stayed at Castle Terrace, but Jock was diagnosed with TB and died some time around 1930. Tibby returned to Moray and stayed with her father, who had moved to the family farm of Glasterim in 1920, on the death of his brother. In about 1936 the two moved to Balnageith, near Forres. After her father's death in 1939, Tibby stayed with her sister Jean and Jean's husband, John Robertson, in Portgordon, where she remained after Jean's death. Tibby died at the age of eighty-five, in 1970, in Dr Gray's Hospital, Elgin.

Tibby's nephew, Hugh Robertson of Forres, son of Alice, remembers Aunt Tibby as 'a pleasant woman, always tolerant, and with a good sense of humour. She smoked like a chimney – Churchill No. 1 – and enjoyed clothes'. Tibby never spoke to Hugh about her time in Serbia. It was perhaps, after the war had passed, a time to

Tibby beside her husband Jock, with a neighbour. Tibby's sister Alice is on the left (Hugh Robertson)

keep private because only those who had experienced it could understand the hardships endured. It is fortunate though, that Tibby gave a report of her adventures to *The Courant* on her return from Serbia, because we should not forget such moments in history, and the personal cost involved. Only one SWH woman died on the great retreat, but of the 30,000 young Serb boys who were evacuated at the same time, only 15,000 got over the mountains, and thousands more died before reaching safety. Tibby saw not only the tragedy of war but also some of the chaos that it brought in its wake. (SB)

# Clara Main

*Clara Gordon, born Lossiemouth, 19 March 1886; married Daniel Main, 1908; died Spynie Hospital, Elgin, 16 October 1975.*

Clara Gordon Main was a stewardess on the SS *President Harrison* when it was captured by the Japanese in 1941. She became one of the first American prisoners of war and was awarded the Meritous Service Medal, the Merchant Marine Combat Bar, the Merchant Marine Defence Bar and the Pacific War Zone Bar.

Clara Gordon was born in Gordon Cottage in the parish of Drainie, one of the six children of Mary and carpenter William Gordon. When still a teenager, Clara left home to earn her living. At the age of twenty-one she married Daniel Main from Burghead and settled down to raise a family. The marriage was not a long one. Daniel died in 1927 leaving Clara with three children to care for. A few years later, in search of better opportunities, she moved to America. She worked for five years on board ship as a stewardess and in October 1941, aged forty-five, she was on board the SS *President Harrison* (formerly named the SS *Wolverine State*) bound for Honolulu, Shanghai, Hong Kong, Singapore, Penang, Ceylon, Bombay and Ca-

Clara Main (*The Northern Scot*)

petown. Britain was already at war but passengers and crew of the American vessel had no inkling of trouble ahead on their journey. At Honolulu there was not the usual band to greet the ship, but Clara Main went ashore as normal, visiting the post office, doing some shopping and visiting an optician, enjoying tea in a hotel before reboarding. However, when the ship arrived in Manila the captain received orders to proceed to a Hong Kong shipyard, where the ss *President Harrison* was converted into a troop transport ship. She was then sent to Shanghai where, on 28 November 1941, passengers and cargo were unloaded and 300 men and their equipment were evacuated to be transported secretly to Manila. The officers and crew were informed of the situation and the captain sent a message to say that Clara could remain behind but she replied:

> Unless the captain thinks I'd better remain, or orders me to do so, I'd rather sail with the ship.

Unfortunately, the Japanese were aware of the destination of the ss *President Harrison* and when the ship was ordered back to north China from Manila to evacuate us marines from Peking (Beijing) a Japanese cruiser was waiting.

If captured, the American ship could be loaded and used within hours against United States forces in the Far East. On 7 December the master of ss *President Harrison* did everything he could to avoid capture. Dive bombers dropped notes demanding surrender, but knowing there was no escape, the captain ignored these and made an effort to beach the ship on the rocky island of Shaw-Wei-Shan in the Yellow Sea and tore the bottom out of her. Currents swept the ship off the rocks and the crew was ordered to abandon ship. As the lifeboats were lowered they came un-

Map showing Shaweishan Island (*MAST*, the magazine of the US Maritime Service)

der machine gun fire. There were 156 people on board, including the captain, and the only woman, Clara Main. In the darkness on 7 December – the morning of Pearl Harbour – the Japanese captured ss *President Harrison*. The Marine war information record states:

> Mrs Main displayed a courage and calmness exceeded by no other member of the crew. While the bomber power-dived, threatening the ship with bombs and sending bursts of machine-gun fire into the bridge, she remained, at least outwardly, entirely unexcited. Before Mrs Main could enter her lifeboat, the bomber returned and again fired into the bridge, hitting very close to where she was standing. When told to take cover down in the ship her reply was 'Why should I? I had enough trouble getting here.'

One lifeboat was thrown by the current and the wind into the ship's screw and broken in half. Three men were killed and several badly injured, including the chief steward. As she left the ship in the last boat, Clara had the foresight to collect some medical supplies and first-aid materials. Within the space of one morning the crew had learnt of the attack on Pearl Harbour, the American declaration of war, and had been captured by the Japanese.

While the Japanese ordered the crew to return to the ship, Clara was allowed to stay on the cold and windswept rocky island for a few days and nurse the injured, before they rejoined the rest of the crew on board the badly damaged vessel. She continued to nurse the chief steward. One of the crew stated:

> During the time we remained on the half-sunken ship, Mrs Main was a steadying influence on the crew, and contributed towards calming those given to excitement and worry over the constant threat of the Japs.

The crew was captured, and twelve crew members died, but it took more than a month before the ship was repaired enough to be taken by the Japanese to Shanghai. For forty days Clara Main nursed Chief Steward JL McKay and undoubtedly ensured his survival. The ship was patched up with quilts, cotton and wood and eventually refloated. On 19 January,

ss *President Harrison* (MAST, the magazine of the US Maritime Service)

with no lifeboats, the ss *President Harrison* made for Shanghai. The marines who were to be picked up by the ss President Harrison also became prisoners of war. Included in the cargo which was to accompany them were the fossils known as 'Peking Man'. The whereabouts of these fossils remains a mystery.

At Shanghai the prisoners were moved from place to place until, in February 1943, Clara Main was interned in Chapei Internment Camp, along with 1,500 other prisoners. The building had been bombed and was filthy, but the prisoners cleaned it as best they could. There was insufficient nourishing food, several epidemics, and 'campitis' – so called because the doctors could find no better name for it and nearly everyone was affected. Clara worked long hard hours in the hospital, apart from the eleven weeks when she too succumbed to 'campitis'. She was eventually repatriated when 1,300 prisoners were exchanged for a similar number of Japanese who had been taken prisoner by the Americans. The transfer took place on a glorious sunny day and Clara recalled:

Mrs Main at the time of capture (*MAST* the magazine of the US Maritime Service)

> With that happy feeling of freedom, and the knowledge of meeting your old friends and loved ones, it truly made one glad to be alive.

Once she was safely back in America, Clara did not forget her comrades on the ss *President Harrison*. She wrote to and visited relatives of the men who had been left behind, saying it was the least she could do for those who had been so good to her. She then went back to her work at sea and was on the first ship which came to Britain to collect the war wives and babies. Clara retired in 1955 and, having maintained contact with her friends and relatives in Lossiemouth, she returned to spend her final years quietly in her old family home, in a cottage in School Brae, not far from the sea. She died in 1976, aged eighty-eight. (JM)

# Olga Byatt

*Olga Margaret Campbell, born Edinburgh, 1891; married Sir Horace Archer*
*Byatt 1924; died Wester Elchies, Aberlour, 10 September 1943.*

During the First World War, Olga Byatt worked as a quartermaster in the suffragist Women's Hospital Corps in France and then in Endell Street Hospital in London. In the Second World War she worked with refugees and evacuees, and served on a tribunal for 'enemy aliens'.

Olga Byatt, the daughter of James Arthur Campbell and his wife Ethel Margaret Bruce, was brought up at Arduaine on Loch Melfort, south of Oban. Here her parents had built a house and planted a beautiful rhododendron garden which is now in the hands of the National Trust for Scotland. She joined the Women's Hospital Corps in September 1914 along with her aunt-in-law, Dr Flora Murray. At the start of the First World War the Royal Army Medical Corps (RAMC) did not accept women doctors, so Dr Murray and her friend Dr Louisa Garrett Anderson turned to France and offered a fully equipped surgical unit to the French Red Cross. It was accepted and the unit travelled to Paris where a hospital was set up at the newly built Hotel Claridges on the Champs Elysée. Olga Campbell went with the unit as an orderly. They arrived in Paris at 10 o'clock at night after a slow train journey. Flora Murray wrote:

The Gare du Nord was dimly lit and there were no porters on the platform. A male representative of the French Red Cross who met them told them that rooms were reserved in the Station Hotel. He watched in silent astonishment while Orderly Olga Campbell and Orderly Hodgson commandeered a large luggage trolley, loaded it with all the bags and wraps and proceeded to trundle it out of the station. The station entrance to the hotel was locked, the lifts were not working and the *cuisinier* had been mobilised. There could be no supper.

Olga Byatt c.1935 (GM Tyrell, Elgin)

In spite of this somewhat inauspicious introduction to Paris, the Women's Hospital Corps made an outstanding success of the hospital at Hotel Claridges. Builders' dust and debris were rapidly removed and within two days they were receiving casualties by taxi from the first Battle of the Marne. Flora Murray wrote:

> The hospital brought help to the wounded at a time when such help was greatly needed. It gave women doctors the opportunity to show their capacity for surgery under war conditions. It was one of the outstanding pieces of work done by women in those first months of war.

After two months most casualties were arriving in Boulogne where hospital facilities were severely overstretched. Dr Murray and Dr Anderson were interviewed there by two colonels of the RAMC and asked to set up a surgical unit. Dr Flora Murray wrote that the senior of two colonels asked 'Have you a quartermaster?' 'Yes, we have one,' Dr Garrett Anderson replied, mentally appointing Orderly Campbell to the post as she spoke. The newly appointed quartermaster was sent as an understudy to the quartermaster of the military hospital in the Grand Hotel, Boulogne, taking with her an official document issued for her use, the very first recognition that women were able to run a hospital:

> To O i/c Supplies.
>
> The Women's Hospital Corps have established a hospital at the Château Mauricien at Wimereux, and is recognised by the War Office. (Signed) D.D.S.—, Lt.-Col., for A.D.M.S.
> 5th November 1914

Armed with this, Quartermaster Campbell assumed her duties, and, accompanied by her [role] model from the Grand, sought out the supply depot. She returned with the most superabundant rations, the male quartermaster apologising and puzzled; for he could not understand how or why they had got so much. Miss Campbell's account was:

> An orderly asked me if I would like a side of bacon, and when I said yes, he put one in the car. And another said a case of peaches would be useful and put it in. And someone else brought the jam and the cheese, and they said a bag of tea and another of sugar would not come amiss. And just as we were leaving, a sergeant threw in two hams... So there it all is' [she ended gleefully].

The hospital was ready for occupation on the following day and the beds soon filled up. The women

> felt strangely near the Front, for the men came down from the lines in a few hours, and their tales of the mud and the wet in which they were standing almost up to their waists, the agony of frostbite, the terrible shortage of ammunition, and the superiority of the German guns made pitiful hearing. The anxiety and strain of the severe cases was as nothing to the pathos of the slight cases which had to be sent straight back to the Front.

By February 1915 the work at Wimereux had become lighter. Conditions at the front had made any advance impossible for weeks to come and the hospital acted more as a clearing station for medical cases being sent back to England. There was a proposal to set up 50,000 additional hospital beds in England and the organisers had to consider whether the Women's Army Corps could be of greater service in England. Drs Murray and Anderson were given the St Giles Union Workhouse premises in Endell Street, London, and invited by the director general of the RAMC, Sir Alfred Keogh, to run a large official military hospital there. Thus Olga Campbell in her early twenties became the quartermaster of a hospital of some 573 beds which cared for over 24,000 patients from May 1915 until December 1919. She involved her father as carpenter and he made 'the latest forms of apparatus' for treatment of compound fractures of the thigh. In 1917, there were 154 of these cases of compound fracture in the wards at the same time, and so he must have been kept very busy.

Olga Campbell never mentioned her connection with suffrage work to her three sons, but Flora Murray and Louisa Garrett Anderson (daughter of Elizabeth Garrett Anderson) specifically linked their military work with suffrage work, using the motto of the Women's Social and Political Union 'Deeds not Words'. An American feminist, Marion Dickerman, who worked at the hospital as an orderly, recorded that it was drilled into them:

> You have not only got to do a good job but you have got to do a superior job. What would have been accepted from a man will not be accepted from a woman. You have got to do better.

Quartermaster Campbell checking in stores at the Endell Street Hospital (Byatt family)

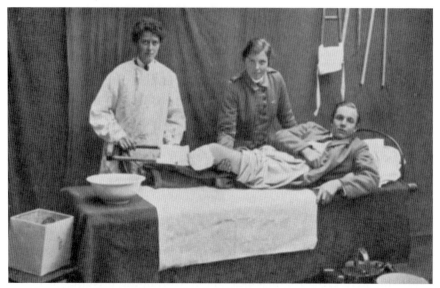

Quartermaster Campbell (centre) and Orderly Cook making 'plaster pylons' – limb supports
(Byatt family)

Whilst the work must have been full of stresses and strains, it seems also to have been full of fun and excitement. Dr Flora Murray wrote:

> In the Quartermaster's offices there was a young team, full of good spirits and ready for any enterprise. They fed and clothed and administered the hospital, and were ready for every entertainment and piece of fun. They prepared extra teas and extra suppers; rehearsed and performed, if need be; danced or sang, or carried tables and handed refreshments, with equal vigour and enthusiasm. Men who had left would write with confidence to the quartermaster for jerseys, socks, cakes, musical instruments, belts and other wants, and in answer she constantly sent parcels to France and Salonika.

Quartermaster Campbell at her desk
(Byatt family)

Government departments tended to economise where salaries were concerned and the rank or position of the women remained ambiguous. Although the quartermaster was graded and paid as a sergeant-major and the store keepers as sergeants, the doctor-in-charge was informed that these members of staff were NCOS, RAMC,

paid under royal warrant, and
could not claim a bonus after two
years' service, as civilians did.

The Endell Street Hospital received high praise from the director general of the RAMC. Writing in
January 1918 to the principal surgeon, Dr Louisa Garrett Anderson, Sir Alfred Keogh said:

Quartermaster Campbell being presented to Sir
Alfred Keogh (Byatt family)

> I was subjected to great pressure
> adverse to your movement when
> we started to establish your Hos-
> pital, but I had every confidence
> that the new idea would justify
> itself, as it has abundantly done. I think your success has probably done
> more for the cause of women than anything else I know of, and if that
> cause flourishes, you and I can feel that we have been sufficiently re-
> warded for our courage.

Olga Campbell was awarded the MBE for her war service at the Endell
Street Hospital. When the hospital was finally closed at the end of 1919,
many of the young girls who had been employed there were faced with the
prospect of exchanging the joy of work and responsibility for the inactivity
of home life. Olga Campbell wrote to an American friend who had also
worked at Endell Street 'I enjoy playing and having a good time enormously
when it is an accompaniment to work but as a sole occupation it bores me
stiff.' She set up a flat in London with three other women, complete with
cook and housekeeper.

It was during a dinner party that she met Sir Alan Anderson of the
Orient Line who was complaining about the time it took to turn around
the ships at Tilbury. 'What you need is a woman' was her reply. After some
thought Sir Alan replied 'My dear, I think you're right' and so it was that
she became chief housemaid of the Orient Line at Tilbury, a position she
held till her marriage in 1924. Her boss at home in London was the marine
superintendent, Captain Baynham, and in a letter she wrote from Nice to
her American friend she said:

> Captain Baynham nearly had a fit when the Managers told him I was
> coming and that I was to have a free hand and be under no-one but
> himself.'

She went on:

> He wanted me to see ship life at sea before I began any work in the
> docks. I was sent off in the Orvieto to Toulon as a 1st class passenger.
> I have a week to wait and then return with the next ship, the Indarea.
> I am armed with letters of introduction to the Captains of the ships
> instructing them to give me every facility and allow me to see any part
> of the ship and its workings that I desire to. Also a letter to the
> Company's Agents in Toulon telling them to give me every assistance
> while on shore.

Olga described herself as 'a post war innovation':

> There has never been a woman in the job before. All the officers are
> hugely intrigued to know what I am going to do… It would tickle you
> to death to see me being taken round by the Chief Steward and Chief
> Butcher and Baker and Linen Steward etc.

Olga quickly made her mark. On one occasion when a board meeting
was held in a cabin she invited the members to try out the crews' pipe cots
in the fo'castle. '*Now* what do you think of them?' she is quoted as saying.
There were groans all around and the uncomfortable beds were changed.

In 1924 Olga Campbell married Sir Horace Archer Byatt whom she
had known for some time. He was then governor of Trinidad and Tobago
and she took on yet another role, that of governor's wife. They had three
sons, all of whom were educated at Gordonstoun School. The two eldest
sons followed their father into the Foreign Service and became ambassadors.
The youngest son later returned to Gordonstoun as Second Master.
Horace's father had been headmaster of Midhurst Grammar School, so
teaching was not an unknown profession to the family.

Horace Byatt retired early through ill health and the family lived at
Meesden Hall, Hertfordshire, from 1929 to 1933. He died in 1933. A year
later, Olga Byatt came north to live in Elgin at the North College, beside
the ruined cathedral. Her brother Keir Campbell was teaching at the newly
founded Gordonstoun School. She had already met the founder, Kurt
Hahn, when he had stayed at her parents' home in Argyll and she had
visited his previous school at Salem in Germany. Her son, Robin, remembers
Mr Hahn (as he then was) coming frequently to lunch in those early years
of the school; not to a lunch party but to talk one-to-one with his mother.
Presumably he valued her judgement on his current problem. But her
association with Germans had its downside and led to the rumour in the

locality that she was a spy. When war broke out in 1939, Kurt Hahn, a naturalised Briton, remained free but Olga's German acquaintances on the staff at Gordonstoun were interned as 'enemy aliens' and sent to the Isle of Man and Canada until the risk they posed to national security had been assessed.

Olga Byatt's sister-in-law had married an Austrian Jew, Fay Wärndorfer, and Olga offered him and his family a home in the North College. She acquired tickets for them and got them out of Austria just ahead of the Anschlüss, the annexation of Austria into Greater Germany in 1938. After the outbreak of war, Olga was asked to serve on a tribunal for 'enemy aliens', and Fay Wärndorfer's sons Wau and Rikki had to appear before it. Presumably they were assessed as Category C, refugees from Nazi oppression, as Wau was allowed to join the Army Pioneer Corps as a private. He was sent into enemy territory as a native speaker to help with the resistance and was captured and killed by the Gestapo.

In September 1939 Elgin was to receive 1,038 children and 194 expectant women evacuees from the central belt. Olga Byatt was designated as a 'billeting officer' and as such was to find places for the evacuees. She was convenor of the 'Domestic Help Committee', consisting of women who didn't actually take evacuees but would help those who did. In the event, only 299 evacuees arrived, mostly from Granton, Edinburgh. *The Elgin Courant and Courier* of 8 September 1939 printed an appeal for clothing, sheets, bedsteads, camp beds, prams and go-carts for the evacuees... 'Any of the above may be delivered to Lady Byatt, North College'. In March 1940 it was reported that another 425 children might be coming to Elgin and a large advertisement was printed asking for volunteers to take a child. Last time the children had arrived 'like a flock of sheep at a late hour, not knowing where they were to go to'. This time it was hoped that they could be allocated to a home before they arrived. At the end of March there was still no home for two boys. Could they be Stewart and Harry Sangster from Edinburgh, known to have been housed by Lady Byatt herself? She housed others too and set up a room in a wing of the house where soldiers on leave from the army camp at Pinefield could stay. It was always known to the family as the 'men's leave bedroom'. Various people at risk from air raids down in England also stayed with her at the College.

Her untimely illness in 1943 cut short a valuable life. She was a warm-hearted and engaging character with endless time for people in need. During her last days she was invited to stay at Wester Elchies, Aberlour, where her two youngest boys were at school, so that she could be near them. Past pupils remember 'Lady Byatt's room' at the end of a passage. She is buried in the churchyard at Knockando.

On 7 November 2008 a memorial plaque was unveiled on the wall of the block of flats now occupying the site of the Endell Street Hospital. The address was given by Colonel Hilary Hodgson, Consultant Adviser in general practice to the army and the most senior woman in the army medical service. The assembled company were all descendants of those pioneering women of the First World War. Many were wearing ribbons of the colours of the suffragettes, violet (votes) fern (for) white (women). (MB)

# Helen Cattanach

*Helen S Cattanach, born Knockando, 21 June 1920; died Woking, Surrey,*
*4 May 1994.*

Helen Cattanach was matron-in-chief and the first director of Army Nursing Services in the Queen Alexandra Royal Army Nursing Corps (QARANC). To mark Remembrance Sunday 2011 the Royal British Legion honoured her by including her in their *90 Years of Heroes* tribute book.

The sixth child of Frank and Marjory Cattanach, Helen grew up near Tamdhu Distillery in Knockando; she enjoyed the rough and tumble of rural life both at home and at Knockando Primary School. She was a bright child and went off to Elgin Academy, twenty miles away, to complete her education. It was there that a maths teacher noticed her quiet compassion and dedication to hard work and suggested she took up nursing. In 1938, at the age of eighteen, she went to Woodend Hospital, Aberdeen, to start her training. Helen sat her State Registration Examinations in October 1941 and a month later she was issued with her registration number: 20162. With the Second World War under way she left the hospital to join the recently set up Civil Nursing Reserve who were employed registered nurses with the power to organise and control their own professional work. Many general hospitals had become militarised and there was an appeal in the *British Journal of Nursing* (June 1940) for trained nurses to step forward 'provided they were not already nursing in hospitals or engaged in public health work'. They were tempted with the offer of £90 a year plus board, lodging and laundry. Helen fitted the bill perfectly; she was newly trained and ready to do her bit. She nursed in various hospitals around Britain throughout the war.

As the war was drawing to a close, members of the Women's Army Nursing Service, QAIMNS, who had worked in all the trouble spots in gruelling conditions, were looking forward to demobilisation. Nurses were needed to fill the hiatus and, in June 1945, Helen applied to join up. Keen though the service was to recruit, it was concerned that only the right sort of girl should enlist. These tended to be middle-class, English young ladies. Helen would have been subjected to intensive interviews to ensure that she would 'fit in'. Apart from the required nursing qualifications of four years' training, a 'good' education was desirable and the ability to play tennis an asset. Helen's prowess on court is unknown. She passed the scrutiny and became a member of the elite force as a reserve. For many civilian nurses, military hospitals in peace-time had a more leisurely approach to nursing and an extremely rigid hierarchy which was difficult for some to take. They also had to learn new meth-

Helen Cattanach by Bassano
(National Portrait Gallery, London)

ods very quickly. Field nursing was very different and an essential part of their work. Helen quickly took to her new working conditions and, as peace-time saw more and more military nurses being demobbed, she applied to enlist as a regular nursing sister in the newly named QARANC. The training centre was at Anstie Grange near Dorking in Surrey where essential skills included marching and saluting as well as remembering to correctly address her superiors as 'ma'am'.

Within a few weeks Helen left for India on her first posting abroad. This was followed by tours of duty in Singapore, Java, Germany, Egypt and Germany. Post-war conditions were desperate in these countries and nursing included treatment for tropical diseases that she had not met before, for malnutrition in young and old, as well as for war wounds and what would now be called post-traumatic stress.

Twelve years later, in 1958, with a wealth of experience under her belt, Helen became a staff officer in the Army Medical Directorate at the War Office in London. She was thirty-eight years old. Three years later she was appointed the first QA officer in the Recruiting Branch, a post she relished. She was not finished with on-the-job nursing and foreign locations; however, and her next posting was to British Military Hospital Hong Kong – the hospital where Annabella Ralph had previously been placed. Based in the

Brigadier Helen Cattanach at Buckingham Palace 1976, after receiving the insignia of Companion of the Order of the Bath. She is accompanied by her sister Janet Petrie, and brother-in-law Bill Petrie
(*The Northern Scot*)

bustling metropolis of Kowloon, the hospital looked after the military personnel and their families and was a dream posting for many. Helen never forgot her roots and thriving Caledonian Societies were part of a lively social life.

On promotion to matron she spent a year at BMH Munster in Germany followed by three at the Cambridge Military Hospital. She was promoted to brigadier, the highest rank then available to women. She was appointed matron-in-chief and Director of Army Nursing Services in 1972. One of her most notable achievements was setting up the regimental headquarters and museum in Camberley, Surrey. Her legendary administrative skills enabled her to look after a full-time staff and develop recruiting and welfare strategies and new opportunities for nurses. She remained interested in the welfare of QAS for the rest of her life. Throughout her career her compassionate style, ready sense of humour and capacity for hard work had won her friends and awards. In 1963 she received the Royal Red Cross Medal. Ten years later she was appointed queen's honorary nursing sister (QHNS). She served in this capacity until 1977 when she was appointed colonel commandant QARANC until 1981 when she was sixty years old. Her involvement with many voluntary organisations led to her investment as an officer (sister) of the Most Venerable Order of the Hospital of St John of Jerusalem. She was promoted to commander in 1977.

She spent her retirement in Woking, Surrey, where she continued her charity work with the Not Forgotten Association and the Royal Scottish Corporation Charity. She was a long-time member of the Clan McPherson Association; her obituary in *Creag Dubh* in 1995 noted her many achievements, her sense of humour and concluded that: 'To the dismayed she was a daughter of consolation.'

Brigadier Cattanach's portrait, taken in 1976 by the noted Bassano Studio, hangs in the National Portrait Gallery, London.

Helen Cattanach's funeral took place in Knockando Kirk just across the brae from Crofts Farm; she lies at a spot in the graveyard from where there is a perfect view of her family home. (AO)

CHAPTER EIGHT

# Across the World

*Travellers are privileged to do the most improper things with perfect propriety*
Isabella Bird[1]

ON THE SECOND of June 1894, the *Banffshire Herald* carried a short article about a chemist's daughter from Keith. Mrs Paul Bert had just been awarded

> the insignia of the Order of the Sapeque d'or (gold sapeque) with silk cord, in commemoration of the services rendered to the Annamite Government by the Resident General, Paul Bert.[2]

Josephina Clayton (known as Finnie) was born in Keith in 1846. At the age of fifteen she went to Auxerre, near Paris, to perfect her French so that she could earn her living as governess for distinguished families. In Auxerre, she worked as a maid at a school for young ladies.[3] It was there that she met Paul Bert, eminent scientist, politician and educationist, whom she married at the age of nineteen. She acted as secretary to her husband. When he was appointed the first French governor general of Vietnam, in 1886, she and her grown up family accompanied him there and spent some time travelling about the country:

> In Tonkin [northern Vietnam] the whole family were so fearless that their friends were perpetually uneasy lest they should be waylaid and carried off by natives.[4]

On his death in Hanoi, in November of the same year, Josephina returned to France where she was appointed lady principal of the Female Colleges of the Legion of Honour at Écouen and Saint-Denis.[5] Her mother and sister also went to live in Auxerre.

Reading the newspaper articles of the time, it is difficult to separate Josephina's achievements from those of her husband. However, to venture abroad by herself, at the age of fifteen, required some spirit. Her many translations of her husband's researches are testament to her intellectual abilities. One of her translated books is still in print today.

Josephina Clayton chose Auxerre because a relative lived there. Women who travelled often had connections to lure them abroad. Eka Gordon Cumming, lacking a 'home' in Scotland, found relatives and introductions around the world; Elsie Watson had relations in Australia and in Southern Africa, but went solo on her adventure across South Africa, as did Anne Hardie in her exploration of Tibet and Central Africa. Margaret Hasluck and Sylvia Benton went to Athens as academics. Georgiana and Andrew McCrae emigrated to Australia, and, like the Hossacks and the Findlays from Knockando, they were part of the great Scots diaspora – people seeking new opportunities across the world. The women emigrants were equal partners in the pioneering stages of colonial expansion. Whatever their station in life they needed to be tough and fearless. There was land to improve; there were houses to build and new communities to be forged. The children they bore helped to swell the population of the growing towns and villages.

Whatever their reasons for travelling, all the women presented in this chapter had a spirit of adventure. Even Margaret Chrystie and her sister, the tourists who appeared to have travelled in style, were adventurers – few teachers, male or female, ventured abroad for their holidays at this time.

Although this chapter looks at the lives of just a few, many of the other women featured in this book travelled abroad at some point in their lives, sometimes finding adventures beyond imagination. And wherever they went they usually remembered their Moray roots and many returned regularly to refresh the spirit.

# Georgiana McCrae

*Georgiana Huntly Gordon, born London, 15 March 1804; married Andrew Muirison McCrae, 25 September 1830; died 24 May 1890.*

Georgiana Huntly Gordon, artist and diarist, made an important contribution to the culture of the early colony of Melbourne, Australia.

Georgiana's mother, Jane Graham, was one of seven children of a minor Northumbrian landowner and it is probable that she was an actress. Georgiana's father, George, Marquis of Huntly, son of Jane Maxwell, was a descendant of James 1 of Scotland and heir to the dukedom of Gordon. He was the first colonel of the Gordon Highlanders, the renowned 'Cock o' the North' and romanticised as 'the Highland Laddie', in the song 'Oh

Self-portrait by Georgiana Huntly Gordon aged twenty (The State Library of Victoria, Australia)

where tell me where has my Highland Laddie gone?'

Georgiana was born in London and, despite her illegitimacy, her father acknowledged her as his daughter and she was baptised a Gordon in St James's Church, Piccadilly. Georgiana grew up with her mother in Somers Town, a lively neighbourhood which thirty years previously had given sanctuary to French émigrés, aristocrats, radicals, writers and artists. With financial support from her father, Georgiana began her education at the hands of émigré French Catholic nuns and also protestant liberals. Concerns about Catholic revolutionary influences resulted in her moving schools to Fulham and at New Road Boarding School she became fluent in French as well as studying Hebrew and Latin. However, she eventually received education at home with a series of tutors and her true potential soon became evident.

In 1813 her father, now aged forty-three, married the very wealthy nineteen-year-old heiress Elizabeth Brodie, a devout woman who did not manage to bear a Gordon heir. Georgiana continued her studies of art and music and learnt to play the piano. When she was eleven she received lessons in watercolour painting from John Varley, the landscape painter and astrology teacher, and at the age of twelve she had a landscape accepted by the Royal Academy. Having proved her ability, she was then tutored by Dominic Serres, and John Glover. Charles Hayter taught her the skills of miniature painting and she studied at the Royal Academy.

An accident with a bolting horse resulted in Georgiana's mother falling out of a pony chaise, fracturing her skull and becoming severely disabled. Georgiana had visited Gordon Castle each summer and, by the time she was sixteen was invited by her grandfather to make it her home as her mother was no longer able to care for her. In 1821 when she was seventeen, her portrait of her grandfather the fourth Duke of Gordon won Georgiana a silver medal from the Society for Promotion of Arts. The following year she won the silver palette award for the most promising young portrait painter in Britain and between 1828 and 1829 she painted fifty portraits, fifteen at Gordon Castle, thirty-five in Edinburgh. Her grandfather, Duke Alexander, a patron and friend of Robert Burns, had retired from the intense social whirl favoured by his first wife and eventually married a Fochabers lass, Jean Christie, who died in 1824.

With her lively company, her beautiful singing voice, competent piano playing, linguistic skills and intelligence, Georgiana was overqualified to become a governess or to teach polite young ladies the art of painting, but she was fortunate in becoming her grandfather's favoured companion until his death in 1827.

With Duke Alexander's death Georgiana's father, George, became the fifth Duke of Gordon and his duchess, the young Elizabeth, took charge of Gordon Castle and family business. Georgiana attracted several suitors but she fell deeply in love with a distant Gordon relative, a Roman Catholic, but this romance was frustrated by the bigoted duchess.

Georgiana was encouraged by friends of her father to make her living painting portraits. She went to live in Edinburgh where she specialised in painting fashionable miniatures of women and children, earning herself £250 for the thirty-five painted in 1829–30. With hopes of marrying her Catholic laird blighted, Georgiana was persuaded by the duchess to marry a distant kinsman, impecunious Edinburgh lawyer Andrew Muirison McCrae. Andrew's father, an abolitionist, had been disinherited by his slave-owning father. Andrew and Georgiana married at Gordon Castle in 1830.

Years later she recorded the event – 'left my easel and changed my name'. As was the custom in those times, her money and her talents were subordinated to the wishes of her husband. The couple moved to Westminster in London and she was soon absorbed in motherhood, suffering the sorrow of losing her first child, aged two, in 1834. Her mother died around this time and within the next few years Georgiana had four sons and, understandably, she had less time to paint.

In 1836 her father, the last Duke of Gordon, died in London of stomach cancer. His will was in the process of being drawn up in Edinburgh and was unsigned. His widow, the Duchess Elizabeth, had no children of her own and remained preoccupied with evangelical causes and showed little interest in illegitimate Gordon offspring.

Georgiana's husband, a Writer to the Signet and a parliamentary lobbyist, was not very successful in business ventures and by 1838 he had decided to seek his fortune on the other side of the world. By then Georgiana had given birth to her fourth child and post natal complications prevented her sailing to the new colony with her husband. While remaining in London, Georgiana resumed her portrait painting. Eventually, in 1840, with some financial help from the Duchess Elizabeth, Georgiana and the boys set sail for Australia. She took a large amount of luggage and 'a box of Elgin oatmeal', intending to join her husband and begin a new life on the other side of the world. She was never to return to her homeland or see Gordon Castle again.

In March 1841 Georgiana and her four sons squelched ashore at Port Phillip in the Australian autumnal rains after almost five months at sea. There were no paved roads in the barely established squatter settlement. Andrew began practising law in Melbourne and soon Georgiana had made many new friends. Her social circle included Governor Charles La Trobe who introduced her to the native flora and fauna and to new like-minded friends.

The McCraes' first daughter was born in 1841 and the family moved to a larger house. Three more daughters completed the family. Andrew McCrae was not one of those to make a fortune in the new colony and his ventures into land speculation were unsuccessful. When the Bank of Australia failed in 1843, many immigrants were ruined and Andrew was in debt. He remained proud and optimistic and, despite his wife's reputation and talent as the most skilled portraitist in Melbourne, he expressly forbade her from receiving paid commissions for her work. Instead, he gave up his law practice and purchased a squatter's run of 12,000 acres on Mornington Peninsula. Georgiana had accompanied her husband on horseback to inspect the property in 1844 when she was four months pregnant. She wrote in her journal:

> He says he can't afford to pay for a conveyance, so I and mine must take our chance... [we arrived] wearied to death by an uneasy saddle and the chafing of a too long stirrup-leather.

Georgiana designed their new house and, after months of building, the

The restored McCrae homestead built at Arthur's Seat 1844, one of the earliest pioneering homesteads on the Mornington Peninsula. Rear of the homestead showing detached kitchen and bread oven (postcard: National Trust of Australia)

family moved from Melbourne in 1845 into their new home, named Arthur's Seat. The Mornington Peninsula area is now a popular Sunday afternoon run for Melbourne city folk, but at that time it was wild and difficult to access. The house which Georgiana designed still stands. It is built of massive gum tree slabs, and is now the property of the Australian National Trust. Inside the front door are two watercolours – one of the damaged Spey Bridge at Fochabers after the great 1829 floods, and the other of Gordon Castle at that time. The house still contains original family furniture, some of which came from Gordon Castle.

Georgiana's 'sanctum' at Arthur's Seat (postcard: National Trust of Australia)

Georgiana proved herself useful at droving cattle and horses and was renowned as a 'medicine woman' amongst the native Bunurong tribe. At a time when some tribes were experiencing severe persecution from colonialists she had no qualms about her children growing up amongst the aborigines. She drew portraits of some of the tribe and they would squat on the veranda listening to her play lively Scottish airs which 'delighted them exceedingly'. Later one of her sons, George, was to write the first Australian poems of any importance which dealt with the aborigine life.

From 1845 Georgiana reared her children, wrote her journal, sketched, painted and sang old Jacobite songs to her children in her beautiful mezzo-soprano voice. The Arthur's Seat venture proved short and unsuccessful, and the family returned to Melbourne in 1851.

This was the advent of gold rush, and Andrew obtained various positions as police magistrate in different areas, eventually working for seven years as warden of the goldfields, deputy sheriff and commissioner of Crown lands. Georgiana did not join him but remained in Melbourne. The marriage was by then virtually over and the McCraes were living separate lives. The gold rush attracted an influx of emigrants and visitors, and Georgiana was socialising with many influential artists and poets at this time, but in 1854 her youngest child, three-year-old Agnes, died of complications following a bout of measles – twenty-two years after Georgiana's first daughter had died in London.

Georgiana never regained her former creativity after this tragedy, however, she did exhibit with the Victorian Society of Fine Arts in 1857. She was partly disabled by a hip injury in 1859 and remained estranged from Andrew until his retirement in 1866.

In 1864 the Duchess of Gordon died, and Georgiana discovered that, despite her late father's wishes, her promised legacy was not to materialise.

However, she was enjoying a wider social life than before, free to travel and paint, as well as writing her journals and continuing to correspond with friends in Scotland. In 1867, after thirty-seven years of marriage, Andrew McCrae returned alone to England where he stayed for seven years. He returned, a sick man, in 1874, to be nursed devotedly by Georgiana and her daughters before his death a few months later. Georgiana was now seventy and becoming increasingly dependent upon her family. She continued to travel, paint and write but by 1886 she was living with her daughter. She saw the centenary of white settlement in Australia in 1888 before her death in 1890.

Her influence lived on as several of her children published poetry, or became artists, musicians and writers of short stories. The girl who had known the splendour of a great castle was not daunted by a change in her fortunes but did the best she could in the circumstances. In a strange new world Georgiana ensured her nine children had a good standard of education while she learnt as much as she could about her new homeland. She earned the respect of the local aborigines through her empathy and kindness and encouraged her children to respect their culture at a time when many tribes were despised and persecuted by colonialists. An obituary by historian Henry Giles Turner concludes:

> It was largely due to the influence of such women as Mrs McCrae that ideas of refinement and principles of taste were kept alive during the 'dark ages' of our colonial history. She was an admirable specimen of one who fulfilled her mission in life, and who in the fullness of time passed away, leaving the fragrant memory of many life-long friendships, and in her children and grandchildren a material contribution towards the building up of a thoughtful and cultured community.

The influence of her strong personality extended well beyond her family and, while she remains relatively unknown in her homeland, the duke's daughter left a legacy of her journals and art and made a remarkable contribution to the development of cultural life in Australia. (JM)

# Penuel Hossack

*Penuel Findlay, born Knockando, 2 April 1821; married James Hossack, Knockando, 1850; died Orbost, Australia, January 1921.*

# Helen Findlay

*Helen Symon, born December 1829, married John Findlay, Elchies, 7 July 1853; died Australia, 23 November 1879.*

Penuel Hossack was an Australian pioneer who despite hardship and setbacks flourished there. Helen Findlay, her sister-in-law, followed a few years later; though with a similar work ethic and circumstances she and her family struggled for survival.

Penuel's parents, James and Janet, were tenant farmers at Heathfield on the Wester Elchies estate. She grew up there with her eight siblings, attending the kirk at Knockando and the Girls' School in Archiestown. Her life centred round her family and neighbours. There were regular social events. They were a musical family; church music as well as concerts and ceilidhs were part of the fabric of their lives. There was not enough of a living on the farm for all of them, so her brother James took over the farm while siblings Alexander, George and John moved to the nearby cottage, Woodside, as storekeepers and shoemakers.

Penuel married James Hossack, son of another local tenant farmer in 1850. The marriage took place at Woodside, where she remained after the wedding as housekeeper to her brother John. James got work where he could. He was an agricultural labourer at Bogfearn, Elgin in 1850 and Blackhills, Elgin, in 1851. Penuel gave birth to a stillborn baby during this time.

Penuel Hossack

The *Elgin Courier* headline on April 12 1852, 'Gold in Australia', must have excited James and Penuel and been the subject of much discussions with friends and family. There were many leaflets and pamphlets around which gave advice on emigration:

Young unmarried women, unacquainted with any kind of farm or agricultural occupation would be of little use to the new colony... should an intending emigrant be married, so much the better, providing the wife be frugal and industrious.

Penuel and James were perfect candidates. Only a few months later their brother John took them to Lossiemouth and waved them off on the first part of their journey. John started a journal on that day:

> This 20th day of August 1852 commence a Journal of every day's proceedings having parted with a number of my dearest relatives at the harbour of Lossiemouth at 12 o'clock noon, per Duke of Richmond Steamer so far on their way to Melbourne, Victoria, Australia.

Penuel and James did not go alone; her brothers Alexander and George were with them along with George's wife, Penuel Grant, their young son Patrick and her sister Ann, as well as George and James Stewart from a nearby farm. It would be many months before relatives at home heard of their safe arrival on Christmas Day. On 4 April 1853 John recorded: 'received intelligence that all the Emigrants are safely landed'. John regularly sent copies of his journal to the pioneers to keep his far-flung family up to date with events at home.

From Lossiemouth, Penuel and her husband went to Liverpool, which they left on 1 September aboard the *Ann Thompson*. Tickets cost £16 14s 9d. There were 235 passengers including a schoolmaster and matron for the eighty children travelling with their parents. Five more were born on the voyage. Penuel's brother George and his wife Penuel Grant lost a son born prematurely just days before they docked at Geelong; poor water supply was suspected. Twelve children died on the voyage. The captain's official report of the voyage noted the ship to be 'well adapted for migrants. Arrangements greatly satisfactory. Immigrants expressed themselves in general well satisfied with treatment received.'

Helen Findlay

They landed at Geelong on Christmas day. James Hossack immediately set about finding work on a farm and was quickly taken on by J Battey at Cowie's Creek. Fortunately there was a house for the family and £60 a year. Penuel was relieved to have space to do the laundry after a 115 day trip as there were no facilities on board. James and his brother-in-law soon started a carting business, with a cart and four bullocks; they had plenty of work and eventually delivered to the gold diggings in Ballarat. James was also commissioned to transport troops after the Eureka gold riots in 1854. Miners had to buy a licence whether or not they found gold. Government officials were over-zealous about checking the licences and the miners' anger boiled over; troops were sent in to quell the riots.

Though they were making money, Penuel and James no longer had a house; like most of the pioneers they set up home in a tent, waiting until they had enough money to lease land. Their daughter, another Penuel, was born in the tent in 1856. This was also the year when they became landowners in Learmonth.

James and Penuel were founder members of the Presbyterian Church at Learmonth; James was on the committee to consider building a church, manse and schoolhouse in connection with the Free Church of Scotland in 1857. When the church was built James was an elder; Penuel was an active member for eighty-five years.

John Findlay and his wife Helen Symon had been left behind at the family home, Woodside, to run the store and care for their ailing parents. By 1856 they were encouraged to make the long journey to join their family, who it appeared, were doing well in their new world. Helen's sister Jane had travelled alone to Australia in 1854. Her ship *The Covenanter* had had to return to Birkenhead owing to a cholera outbreak on board. She eventually arrived safely. John and Helen took their two young children, John's sister Isabella and his sixty-seven-year-old mother with them. Unlike the previous pioneers who travelled by ship from Lossiemouth to Birkenhead, they set off on the new train service from Huntly to Aberdeen and then to Edinburgh and Glasgow. They then joined the ship *Vanguard* for Liverpool, enduring a fierce storm on the way. Eventually they paid £10 for their passages to Australia on the *Shooting Star*. Their luggage was lost for a time when they first joined the ship. John Findlay noted in his journal that his wife Helen and his mother were both very unwell at the beginning of their voyage, the children were particularly ill; this continued with little respite throughout the voyage. After a journey of 104 days they arrived at Geelong on 28 February 1857 and were met by John's sister Ann. They stayed in lodgings for a fortnight, allowing the womenfolk to do four months worth of laundry while John explored Geelong.

They were then transported by bullock dray to the Hossack farm at Burrumbeet where it took several days to erect and sort out a tent for the family near the Hossack family tent. John also made some furniture. He worked for the Hossacks on the farm for several years, carting items to the diggings and working the land. In May he helped dig the footings for Penuel's first house in Australia. She named it Heathfield after her childhood home. Helen was attending to the children and her mother-in-law and helping with the farm. On 24 November, just nine months after their arrival she was, according to her husband's journal, 'very unwell' and went to bed in the tent; a week later she produced a daughter, Esther Anderson Findlay, named after their neighbour, Mrs Anderson, who acted as midwife. The growing family remained at this farm for sixteen years. Helen went on to produce nine more children – twelve in all.

Like all the women in the family Helen was active on the farm and in the community. They all carted butter, eggs and other produce from door to door. In 1873 the Farmers Wives and Daughters Petition for a regular market to be held in Ballarat was signed by Helen and two of her daughters, as well by as her mother-in-law and 'Penuel Findlay'.

Helen and John built their home on leased land in 1858. A few years later John bought land on the outer edges of the settlement. Their first child, Jessie, was nineteen years old; she bought a neighbouring allotment, as did her brother John. The settlement, West Charlton, was remote and the work hard; they paid a heavy toll when the rabbit plagues and droughts decimated their crops. Jessie and her father wrote letters to the Crown officials when they could not make their payments. Helen meanwhile was still producing babies, including twins in 1863. The final two were Grace, who lived only a year, in 1873, and Alexander, in 1875.

Helen died of pneumonia in 1879 at the age of forty-nine; she left eleven children, three under the age of ten. The following year husband John was killed in an accident with a young horse. The family sold the land and went their separate ways.

Penuel Hossack and her family moved to Orbost in 1884 where they became substantial landowners. James died in 1894 at the age of sixty-eight. Penuel remained active in her community for many years; she moved in to her daughter's home where she died in January 1921, just a few weeks short of her 100th birthday.

Penuel Hossack was the first of the Findlay family to embark on the long journey across the world to make a better life. She and her husband James succeeded in their aims. They had three children, worked hard, invested wisely and supported their new community. They were able to weather the setbacks which devastated Helen Findlay and her family.

Helen's life was different. She and John worked hard too; they moved to a remote farm where they struggled financially. Helen was pregnant or feeding a baby almost continuously for twenty years. She died at the age of forty-nine, less than half the age that Penuel reached. (AO)

# Eka Gordon Cumming

*Constance Frederica Gordon Cumming, born Altyre, Forres, 26 May 1837; died College House, Crieff, 4 September 1924.*

From 1868–1880 Eka Gordon Cumming travelled the world. She published many accounts of these travels, as books and magazine articles, illustrated from the vast quantity of her very competent watercolours. In China she met, and was influenced by, William Hill Murray, founder of the Beijing School for the Blind.

Eka was the fourteenth child to survive infancy born to Sir William Gordon Cumming of Altyre and Gordonstoun and his first wife Eliza Maria Campbell of Islay and Shawfield.

When only six hours old, Eka was sent from Altyre to stay with her father's unmarried sisters at Moy to escape the scarlet fever from which her brother Walter Frederick and sister Constance had died. She was named for them but as her mother could not bear to address her as Constance, she was known in the family as Eka. Before she was five, her mother was dead.

Eka then went to live with her eldest sister, Anne (Seymour), at Cresswell Hall and later Harehope, in Northumberland. Seymour had asked for her 'as a bit of young life in the great house'. In 1847 Sir William remarried, to Jane Mackintosh of Geddes near Nairn. There were three half siblings from this marriage.

School from the age of ten to fifteen was a Fulham boarding school, but there were glorious summer holidays with the family in Moray. She travelled from London on the *North Star* which put in at Burghead where passengers and cargo were fetched ashore by fishers' boats.

For Eka's generation of Gordon Cummings, the main house was Altyre near Forres. Gordonstoun, near Duffus and semi-derelict at this time, was used in the summer months as a base for access to the beach a mile and a half distant. A recurrent theme in Eka's accounts of her life is bathing, starting with the sandy beach at Covesea when the family was at Gordonstoun and the peaty Findhorn when at Altyre.

Between leaving school in 1853 at the age of sixteen and 1868, Eka's life revolved around visits to her large extended family and their friends in England and Scotland, often in their titled houses, nursing members of her close family, many of whom died young, and attending balls such as that for the Inverness Northern Meetings. She survived rheumatic fever with no after effects. Northumberland was her base until Seymour died in 1858. Thereafter, sister Nelly's place was home, first in Aberlour, then in Comrie, and finally in Crieff.

In 1868, Eka spent a summer
on the west coast of Scotland,
starting with an Easter holiday
with her half-brother Fred, on the
Mull of Kintyre and a yachting trip
round Skye in the *Gannet*. She
swam, and sketched and then
stayed on alone in Skye until
October. She later wrote:

> From Sligachan [Inn] I made fully
> half-a-dozen expeditions to
> sketch dark Loch Coruisk and its
> green sea-loch Scavaig... each
> expedition involving fully twelve
> hours of hard toil, always
> accompanied by Alfred Hunt, the
> artist – most delicate interpreter
> of mountains and mists, and a
> thoroughly congenial spirit.

Miss CF Gordon Cumming in 1887
(photograph by W Crooke)

By November of 1868, Eka was en route to India to visit Emilia (Emmy)
Sergison, a half-sister, who had gone to India with her husband. Eka was
asked to join them before they retired to Britain. Thus began Eka's 'twelve
years of enchanting travel', with its mix of serendipity, letters of introduction
and welcome by an international network of family and friends. Eka sailed
on the *Pera*, via the Mediterranean to Alexandria, across the desert by
train to Suez and on to Calcutta on the *Candia*. For the rest of 1869 she
travelled in India with her sister, or with friends, to Delhi and the Himalayan
foothills. They took the new train to Bombay and sailed home on HMS
*Simoon*, which was doing duty as a troop ship and captained by a naval
friend. Eka stopped off for a month in Malta, returning to England with
'well-filled portfolios'.

The Episcopal minister of Forres, near Altyre, was appointed Bishop
of Colombo; in 1872, he and his wife invited Miss Gordon Cumming to
join them in Ceylon (now Sri Lanka). The *Hindoo* left from Tilbury, but
in a Channel storm, lay off the Eddystone Light, firing distress rockets.
Eka 'never spent a more interesting night' than that allowed her by the
captain in the corner of the wheel-house. She finally arrived in Ceylon in
the *Othello*. In *Two Happy Years in Ceylon* (1892) Eka wrote of 'one
prolonged delight' – the journeys she made with the bishop and his

daughter, and the 'long days of solitary sketching'.

In 1875 Eka became part of an improbable event in the South Seas: the donation of the Fijian Isles by the chiefs to Queen Victoria. Rachel, Lady Gordon, the wife of the recently appointed first governor, Sir Arthur Hamilton Gordon, invited Miss Gordon Cumming to accompany her to Fiji, then still known as cannibal islands. The new government party crossed to Boulogne, then went by train to Marseilles, through the Red Sea (Eka wearing her preferred navy serge dress and pilot-cloth jacket), via Ceylon and old friends, and Malaysia, to Sydney. Her host there took the gentlemen of the party on to Fiji, leaving Lady Gordon, Miss Gordon Cumming and the children to await preparation of a suitable home. Within three months, the boat's commodore was dead from wounds from the poisoned arrows of Santa Cruz islanders.

On passage to Fiji, Eka made great friends with Rev. Fred Langham, the superintendent of the Wesleyan mission. Much of her voyaging in the Fijian Archipelago was with Langham and his wife in the mission-ship as they visited the scattered native clergy.

Baron Anatole von Hügel, later the first curator of the Cambridge University Museum of Archaeology and Anthropology, also arrived in Fiji in 1875. Many of Eka's drawings of pots and other native artefacts contribute to the outstanding Fijian collection in Cambridge. Von Hügel was twenty-one when he recorded in his journal his first impressions of Miss Gordon Cumming, then aged thirty-eight:

> She certainly is a character – very tall lanky, and pronounced ugly, though clever features; of exorbitant dress, a large anchor-bespangled yachting costume of bathing dress cut, looped up with jet chains, which also clasp her throat and bind her bosom. Her hair, rough and scratched off her forehead, is covered on the back by a 'perky' velvet hat.

Von Hügel at first thought Miss Gordon Cumming bumptious and he disagreed with her view of the missionaries, but he softened towards her and later found her 'capital company' and 'a dear soul'. Eka's two years in Fiji were later recorded in *At Home in Fiji* (1881), as letters home.

When she was in Fiji Eka's first book was published – *From the Hebrides to the Himalayas* (1876). Because Eka was travelling, the book was proof read by Isabella Bird, another traveller. The Scottish section was republished in 1883 as *In the Hebrides* 'omitting all dryer matter'. Despite this declared editing, as in all her traveller's tales, the basic and intrinsically engaging account is obfuscated by lengthy comparisons of religious iconography, practice and belief.

Elizabeth Fitzgibbon, painting by John Aubrey (Elizabeth Fitzgibbon)

Hopeman Harbour, looking west, by Sophia Dunbar c.1850 (A Dunbar)

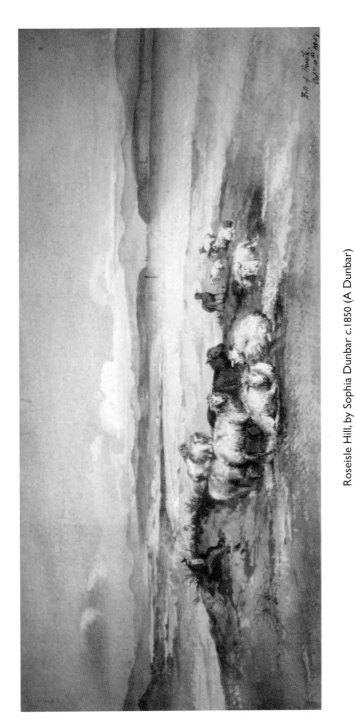

Roseisle Hill, by Sophia Dunbar c.1850 (A Dunbar)

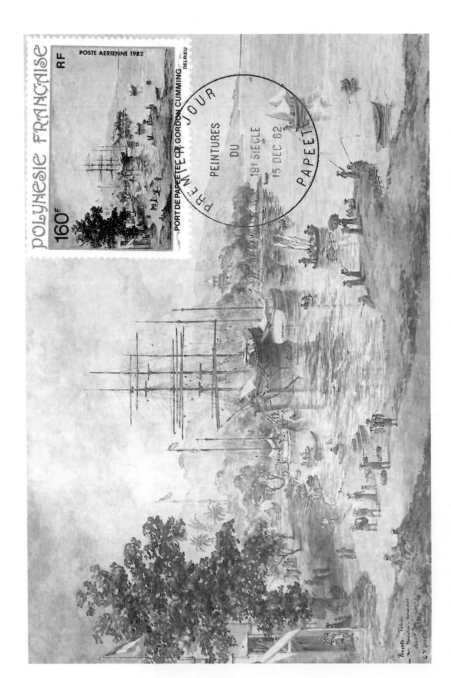

First day cover, 15 December 1982, 160F stamp on postcard, Port de Papeete, Tahiti, by CF Gordon Cumming

Interior of the Watts Memorial Chapel, Compton, by Mary Seton Watts (Susan Bennett)

The river at Lossiemouth 1906, by Emma Black (Jennifer Shaw)

Loch Ben Tigh, Eigg, by Dorothy Brown (Elgin Museum)

Alexander, fourth Duke of Gordon,
by Georgiana Gordon
(The State Library of Victoria,
Australia)

Page from Isabella Gordon's
Millport notebook (© The Natural
History Museum, London)

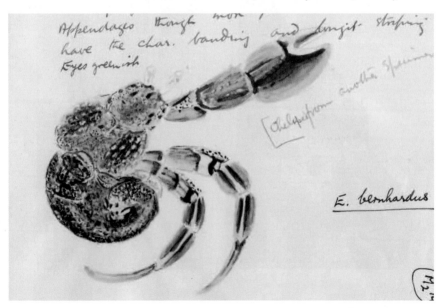

'A Chief's Kitchen' from *At Home in Fiji* (1881) by CF Gordon Cumming

In 1877 a French man-of war, *Le Seignelay*, came in to Fiji to take the Roman Catholic bishop of Samoa on a tour of his mission. The captain invited Miss Gordon Cumming to join them to Tonga, Samoa and Tahiti. In Tonga she stayed in a convent and visited various kings, queens and chiefs of the Friendly Isles, but Samoa was in the grip of civil war and so she continued with the mission to Tahiti. An unexpected meeting in Tahiti was with a high chiefess, Princess Titaua, the 'delightful *demi-blanche*' widow of a Brander of Pitgaveny, near Elgin. This South Seas trip was detailed in *A Lady's Cruise in a French Man-of-War* (1882).

At Easter 1878 Eka sailed through the Golden Gate into San Francisco Bay in the brigantine *Paloma*, six weeks out from Tahiti. For her six months in California she lived most of the time in the Yosemite Valley which she described in *Granite Crags* (1884). Her next stop was Japan, and from Nagasaki she passed on to China, where she spent six months, arriving on Christmas Eve in Hong Kong 'to witness an appalling but magnificent fire'.

It was in Peking that Eka met William Hill Murray, a one-armed colporteur of the National Bible Society. Eka accompanied Murray on his attempts to sell religious books to the retainers of Tartar nobles near the Imperial Palace. When she returned to Scotland she renewed this connection with Murray and spent much energy on raising money for his blind mission. She wrote:

The Inventor of the Numeral Type for China… I understood why I had
been constrained to end my twelve years of pleasant aimless travelling
by making the journey to Peking so entirely against my own inclination.

Murray had developed a system that reduced the complex Mandarin
language to numbers that could be more easily read by the blind (in Braille)
and the illiterate. The mission, founded by him in 1874, became what is
now the Beijing School for the Blind. Eka's travels in China eventually
resulted in *Wanderings in China* (1886).

Another near shipwreck in a calm off the Goto Isles, and she was back
in Japan for a further three months. Her excursions and experiences in
Japan sound tamer than in other countries, apart from an ascent of
Fujiyama. While staying with Sir Harry Parkes at the legation in Tokyo,
she met General Ulysses Grant. Miss Gordon Cumming and party had
excellent seats in the grandstand when The mikado made a rare public
appearance at a festival to show the general something of old Japanese
feats of arms.

The Grants, 'the American Wellington and his wife', invited her to
return to San Francisco from whence she spent two months in the Hawaiian
Islands, painting the volcanoes described in her *Fire Fountains of Hawaii*
(1883). She then made her way across America, spending time with her
nephew, Alastair, in Maryland, meeting Oliver Wendell Holmes and
Longfellow, and visiting a 'medium' in Boston.

She returned to Britain in the *Montana* from New York in 1880. One
last shipwreck awaited her when the ship ran aground in thick fog on the
cliffs of Holyhead Island, off Anglesey. The women and children were
rowed ashore in a leaky tender, but Eka was allowed to stay with her
'precious portfolios' and that afternoon she and they were transferred to a
tug and taken to Liverpool. Once settled back in Crieff, in College House,
she began writing for publication; this brought much needed income, for
her own support and that of her charities, and an alternative to exasperating
her relations. She was in her early forties; with her travelling more or less
over, the second half of her life was devoted to writing, including her
autobiography, *Memories* (1904).

Eka's written works suggest prodigious amounts of research on a wide
range of topics, including and beyond those immediately related to
wherever she was travelling. She wrote extensively about the history of
Moray. Magazine articles and appendices to her books cover, for example,
leper hospitals in Britain, the beneficial effects of pouring oil on rough seas,
the Crofters' Commission of 1883 and the dangers of 'the daily dose of
alcohol'. Her hundreds of watercolours, mainly landscapes, and drawings

are scattered about the world, in museums in Tahiti, Fiji, Honolulu, California, Forres, Elgin, Cambridge and in her family's homes. Some of her Fijian pots are in museums in Cambridge, Edinburgh and Elgin. She regretted she did not have the funds for a permanent place of display, like her friend Miss Marianne North, but arranged many temporary exhibitions usually for charity. Of local interest is the display of 200 of her paintings in the Town Hall, Lossiemouth, in 1895, in 'the furtherance of the movement to establish a sick nurse for the poor of Lossiemouth', opened by Sir William Gordon Cumming, Elma Napier's father. Miss Gordon Cumming gave an interesting address 'in a racy and instructive manner'.

She was awarded a Civil List pension in 1888 of £50 a year in consideration of her many services to literature. Newspaper reviews were generally favourable; she is mentioned in several nineteenth century reviews of contemporary achievers and had an obituary in *The Times*. The Royal Geographical Society made her a life fellow in 1914, but in their obituary it was made clear that while they could not ignore her passing, her fame came from her being a 'lady-traveller' when they were far less common in outlying parts of the world.

In recent years there has been a great interest in women travellers. Eka and her friend Miss Marianne North and acquaintance Miss Isabella Bird (later Mrs Bishop) are usually referred to, and Eka in 2010 featured in the

Constance Frederica Gordon Cumming by
Herbert Rose Barraud, 1893
(National Portrait Gallery, London)

Museum of Scotland exhibition *Treasure*. The *DNB* is particularly scathing of the writing of 'Gordon-Cumming', describing it as turgid, which it is compared with modern travel writing. *The Biographical Dictionary of Scottish Women* (2006) and *The Scotswoman at Home and Abroad* (1999) are more generous. A reviewer of *Off the Beaten Track: Three Centuries of Women Travellers* at the National Portrait Gallery, London, in 2004, comments on the way in which Victorian women travellers sat for their portraits, perhaps wishing to present themselves as women of moral substance lest their exploits expose them to charges of moral looseness. He contrasts 'Contance Gordon Cumming' in her portrait by Herbert Barraud (1893) with the woman who bathed naked in the sea in Fiji.

It is said in the family that Eka never married because two brothers loved her and tossed up as to which would propose, the loser to disappear – and he was the one she loved. Strong and capable, she believed firmly in the family and felt the loss of her siblings very deeply. Eka was ill for two years before her death at the age of eighty-seven. She is buried, not at the Michael Kirk, Gordonstoun, but with her sister Nelly and brother-in-law George Grant at Ochtertyre, Crieff. (JT)

# Margaret Chrystie

*Margaret Chrystie, born 7 September 1860; died, St Helen's, Fochabers,*
*25 February 1941.*

# Jean Chrystie

*Jean Chrystie, born 7 September 1874; died, St Helen's, Fochabers,*
*25 February 1957.*

Both Margaret and Jean Chrystie taught in Fochabers for over forty years. During the school holidays they travelled the world.

Maggie Chrystie was the second of six children of Gordon Campbell Chrystie and Margaret Asher. The family lived at St Helen's, a house on Fochabers High Street. Gordon Chrystie was inspector of the poor for Bellie. The family attended the Free Church of Scotland in the village.

The children were educated at Milne's Institution and though three died young, Margaret, her brother Alex and her youngest sibling Jeanie, all became teachers. By the age of fifteen Maggie was a pupil-teacher at Milne's. At nineteen in 1879 she is recorded as being a member of Class VI at the Aberdeen Church of Scotland Training College. She spent part of her probation as assistant at the Aberdeen Practising School. Her long teaching career at Milne's began in November 1881; she received her teaching certificate in 1883.

Though Maggie remained at Milne's she continued to add to her qualifications and broadened her knowledge throughout her life. The rector records in 1887 that teaching of sewing was particularly successful at the school and he had sent Miss Chrystie on a ten-session sewing department course at Keith in order to secure a grant. She was successful in her endeavours and the school obtained various items of equipment to enable them to carry out the requirements of the sewing schedule. In 1900 her sister Jean-

Margaret Chrystie c.1912
(*The Northern Scot*)

ie joined the school as infant teacher and to assist with needlework.

A few years later Maggie received £5 towards the cost of a geography course in Oxford. By 1906 she was transferred to the higher grade department. Her sister Jeanie took a course to qualify as a domestic science teacher. Maggie was teaching drawing, history, geography and English to the second year class.

The Royal Scottish Geographical Society awarded Miss M Chrystie, Milne's Institution, a diploma of fellowship of the society. As the main aim of the society was to advance the study of geography in Scotland, it may be assumed that Maggie saw her travels as educational for the benefit of her pupils. The Misses Chrystie were well remembered for their holiday adventures. On the last day of the summer term pupils would gather outside St Helen's to see their teachers emerge dressed in holiday, sometimes tropical, gear with luggage piled high to await the taxi to the station.

The sisters travelled throughout Britain buying postcards and photographs to stick in their albums. They also embarked on many cruises. One album is embossed with: 'the compliments of the Chairman and Managing Director of P&O SN Co.' and included a photograph of P&O Turbo Lines *Viceroy of India*. On this occasion their visits included Hamburg and Gdansk. Among the places they visited in 1927 were Bali, Malaya, India, Africa, Jamaica, Australia, Hawaii and Java. A farewell dinner menu in August 1928 on the SS *Lancashire* was signed by the captain and others on his table including their neighbour Rosamond Gordon Lennox.

Margaret Chrystie was secretary of the Milne's Institution Former Pupils Reunion Committee and in 1912 she wrote to the governors suggesting that a former pupils' club be formed with the intention of raising funds for the institution. A year later, as secretary, she presented the governors with a Union Jack and flagstaff in recognition of the inauguration of the club. She was secretary for many years; and later shared the post with her sister Jeanie. The club was suspended for the duration of the First World War. In December 1918 Margaret wrote to members asking them to

Maggie and Jeanie on a London bus in the 1920s

work towards providing a memorial to those former pupils who had fallen. The war memorial, placed near the main door to Milne's was unveiled on 27 August 1921.

Margaret Chrystie was a 'teacher of distinction', according to the memorial on her tombstone, for forty-five years. Records show that she was dedicated to the school and its pupils; she also recognised her worth; there are frequent instances of requests for salary increases, often successful, sometimes not. By March 1919 she was earning £142 10s; her sister as assistant teacher earned £120, which included £10 for teaching cookery.

Margaret Chrystie retired in 1920 and Jeanie, who notched up forty years as a teacher, in 1934.

Though they remained in Fochabers at Milne's and lived all their lives at St Helen's, the albums of postcards and photographs from around the world are testament to their adventurous spirit. The Chrystie sisters are still remembered in Fochabers for their teaching skills and their travels. (AO)

# Elsie Watson

*Elsie Watson, born Elgin, 1 April 1870; died Cheltenham, 17 January 1945.*

Working variously as a journalist, teacher and writer, Elsie Watson travelled a great deal, notably to Australia. In 1912 she embarked on an epic motor cycle trip through South Africa.

Elsie's parents were Elspeth (Elsie) Wink and James Watson. There were at least ten siblings. When Elsie was four, three of her sisters (aged two, seven and ten) died within ten days of each other, possibly of diphtheria or one of the other infectious diseases prevalent at the time. James Watson ran a successful business as a bookseller and stationer, using the same premises for over fifty years under the Assembly Rooms in Elgin (at the eastern corner of the High Street and North Street). Thomas Russell became his partner for a few years, and they started a printing business in addition to bookselling. Together they published a guide entitled *Morayshire Described* in 1868, James being one of the authors. After Thomas Russell's death, James Watson founded the *Moray Weekly News*, a single-sheet paper, a forerunner of *The Northern Scot*.

Elsie was enrolled at Elgin Academy. Education was highly valued and encouraged – for the daughters as well as the sons of the family. When she left the Academy at the age of seventeen Elsie was awarded the Allan Rewards in English and mathematics. In addition she won the Jubilee medal for an essay on 'The Life and Reign of Queen Victoria'.

Elsie Watson (Lorna Glendinning)

During the next two years Elsie studied for the Lady Literate in Arts (LLA), awarded by the University of St Andrews. At the time, 1889, she was the youngest woman to be admitted to this degree. She sat examinations in Aberdeen and London after studying by correspondence, passing in physiology, maths, French, education, history and English. Three months after passing all the exams, the women were allowed to buy their certificate, sash and silver badge of St Andrew to allow them some kind of academic dress.

As a governess to an Elgin family, the Browns of Dunkinty, Elsie enjoyed teaching so much that when she was advised to go abroad after a spell of ill-health, it was to take up a teaching post in Australia. At the Presbyterian Ladies' College, in Croydon, New South Wales, she taught art, music and mathematics. In later years when she did not have regular earnings, she supplemented her income by writing arithmetic text books, drawing on her experience in teaching posts she had held.

As a result of increasing deafness Elsie was asked to resign from her position as assistant teacher. She returned to Britain to take up another post teaching maths at Norwich Academy. While there, perhaps inspired by her father's publications, she wrote a guide to the city of Norwich.

After this spell of teaching Elsie returned to Australia where she took up her main career as a journalist, with a special interest in agriculture. On one of her trips to Australia, she was engaged by a London daily newspaper to describe the voyage, accompanying emigrants travelling steerage on cheap assisted passages; she did not enjoy this assignment.

Back in Britain Elsie became private secretary to Seebohm Rowntree, a member of the famous Quaker and chocolate making family. Rowntree was a pioneer sociologist. Elsie travelled around

Staff of the Presbyterian Ladies' College, Australia, 1892. Elsie is sitting on the steps third from left (Presbyterian Ladies' College Sydney Archives)

Europe to collect the material for Rowntree's book on social and housing conditions at home and abroad. This project took several years and included research using her employer's private library in York.

In 1903 Elsie was engaged in a stunt for the *Daily Express*. She was required to be a 'Missing Lady'. Every day she had to wear the same clothes, move around London in an obvious manner and eat her meals in the public eye. The reward for the finder was £100. Each evening she would write up her movements and have a photograph taken for publication the next day. It was about ten days before she was 'spotted', and the reward duly paid to one Mr Higgs. She wrote a final piece on her experiences when she was 'captured' and was then able to read some 400 letters written to the editor, claiming to have seen her in various parts of London.

Elsie became involved in the suffrage movement and spent some time in jail. In a letter to a family member, she refers to her time in prison in October 1910 when her bed was next to a harmonium used for playing hymns. Little is known about her suffrage activities.

In 1911, at the age of forty-two, Elsie looking for more excitement. She decided to journey across South Africa. She considered herself to be the first woman to bicycle in Australia, and now she wanted to be the first woman to make a long trek on a motor cycle through Africa. She intended to pay for the trip by writing articles for the magazine *Motor Cycle*. Leaving Britain in February would catch the most favourable weather. The practical arrangements were endless. A will was needed. How was she to carry her funds? Elsie's answer was 'sewn in her "trowsies"'! Elsie had initially planned to wear skirts to ride the bike but realised that these would not be practical, and so arranged to have khaki trousers made with a pocket for her revolver. In due course she had her Motosacoche Cycle (the engine was made in Switzerland) crated up to travel with her on the ss *Marathon*, leaving London on 17 February 1912.

From Cape Town Elsie had planned to travel 1,500 miles, passing through Kimberley, Johannesburg, Pretoria, Ladysmith and Pietermaritzburg to Durban. Apart from travelling on her own, some nights she faced a lack of any kind of shelter. It was hard to plan for every eventuality. Ultimately Elsie took with her a small suitcase, spare tyre, spare engine parts, extra petrol in cans, an overcoat and her revolver for protection. Her provisions consisted of tea, sugar and the equipment for brewing.

Along the route Elsie met up with and accepted hospitality from members of local motor cycle clubs, as well as other contacts. Some of these stops were pre-arranged and some were totally unexpected. Outside towns the going could be very rough. Potholes, mud, sand, boulders, sharp turns as well as rivers and gates all had to be negotiated. Much of the road system was little more than cart tracks. Indeed at one point she found herself riding up a dry river course and another time over a bridge of two planks held together by barbed wire. Not ideal for pneumatic tyres. She met up with fellow cyclists who were following her exploits in the *Motor Cycle*. Elsie wrote articles over a period of three months giving details of her adventurous journey.

Elsie sent this postcard of herself from her sister's house in Tongaat, Natal. The photograph was taken in Capetown at the start of her 1,500-mile trek (Lorna Glendinning)

The machine itself kept needing repair as well as maintenance, but it held its own until nearly the end of the trip when the screws holding the carriers on the back fell out again allowing one of the stays to get wrapped around the axle of the back wheel. No sooner had this problem been solved, than the chain broke. Elsie had not mastered a running start and her pedal start was now not possible. Nevertheless, in her concluding article in *Motor Cycle*, she extols the virtues of her machine. There had been criticism of her using such a lightweight model but a heavier one would have much more difficult to push through the sand. The Motosacoche (literally 'motor in a bag') engine withstood all that was asked of it and arrived in Durban in very good working order, unlike the frame – and the rider – both battered and bruised!

By September 1912 the trek was over. Including the planning, it had taken over one and a half years. Before going to stay with her sister in Tongaat, Natal, Elsie went by train up to the Zambezi Falls. Here she managed to collect some water from the Zambezi to be sent back to Scotland for her great-nephew's baptism. Family legend has it that she was lowered by a rope to fill the bottle.

The news of Elsie's trek through southern Africa spread across the globe. The *New York Times* reported on her journey mentioning (maybe incorrectly) that Elsie had also travelled in America.

By 1913 Elsie was back in Britain, initially visiting friends in Norwich. She started to write another book, this time about South Africa 'in transition' drawing on her experiences there.

Another trip to Australia followed, this time to be a delegate at a science congress working for the *Daily Despatch*. 1914 saw the outbreak of the First World War and it was with difficulty that Elsie secured a passage home. She left Australia in the company of many who were desperate to support Britain in its hour of need. At first the passengers were more scared of sea-sickness than torpedoes but once they had passed the wreck of the German ship SMS *Emden* scuttled by the Australian Navy on North Cocos, the war seemed more of a reality. On board the ship, many of the men started drilling; most of them were planning to join up.

Probably deafness prevented Elsie from taking an active role in the war. Writing suited her much better. After the First World War she spent the rest of her working life as London correspondent for the New Zealand Press Agency and the Brisbane *Daily Telegraph*. She wrote articles for other newspapers and magazines whenever she could get commissions.

Later, Elsie Watson moved to Cheltenham where she died in 1945 after a life full of travel and adventure, spurred on by a constant willingness to break through the barriers faced by women during her lifetime. (LG)

# Isabella Kerr

*Isabella Gunn, born Gollachy, Enzie, 30 May 1875; married George McGlashan Kerr, 16 September 1903; died Dichpalli, India, 22 December 1932.*

Dr Kerr pioneered treatment for leprosy in Dichpalli, Nizamabad, India.

Isabella Gunn, always known as Isabel, was born in Gollachy, near Portgordon, but brought up on the family farm at Kilnhillock House, just outside Cullen, then in Banffshire and now in Aberdeenshire. Her father, John Bain Gunn, died soon after her second birthday when her mother Mary was pregnant with her brother William. Mary continued to run the farm. There followed a catalogue of losses: Isabel's five-year-old sister Maggie died of scarlet fever, her sister Helen and brother Alexander both died of diphtheria.

Isabella Kerr (Centre for the Study of World Christianity University of Edinburgh)

The progress of Isabel's education has not been easy to determine. She may have been educated privately. In 1894, aged nineteen, she took her first Lady Literate in Arts (LLA) examinations in Elgin, passing in French and German. Elgin Academy was running classes for LLA pupils at this time; it would have been possible for her to take the train from Cullen in order to attend, or she may have boarded in Elgin. A year later she passed in education and history honours, again in Elgin. Records show that she took correspondence classes at St George's College in Edinburgh. Isabel also studied in Germany, taking French honours and German honours in Cassel in 1896 and French honours again in Frankfurt in 1897. By 1899 she was in Aberdeen sitting chemistry, and in the same year she received her LLA certificate from St Andrews University. Thereafter she studied medicine at Aberdeen University where she graduated as a doctor at the age of twenty-eight in 1903.

George, Isobel, Isabel and Eric
(Centre for the Study of World Christianity,
University of Edinburgh)

Isabel's mother died at the end of June that year. Isabel married George Kerr in September at Kilnhillock. He had studied divinity and medicine at Aberdeen University and had been working in Rhodesia as a Wesleyan missionary.

The couple moved to a Methodist Church in England until the Wesleyan Missionary Society sent them to Hyderabad in India in 1907. Isabel learned the local dialect, Telugu, and then set up dispensaries on the roadside in the Nizamabad district and travelled from village to village by bullock cart. She also worked in the local hospitals while her husband was superintendent of the Industrial School. Isabel became increasingly concerned about the plight of leprosy sufferers in the area and provided what care she could. By this time the couple had a son, Eric, and their daughter, Isobel Frances, was born in 1910.

Raja Narsa Goud, a wealthy philanthropist who built the first girls' school in Nizamabad, was impressed by Isabel's work and donated sixty acres of land plus financial backing for the building and the running of a permanent treatment centre in Dichpalli. The first patients entered the leper home in 1915. One of the earliest leper centres in India, it served every caste and religion. Isabel, delighted with the building, wrote:

> our beautiful new Leper Home is so manifest a witness to Christ... from a medical point of view it is heartbreaking work. It can only be palliative treatment.

But all that was about to change. While the family was in Britain on furlough, Dr Edwin Muir and Sir Leonard Rogers of the Leper Research Centre, Calcutta, had discovered the effectiveness of injections of hydnocarpus oil in curing the disease. In March 1921 Isabel was able to launch a pioneering programme of injections in Hyderabad. The government provided the clinic and Isabel handed over some of her duties at Dichpalli to Dr John Lowe. She took an overnight journey of more than 200 miles twice a week to attend patients at Hyderabad. The sixty or seventy patients had also travelled long distances to receive the restorative injections. She spent the mornings in the clinic and the afternoons in the zenanas and palaces where Muslim women suffering from leprosy lived in seclusion. About eighteen months after the new treatment had started Dr Kerr met with a group of patients on a particularly hot day. On enquiring why they appeared so happy one replied: 'we are rejoicing because once more we are enjoying the sensation of prickly heat', proof that the treatment was working and restoring feelings to their bodies. On the long journeys home Isobel spent her time with embroidery, embossed leatherwork or weaving on a tiny loom, all with a view to introducing more crafts to the patients at Dichpalli.

The work of Dr Kerr and her husband was spreading; a report in the *Hyderabad Bulletin* on 18 March 1922 noted that at a public meeting His Exhalted Highness, the Nizam of Hyderabad, allocated government funds for the building of new wards and accommodation at the new clinic. Dr Kerr treated around 2,800 patients at Dichpalli and Hyderabad. Around half saw the progress of the disease arrested as a result. For her services she was awarded the Kaisar-I-Hind Gold Medal, First Class. The medal had been established by Queen Victoria in 1900 to reward individuals who rendered distinguished service to the British Raj. George also received this medal.

In 1925 Isabel and George returned to Europe to visit relatives in the Moray area, to see their daughter settled in Geneva and be with their son Eric who was ill. Their fears for Eric were allayed and they returned to Dichpalli to help with the work on the gardens surrounding the new buildings and to encourage the setting up of cottage industries such as copper work. The Girls' Life Brigade was established to tackle the inertia and apathy engendered by leprosy. The girls took part in physical training and learned home nursing, hygiene, cooking and needlework. Later a similar group was formed for the boys.

By 1926 the British Empire Leprosy Relief Association was recommending Dichpalli as the centre for regular instruction courses for all doctors in South India. Doctors also went from Egypt, Siam, the Philippines, Basutuland and Ceylon.

In November 1928 the 'Great Day at Dichpalli' took place. The Victoria Treatment Hospital was declared open by the prime minister of the state,

Maharaja Bahadur Sir Krishen Pershad. A special train was run from Hyderabad to Dichpalli bringing distinguished guests and a multitude of citizens. It is possible that Anne Hardie, head teacher of the Mahbubia Girls' School at the time, also attended as the school had gifted two special sick wards for women. Anne Hardie was also Moray born, and a fellow graduate of Aberdeen University.

Isabel Kerr memorial chapel, Dichpalli
(Centre for the Study of World Christianity,
University of Edinburgh)

Isabella Kerr contracted pneumonia and died suddenly in December 1932. She was buried in the heart of the colony that she had made her life's work. A memorial chapel was built for her. She was remembered for her 'restful quietness', her hospitality and her 'great bowls of glorious roses'. Her garden was enjoyed by many; Rev. Leonard Simpson wrote:

> Roses in a Leper Hospital? Dichpalli was and is a veritable Garden of God, where love, and beauty, and hope are replacing ugly disease and despair. It all bears the impress of Mrs Kerr's personality. The fragrance of her life will outlive that of roses.

Her work at Dichpalli was carried on by her husband George until he retired back to Cove near Aberdeen in 1938. Their daughter Isobel Frances married Alexander Gunn Graham in 1941 and was living in Greenock when her father died in 1950. Isabel's son Eric appears to have died around 1930.

Isabel's brother William graduated as a doctor in 1904. He joined the Royal Army Medical Corps at the outbreak of the First World War and was killed in 1915.

Isabel Kerr's early life was dominated by sickness and death. She devoted her life to easing pain and providing pioneering treatment to the poor and desperate in a country far from home. (AO)

# Margaret Hasluck

*Margaret Masson Hardie, born Drumblade, 18 June 1885; married Frederick W*
*Hasluck at Pluscarden, 26 September 1912; died Dublin, 18 October 1948.*

Margaret Masson Hardie – classical scholar, archaeologist, traveller, ethnographer and spymaster – was born, the eldest of nine children, on the farm of Chapelton, Drumblade, near Huntly on 18 June 1885. By 1886 the family was settled at Westerton, near Pluscarden, in Moray.

The Hardies were a high-achieving family. David Hardie, Margaret's uncle, graduated in medicine, established himself as a surgeon in Forres, emigrated to Australia and was instrumental in establishing the health service in Queensland. He was knighted in 1913. Margaret's sister Anne became head of a ladies' college in India and was one of the first European women to visit Tibet. Margaret was a brilliant classical scholar. On leaving Elgin Academy she attained the equivalent of first class honours in classics at Aberdeen University, received a scholarship to Newnham College, Cambridge, where, in 1911, she earned a first in the classical tripos, and won a studentship at the British School at Athens (BSA). she was the first woman to win a post at this elite institution for classical and archaeological scholarship.

Within a year of arriving at the BSA, she was married. Seven years older than his wife, Frederick W Hasluck was assistant director of the school and a scholar of international reputation. They were married in the Church of Scotland at Pluscarden on 26 September 1912. On returning to Athens, the couple travelled widely in the Balkans and in Turkey, working together on archaeological and ethnographical projects. They worked on the Roman remains in Anatolia with two of the most distinguished archaeologists of the day, both later knighted – William Calder, who came from Dunphail, and William Ramsay. However, the scholarly idyll was shortlived. War intervened and in 1915 the Haslucks left the BSA and began to work for British Intelligence, Frederick in Athens and Margaret in London. Frederick worked with Compton Mackenzie in compiling a list of 'suspect persons'. In April 1916 Margaret joined Mackenzie's unit in Athens but Frederick's health declined. He contracted tuberculosis and, in November 1916, he and Margaret left Athens for a sanatorium in Switzerland. In *Greek Memories* (1932) Mackenzie describes his loss as 'irreparable':

We were never again to have the services of such an accurate, patient and logical mind to put into shape the inaccurate, hasty and haphazard information that reached us about people, places and events.

Following her husband's death, aged forty-two, in February 1920, Margaret organised the mass of notes and manuscripts he had left into a series of books under his name. The most significant of these, *Christianity and Islam Under the Sultans* (1929), is an authoritative work on the ethnography of the Balkans. In 1921 she received the first of two Wilson Travelling Fellowships from the University of Aberdeen, travelled to the Balkans in deepest winter and set about establishing herself as the principal authority on the customs and folklore of West Macedonia and Albania. What drew her to that part of Europe is unclear. It may have been, in part,

The young Margaret Hardie
*(Aberdeen University Review 1949)*

through loyalty to her husband's work in the area, but she was a professional scholar and she saw the potential for scholarship in this little-known area. The Balkans at that time were just emerging from what Rebecca West, in *Black Lamb and Grey Falcon*, calls 'the grim Ottoman night'. Albania, a country that did not exist until 1913, was a distant outpost, rugged, inaccessible and the victim of serious neglect for centuries. There was no governmental infrastructure; roads inland from the coast were non-existent; tribal law prevailed. The tribal organisation absorbed Margaret Hasluck and it became the subject of her most important work, *The Unwritten Law in Albania*, published posthumously in 1954. Her first ten years or so in the Balkans she spent in constant travel, moving by donkey from village to gypsy encampment, sleeping in native dwellings, on carpets amongst the other women and the children, or alone in her tent. She describes, in her reports to the Trustees of the Wilson Fellowship, the problems she encountered in working and travelling alone in the Balkans at this time:

> To get accurate texts I once proclaimed that I had marbles to give to industrious small boys who would write down folktales for me.

Unfortunately I had underrated the Macedonian boy's passion for marbles, and to the utter ruin of my peace a trail of children as long and eager as the Pied Piper's beset my footsteps from dawn to dusk until I fled the town...

It is hard work extracting charms from the old ladies. They are toothless and their minds chase every mouse that runs. For this reason, never let them boil an egg for you! They are supposed to count up to a hundred as it boils, but if a neighbour happens to look in in the middle, they stop to pass the time of day with her, ask how she and all her children and other relatives are, and give similarly thrilling information of their own family: then, with a hasty recollection of your egg, they resume their counting exactly where they left off five minutes before...

One remote village near Mt Olympus feared the brigands so much that they feared to lend or hire me a horse and sent me off on a donkey as being less useful to brigands. As a result I had nine hours' ride under a blistering sun through a scrub oak forest just high enough to exclude successfully all air; it scratched and tore my face and my belongings and produced the most annoying type of horse or donkey fly known. For sheer misery such a ride is hard to beat. It aggravated matters that, when a prodigious wriggle of the donkey smashed my thermos, leaving me waterless, I was perched so high on the wooden frames they use for saddles that I could not even kick him satisfactorily. These saddles are the torment of Levant travel...

All the time she was probing the customs and the culture, measuring, interviewing, taking notes and writing papers for periodicals on subjects as

Mirdite woman, Scutari, Albania 1923 (Margaret Woodward and UCL School of Slavonic and East European Studies Library)

diverse as 'Measurements of Macedonian Men' (*Biometrika*, 1929) and 'Bride-price in Albania' (*Man*, 1933). In particular, she was absorbed by the laws governing the bloodfeud. She became the recognised expert on Albanian gypsies. In the period from 1921 to the outbreak of the Second World War in 1939, she published some forty articles, papers and items of correspondence as well as gathering material for *The Un-*

*written Law in Albania.* She published in 1932 an *Albanian–English
Reader with Two Grammars and
Vocabularies.* This textbook, based
on Albanian folktales, remained in
use for more than fifty years. She
sent back to the Wilson Museum
(later the Marischal Museum) of
Aberdeen University a large and important collection of Balkan textiles
and other ethnographical artefacts
and curiosities. She also compiled a
very important collection of photographs of aspects of the life of
the Balkan peoples in those years.

Nixolle Gjeta and family, Breg Mates, Albania 1934
(Margaret Woodward and UCL School of Slavonic
and East European Studies Library)

From the early 1930s it was Margaret Hasluck's intention to settle in
Albania and she had built, by 1935, a substantial property in the central
city of Elbasan. Her choice of Elbasan was influenced by the presence
there of Lef Nosi, a distinguished Albanian Nationalist and ethnographical
scholar. Her relationship with Nosi was of enormous importance to her.
They shared academic specialisms. A close collaborative friendship
developed. On the Italian invasion of Albania in April 1939, Hasluck was
forced to leave Elbasan for Athens. She left her home, of which she was
intensely proud, and her 3,000-volume library, in the care of Lef Nosi.
She took with her only some notes and the manuscript of *The Unwritten
Law in Albania.* She never saw her home, her books or Lef Nosi again.
Nosi was appointed by the Germans to the Albanian High Council in
1943 and was executed as a traitor by the Communist government in
1946.

In Athens Margaret Hasluck returned to the British School which was
becoming, as the Axis powers took control of the Balkans, an enclave of
British expatriates. She was probably engaged in some small scale
intelligence work in Athens. In 1942, she moved to Cairo and was employed
as head of the Albanian section of the Special Operations Executive (SOE).
Her job was to recruit Albanian exiles as agents, to sift intelligence emerging
from Albania and to brief British agents about to be parachuted into
Albania to work with the Albanian resistance. She also had to write
fortnightly reports on the developing situation for SOE HQ. No one was
better placed for the briefing role. Her knowledge of the language,
topography, culture, of the complex web of family and tribal connections
was unique and invaluable. The situation, however, was strange. A woman

academic in her late fifties had the task of briefing men less than half her age for military duties of intense danger in an unknown land. In communicating her knowledge of Albania's geography, customs and language, she inspired affection and loyalty on the part of the agents she called her 'boys'. The 'boys' were keenly aware of her energy, her enthusiasms and her eccentricities. They referred to her as 'Fanny', the name they commonly used for their mules. She worked without rest, to the detriment of her health.

Difficulties arose for Margaret Hasluck and for her superiors in SOE as the war in the Balkans progressed. She was dedicated to Albania. Her home was there. She had seen the country develop in the last twenty years to a state of relative peace and prosperity. She now contemplated Albania's collapse. Whilst she was completely committed to defeating the Germans who had invaded Albania in September 1943, when it became clear that the Italian appetite for the war had disappeared, she found the growing Soviet influence on the resistance movement very hard to stomach. She was utterly opposed to Communism and predicted at an early stage that Albania would become a satellite republic of the Soviet Union. It was the British government's policy and that of SOE to work with and support the communist guerillas.

Margaret Hasluck's sympathies lay with the diminishing band of non-communist, Nationalist resistance fighters. She urged SOE to engage with the puppet government of Albania of which her great friend (and, perhaps, lover) Lef Nosi was a member. Her passionately held views began to affect her judgement. Her fortnightly reports for GHQ began to bear less and less relation to what senior staff knew was going on in the field. She was accused of falsifying intelligence in order to suit her political views. Matters came to a head: differences were irreconcilable. She disagreed fundamentally with the government's handling of the Albanian situation. She left the section in January 1944.

There was a sad coda to Margaret Hasluck's work in the war. In September 1944 she was awarded the MBE. The citation read:

> In briefing and advising agents who were infiltrated into Albania [her] work has been of the highest order, and distinguished by her outstanding gifts of intellect and personality.

However, because the Foreign Office had apparently lost track of her whereabouts, it seems she died unaware of the honour.

Margaret was diagnosed with leukaemia in London in May 1944. The next four years were spent partly in Cyprus and Switzerland, where she found conditions suitable for her state of health, and partly in London, with regular visits to her family in Moray. She wrote a few articles and worked on *The Unwritten Law in Albania*, which was not published until six years after her death. She tried to return to visit her home in Elbasan, but with no success. She maintained contact with some of her 'boys' after the war. Some of these, hearing of her financial difficulties, made anonymous payments into her bank account. One such was the actor Anthony (later Sir Anthony) Quayle. When she knew that the end was near, she went to Dublin to live. She did not want to be a burden to her family and she admired the reputation of Irish nurses. She wrote regularly to her family from Dublin but she did not want visitors: we can assume that she wanted to be remembered as fit and healthy. She survived in Dublin only a few months and died on 18 October 1948. Her ashes were interred in Dallas cemetery.

In the novel *Friends and Heroes*, the final volume in *The Balkan Trilogy*, Olivia Manning presents the character of Mrs Brett. It is generally agreed that Mrs Brett is based on Margaret Hasluck, whom Manning met in Athens in 1941. It is an essentially comic and unsympathetic portrait. Mrs Brett is rude, arrogant, garrulous, theatrical, manipulative, at times 'dotty', at other times 'verging on lunacy'. Mrs Brett's husband had been director of 'the School' in Athens. He had been ousted by treacherous forces and had died of typhoid. There is no mention of Albania, but Mrs Brett has dealings with Australian troops whom she 'knows how to deal with'. She is indefatigably curious and she is courageous. The last we see of Mrs Brett is on board the rusty freighter that is to take the ex-patriates from Athens to Egypt on Greece's entry to the war:

> The bunks were wooden shelves... sticky to the touch and spattered with the bloody remains of bugs.
> 'Like coffins,' said Mrs Brett. 'Still it's an adventure.'

Manning's portrait, while some features will have struck a chord with those who knew her, barely hints at the passions, the achievements and the tragedies, of Margaret Hasluck's life. She gave herself heart and soul to Albania. She was a scholar of international significance in her chosen field of ethnography and had made important contributions to archaeology and the study of the language of the Balkans. She lost her husband at the age of thirty-four, had rebuilt her life and established her academic reputation in Albania over the next twenty years. Everything changed in 1939. She lost a great deal in the war, including her close friend Lef Nosi. After the war she battled ill-health until she chose to die alone, far from family and friends.

In a tribute published in 1949, JM Reid, the editor of *Aberdeen University Review*, writes:

> I remember Margaret Hardie as a student at King's... girl undergraduates were still diffident, even demure, and their dress was decorously ankle-length... she brought a flutter of tempestuous petticoat. Hardie by name, she was hardy by nature. She was cast in heroic mould, and all her store of Greek... seemed but a preparation for the dramatic role she was to play in the fight for Greece in two world wars. I like to think of her defiant of GHQ. That was just our Margarita *contra mundum*.

A building on Margaret Hasluck's property in Elbasan now houses the Home of Hope Orphanage, a school for Roma children, run by an Anglo-American charity. On 18 June 2010, the 125th anniversary of Margaret Hasluck's birth, a ceremony took place at the school. It was attended by the British Ambassador to Albania, many distinguished Albanian guests and by members of her family. After a presentation on her life and work a plaque was unveiled, and family members were presented with a certificate awarding Margaret Hasluck the status 'Citizen of Honour', for her 'outstanding contribution to the public sphere of the city of Elbasan'. The inscription on the plaque reads in English and Albanian:

> This house was built by Margaret Hardie Hasluck from Dallas in Scotland 1885–1948. She understood and was deeply attached to Albania and its peoples for whom she worked in peace and in war.

(RB)

# Sylvia Benton

*Sylvia Benton, born Lahore, 18 August 1887; died Inverness, 12 September 1985.*

Sylvia Benton was a classicist who later trained as an archaeologist, working for many years with the British School at Athens. She carried out the first formal excavation at the Sculptor's Cave at Covesea in Moray.

Sylvia's father, Alexander Hay Benton, was educated at Keith Grammar School. Her mother, Jane, was a daughter of William Rose, farmer at Sheriffston, near Lhanbryde, and it was to Moray that Sylvia returned throughout her life. Sylvia was the youngest of their four children, and when she was born, in 1887 in Lahore, her father was chief judge in the Punjab. The family left India in 1894 and settled in Polmont, Stirlingshire where Sylvia attended St Margaret's School. Sylvia's mother died in 1901, and they moved again, to Surrey, and Sylvia went to Wimbledon High School. In 1907, she went up to Girton College, Cambridge, to read Classics, a subject dear to her father. Sylvia reveals an aesthetic side in a letter to a Girton friend in later life:

> I started my pursuit of beauty in 1899, sitting in the sun under a hedge, looking at one of our tree-studded policies in Polmont Bank, a Ruskin on my knee. I continued it in Wimbledon High School garden, Ruskin replaced by Homer. The next step was taken when I opened the door of the magnificent Girton library, and said to myself, 'This is now *my* library'.

Sylvia did not do as well academically at Cambridge as might have been expected, gaining, in 1910, only a low second class degree. It is suggested she may not have got on well with her tutor, 'Kits' Jex Blake, both being of strong minds. Playing hockey and tennis for her college and the university probably did not help either. For the next fifteen years she taught in girls' schools in England, having taken the teacher training certificate in Cambridge in 1912.

It was not until after the death of her father that Sylvia embarked on her career as a classical archaeologist. In a contribution to the obituary of a friend and contemporary at Girton, Phyllis Tillyard (née Mudie-Cooke), Sylvia mentions that 'A trip round Greece with the Tillyards was my introduction to archaeology' – and also describes a collision with the sluice gates in a canoe with Phyllis, and slime at the bottom of the Granta being bad for best dresses.

She was first admitted a student at the British School at Athens (BSA) for the session 1927–28, when she was already forty. This was to be a life spent in the BSA student hostel or tents, excavating in arduous, wet and dirty conditions, often in caves; in fact, her time spent in the Sculptor's Cave

Miss Benton with the certificate of her honorary membership of the Elgin Society, later the Moray Society (Elgin Museum)

at Covesea may not have been dissimilar, apart from the fact that life at the Greek seaside would have been warmer. Much of her earlier exploration in Greece was alone, and often on foot. She was not readmitted to BSA for the 1928–29 session, after disobeying the orders of the director, Arthur Woodward, and climbing alone Mount Taygetus (2407m) in the Peloponnese, cutting steps in the snow with her stick. However, the same director also encouraged her to acquire further qualifications for work in Greece; supported by Professor JL Myres, she read for the Diploma in Classical Archaeology, at Lady Margaret Hall, Oxford. She followed this in 1934 with a dissertation on the Barony of Odysseus, for a BLitt.

Her excavation at the Sculptor's Cave, on the beach west of Covesea Village, followed a visit there in 1928 with a tennis friend from Lossiemouth, Miss Mollie Hair (later Mrs Scoular-Buchanan), who 'called her attention to the fact that the floor was strewn with human bones'. They had gone to see the Pictish carvings on the walls, so it is all the more remarkable, that her most detailed and immediate report of the excavation for the Society of Antiquaries of Scotland included scant consideration of the carvings or the bones. Although the dig was hers, it must have seemed peripheral to her main focus at that time as she prepared to start her real career in Greece. The report is typical of Sylvia's writing, combining wide-reaching academic analysis with her own wit and down-to-earth approach. Referring to the range of puzzling bronze items discovered, she wrote:

> I do feel rather strongly that none of these articles are really suitable for cave-dwellers. Perhaps I am prejudiced by the extreme difficulty we had in detecting the bronzes. We kept losing excavation knives and entrenching tools. How would these people have kept nail-cleaners and tweezers, and who would have the heart to clean nails in the Sculptor's Cave?

This she ties in with Professor Myres' suggestion that 'the expedition of Severus in 210 AD caused the ladies of the Laigh to seek sanctuary, and that they died at Covesea with their trinkets upon them.'

The landowner of the Sculptor's Cave was Sir William Gordon Cumming (father of Elma Napier) of Gordonstoun. He was sympathetic to their further examination of the cave, as was his son, Alastair, in 1929 and 1930, lending tools and five men from the estate. Sylvia was not only able to call on help from a prodigious number of experts in the assessment of the finds from the dig, but also have them respond in time for her post-excavation lectures and publication. She was much encouraged by Professor V Gordon Childe, who appreciated her European approach, and disparaged by JG Callander, which would not surprise anyone familiar with the political history of archaeology in Edinburgh. The original lists of the some 2,000 human bones recovered have survived, with Sylvia's letters to Professor Alex Low, Aberdeen, although most of the bone is lost; her correspondence with another remarkable woman, the pioneering fossil-hunter who helped Sylvia with animal bone identification, Miss Dorothea Bate, is in the Natural History Museum, London – as is a beaver tooth from the Late Bronze Age layer, retained by the Museum.

Her archaeological work in Greece is more fully chronicled in the obituaries, for example, of Waterhouse and of Cook, both associated with BSA, and in her own and others' excavation reports and the records of the BSA. Lady Waterhouse's daughter, Eleanor Bodger, remembers Sylvia 'only as a frequent visitor to our house when I was a child. As she disliked both children and our cat, she was extremely memorable.' Before the war Sylvia worked in Macedonia, and later the Ionian Islands, discovering a Minoan colony on Kythera (Kithira), and at sites including a cave at Astakos, and in Ithaca, at Aetos and Polis Bay. At the latter site, she worked in a bathing dress and largely under water and was renowned for swimming across the bay daily after work at Stavros.

In late August 1939 she caught the last boat back to England from the eastern Mediterranean. During the war, she worked in naval hydrography on a *Gazetteer of Greece* and a *Glossary of Modern Greek*, and then in the Uncommon Languages Department of Postal and Telegraphic Censorship. By night she was a fire-fighter, but was badly injured in the bombing in London in 1945. By spring 1947 she was back in Ithaca, and continued to spend long periods working there for another twenty-five years, although based in Oxford until her retirement to Lossiemouth in 1970. Devastating earthquakes shook the Ionian Islands in 1953 and Sylvia was quickly on her way to help in the ruined Vathy Museum – diving into the water from the Grecian minesweeper, rather than waiting for the ladder. She was back in the new museum at Vathy and elsewhere in Ithaca, working with students and the BSA vase-mender in 1964–66. In the later 1950s her attention turned to the study of birds and winds in Greek art, and the more general view of the ancient Greeks on nature. She resisted wearing reading glasses, despite failing eyesight. A drawer of her mainly unpublished work from this time languishes in the Ashmolean Museum in Oxford, in the archive of Sir John Beazley, a scholar she particularly valued.

In retirement at Four Winds, her home near St Gerardine's Church on the cliff in Lossiemouth (her late sister Rose's house), Sylvia had several friends and correspondents, a continuing interest in cricket and crime novels, and latterly a devoted carer, Katie Tulloch. She visited Elgin Museum, was elected an honorary member and was for a short time, honorary curator. She was very proud to be sent a sonnet in Greek for her ninetieth birthday, written by GL Huxley, who had dug at the Minoan site she identified at Kythera. She wrote to a friend, 'I wish my father could have known what I have done and my reward'.

Very exciting for her was the new excavation of the Sculptor's Cave, by Ian and Alexandra Shepherd, in 1978, which concentrated on the two strips deliberately left by Sylvia for posterity. Her first question to them was: 'What about the bones?'. Sylvia would have been thrilled to learn of the current scientific examination of the twenty or so surviving bones, using techniques unknown in 1930. The Shepherds' excavation

Sylvia after descending the scaffolding to the Sculptor's Cave, 1979
(courtesy of Alexandra Shepherd)

was a properly funded venture, with the ninety-foot cliff covered with scaffolding for access. Just before they started work, Sylvia at the age of ninety-two, was subjected to a horrific assault in her home, in which her arm was broken. This did not deter her from descending to 'her' cave. On the way back up she scampered 'like a hamster', almost faster than they could coil in the safety rope.

Her last years were spent in Kincraig, being cared for by her great-niece, Mrs Elizabeth Neill, whose father Lt. Col. Benton, Sylvia's nephew, had died unexpectedly three weeks before Sylvia's attack. Sylvia died in Raigmore Hospital, Inverness, after a fall, with a fund of stories to tell almost to the end.

Sylvia's sister Rose, also unmarried, is said to have been wild, dancing on the beach at Lossiemouth, and a friend of Isadora Duncan. In occupied France during the war, she was involved in the escape through Spain of an injured officer, later an Aberdeen lawyer, and a sergeant. The latter had a metal ankle, and oil from tinned sardines supplied by Rose stopped the tell-tale squeak. Mary, her other sister, had a single-figure handicap at the Moray Golf Club for over thirty years, and in 1914, played for Scotland.

Sylvia was not always proved right, but she had the vision to propose ideas and go out and test them. On at least one occasion she confessed her mistake – for example, in a letter to *Man* in 1933. She had approached various experts for help with identification of an object ostensibly from a wheelbarrow of clay at the Sculptor's Cave. It turned out to be the top of a hot water bottle, and a doubly humiliating incident as it tended to throw doubt on her competence in controlling the stratification of her excavation. Checking later with the foreman, he said 'I dinna mind far I got yon, but it wisna frae the barrow'.

There are difficulties in doing justice to many of our Moray women who lived such long, varied and active lives. Miss Benton is one such. Although she is still remembered by the living, for the most part, this is necessarily when she was beyond her prime. Although she has not yet been included in the *DNB*, along with the zoologist Dr Anna Buchan she has the distinction of being a woman recorded in the *Third Statistical Account of Scotland*, in the Rev. Malcolm Corner's entry for the parish of Drainie. The number and content of her obituaries testify to a woman who attracted professional respect for her archaeological work, stamina and determination, and also affection. (JT)

# Anne Hardie

*Anne Hardie, born Pluscarden, 13 January 1888; married Hubert Johnson, July 1927; died Kitwe, Zambia, 24 August 1974.*

Anne Hardie was awarded the MBE for her work in the War Office during the First World War. Afterwards she was appointed headmistress of Mahbubia Girls School in India from where she travelled extensively during the school holidays. Later she farmed in Rhodesia.

Born at Westerton, Pluscarden, to farmer John Hardie and his wife Margaret Leslie, Anne had eight siblings, including elder sister Margaret (later Margaret Hasluck), whom she followed to Aberdeen University, graduating with an MA in modern languages in 1910. Anne rarely talked about the past, and unfortunately she burnt her letters and diaries. Recently, however, her son Andrew related what he knew of her to a relative, and it is mostly his memories that are used in this article.

At the start of the First World War Anne was in Germany and it was only by posing as a local that she was able to find her way over the border and thus home. On return to Scotland she taught in Motherwell. When her fiancé, another graduate of Aberdeen, was killed in the war Anne took a passage to Canada, where she taught for a while but returned to work in the War Office in London just as this government department was beginning to allow women through its portals; by 1918 there were more than 22,000. Anne was superintendent of the Mobilisation Department's press section for a while before moving to the Women War Workers Resettlement Committee where she was secretary. As the men began to return home to reclaim their former jobs this committee was set up to help more than a million women who had stepped into 'men's jobs' throughout the war. They were encouraged to return to their former positions in the home.

But Anne did not return to the family farm when she left her post in 1919. She travelled to Hyderabad, India to take up the position as headmistress of Mahbubia Girls' School. Women in India were beginning to find a voice with the foundation of such schools, which provided good education while observing strict Purdah. Most girls up until the 1940s were still educated at home. Mahbubia Girls' school was a former zenana school founded in 1907; its aims were to provide high quality education in the British style for Muslim girls. The staff were local and the head teachers British. Anne was the third principal and remained there until 1930. She enjoyed a glittering social life with the Nizam and his wife, the British Resident (an adviser to the Nizam) and officers of the Indian Civil Service. Under her headship, in 1928, the school was able to gift two special sick wards for women at the leper hospital in Dichpalli, about 100 miles away. Dr Isabel Kerr ran the hospital and visited Hyderabad regularly. Like Anne Hardie she was from the North-East of Scotland.

While teaching in India, Anne took advantage of the holidays to travel. One journey took her to Tibet where she travelled over the Himalayas with a team of mules and muleteers, but no other westerners, reaching as far as Shigatse. She was well received by the monks in the monasteries where she stayed. Her attempt to reach Lhasa was thwarted by a British political agent, because her visa did not allow her to visit that city.

Anne Hardie, thought to be taken at Easterton, Moray (Margaret Woodward)

Another solo trip took Anne to Africa. She went by boat to Mombasa and travelled by train into Uganda. It was her wish to cross Africa from east to west. Since there were no roads between the Ruwenzori mountains and the

Congo river she hired donkeys to enable her to make it through the incredible landscape that is now part of a World Heritage Site. Eventually she found river transport in the Belgian Congo. It was there that she became seriously ill with malaria. It being a small world, where Scots could be found anywhere and everywhere, it is of only slight surprise that Anne, born and bred in Moray, was nursed back to health by missionaries from Lossiemouth. It was because of her illness that Anne met Hubert Johnson, her future husband. Hugh, as he was known, was working as an agent for Lever Brothers' palm oil plantations. The missionaries asked Hugh to take Anne down river and as he was going on leave he accompanied her all the way to Britain.

Anne and Hugh were married in London in 1927. They spent their honeymoon in Abyssinia (now Ethiopia). Afterwards Anne returned to India and Hugh returned to Africa; they both had contracts to fulfil.

Britain in the early thirties was suffering from economic depression and when the couple reunited in London they were unable to find employment. There was opportunity in Africa, but the Congo was not a healthy place to live. Rhodesia, a Commonwealth country, had more appeal.

Having decided on Africa, the Johnsons bought a farm, Baguta, about eighty miles from Salisbury (now Harare). It was a far different call for Anne from her life in India. She knew something of farming in Moray but that was a world away from Rhodesia. Hugh was a Londoner who served in the army and then as a pilot in the Royal Flying Corps. He had no farming background, but did have experience of Africa. They threw themselves into the new venture with enthusiasm. A son, Andrew, was born. The Johnsons had a deep love of Africa. They stayed in Rhodesia for over thirty years and found much happiness. Sensing the political changes that were coming they returned to Moray in the early sixties, before UDI and the birth of Zimbabwe. They had to leave their assets behind. Hugh died in Dufftown in 1969. Anne then returned to Africa and was able to regain some of her money through South Africa. She lived for several years in Pietermaritzburg before moving to Zambia where Andrew was working as a doctor. When she died in 1974, her body was cremated on a pyre of logs in the bush. Andrew says that she would have approved. Her ashes were returned to Dallas cemetery to be beside those of Hugh.

Andrew considers that his mother was the first western woman to cross Central Africa from east to west and the fifth recorded western woman to reach Shigatse in Tibet. The stories that remain of Anne Hardie's life raise many questions; one can only regret the loss of photographs and letters that would have illustrated a long and interesting life spent on four continents. (AO and SB)

# Elma Napier

*Elma Gordon Cumming, born Sanquhar House, Forres, 23 March 1892; married
1) Maurice Gibbs, 1912, 2) Lennox Napier, 1924; died Antrim, Dominica, West
Indies, 1973.*

Elma Napier, much travelled throughout her life, set up home with her second husband in Dominica where she lived for more than forty years. She was the first woman to be elected a member of a Caribbean Legislative Assembly and was a published author of novels, three volumes of autobiography, travel stories and newspaper articles.

Elma was the eldest child of Sir William Gordon Cumming of Gordonstoun and Altyre and his wife, Florence Garner. Lady Eliza Gordon Cumming was her great grandmother and Constance (Eka) Gordon Cumming her great aunt.

In 1890 Sir William was accused of cheating at baccarat at a house party at which the Prince of Wales (later King Edward VII) was present, the 'Tranby Croft scandal'. Ill-advised, Sir William lost the case for slander that he brought against his accusers. His fiancée, daughter of the late commodore of the New York Yacht Club, married Sir William, who was twice her age, the day after the verdict. The couple retired to their Moray estates, financed for a while at least by income from her inheritance. The disgrace of her father, in the eyes of society and his regiment, affected Elma throughout her life: she was never personally aware of discrimination against herself or her siblings, but later in life she understood its effect on her parents, and the event continues to evoke curiosity.

Elma's first volume of autobiography, *Youth is a Blunder* (1948) tells of her upbringing on the edge of Edwardian society, and life as the unsatisfactory daughter of a mother trapped in an unhappy marriage. It was also a childhood spent on the contrasting estates of Gordonstoun and Altyre, with thrilling rides on the beach at Covesea or high above the River Findhorn. Parenting swung between leaving her at the age of six weeks in the care of a nurse who gave her gin to quiet her crying until she turned yellow, to outrage that she should appear aged twelve, in a skating photograph taken by the rector's wife with the rector's arm round her to steady her.

Elma's education was haphazard and unsettled: whereas her brothers went to Eton, Mademoiselle arrived when Elma was six, followed in 1901 by two terms at a boarding school. The next two years were mainly a misery under the grim totalitarian rule of Fräulein, with relief a homesick year again at boarding school. One quarter in 1906, Florence's cheque from

Elma Napier
(photograph: Dorothy Wilding)

America didn't arrive. Garner had tied up the family money in the hands of trustees lest, as happened, his girls should marry titled foreigners 'who thought that money was something that cads made for gentlemen to spend'. Economies had to be made, and the family left Altyre for Dawlish in Devon when Elma was fourteen. Here she briefly attended a Catholic convent, until the summer of 1908, when Florence decided Elma would have to earn her living. Elma chose the stage, and spent a year at Miss Fillipi's in Covent Garden, until told she had to give up 'this pleasant useless life', and prepare to come out. While she could not have been presented to Edward VII, this was George V's Coronation year.

Just before this, Elma met her first husband, Maurice Gibbs. He was twenty-three, and much sought after for parties. Elma was flattered by his attention at a time when she was still bruised by an innocent attraction to a married man which had been revealed to all by her maid. Neither mother thought the match good enough. A dinner was held 'and the two sides met as might combatants at an armistice'. Altyre was lavishly opened up, and the wedding took place in January 1912, at the little red estate church, and the couple honeymooned at Burnside, near Gordonstoun.

Soon pregnant and ill for the first three months, early married life was not easy for Elma. Her mother was often not speaking to her, and the couple were pushed by their families into living beyond their means. In 1913 one of Elma's 'nice uncles', Walter, left her £5,000 so that she might be independent. Fortunately, after two years, the family firm sent Maurice to Australia. This phase of Elma's life is told in *Winter is in July* (1949). Initially they were based in Melbourne, with their daughter Daphne (who had survived emergency surgery for intussusception), Nannie and the lady's maid, Miss Hughes, whose work later had to include putting to bed the drunken cook and rounding up the 'rations' sheep. Elma considered that she grew up in Melbourne, where life was gay and leisured and the social round included many people of consequence, including another Edward, Prince of Wales; she also experienced the 'dawning of political thought', and began to write, and be published in local newspapers and magazines.

Three months after their arrival in Australia, the First World War began; Maurice's work was 'protected'. Elma describes her 'war work' in her self-deprecatory but incisive way: selling programmes at war charity matinees, using her sewing machine for the Comforts Fund. In 1915, because Maurice had TB, he was sent to Japan, which was on the side of the Allies, and then, less logically, to one of the company's remote and primitive stations in Queensland, where they arrived after three days of rain following three years of drought.

Ronald was born just before the Armistice and in 1919 the family returned to Britain, mainly to see their families. It was on the voyage back that Elma met Lennox Napier who was to be the love of her life, and her second husband. Lennox had been at Rugby and Cambridge with Rupert Brooke, and having been inspired by Brooke to visit the South Seas, was en route for Pago-Pago. Elma and Lennox would meet again briefly in Melbourne and then not for two years, by which time Elma's first marriage had all but died. In 1922, Maurice was moved to Perth, Western Australia, and Elma went home to her ailing mother who had moved to Pitmilly, Fife. After the funeral at Gordonstoun, Elma returned briefly to Perth, with her eighteen-year-old sister Cecily, Nannie and the children, but soon realised this was a mistake. In 1923, after nine years in Australia, Elma left with Cecily, and Lennox met them in San Francisco.

Daphne and Ronald were not allowed to go with Elma; later Daphne was able to choose to live with her mother, but Ronald stayed with his father's family. Adultery could be condoned, but divorce was unacceptable, and the Gibbs family wanted nothing to do with Elma. Later there were reconciliations. After his second wife died, Maurice came to live on Dominica with Daphne's son and was a frequent visitor at Pointe-Baptiste. Ronald was killed in 1942, in the air, during a German raid on Canterbury.

Elma's new mother-in-law, Lady Napier, was most welcoming. In 1924, now married, Lennox and Elma went on a business tour of the Far East, Italy and then South America. They settled in Manchester where Patricia was born in 1925 and Michael in 1928. These were happy days although Elma never felt part of the place; here she developed politically and 'became essentially of the world that reads the *New Statesman*'. A sad mistake was made about this time – Lennox had been diagnosed with TB, but a second opinion from Sir William Osler refuted this, and the opportunity to move sooner to a more suitable climate was missed. He continued his busy business career in London, with many Continental journeys for work and holidays. Elma was often in Scotland in the 1920s, until her father died in 1930.

The next volume of memoir, *Black and White Sands*, Elma wrote in the

1960s but it was not published until 2009. Their first visit to Dominica was in 1931, on a voyage to the West Indies for Lennox's health. Before they left the island, negotiations to buy a piece of land were completed and by November 1932, they were back for good with Daphne (twenty), Patricia (seven) and Michael (four).

Michael particularly recalls the early days: the rain, mud and grey seas, the dislocation. The children were not initially impressed by their mother's 'desert-island fiction come true'. Eventually the sun came out, the Small House was ready to move into, Lennox started his garden and the land was cleared for the Big House at Pointe-Baptiste, which would be built to his design. At this time, the north-east coast, the Atlantic shore, was connected to the capital, Roseau, by launch up the west coast as far as Portsmouth, so the pitch pine timbers that have survived so well all came in by sloop to the beach below the house, while the furniture from London made the last part of the journey on the passenger bus. The house today is little changed, with its magnificent, seventy-foot balcony looking out over the colourful garden and the sea towards Marie Galante, although, after Elma's death, Michael installed electricity, running water and indoor sanitation.

Lennox died in 1940, just four years before the first use of streptomycin. Their shared interest in island politics had begun in 1932, and when he was dying, the voters of North Eastern District petitioned Elma to take his place on the Legislative Council. Elma thus became the first woman in the Caribbean to be elected to parliament. Promoting village boards and various self-help programmes were her main contributions, and she was a leader of the campaign for a motorable Transinsular Road, speaking up as a lone voice at a crucial meeting when the money was almost reallocated. Visiting her scattered constituents and attending meetings in Roseau meant long days on horseback, in the launch or in unreliable cars on unmade roads. She continued in the Council with a nominated seat until 1954, when at the height of the Mau Mau campaign she represented Dominica in Nairobi at a conference of the Commonwealth Parliamentary Association.

Many well-known people made Pointe-Baptiste the object of a visit while on Dominica: Patrick Leigh Fermor, Alec Waugh, Somerset Maugham, Charles Morgan, Noel Coward, Princess Alice of Athlone

1980s Decade for Women stamp. The small print reads 'Elma Napier 1893–1973 First Woman Elected To Legislative Council In British West Indies 1940'

and Princess Margaret. Despite the sub-title of her Dominican memoir, *Black and White Sands* (2009), she and Lennox were not Bohemians, although visitors and house-parties were frequent. When they arrived on the island, they did not have much time for the conventional expatriate society, which anyway was physically distant from their chosen remote corner, and their friends were not confined to any colour or creed. Of the two contemporary white women novelists, Elma had more in common with Phyllis Shand Allfrey, but they lived on opposite ends of the island, and Elma seems not to have had a high regard for Jean Rhys. Most analyses of Caribbean writing include references to all three.

Wherever Elma was living, she would immerse herself in the locality, and take every opportunity to explore, often alone, on foot or on horseback. She refers often to scenes reminiscent of Moray, and marvels at the flowers that are at home garden treasures, but seen elsewhere growing wild. Another recurrent theme is books: what she or those around her were reading, her parents' choice having been somewhat restricted; her library is still there at Pointe-Baptiste. Her own work, including her biographies, two novels and numerous newspaper and magazine articles, was largely written after she was widowed. *A Flying Fish Whispered*, a novel first published in 1938 under her pen name, Elizabeth Garner, has just been (2011) reissued in Caribbean Modern Classics.

As she grew older she lived alone, sewing and reading on the verandah by oil lamp, with devoted servants, and with the families of her two daughters growing up on the island. She visited her son, an engineer in Turkey, and he and his family continue to holiday on Dominica. One of her grandsons, Lennox Honychurch, is a leading anthropologist and historian on Dominica, and although Pointe-Baptiste is still in the family's ownership, it is now available for holiday lets. In the 1980s 'Decade for Women', Elma appears on the Commonwealth of Dominica 10c postage stamp. She is buried near Lennox in a grove on the estate. (JT)

CHAPTER NINE

# Running a Business

*Lady Onlie, honest lucky,*
*Brews gude ale at shore o' Bucky;*
*I wish her sale for her guid ale,*
*The best on a' the shore o' Bucky.*
Traditional drinking song,
collected and tidied up by Burns in 1787

LIKE BURNS' LADY ONLIE, landlady of a Buckie inn, Mrs Innes of the White
Horse Inn, Elgin, was celebrated in verse. According to Will Hay, Elgin's
poet, Mrs Innes was the perfect business woman – 'The same right-hearted,
good gudewife, the pride o' Elgin toon!' She kept a clean house, good
whisky, ale and wine, was bonny, charming and good at sorting out disputes
– in her 'house' there was always mirth and pleasantness.[1] Not much is
known about Mrs Innes, except that Elgin generally held her in high regard.
After about fifty years as innkeeper, the town presented her with a portrait
in a 'gorgeous frame bearing a suitable inscription'. She died in 1840 at the
age of sixty-nine. Isabel MacKenzie too, had been an innkeeper who was
held in high esteem. Innkeeping, it would seem, was a suitable occupation
for a woman in the eighteenth and early nineteenth centuries.

In 1726 Mrs Jean Hay, servant to Hon. Lady Braco, applied for
membership of the tailor's craft as mantua maker (dressmaker) and
designer. She was admitted to the 'Freedom of the Craft'.[2] Jean Hay was
unusual; women with sewing skills often set up in business as seamstresses,
staymakers and milliners, but they were rarely admitted to the tailor's
craft. More common in Scotland was the passing of a dead husband's
membership of the craft to a new husband.

Whilst women's businesses were most likely to rely on domestic skills,
like cooking, brewing and sewing, women had long been helping out with
their husbands' businesses in many different trades. Some, like Ethel Baxter, may have been at the root of the business success. Consequently, it was
not uncommon for a woman to take over a business on the death of her

husband. Widows like Elizabeth Cumming had, since medieval times, a high status in society. A woman who could continue her husband's business would not be dependent on charity for survival or be a burden on society.

Occasionally circumstances were such that women inherited businesses because there were no sons. Isobel Brown's life in farming might have been very different had she had brothers. As a farmer, albeit with a grieve to run much of the business, she was able to take an active part in community matters relevant to rural society.

On the whole, running a business gave women an enviable position. They might have to work hard, but they were in charge, able to take

Mrs Innes of the White Horse Inn, Elgin c.1840
(Elgin Museum)

decisions and, if successful, watch their businesses grow. Since native wit, rather than a formal education, was required to become an entrepreneur, women were as likely to succeed as men, provided that they had the opportunity to test their ideas and organisational skills. Inevitably, in a patriarchal society, such opportunities were limited until the later years of the twentieth century.

Two of the women featured in this chapter, Elizabeth Cumming and Ethel Baxter, left a legacy of business expansion in companies that are today of international standing.

# Elizabeth Cumming

*Elizabeth Robertson, born Knockando, 12 May 1827; married Lewis Cumming, 20 July 1859; died Knockando, 19 May 1894.*

Elizabeth Cumming was a successful distillery proprietor and compassionate employer.

Elizabeth Robertson was the youngest daughter of farmer Lewis Robertson and his wife Jane Inkson. By the time Elizabeth was nine months old her father had died at the age of fifty-three. She lived at the farm of Claggan, Elchies, in Knockando Parish, with her mother, brother James and sisters Jane and Elspet. Jane was born two years before Elizabeth; she only lived for ten years.

Little is known of Elizabeth's early life; it is likely that she attended the nearby Elchies School, and Knockando Kirk. Her mother and brother James were running the farm and probably Elizabeth was doing her share. She stayed on at Claggan with her mother and brother until her marriage in 1859.

Cardow Farm, a few miles away, was home to the Cumming family. The Excise Act of 1824 had allowed John Cumming to take out a licence to distil at Cardow, thus continuing what he had been doing illicitly since 1811. John's wife Helen was an active partner in the business; her talents for outwitting the excise men were legendary in the area. When these men were visiting Knockando she invited them to stay at Cardow Farm. While they were tucking into a meal she would excuse herself and go into the barn to raise the red flag as a warning to all the other distillers that the excise men were about.

Lewis Cumming, John's son, took over the running of the distillery in 1832 after John's death. He was twenty-seven; his young neighbour Elizabeth Robertson was just four years old. The new road from Elchies to Knockando (built in 1827) provided quicker and easier access to Knockando – Cardow Farm was then just a couple of miles away from Claggan. Elizabeth probably knew the Cumming family all her life, but she did not marry Lewis Cumming until she was thirty-two.

Helen, Elizabeth's mother-in-law, remained active in the farm distilling operations, and died at the age of ninety-seven. Following her marriage, Elizabeth set about learning the business while looking after her growing family. By the time her husband died in 1872 she was an astute businesswoman and expecting her fourth child.

This dramatic interpretation of Elizabeth Cumming, with Cardhu Distillery in the background, was painted for a descendent's sixtieth birthday in 1956 by Doris Zinkeisen, Scottish official war artist (Sir Alistair Irwin)

She decided that she was well equipped to run the distillery herself.

The railway came to nearby Carron in the 1860s; this benefited the distillery as demand from the south was growing. Easier transportation meant that the business flourished. Eventually Cardow Distillery became a victim of its own success as it was having difficulties keeping up with that demand. Elizabeth decided to acquire the perpetual lease of land within 300 yards of the old building and to erect a new distillery with thick stone walls and slated roof which would be capable of producing three times that of its predecessor.

Elizabeth Cumming (Cardhu Distillery)

Elizabeth's eldest son, Lewis, worked with her in the business; he died in 1886 at the age of twenty-five. Her second son, John Fleetwood, gave up his medical studies to help his mother during the boom years. There were many whisky blenders operating in Scotland at the time who were keen to buy distilleries even at inflated prices; Elizabeth resisted them all until February 1893 when she was sixty-five years old. She decided to sell to John Walker & Sons of Kilmarnock for £20,000 including shares valued at £5,000. She still had a keen eye for a good deal; as a condition of sale her son John was appointed to the board of the new company.

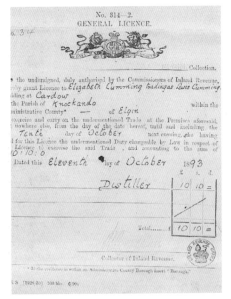

Cardow licence 1893 (Cardhu Distillery)

Elizabeth was a generous woman and her welcoming attitude to friends and strangers was appreciated. When author Alfred Barnard visited Cardow in the late 1880s he noted that his appetite, sharpened by the mountain air, 'was soon allayed by the well-known hospitality of Mrs Cumming, the proprietress of the distillery'.

Before Elizabeth settled into retirement she built another warehouse, and cottages with running water for distillery employees. It would be more than half a century before most of the local area was on mains water.

She had taught her son well. Her good business practice meant that he was able to expand production for Walkers; by 1898 the output had doubled. Elizabeth was not to see these fruits of her endeavours; only a few months after the sale she had a stroke and died just a few days after her sixty-seventh birthday.

Elizabeth Cumming's hard work, business acumen and daring, a century before it became acceptable for women to take on the boardroom, meant that the distillery continued to flourish and by 1982 the brand was selling all over the world. She had, perhaps, learned from two strong role models, her widowed mother who ran the family farm and her mother-in-law who remained an active partner in the distilling business well into old age. (AO)

# Ethel Baxter

*Ethelreda Adam, born Cummingston, 1883; married William Baxter, November 1914; died Elgin, 1963.*

Ethel Baxter founded the Moray family business which has become the internationally renowned food manufacturers, Baxters of Speyside.

Ethel was born in 1883 to Andrew Adam, grieve of Meadowhillock farm on the Roseisle estate, and his second wife, Elizabeth Farquhar Adam. She was a strong, independent child and resented being sent to school. She walked three miles to Keam School, Duffus, in all weathers. There she was taught by an unpleasant schoolmaster who threw chalk and slates around. She bore a scar all her life where a slate had hit her on the chest. In spite of all the unpleasantness, she gained

Nurse Ethel Adam in Kent (Gordon Baxter)

sufficient qualifications to be accepted by Aberdeen Royal Infirmary to be trained as a nurse. She specialised in midwifery and moved to the Northern

Nursing Home in Albyn Place, Aberdeen, run by a Miss Elphinstone.
Here she nursed special surgical patients and was also called upon to
nurse patients nearer home that could
afford a private nurse. She turned increasingly to private nursing and
spent lengthy periods in fine houses
in northern Scotland and even as far
away as Kent. The photograph of her
in nurses' uniform was taken in Fa-
versham, Kent, where, in 1912, she
nursed the mother of Sir John Reith,
later Lord Reith, the first director
general of the British Broadcasting
Corporation. During this period of

Nurse Ethel Adam in travelling uniform
(Gordon Baxter)

her life she learnt what the rich liked to eat and where they bought it.

In March 1914 Nurse Adam had just arrived back at the Northern
Nursing Home when she received a telegram from Dr Taylor of Elgin asking her to call him in his consulting rooms that evening. He asked her if she
would be willing to nurse two middle-aged bachelor brothers who both
had septic throats and were 'nervous about themselves'. They were William and George, sons of a high class Fochabers grocer, William Baxter. Dr
Taylor said they were 'nice patients' and he 'hoped she would be happy'.
Little he did know that this was the introduction that would result in the
setting up of a world-wide food business. Nurse Adam found that the pair
had been advised to use an inhaler stuffed with two or three poppy heads
and that as they had been inhaling too frequently they were suffering from
opium poisoning as well as septic throats. They had been seeing all sorts of
faces and creatures around them. No wonder they were worried. Within
two weeks she had them restored to health and left them 'in the care of
their dear old housekeeper' and returned to Aberdeen.

A little later in 1914 Ethel was invited by the Baxters to Highfield
House, Fochabers, and she cycled over from Cummingston. She noted that
William had got rid of the beard which he had grown whilst ill, was well-
dressed and 'with plenty of hat-doffing was altogether quite attractive'.
After tea in the drawing room, William wanted to show her some of the
beauty spots of Fochabers. They climbed the hill behind the house through
eighty-foot Scots pines that were soon to be felled for war use. After admiring the view from the top they descended to the Spey where there was a
one-foot-wide plank, twelve foot long, across a deep stagnant pool. Wil-

liam was keen for her to cross it first before he would risk it – surely a foretaste of the relationship to come. They returned to Highfield via the road bridge and Ethel cycled the eighteen miles home again to supper.

Then another call from Fochabers came to Nurse Adam, now back in Aberdeen. This time it was from the Rev. Dr Birnie of the Red Kirk manse, Speymouth, who had a guest suffering from a bad accident in his house. The patient was a fourteen-year-old boy who had been cycling home, head down into the wind, when he'd been hit by a gig driven by a drunken farmer. The shafts had gone into his abdomen. After two weeks at the manse the boy was well enough to return to Fochabers School where he was a boarder. Nurse Adam returned with him. William Baxter soon heard that she was back and invited her to come to see him when he was off duty. The shortest way was across the fields of Stynie Farm and she could see a white handkerchief waving at her in the distance. She also knew that there was a bull in the field. She got safely across and he didn't attempt to meet her half way. They were able to meet for three afternoons only, but thereafter 'things got feverish' and she was bombarded in Aberdeen by two or three letters a week which she had not time to answer.

In November 1914 Ethel Adam married William Baxter. He had not been accepted for war service having had a major operation for a duodenal ulcer. They lived first at Ford Cottage, Fochabers. Soon Ethel was involved in the family business, making large quantities of marmalade. For this she would use three coke furnaces with three copper pans each three feet deep. The pans were on an endless chain which had to be pulled up and down and Ethel had to mount three steps to stir each one. The marmalade was required for William's fishing boat orders, extending from Peterhead to Hopeman. When the boats returned home with their haul of fish, the Baxters had to be quick in claiming their money as it was soon spent by the fishermen themselves.

It became apparent that the three Baxter partners were not going to work well together and Ethel encouraged William to ask for 'a dissolution' and to withdraw his share so that they could start out on their own. When the old Duke of Richmond and Gordon heard the news he said: 'Baxter, meet me at three o'clock on the Spey Bridge to choose a site'. And so it was that the site on

Ethel and Willie Baxter (Gordon Baxter)

the banks of the Spey of the now famous factory was chosen and 'marked out with a piece of string'. In 1916 Ethel and William borrowed enough money to set up a small jam factory. Within two years they had paid back that money and were never in debt again. Ethel's son Gordon refers to her as 'a frugal Dougal'. Shortage of male workers during the First World War meant that Ethel herself was responsible for firing up the boilers and shovelling coal to keep them going. She is reputed to have made three tonnes of blackcurrant jam two days before the birth of her first son Gordon in 1918 and he says he was breast fed amongst the coal. Ethel worked from 8am to 8pm, with a half hour break at midday. The jam was put into stone jars and had to be cool enough to cover with wax paper circles before she went home at night. Meanwhile her husband Willie, the natural salesman, was marketing and selling the jam.

In the early 1920s they started their first canning machine, preserving raspberries and blackcurrants. Ethel kept the machinery going and hitched up her skirts to climb into the rafters and oil the wheels which ran the pulleys of the belts. Resourceful and practical, she was even known to have carried out electrical repairs. In 1929 Willie discovered on his travels that the deer shot by stalkers around Aviemore were being buried on the hillsides for lack of a market. He asked Ethel if she had a recipe for game soup, and, sure enough, she found a traditional recipe and started making the well-known Baxters Royal Game Soup. She had inherited from her mother, Elizabeth Adam, the ability to make fine Scotch broth, hotch-potch and cock-a-leekie and so she soon began to can other soups as well as the highly successful Royal Game. Preservation of beetroot was introduced in the early 1930s. The source of beetroot was the Oakbank Reformatory School in Aberdeen where recalcitrant boys were made to grow them. Ethel discovered that neat vinegar preserved the beets but was unpalatable, so she experimented until she found the right dilution. Today, fifty tons of beetroot are prepared daily for bottling.

The depression in the 1930s meant that Willie had to travel further afield to sell his wife's products. Ethel had learnt in her private nursing days that Harrods was the place where the wealthy bought food and so Willie went off to London. Having gained a market at Harrods, Baxters foods were soon sold at Macy's in New York, Marshall Field's in Chicago and HJ Thrupps in Johannesburg. They are now sold throughout the world.

Ethel was a tall, quiet woman with a warm heart. Described as a 'kindly matriarch', she ran the factory with strict military discipline but great concern for the welfare of the workers. Standards of hygiene and morality were important to her and she warned her female workers not to get pregnant when soldiers were stationed in the area during the Second World

Ethel in later years
(Gordon Baxter)

War. She had been born into a devout presbyterian family but became an Episcopalian on her marriage to Willie. Services were held in the Gordon Chapel, Fochabers, owned by the Duke of Richmond and Gordon. On the death of the seventh duke in 1928, the family were no longer able to maintain the chapel and it became the property of the Crown Estates. During the Second World War it was used to station soldiers and was then threatened with being turned into a cinema. Ethel, outraged at this idea, raised the money to save it as a chapel and to have it restored and refurbished. The chapel was bought from the Crown Estates Commissioners in 1950 by the local congregation of the Episcopal Church of Scotland and rescued as a place of worship. Within the Gordon Chapel are the lovely Burne-Jones stained glass windows, arguably still the most important art works in Moray. Although her work as a nurse had ended in 1914, Ethel kept her allegiance to nursing throughout her life and raised money to support the Scottish Nursing Association.

Ahead of her time, Ethel Baxter, handsome and independent, created with her husband one of Scotland's most successful business partnerships. In the words of her son Gordon, she was 'the pillar and the architect of the firm'. Having resisted more than 150 takeover bids, it remains a family business and now has an annual turnover of at least £50 million. (MB)

# Isobel Brown

*Isobel Brown, born Moray 1900; died Dipple, Fochabers, 2 March 1985.*

Isobel Brown spent her formative years growing up with her sister, Agnes Christian, on the family farm at Dipple. Following the First World War, manpower was in short supply and, as there was no son to take over the running of the farm, Isobel took on this responsibility when her father died.

The ancient parish of Dipple lies beside the Spey where once the bishops of Moray held the fishing rights. The farmland is fertile and when James Paterson Brown married in 1899 and eventually acquired the lease of Dipple Farm, he hoped to be able to pass it on to a longed-for son. In the early years of 1900 it was not considered likely that a woman could

manage a farm but the outbreak of war changed many such perceptions.
James Brown was secretary of the Northern Auction Mart Company, Elgin
for twenty years and gained a reputation as an excellent agriculturalist.
The loam of Dipple Farm was recorded as being the best-conditioned soil
in the district. He was secretary of the Northern Stud Company, was in
demand as a judge of horses, and frequently exhibited his Clydesdales at
shows throughout the north. For many years he was also secretary to the
Morayshire Farmer (sic) Club.

James Brown and his wife Isabella seriously considered adopting a local
boy to take over the farm – a not unusual practice at the time and Isabella
made several attempts to persuade an impoverished local family to part
with their baby son. This scheme never materialised and so the Brown of
Dipple family consisted of just two girls. Their youngest daughter, known
as Chrissie, was to marry the manager of a sugar company and spend most
of her married life in Trinidad before retiring back home to Moray. Isobel,
known as Tibby to her close friends and family, was to spend her life devoted to Dipple Farm and to her work within the community.

Educated at Elgin Academy, she finished her final year of schooling at
Milne's Institution, Fochabers before leaving in June 1915. Isobel and her
sister were among the founders of the Fochabers Girl Guides when the
company was set up in 1924, with Chrissie as the lieutenant. In 1927 the
first annual report of the group records:

Miss I. Brown has been giving a course of practical demonstrations on
cookery this week and a majority of Guides hope to try this badge soon.

---

*Walnut Bread*

| | |
|---|---|
| *4 cups flour,* | *4 teaspoons of baking powder* |
| *1 small teaspoon of salt* | *1 cup of sugar* |
| *1 cup of walnuts chopped fine* | *1 cup of milk (sweet)* |

*1 egg*

*Mix the dry ingredients together then mix with the milk and egg.*
*Place in buttered tins or tin and let stand for twenty minutes in a warm*
*place before putting in the oven.*
*Bake in a moderate oven for about ¾ of an hour or more.*

---

Recipe from Miss I Brown of Dipple in the Bellie Parish Church calendar of recipes printed in 1934
'To Recall Old Days and Happy Memories'

Thanks to good leadership, the Fochabers Guides group kept going throughout the war.

By the time her father died aged sixty-six in 1936, it was evident that Isobel had no plans to marry. Her mother, Isabella Reid, was a protective and strong mother by all accounts, giving short shrift to a gentleman caller who, shortly after the Second World War, expressed an interest in Tibby. Although hampered by a severe limp, Commander Marsden had a very elegant demeanour, dressed in frock-coat with tails, and wearing a half-tile hat, he drove around the district in a black Austin 16 which had been specially adapted for his disability. He took lodgings in Fochabers village and professed to be writing a book on shorthorn cat-

Miss Brown of Dipple
(Fochabers Heritage Centre)

tle, but Tibby's mother discouraged any close involvement. She died in 1953 at the age of eighty-one leaving Isobel to continue on the farm alone.

The First World War – called 'the war to end all wars' by some optimistic folk – had decimated the male population and manpower was scarce. Isobel had been taking a serious interest in agriculture and, with the help of her mother, was to prove herself more than capable of managing the large farm. As well as a grieve to supervise work, there were several farm labourers living in the six farm cottages, plus a gardener who took care of the grounds around the house itself.

Isobel was a member of the local agricultural executive committee and was the last president of the now defunct Morayshire Farmer Club which had done so much to improve agricultural practices since its formation in 1799. As well as the Girl Guides, Isobel was involved with the local Red Cross and also served in the Land Army during the Second World War. Although a strong-minded businesswoman, she was known for her kindness – giving one of the farm cottages to a small family who had been ruined and driven out of their Cabrach home by a severe winter. Isobel became a leading member of Speymouth Church and in 1962 was appointed an officer of the Order of St John of Jerusalem. Membership of this charitable royal order of chivalry is by invitation only; those selected having acted to promote humanitarian and charitable work – its largest service organisation being that of St John's Ambulance.

Isobel worked unstintingly for the Woman's Rural Institute (WRI). The Women's Institute had been founded in Canada in 1897 and the movement spread swiftly to Europe, the first in Scotland being set up in Longniddry in 1917. It proved an invaluable support group for many isolated women, especially during the challenging war years, and enabled the spread of new ideas and the sharing of many skills. Having founded the first Rural in Moray at Cranloch in 1924, Isobel became the first secretary of the Moray & Nairn Federation of the Scottish Women's Rural Institute, a position she held for forty-five years. This organisation now covers an area from Fochabers to Nairn, and the Spey Valley from Cromdale to the Spey estuary, with twenty-four institutes in the area.

Despite occasional financial problems Miss Brown became known as a successful breeder of pedigree shorthorn cattle and often attended the Perth bull sales. She became one of the directors of the Scottish Beef Shorthorn Society and as such her photograph appears in the 1971 Christmas Number of the local paper, *The Northern Scot*. She also enjoyed rearing Muscovy ducks. Potatoes and other vegetables were grown on Dipple Farm and in early autumn the local school children could earn pocket money by helping with the 'tattie' harvest. Miss Brown was frequently invited to local schools to give speeches and hand out prizes at the end of term.

Isobel's interests were not confined to farming; she was a skilled needlewoman, well versed in local history, and she collected agricultural antiques. On discovering that a 'feeing stone' was situated outside historic Dipple churchyard, she insisted that the local council keep this remnant of olden times clear of vegetation and easily visible. Sadly it has once again become overgrown and difficult to detect. She was also instrumental in assisting the past president of the Society of Antiquaries of Scotland in rediscovering a tombstone of significance at Bellie churchyard. This stone had been discarded, along with many others, in the late eighteenth century during the improvements to Gordon Castle and the consequent destruction of the original ancient church at Bellie. The stone commemorated a past minister who had been born in 1556, ministered for fifty-six years and died at the age of 107. Thanks to Miss Brown this fascinating part of local history has been restored.

As well as serving on several committees, Isobel found time to work as a justice of the peace. At a time when the local hospital in Elgin, Dr Grays, was threatened with restructuring and 'improvement', she put up a determined fight to preserve its neoclassical architecture. Consequently, while many changes have since been made to the building, the distinctive and picturesque frontage remains.

Miss Brown of Dipple, as she was respectfully known, became a familiar sight driving around the county in her black Lancaster car; she was rarely seen without her hat and gloves, as befitted a lady of her standing. She had a good sense of humour and was firm friends with another like-minded woman, Miss Isobel Wharton-Duff of Orton. Both were highly respected members the community, similarly committed to the WRI.

Miss Isobel Brown attended her last official engagement – the twenty-fifth anniversary of Mosstodloch WRI – a week before her death in 1985. She had been born in 1900 before women were allowed to vote and when their career opportunities were generally limited to marriage, teaching or nursing. At a time when she could have expected to marry and raise her own family a whole generation of possible partners had been slaughtered in the fields of Europe. Isobel Brown turned her focus from her own needs to the needs of her community. During the Second World War she contributed to the war effort by her Land Army work and also by keeping the farm going productively. Although her parents had hoped for a son to continue the family line, and Isobel may not have travelled far or her name be universally known, within her home patch her steadfastness of purpose and sense of community spirit touched many lives, making a huge difference to the people around her. She is buried near some of her forebears, at Urquhart cemetery, where the adjacent farm fields stretch towards the distant hills. (JM)

CHAPTER TEN

# Breaking into Science

*During the drive home had some amusement with my sketchbook – an old one,*
*which Contained among other things a Copy of Sir Roderick's [Murchison]*
*Section of the Findhorn made for Lady Gordon Cumming – From this text he*
*[Murchison] preached a capital sermon, to the apparent delight & Edification of*
*the ladies, who resolved to become Geologists.*

Letter from James Joass Maxwell to George Gordon 24 August 1865[1]

MORAY WAS A FOCUS for a great deal of scientific interest in the nineteenth
century. George Gordon of Birnie (1801–1893), Church of Scotland
minister, was part of a network of enthusiasts. The network was extensive
and comprised of different groups: local naturalists, such as W Alexander
Stables, factor at Cawdor, John Innes, doctor in Forres, and James
Macdonald, teacher at Elgin Academy; Gordon's friends and acquaintances
from university days in Edinburgh – Robert Graham, William Hooker, HC
Watson, John Hutton Balfour; and geologists like Roderick Murchison,
Louis Agassiz, TH Huxley, Charles Lyell, and Archibald Geikie. Charles
Darwin wrote to Gordon asking for orchids and John Lubbock came to
look at kitchen middens. Few women ventured into this arena; it was the
domain of men. Of the 1,300 letters of George Gordon's correspondence,
cared for by Elgin Museum, only a handful are from women, and of those
only one is about science or natural history: Catherine Ross wrote from
Rhives, Ross-shire about shells and mosses.[2] Botany was an acceptable
occupation for women – a female assistant could be useful. Mary
MacCallum Webster makes a brief reference to a Miss Robertson of
Thornhill House, Forres.[3] Miss Robertson and her brother ran an academy
for young gentlemen and it was at Thornhill House that Thomas
Edmondston (1825-1846) stayed in the summer of 1844 when he was
giving botany lectures in Moray. Miss Robertson appears to have been one
of those useful botanical assistants. Any other early female botanists in
Moray seem to have gone unrecorded.

Eliza Maria Gordon Cumming was one of the few women drawn into
the geological debate. Like Jane Maxwell, Lady Eliza Gordon Cumming,

238

Grisel Dow's University of Aberdeen geology excursion, Newmachar 1910 (Marjorie Whytock)

half a century after Duchess Jane, provided a social environment where great intellects could meet. Her talents in horticultural and geology were tested in the gardens and quarries of the Altyre estate. By the time Eliza Gordon Cumming was finding fossils, the Enlightenment was over, but it was in part the discovery of the Old Red Sandstone fossil fishes and the Permo-Triassic reptiles that stimulated the growth of intellectual society in the north of Scotland. Eliza Gordon Cumming was part of that society, until her early death ended her contribution. Her legacy today is her fossil collection, to be found mostly in Neuchatel, London and Edinburgh.[4]

At Findhorn, just down the road from Altyre, Grace Milne was also drawn to geology. The niece of Hugh Falconer, she had learnt geology at his knee, and, when her first husband died, she travelled abroad with her uncle, acting as his assistant, and becoming very knowledgeable. Talented in many ways, she wrote novels and concerned herself with women's education, being involved in the establishment of Somerville College.

By the twentieth century more was on offer: women could go to university and study science. It was not necessarily an easy path to follow, especially without a wealthy father to offer support, but, as zoologists Isabella Gordon and Anna Buchan demonstrated, it was achievable and more. Who would have thought in 1901 when Isabella, a labourer's daughter, was born that she would be a guest of honour at Emperor Hirohito's sixtieth birthday celebrations in the 1960s? Anna Buchan, born into the fishing community of Rosehearty, was able to study as a mature student when in her thirties, ultimately gaining a PhD.

If zoology was difficult for women to access as students, engineering was almost out of bounds. Lesley Souter of Elgin had her family's experience for support, but ultimately it was up to her to fight the prejudice, and to do that she had to be first class – only in that way could she win through to the male precinct.

There has long been a tradition of amateur naturalists building up impressive knowledge of their local area. Mary McCallum Webster was one of those amateurs, who put in a prodigious amount of work, organising local support, and finally producing, in 1978, one of the first modern local floras in Scotland. No one would call her *Flora of Moray, Nairn and East Inverness* an amateurish affair. She may have started off as an amateur, but she became a professional along the way.

# Eliza Gordon Cumming

*Eliza Maria Campbell, born probably Inveraray, c.1799; married Sir William Gordon Cumming, 11 September 1815; died Altyre, 21 April 1842.*

Eliza Maria Campbell was known for her great beauty and many accomplishments, including gardening, painting and salmon fishing, and is remembered particularly for her fossil collecting and collaboration with some of the leading palaeontologists of her day.

Eliza's parents, Colonel John Campbell and Lady Charlotte Maria Campbell, owned the island of Islay, and Shawfield, a small estate on the banks of the Clyde, in the parish of Rutherglen and county of Lanark. Their marriage sounds from correspondence to have been a miserable affair. Eliza was the second daughter and had five sisters (Beaujolais, Julia, Emma, Constance Adelaide and Eleanora) and two brothers (Walter and John). Several of her siblings' names she gave to her own children. Her father died in 1809, and in Walter's charge, Islay and Shawfield had to be sold as the family fortune had 'melted away in the hands of his agents'. Eleanora married in her sister's sitting room at Altyre in 1819.

Lady Charlotte, Eliza's widowed mother, was travelling in Italy in 1814 'with some of her beautiful daughters' when the romantic meeting of this daughter and her future husband took place. Shortly before this happened, Eliza had been persuaded to have her fortune told by an Italian lady who predicted that the political troubles already brewing in Florence would worsen while they were there, to their danger. They would be rescued by two fair-haired Scots brothers, and she would marry the elder. And so it came to pass, that William Gordon Cumming and his younger brother Charlie, on their Grand Tour, heard of the ladies' plight, and escorted them to safety in Switzerland. The marriage took place in the house of the British Envoy in Zurich the following year, when Eliza was seventeen. Initially her name became Lady Comyn-Gordon, until later the order of the family names was reversed.

The beauty of Eliza ran in the maternal line of her family. Her mother, Lady Charlotte, in old age was still 'stately and fair to see', and her grandmother, Elizabeth, was one of the three beautiful Miss Gunnings 'whose combined loveliness set first Dublin and then London crazy'. Eliza's painting by Raeburn was sold by her grandson, Sir William, at Christie's in 1920 for £1,470. It was said to have been painted in 1817, and in the accompanying letter, the artist states it is 'the handsomest female picture I have yet painted'. Her youngest daughter Eka recalled in

Eliza Maria, Lady Gordon Cumming of Altyre, painted by Saunders c.1830

her autobiography, *Memories*, her mother's 'glorious masses of hair falling in clustering ringlets far below her waist'.

Lady Charlotte outlived her daughter Eliza, and did not die until 1861. Her second marriage was extremely controversial and contributed to the rift with Eliza.

During Eliza's lifetime, major changes were taking place in agriculture in Scotland, and in the management of the Gordon Cumming lands. Her husband's father, Alexander Penrose, and first baronet of Altyre and Gordonstoun, had died unexpectedly in 1806; he had already begun improvement of the farm land, guided by his factors, who continued to advise the new young laird. In the early years of marriage at least, Sir William saw his property as a source of income to finance his life abroad. Home was Altyre, but the couple were often away on the continent and their first daughter (Anne) Seymour was born in Naples in 1818. The season was spent in London, or as Eka recalls, sometimes Paris, where Eliza and her older daughters were granted a special permit to copy paintings in the Louvre.

Despite the size of the estates, and the improvements made, Sir William lived his whole lairdship beyond his means. The rents never met the expenses, there were outstanding debts from the legal costs of the disputed inheritance of Gordonstoun and they spent lavishly on the restoration of that neglected mansion. In addition, there were many daughters, either unmarried or requiring dowries, and an heir who took up an expensive career in the cavalry and married without himself securing a usable dowry.

In 1829, the year of the Muckle Spate, there was severe flooding in Moray and surrounding areas. Sir Thomas Dick Lauder tells of the great damage done at Altyre:

> the current was running furiously among the hothouses and pineries, and actually carried off the gardener on one of his melon frames, to take an aquatic excursion among his gooseberry bushes and cauliflowers.

Lauder goes on to describe the damage done by the River Lossie to their estate at Dallas, with the water level at three feet in the village houses, seventeen families left destitute and the Gordon Cummings' loss on the two estates 'no less than £8,000'.

The following year Sir William had to apply to sell off as much of the entailed lands of Gordonstoun, Dallas and Altyre as might be necessary to pay off the debts affecting the lands and estates. This involved an act of parliament, in the reign of King George IV. There is a clause that states that if lands over which Lady Gordon Cumming's annuity (£1,000) is secured be sold, other lands are to be substituted in security; sadly this would prove an unnecessary precaution, because she died young. It remains a fascinating document for the detail of description of the estate, the names of farms and tenants, and the debts.

Eliza's greenhouse at Altyre was the first in Moray. She not only delighted in the garden she created, and the colour and fragrance of the flowers, but carried out experiments in plant breeding and corresponded with the botanist, WJ Hooker. She ensured her staff had access to the best books on botany and horticulture, 'and many successful gardeners scattered over the world owed their start in life to her encouragement'.

With her daughters she shared her skills in needlework and art, and with her sons, her passion for salmon fishing – she was an expert fly tier. Fishing was an unusual interest for a woman of her time. Her difficulties when faced with one of the Findhorn's notorious flash floods can be imagined as she leapt for her life over the rocks, from her stance midstream to the safety of the bank. She may have passed on to her children her taste for travel too: Roualeyn, 'The Mighty Lion Hunter', William, tiger hunter in the Indian subcontinent, and Eka, world traveller, all of whom published accounts of their adventures; three other sons spent long periods abroad and Ida (Adelaide) went to the Crimean War with her husband. Family letters suggest she was much loved by all the family, although the children (she had fifteen) were often left to their own devices while their parents were abroad.

It is for her part in the story of the discovery and description of fossil fishes in Scotland that Eliza deserves particular recognition. It was probably Dr John Malcolmson, formerly of the Honourable East India Company and home on sick leave for two years from Madras, who introduced Eliza to fossils and their collection, while staying with his mother in Forres. They may have met when Malcolmson was exploring the rocks in the Altyre Burn, but she does not seem to have become enthusiastic about fossils until after he introduced her to the beautifully preserved fish fossils from Lethen Bar. This was a limestone quarry some ten kilometres west of Altyre, by the Sluie Ferry over the Findhorn, and a new find site for fossil fish of the middle Old Red Sandstone. Malcolmson, with his friend Stables, factor of Cawdor, made the discovery in March 1839. By autumn 1839, Eliza and her eldest daughter Seymour were making pen and water colour sketches of the fossils which Malcolmson hoped to use for what would have been his ground-breaking memoir. Unfortunately it was not completed before he returned to India in early 1840, where he died in 1844.

Through Malcolmson, Eliza's collection and illustrations came to the attention of many other geologists, amateur and professional, who corresponded with her or visited Altyre. In September 1840 the British Association for the Advancement of Science reunion was held in Glasgow, and not long before this, the voracious collector, Lord Enniskillen was at Altyre and received a most generous donation of fossils from Eliza. The BA meeting was also attended by Professor Louis Agassiz from Switzerland, the Reverend William Buckland, president of the Geological Society and Sir Roderick Murchison of Tarradale and director of the Geological Survey; the former two gentlemen visited Altyre very soon afterwards, and Murchison possibly sometime later – after a letter to Eliza describing the BA

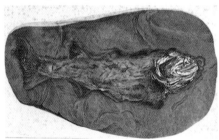

meeting and signing himself 'your Ladyship's geological slave'. She was able to show new fossils to Agassiz and these and her drawings contributed significantly to his *Monographie Des Poissons Fossiles Du Vieux Grès Rouge* (1844–1845). Nodules from Lethen Bar were being brought back by the cartload, and when the house was overflowing, fossils were stored under a verandah, thanks to, as Buckland put it: 'Sir William... supplying the necessary Corps de Mineurs for your subter-

Lithograph used in *Monographie Des Poissons Fossiles Du Vieux Grès Rouge* 1844–1845 by Louis Agassiz, from Eliza Gordon Cumming's painting of a fossil fish, *Cheirolepis cummingiae,* found at Lethen Bar on the Altyre Estate. The fossil is now in the collection of National Museums Scotland (Falconer Museum, Moray Council Museums Service)

ranean fishing...' Hugh Miller, the Cromarty stonemason and editor of *The Witness*, recorded that he last saw Eliza and a new fossil 'a few weeks previous to her lamented death', although this timing is unlikely, given her state of health.

Through her lavish donations and subsequent sales, the 'Altyre' fossils have ended up in various collections, including Agassiz' university at Neuchatel and the National Museums Scotland in Edinburgh. The late Dr S Mahala Andrews of the Royal Scottish Museum examined many of the 'Altyre' fossils and published two very detailed papers in the 1980s about the discovery of fossil fish in Scotland, in which Eliza features both for her collecting and for her social role in promoting the exchange of fossils and scientific ideas. More recently, the Geological Society published *The Role of Women in the History of Geology*, in which the contributions of nineteenth century women, including that of Eliza, are assessed, especially in the field of palaeontology. Charlotte Murchison, Mary Buckland and Grace Milne also took an active role as field geologists and recorders, as assistants to their husbands, and independently.

From letters written by Seymour to Murchison, in the days before and after her mother's death, it sounds as if Eliza was regretting having given away their fossil illustrations, as she hoped to publish them under her own name, or possibly as an insert in Murchison's *Siluria*. Seymour was also anxious to put the record straight that some of their fossil drawings are a compilation of incomplete specimens, and another acquired an extra fin in a preference for symmetry!

All this beauty and action came prematurely to an end when Eliza died in her forty-fourth year, less than a month after her last child was born. It seems she had not recovered from injuries received some time previously in stopping a bolting horse attached to a gig carrying a terrified woman. The introduction of anaesthetics was still four years away; she was kept 'soaked in laudanum' which, while it did not completely dull the pain, may have impaired her unborn baby and 'festered itself upon her constitution'.

The *Forres Gazette* obituary is full of praise for this 'excellent and distinguished lady'. It tells of the 'mournful cavalcade' accompanying her on foot, by conveyance and on horseback for the sixteen-mile journey from Altyre to the family resting place at Gordonstoun. Business was suspended in Forres, the streets were lined with mourners while tenants, gentlemen and clergy 'both established and dissenting' accompanied the coffin. She is described as a 'ministering angel'.

Her death is recorded on the Gordon Cumming memorial tablet in the Michael Kirk, Gordonstoun, then still a mausoleum, and she was interred in the vault. Her husband married again and died in 1854. (JT)

# Grace Milne

*Grace Anne Milne, born Findhorn, 18 December 1832; married 1) George McCall, 18 October 1854; 2) Joseph Prestwich, 26 February 1870; died Shoreham, 31 August 1899.*

A respected geologist and also author and biographer, Grace Milne supported the right of women to be educated at university and wrote valuable biographies of her famous uncle, Hugh Falconer, and of her husband.

Grace was the eldest of four children; her mother, Louisa Falconer, came from a Forres family of merchants. Her father, James Milne, was a hard working ship owner at Findhorn who died in 1853 aged fifty-four at the family home of Abbeyside.

Grace was a bright child; by the time she was four, she was able to read the New Testament with competence and she enjoyed a happy childhood within a loving family. She was twenty when her father died. It seemed as if her future would be secure when, on 18 October 1854 at Abbeyside, she married George McCall, a Glasgow merchant. The young couple moved to 300 Bath Crescent Glasgow, doubtless full of happy and high expectations.

The marriage was short-lived. In March 1856 George McCall died at home and two months later their infant son James died, also in Bath Crescent. Within three years Grace had lost her father, become a widow and then a bereaved mother. She had a supportive family and was helped through her understandable depression by her mother and younger sisters. From then on her mother's younger brother, Hugh, was to play a most important and defining role in her life.

Hugh Falconer, born in 1808, was a multi-talented scientist. He had graduated in medicine and in natural history and had spent much of his working life in India, beginning work as an assistant surgeon for the British East India Company in Bengal. While there he had developed his reputation as a botanist and for his research into fossils and geology. He had been elected a fellow of the Royal Society in 1845 and enjoyed close connections with Charles Darwin, supporting him in his theory of evolution. Although ill-health forced him to leave India, he returned a few years later as superintendent of the Calcutta Botanical Garden and as professor of botany in the Medical College, Calcutta, near his older brother Alexander who was a merchant there. While in Calcutta he wrote frequently to his niece Grace, describing his expeditions and discoveries. Frustratingly, ill health once again forced him to return to Britain in 1855, just a few months before Grace was widowed and endured the loss of her child.

Grace Milne, date unknown (Moray Council
Museums Service)

Grace had always been keenly interested in science and by 1858 she had begun to work closely with her uncle. They had exchanged many letters about scientific theories and discoveries and she was able to help him with drawings and classifications of specimens. Because of his poor health, Hugh's research was now confined to Europe.

Grace travelled with him during his European excursions, proving herself to be an able assistant. On these trips she met many interesting people, including the Italian revolutionary, Garibaldi. One of Hugh's scientific friends was the inspirational Scotswoman Mary Somerville, a self-taught mathematician and theoretical physicist who, for the sake of her husband's health, had settled to live in Italy. Despite the personal tragedies of the death of three of her six children, Mary Somerville had been deeply involved in London intellectual circles and hers was the first name on the petition for female suffrage presented to parliament by John Stuart Mill. In her late fifties she began her output of science writing and her '*Molecular and Microscopic Science*' was published in 1869 when she was in her eighties. She was fifty-eight years older than Grace, and was a determined advocate for higher education for women at a time when women were not allowed in universities. Meeting her would have been a stimulating experience for Grace. Like Mary, Grace was deeply concerned about female education and in later years was to be one of the patrons of a new college for women.

Grace dealt with much of the correspondence between her uncle and prominent scientists, including that with his friend the gifted amateur fossil and geological enthusiast, Joseph Prestwich. By 1863 Grace was staying in Edinburgh and, as well as pursuing her own interests, she continued her involvement with her uncle and his work, copying out and forwarding scientific articles on his behalf. Her uncle encouraged and advised her with her own writing, as well as exchanging information about the latest research and the controversy it had engendered. In a letter to her from

London he commented on the 'Moulin Quignon jaw' and his work with Prestwich, as well as enquiring about her move to a new home at 4 Chester Street, Edinburgh. Hugh Falconer's last project included an investigation of the Gibraltar cave finds in 1864 and Grace must have been amused by his letter to her from Gibraltar describing the governor's wife who, on religious grounds, disapproved of geology!

Hugh died in 1865, a month before his fifty-sixth birthday. His botanical notes, specimens and drawings were given to Kew Gardens but he had never forgotten his roots in Forres and, like his brother Alexander, left a bequest for a museum in that town, as well as bequeathing some of his important fossil collection to be housed there. The Falconer Museum in Forres eventually opened its doors in 1872.

Grace was then still a young woman of thirty-three with a passionate interest in science and geology. The death of her uncle did not mean the end of her involvement with the scientific innovators of the day. In 1870 she married Joseph Prestwich who had been a friend and colleague of her uncle for many years.

Born in 1812, Joseph was of financial necessity a wine merchant but he had been well educated in Paris and London. As well as being interested in many branches of science, he was a keen mineralogist and geologist, and in 1865 had been awarded a medal by the Royal Society for his research. The following year he was chosen as a commissioner by the society to inquire into coal fields and produced several reports on the subject. Having built a country home in Shoreham, Kent, in 1869, he married Grace, retired from business in 1872 and was able to concentrate fully on his 'geologising'. Two years later he was invited to take the chair of geology at Oxford, a post he occupied until 1887.

Although nearly twenty years younger than her husband, Grace with her intelligence, social experience and understanding of geological research, was the perfect companion. The couple divided their time between their house in Shoreham and Oxford University. With the encouragement of her husband, Grace developed her writing skills, contributing many articles to Blackwood magazine and to magazines designed for the prosperous middle classes. She was an extensive communicator, writing articles and novels to illustrate a way of life and essays to inform and educate. In 1875 she published her first novel *The Harbour Bar*, a descriptive work set in her native Findhorn and revealing her intimate knowledge of the fisher folk and the local area with intense descriptions of the local scenery of Forres and Altyre.

As well as travel articles and scientific papers Grace also helped her husband in the preparation of his own lectures and diagrams. She worked as his able assistant, travelling with him on his excursions, recording and writing essays which included important reports on the complex geology of the Chesil Bank and the area of the future Channel tunnel. She was also actively involved in the production of his standard work on geology. Grace was acknowledged as a geologist in her own right, respected by the fellows of the Geological Society and recorded as an endearing and friendly character and 'a good and highly cultured woman'.

Not only concerned with geology and literature, Grace was very aware of the difficulties faced by women in achieving their full potential. She concerned herself with the first attempt to initiate university education for women when, in 1873, a group of Oxford dons and their female relatives began the Association for Higher Education for Women. The idea was ahead of its time, those dons opposing the concept insisting that serious study would put a strain on the female constitution and lead to mental and physical debilitation – possibly leading to infertility!

Opposition was eventually overcome and the association was instrumental in the foundation in 1879 of Somerville College at Oxford University. This was the first college which at last gave women a chance for a university education and was named after Mary Somerville, whom Grace had met many years earlier in Italy.

Joseph continued, with the help of his wife, to produce papers about his researches. He was knighted in 1896 and Grace became Lady Prestwich, but Joseph died just a few months later. Although by then she was in delicate health, Grace was determined to ensure a proper record was made of her husband's achievements. With the help of her sisters, Isabella, Margaret and Louise, she was able to complete his biography and published *Life and Letters of Sir Joseph Prestwich, edited by his Wife* two months before she died aged sixty-six, at her home in Shoreham in August 1899. Her book about Hugh Falconer *Essays, Descriptive and Biographical, by Grace, Lady Prestwich* was edited by LE Milne and published in 1901 after her death. The biography of Joseph Prestwich by Grace, and also a biography of Grace by her sister Louise are in the Falconer Museum, Forres. Grace never forgot her birthplace and, following the example of her uncles Hugh and Alexander, left a bequest to the Forres museum in Moray. (JM)

# Anna Buchan

*Anna Buchan, born Rosehearty, 2 September 1897; married Edward Arthur Suckling, 2 April 1937; died Aberdeen, 19 July 1964.*

Anna went to Aberdeen University as a mature student, and gained a PhD in zoology. She worked on the curatorial side in the Marischal Museum, Aberdeen and in Elgin Museum.

Anna's father, Alexander, was a fisherman at Rosehearty; in 1907, the family moved to Elgin. He worked for fifteen years at Low's net makers, and then became foreman at Hamilton's Nets, not retiring until 1946, in his late seventies. He was also an elder of Elgin High Church.

The First World War broke out soon after Anna left school, and she went into munitions work. After the war, she worked in an office. She had three brothers, and when her youngest brother was working for his BSc at Aberdeen University, he persuaded her she was well able to study for a science degree herself. She graduated BSc in 1930, with honours in 1931 and obtained her PhD (zoology) in 1935, for which her supervisor was Professor James Ritchie – who also examined some animal bones excavated by Sylvia Benton at Covesea.

Anna's thesis is titled *Investigation of the Glacial and Postglacial Deposits of Spynie.* Her field work was carried out in the old clay pits between what is now the disused railway line, and the road from Elgin to Lossiemouth, near Windyridge. At that time, the pits were in use during the summer, which is when she unearthed the remains used in her paper. The pits were first opened for the working of clay in 1897, and fossils had been found there over the years, including a couple of brittle stars (ELGNM 1978.943C) on display in Elgin Museum, probably donated by one of the Christie family, owners of the Morayshire Brick and Tile Works. No detailed observations were made until Anna's preliminary investigation in 1931, and

Anna Buchan aged about twenty-five years
(Dr Alison Hoppen)

Anna researching for 'Lamps Through the Ages'
(Dr Alison Hoppen)

her work is cited by JD Peacock, principal author of *The Geology of the Elgin District* (1968), in a paper in 1999.

Her conclusions on the story of climate and environmental change in the Spynie area are based on study of the stratigraphical and palaeontological evidence from her own observations. The deepest layers in the pits are boulder clay from the time Moray was covered with an ice sheet of great thickness. As the glaciers began to retreat, which took place in a series of readvances and retreats, a depression of the land took place by at least 100 feet, so that an ice-bound land surface was replaced by an Arctic-cold sea. Gradually, as deduced from the nature of the plants in the peat layer, land emerged from the former sea floor. A more temperate climate next prevailed, and Anna found the remains of red deer, elk, horse (*Equus caballus*) and long-fronted ox (*Bos longifrons*). The peat is overlain by marine sand and shells from the time when the sea level rose again, and the current surface deposits of wind-blown sand and soil relate to the final retreat of the sea and elevation of the land to their present levels.

Working conditions were not easy. Anna describes difficulties with boring for samples: getting permission to dig, and then boring to a depth of forty feet, working in water and using handtools. Many pounds of clay from different parts of the pits were washed and carefully examined for fossils, the earliest being pre-glacial and these mainly from the Jurassic period.

In 1937, when Anna was nearly forty, she married Edward Suckling, in Glasgow. He was ten years older than her and born in Takeley, Essex; they had no children. During the Second World War, Edward was a conscientious objector. Another Anna, and her brother Samuel, children of District Pastor McKibben of the Apostolic Church in Aberdeen, remember the couple there during the war. (The church seems to have had its origins in the Welsh Revival of the early twentieth century; its first convention was held in Glasgow in 1920.) Edward had recently learned to drive, and was willing and able to be overseer for their church in Peterhead. He had trained in London's Bond Street as a hairdresser and had businesses in Rosemount, Aberdeen and in Inverurie. They remember Anna's relationship with them as 'special', and that she was 'such a gentle lady'.

Anna worked as a museum assistant in the Anthropological Museum, Marischal College, Aberdeen University from 1946–48. An illustrated article under her married name is published in the Aberdeen University Review of Summer 1947, entitled 'Lamps Through the Ages'. Some 200 lamps from

Anna and her husband Edward Suckling
(Sheila Dick)

around the world had been donated to the Museum by George Johnston, of a family of paper makers. Anna judged the most remarkable historically to be a red clay lamp dated to about 4777 BC, when Egypt was ruled by Mena, its first king. Researching the collection was probably the stimulus for writing this broader article about the history of artificial lighting, in which she also describes the development of the Scottish cruisie.

Her mother, also Anna, died in Dr Gray's Hospital in 1948, and Anna moved back to Elgin to look after her widowed father. Her husband opened a hairdresser's business at 22 South Street. He was also pastor of the Apostolic Church at 31 Academy Street. Their nephews and nieces recall happy holidays as children spent with them in Elgin, with visits to the beach; Anna 'had a very gentle and charming personality', but her husband, 'a dominant man', tended to be over-zealous in forcing his religion on them.

Anna was active in Elgin Museum from at least 1948, perhaps even before she left the Marischal. She is mentioned in the minutes of the Elgin and Moray Literary and Scientific Society (forerunner of the Moray Society) variously as Mrs or Dr Suckling. In February 1948:

> The Curator drew attention to the condition of the geological department in which the various objects had been re-arranged, principally by Mr Christie, under the guidance of Dr Anna Suckling... The Secretary was instructed to thank Dr Suckling for her 'good efforts in this matter'.

In June the following year, she is 'Mrs':

> It had been agreed at a previous meeting that no honorarium was necessary in respect of work done by Mrs Suckling but she had been sent a letter of thanks. It was now agreed to send £5 to Mrs Suckling in recognition of her work.

Later in 1949, Anna became a director of the society, and in 1951, she was appointed honorary joint curator with WE Watson, of the wood and sawmills in Elgin. Again Anna was at work on the internationally important geology collection and is recorded as cleaning, reviewing and rearranging the specimens in the store and on display. Watson resigned in 1952 and died soon after, and Anna was then sole curator, until she resigned the following year. Her father died in 1954, aged eighty-four. In 1961, Anna was again appointed to a post in the museum, as museum keeper, but she withdrew the same day in favour of her friend Miss AC Kennedy.

Within Elgin Museum, Anna is remembered in the alcove 'Where are the Women of History?' in the *People and Place* exhibition about the past 1,000 years of life in Moray. Dr Alison Hoppen, daughter of the brother who suggested Anna go to university, was very proud of her aunt, and donated a folder of Anna's anatomical zoological drawings (ELGNM 1998.1) which probably date to her undergraduate study. One of these, of the skeleton of a frog, is in the display. Also mentioned in this area of the museum are Mary McCallum Webster, Jessie Kesson and Sylvia Benton.

Anna was widowed in 1963. She died the following year at the age of sixty-six in Foresterhill Hospital, Aberdeen, from bacterial endocarditis, having had no previous heart problem. Just before she died 'she was as usual solicitous of other members of the family'.

The headline of her obituary in *The Elgin Courant* reads 'was widow of an Elgin hairdresser'. (JT)

# Isabella Gordon

*Isabella Gordon, born Keith, 18 May 1901; died Carlisle, 11 May 1988.*

Isabella Gordon was the first female full-time permanent member of staff at the British Museum (Natural History). Her researches into crabs and shrimps took her all over the globe. A high profile visit to Japan to meet Emperor Hirohito was public evidence of her international standing.

Isabella was the daughter of Margaret Lamb, a servant, and James Gordon, a labourer. Though unmarried at the time of her birth, her parents married later, and Isabella had two younger brothers, John and James. Isabella did well at school and gained a bursary of eight pounds a year to enable her to stay on at Keith Grammar School until the sixth year. A further bursary led to her matriculation at the University of Aberdeen.

After the First World War, the University of Aberdeen was flooded with ex-service men. The first year medical students numbered about 180. Isabella, still a student herself, demonstrated to the zoology classes, and the money she earned helped her vulnerable financial position. She graduated, in 1922, BSc with special distinction in chemistry, botany and zoology – the equivalent of first class honours. Appointed senior demonstrator in zoology at the university in 1922, Isabella also attended classes at Aberdeen Training College, becoming qualified to teach at secondary level. But biology was not taught in the North-East and she needed to look elsewhere for a career.

The newly funded Kilgour Senior Scholarship, a competitive exam, provided the answer, with an opportunity to work on corals under Professor J Arthur Thomson at Aberdeen, followed by a postgraduate research scholarship under Professor EW MacBride in London studying echinoderms (sea urchins and their relations). The scholarship was extended to three years, and four papers were produced. Throughout her working life Isabella contributed papers in zoological journals; altogether she published over 130 articles. Following the award of her PhD (University of London) in 1926 she gained a Commonwealth Fund Scholarship and visited the United States of America.

We can only guess how exciting the trip to the States was for Isabella, a working-class girl from Keith. In Britain 1926 was the time of the general strike; a woman could not expect to have a career.

Dr Gordon spent two years in the States working on echinoderms and making important professional connections. Initially she was based at Woods Hole at Cape Cod, on the eastern seaboard, but during her time in America she visited laboratories in California, Washington and Connecticut,

Isabella Gordon
(The Natural History Museum, London)

and also made a trip to Jamaica.

In 1928 Isabella was awarded a DSc from Aberdeen. She was now an experienced zoologist, able to look at the intricate details of the invertebrates she studied and to differentiate closely related species one from another. WT Calman, keeper of zoology at the British Museum (Natural History), was keen to appoint Isabella as a member of his department, and in 1928 she returned from America and was appointed assistant keeper 2nd class. She was in charge of crustacea and pycnogonida under Calman, at what is now called the Natural History Museum – that impressive building, decorated with buff and blue terracotta, in South Kensington. By 1946 she was principal scientific officer.

There are over 40,000 species of crustacea in the world and Dr Gordon's task at the museum was to study as many as possible, to understand the relationship between different groups, to name new species and to publish papers about her researches. She visited various museums and marine laboratories in her quest to learn more. In 1931 she was granted ten days leave to study Pycnogonida (spider crabs) in the museums of Paris and Hamburg.

Dr Gordon's notebooks are full of delicate and intricate watercolour paintings of crabs and shrimps; her papers are illustrated by her own drawings. Some of her illustrations were done at Millport on the Isle of Cumbrae, where the weather in September 1950 was 'so bad that hardly any new things came to hand'. Besides the research and publications, there were enquiries to answer. The British Museum enquiries about crustaceans were many and varied, from across the world. On one occasion in 1958 a physicist from the Atomic Weapons Research Station at Aldermaston enquired about the deposition of calcium in the Christmas Island crayfish. Dr Gordon answered all enquiries diligently, often including drawings to illustrate relevant details. She regularly travelled abroad, attending meetings such as the International Congress of Zoology in Lisbon (1935), Paris (1948) and Copenhagen (1958).

Around 1960 the keeper of zoology, FC Fraser, applied to the museum panel for the special promotion which would give Isabella due recognition:

Dr Gordon is in the first class of taxonomists working on Crustacea. She is the most senior Principal Officer in the Zoology Department and is of an age and scientific stature comparable with others who have been selected for Special Promotion. Her status is recognised internationally by the eminent carcinologists of the world and she is a leading member of a small but distinguished group of world authorities on the Decapoda (see attached leaflet). She is also editor of a newly established journal dealing with crustaceans.

The application was unsuccessful and FC Fraser was 'personally extremely disappointed'. Dr Trewavas (a woman) had also recently been refused Special Promotion and Dr Fraser wondered why the two had failed – was it because of their age? He had been sure that Dr Gordon would have been successful. He expressed his thoughts to Dr Morrison-Scott on 1 June 1960:

> In my opinion she is really of FRS standing and is a much better zoologist than many FRSs I could name. Is it, again, that taxonomists are regarded generally as in a rather lower stratum in the zoological world and that the Panel has just got no idea of the sort of work that the Museum tries to do?

Despite the lack of recognition from the panel, Dr Gordon's expertise was called on across the world, with invitations to attend conferences and symposiums. The host country was usually willing to pay her expenses for these trips.

In April 1961 Japan was celebrating the sixtieth birthday of Emperor Hirohito, himself a marine biologist, and Dr Gordon was asked to join in the celebrations as a special guest. Besides a two-hour meeting with the emperor, she gave a public lecture to a large audience, spent some time dredging in Sagami Bay and visited various universities. She also attended the inaugural meeting of the Carcinological Society of Japan, when she was elected as one of three honorary founder members. The Japanese wished to honour her with the Order of the Rising Sun, but the British Government would not allow this. The British press made something of this refusal, but Isabella deplored the fuss. On arriving home an exhibition of her Japanese collection was arranged for the trustees of the British Museum. It was in November of 1961 that she was awarded the OBE.

Six days' leave were granted to Dr Gordon in order to attend the symposium on evolution of crustacea at Harvard in 1962. An awe-inspiring 713 specimens were brought back from America in 1966 after attending a conference in New Orleans and visiting Washington; somehow she had to organise and study these specimens.

A major visit to Africa took place in 1964 at the invitation of Conseil Scientifique pour l'Afrique to attend a meeting in Zanzibar. Dr Gordon was invited for ten days, but saw the sense in extending the trip. FC Fraser was willing to grant thirty-five days additional leave and he managed to raise the funding required:

> I should say that Dr Gordon is one of the foremost zoologists in the world in her particular specialisation and has in the past been consulted not infrequently by the people in East Africa concerned with commercial shell fisheries and also by the medical people concerned with River Blindness.

Dr Gordon visited various places in Kenya and Uganda and reported back on visits to fish farms and laboratories. River blindness was, and still is, one of the pressing problems of Uganda. It is carried by black fly larvae which attach themselves to river crabs. Dr Gordon reported:

> The naming of River Crabs in the Museum is exceedingly difficult, and I thought that it would perhaps help matters if I could see some of them alive in their natural habitats. It was not possible to visit all the scattered areas of Uganda, but live specimens were brought in from streams in the Mount Elgon region to Kampala. Then I was able to do some actual collecting from rivers in S.W. Uganda, from the Budongo Forest near Lake Albert, to the Kagera River on the Tanganyika border. These crabs, together with those from Mount Elgon and other areas, will be examined as soon as possible, so that the entomologists may have names for them.

A visit to a part of Kenya where the river blindness had been eradicated was also useful. Dr Gordon commented:

> Now that I know a little of local conditions, and the surprising lack of knowledge of the economic Crustacea, I am better able to assist with information and literature.

Certainly Dr Gordon was an academic, but she was not confined to an ivory tower. Her willingness to communicate and assist others was part of her success. There was, however, a touch of the absent-minded professor about Isabella.

FC Fraser defended her on more than one occasion:

Isabella in the laboratory at the British Museum (The Natural History Museum, London)

I have long ago abandoned any idea of keeping up with the way that Dr Gordon arranges what should be, more or less, routine matters. [1962]

and

> her brilliance as a zoologist and particularly as a carcinologist is nearly equalled by her lack of concern about doing the ordinary run of things in an orthodox way. [1963]

Isabella was fortunate in her colleagues WT Calman (1871–1952) and FC Fraser (1903–1978), the two keepers of zoology whom she worked under for the greater part of her career. The British Museum was very much a man's world, largely old-fashioned and ridden with class and gender prejudice, but their backgrounds were not dissimilar to hers. WT Calman came from Dundee, where his interest in biology was fostered at Dundee High School. He left school at sixteen and continued his biological studies through the Dundee Working Men's Field Club and the Dundee Naturalists' Society. A job as a laboratory assistant enabled him to study for a degree. FC Fraser, two years younger than Isabella, attended Dingwall Academy and Glasgow University. Both men were known for their good humour, as was Isabella. Her sense of humour is illustrated by an exchange of limericks following the publication of a book review she had written on 'A thermophilous shrimp from Tunisia'. AJ Bateman, geneticist at Manchester, sent her the following rhyme:

> A thermophilous shrimp from Tunisia
> said: when it gets cold I get busier
> I dig a hole
> and fill it with coal
> then there's nowhere as warm as it is 'ere.

To which Isabella replied:

> The idea's OK – but Aplysia
> is the rhyme I would choose for Tunysia
> A purist and Scot
> I simply could *not*
> pronounce it to rhyme with 'it is ier-r-r!!

Although Dr Gordon retired in 1966 she did not stop work altogether and she was able to retain a room in the museum. In 1967 she attended an FAO World Conference in Mexico City on behalf of the museum. She continued her work on the editorial board of the journal *Crustaceana*, and she remained a member of the curatorial committee of the Linnean Society until 1981, by which time she was known as 'the Grand Old Lady of Carcinology'.

All her life Isabella suffered from ill health; flu, tonsillitis and bronchial ailments were constantly battled against. In 1983 she suffered a stroke which partially disabled her. She managed to live by herself until 1987 when she went to live at her nephew's home in Carlisle, where she died a year later.

In the obituary by two of her colleagues, LB Holthuis and RW Ingle, Isabella is described as a 'delightful person, always ready to help others'.

The study of biodiversity and ecosystems, the consideration of major conservation issues and the understanding of the effects of climate change are all dependent on a knowledge of the individual species that inhabit the planet. The knowledge that our present-day taxonomists have is built upon the scholarship and dedication of people like Isabella Gordon. (SB)

# Mary McCallum Webster

*Mary McCallum Webster, born Sussex 31 December 1906; died Forres,*
*7 November 1985.*

Mary, a self-taught botanist, became a leading field botanist in the British Isles. In later life she researched and wrote her *Flora of Moray, Nairn and East Inverness.*

Mary McCallum Webster was born in Sussex to Scottish parents, Alexander McCallum Webster of Old Meldrum and Norah Kathleen Gray. They were married in Paddington in 1904 and Mary was born two years later. She was just four when she was captivated by an unusual white violet growing in a Sussex ditch and she joined the Wild Flower Society as early as 1915 when only nine years old. Her paternal grandmother, Mrs ML Wedgewood, was a keen botanist and undoubtedly had a profound influence on her granddaughter. Mrs Wedgewood had established a herbarium at Marlborough College and had had a bramble *Rubus wedgewoodiae* named after her. She is known to have botanised in Moray towards the end of the nineteenth century with Dr GC Druce.

Mary was educated at home until the age of fifteen by a procession of governesses: nineteen in seven years. After that she achieved her ambition of going to boarding school 'to play games and wear a gym tunic'. She went to West Heath and then Ham Common before attending a finishing school in Brussels.

Though botany was always Mary's best subject at school and became a life-long interest, she was also both artistic and athletic. She played hockey for her district, became a distinguished tennis player and was invited to play at Wimbledon in 1925 but didn't go for lack of funding. Later she won the North of Scotland Ladies Singles for four consecutive years in the early 1950s and was allowed to keep the silver cup which later stood gleaming on her mantelpiece at Rose Cottage, Dyke. She continued to play tennis well into her seventies and those that played with her remember her acid comments when she was presented with a drop shot that she could no longer reach. The only time that botany took second place in her life was during the Wimbledon fortnight when she remained glued to her television.

Before the Second World War Mary was a children's nurse, but when war broke out she joined the Auxiliary Territorial Service. For seven years she was attached to the 10th Batt. Gordon Highlanders and was sent to train at the cookery school at Aldershot. From there she was posted to Orkney and then to Shetland, where she was cook-sergeant at the time of the battle of Narvik. After training cooks at the Bournemouth Officers'

Cadet Training Unit she ended up as a staff captain in Field Marshal Montgomery's HQ in Germany. After the war she became a cook in up-market hotels and for private clients, including at Balnakeilly, Pitlochry, from where she wrote a report for the *Irish Naturalists' Journal* of January 1953 on an outing to County Kerry. She had led this outing for the Botanical Society of the British Isles in June 1952.

Although an excellent cook, love of plants took over and Mary decided to work in the winters only and to spend the summers botanising. When the mapping scheme of the Botanical Society of the British Isles (BSBI) was in progress for the *Atlas of British Flora* she walked a hundred miles a week for several summers, recording plant species in 266 grid squares in the north of Scotland.

In 1958 she went out to Natal to visit her brother. She travelled out on the ss *Braemar Castle* in November 1958, crossing the equator on 23 November with the usual pomp and ceremony. Apart from the certificate awarded her for the crossing, one other piece of remaining memorabilia is a race card for the Equatorial Cup. Mary was entered as 'Aberdonian out of Sixpence' and she was partnered by Mr CE Hubbard, Keeper of Graminae at the Royal Botanic Gardens, Kew. The race consisted of cutting a tape along its length as fast as possible, with the partner holding the far end. History does not relate how she fared in the race!

Mary's friendship with Mr Hubbard resulted in a keen interest in grasses. From Natal she went on a seven-month botany safari in Northern Rhodesia and Tanganyika where she collected 5,000 plant species for the Royal Botanic Gardens at Kew. Mr Hubbard corresponded about the grasses that she had collected. Her collection included a holotype for a new species *Digitaria melanotricha*. (The holotype is a single specimen chosen to represent a new species by the first author to describe it.) The next three winters were spent at Kew, helping to identify her collection, living at 57 Priory Road, Richmond.

Mary's prowess in the botanical world led on to four winters at the Botany School in Cambridge where she worked in the herbarium, turning it into a hive of activity. She was intolerant of slackness in others and thought the technicians weren't working hard enough. Her day started at 8.30am and ended at 10pm and her productivity was said to be frightening. She filled in cards for the *Hieracium* maps for the *Critical Atlas* and was also given the task of sorting out Charles Darwin's plant specimens collected in the Galapagos. She later commented that she found his notes very hard to decipher, being cross-written in two directions on scraps of paper, in poor handwriting.

The year 1960 saw Mary botanising in Yugoslavia with a friend, travelling around by local bus. Her diary is full of plant lists, many species being described as 'old friends'. A keen member of the BSBI, she often corresponded with the honorary secretary, Mary Briggs, who was another famous amateur botanist. On one occasion in 1961, Mary Briggs wrote, 'Your flora was the belle of the ball, by far the most attractive and the centre of interest at the BSBI meeting.' This was many years before the publication of Mary's real masterpiece, her *Flora of Moray Nairn and East Inverness*.

In 1966 she came to live permanently in Moray and made Rose Cottage, Dyke, near Culbin, her home for the rest of her life. From there she documented the

Mary McCallum Webster on the publication of her flora in 1978 (*The Northern Scot*)

flora of the area, spending many hours out in the wilds, complete with woolly hat and Gertrude Jekyll boots. She carried a card in one hand, pencil in the other and a poly bag of 'doubtfuls'. Those that botanised with her found it taxing; her eyes were always on the ground and she didn't miss a thing. Her knowledge was prodigious and though she was generous with it, she did not suffer fools gladly. Her attitude was 'Surely everyone should be able to name wild flowers'! When interviewed by the BBC about the newly re-constituted Moray Field Club for which she was the botany recorder, she was asked if the future president beside her knew anything about wild flowers. 'No. She doesn't know a daisy' was her reply.

Mary was elected a fellow of the Botanical Society of Edinburgh in 1955 and was a fellow of the Linnaean Society of London from 1960 to 1974. A member of the BSBI since 1936, she served on its council between 1960 and 1964 and was the society's recording officer for vice-counties 94 (Banff), 95 (Moray) and a portion of 96 (Easterness). One of her favourite places was Culbin State Forest, an area of sand-dunes which had been stabilised by afforestation after the First World War. In 1968 a comprehensive checklist of the area was produced, the result of many hours of patient field work. Mary was a faithful member of the Wild Flower Society from childhood and became secretary for the Scottish branch in 1968, keeping plant lists of all the counties in the north of Scotland. She became a member of the Inverness Botany Group in 1966 and its president from 1973 to 1976. She was also a keen member of the Moray Field Club. Another of her interests, the introduction of aliens, made her a founder member of the Shoddy Club whose first bulletin was produced in 1973. When *The Moray Book* (ed. Donald Omand) was published in 1978, she was one of only three female contributors amongst fifteen men.

Mary belonged to that generation of women that never married as a result of the losses of the First World War, but her life was full to the brim and she never gave less than 100 per cent, at work or play. Her hospitality was renowned and on one occasion on New Years Eve she is said to have pulled the cork from a bottle of whisky and thrown it out of the window saying. 'We won't need *that again.*' She held mini fetes in her garden for charity (often the World Wildlife Fund) and ended the day with a meal for her friends in Dyke. Her cottage was festooned with bunches of dried flowers collected from gardens of her many friends as well as from her own. Some of these flowers she used to make dried flower pictures which won her first prizes at the Royal Highland Show. She sold others for charities, along with dried flower arrangements on driftwood collected from the shore. Mary's garden at Rose Cottage was unique. It was not for show; Mary needed it for her creative energy. As well as material for her intricate pressed flower arrangements there were botanical treasures, common weeds, massed gentians and cabbages hugger-mugger amongst the flowers.

Mary's botanical dried specimens are divided between the herbaria of Aberdeen and Cambridge universities and of the Royal Botanic Garden in Edinburgh, with a few in the Elgin Museum. Her most outstanding contribution to botany was her *Flora of Moray, Nairn and East Inverness* which was published by Aberdeen University Press in 1978, funded by her life savings and financial help from two friends. It was a very thorough publication in that it told the reader exactly where each species could be found and gave history of the sites. Mary felt justified in its unusual layout and said that it 'sold like hot cakes'. The first 800 copies covered all her expenses and allowed her to make two visits to Western Australia where she took great delight in exploring an entirely new flora towards the end of her life.

After her death in 1985 her ashes were scattered in Culbin forest as she had requested, in the direction of Buckie Loch, at map reference NJ 002632. A stone memorial to her, decorated with her favourite flower, the one-flowered wintergreen *Moneses uniflora,* was erected on the site in 2003. Mary McCallum Webster gained an intimate knowledge of the wild places of Moray and cared deeply about the loss of country places to rural development. Most of her life was devoted to the love of plants. She was a unique character, enthusiastic, steadfast and often stubborn, with an untiring appetite to learn and learn. Known by other botanists as 'Lady Mary of Moray' for her direct speaking and botanical exactitude, she also had gruff warmth and an ever open door. (MB)

In memory of
**MARY MᶜCALLUM WEBSTER FLS**
1906 - 1985
A botanist who was an expert on the plants of the Moray area and wrote The Flora of Moray, Nairn and East Inverness. Her ashes were scattered here, at her own request, in the Culbin Forest she knew so well and among the wintergreens, her favourite plants.

Moray Field Club 2003

Memorial stone inscription in Culbin Forest
(Mary Byatt)

# Lesley Souter

*Lesley Scott Souter, born Elgin, 25 October 1917; died Rugby, 21 April 1981.*

Lesley Souter became the first woman associate of the Royal Technical College of Glasgow. She proceeded to work on secret research in connection with the Second World War, and continued her post-war career by researching into the new field of solid state physics.

Lesley's parents were Beatrice Gordon Edgar and James Stephen Souter. Her maternal grandparents had run the Gordon Arms Hotel in Elgin and, later, the Craigellachie Arms in Craigellachie. Her paternal grandfather had established the Souter engineering business situated off Greyfriars Street, Elgin. This business was originally a foundry, and the family house, which had been part of the business premises, was known as The Foundry, but later called Rose Cottage. Stephen, as Lesley's father was always called, was an engineer and inventor who worked in the family firm. Lesley was one of three bright sisters and her interest in engineering began as a small child. Dolls were dismantled to find out how they worked and, at the age of nine, Lesley adapted a small engine that ran on methylated spirits and powered a circular saw made from the lid of a cocoa tin. She appeared to have inherited her father's genius for invention. Stephen Souter was forever inventing things: anything from propelling pencils to diesel engines. He even made his own car, built from scratch and registered as SO5 in 1904. Years later Lesley used the number for her own car, although she was obliged to add a letter making it CSO5. In this childhood environment Lesley was able to develop her natural talents. She often accompanied her father around rural Moray when he went out to visit his clients – mostly farmers needing their machinery fixed. Phyllis, Lesley's younger sister, re-

263

members a happy childhood, the highlights being trips to the beach at Lossiemouth, and camping with the family and with the Girl Guides. School too, held good memories for all the sisters; Tresta was talented in languages and Phyllis shone at mathematics.

Lesley attended the West End School and then Elgin Academy. She was joint dux, with Coral Smith, in 1936. She then went to Glasgow where she took a 'thin sandwich' course at the Royal Technical College, an extra-mural college of Glasgow University. There she suffered the indignity of listening to the lecturer address the class as 'Gentlemen'. The course involved industrial training which was done partly with the family firm in Elgin

Lesley Souter after graduation with first class honours from Glasgow (Phyllis Titt)

and partly with The General Electric Company (GEC) in Wembley. Despite being ignored by the lecturer, Lesley graduated with first class honours in 1940, whilst writing a thesis concurrently.

After her degree, Lesley continued to work at GEC. In Wembley her research was initially connected with the radio proximity shell, which was developed as an anti-aircraft device to blow up the flying bombs or doodlebugs of the Germans, and the Japanese suicide pilots. These radio shells used special valves to throw out radio waves that picked up signals from the enemy bombs. The radio shells then were attracted to the enemy bombs and planes and, when within lethal range, exploded. It was Lesley who worked on the valves. To do this she took a glass blowing course so that she could make the valves for her experiments. Aside from work, she was a regular fire watcher during the war – an important home front duty, especially in Wembley.

Following the war, Lesley was made an associate member of the Institute of Electrical Engineers, an honour of some importance. During the 1950s her work moved to research in solid state physics, the focus of which was crystal study. This study is relevant to the electronics world that we are so familiar with today. A description of her work may be difficult for the layman to understand, referring as it does to gas discharge devices, fermi level calculations, and germanium and silicon crystal growing methods, but a good story is told of her capabilities in connection with electric cookers. The director of the domestic products division at GEC was at his wit's end one summer because the heating elements on the cookers on the production line were all burning out and no one could understand why. Much of the staff were on holiday so the director sent for help from the research section, and was very disgusted when a woman turned up, and a theoretician at that. However, after discussing the problem with the staff and spending some time working in the library, Lesley was able to pinpoint the problem, and all was resolved.

Lesley left GEC in 1955 and worked for a while with Mullard Research Laboratories in Redhill, Surrey, and with Radiation Group Electrical Laboratory in Luton. In 1958 she moved to Harlow, Essex, and worked with Associated Electrical Industries Ltd. (AEI), where she was able to participate in the organisation of the new research laboratories as well as being the leader of the Magnetic Materials Section. She moved with the firm to Rugby in 1963 and lived there until her death. Lesley often travelled abroad, going to the States, Holland, Poland and Japan to attend conferences and give papers.

Always keen to help other women along the road to an engineering career, Lesley wrote a book on the subject and gave interviews on radio. She was a member of the Women's Engineering Society and acted as its careers and training advisory officer for many years. In 1960 she and Rosina Winslade, were awarded a Caroline Haslett Memorial Trust Travelling Scholarship to enable them to study training, employment and prospects for women engineers in the USSR. The two women travelled to Russia, visiting Moscow, Leningrad, and Kharkov in the Ukraine. During the two weeks they were there they interviewed many women engineers. One in three engineers was a woman in Russia at this time, partly due to the imbalance of the sexes, but also because there was equal opportunity for men and women. In Britain there was only one woman to 1,000 male engineers, largely because of male intolerance.

As well as work there were personal interests: Wembley Philharmonic Orchestra needed a cellist and, later, the Rugby Soroptimists a secretary. The Soroptimists is an international organisation for professional women committed to the advancement of the status of women, and to human rights. Holidays were often spent in Moray, visiting the family. Some time after Lesley's father died in 1954, her mother moved south to stay with Lesley.

Lesley's main interest, outside work, arose from her experiences as a single, professional woman. Finding decent accommodation had always been a problem. People were suspicious of single women living alone. At one time it was not possible for a woman to buy property without a man's guarantee. So when Lesley inherited a house in Forestgate in London, in 1956, she decided to use it for lets to single women. Single teachers particularly were desperate for accommodation during this time of housing shortage. Large rooms available as bed-sits, with shared kitchen and bathroom were the ideal solution. The letting laws were difficult, but the problem was resolved by one of the tenants acting as the official tenant. Thus, when Lesley became a Conservative councillor for Rugby Borough Council in 1976,

Lesley the engineer (Phyllis Titt)

she had good relevant experience to offer the housing committee.

Her last battle, as regards housing, concerned sheltered housing in Rugby. The council wished to build a complex in a quiet place out of town. Lesley said 'there will be enough quiet times in the cemetery', and she fought hard to have the complex built nearer the town where the residents could walk to the shops and readily have visitors. Sadly, she did not live to see this housing development completed, but it was named after her as a token of regard for the work she had done for the community. A fellow councillor remarked that 'her main interest was people and that is why she did such a good job as housing chairman'. Rugby Borough Council joined her family and friends at the funeral in 1981, wearing full civic robes to show its respect.

As a woman, Lesley Souter had to make her own road in life, both in her career and in her personal life. She never forgot the college lecturer who ignored her and addressed the class as 'Gentlemen'. She did not falter on the way, and neither did she forget those who followed. She was a brilliant scientist, but she was not just a boffin; she fought for women's rights and for the elderly. In Rugby the sheltered housing complex, Lesley Souter House, stands as her memorial. (SB)

CHAPTER ELEVEN

# The Creative Life

*A woman must have money and a room of her own if she is to write fiction.*
Virginia Woolf, 1929[1]

WHEN EKA GORDON CUMMING and her half brother set off for the Hebrides in 1868 they had no particular itinerary in mind:

> Our only plan was to spend some quiet weeks in the most out-of-the-world place we could find; one where my pencil might keep me busy, where my brother could rejoice in perfect idleness after a course of hard reading...[2]

For those with talent and money there seemed no limit to what they might achieve. Space and time are important requirements for living a creative life – space to write or paint in peace; time to master techniques, to explore the imagination. Good tutors help, too: Georgiana McCrae, daughter of the fifth Duke of Gordon, benefited from the teachings of John Varley; Mary Seton Watts trained in London and various establishments in Europe; Mary Symon, the saddler's daughter from Dufftown, was sent to the most prestigious girls' school in the country; and many of the other women in this chapter received a privileged education. These women also enjoyed some sort of financial support when they were adults and most were able to take the time to paint or write because they did not need to earn a living. Painting had long been considered a suitable activity for women with time on their hands. Generally, watercolour was the favoured medium. Oil painting – a smelly, messy medium – tended to be a male preserve.

The Society of Women Artists (SWA) existed from around 1855 to give serious women painters the opportunity to exhibit. Until 1855, the art world had been dominated by the Royal Academy, founded in 1769, and the Royal Watercolour Society, founded in 1804. Both were for male artists; there were no female academicians until after 1918, apart from two

'Findhorn' by Emma Black from *Impressions of Moray* (1931)

founder members of the RA. A desire to make the participation in the arts easier for all took root in society in the late nineteenth century. Mary Seton Watts became a pioneer in the Arts and Crafts movement – a movement that was democratic in its philosophy.

As well as painting attractive watercolours, Sophia Dunbar, Eka Gordon Cumming, Dorothy Brown, and Emma Black left valuable records of the landscape of Moray before the first and second world wars; a landscape that has since changed immeasurably.

Veronica Bruce, the ballerina, also benefited from good teaching; in her case an aunt by marriage, Madame Karsavina, a famous Russian dancer. The poets Mary Symon and Margaret Winefride Simpson, both highly educated, left a legacy of importance to the Scots language.

Other women were less cushioned by wealth. Isabel Cameron's teaching career came to an end when she got married – married women were not allowed to teach. Immensely popular, her stories were eagerly awaited by her readers. The financial reward kept the stories coming and was a welcome addition to the United Free Church stipend. Elizabeth Macpherson's journalism pieces about life on the Dava Moor provided some extras to the living wrung from an upland farm. John Aubrey spent time working in a bank when the war disrupted her career as an artist. Jessie Kesson's storytelling talents, fostered by a wayward mother and encouraged by a good teacher, had no easy blossoming. She might have written more with 'money and a room of her own'.

Whilst Moray does not appear to have produced any outstanding women musicians, there have been women who made significant contributions to the music scene. The first music festival to be held in Elgin was inspired by a visit of the Glasgow Orpheus Choir in 1922. During the Second World War the festival lapsed, but was revived in 1955 as the Moray Music Festival. It gave children and adults a rich musical experience as they competed as soloists and in choirs and orchestras, encouraged by devoted teachers such as Kim Murray, Ella Taylor and Sister Mary Winefride.

Of the women in this chapter, three are internationally famous: Mary Seton Watts and Veronica Bruce were born to privilege; Jessie Kesson was born in the poorhouse.

# Sophia Dunbar

*Sophia Orred, born 1814, Cheshire; married Archibald Dunbar 1840; died Duffus House, by Elgin, 2 June 1909.*

Sophia Dunbar was an accomplished amateur water colourist, exhibiting at the Royal Scottish Academy. She shared with her husband an interest in local antiquities and Continental travel.

Sophia's father was George Orred Esquire of Tranmere Hall, near Birkenhead, Cheshire, and her mother was Elizabeth Woodville. Sophia was their youngest daughter and had two brothers and three sisters. It seems they were a close family as Sophia's relatives were frequent visitors to Duffus during her married life, and her brother George even took up residence at Grant Lodge, Elgin for a time.

Sophia came to Moray as the second wife of Archibald Dunbar who in 1847 became the seventh Baronet of Northfield. (This Archibald, through his mother, Helen Gordon Cumming, was the nephew of Eliza Gordon Cumming, and cousin of Eka Gordon Cumming.) They married at St Oswald's Church, Chester in 1840, when Sophia was twenty-six and Archibald ten years older. A fine portrait by the Glasgow artist, John Graham-Gilbert, depicts Sophia in her wedding dress. The dress is said to be a copy of Queen Victoria's; she had married earlier that year.

Home in Moray was Duffus House, built as a replacement for Duffus Castle. The House dates from the seventeenth century – with additions by William Robertson in 1835. It is situated in woodland on the southern outskirts of Duffus village, and stands very close to the boundary with Gordonstoun, a former home of the Gordon Cummings. Northfield (now

Highfield) was the Dunbar town residence in Elgin until the mid-nineteenth century.

Archibald's first wife, Keith Alicia Ramsay, died in 1836 and left four children: Archibald (known as 'Young Archie' until his seventies when he became eighth Baronet), Jeanie, Agnes and George. It seems their father was rarely at Duffus during his three and half years of widowhood.

When nearly eighty, Agnes was asked by her niece, daughter of Jeanie, to put down anything she remembered of her childhood. The notes were transcribed by the niece in a beautifully legible hand (in marked contrast to Lady Sophia's scrawl) and are now a valuable family and social record. The children, especially Jeanie, aged twelve, had been anxious about the arrival of their new stepmother, but:

Sophia, Lady Dunbar from the catalogue of 'From Elgin to the Alhambra' exhibition at Aberdeen Art Gallery, December 1987 – January 1988. Painting by John Graham-Gilbert, about 1840 (Aberdeen Art Gallery and Museums Collections)

> she was nice and we liked her... I don't think in our lives we were ever jealous of each other, and so we failed to see that the absence of jealousy was a great virtue in our Stepmother.

The children called Sophia 'Mama' and were in time joined by three stepbrothers: Randolph, Charles (ninth Baronet) and William. Sophia dreaded the birth of Willie in 1850. She went to Edinburgh to be under the care of Professor (later Sir) James Y Simpson, and took leave of the family as if she did not expect to return home. Agnes remembered:

> Her sisters were with her and for the first time she had a modern and thoroughly trained monthly nurse and had chloroform at the worst, and recovered wonderfully.

Sir Archibald, his brother Edward Dunbar Dunbar of Sea Park, Kinloss, and their neighbour, Sir (Alexander) Penrose Gordon Cumming (eldest brother of Eka) were all keen antiquarians, as was her obstetrician.

Professor James Y Simpson was President of the Society of Antiquaries of Scotland from 1861, and was particularly interested in ancient carvings on stones, such as the Pictish carvings in the caves at Wemyss, Fife, and he and colleagues had been making enquiries for any in the coastal caves at Covesea, near Duffus. In Sophia's letter to Simpson of 22 May 1866 she says she was 'lately so fortunate as to discover some small remains of ancient sculptures in a cave at Covesea'. On the strength of her preliminary drawings, which recently resurfaced at the Royal Commission on the Ancient and Historical Monuments of Scotland (RCAHMS), John Stuart sent a Mr Gibb to make the drawings used in his second volume of *Sculptured Stones of Scotland*. The Sculptor's Cave, Covesea, thus became well known for its Pictish carvings, and this was the attraction for Sylvia Benton, who carried out the first formal excavation in 1928–30. From a couple of entries in *The Elgin Courant* in 1868, it seems that the Dunbars did some amateur digging at the Cave: a variety of finds, all now lost, including a human lower-jaw bone and part of a human skull, were donated by them to Elgin Museum.

Sophia's letter to Simpson is primarily about a number of Bronze Age cist burials the Dunbars had excavated in the neighbourhood from Burghead to Covesea. She included a sketch of the most recent cist to be found, in which there was an urn – which the herd boy let fall, some of the neighbours removing the fragments as curiosities. As was common with nineteenth century antiquarians, they dug many cists, the contents of which have rarely survived. Two cists they reassembled at Duffus House, and several of Sophia's watercolour and ink sketches of local cists and jet necklaces are now in the archives of RCAHMS and Aberdeen Art Gallery.

Sophia's artistic accomplishments merited a whole chapter in Ellen Clayton's *English Female Artists* (1876). Ellen, a feminist, wrote the book based on questionnaires sent out to the artists. A more recent appreciation appears in the catalogue of an exhibition of Sophia's work, *From Elgin to the Alhambra*, held at Aberdeen Art Gallery in 1987/88. She is said to have been fond of sketching from nature from early childhood. As a young woman, art as a profession, or even formal training in it, would not have been an option; her chief means of study would have been

Sophia Dunbar's preliminary sketches of the Pictish carvings in the Sculptor's cave
(© Courtesy of RCAHMS)

271

looking at and copying the works of others and picking up hints from art-ists she happened to meet.

The Dunbar family were in Jersey in 1844 for Sir Archibald's health, and Agnes attended school there. It may have been then that Lady Dunbar received lessons from John Le Capelain, a local marine and landscape artist. A self-taught artist, Le Capelain came to some prominence as a painter who captured the atmosphere of Jersey, from the mists of sunrise to the glowing colours of the setting sun. A painting of Burghead dated 1846 is one of several of her paintings that suggests Le Capelain's influence.

While in Seville, Sophia made the acquaintance of two well-known artists, Edward Cooke, RA, FRS, FSA, FZS, FGS and John Phillip, RA. Cooke was not only a marine artist, but a polymath. According to Ellen Clayton 'Several rambles in search of the picturesque were enjoyed by her with Mr Cooke', as is attested by her paintings from this time. While in Barcelona, a reference to 'Prout-like houses' suggests she was familiar with the works and instructive art manuals written by Samuel Prout for such ladies as her. At the Alhambra she met a Russian artist, Monsieur Bachan, whom she considered a first-rate artist for his views of architectural subjects and costumes of the peasantry.

A winter spent with easel and brushes in southern Europe is described by Sophia in her journal published by Blackwoods: *Tour of a Family round the Coasts of Spain and Portugal during the winter of 1860–1861*, with 'a wish to realise a few pounds for a charitable purpose'. They had previously spent a few winters at Nice, and the railway guides suggested Barcelona would be as easy. However, in the first of their travel traumas, they had to take a diligence from Perpignan, which overturned. Their inestimable, English-speaking, Spanish maid 'made a flying somerset over the mules'.

Her account is full of details about hotels to avoid, the price of wines or a full suit of clothes for a matador, as well as detailed and often very personal observations on art, architecture and people encountered. They take in Gibraltar and cross the Straits, meet Moors and Jews and English Consuls, see a prisoner being flogged near to death in Tangier and visit a foundling hospital where the infants' eye complaints are treated with bleeding. One is left marvelling at the pace of the activity and experiences, at the belittling of the discomforts and uncertainties of the journeying, and at the resulting art work.

Ellen Clayton records that it was after a series of bereavements in 1862 that Sophia took up painting seriously, finding solace in her art. This was the year in which her son, Randolph (20), and stepson, George (30) died. Sophia first exhibited, with the Society of Female Artists, Conduit Street, London in 1863.

Her first painting exhibited at the Royal Scottish Academy, in 1867, was a view of the Bay of Algiers. While in Algiers, Sophia made a friendship with Mme Barbara Bodichon, an artist of a very different background from herself. Barbara was the daughter of a Radical MP, Benjamin Leigh Smith and his young common-law wife, Anne Longden. A prime mover in campaigns to improve the rights of married women, Barbara was also active in the suffrage movement and instrumental in the founding of Girton College, Cambridge, owners of a number of Sophia's watercolours.

In Duffus, Sophia's artistic interests were recognised in the planning of the new Duffus Church (architects A and W Reid). An article in the *Elgin Courant* in 1868 stated:

Lady Dunbar of Duffus House, whose abilities as an artist are well known, has taken a great interest in the preparation of the plans of the church. The Heritors did well in allowing her highly-cultivated taste to guide them to a great extent in the character of the church... though they will no doubt involve considerably more expense than four square walls and a roof would have done.

By the time she exhibited for the last time at the RSA in 1888, Sophia had shown forty-two paintings. She rarely gave titles to her works, other than the name of the place, and most of her paintings are watercolours of landscapes, with only occasional and incidental people. They were painted at home in Moray, pastoral scenes in the Laigh and on the coast, and in Aberdeenshire, and on frequent journeys abroad, especially to the Mediterranean. Apart from their considerable aesthetic merits, these pieces are records of places little visited by foreigners at the time, or in the case of her antiquarian sketches, the only record from a period when photography was in its infancy. These sketches are still regarded by archaeologists as valuable records of objects and locations.

At the time of their Golden Wedding Anniversary in 1890, Sophia had been in very poor health, although the Baronet was 'hale and healthy'. She gave a short response to the address of thanks and praise given them by the tenantry, crofters and feuers but did not attend the celebratory bonfire with her husband. Elma Napier (née Gordon Cumming) recalled from about this time: 'everything in the drawing-room was old and queer and smelt of pot-pourri... In a wheeled chair, under a mob cap, sat Old Lady Dunbar, wife of Old Sir Archie'. She died nearly twenty years later in 1909, eleven years after her husband, aged ninety-five, and is buried in St Peter's Churchyard, Duffus.

In 2008 the RCAHMS and the Scottish Portrait Gallery joined forces to present an exhibition entitled *Faces and People*. Lady Sophia, described as a skilled archaeological illustrator, was one of twenty individuals chosen as key figures who have contributed to Scotland's built heritage, in her case, by recording Scotland's past. (JT)

# Mary Seton Watts

*Mary Seton Fraser Tytler, born Ahmednaggar, India, 25 November 1849; married George Frederick Watts, 20 November 1886; died 6 September 1938.*

Mary Seton Watts drew on her Celtic heritage to develop her artistic talents. Her design and decoration of the Watts Memorial Chapel in Compton, Surrey, is a lasting tribute to her place in the arts and crafts movement and the Home Arts and Industries Association.

Mary was born in India where her father, Charles Fraser Tytler, was employed by the Honourable East India Company. She was the youngest of four sisters. Her mother, Etheldred (maiden name St Barbe), died when Mary was eighteen months old and consequently the children came to live with their grandparents at Aldourie Castle, about six miles to the south of Inverness. When Charles retired in 1861, the family, including Charles's second wife, moved to Sanquhar House on the outskirts of Forres. Following extensive alterations in 1863, the house (demolished 1974) was described in 1868 as having 'a beautiful conservatory, two storeys high and fitted up with exquisite taste'. The grounds were terraced with flower gardens, gravel walks and fine park trees. The kitchen garden contained a peach-house, vinery and forcing-house. To the north was an artificial lake and fine views over the town of Forres. The family, with a literary background, encouraged the sisters to be artistic, and it is thought that Mary might have attended an art college in Inverness.

Meanwhile Julia Margaret Cameron had set up her photography studio at Freshwater, on the Isle of Wight. Possibly there was a family connection through India, but for whatever reason, Mary's sisters were sitting for the photographer and coincidentally meeting the artist, George Frederic Watts. GF Watts was known for his scandalous separation from his young wife Ellen Terry.

By the age of eighteen Mary had also visited Freshwater where she met the poet Tennyson who lived next door to the Camerons. The four Fraser Tytler sisters posed for one of Julia Margaret Cameron's photographs, *Rosebud Garden of Girls* (1868) – a classic Pre-Raphaelite composition inspired by Tennyson's *Maud*. After travelling on the continent and studying art in Dresden and Rome, Mary continued her studies at the National Art Training School in South Kensington. In 1873 she attended the newly opened Slade School of Art. There she worked under Aimé-Jules Dalou, the sculptor, from whom she took private lessons and learned the use of clay. Both oil and watercolours were used as a medium for her portraits of herself and her family.

Self-portrait by Mary Seton Fraser Tytler 1882
(Courtesy of the Watts Gallery)

Emotionally, Mary's life was difficult. She suffered from failed love affairs in Germany and in Italy. In Britain she was increasingly influenced in her painting by GF Watts, known as 'Signor', who had, by this time, built a house in Freshwater. George Paul Chalmers, who painted a portrait of Mary in 1876 in Edinburgh, was for a while the object of her love. Her love of artists seemed to be closely tied up with her love of their art. In the south she could not escape the influence of Signor. Watts (finally divorced from Ellen Terry in 1877) rejected her love, calling her a 'silly child', although he was happy to work with her and they had much in common regarding their art.

Mary's father died in 1881, but Mary, who moved in with her stepmother in London, retained her studio in Sanquhar House. A photograph of the studio in Forres is full of easel paintings, mostly portraits; the central framed oil painting is a self portrait painted in 1881.

In 1883 Mary Fraser Tytler began teaching clay-modelling in the slums of Whitechapel. This pioneering move developed, along with other artists' projects, into the Home Arts and Industries Association. It was this conviction that art should be available to everyone that was the basis of the arts and crafts movement. The creation of beauty was possible in all walks of life; anyone could make beautiful things and in the process be enriched. In practice, the movement appealed most to the middle classes.

On 3 July 1886 GF Watts, then aged sixty-nine and one of the most revered figures in British art, proposed to Mary, apparently being afraid that she was becoming too involved with one of her sitters. Mary was only thirty-six. She understood that she would need to give up some of her own ambitions, but the offer of helping him in his work was enough for her to accept his proposal. The couple were married in November and travelled to Egypt and Greece, spending six months studying art and 'all that is beautiful'.

The Watts Memorial Chapel in Compton graveyard
(Susan Bennett)

On returning home Mary Seton Watts benefited from the artistic connections of her husband, but felt frustrated by her submission to his wishes. She did less painting, but spent more time working with clay. 'Limnerslease', the house they built in Compton, near Guildford, saved Mary's individuality as she became increasingly absorbed with its decorative design. She designed and decorated ceilings, side panels, fireplace surrounds, reading alcoves and bay windows, using clay and gesso, a fibrous plaster. As the work progressed the inspiration she derived from studying Celtic manuscripts became more evident. She wrote, 'The Celtic seems in character the most decorative symbolic style there is'. The flamboyant and intricate reading alcove that Mary designed for Signor is lost, but most of the other decorative features of Limnerslease remain.

About 1894, Compton Parish Council purchased land near Limnerslease for a new burial ground. It was then that Mary started designing a mortuary chapel which would be built of local clay by local people, and paid for by the sale of GF Watts's paintings. Lucinda Lambton (1998) describes this Watts Memorial Chapel as:

> A brilliant beacon of a building – seemingly aflame with the redness of its brick – that has been most surprisingly wrought into the ancient forms of a Greek cross with Romanesque motifs and a cacophony of Celtic decoration.

Mary decided, against her husband's wishes, to set up the Potters' Art Guild in Compton and at Aldourie. In Compton her new apprentices worked on the interior of the chapel and outside memorials. Both potteries produced garden ornaments, such as sundials and pots, all of which were in great demand for the gardens designed by Gertrude Jekyll and Edwin Lutyens. The ornaments were sold by Liberty's. Jekyll wrote of the pots:

Some delightful garden pottery of subdued reds and greys is made by the Potter's Arts Guild at Compton, Surrey, the enterprise of Mrs GF Watts.

In 1903–04 the Watts Gallery was built across the road from Limnerslease. It was an early concrete construction designed to exhibit GF Watts's paintings. This gallery featured, some years ago, in the BBC programme *Restoration*. It came second in the contest and, at the time of writing, after major restorative work, had just reopened.

GF Watts died in 1904. Mary devoted much of her time to bolstering his achievements, interpreting his life and maintaining the Watts Gallery. She was criticised for her possessive attitude to his work. Busy also with her own projects, she designed and oversaw the production of a frieze and altar decoration, in painted gesso, for the Cambridge Military Hospital at Aldershot during the First World War. Although pottery was Mary's main medium, she also designed, in the art nouveau style, such items as book covers, carpets and wall hangings.

A visit to the Watts Gallery at Compton is necessary to see most of Mary's work. The gallery also holds a large archive relating to Mary Seton Watts, including her diaries dating from 1870–1908. The Watts Memorial Chapel in the Compton Church graveyard is readily accessible and usually open. Visitors can hardly fail to be impressed by the intricate designs and craftmanship, whether or not the style is to their taste. The graveyard is full of tributes and gravestones that reflect the work of the Compton Pottery.

The Celtic influence on the chapel is most striking. The eagles that decorate the north-east side of the chapel are copied almost directly from the Book of Kells, and represent St John. Celtic knotwork is everywhere. Every detail of the design has symbolic and spiritual meaning. Mary wrote of the angels on the ceiling of the chapel:

The encircling group of winged messengers, alternatively presenting the light and dark of all things, 'made double one against the other,' [Ecclesiasticus 42:23] would suggest the earthly conditions in which the soul of man

The eagle, representing St John, shows the influence of the Book of Kells (Susan Bennett)

finds itself. The face of the angel carrying the symbol of light is seen, but the face of the angel carrying the symbol of darkness is unseen.

A woman from a wealthy background with every opportunity to develop her talent, Mary Seton Watts was committed to bringing art into ordinary lives. If her most important legacy is the Watts Memorial Chapel, it is because it embodies not only her own impressive work, but also the work of the people of Compton – people who were neither privileged nor exceptionally talented, but who nevertheless contributed to a masterpiece. (SB)

# Mary Symon

*Mary Symon, born Dufftown, 25 September 1863; died Dufftown, 27 May 1938.*

Mary Symon, born in Dufftown, was a poet and author of national importance and a passionate advocate of the use of the Scots tongue.

The elder daughter of John Symon, proprietor of the family saddler's business on Church Street, and of Isabella Duncan, from Drywells in the Cabrach, Mary was educated at Mortlach Female School, and, from the age of fifteen, at the Edinburgh Institute for Young Ladies (later, to become Edinburgh Ladies' College and, later still, the Mary Erskine School). In Edinburgh she came under the influence of two key figures in the development of education for women: James Logie Robertson (better-known under his pseudonym, 'Hugh Haliburton') and David Masson, Professor of Rhetoric and English Literature at the university. Robertson was an inspirational teacher of literature and an accomplished practitioner of vernacular verse. Masson, born and educated in Aberdeen, was a founding figure in the Edinburgh Association for the University Education of Women which offered the first university-level lectures for women from 1868. Mary Symon attended Masson's lectures on English and Scottish literature. On leaving school, she returned to Dufftown and undertook the Lady Literate in Arts (LLA), a qualification offered by correspondence by the University of St Andrews in the decade or so before women were admitted to degree courses. In 1889, her father, now provost of Dufftown, purchased Pittyvaich House and the 128-acre farm. He later established Pittyvaich Distillery on the site of the Pittyvaich Mills. Equipped as she was with an expensive modern education, as the unmarried daughter, Mary's responsibility was the care of her aging parents. Her father died in 1908; her mother in 1924. From the early 1890s, Pittyvaich was Mary Symon's

Mary Symon from a photograph given to Robert
Gordon's College Aberdeen in 1938
(Robert Gordon's College)

home until her death in 1938.

Her work in verse and prose had, from the 1890s, appeared in a variety of publications including the *Scots Magazine*, *New Century Review* and the *Aberdeen Journal* when, in, February 1916, 'The Glen's Muster Roll: the Dominie Loquitur' was published in *Aberdeen University Review.*

Colin Milton describes the poem as 'perhaps the finest vernacular elegy to come out of the Great War'. No other poem evokes so effectively the sense of the loss to a community of a whole generation. Symon's stroke of genius is in the creation of the voice of the dominie – drily humorous, fiercely proud, democratic, rooted in the community that he has served for so long. He has taught every one of the young men whose names, 'near han a hunner', make up the muster roll. The dominie remembers and reflects on the fate of a representative eight of his 'loons', leading to the final individual tragedy of Robbie, the dominie's star pupil, the lad o pairts, the first year classical scholar – 'a sowle an brain fae's bonnet till his beets' who joined up out of principle and whose fate is worst of all. Robbie will return to the glen destroyed in body and mind. The dominie is 'waitin till [he] a puir thing hirples hame'. This is a rich, multi-layered poem. The detailed references to the events of the war evoke both the 'foreignness' of the action to the loons and at the same time the familiarity of these names as the daily currency of ordinary people in those appalling times. The vignettes of the individual loons extend our understanding of the dominie's character and of the life of the glen. There is telling detail – Davie's 'moo fae lug tae lug', Robbie's 'chappit hannie grippin ticht a Homer men't wi tow', the gaup who offers a 'lang sook o a pandrop' for the meaning of a Latin tag and the two loons who beg, 'Please-sir-can-we-win-oot-tae-droon-a-fulp?' In the final stanza the dominie has a hellish vision of the dead and the wounded returning to the school room:

Ye're back fae Aisne an Marne an Meuse, Ypres an Festubert:
Ye're back on weary bleedin feet – you, you that danced an ran –
For every lauchin loon I kent I see a hell-scarred man.

The closing lines express the hopelessness of the dominie, the representative of the establishment that authorised the war, confronted by the ultimate question posed by his ghostly visitors: 'Ah, Maister, tell's fit aa this means'. His only reply is in the 'bairns' words' that they used to use in response to his questions on The Rule of Three or Latin declensions or the Catechism: 'I dinna ken, I dinna ken. Fa does, oh Loons o Mine'.

This poem instantly struck a chord in the hearts and minds of the people of the North-East. It was much reprinted and anthologised and it, along with a handful of other 'war' poems, most of them monologues with distinctive and beautifully realised voices – 'The Soldier's Cairn', 'After Neuve Chapelle', 'A Recruit for the Gordon's, 'A Whiff o Hame' – established Mary Symon's reputation as a poet of national importance.

A key figure in the later part of Mary Symon's story is William Will. Born in Huntly in 1863, Will began work for the *Huntly Express*, moved to London and rapidly distinguished himself in the world of journalism. He was editor of *St James's Gazette*, *Sporting Life*, managing director of *Graphic* publications, manager and director of Allied Newspapers, chairman of the Press Association and deputy chairman of Reuters. In 1940 he was appointed chairman of the Committee of National and Provincial Newspapers established to act as liaison between newspapers and government departments in reporting the war. He was also secretary of the Vernacular Circle of the Burns Club of London, an influential body in those days when the use of vernacular Scots was under threat. The aims of the circle were 'to remove from the minds of simple people that only vulgar people speak the Doric' and 'to convince the Scottish Education Department that "classical Scots" must be taught in schools or at least be encouraged to be read in the classroom'.

Will and his friends of the Burns Club of London are contemptuously dismissed by Hugh MacDiarmid in the opening section of *A Drunk Man Looks at the Thistle* (1926):

> Croose London Scotties wi their braw shirt fronts
> An a their fancy freens...
> toastin ane wha's nocht to them but an
> Excuse for faitherin Genius wi *their* thochts.

MacDiarmid had expressed extreme antipathy to the Doric movement promoted by the Vernacular Circle. He wanted a Scots that could express complex modern ideas and he considered their attitude to be essentially nostalgic and backward-looking. However, some differences were reconciled, and MacDiarmid published the work of Murray, Jacob and

Symon in *Northern Numbers* (1920–22) – the influential anthologies that record the first stirrings of what came to be called the Scots Literary Renaissance.

From just after the war to the end of her life Mary Symon engaged in a passionate correspondence with William Will on the state of Scots language and literature. She was by this time a well-known and respected poet of more than local significance. By the publication of her own verse and prose and by her proselytising through public speaking and reading, she had become an important figure in the promotion of Scots for literary and for everyday use. In one letter she refers to the propensity of the growing middle class in the North-East to

> frenziedly hustle southward their Jockies and Jeanies to acquire fine English – the soaring ambition of the Fain-would-be folk among us, and will be until Doric receives the academic imprimatur in some fashion…

Symon contributed some 'bitties' to be read and circulated at meetings of Will's circle in London. They were well-received, but for many years she resisted Will's persistent urging for their wider publication – 'it's the War Loan to a weskit button', she says at one point, 'that Mary Symon won't be worth a small-sized Bradbury to anybody'. She was, of course, wrong. In 1933 when *Deveron Days* appeared, published by Wyllie of Aberdeen, it sold out within a week, was immediately reprinted and sold out again. A second edition with seven additional poems was published in 1938.

The vigour with which she expressed her views on the promotion of the Scots tongue put her on the same side of the language debate as MacDiarmid. Her hero, however, was Charles Murray, a close friend. Of other poets – David Rorie, Elsie S Rae, Violet Jacob, for example – she could be scathing. Describing some recently published work as 'platitudinous havers for the most part, walshach and dweeble beyond belief', she writes:

> [regarding our project] my heart by no means loups so licht as once it did. I have had the most appalling letters from so called Burns enthusiasts – self revelations of smug imbecility and pretentious vanity – which have considerably dashed my optimism.

She goes on to say that:

> an infinitude of harm is being done to Doric and all it stands for by the feeble drivel which upsettin bodiekins at every burnside and braefoot are turning out day after day. Our local papers offer perfect orgies of

ineptitude – drop your 'g's and say 'fa' and 'fan' and 'foo' – and 'a' for
'I' and you are as good as Charles Murray!!! That is the recipe in its
entirety.

Her delight in Scots –'our glorious birthright' – is always evident, and it is
the language of her past and of her own locality that she turns to. In 1930
she writes:

you have given me back out of the limbo of forgotten things a joyous
word – 'maindle'. I think of it – I had tint it – clear tint it. Have not
encountered it, spoken or written it for several decades. – 'A swarrach
o geats, I'se warran' eh?' 'Oh aye, a fair maindle'. That comes back to
me over the years with the sough of the Deveron, the guff of peatreek
– and my old grandfather colloguin wi a crony on the Cabrach road.

Her relationship with William Will was of great importance to Symon.
In 1924 she writes: 'although I have never seen you, I count you among my
friends'. She often expresses a wish to see him in her own home:

How I longed for a half hour's chat over it – four feet on the fender.
That would take us further than reams of 'write'. Enthusiasm burns low
by the lonely ingle.

In the autumn of 1930, Will visited her at Pittyvaich:

I cannot tell you the pleasure it was to me to see you under my own old
rooftree the other day. I am still sitting out of doors but the nichts are
creepin in and the footsteps up the brae an ower the brig are growin
fewer – I have blithe memories though.

The letters of her later years are marked by melancholy notes:

since my mother's death [in 1924], the fateful doctrine of 'nothing
matters' has got hold of me – what's the use? Cui bono? – and so on.

Her spirits were lifted by the impending publication of *Deveron Days*
in 1933 and then by its immediate success. It is clear, however, that her
work would never have reached book form without the persistent 'prigging'
and 'deaving' of Will over a number of years. It was her natural reticence
and modesty and her growing sense of 'the shadow of the cypress trees'
and the passing of 'the ruthless mourning years' that delayed its coming to

press. Nevertheless, she took an active part in the publication. There would be no introductory foreword by a famous literary figure – the poems must 'speak for themselves'; she would compile the glossary of Scots herself – she did not trust anyone else; and she would be entirely financially responsible for the publication – she should 'feel besmirched' otherwise.

As the book approaches publication, she writes:

> I am still greetin in helpless bewildered gratitude over everything you are doing... Since ever I have known you, you have always stood to me as the best representative of this Northland that I love, This is not exaggerated rhetoric – mere vacuous dithyrhambics – my enemies would admit my honesty – you epitomise Celtic fineness and idealism with forcefulness and practicality – a very rare combine.

*Deveron Days* is dedicated to 'That Scot of Scots – William Will'. Finally the book is published: 'First impression – Dec 1933; Second impression – Jan 1934. Sounds grand indeed, well, well!' Typically, she undercuts her own pleasure at the book's success:

> The sales reminded me of the wifies's shoppie in the Cabrach where you stopped in and bought 'pints' and 'trappin' and conversation 'lozengers' for the Kirk.

Her funeral on 30 May 1938 in the churchyard of Mortlach was a remarkable occasion. Apart from Dufftown friends who had gathered to honour Miss Symon of Pittyvaich, her close associates of the North-East's literary and academic worlds, were present. Pall bearers included David Rorie and Sir Charles Murray. Tributes were paid by Sir John (later Lord) Boyd Orr and William Will of London. Her obituarist in *The Dufftown News* of 4 June 1938 writes:

> Mary Symon was a woman of extraordinarily wide culture... She was never happier than when acting as hostess to a party of her friends. On one memorable day three Fellows of the Royal Society sat together at her table, and she revelled in the keen interplay of their brains, in which she took the competent part... Her love of Scotland was no mere artistic sentiment but her creed, and it was that sincerity, projected into her poetry and her conversation, that made her words memorable.

The poem 'The Glen's Muster Roll', with a glossary of Scots words, is printed in full in Appendix 1. (RB)

# Emma Black

*Emma Williams, born c.1870; William Rose Black, married Liverpool,*
*12 September 1900; died Leuchars House, by Elgin, 15 December 1945.*

Emma Black was a gifted watercolour artist who painted Moray scenes and sold them for charity. She published two books of her works: *Impressions of Moray* (1931) and *Glimpses of Moray* (1937).

Emma Williams was the daughter of Owen Hugh Williams of Fulwood Park, Liverpool, and of Ann (Annie) Birch. She became a close friend of Edith Scott (Mrs Livingstone), grandmother to the current owner of Leuchars House near Lhanbryde, and went with her to a finishing school in Dresden. There she would have been schooled in drawing and painting, whilst her friend, a gifted singer, followed musical pursuits. Girls of her background were not expected to earn their own living in those days and she did not go on to art school. But she was determined to excel in art and it was of great benefit to all her subsequent charitable work.

It is not known how Emma met Col. William Rose Black. He was several years older than her and already a prominent solicitor in Elgin. They were married in St Andrew's Church, Liverpool on 12 September 1900 and lived at Oakbank in Bishopmill, Elgin, before moving to Leuchars House.

In the early 1920s, William Rose Black negotiated the purchase of the lands of Leuchars and Calcots for George Douglas on the understanding that Black would buy Leuchars house and the farm from Douglas. Leuchars House became Black's property in 1922 and he and Emma took up residence there. They never had any children and Emma's life was given to the support of local charities through the sale of her paintings. One of her earliest achievements was the setting up of the Lhanbryde & Urquhart bowling green in 1911 on Burnside Road, Lhanbryde, paid for by the sale of paintings. It was opened on 2 August 1911 and she was presented with a commemorative trophy in the form of a silver dancing lady holding a silver bowl. No doubt she also supported the building of

Emma Black, thought to be taken at the time of her wedding in 1900 (Jennifer Shaw)

a new pavilion at the bowling green twenty-one years later. When it was opened in 1932 she was presented with the original jack. Emma was a prolific and popular artist, and her paintings of Moray were sold in London, Elgin and Lochinver. She exhibited in the Elgin Library at Grant Lodge in 1922. Some years later a particularly charming set of watercolours of the old mills of Moray was published in the 1931 Christmas Number of *The Northern Scot*. Her first book of paintings, *Impressions of Moray*, was also published in 1931 and went to a second edition. In the introduction Emma wrote:

> It has been a great joy to me to live in the beautiful county of Moray, this land of my adoption, and I feel it will give me untold pleasure to paint and write my impressions of it... I am trying to depict our county 'atmospherically' and in some of its changing moods. If I have brought some of our beauty spots to mind in ever such a slight degree, I shall feel happy. No one realises more fully than I do myself how far short of my ideal these impressions of mine are.

The paintings are accompanied by descriptive text written in the form of a letter, describing Moray to an outsider.

Five years later her work was published in the Christmas number of *The Elgin Courant: Moray Life 1936*. A painting of Speyside and Benrinnes from Dundurcas was used as its frontispiece and a page entitled The Old Town Bell of Elgin was illustrated with five miniature sketches by Emma Black and a poem by DJ Mackenzie.

Emma's second book of paintings, *Glimpses of Moray*, was published in 1937. This book was printed locally, by *The Courant & Courier* office. It was dedicated to Dr Gray's Hospital and all who worked in it. Proceeds from the book went towards a new extension to the hospital, comprising outpatient department, an operating theatre, an X-ray unit and more nurses' accommodation. Emma did not write the text, as in her first book. It was introduced

'The Muckle Cross' by Emma Black, from *Impressions of Moray* (1931)

by Dr Thomas HW Alexander who lived in Lhanbryde and Emma's paintings were accompanied by poems written by local poets such as Margaret Winefride Simpson and William Hay.

Shortly after publication of her second book, Emma retired from public life through illness. She is said to have suffered from 'melancholia' and she lived the life of an invalid for seven years, looked after by a nurse/housekeeper, Mrs Grant. She would walk up and down the Leuchars front drive in a muse, and no one was allowed to use that drive, not even her husband Willie. The house was covered with ivy and surrounded by huge ponticum rhododendrons which were soon to become magic tunnel houses for the delight of the next generation of Blacks. Inside it was full of Victorian and Edwardian clutter, enlivened by Emma's colourful paintings, some graceful furnishings and Col. Willie's military and Scottish artefacts. Emma died there in December 1945. William Rose Black survived her by many years and when he died in the 1960s, the house passed to his first cousin once removed, Brigadier Gordon Black who had since his boyhood been treated by the Rose Blacks as a son; and to whose children Cousin Willie acted as a kind and much loved grandfather.

Nowadays Emma Black's paintings and books are much sought after by collectors. (MB)

# Isabel Cameron

*Isabel Margaret Noble, born Nairn, 1873; married Rev. John Cameron, 9 August*
*1904; died Nairn, 1 November 1957.*

Isabel Cameron (née Noble) was a writer of some success across the world.

She was born at her father's family home, Fern Cottage, Nairn. Her parents moved to Caithness, where her father worked as a tinsmith. Isabel pursued one of the few courses open to intelligent and ambitious girls of that time. She became a pupil-teacher and completed a teaching certificate. She taught in Inverness and was teaching in Thurso, where her family lived, when she met and married John Cameron, Free Church minister in Helmsdale, Sutherland, in 1904. Within two years Elizabeth was born. In 1908 John Cameron accepted the call to the United Free Church charge of Hopeman. This move coincided with the birth of a son, John.

Isabel Cameron had published, in a desultory fashion, stories and reflective pieces in church magazines before the publication of the first 'Doctor' booklet in 1915. Based on the character and the life of a close family friend, the Rev. Robert Cowan, long-serving minister of the High Church in Elgin, the 'Doctor' series was a publishing phenomenon. Initially published privately and distributed by TD Davidson, a bookseller in Elgin, the book was taken up by Lutterworth Press. Half a dozen sequels ensued over the next twenty years; these ran into many editions. The books were translated into German, French, Afrikaans, Scandinavian languages and Braille. They were highly popular in the colonies. A 'Doctor Omnibus' was published in 1954. On Isabel Cameron's death the publishers estimated that over a million copies of the 'Doctor' books had been sold.

Old Doctor Lindsay is the perfect model of Christian wisdom, humility, forgiveness and good humour. Some of the sketches are frankly religious tracts in which the doctor

Isabel Cameron (Jane Yeadon)

helps the blind and the lame find a way through darkness and difficulty to God and light. Some have a social purpose. 'A hungry man is an angry man,' we are told. To mend her marriage a young wife must stop buying baker bread and bake her own scones and oatcakes. No one is better than the doctor at cutting through knots, at seeing lights at the end of tunnels.

The 'Doctor' series represented only a small fraction of Isabel Cameron's literary output. She was a prolific and immensely popular novelist whose name appears in no history of Scottish literature. She published at least twenty works of fiction – novels and loosely linked collections of stories or sketches – between 1933 and her death in 1957. She was very interested in aspects of local history. She published, in 1923, *Helen Rose and the Children*, a tribute to the work of Helen Rose with poor children in Elgin. She published two collections of folklore, dealing with magic, charms and curses, witches and the evil eye: in 1928, *A Highland Chapbook* and, in 1948, *A Second Highland Chapbook*.

In some of her fiction she takes on specific social issues – for example, *New Foundations* (1955) addresses the loneliness of women transported from city and countryside to the new housing schemes of post-war Scotland. (The answer to their problems is, of course, to build a kirk.) However, in the main the novels are romances, some historical, some set in an idealised, just-vanished rural past. Class distinctions are important: the laird is respected but less so than the minister; the dominie and the doctor work selflessly for the good of the folk of the glen; the poor are either diligent and aspire after ownership of their crofts or they are feckless and drunken – but none is irredeemable; the values of the kirk triumph in the end.

Her approach was unashamedly commercial, and she was extraordinarily successful. Despite – or, perhaps, because of – the stilted characterisation and dialogue, the formulaic plots and easy resolutions, novels with titles like *Red Rowans in Glen Orrin*, *The Folk of the Glen*, *White Bell Heather*, *Tattered Tartan* and *Heather Mixture* sold hundreds of thousands of copies. In the 1930s and 1940s, the minister's wife from Hopeman, who had started to write in order to augment the frugal UF stipend, became – to her endless embarrassment – a huge bestseller.

The Rev. John Cameron had transferred to the Church of Scotland at the reunion of 1929. In 1933 he left Hopeman to take up the charge of Carnoch-Strathconon, near his birthplace of Contin in Ross-shire. On his retiral from the ministry in 1936, the couple moved to Isabel's father's family home, Fern Cottage in Nairn. After her husband died in 1943, Isabel continued to write prolifically – both fiction and journalism – up to her death. Always incredulous of her own success as a writer, she had seen, by that time, her daughter, Elizabeth, established as a successful freelance journalist, and her son-in-law, Ian Macpherson, become recognised, before his death in 1944, as one of the finest novelists of his generation.

On 1 November 1957 Isabel Cameron died in the room in which she had been born.


# Dorothy Brown

*Dorothy Brown, born 8 December 1886; died Elgin, 23 August 1964.*

Dorothy Brown was a capable and well known local artist whose paintings are owned by many people in Moray and beyond. As one of many heirs to the Dunbar shipping fortune, she had no need to earn money from her paintings and sold them all for charity.

The daughter of William Edward and Laura Brown, Dorothy was orphaned very young and brought up from about the age of ten by her aunt, May Dunbar-Rivers, née Brown. Her new siblings were Beatrix Justina, Harry and Evelyn Dunbar-Rivers, whilst her true brother, Tim, was adopted separately and died in the flu epidemic that followed the First World War. Harry Dunbar-Rivers was to become her lifelong companion.

Dorothy's early life with her adopted family was spent first at Eastbourne where she made friends with Alice Hudson, later a travelling companion. Subsequently the Dunbar-Rivers family moved to Forres House, situated at the foot of Cluny Hill where the Forres sunken garden now lies.

This was their winter residence and the huge Victorian mansion in Glen Rothes was their summer residence. She studied painting in Germany before the First World War; a war which was to take away her adopted brother Evelyn when HMS *Vanguard* blew up in Scapa Flow on 9 July 1917, as a result of an explosion in a munitions magazine.

The Dunbar shipping fortune was passed down the female line, so when Dorothy's adopted sister Justina married Martin Nasmith, he was obliged to become a Dunbar-Nasmith, and he was known as such throughout his distinguished naval career.

Dorothy Brown (James Dunbar-Nasmith)

Between the wars Dorothy Brown travelled extensively on the continent with her friend Evelyn Pease. Switzerland, Spain and Dalmatia were favourite destinations. Bicycles were sometimes hired, but only to carry the painting gear, not to be ridden. At home in Moray, Dorothy and her cousin Harry now lived at the extended Littlehaugh Cottage on the opposite side of the valley to Glen Rothes, together with their old nanny, Mary Gill.

The end of the Second World War brought Admiral Martin Dunbar-Nasmith and his family home for good. The old Victorian mansion, Glen Rothes, had been requisitioned during the war and was now sold. Dorothy Brown, Harry Dunbar-Rivers and Nanny Gill moved out of the enlarged Littlehaugh (now called Glen of Rothes) to make way for the admiral and his family. They bought an old croft with a steading and some land on the Buinach near Kellas. Here they built a small house, with three downstairs bedrooms and an upstairs studio for Dorothy. Harry, a master craftsman with wood, used the next door croft as a work shop. He had an old diesel engine which drove a circular saw and wood turning machinery in it. The steading was converted into a cottage and lived in by their retainers, first the Clarks and then Mr and Mrs Hugh Munro. In those post war years Dorothy travelled with another friend, Alice Hudson. Dorothy would sit and paint whilst Alice walked.

Dorothy had already created a wonderful garden at Glen of Rothes and now turned her attention to a new garden project. Her garden in front of the house became a riot of colour, particularly in spring. The vegetable garden of the old croft was fenced in by Harry and laid out partly for church flowers, partly for vegetables and partly for caged fruit. A greenhouse was built against the old croft to house a special peach tree and there was a rabbit's tail on a stick for pollinating it. Hugh Munro looked after the car and the policies, whilst his wife cleaned for Dorothy. Dorothy continued to paint Moray's rivers, lochs and moorlands with her car as her studio and the steering-wheel her easel.

Dorothy's adopted brother-in-law, Admiral Dunbar-Nasmith, lived on at Glen of Rothes until his death in 1965. His children David, James and Evelyn all adored their kind and generous Aunt Doe and continued to see her often. A favourite time in the week was Sunday lunch at the Crofts of Buinach, after church at Holy Trinity, in Elgin. James says she gave him his first car. David became an admiral in his own right and moved into Glen of Rothes after his father died. Evelyn became a social worker in Manchester and later took holy orders and became a deaconess.

Dorothy Brown's style of painting was loose, free and utterly convincing. She tended to use a restricted palette and was a master of the wet-in-wet technique. She is known for her watercolour views of upland Moray, particularly in autumn colours. Her life as a painter was not without certain health handicaps. She first lost the use of her right hand and had an operation on her wrist. At this point she taught herself to paint with her left hand. The trouble was really the possession of two extra ribs at shoulder level (cervical ribs). They pressed on the nerves of her arms and were removed in two separate operations in later life.

On the professional front, Dorothy Brown was a member of the Royal Watercolour Society (RWS), of the Royal Scottish Society of Painters in Watercolour and of the Society of Women Artists (SWA) where she exhibited two landscapes in 1917.

Nanny Gill and then cousin Harry both died before Dorothy. She moved to the front bedroom in the house from where she could see her beloved garden from her bed. Outside her ground floor bedroom window was an area covered with spring flowering bulbs and each gap had to be filled by Hugh Munro year on year. Munro now became her driver, taking her out to paint her favourite autumn colours.

Dot Brown (as she was known) was also a member of the Soroptomists Club of Elgin and was well-known for her charitable works. These included being a member of the governing body of the Aberlour Orphanage, of the Elgin Venture Club and of the County and District Nursing Association. She raised money for Holy Trinity Church, Elgin, through sale of her paintings. Dorothy Brown's paintings remain as her legacy and continue to delight the discerning eye. (MB)

# Margaret Winefride Simpson

*Margaret Winefride Simpson, born Buckie, 23 May 1893; died Elgin,*
*8 June 1972.*

Margaret Winefride Simpson, poet, author, artist, musician and early Scottish Nationalist was well known locally.

She was the daughter of John Simpson, justice of the peace, bank agent and town chamberlain of Buckie, and of Margaret Stuart of Keith. Miss Simpson was educated in Brussels, where she studied music, painting and classical and modern languages. She gained musical diplomas both at home and from the Brussels Conservatory. As the only child of a prosperous couple, she had received a privileged education. She returned home on the threat of war in 1913. Her father retired in 1922. The family moved to Friars House, Institution Road, Elgin. John Simpson died in 1945, his wife, Margaret, in 1959, at the age of ninety-seven.

Margaret Winefride Simpson belonged to that generation of women that reached maturity in a world bereft of men. Four million men were at war between 1914 and 1918; the census of 1921 identified a total of two million 'surplus' women. As a cultivated young woman of wide interests and independent means, eager to participate in the life of a world where women were positively discouraged from seeking employment, what was she to do? In the years following the First World War, she devoted herself to charitable works, those charities associated especially with the local regiments, the Seaforths and the Gordons and with the Red Cross. She developed her knowledge and understanding of Gaelic and helped to found the Elgin branch of An Comunn Gaidhealach; she formed and trained an orchestra and choir which she called Clann Alba – the children of Scotland; she became an ardent Nationalist and, from 1930 to 1932, she was president of the Moray and Nairn branch of the Scottish National Party. She was an accomplished artist and often exhibited her oil paintings, drawings and work in tapestry and embroidery.

She was, however, best known as a poet and writer. Between 1923 and the end of her life she published ten volumes of verse and innumerable individual and occasional poems that regularly appeared in publications from the *Times Literary Supplement* and the *Manchester Guardian* to the *Press and Journal,* the *Scots Magazine* and the magazine of the London Morayshire Club. Her work was ever present in the *Northern Scot* Christmas Number for forty years.

Miss Simpson was a considerable linguist and translated poems from French, Spanish, Italian, German, Portuguese and Gaelic into both Scots

Margaret Winefride Simpson (*Moray Life*)

and English. She was technically very skilled and her best work reveals a sure and delicate lyrical touch and an excellent ear. Her best work is probably in Scots. There are strong devotional and patriotic thrusts to her verse. There also emerges an intense love for Moray – for the changing faces of its seasons and its landscape and its folk. During the Second World War she published two volumes of verse, the proceeds of which went to military charities.

Although her work was much admired and appeared in major anthologies, including *The Oxford Book of Scottish Verse*, it is now regarded as being essentially nostalgic and of minor interest. In a decidedly cool introduction he had been invited to contribute to *Day's End* (1929) Sir Compton Mackenzie writes: 'I want to hear no more Songs of Exile (the title of a section in the book), because I dread the easy outlet they provide for a barren sentimentality.'

A devout Catholic, in 1971, the year before her death, Miss Simpson made a significant gift of ecclesiastical silver to Pluscarden Priory (as it was then), in the form of a chalice and a monstrance made from her family silver and incorporating many jewels and semi-precious stones that belonged to her and her mother.

She is buried in St Ninian's Churchyard, Enzie, alongside her mother and father. (RB)

# Kim Murray

*Kathleen Ida Murray, born 1902; died Avenue House, Duff Avenue, Elgin, 19 December 1985.*

Kim Murray was a gifted musician and conductor who championed the cause of the Moray Music Festival and is remembered by generations of musicians.

Dancing teacher Robert Hadley and his wife Agnes started a music festival in Elgin in 1922. The impact it made in Moray was noted in a speech made by the former Lord Provost Edward Stroud Harrison in 1964. When he was awarded the freedom of Elgin on 7 October that year he noted that the festival was the forerunner of the 'polished music of Kim Murray and Sister Mary Winefride and the schools'.

Miss Ida Bruce, Kim's mother, had set up business as a private music teacher in Seafield Crescent, Elgin, in 1892 at the age of twenty. Following her marriage to auctioneer William Murray she moved to Avenue House, Duff Avenue, Elgin. Avenue House was to become a place of music for decades, and well-known to generations of children from throughout the area. Ida was on the committee of the music festival from the early days, as was her daughter Kathleen, or Kim, as she was universally known. Kim was a violinist and conductor for most of her life. By the time she was twenty-one she was advertising her services in the local press as a music teacher. As a preparation for this she began giving violin recitals around the district. In October 1923 a recital in the Mechanics Hall was well received by audience and critics. Assisted by Madame Rene Black she provided 'a recital of a quality that Forres is seldom privileged to hear'.

By the 1940s Kim's business was flourishing and she took on Isabella, or Ella, Taylor from Forres as an additional teacher to meet demand. Most pupils from many of the schools in the district including Gordonstoun took their music lessons at Avenue House. Kim trained many of them for the music festival. Pupils at St Syl-

vester's Roman Catholic School had their own music teacher in Sister Mary Winefride whose lessons were given at Greyfriars Convent, Abbey Street, just round the corner from Avenue House. Few former pupils have forgotten this trio of formidable women. They were deemed to be strict and slightly eccentric but their musical talent shone through and they were able to get the best out of their sometimes reluctant pupils. John Mustard, a noted Moray cellist, recalls playing at Kim's golden jubilee concert in April 1978 when she conducted and performed at the age of seventy-six.

Kim Murray was awarded the

Kim Murray (Elgin Museum)

Sister Mary Winefride (right)
(Elgin Museum)

MBE in the New Year Honours List 1971, for service to the community. Sandy MacAdam of Dufftown, still a keen fiddle player, remembers his trips to Avenue House with affection. He was a pupil of Ella Taylor from the age of twelve until he was eighteen. He found both women strict but no more than any other adults of the fifties and sixties. He respected both ladies. A generation later he had no qualms in sending his own son there. Prince Charles learned to play the cello through the auspices of Avenue House. Ella Taylor is thought to have conducted the lessons. The Moray Music Festival flourished during their years at the musical helm. All three women entered their pupils in the competition and helped make it a continual success.

Kim died in 1985 at the age of eighty-three just a year after Sister Mary Winefride. Ella Taylor died in 1992 and a musical phenomenon in Moray was silenced. (AO)

# Elizabeth Macpherson

*Elizabeth Cameron, born Helmsdale, 2 April 1906; married 1) Ian Macpherson, May 1931; 2) George Bremner, 1949; died Nethybridge, 10 April 1998.*

Elizabeth Macpherson was a gifted writer of fiction and memoir.

Daughter of the popular writer Isabel Cameron, Elizabeth was educated at Hopeman School and at Elgin Academy, graduated MA with honours in English from the University of Aberdeen in 1928, trained as a teacher and obtained a post at Strichen Senior Secondary School in 1929. What happened next can be left largely to her own words:

> I was miserably unhappy teaching in a dreich Aberdeenshire townlet. Indeed I never wanted to teach, but there didn't seem anything else to do with my nice expensive Arts degree. Perhaps if I'd landed in any other school things might not have been quite so grim, but it was my luck to go to one of those Leaving Certificate factories of which Scotland is so proud. Ever since I was ten I seemed to have been living with one eye on the calendar for the next exams., and now, with the university behind me, found myself paid to force a younger generation through all

the worry of my own childish days. All that year I felt trapped and desperate, and the nearer it came to the time of the Higher Leaving Certificate exams, the worse it got. An appalling energy drove us all on, children and teachers alike, to reduce all culture, all learning, all loveliness, into spotters for the wretched examinations.

Thus, the opening paragraph of *Happy Hawkers* (1937), a delightful account of the first year of married life of Elizabeth and her husband, Ian Macpherson. The story of their marriage is remarkable for the time. Ian was, whilst waiting to go to Cambridge to take a second degree, assistant to the professor of English and becoming progressively more certain that he was not suited to the academic life. They 'said goodbye to caution' and burned their boats. One Saturday in May 1931, they set off to Dundee with a cheque for two guineas and friends to act as witnesses and were married by a commissioner for oaths. Ian had given up *academia*, and, Elizabeth, as a married woman, was disqualified from teaching. The plan was to buy a car and a caravan and to hawk crockery around the villages, farms and estates of the central highlands. The car they purchased was a vast, twenty-five horse power, pre-war Chalmers with broken springs; the caravan a wooden, gypsy-type van built upon an old car chassis.

*Happy Hawkers* does not recount the reaction in the manse at Hopeman to this bohemian approach to marriage and career. Elizabeth's description of her behaviour as 'partly reaction to all the respectability we had around us' suggests that rifts occurred. Ian was blamed. The rifts took time to heal.

The projected marketing of dishes soon fell through and the couple settled on selling fruit and vegetables around the upper Spey Valley. They parked the caravan at Culreoch between Grantown and Nethybridge. They were innocents to the retail trade. They made huge mistakes, learned quickly to react to need and to diversify and discovered a ready market for their wares and services. By October, they had rented (for £1 a month) an isolated cottage – Halfway House – on the high road between Dalwhinnie and Laggan. They remained there for six years.

In their first year of hawking, they had volunteered their services as local 'news reporters', including as weather reporters, to a number of newspapers. After the grouse season began, Ian became an 'estates correspondent', reporting on 'bags' throughout Badenoch and Strathspey. The years that followed at Halfway House were a period of intense creativity for Ian. His first nov-

Elizabeth Macpherson
(Jane Yeadon)

'Ian always had a preference for the more desperate course' – illustration by Mildred R Lamb from *Happy Hawkers* (1937)

el, *Shepherd's Calendar*, had been published in 1931 while he was still in Aberdeen. Now, in a period of six years, in addition to writing regularly on aspects of country life, in particular for the *Glasgow Herald* and for the BBC, Ian completed three novels, *Land of Our Fathers* (1933), *Pride in the Valley* (1936) and his greatest work *Wild Harbour* (also published in 1936).

Elizabeth, too, was busy writing. As well as *Happy Hawkers*, which, though published under both names, is clearly Elizabeth's book, she published regular journalism and two gently amusing volumes about life in fictional communities – *Letters from a Scottish Village* (1936) and *Letters from a Highland Township* (1939).

In 1938 the Macphersons took up the tenancy of Tombain, near Edinkillie, on the northern edge of the Dava Moor. They devoted themselves to the hard tasks of upland farming and raising a family. Two daughters were born, Elizabeth in 1942, Jane in 1944. The new parents were both now established journalists. Ian's wartime writings suggest that he and Elizabeth had found contentment in a way of life that suited both of them. In a 'Letter' to *Aberdeen University Review* (spring 1942), Elizabeth wrote:

> We came to our croft two years before the war began. It stands high, and seen from the road as you come towards it, it looks as if it were about to topple down into the fertile Laich of Moray and roll on into the firth, beyond which, in the distance, lie the hills of Sutherland. The views, of course, are superb; the land just hill-ground of the sort where heather grows and sheep graze...

Elizabeth at Tombain with daughter, Jane, and Nell the dog (Jane Yeadon)

> She admits that they took on the farm 'for fun' but,
>
> quite insensibly we found ourselves growing into the remorseless routine. The seasons became

our masters and the inexorable succession of seed-time and harvest taught us humility. We were taking part in something that had gone on long before us and would continue long after us. As individuals we felt ourselves of no importance and yet we knew that all we did was important because our sins of omission or commission must show for years – perhaps for generations – on the faces of our fields.

On 15 July 1944 Ian Macpherson was killed in a motorcycle accident not two miles from Tombain. Elizabeth continued to work the farm with the assistance of a land girl, an Italian prisoner of war and, later, a grieve, George Bremner, whom she married in 1949. From 1945 until she and George retired to Nethybridge in the early 1970s, she wrote a weekly column on farming and country matters, first for *The Bulletin*, and, when *The Bulletin* ceased publication, for the *Glasgow Herald* and the *Press and Journal*. Two recently published selections of these columns, *Leaning on a Gate* (2005) and *An Upland Place* (2007) provide evidence of the quality of Elizabeth's style and approach. The pieces cover aspects of agricultural politics, the problems associated with the steady amalgamation of crofts into larger units, increased mechanisation and changing practices in agriculture. She was intensely aware of what we now call 'environmental issues'. Completely unsentimental, the articles, polished, economical, literary, provide a detailed record of a way of life and of a community undergoing change and, at the same time, convey an almost visceral sense of the hardships and the pleasures, the bitterness and the beauty, of farming 'on the heather line'.

Elizabeth Macpherson died at Nethybridge on 10 April, 1989. (RB)

# John Aubrey

*Isabel Margaret Chalmers, born Nottingham, 1 May 1909; died Lossiemouth, 9 June 1985.*

Isabel Chalmers, a portrait artist who exhibited at the Royal Academy, was also an important figure in the Moray Arts Society.

Isabel Margaret Chalmers, who painted under the name of John Aubrey, was born in Nottinghamshire in 1909. The year before her birth her father, George, working as a GP, had moved from Huntly to Beeston, Nottingham. Isabel studied painting for three years at Nottingham School of Art, and a further five years at the Royal Academy Schools. At that time the reputation of the Slade was high and it was considered the best training ground.

Henry Tonks and his friend Philip Wilson Steer were influential teachers there. Their approach was opposed to the conservative method of instruction followed at the Royal Academy Schools and they encouraged their students to work directly and spontaneously from the model. Almost all the major British painters of the late nineteenth and early twentieth centuries were students of the Slade School of Art. However, whether through direct contact or simply innate preference, Isabel Chalmers painted more like a product of the Slade than the Royal Academy Schools. What she did benefit from in the latter establishment was a firm grounding in drawing which stood her in good stead throughout her career.

During the 1930s London was one of the most exciting places to be in the world of art. 'England', as Barbara Hepworth wrote 'seemed alive and rich' – the centre of an international movement in architecture and art. The closure of the Bauhaus by the Nazis in the mid 1930s saw an influx of creative talent from Germany, strengthening the trend towards abstraction and constructivism. Manifestos were produced by some of the great names of the day, and many leading German painters arrived to enrich the cultural mix. In 1936 Roland Penrose put on his ground-breaking exhibition on Surrealism, sending shock-waves through the artistic community. Students naturally identify with the newest trends, and Isabel Chalmers did produce some work in the modern style in which clusters of buildings were simplified to bold outlines and interlocking flat shapes. While these works were stylistically strong, they proved isolated experiments. The modern manner was alien to her. She was an acute observer and natural painter at her best when confronting her subject directly from the business side of the easel. In an early talk she gave about the confusion of influences troubling modern art, she began by stating that 'The art world today is in a fluid state, a state of turmoil...' Her words reveal that she was more on the side of the traditionalists than the innovators and would have approved of Augustus John's comment that the new practitioners were all, 'Cubists, Voodooists, Futurista and other Boomists'.

In 1938, having gained her diploma at the Royal Academy Schools, she exhibited *Grey Lady* at the Royal Academy. It is a portrait of modern clarity and edginess, distinguished by a masterly design, less sensually appealing than the work of later years but haunting. If the war had not come along her career might not have stalled. As it was she moved to Fochabers in Moray where she earned a living as a bank clerk. After the war, when she returned to painting from her base in Lossiemouth, she seemed to try hard to make up the lost ground. She exhibited at the Royal Academy, the Royal Scottish Academy, the Royal Society of Portrait Painters, the Royal Scottish Society of Painters in Watercolour, the Royal

Viewing John Aubrey's portrait of Elizabeth Fitzgibbon. Jess Milne on the left, Isabel Chalmers and John Aubrey on the right, Miss Anderson behind (Elizabeth Fitzgibbon)

Society of British Artists and the Royal Glasgow Institute of Fine Arts. Over the years, she held several solo shows, mainly in Edinburgh. In 1960 she was made a Fellow of the Royal Society of Arts. The steady flow of work submitted to the various societies and academies demonstrated her determination. The logistical difficulties in keeping in contact with the cities from the distance of Moray are enough to put weaker spirits off. Life would have been easier had she located in Edinburgh or London. And that is where the opportunities were for her – a gifted portrait painter who could capture a likeness with apparent ease. She might even have branched and entered the world of theatre design for which she had a particular flair. Her costume designs for ballet were executed with delightful panache in keeping with the flamboyance of the stage. There were few opportunities for any of that in Lossiemouth. Painting classes helped with the finances. A series of life classes, held in Elgin Museum Hall, in the 1970s is well remembered, not least because the model's flesh turned from shades of blue to shades of pink as the hall warmed up – most disconcerting for the budding artists.

Isabel Chalmers' interest in arts went beyond furthering her own career. In 1962 with Henry Gordon, she founded the Moray Group, a society of

THE STUDIO SALE OF JOHN AUBREY
& OTHER OIL PAINTINGS & WATERCOLOURS
Thursday 22 May 1986 at 11.00 a.m.

CHRISTIE'S
SCOTLAND

CHRISTIE'S & EDMISTON'S LTD
164-166 Bath Street, Glasgow G2 4TG. Telephone 041-332 8134

John Aubrey sale catalogue
22 May 1986 (Christie's)

ten local artists with whom she exhibited on many occasions and who must have found their work distinguished by her presence. She was also a powerful voice in the Moray Arts Club, which, with her companion Miss Anderson, she virtually ran as her own benign fiefdom for many years. Although she could be defensively crusty at times, she was quite capable of taking promising students under her wing and helping to give a start to their careers. Proof of her love of arts in general was revealed on death by a collection of some hundred watercolours and oils she had amassed over a lifetime of gallery going. Her own work has made its way into major collections worldwide including Loughborough College of Technology, the Royal Academy of Music, London, and HRH Prince Philip's Collection, Holyrood House, Edinburgh.

In Moray, Isabel Chalmers was a big fish in shallow water. Her use of the pseudonym, John Aubrey, may have some bearing on the way her life developed. The academic art world has always kept its doors open to aspiring women artists. The prejudices that women had to overcome in the recent past in order to pursue a professional career of their choice were not so apparent in the arts. There was no shortage of women artists in the early twentieth century making a successful career in the arts without feeling the need to adopt a male persona. Vanessa Bell, Ethel Sands, Dame Laura Knight, Barbara Hepworth and Dame Ethel Walker were some of the great names she might have encountered in the London art scene of the 1930s. There is no suggestion any of them were disadvantaged by a prejudice against their sex. They were trail-blazers and exemplars for any up and coming portrait painter. There was a background of artistic endeavour in Moray but it belonged more to the old school of ladies' accomplishment through the fine watercolours of Dorothy Brown and Emma Black who put their talents to the service of charitable organisations. Miss Chalmers was a traditionalist by temperament and a modern woman by feeling. She was often to be seen at Moray Arts Club exhibitions, standing at the door by the cash-box, a short, robust figure in a corduroy jacket, a fag dangling at her fingers, while Miss Anderson, her long-term companion, watched over her shoulder.

Having achieved so much it may be wrong to suggest Miss Chalmers could have achieved more or been better recognised. Her studies of children are executed with the expressive sympathy of a Joan Eardley. Her portraits of young women consistently show a painterly penetration into character. Her textual enrichment of surfaces carries a hallmark of real merit. Ian Fleming, RSA, Head of Gray's School of Art, Aberdeen, was greatly impressed by the maturity of her style. In 1958 he wrote:

> Her drawing is always evident, yet that drawing is not forced to the front, but is realised largely in paint. She concentrates largely on portraits and in these portraits she reveals the strengths of the subtleties of colour, tone and drawing that would defeat the amateur.

His commendation would have been more positive and true if he had thought to add, 'and that indicate the hand of an assured master'. (WS)

# Veronica Bruce

*Veronica Mary Bruce, born Wiltshire, 15 May 1911; died Forres, 24 January 2000.*

The Hon. Veronica Bruce was a ballerina who set up the Intimate Ballet Theatre at her home, Glenerney, Dunphail, where she ran the annual Glenerney Ballet Festival from 1961 to 1974. She also created the Cygnet Ballet Dancing School in Forres for local children.

Born in Wiltshire, Veronica was the elder daughter of Major the Hon. Robert Bruce, second son of the ninth Earl of Elgin; her mother was Mary Katherine Lindley. She spent most of her youth in England but always had a soft spot for the family's Scottish home, Glenerney, Dunphail. She was both artistic and musical and opted for dance in her teens, having been inspired by Anna Pavlova at the age of five.

Veronica had the perfect introduction to ballet; her uncle, Henry Bruce, a diplomat in Russia, had married the famous Russian ballerina Tamara Karsavina in Moscow in 1919. They fled to London and, afterwards, Karsavina had continued to dance with Diaghilev's Ballets Russes in Paris. So Veronica went to Paris to train under her aunt. Her obvious talent and aptitude developed quickly under Madame Karsavina and also Madame Cleo Nordi, soloist with Pavlova's company. She took the stage name Maria Nadezdinova and was about to embark on a career with the Ballet de la Jeunesse, founded in 1937 by Karalli, another of Diaghilev's dancers.

When the Second World War broke out, Veronica returned to Britain and made Glenerney her home. She teamed up with the pianist Kathleen

Bannerman and with the actress Nan Scott (who lived in Garmouth) and toured Scotland entertaining military and civilian audiences, under the auspices of the Entertainments National Service Association (ENSA) and the Committee for the Encouragement of Music and the Arts (CEMA), the forerunner of the Scottish Arts Council. After the war she formed the Cygnet Ballet to help give employment to young professional dancers and toured for seven years all over Scotland and as far as London and Guernsey. At the same time she was dancing all over Britain with the International Ballet Company, alongside artists such as Moira Shearer and Maurice Bejart.

Veronica Bruce at eighty-two, with pupils preparing for a Highland Hospice gala evening in Forres Academy (*Forres Gazette*)

When the onset of arthritis curtailed her own dancing in the early 1950s, she turned her hand to choreography and produced a ballet called *The White Moth* for Margaret Morris and the Scottish National Ballet. Worsening arthritis forced her to return home to Glenerney where she helped her father with the affairs of the estate. In Forres she set up the Cygnet Ballet Dancing School. She was an immensely popular teacher with local children. With Jim Hastie and Robin Anderson she started the Glenerney Ballet Festival in 1961. Performances took place over several weeks in the Intimate Ballet Theatre at Glenerney, a former squash court converted to a theatre by Robin Anderson. The soloists were young professional dancers and the corps de ballet was formed from Veronica's own local students. Several went on to the Royal Ballet School and from there to international careers.

The Glenerney Ballet Festival lasted until 1974, when Veronica underwent two hip replacements at the same time. She astonished her surgeon by prescribing and providing her own physiotherapy, something she was able to do through her training as a dancer.

Veronica's talents were not limited to music and dancing; she also wrote poetry, publishing a book of poems and prayers in the 1980s. She was a regular attendant at St John's Episcopal Church, Forres and her deep faith was important to her. Empathy with animals was another of her gifts and she kept dogs and ponies all her life. She bred donkeys and horses at

Glenerney, including one hunter that evented all over Scotland and qualified at Stoneleigh, Warwick, the principal eventing site for Britain.

Veronica moved in 1983 to Finlarig, Rafford, for the rest of her life. She continued to teach ballet at the twice-weekly Cygnet School in Forres, based at Forres Academy. In 1992 her pupils took part in a gala evening at Forres Academy in aid of the Highland Hospice. She died in Rafford in 2000.

In 2001 her sister Ursula established the Veronica Bruce Memorial Fund. This fund, administered by Scottish Ballet, was set up to provide financial aid to young dancers. Grants are allocated according to needs. In 2010/11, twenty-one young people received very significant grants towards the cost of training to become professional dancers. (MB)

# Jessie Kesson

*Jessie Grant MacDonald, born Inverness, 29 October 1916; married John Kesson, 1937; died London, 26 September 1994.*

Jessie Kesson is the most celebrated author and broadcaster associated with Moray in modern times.

Jessie was born on 29 October 1916 at the workhouse at 28 Old Edinburgh Road, Inverness, to Elizabeth (Liz) MacDonald, a member of a large farming family in the Alves–Mosstowie area of Moray. Her mother was thirty-one when Jessie was born.

'There has been', writes Isobel Murray, 'endless debate on the question of Jessie's paternity.' Jessie came to believe, later in life, that her father was John Foster, sheriff clerk of Moray, author of the popular historical romance *The Bright Eyes of Danger* and occupant of Ladyhill House in Elgin. However, in applying for poor relief to the inspector of the poor for the parish of Alves, Jessie's mother, on three occasions, identified her daughter's father as John Smith, woodcutter, widower (forty-one), of Redbog, Lhanbryde. According to Liz, John Smith's origins were in Dallas. Liz's parents, Robert and Jessie MacDonald, had lived at Badentinan, Redbog, Lhanbryde from 1910. After giving up farming at Cardenhill, Alves, Robert had acquired the wood contract for Jones Brothers of Larbert, employing men from all parts. Some of the workers no doubt lodged in the vicinity of Badentinan – perhaps even with the MacDonalds.

The extensive range of applications for poor relief during Jessie's early years makes depressing reading. On the day before Jessie's birth, her mother presented herself to the parochial board of Alves to seek relief. She is de-

Jessie Kesson c.1987, the year she received a DLitt
from the University of Aberdeen
(*The Northern Scot*)

scribed as 'Partially Disabled'; the description of the 'disablement' – 'Pregnant'. Liz was sent back to the workhouse in Inverness and, three weeks after the birth, mother and daughter were admitted to the Elgin poorhouse at Craigmoray in Bishopmill, where they stayed for about four months. Jessie was Liz's second child. The first daughter, Peg, was absorbed into the large MacDonald family, but Liz's father could not accept his daughter's second 'mistake', nor her feckless lifestyle, with the result that Liz and Jessie were cast out to fend for themselves. The next ten years were marked by erratic school attendance, by a succession of appeals for 'Outdoor Relief' and by admissions of mother and daughter to Craigmoray. At one point the inspector of the poor for Alves observes, 'She has led an unsettled life'. In fact, Liz's life was one of desperate poverty, small time prostitution and growing dependence on alcohol. She neglected Jessie who, at the age of ten, was taken from her mother at the instance of the Scottish Society for the Prevention of Cruelty to Children and admitted to Proctor's Orphan Training Home at Skene, Aberdeenshire. She stayed there until she was sixteen. In *Writing her Life*, Isobel Murray states:

> almost all the extant evidence of Jessie's life is in her own papers, her writing, her letters. The biographer is forced back on this 'evidence' and must use it, even when not reliable in the strictly factual sense.

She writes of Jessie's need to 'work over and over her early years... to construct the necessary myth of her life'.

Central to the emotional impact of her first novel, *The White Bird Passes* (1958) is the presentation of Liza, the mother of the central character, ten-year-old Janie. Liza has all the faults and weaknesses of Jessie's own mother, and Janie is devoted to her.

Liza had always leapt burnished, out of her surroundings. And in the leaping had made the dim world bright.

All the things I know, she taught me, God. All the good things, I mean. She could make the cherry trees bloom above Dean's Ford, even when it was winter. Hidden birds betrayed their names the instant she heard their song. She gave the nameless little rivers high hill sources and deep sea endings. She put a singing seal in Loch Na Boune and a lament on the long lonely winds. And the times in the Lane never really mattered, because of the good times away from it. And I would myself be blind now, if she had never lent me her eyes.

In an interview with Isobel Murray and Bob Tait (*Scottish Writers Talking* 1996) Jessie says:

> it was my mother... she was the one that had the poet in her – she really had – it wis her gave me my great love for all o' it, it really was.

At the orphanage, Jessie came under the influence of Donald Murray, dominie of Skene Central School. He recognised her gifts and her spirit, encouraged her reading but was unable to persuade the trustees of the orphanage to finance her staying on at school to take the leaving certificate and to go, perhaps, to university. For the rest of her life, Jessie harboured resentment at being thus deprived of the chance of university education. In 1932 Jessie had to leave school to take a job as 'kitchie deem' at a neighbouring farm. She dedicated *A White Bird Passes* to Donald Murray.

The next few years were very difficult for Jessie. She left the farm, lived in a women's hostel in Aberdeen, worked in Isaac Benzies department store and attended 'commercial' classes at the Central School. She suffered a major breakdown and spent a year in the Royal Cornhill Mental Hospital in Aberdeen. She was, in the spring of 1936, 'boarded out' as a 'patient' with an old woman in Abriachan, high above Loch Ness. In Inverness, she met and married Johnny Kesson, eleven years her senior, in 1937.

Their eldest child, Avril, was born in 1938. From 1939 till 1946, the Kessons, like hundreds of other cottar families, traversed the north of Scotland from year to year from farm to farm from Rothienorman, near Inverurie, to Poyntzfield on the Black Isle, before settling in the Elgin area, under the patronage of farmer Hugh Kellas, first at Coulardbank near Lossiemouth then at Wester Calcots, then at Linksfield, on Elgin's northern fringe. The second child, Kenny, was born in 1946. Jessie's mother, Liz, died of syphilis in Craigmoray in 1949. The family left Moray for London in 1951.

Throughout the 1940s Jessie was writing for publication and broadcast. She wrote poems, reflective pieces of prose, stories and radio plays. These were published in the *Scots Magazine*, *North East Review* and aired on the Scottish Home Service of the BBC and on the third programme. In her writings she strove to come to terms with the difficulties and the paradoxes of her own life: the childhood neglect, the complex relationship with her mother, her experiences in orphanage, hostel and mental hospital, the privations and insecurities of cottar life. She was also working – over a period of sixteen years – on the text of *The White Bird Passes*.

Life in London was not easy for the Kessons. Johnny found work on the roads and with builders; Jessie's work ranged from cinema cleaner to Woolworth's assistant to life model. Later, she had difficult – and very responsible – jobs working with young people and with the elderly – often the mentally handicapped and the disabled. Johnny had serious heart attacks in the early sixties, and his earning capacity declined. *The White Bird Passes* was published in 1958 to enthusiastic reviews.

The novel deals with the life of Janie from eight to fifteen, first in an Elgin close and then in the orphanage at Skene. The novel explores, in an impressionistic series of short episodes and fragments of song and storytelling, the adult worlds into which Janie is growing. Our Lady's Lane is a land of misrule, dominated by women: Poll Pyke, Battleaxe, The Duchess, Annie Frigg and the small-time prostitutes, Mysie Walsh, and Janie's mother, Liza. The lane is full of singing, tales, games and fighting. The world outside the lane is dominated by patriarchal figures: the cruelty man, the sanitary man, the free boot man. It is only when she is removed from her mother to Skene that she discovers in the mannie who helps run the orphanage a sympathetic male figure. Janie is an 'ootlin'. In her 1985 interview with Isobel Murray, Jessie declares: 'Every work I've ever written contains ae "ootlin". Lovely Aberdeenshire word. Somebody that never really fitted into the thing.'

At the end of the novel, Janie, having had her hopes of a university education dashed, rejects the offers of jobs in shops and service and confirms her status as an 'ootlin': 'I don't want to dust and polish and I don't want to work on a farm. I want to write poetry. Great poetry. As great as Shakespeare.' *The White Bird Passes* is, of course, Jessie's own story. In the novel, which was a long time in the making, she strove to come to terms with, to try to resolve, perhaps, some of the difficulties of her life.

*Glitter of Mica*, Jessie's favourite of her novels, appeared to mixed reviews in 1963. It is an extraordinary piece and impossible to summarise. The central character is a man, Hugh Riddel, another 'ootlin', denied education but a valued farmworker, risen on merit, respected by the hierarchy of the parish of Caldwell, and so suspected by his peers. Much of the novel focuses on the lives of Hugh's wife, Isa, his daughter, Helen, and his mistress, Sue Tatt. The whole parish is characterised – in its social structures, its prejudices, its tensions, both public and private, and in the limitations it places on women's lives. There is a political dimension to this novel. Hugh Riddel is invited to present the immortal memory at the parish Burns supper. He identifies the people of Caldwell with the 'unco guid' of Mauchline in Burns's day. He 'deprived [his audience] of the comfort of myth' and 'flung, as it were, all the little statues of Highland Mary off their mantelpieces and left them lying in broken pieces'. The novel can be seen as a sustained attack on the sentimental picture of the cottar's life that Burns presented to the Edinburgh gentry in *A Cottar's Saturday Night* and at the same time as a memorial to the victims of the oppressive system that Jessie and her family escaped in their departure for London in 1951.

Publication of the two novels and the praise that followed brought no real easing of financial worries. Jessie wrote much for the BBC. Plays and 'talk' pieces were produced, but she strove for a job, particularly with *Woman's Hour*, however, nothing permanent was forthcoming. In the early Seventies the Kessons spent about four years in East Lothian, Jessie working in a List D School for girls. They returned to London in 1976. Jessie was writing stories and adapting them for radio and, importantly, helping Michael Radford in preparing the script of *The White Bird Passes* for television. The film was produced in 1980 to publicity, acclaim and awards. There was money too. Jessie, at the age of sixty-four, was, at last, able to give up the 'hard jobs'. Further success followed in 1983 with the publication of the novel and the release of the film *Another Time, Another Place*.

In this novel Jessie revisits her own experience of forty years earlier. Recently married, she and Johnny had fee-ed at Udale on the Black Isle. Jessie was given responsibility for providing a modicum of care for the Italian prisoners of war who occupied the bothy next door. The young woman of the novel is an 'ootlin' in several senses. Town bred, she is alien to the culture of the cottar system; childless, she is the odd one out in the row of cottar houses; she is isolated, too, in her marriage, from the kind, older man with whom she has nothing in common. She is excited both sexually and imaginatively by the presence of the Italians. They represent a possibility of escape, but her brief adventure with Luigi, the Neapolitan barrow-boy, ends in shame, guilt, loss of dignity. She is left with very little when the Italians leave:

a ship in a bottle and a note –
Dina
*Con amore e molte felicitas*
Paolo     Umberto     Luigi

They had never known her real name, she remembered. And had bequeathed her with a name of their own choice.

With the success of the book and the film, Jessie Kesson was a household name in Scotland. Her collection of stories, *Where the Apple Ripens* was published in 1985. She received honorary doctorates: from Dundee University in 1984 and from the University of Aberdeen in 1987. She was still writing for the BBC. She was now sought after as a speaker and as a judge of literary competitions. She was a star turn at the annual Edinburgh Book Festival. In a piece for *Woman's Hour* in 1957, Jessie wrote:

I think perhaps I've got to the core of the reason why I can't go back. It is our dreams and plans that make day to day living bearable. These dreams and plans are stronger in our youth, and in the places where our youth is spent, but we usually have to go away to fulfill them. Once we have done so, there is nothing to go back for.

Elgin was always important to Jessie. She remains an important figure in the local consciousness. She is remembered as a 'character' in the town: bold and outspoken, complex and paradoxical. Stories about her behaviour abound, from mildly humorous tales of her eccentric dress sense and her failures as a housekeeper to scurrilous accounts of her drinking habits, her treatment of Johnny and of her allegedly casual way with other people's money. After moving to London, Jessie maintained contact, through letters and visits, with a wide range of old friends and neighbours.

Jessie Kesson's literary output amounted to three slim novels, a collection of short stories and an unknown number of radio plays – possibly more than a hundred – many of which are lost. Other work for radio and magazines included stories and reflective and autobiographical pieces and a handful of fine poems.

Her work is not easy. It treats big and difficult subjects. It deals with lost chances, with the death of hope, with the powers that stunt the growth of ordinary people. It never seeks the easy way out. It is harrowing and often tragic. Kesson is passionate in her commitment to her notion of 'the sma perfect'. There is no superfluity. Language and narrative are pared down, sharpened to maximum effect. She takes great risks, for example with the handling of time in her fiction and with the significance of what is left unsaid.

All three novels and the collection of stories are in print. Two publications by Isobel Murray of previously uncollected radio and magazine work are available. Jessie Kesson's place in the history of Scottish fiction is secure.

By the nineties, both Jessie and Johnny were ailing. Jessie's time was divided between writing for the BBC and caring for Johnny. He had further heart problems and a succession of strokes; she suffered from bronchitis and angina. In the autumn of 1994, Johnny died. Jessie died of lung cancer less than two months later. They were both cremated, and their ashes scattered at Abriachan where they had first met. (RB)

## CHAPTER TWELVE

# Sporting Success

*To those who had never seen lady golfers of the champion class play, their*
*performances were astounding, and to most mere men players somewhat depressing.*
Report on the Scottish Ladies Championship, Nairn, 1910[1]

IN JANUARY 2009 Louise Richardson, an Irish born American, was appointed as principal of the University of St Andrews. The Royal and Ancient Golf Club (R&A) of St Andrews had always been in the habit of granting honorary membership to the principal of the University, but no such offer was forthcoming to Louise Richardson because the R&A does not admit women.[2]

For hundreds of years commonly held beliefs about the physiology of women's bodies, the fashions of the day and the expectations that women were encouraged to hold for themselves militated against their participation in hard physical exercise for pleasure, with the possible exception of the traditional country sports of the landed gentry – hunting, shooting and fishing. Even when sports such as bicycling, tennis and golf became popular towards the end of the nineteenth century, they tended to be the preserve of the middle classes. The keep fit exercises of the 1930s, promoted by the Scottish Fitness Council, were genteel and restricted to 'those of a rhythmic nature for use with music'. There was a suggestion that women should conserve their energies for childbirth.

There were tennis clubs in many of the villages and towns of Moray by the end of the nineteenth century – over a dozen are listed in Libindx. *The Northern Scot* Christmas numbers contain photographs of women on the tennis courts from the first decade of the twentieth century. Nora Mackintosh of Dufftown won the Scottish National Girls' Championship in 1926, and the British Girls' Championship at Wimbledon in the following year.[3] Women were prominent in the Moray Mountaineering Club from its beginnings in 1932, Miss H Harrison being vice president in 1935. These women took to the hills with alacrity, as can be seen from Ethel Fraser's diary. Ethel, a book-keeper with the Elgin Dairy, was an

Scottish Ladies Golf Championship, Lossiemouth 1912 (*The Northern Scot*)

active member of the club for many years and a good amateur photographer. During a weekend in the Cairngorms, when ice axes were needed, she made it down to the Shelter Stone by Loch Avon. Another weekend, in July 1938, saw Ethel, Miss Hood, Bess Anderson and Rita Fraser leave Elgin by train for Aberdeen, then take the bus up Deeside. Starting from Braemar at 8.45pm they walked through the Lairig Ghru, reaching Coylumbridge sometime the next day. After a night at Coylumbridge they took the train home from Aviemore. All this in tweed skirts. [4]

The Moray Golf Club in Lossiemouth was happy to admit women, almost from its beginnings in 1889. By 1897 there were eighty-five women members – over a quarter of the membership. There were restrictions, however: the women could not start playing until 10.30 am and they were required to let the men pass them on the course.[5] The popularity of the women's game nationally can be judged by the gathering in Lossiemouth of women golfers in 1912 for the Scottish Ladies' Amateur Championship, seen in the photograph at the head of this page.[6] As the county club with a championship course, Moray Golf Club acquired a prestige above that of the other local clubs. Its membership was described by John McConachie (1988) as consisting mainly of 'Elgin gentlemen, and later, English and London gentlemen and their ladies'.

Mary Benton (sister of Sylvia) was Ladies' Champion of the Moray Golf Club six times between 1906 and 1919. In a photograph taken at the Scottish Ladies Championship at Nairn in 1910, Miss Benton is shown taking a swing in a long white skirt, and with a wide hat held in place by a chiffon scarf.[7] A framed text found in Moray Golf Club stated that she played for Scotland. In 1936, then in her fifties, she was playing off a handicap of four.[8] Women at the Moray Club still play for the Mary Benton Quaich that she presented in 1949.

George Smith, Meg Farquhar's mentor, was an important professional at Lossiemouth. Scottish Professional Champion in 1922, and Scottish

Meg Farquhar – the occasion and the people are unknown (Farquhar Thomson)

Internationalist in 1932, his training facilitated the success of Hilda Cameron and Kathleen Macdonald, who did well in competitions throughout Scotland in the 1920s and 1930s. In 1928 Kathleen, the youngest Scottish cap, played in the Home Internationals at Hunstanton and won all her matches.

Peggy Ramsay, another of Smith's pupils, came to Lossiemouth from Northumberland each summer for the golf. Her father built Hillhead, a house in Dunbar Street, as a holiday home. She made it to the final of the Scottish Ladies' Championship on two occasions.[9] Indeed, because of the golf, Lossiemouth was an attractive holiday destination and hotels like the Stotfield and the Marine were built to cater for the tourists' needs. A book for children written in 1938 tells the story of a family motoring to Scotland for a golfing holiday in Lossiemouth, the children playing on the relief course.[10] The author, Eleanor Helme, reporter on *The Morning Post*, was a member of Moray Golf Club and champion there in 1914.[11]

Ramsay Macdonald's pacifist views caused controversy in the 1920s and he was black-balled by the club. Interviewed in 1924 for the *Strathspey Herald*, George Bernard Shaw commented:

I felt I must see a place which has simultaneously produced the best Prime Minister of our time and the most stupendous collection of golf snobs known to history.[12]

John McConachie's history of the Moray Club concludes:

> Gentlemen in stiff shirts with dinner jackets, no longer stroll over to the
> Moray Golf Club on a summer evening after dinner in the Stotfield or
> Marine Hotels while the inhabitants of Lossiemouth look on in wonder.

Although the links have always been part of the Moray scene, they
were not always accessible to the Lossiemouth locals. It remains remarkable
that Moray's most significant sportswoman, born a hundred years ago,
was the daughter of a Lossiemouth fisherman who taught herself golf
while caddying for the gentry.

# Margaret (Meg) Farquhar

*Margaret Farquhar, born Lossiemouth, 29 April, 1910; married John Alex Main*
*1947; died Lossiemouth, 9 November 1988.*

Meg Farquhar, at the age of nineteen, became the first woman assistant
professional golfer in Britain. Reinstated as an amateur in 1949, she had a
distinguished career in the game, representing Scotland twice in the Home
Internationals.

Meg Farquhar, the daughter of Jane McLeod and Robert Farquhar,
Baptist fisherman, was born in Lossiemouth and lived in the town all her
life. A younger sister, Isabella, trained as a nurse and died in 1936, at the
age of twenty-three. Meg taught herself to play golf whilst caddying for the
London gentry who spent their summers in the town. She showed a natural
aptitude for the game and rose to the top, despite golf being regarded as a
sport for wealthy males, and most golf clubs restricting or forbidding
female members.

In 1929, when she was nineteen, her playing skills were brought to the
attention of Johnny McAndrew who ran a golf school in Glasgow. Because
Meg's parents did not like the idea of her going to Glasgow, her father
contacted George Smith, the professional at Moray Golf Club, who offered
her a job as his assistant. Despite her ambition to be a nurse, she accepted
this offer and so became the first woman professional in Britain. Under
George Smith she received training in all the skills that a golf professional
needed, such as making and repairing clubs and giving lessons.

The Scottish Professional Championship was played over the Moray
Links in 1933 and, encouraged by Smith, Meg Farquhar entered and was
accepted to play. Thus, she became the first woman to play in what was

Meg Farquhar, Scottish Professional
Championship 1933 (Moray Golf Club)

normally an all male national championship. She had a vociferous following of blue-ganseyed local fishermen on the course. She regularly outdrove her playing partners off the tee and threatened to cause an upset when she finished her first round only four shots behind the leader. Unfortunately, she did not fare so well in the three subsequent rounds, slipping to fiftieth place but still ahead of many of her male contemporaries.

Despite the fact that steel-shafted clubs were legal in Britain by this time, she had played with hickory-shafted clubs, which put her at a distinct disadvantage. After the tournament, the True Temper Corporation of America presented her with a set of steel shafts which were made up for her by Nicoll of Leven, in recognition of her brave performance.

She remained as a professional at Lossiemouth for another five years and established a significant reputation as a teacher. An advertisement for George E Smith's Sports Emporium in Batchen Street, Elgin (in *Moray Life*, 1935) states that 'Miss Farquhar is in charge at Elgin and gives lessons at 2/- per half-hour.' Of course, it was very unusual for lady golfers to be able to get lessons from a professional of their own sex. Indeed, such was the prestige of Moray Golf Club in the 1930s that it was very unusual for a local resident, never mind a woman, to enter the clubhouse. The Second World War changed all that.

After the war, by now married, playing as Meg Farquhar Main, and tired of being the only female in all-male competitions, Meg was reinstated as an amateur. In 1949 she reached the semi-final of the Scottish Ladies' Amateur Championship at Troon, losing to the eventual winner, Jean Donald. In 1950 she played for Scotland in the Home International Championship in Newcastle, County Down, winning all of her matches. She travelled to this championship with the Irish internationalist Chrystal McGeagh, who lived in Huntly House, Lossiemouth – at that time a private home. The two players went by train from Lossiemouth to Elgin, then to Glasgow, where they caught the steamer to Belfast. After a three-day journey, they arrived to find that they had to play against each other. Meg won this match 5&4 and went on to win all her matches in the tournament. It was unusual for two internationalists to be living in a small town like Lossiemouth; Meg from a local fishing family and Chrystal from a wealthy Irish family. As far as is known they are the only two ladies to have played in the prestigious Moray Open Tournament, which still takes place at Lossiemouth every year and, as its name implies, is open to all.

Meg played for Scotland again in 1951 and won all her matches at Broadstone in Dorset. She did not play for Scotland thereafter, but maintained a high standard of golf, playing to a handicap of plus one in 1957 at the age of forty-seven – a remarkable feat unlikely to be repeated. Although she did not play in amateur competition until she was thirty-nine, she was ladies' champion at Moray nine times and won the Northern Counties Championship five times.

At the time of her death, Meg had the distinction of being the sole woman honorary member of Moray Golf Club.

Whilst she is known and respected as the first lady professional golfer, her amateur career was more illustrious. In an interview in the *Press and Journal* in 1988, the year of her death, she reflected,

> as a teenage girl I did not realise I was cutting myself off from amateur golf completely. I did not even have a handicap. I really should have achieved something as an amateur before getting a job as a professional …Maybe I could have become a famous amateur player before World War II if I hadn't taken the job as an assistant professional… if I had my time over again, I would have gone in for nursing.

For all that, Meg Farquhar Main is still the finest lady golfer that Moray has produced. She continued to play golf to a high standard well into her seventies. She died at the age of seventy-eight and is buried in Lossiemouth Cemetery. (SM)

CHAPTER THIRTEEN

# Tradition and Memories

*The women were the worst rioters. One of the special constables was Robert Murdoch, a shoemaker. As he came out of the hotel, three women followed him with their aprons filled with stones and bottles.*

JJ Dawson recalling, in about 1931, memories of 1846[1]

IN THE MID-NINETEENTH CENTURY an economic crisis hit Moray, resulting in desperate poverty. Whilst not so devastating in Moray as in Ireland and the highlands, the potato famine of 1846 caused an increase in the price of grain across Scotland. Ordinary people could no longer afford enough oatmeal to sustain their families. And yet, along the coast of Moray, ships continued to export grain. As the inhabitants of Findhorn, Burghead, Garmouth and other villages watched the shipments being loaded, resentment grew and spilled over into the riots of January 1847. Sometimes men led the riots, sometimes women. Elizabeth Grant and Janet McIntosh led a mob that prevented three ships, *Ceres*, *James* and *Jessie*, from loading at Burghead. In panic, the government sent 100 soldiers of the 76th Regiment from Edinburgh to quell the rioters, and the two women were imprisoned in Elgin jail. Meanwhile, along the coast at Findhorn, porters were refusing to load the ships. When carts and labourers were brought from Gordon Castle to do the porters' work, the troops had to protect the labourers from a threatening crowd. This time Margaret Macdonald, or Murray, and Isabella Brown were arrested and escorted by the troops to Elgin jail. Some of the men who were arrested were sentenced to transportation. Hearing of Queen Victoria's tour of the highlands, a group of fisherwomen from Burghead and Hopeman decided to seek an audience with the queen to plead against the transportation. These women walked to Ardverikie, the castle by Loch Laggan where the queen was staying during September 1847. The distance from Hopeman to Ardverikie is a round trip of nearly 200 miles. They did not see the queen, but they met Earl Grey, who advised them to return home, to gather a petition, and to post it to the queen. This they did, and the men were later released.[2]

This story is remembered in Hopeman today, although sometimes it is

316

said that the women walked to Balmoral. However, the Queen's first holiday at Balmoral did not take place until 1848; the castle was purchased by Albert in 1852. Whilst details may have changed in the telling, the gist of the tale stands to remind the fishing community of the strength of its womenfolk.

This chapter is about tradition and memory. Christina Munro's story cannot be validated, but that does not mean that it should be forgotten. Someone in 1888 remembered the hanging. Of course stories change in the telling, but the theme of the story may be more important than the facts. The story of the grain riots is a tale about injustice. The location of the Queen does not change the purpose of the memory.

Travellers no longer camp in bow tents in the Lhanbryde belts, and fishwives no longer carry their men out to the fishing boats because there is no decent harbour, but it is important to remember and record such history and to recognise the part that women played in the community. If the women had not carried their menfolk out to the boats, the fishermen, with their thick woollen socks, could have had wet, cold feet for their whole trip.

Talk to local people about memories and they will mention teachers who were loved and/or feared and revered district nurses. They will remember Fanny Baxter who taught the piano and 'Tihi' Dunbar the dancing teacher. And they will recall characters like big Joanne McCulloch, wearing her spotless white pinafore, and on occasion swearing and cursing at the police. Was she the same person as the Joanne who sold pegs around by Spey Bay, who was always clean and polite, but was known to swear like a trooper? This Joanne knew that the sweetest water came from the

Women carrying their men to the boats, Moray Firth, date unknown
(Buckie Heritage Centre)

well at Alves. She would take away old clothes, but always gave something in return such as a fruit bowl.

On other occasions reminiscence will turn to fortune tellers: Mrs Plummer, from a single end in Bishopmill, who might tell of the tall dark stranger, and the Batchie from the Batchen croft near Miltonduff. People have differing memories of the Batchie. Was her name Annie Dean? Most agree that she had a goat. Teenie Webster might be called to mind; she collected unwanted items from houses and made a small income from selling to others. The travelling shows brought colour and excitement to Moray every year. In Elgin the travellers set up camp on the Lossie Green. Their children went to local schools when the showies were in town. The musical family, the Stewarts of Blair, came to Moray every summer, the children cockling on the shore with their mother whilst their father did business with Williamson the scrap metal dealer.

People who record the memories, either in tales or legends or as curators and historians, are also keeping the stories in circulation. The London Morayshire Club collected stories about local characters. *Old Morayshire Characters* and other books of a similar nature are based on local memories, but few women feature.

In the nineteenth century, the term 'worthy' acquired a touch of irony and is now generally used to denote a strong personality, 'a character'. This chapter includes some worthies and some who are remembered only for their misfortune, but about whom relatively little is known. However, their stories give an insight into the community of their times and attitudes towards impoverished women. The women in this chapter have not made great discoveries or travelled far (excepting Mrs Levack), but readers will recognise their place and their importance. Our collective memories of such women helps to give Moray its identity.


# Christina Munro

*Christian Munro, born Ross, date unknown; died Elgin, date unknown.*

Christina was a farm servant and seer in the Duffus area, and convicted of the murder of her infant. Legend relates that the child was killed by his father.

There is a green hill at North Covesea Farm on the Moray coast known as 'Christina's Knock'. Christina was engaged as a half-yearly domestic servant to a farmer in the neighbouring Parish of Duffus, and the story goes that from this hill, the young woman would gaze longingly across the

Elgin Tolbooth from Rhind's *Sketches of Moray* (1839)

Firth towards her home in north-eastern Ross.

Credited with the second sight, Christina saw a shadow, a corpse-like tinge that foretold her doom. At the start of her second engagement, at the Martinmas term, the shadow of a fellow-servant crossed her path – she became pregnant and the father did not marry her. From here on, the reason why Christina's story persists becomes more obvious: the man apparently so grudged the miserable amount he was compelled to pay in support, that he nipped, pinched or strangled the child during a visit, so that it almost immediately died. There were no witnesses, and, within forty-eight hours, Christina had been tried and executed in Elgin.

The inhabitants of the West End are said to have protested at this haste by shutting their doors and covering their windows as she was led by the hangman from the Tolbooth to the Gallows Green. However, it would seem there was also a good turn-out at the gallows as what happened next was still recounted by older inhabitants in 1888. At the twenty-foot scaffold, she underwent a change from 'the poor yellow-haired, child-like girl' with 'the shrinking demeanour of those about to suffer the last dread penalty of the law' and made this curse:

Ho, dwellers in a city of kirks and manses, ye have come up making holiday over the destruction of the innocent, and he who has sworn my life away stands in your midst, flaunting in ribbons and ruffles, but the heritage of the destroyer shall not stand, nor the chief of the arraigners or the suborners of a lie escape, for the winged ones of the air shall be my witness, and the Judge of all the earth my defence, before God and this great assembly.

The sight of the girl's dead body being torn apart by the dogs of the town, in the presence of the representatives of the law, had a lasting effect on the future conduct of 'hanging cases' in Elgin.

The detail of the story suggests it is history, but corroboration is difficult without a confirmed date. As the tolbooth was demolished in 1843 this gives a terminus post quem for her death. A ballad by Andrew Watt, schoolmaster, was published in *The Elgin Courant*, about 1858, and may be the origin of the tale. To put this execution in some context, the last fully public hanging in Scotland was in March 1868, two months before Parliament passed the Capital Punishment (Amendment) Act. (JT)

# Jean Carr (or Kerr)

*Jean Carr, born c.1770, died 1830.*

There are not many detailed facts about Jean Carr's tragic life but local legend tells of a young girl at the mercy of a demented father who chained her up in their home in Garioch. Jean managed to escape and, for a short time, lived the life of a vagrant travelling the country between Banff and Fochabers. She soon gave birth to a son, but the baby was taken away from her by the authorities who were concerned for his welfare.

The baby was called John and given the surname Banff – the name of the town in which he was born. Jean desperately tried to get her baby back but was thrown into jail for her efforts. John died after a few short months of life and an unreferenced notification of this event is given as:

1785, John Carr, natural son of Jean Carr, idiot, died on 9th August, aged 15 months, buried at the back of the shoemaker stair, north side of the church.

Which church is not now known, but presumably it was in Banff. This tragedy proved too much for Jean, and there was no medical or social support for people like her with special needs. However, the community around Fochabers tolerated her, despite the belief that that she would try and steal young children. When she appeared in the village the warning cry would ring out – 'Lock up your bairns, Jean Carr is in town'. It was rumoured that she had murdered one child by throwing it into the river Spey from the old Fochabers bridge, but this may have been just a story used to frighten naughty children into obedience.

Doubtless relying on handouts, Jean spent her nights in the woods around Fochabers, sheltering under a huge stone and surviving as a vagrant until she was a relatively old woman. She was found dead under the stone in 1830, and her ghost is reputed to haunt the area still. This stone in Slorach's wood on Ordiquish hill is now known as Jean Carr's stone, perpetuating the memory of her unfortunate and desperate life. (JM)

# Lucky Jonson

*Lucky Jonson, date and place of birth unknown; lived in New Elgin in the early to mid-1800s.*

Lucky Jonson was one of the oldest residents in Middle Street, New Elgin, during the mid 1800s. Her story appears in an obscure book written by a local minister of the time who believed the lives of some of his more colourful parishioners should be recorded. Thanks to his little book we can appreciate the tribulations of a woman who was reputed to be a witch.

Lucky Jonson was a cranky old maid who wore an old-fashioned white muslin mutch on her head and, as a consequence of continually grumbling about the world going to the dogs, had very few friends. Her past was a mystery and it was thought that she came from either the Cabrach or 'over Rafford way'. She lived in two rented rooms and for many years had daily battles over the fence with her neighbour John Oggle. As she grew older, Lucky gained a reputation as a witch and was blamed for casting bad luck spells on people that passed her door. When Andra Adams the carter broke his leg on the way to Portknockie with a load of wood, he blamed it on Lucky because she wished him good morning on the day it happened.

She was blamed for the death of a valuable pig. Sammy Boggs, a plasterer's labourer fell off a twenty-foot high scaffold and injured his back. He was carried home lying flat on a door and blamed Lucky for his accident.

Her neighbour John Oggle wouldn't go to the wood for sticks for his fire if Lucky was near her door for he knew from bitter experience that some evil would overtake him before he got home again. He had been chased by 'gammies' (gamekeepers) and had to return home without a 'fir reet' to light his fire because of her – or so he believed.

Lucky couldn't see well in the dark, so the local lads would get her on the warpath then hide behind a hedge and call out names to enrage her. Sometimes they would kick her door – until the day she grabbed one tormentor and beat him so badly that they stopped the teasing. People became convinced that Lucky was a witch with a broomstick which she rode at night and she fostered the idea for her own profit. Kenny the horse-dealer, always gave her a shilling to 'buy tea' when setting out to horse trade in order to avoid her evil eye. This sort of money was a vital help to the impoverished Lucky. Her battles with her neighbour came to a head when her hens caused havoc in his onion patch. Enraged, John Oggle killed her eleven hens 'with saut and meal'. When her hens were destroyed Lucky was devastated, mourning for them and falling into a decline. Even the remorseful John Oggle's wife could not tempt her to eat and, never recovering from her loss, Lucky died soon afterwards. Despite the rumours of a hoard of silver, none was found, and Lucky's meagre furniture had to be sold to pay her debts.

It is a sad but not unusual story of poverty and of prejudice towards an elderly, somewhat irascible lonely old woman. If Lucky had been living in an earlier era there is a strong possibility that she would have been burnt, strangled or drowned after being accused of witchcraft by superstitious neighbours. (JM)

# Jeannie Shaw

*Jeannie Shaw, mid 19th century.*

The latest cemetery extension in Elgin took place in the 1960s when an area of land on the north side of Linkwood road was utilised. Previously this land had been an area of scrubby trees, gorse bushes and sandy hillocks. It was much enjoyed by youngsters of New Elgin who ran around playing a variety of childhood games amongst the dunes until the siren from the bacon factory on Linkwood Road sounded, reminding them to run home for their dinner. The ground was called 'Jeannie Shaw's widdie' by all the New Elgin locals. During the Second World War, it was a favourite meeting place for soldiers from the nearby Pinefield camp and the local girls. After the war local children continued their adventure games at Jeannie Shaw's and sometimes the Brownies would be taken there for picnics.

Nowadays the area has been landscaped and tidied and the gorse and sandy hillocks have been replaced by grass and granite headstones. There are still a few local folk who, when referring to departed friends, state that they are 'playing in Jeannie Shaw's wood', but this phrase is fast being lost. One very aged local describes Jeannie Shaw as small woman dressed in black who used to keep her cow in the area. She must have been a memorable character within her community in order to have an area of land named after her. Now, a few generations later, nothing is left but her name. (JM)

# Janet Levack

*Janet Taylor Brander, born Lossiemouth 1842; married Captain John Levack; died Lossiemouth 21 Jan 1927.*

Mrs Levack was an imposing Lossiemouth figure who made a name for herself by telling stories in the local dialect. She sailed to the Far East, Australia and New Zealand with her husband.

Janet was the daughter of Robert Brander, the first provost of Lossiemouth after it was resuscitated as a municipal burgh at the end of the nineteenth century. Robert Brander was a Lloyds agent and a well-known ship owner and grain merchant. He built Rock House where Janet lived for most of her life. Brought up surrounded by shipping and trade it was not surprising that Janet should have married into that world. She married

Captain John Levack of the mercantile marine, who commanded a ship that was one of the first ships to enter a Treaty Port after Japan ended its trade isolation in 1859. Janet accompanied her husband on his voyages to the China Sea, Australia and New Zealand during the first two years of their married life, collecting stories and *objets d'art*, many of which were given to the Elgin Museum.

From February 1870, Captain John Levack made eight trips to New Zealand in command of a smart little iron barque of 580 tons, named *Schiehallion*, of the Shaw Savill Line. Emigrants and various items of cargo, including railway plant and gun powder, were taken from Britain to New

Portrait of Mrs Levack, Studio Tyrrell, Elgin (Elgin Museum)

Advertisement for the barque *Shiehallion*
(*Papers Past: Otago Witness* 1876)

Zealand and the ship returned with a cargo of wool, leather, tallow, kauri gum and sometimes even gold. The emigrants were not the easiest of people and in 1874 had mutinied on arrival at Napier, New Zealand, and had locked the captain and mate into their cabins and helped themselves liberally to grog. *Schiehallion* was wrecked in fog off the Isle of White, on a return voyage from Auckland in 1879. The Levacks' first child, Margaret, was born in 1870 in Newcastle, New South Wales, Australia. The date suggests that this was during the first of Captain Levack's eight voyages in the *Schiehallion*. The ship sailed from Gravesend with twenty-one passengers on 25 February 1870 and rounded the Cape of Good Hope on 28 April. She passed by Tasmania on 30 May, sailed through two 'heavy' NE gales in the Tasman Sea, reached Cape Maria Van Diemen on 9 June and sailed down the coast to Auckland, arriving on 6 July 1870. Two weeks later, the *Schiehallion* left Auckland, bound for Newcastle, New South Wales, where she took on board 800 tons of coal bound for Hong Kong and where the captain's first child was born. *Schiehallion* left for Hong Kong on 7 October 1870, presumably with a very small baby on board.

Thereafter Janet Levack spent two years living in London from where her husband usually sailed, and then returned for the rest of her life to Rock House, Lossiemouth. They had four daughters and one son: Margaret (b. 1870), Annie (b. 1872), Ethel (b. 1874), Jane (b. 1875) and Robert (b. 1880). Margaret married a school teacher, moved south and died in Winchester, Annie remained single and died in London aged eighty-three, Ethel stayed in Lossiemouth where she started the Lossiemouth Girl Guides, Jane died aged just five and Robert worked in Paris for Cable and Wireless, marrying a French girl Thérèse.

When steam supplanted sail, Janet's husband became a part-owner of a steamer, still trading with the Far East. He brought home a Japanese cabin boy who became a servant in the Levack household and was known locally as 'Jap'. Captain Levack later took the Board of Trade examination and became the first of his race to become a master mariner. He traded latterly with ports of continental Europe and died in 1887 at the strongly fortified port of Cronstadt, on a Russian island at the mouth of the River Neva, aged fifty-four.

During the First World War, Janet Levack used her story-telling powers to raise money to provide 'comforts' for the men at the front. She was one of the organisers of a work party which knitted countless garments for soldiers and sailors. She became a member of the War Pensions Committee, doing valuable service for the claims of widows and orphans. A member of the Morayshire Asylum Board, she was one of first two lady visitors to be appointed visitor

Rock House, Lossiemouth
(Susan Bennett)

to the asylum at Elgin. Perhaps this says something about the good nature and warm heartedness of this remarkable woman. Her interests were diverse but always with the well-being of others at their centre. She was one of the promoters of the plan to construct a wooden footbridge over the river Lossie near its mouth. Later on she was a member of the first local Association of Girl Guides in Morayshire, the committee responsible for forming the Lossiemouth Girl Guides which were started by her daughter Ethel.

Janet Levack was a storyteller, endowed with remarkable powers of observation, an exceptionally retentive memory and a rare sense of humour, even about herself. She was able to relate stories in a vivid and dramatic way so that characters of the past came alive again and would not be forgotten. *Stories of Old Lossiemouth as told by Mrs Levack* was published after her death (three of these stories appear in Appendix 2). (MB)

# Jessie Pozzi

*Jessie Paterson, born Elgin, 14 November 1855; died Cathedral Lodge, Elgin,
31 August 1943.*

Jessie Pozzi was the keeper of Elgin Cathedral for thirty-one years.

She was born Jessie Paterson, seven years before her mother married James Pozzi. Her mother, also named Jessie Paterson, was a domestic servant from Rafford and for a while young Jessie lived with her grandparents at Sheriffston and was educated at St Andrews, Lhanbryde. James Pozzi was a tailor with a clothing business at 40 High Street, Elgin, just east of Red Lion Close. He married Jessie's mother on 24 October 1862. The 1881 census lists the Pozzi family as living at 40 High Street,

Jessie Pozzi in Elgin Cathedral grounds
(*The Northern Scot*)

Elgin, along with their daughter Jessie and five younger sons. Jessie was working there as a milliner. About that time, James had to give up the clothiers on account of ill health and was appointed caretaker of the cathedral. The family moved to Cathedral Lodge (now the Cathedral shop). Jessie helped her father to show people round and read avidly about the history of the place, the local families and heraldry. She became a walking encyclopaedia.

James Pozzi and his daughter Jessie were, between them, custodians of the ruins for over sixty-five years. James died in 1912 and presumably Jessie took sole charge from then on. She became a legendary figure, dressed in a long black cloak with a hood, out of which peered a thin white face – a somewhat witch-like appearance, added to by the ever-present cat that stalked behind her with 'back arched and tail held high'. But Jessie was in reality a kindly soul, thoughtful and altruistic, with a passionate love of the venerable ruins of Elgin Cathedral and a way of passing on the excitement of the cathedral's history to the town's children which they never forgot. Her self-taught, intimate knowledge of this history enthralled people and her accounts were said to be racy and interesting. She showed round tens of thousands of people from all over the world, including royalty (Queen Mary) and nobility (Lord Oxford). Her brother said that she hardly left the place for a single night and vowed she would die if taken away from it.

The following poem about the cathedral was written for her:

> Still in thy ruins thou art strong.
> What though ivy creeps along
> Thy roofless walls? Thou hast the power
> To show the world 'twas not an hour
> That raised thee, nor a century lone
> That changed thee into mouldering stone.

Jessie died aged eighty-seven at Cathedral Lodge, Elgin, on 31 August 1943 and is buried with her parents and grandparents near the cathedral's south tower in grave number 820. (MB)

# Christina Macdonald (Joyful)

*Christina Farquhar, born Farr c.1857; married James Macpherson; died Morayshire Union Poorhouse, Bishopmill, Elgin, 1927.*

Joyful and her husband 1927
*(The Northern Scot)*

Christina was the daughter of Joan McKay and James Farquhar, a pedlar. Joyful's story is told in a two-column newspaper article subtitled 'Sad Passing of a Well Known Street Singer'. She and her husband James eked out a living in Lossiemouth and Inverness with a limited repertoire of hymns of which their favourite was 'Oh that will be joyful'. He is described as having been a chimney sweep but was practically blind and in receipt of a pension at the time of his wife's death, an event hastened by her fear of the poorhouse. They had been living for the previous nine months with their daughter and a dog under Covesea Skerries Lighthouse in one of the caves which they had lined with straw and sacking. Joyful became unwell, but when visited by Dr Brander from Lossiemouth and the local inspector of poor, Joyful was adamant she would not go to the poorhouse. It seems that in the night she resolved to go to Inverness. Despite being more or less bedridden and it being February, she made it alone to Lossiemouth where her family, aided by the dog, found her numbed with cold and speechless in Stotfield. As Dr Brander then had Joyful removed to the Morayshire Union Poorhouse, it is to be hoped she did not regain consciousness before dying there later that day. The dog, of which she had been very fond, and which had tried to savage the Police Sergeant, was taken to Elgin and exchanged for another with '1s 6d thrown in!'. His mistress was buried in Lossiemouth Cemetery, and the cause of death registered as exposure and myocardial degeneration. (JT)

# Betsy Whyte

*Betsy Whyte, born Mortlach, 14 September 1879; married 1) George Williamson, c1898; 2) Thomas Wilson, December 1908; died Lossiemouth, 1971.*

Born in Dufftown, Betsy Whyte's biography tells of a traveller's life. She and her family eventually settled in Lady Lane, Elgin, in the 1920s.

In Mortlach, Banffshire, on the 14 September 1879, Georgina Mcphee and Duncan Whyte welcomed the ninth of their twelve children into the world. They named her Betsy. In many ways this was a very ordinary brood, except that none of the children were born in the same place. The Whytes had been a travelling family for centuries. The first thing Betsy would have seen when she opened her eyes, was the canvas roof of her mother and father's bow-tent.

On her birth certificate, Betsy's father is referred to as a 'Travelling Tinsmith'. On other records he occasionally becomes a 'Pedlar', or an 'Itinerant Tinsmith', but most often he is recorded as being a 'Hawker'. This is how he is described on the birth certificate of his youngest child, a son, in 1887. Betsy no doubt remembered the birth of her brother, Duncan. He was born in the ominous sounding Hell's Hole Cave, near Hopeman, at four o'clock in the afternoon on 1 February. Other events within the family had been recorded in these caves, usually during the winter, suggesting that the Whytes stayed there in colder weather. In the summer they would have travelled with their tents, and they are recorded as far south as Linlithgow, west to Inverness, and east to Aberdeenshire. Although there are few facts to go on, the family photograph album and rumours handed down suggest they made a living in a variety of ways: trading horses, weaving baskets, pearl fishing, tinsmithing, agricultural work, and boat building. These were all typical activities for travelling families in Scotland.

The 1891 census for the 'White' family (spellings were variable) shows that the children of Georgina and Duncan were all born in different places: Renfrew, Crathie and Birse on Deeside, Mortlach and Inveravon in Banffshire, and Duffus in Moray. In the census records, the Whytes are often sharing campsites with other families of travellers, in particular the Williamsons. Several marriages between Whytes and Williamsons suggest that they were close and friendly with each other. Betsy spoke a mixture of English, Scots and Cant, a language used by travelling people, and the camps were probably filled with colourful, inventive language. According to the 1881 census, the Whytes were also Gaelic speakers. Amusement came in the form of storytelling, music, singing, and a good dram. Betsy's brothers were pipers, and later in life Betsy played a small organ which sat in her living room. She was very fond of music and encouraged her children and grandchildren to play. Betsy's grandson-in-law won the approval of the Old Woman (as Betsy was known by then) with his musical skills. Initially he was terrified of her stern appearance, pipe-smoking, weather-beaten face and strong, tall physique, but when he got a tune out of the organ she came over and hugged him.

Betsy had ten of her own children, the eldest born when she was nineteen. With her first husband, George Williamson, she had five children. Only three survived infancy. Then, in 1906, George passed away in suspicious circumstances while returning from a horse fair. The family story told that he was killed in a brawl, but, according to local newspaper archives, George was suffocated. His body was discovered by the rural postman on the road between Urray and Muir of Ord, near Beauly. The article erroneously refers to George's wife as 'Jane Whyte'. It is possible that Betsy didn't want her real name recorded in connection with the death.

Betsy remarried in December 1908. Her second husband was Thomas Wilson, a traveller from Sutherland. They had four daughters and one son before moving into a house at 8 Hill Terrace, Elgin, in the early 1920s. Local tax records reveal that just one year earlier, one of the Williamson family had purchased the scrap metal yard around the corner. It was this business that employed the men of the family for decades, and the chance of stable employment was almost certainly the reason the family settled in Elgin.

In the 1920s Hill Terrace was known as Lady Lane. Betsy's children were likely to have been playmates with Jessie Kesson, the well-known author who wrote about her childhood experiences in Lady Lane. They would have been growing up around the lane at the same time.

Betsy Whyte and her descendants were residents in the lane for over thirty years. Betsy's granddaughter was born in 1943 and lived in Hill Terrace till she was nine. She remembers two rooms upstairs and two below, each inhabited by aunts, uncles and cousins, with Betsy herself in one room on the bottom right of the stairs. Betsy was the matriarch of a very large brood, but despite the joy of having her family and grandchildren close, there was also sorrow between those walls. Betsy's second husband died in 1928, just one year after her son, Jock, died of tuberculosis at the

Betsy Whyte with her granddaughter in 1943
(Thom family)

329

age of twenty-one. Daughters Jeannie and Elsie were lost also, the latter in her early twenties, of a complication of pregnancy. Finally, in 1951, her son Duncan died at the age of thirty-five. He was arrested one night for being too drunk to put his shoe on, and he never returned from the cell. Understandably, the family were suspicious of how Duncan died. Travellers had always been unpopular with the police. The family pushed for an inquest, and both Betsy and her daughter-in-law gave long statements in Duncan's defence. After a dozen other statements by police, doctors and witnesses, the court found that Duncan had died of heart failure.

Betsy has many descendants and relatives. A large number have remained in Scotland, though all but a few have given up their traditional way of life. Those who remember Betsy describe her as follows: a superstitious person; having second sight; a Catholic. She seems to have had many friends – her door was always open.

Eventually Hill Terrace was condemned by the local council. All the tenants were ordered out so that the buildings could be renovated, and Betsy relocated with relatives in Lossiemouth. A family photograph shows her in her garden in her old age, sitting in a wheelchair with a red tartan rug over her lap.

A hundred and thirty years after Betsy's birth, her life story was used as inspiration for a fictional character in the novel *The Tin-Kin* by Eleanor Thom, her great grand-daughter. Betsy had passed on very little about the travelling tradition into which she was born, preferring or feeling the need to keep quiet about the first forty years of her life, but the archives held something of her history in safe-keeping. Like everyone else, travellers recorded births, deaths and marriages, and were usually included in the census. Maybe in the present climate, Betsy would be proud to speak of the remarkable life she led.

Betsy Whyte Wilson died in 1971 at the age of ninety-two. She is buried with her daughter, Jeannie, and son, Duncan, in Elgin cemetery. (ET)

# Joanne McCulloch

*Joanne McCulloch, born c.1890, died c.1960.*

Big Joanne was thought to be the widow of a soldier. She lived in a woodland area between Bishopmill and Lesmurdie, beside the local 'tinker' families. Despite having no running water, Joanne would always be seen wearing a spotless white apron. She was a hard worker, doing odd cleaning and washing work for folk. She earned her notoriety due to her lapses from sobriety – when drunk 'Big Joanne' turned into a veritable Amazon and it took several policemen to restrain her. However, these frequent lapses were put to good use. Joanne would be wrestled into a police cell and, as she sobered up, would be given the task of cleaning the cells and washing the blankets before being released without charge. At a time before reams of paper work, records and referrals were required by officialdom, this common-sense arrangement proved satisfactory to both parties. Big Joanne was considered to have provided a much needed service to the community at minimum expense. By the time the new police station was built in 1963 a new era had arrived and these unofficial, but satisfactory community service arrangements, and Big Joanne, had vanished from the scene. (JM)

# Ida McPherson

*Ida Jones, born Halton, Wales, 2 April 1910; adopted as Ida MacPherson 5 November 1915; married Thomas Sutherland Murray 1931; died Forres, 15 July 1998.*

Although born many miles away from the fishing villages of Moray, Ida Jones was to spend her life amongst the fishing community of Hopeman. For a few years she worked in Yarmouth with the fisher lasses who followed the herring fleet. After her marriage she settled in Hopeman and devoted her life to the North-East coastal community.

Ida's mother was Nellie Jones, born in 1883, one of six children of Walter and Sarah Jones of Halton, Wales. Walter was a shop-keeper and a son of a Welsh cattle drover who, his family believed, had descended from a family that migrated to Wales from the Dee valley in Scotland. Cholera was endemic at the end of the nine-teenth century and childhood a hazardous time – of the six children born to Sarah, only two, Nel-lie and Katie, survived beyond the

Ida McPherson (family archive)

331

William and Isabella McPherson with their adopted
daughter Ida (family archive)

age of five. By 1891 Sarah had died and Walter had married again, to Mary Mair, fifteen years his junior. By this time Nellie and her older sister Katie were working away from home in service.

When, in 1903 at the age of twenty-eight, unmarried Katie gave birth to a boy, Thomas, the child was left in the care of his grandfather Walter and his wife Mary while Katie continued to work. Three years later twenty-seven-year-old Nellie, also unmarried, gave birth to Ida at her father's home and had no option but to leave the child in the care of her father and step-mother and return to work.

Ida grew up alongside her cousin Thomas in the row of back-to-back houses built for colliers of the nearby Black Park mine. Her grandfather Walter ran a grocery and bakery shop from his house but times were hard and when Ida was five years old she was sent away to an orphanage in Liverpool. When she discovered what had happened to her daughter, Nellie was devastated. She kept Ida's birth certificate, never married and continued to search for her daughter for the rest of her life – but in vain.

Ida was only in Liverpool for a short time before she was transferred to another orphanage in Stirling, possibly to prevent discovery by Nellie. It was from here that, on 5 November 1915, Ida was officially adopted by William McPherson of Hopeman and his wife Isabella.

The McPhersons were a childless couple in their forties when they adopted Ida Jones. William McPherson had been skipper of the fishing boat *Embrace* and was a well-respected member of the fishing community, known for his kindness and willingness to help others less fortunate than himself. Ida was their only child and she grew up in a close-knit, interdependent community at a time when fortunes were fluctuating in the herring industry.

At its peak in 1913, the Scottish herring industry exported 1,886,596 barrels of cured herring, mostly to Russia and Germany, but this flourishing trade was severely affected by the First World War. The diminished trade continued after the war and by the time she was seventeen Ida had joined the large number of fisher lasses that followed the herring fleet to gut and salt the fish as the fleet travelled around the east coast. At the start of the herring season in May, the herring boats moved from the Hebrides to Shetland and by September gradually moved south down the east coast of Scotland. By autumn the fleet, and the accompanying gutters and curers, would be following the migrating fish south to Lowestoft and Yarmouth.

There had been 1,000 registered Yarmouth drifters when the herring industry was at its height and when these were joined by nearly 2,000 of the Scottish boats it was possible to walk from one side of Yarmouth harbour to the other across the boats. In the late 1920s Ida was amongst the hundreds of Scots girls arriving in Yarmouth by train and lorry to work gutting herring. A shop on South Quay stayed open until ten or eleven at night and was crowded with girls buying oilskins, boots and aprons and other necessities.

Herring is a very perishable fish and the processing of the catch required a substantial mobile workforce. The scale of work required at the herring stations exceeded the scale of employment in large-sized factories. Ida was required to work with skill and speed in a smelly and unpleasant environment. She wore a headscarf and a waterproof skirt, boots and an apron which was hosed down at the end of the day. Working outside on the harbour quay, she and the other the gutters wrapped their fingers with strips of cotton to protect themselves as much as possible against the inevitable cuts to their cold fingers from their short sharp knives. Salt water got into these cuts and was very painful. The girls worked in teams of three, two gutting and one packing the fish into barrels with salt. Ida had to keep pace with the others and the packer had to keep pace with the gutters so good relations were important. Every girl had to work equally hard for the benefit of the team, with no room for unproductive or lazy workers.

Ida worked long backbreaking hours, sometimes until two in the morning, to ensure the fish were packed as freshly as possible. The work was messy and dirty but a team of three could gut and pack 21,000 herring in a ten hour shift. The crew as a whole was paid according to the number of barrels filled, and their work was under constant inspection to ensure high

Ida and friends (family archive)

The wedding of Ida Jones McPherson and Thomas Sutherland Murray at Elgin in 1931 (family archive)

quality before each barrel was sealed and stamped with Crown Brand of approval ready for export. If poorly packed or cured, or if the fish were too small, they were rejected. Monday was usually a half day, the time off used for washing and cleaning themselves, their clothes and their lodgings. At Yarmouth the fisher lasses were given basic accommodation within the town and in these lodgings newspapers were plastered onto the walls to try and absorb the smell of the fish.

Fisher lasses, with their often incomprehensible accents, would appear rough and very strange to inhabitants of the coastal communities where they worked. Their apparent freedom and independence and their ability to earn their own living was alien to the culture of the southern towns of the time. The author, Peter F Anson, noted that these women 'acquired a self-assurance and a knowledge of the outside world that was rare in a woman of another sphere.' Despite the hard work and distaste with which they were viewed by outsiders, the community of fisher girls were a cheerful group. They sang as they worked and, when the fleet came into harbour to rest on Sunday, they met up with their fathers, uncles and brothers who had been working on the boats. Romances were easier to conduct when the girls were so far away from home, and many betrothals took place amongst the peripatetic herring fishing community. The fisher lasses were welcomed home at the end of the season – especially as they usually

brought gifts from the southern ports. Some of the fishermen would return to re-equip their boats for close shore work while others would spend the winter months repairing gear and nets in readiness for the next herring harvest.

By 1931 Ida had met and married a fisherman – Thomas 'Top' Sutherland Murray and the couple set up house back in their

Ida Murray at home in Hopeman, mending the nets (family archive)

hometown of Hopeman. Here the fishing community was bound together by years of hardship and the dangers of the work.

Ida's adoptive father, William, died in 1938. Although it continued, fishing was curtailed by the Second World War as boats were commandeered by the Admiralty and over half of the Scottish fishermen served in either the Royal or the Merchant Navies.

As well as running the home and bringing up their five children, Ida assisted her husband in his work which included mending the nets. Ida never went away with the herring fleet again but, when they were old enough, her children were involved in the ever changing and often dangerous fishing industry. Her marriage lasted for sixty-seven years.

By the time Ida died in 1998, within three months of her husband, many of the east coast harbours were havens for numerous small pleasure craft with only a few small fishing boats or lobster boats. The modern large commercial trawlers could only berth in the bigger harbours.

Following her disadvantageous start in life, Ida Murray witnessed the height of the herring industry boom and the vagaries of an ever-changing, comforting and challenging close-knit fishing community. (JM)

# Appendix 1

# The Glen's Muster Roll

The Dominie Loquitur:–

Hing't up aside the chumley-cheek, the aul' glen's Muster Roll,
A' names we ken fae hut an' ha', fae Penang to the Pole,
An' speir na gin I'm prood o't – losh ! coont them line by line,
Near han' a hunner fechtin' men, an' they a' were Loons o' Mine.

A' mine. It's jist like yesterday they sat there raw on raw,
Some tyaavin' wi' the 'Rule o' Three,' some widin' throu' 'Mensa';
The map o' Asia's shoggly yet faur Dysie's sheemach head
Gaed cleeter-clatter a' the time the carritches was said.
'A limb,' his greetin' granny swore, 'the aul' deil's very limb'
But Dysie's deid and drooned lang syne; the *Cressy* coffined him.
'Man guns upon the fore barbette!'… What's that to me an' you?
Here's moss an' burn, the skailin' kirk, aul' Kissack beddin's soo.
It's Peace, it's Hame – but owre the Ben the coastal search lights shine,
And we ken that Britain's bastions mean – that sailor Loon o' Mine.

The muirlan's lang, the muirlan's wide, an' fa says 'ships' or 'sea'?
But the tang o' saut that's in wir bleed has puzzled mair than me.
There's Sandy wi' the birstled shins, faur think ye's he the day?
Oot where the hawser's tuggin' taut in the surf o' Suvla Bay;
An' owre the spurs o' Chanak Bahr gaed twa lang stilpert chiels,
I think o' flappin butteries yet or weyvin' powets' creels
Exiles on far Australian plains – but the Lord's ain boomerang
'S the Highland heart that's aye for hame hooever far it gang.
An' the winds that wail owre Anzac an' requiem Lone Pine
Are nae jist a' for stranger kin, for some were Loons o' Mine.

They're comin' hame in twas an' threes; there's Tam fae Singapore -
Yon's his, the string o' buckie-beads abeen the aumry door -
An' Dick Macleod, his sanshach sel' (Guidsake, a bombardier!)
I see them yet ae summer day come hodgin' but the fleer:
'Please, sir' (a habber an' a hoast), 'Please, sir' (a gasp, a gulp,

337

Syne wi' a rush) 'Please – sir – can – we – win – oot – to droon – a – fulp?'
...Hi, Rover, here, lad! Ay, that's him, the fulp they didna droon,
But Tam – puir Tam lies cauld an' stiff on same grey Belgian dune,
An' the *Via Dolorosa*'s there, faur a wee bit cutty quine
Stan's lookin' doon a teem hill road for a sojer Loon o' Mine.
Fa's neist? The Gaup – A Gordon wi' the 'Bydand' on his broo,
Nae murlacks dreetlin' fae his pooch or owre his grauvit noo,
Nae word o' groff-write trackies on the 'Four best ways to fooge'
He steed his grun' an' something mair, they tell me, oot at Hooge.
But owre the dyke I'm hearin' yet: 'Lads, fa's on for a swap?
A lang sook o' a pandrop for the sense o' *verbum sap.*
Fack's death, I tried to min' on't – here's my gairten wi' the knot
But – bizz ! a dhubrack loupit as I passed the muckle pot'.
...Ay, ye didna ken the classics, never heard o' a co-sine,
But here's my aul' lum aff tae ye, dear gowkit Loon o'Mine.

They're handin' oot the haloes, an' three's come to the glen –
There's Jeemack ta'en his Sam Browne to his mither's but an' ben.
Ay, they ca' me 'Blawin' Beelie', but I never crawed sae crouse
As the day they gaed the VC to my *filius nullius.*
But he winna sit 'Receptions' nor keep on his aureole,
A' he says is "Dinna haiver, jist rax owre the Bogie Roll.'
An' the Duke an' 's dother shook his han' an' speirt aboot his kin.
'Old family, yes; here sin' the Flood,' I smairtly chippit in.
(Fiech! Noah's? Na – we'd ane wirsels, ye ken, in '29.)
I'm nae the man tae stan' an' hear them lichtlie Loon o' Mine.

Wir Lairdie. That's his mither in her doo's-neck silk gaun by,
The podduck, so she tells me, 's haudin' up the HLI
An' he's stan'in' owre his middle in the Flanders' clort an' dub,
Him 'at eese't to scent his hanky, an' speak o's mornin' 'tub'.
The Manse loon's dellin' divots on the weary road to Lille,
An' he canna flype his stockin's, cause they hinna tae nor heel.
Sennelager's gotten Davie – a' moo fae lug tae lug –
An' the Kaiser's kyaak, he's writin', 'll neither ryve nor rug,
"But mind ye" (so he post-cards), 'I'm already owre the Rhine.'
Ay, there's nae a wanworth o' them, though they werena loons o' Mine.

...You – Robbie. Memory pictures: Front bench, a curly pow,
A chappit hannie grippin' ticht a Homer men't wi' tow
The lave a' scrammelin' near him, like bummies roon a bike.

'Fat's this?' 'Fat's that?' He'd tell them a' – ay, speir they fat they like.
My hill-foot lad! A' sowl an' brain fae's bonnet to his beets,
A 'Fullarton' *in posse*, nae the first fun' fowin' peats.
...An' I see a blithe young Bajan gang whistlin' doon the brae,
An' I hear a wistful Paladin his patriot credo say.
An' noo, an' noo I'm waitin' till a puir thing hirples hame
Ay, 't's the Valley o' the Shadow, nae the mountain heichts o' Fame.
An' where's the nimble nostrum, the dogma fair and fine,
To still the ruggin' heart I hae for you, oh, Loon o' Mine?


My Loons, my Loons! Yon winnock gets the settin' sun the same,
Here's sklates and skailies, ilka dask a' futtled wi' a name.
An' as I sit a vision comes: Ye're troopin' in aince mair,
Ye're back fae Aisne an' Marne an' Meuse, Ypres an' Festubert;
Ye're back on weary bleedin' feet – you, you that danced an' ran –
For every lauchin' loon I kent I see a hell-scarred man.
Not mine but yours to question to question now ! You lift unhappy eyes
'Ah, Maister, tell's fat a' this means.' And I, ye thocht sae wise,
Maun answer wi' the bairn words ye said tae me langsyne:
'I dinna ken, I dinna ken.' Fa does, oh, Loons o' Mine?


Glossary of Scots words
beets (n) – boots
chappit (v) – chapped
chiel (n) – fellow
colloguin (v) – conversing
croose (adj) – smart
deavin (v) – nagging
dow (n) – dove
droon (v) – drown
dweeble (n) – drivel
fa... fan... foo (pro/ adv/adv) – who... when... how
fulp (n) – whelp
geats (n) – children
grieve (n) – farm foreman
hannie (n) – little hand
hirples (v) – stumbles
lauchin (adj) – laughing
loon (n) – boy

lug (n ) – ear
maindle (n) – a fair number or amount
men't (v) – mended
moo (n) – mouth
pandrop (n) – type of mint sweet
pints (n) – laces
sourock (n) – a sulky, sour-tempered person
stouf (n) – clod-hopper
swarrach (n) – swarm
ticht (adj) – tight
tint (v) – lost
tow (n) – twine
trappin (n) – ribbons
walshach (n) – nauseous stuff
win oot (v) – go outside

# Appendix 2

*Three Lossiemouth stories by Janet Levack*

## A Home Thrust

Coming down the Jubilee Brae the other day I overtook an old fisherman with a bundle of wythies under his arm.

Having a garden basket that wanted mending, I thought, 'Now's my chance.'

'Can you mend baskets?' I asked.

'Aye, roch kin' o' baskets, wi sauchs ye ken. Wud that dee ye?'

We chatted a little and I asked his name, which he told me.

'An' wha micht ye be?' he asked?

'Well,' I said, 'my name is Levack now, but probably you might remember me better as Jessie Brander.'

He looked me up and down astonished, sadly shaking his head.

''Od be here! Are ye Mester Brander's dauchter? Weel, I min' on Jessie Brander fan she wis a fine, slim, an' bonny lass, but FAR ARE YE NOO?'

## As Others See Us

At one time I did a little massage and had a few patients in Elgin whom I visited daily.

While waiting for the train I sauntered up and down the platform, passing a seat on which two women were sitting with creels at their feet.

I saw them looking at me with great interest and heard one of them say:

'Fa's yon?'

'Oh!' said the other one, 'divn't ye ken? That's Mistress Levick.'

'Fat's she deein' comin'up and doon tar Elgin ivery day?'

'They say 'at she rubs fowk.'

'Rubs fowk! I aye thoucht 'at she wis a leddy.'

'Eh, na! She's nae a leddy, she's juist ane o' oorsels!'

## The Clockie

A woman came into the watchmakers one day with a clock in her hands.

'I've come tae ye wi' ma clockie, it's a' vrang, an' ma man winna pit up wi't ony langer. I unnstan't fine masel. Fan it strik's ten an' the han's pints tae half-past two, I ken 'at it's 5 o'clock. But my man's nae a coonter an' he winna pit up wi't ony langer.'

# Appendix 3

*Family and friends taken before the wedding of Joseph Stewart (Dovie) and Maggie Ann Stewart, 24 December 1909, pictured p85*

Back row from left: John Stewart, Pat Stewart, Jamie Stewart (Stiff), John McLeod (Johnee), Jessie Stewart, Alex Stewart, Lydia Stewart, Jock Scott, Elsie Stewart, Jamie Stewart, Jane Stewart, Beel McLeod, John Souter, [George McLeod], George Crockett.

Middle row: Jock Bain, Peter Stewart (Dougal), Isa Docher, Annie Stewart (Dougal) Annie Macdonald (Dooser), William Stewart (Beel Loll), Jessie Helen McKenzie, George Stewart (Dodie Bung), Annie Ramsay, Joseph Stewart, Katie Stewart, unknown

Front row: J Crockett, Bell Stewart, Willie Stewart (Wilkie), Jamesina Stewart (Dick), George Stewart (Gycie), Maggie Ann Stewart, Joseph Stewart (Dovie)

# Books Useful for General Background

Abrams *et al.*, *Gender in Scottish History since 1700* (Edinburgh 2006).

Adam, Ruth, *A Woman's Place 1910–1975* (London 2000).

Anderson, Carol and Christianson, Aileen, *Scottish Women's Fiction 1920s to 1960s: Journeys into Being* (East Lothian 2000).

Devine, TM, and Mitchison, Rosalind, (Eds), *People and Society in Scotland: 1760–1830* (Edinburgh 2004).

Dickson, Tony and Treble, JH, (Eds), *People and Society in Scotland: 1914 – the Present Day* (Edinburgh 1998).

Ewan, Elizabeth, Innes, Sue, Reynolds, Sian (Eds), *The Biographical Dictionary of Scottish Women* (Edinburgh 2006).

Forster, Margaret, *Significant Sisters*: *The Grassroots of Active Feminism 1839–1939* (London 2004).

Fraser, W Hamish, and Morris, RJ (Eds), *People and Society in Scotland 1830–1914* (Edinburgh 2000).

*Oxford Dictionary of National Biography* (*DNB*) (Oxford 2004, available online at www.oxforddnb.com).

Gifford, Douglas and McMillan, Dorothy, *A History of Scottish Women's Writing* (Edinburgh 1997).

Leneman, Leah, *A Guid Cause: The Women's Suffrage Movement in Scotland* (Edinburgh 1995).

Lynch, Michael (Ed), *The Oxford Companion to Scottish History* (Oxford 2001).

McCrae, Morrice, *The National Health Service in Scotland*, (2003 East Lothian).

McCulloch, Margery Palmer, *Modernism and Nationalism, Literature and Society in Scotland 1918–1939* (Glasgow 2004).

Mill, John Stuart, *The Subjection of Women*, Foreword by Fay Weldon (London 2008)

Nicholson, Virginia, *Singled Out* (London 2007).

Omand, Donald (Ed), *The Moray Book* (Edinburgh 1976).

Orr Macdonald, Lesley A, *A Unique and Glorious Mission: Women and Presbyterianism in Scotland 1830–1930* (Edinburgh 2000).

Tyrer, Nicola, *Sisters in Arms* (London 2008).

Watson, Norman, *WRVS in Scotland* (Edinburgh 2008).

Wollstonecraft, Mary, *The Vindications of the Rights of Men and the Vindications of the Rights of Woman* (Eds. Macdonald, DL and Scherf, Kathleen; Ontario 1997).

# Notes on Contributors

RICHARD BENNETT was born and brought up in Moray. After graduating from University of Aberdeen he taught English in Dundee and Moray. He is responsible for two recent publications: *Elgin Academy: A Celebration of 200 Years* (2001) and *Willie Macpherson: The Elgin Fiddler* (2006). He regularly contributes articles to the bulletin of the Moray Field Club. He is currently studying at the Elphinstone Institute, University of Aberdeen.

SUSAN BENNETT was born in Manchester and graduated in zoology at the University of Aberdeen in 1965. In 1996 she co-authored, with Michael Collie, *George Gordon: An Annotated Catalogue of his Scientific Correspondence* (Scolar Press). As curator of the Elgin Museum she wrote and curated a lottery funded exhibition, *People and Place*, about Moray's place in Scottish history. She retired in 2003 and now lives in Aberdeenshire.

MARY BYATT was born in Oxford and has lived in Moray since 1971. She has taught science in three state secondary schools in Moray and at Gordonstoun School. After retiring from teaching in 1993, Mary worked as a volunteer in the Elgin Museum for ten years, also serving the management as a board member of the Moray Society. She has written three books about Elgin. The first, *Elgin: A History and Celebration*, was for Ottakar's, and the second and third, *Elgin: The Story of the Closes* and *Victorian Elgin*, were published privately for the Moray Society.

JANET CAROLAN (née Rorke) grew up in Dollar. After graduating MA Hons from St Andrews University, she taught with VSO in Ghana and later worked for an international publisher in Copenhagen. She returned to live in Dollar, has been honorary curator of Dollar Museum from its birth in 1988 and is also archivist at Dollar Academy. Janet has done much research on Lavinia Malcolm, was asked to write her biography for the *Oxford Dictionary of National Biography* and has spoken about her on radio and TV.

LORNA GLENDINNING was born in Harrow-on-the-Hill of Scottish parents. After graduating from Trinity College Dublin with a degree in civil engineering in 1972, she worked in the tunnelling industry building the Jubilee Line in London. Marriage to a British Army officer and two children prevented furthering this career so she took up various teaching posts as she travelled with the flag, including teaching in a prison and tutoring children in maths. Working life ended with a post of deputy manager in a Citizens Advice Bureau, continuing to problem solve, at times specialising in debt.

SHEILA MCCOLL Born in Kirriemuir in 1939, Sheila moved to Moray in 1977 with her husband. After retirement from insurance work in Elgin, she began a course in archaeology at Aberdeen University, and received her diploma in 2003. Sheila was archaeology representative in Elgin Museum for nearly ten years, and was involved in various digs in Moray and beyond, and also in burial ground recording. She was a skilled needlewoman and a member of Moray Embroiderers' Guild and Highland Quilters. Although Sheila was a member of the Moray Golf Club, her game was bowls. Sheila died in September 2011.

JENNY MAIN was born in New Zealand but spent her childhood years living in diverse places. In her late twenties she settled in Moray. For several years she worked as a volunteer with the Moray Society which runs Elgin Museum and was also editor of the *Moray Field Club Bulletin*. She has written five books – *Elgin in Old Photographs* (Sutton 1996), *Elgin People in Old Photographs* (Sutton 1998), *The First Nurse* (Librario 2003), *Elgin Through Time* (Amberley 2009), *The Moray Coast Through Time* (Amberley 2011).

ANNE OLIVER was brought up in Staffordshire. She trained as a teacher when her three children were young. Following the family's move to Moray in 1980 she worked for *The Northern Scot* newspaper, latterly as a sub editor. Anne has lived in Archiestown for twenty-five years and is involved in village affairs. She has written a community book, *Archiestown: The Way it Was*, as well as numerous articles and booklets on local history. She gained a BA Hons from the Open University in the 1990s and is currently studying for her masters degree.

WILLIAM (BILL) SMITH After National Service Bill Smith studied drawing and painting at Edinburgh College of Art. Four years there were followed by a year of teacher training at Moray House. For another four years he painted from his Edinburgh studio before taking up a teaching post at Fochabers, serving as principal teacher for most of his thirty-odd years there. Towards the end of his career he served as principal examiner for his subject. Retirement has brought a return to the carefree life of the landscape painter.

ELEANOR THOM was born in London in 1979. Her novel, *The Tin-Kin* (Duckworth, 2009) is set in Elgin and is based on the story of her mother's Travelling family. It won The Saltire First Book Award in 2009. Eleanor has been commissioned to write for BBC Radio 4, the Edinburgh International Book Festival, *Gutter Magazine*, and *Algebra*, Glasgow Tramway's digital literary journal. Eleanor now lives in Ayr with her husband and young son, Ivor Jupiter. She is completing a second novel and beginning a new project as a PhD student at the University of the West of Scotland. She has a website at www.eleanorthom.com.

JANET TRYTHALL was born in London in 1946. Apart from a few years in Africa, she has moved northwards after qualifying in medicine at Newcastle University. Familiar with Scotland from sailing and hillwalking, she moved to Covesea, overlooking the Moray Firth, when her husband took up a post at Gordonstoun School. Janet worked as an anaesthetist around the highlands and islands, and from 1995 at Dr Gray's Hospital, Elgin. Since retirement in 2007 she has had more time for involvement in various capacities in the Moray Society and Elgin Museum, and the study of local geology, botany, archaeology and history.

# Notes and Main Sources

## INTRODUCTION

### NOTES

1 Elgin 1930, originally published as articles in *The Elgin Courant and Courier.*

2 We are grateful to Lis Smith for information on Annie Maude Sellar. Annie was born in Golspie in 1858. She was resident in Westfield House, Spynie, in 1861. Westfield House was sold by the Sellar family in 1862.

3 Libindx NM131802.

## CHAPTER 1 – MEDIEVAL WOMEN

### NOTES

1 Barnes, Ishbel CM, *Janet Kennedy Royal Mistress* (Edinburgh 2007), p66.

2 Grant, Alexander, 'The Wolf of Badenoch', in Sellar, WDH, *Moray: Province and People* (Edinburgh 1993), p151.

3 Barnes, Ishbel CM, *Janet Kennedy Royal Mistress* (Edinburgh 2007), pp3–4.

4 Ibid, pp4–5.

5 Cramond, William, *Records of Elgin* (Aberdeen 1903), Vol. 1, p24.

6 Ibid, p72.

### MAIN SOURCES

#### GRUOCH (LADY MACBETH)

Cowan, Edward J, 'The Historical Macbeth', in Sellar, WHD, *Moray: Province and People* (Edinburgh 1993).

Davies, Norman *The Isles* (London 1999).

Mackie, JD, *A History of Scotland* (London 1991).

Oram, Richard (Ed.), *The Kings and Queens of Scotland* (Stroud 2001).

Taylor, Cameron, Murray, Alistair, *On the Trail of the Real Macbeth* (Edinburgh 2008).

#### EUPHEMIA OF DUFFUS

Cannel, J and Tabraham, C, 'Excavations at Duffus Castle, Moray', in *Proceedings of the Society of Antiquaries of Scotland*, 124 (1994), pp379–90.

Fawcett, Richard, *Elgin Cathedral* (Edinburgh 1999).

Innes, C (Ed.), *The Book of the Thanes of Cawdor 1236–1742* (Spalding Club) (Edinburgh 1859).

Keith, Agnes, *The Parishes of Drainie and Lossiemouth* (1975).

Mackenzie, David J, 'The Old Church of St Peter at Duffus', in *Transactions of* *the Scottish Ecclesiastical Soc*iety 1924–25, pp36–40.

Platts, Beryl, *Scottish Hazard: The Flemish Nobility and their Impact on Scotland* (London 1985), Vol. 1, Appendix 3.

Innes, C (Ed.), *Registrum Episcopatus Moraviensis* (Bannatyne Club, Edinburgh 1837).

Rose, D Murray, The de Moravia Family *Transactions of the Gaelic Society Inverness* Vol. xxv, 1901–03.

Simpson, W Douglas, *Duffus Castle and Church* (Edinburgh 1951).

Sutherland, Elizabeth, *Five Euphemias* (Edinburgh 1999).

Stuart, John, *Records of the Monastery of Kinloss* (Edinburgh 1872).

Tabraham, CJ, *Duffus Castle and Church* (Edinburgh 1986).

AGNES RANDOLPH (BLACK AGNES)

Duncan, AAM, 'Randolph, Thomas', in *DNB* (Oxford 2004).

Ewan, Elizabeth, 'Randolph, Agnes (Black Agnes of Dunbar), Countess of Dunbar and March', in Ewan, Elizabeth, Innes, Sue, Reynolds, Sian, (Eds), *The Biographical Dictionary of Scottish Women* (Edinburgh 2006).

Mosley, Charles (Ed.), *Burke's Peerage, Baronetage and Knightage* 107th edition 2003.

Watson, Fiona, 'Patrick Dunbar', in *DNB* (Oxford 2004).

ELIZABETH DUNBAR

Alexander, Flora, 'Buke of the Howlat', in Hewitt, David and Spiller, Michael, *Literature of the North* (Aberdeen 1983).

Bawcutt, Priscilla and Riddy, Felicity, *Longer Scottish Poems 1375–1650* (Edinburgh 1987).

Boardman, SI, 'Dunbar family', in *DNB* (Oxford 2004).

McKim, Anne, 'Dunbar, Elizabeth, Countess of Moray', in Ewan, Elizabeth, Innes, Sue, Reynolds, Sian, (Eds), *The Biographical Dictionary of Scottish Women* (Edinburgh 2006).

Mosley, Charles, *Burke's Peerage, Baronetage & Knightage* Vol. 1 (107th edition 2003).

Spalding Club *Miscellany IV* (Aberdeen 1849) p128.

JANET KENNEDY

Barnes, Ishbel CM, *Janet Kennedy Royal Mistress* (Edinburgh 2007).

Barnes, Ishbel, 'Kennedy, Janet, Lady Bothwell', in Ewan, Elizabeth, Innes, Sue, Reynolds, Sian, (Eds), *The Biographical Dictionary of Scottish Women* (Edinburgh 2006).

Mosley, Charles (Ed.), *Burke's Peerage, Baronetage and Knightage* 107th edition (2003).

AGNES (ANNAS) KEITH

Libindx NM119059.

Dawson, Jane, 'Keith, Annas (Agnes, Anna), Countess of Moray, Countess of Argyll', in Ewan, Elizabeth, Innes, Sue, Reynolds, Sian (Eds), *The Biographical Dictionary of Scottish Women* (Edinburgh 2006).

Innes, C, (Ed.), *The Book of the Thanes of Cawdor 1236–1742* (Spalding Club, Aberdeen 1859).

Marshall, Rosalind K, *Queen Mary's Women, Female Relatives, Servants, Friends and Enemies of Mary Queen of Scots* (Edinburgh 2006).

## CHAPTER 2 – POWER AND PERSECUTION

### NOTES

1 Cramond, William, *The Church and Priory of Urquhart* (nd).

2 Cramond, William, *Records of Elgin* Vol. II (Spalding Club, Aberdeen 1908), pp5, 77, 263.

3 Cramond, William, *The Church of Lhanbryd* (nd).

4 Cramond, William, *Extracts from the Records of the Synod of Moray* (Elgin 1906) p120.

5 Lynch, Michael (Ed.), *The Oxford Companion to Scottish History* (Oxford 2001).

6 Henderson, Lizanne, 'Horne, Janet', in Ewan, Elizabeth, Innes, Sue, Reynolds, Sian, (Eds), *The Biographical Dictionary of Scottish Women* (Edinburgh 2006).

7 Mcdonald, SW, 'The Devil's Mark and the Witch Prickers of Scotland', in *Journal of the Royal Society of Medicine*, Vol. 90, Sept 1997.

8 Martin, Lauren, 'Caldwell (Caldall), Christian [John Dicksone]', in Ewan, Elizabeth, Innes, Sue, Reynolds, Sian, (Eds), *The Biographical Dictionary of Scottish Women* (Edinburgh 2006).

9 Bishop, Bruce B, *The Lands and People of Moray, Witchcraft Trials in Elgin 1560–1734* (Elgin 2001).

10 Brodie, Alexander, *The Diary of Alexander Brodie of Brodie 1652–1680 and of his Son James Brodie of Brodie 1680–1685* (Spalding Club, Aberdeen 1863), p296.

### MAIN SOURCES

ISOBEL GOWDIE

Libindx NM066143.

Callow, John, 'Gowdie, Isobel', in *DNB* (Oxford 2004).

McPherson, James, *Primitive Beliefs in North East Scotland* (London 1929).

Pitcairn, Robert, *Criminal Trials in Scotland* (1833).

Pugh, JM, *The Deil's Ain* (Balerno 2001).

Wilby, Emma, *The Visions of Isobel Gowdie* (Eastbourne 2010).

MARY KER

Brodie, A and J, *The Diary of Alexander Brodie 1652–1680 and of his son James Brodie 1680–1685* (Spalding Club Aberdeen 1863).

Brown, KM, *et al.* (Eds), *The Records of the Parliaments of Scotland to 1707*, (St Andrews 2007–2009) at www.rps.ac.uk.

McKay, Margaret, *Some Brodie Ladies and their Times* (Elgin 2008).

Muir, Alison G, 'Brodie [Brody], Alexander, of Brodie, (1617–1680)', in *DNB* (Oxford 2004).

## CHAPTER THREE – WOMEN OF THE ENLIGHTENMENT
NOTES

1 Reynolds, Sian, 'Gender, the Arts and Culture', in Abrams *et al.*, (Eds), *Gender in Scottish History since 1700*, (Edinburgh 2006) pp177–78.

2 Moran, Mary Catherine, 'Between the Savage and the Civil: Dr John Gregory's Natural History of Femininity' in Knott, Sarah, and Taylor, Barbara (Eds), *Women, Gender and Enlightenment* (Basingstoke 2005) p8.

3 Rendall, Jane, '"Women that would plague me with rational conversation": Aspiring women and Scottish Whigs, *c.*1790–1830', in Knott, Sarah, and Taylor, Barbara (Eds), *Women, Gender and Enlightenment* (Basingstoke 2005) p326.

MAIN SOURCES

MARY SLEIGH

Brodie papers, The National Trust for Scotland.

Libindx NM077700; spouse: NM015987; son: NM263107.

Anderson, Mark L, *A History of Scottish Forestry* (London 1967).

Chambers, Robert, *Traditions of Edinburgh* (Edinburgh 1947, reprint).

Douglas, Robert, *Annals of the Royal Burgh of Forres* (Elgin 1934).

Lang, Andrew M, 'Brodie, Alexander, of Brodie' (1697–1754), in *DNB* (Oxford 2004).

McKay, Margaret, *Some Brodie Ladies and their Times* (Elgin 2008).

Sinclair, Sir John, (Ed.), *The Statistical Account of Scotland,* Vol. XVI, Dyke Parish, (Edinburgh 1791–99).

Sleigh, Arthur, *The Sleighs of Derbyshire and Beyond* (privately printed nd).

Tayler, Alistair, and Henrietta, *Morayshire MPs since the Act of Union* (Elgin 1930).

JANE MAXWELL

Letters of the Duke and Duchess of Gordon to Sir William Forbes 1783–1806, Acc. 4796/41, National Library of Scotland.

Libindx NM089365; spouse: NM061308, NM061311; children: NM109534, NM113964, NM117102, NM157162, NM065601, NM049783; Jean Christie NM255277.

Bulloch, John Malcolm, *The Gay Gordons* (London 1908).

Cosh, Mary, *Edinburgh the Golden Age* (Edinburgh 2003).

Forbes, Margaret, *Beattie and his Friends* (Altrincham 1990, reprint).

JW[G], *An Autobiographical Chapter in the Life of Jane, Duchess of Gordon* (Glasgow 1864).

Gordon, George, *The Last Dukes of Gordon and their Consorts* (Aberdeen 1980).

Grant, Elizabeth, *Memoirs of a Highland Lady* (London 1911).

Lodge, Christine, 'Gordon [née Maxwell], Jane', in *DNB* (Oxford 2004).

McKean, Charles, *The District of Moray: An Illustrated Architectural Guide* (Edinburgh 1987).

Tayler, A and H, *Lord Fife and his Factor* (London 1925).

## CHAPTER FOUR – FOLLOWING THE DRUM

NOTES

1 Shuldham-Shaw, Patrick, and Lyle, Emily B, *The Greig-Duncan Folk Song Collection* (Aberdeen 1981) Vol. 1 p256.

2 Miller, David, *The Duchess of Richmond's Ball* (Staplehurst 2005).

3 Black, Jeremy, *Culloden and the '45* (Stroud 1997) p160.

4 Henderson, Diana M, *The Scottish Regiments* (Glasgow 1996).

5 Gordon Cumming, CF, *Memories* (Edinburgh and London 1904).

MAIN SOURCES

MARJORY ANDERSON

Libindx NM001960; son: NM001961.

*Guide to the Ruins of Elgin Cathedral to which is added the History of Marjory Gilzean Mother of General Anderson*, (*Courant and Courier* Office, Elgin 1926, 16th edition).

'Reminiscences of Marjory Gillan', in *The Elgin and Morayshire Courier* 28.2.1851 p3/3–4.

Campbell, Keith, *General Anderson's Institute, Elgin* (1980, LMisc400).

Ray, James, and Grant, W Calder, (Eds), *Annals of the London Morayshire Club* (London 1894).

Wills, Peter R, *A History of General Anderson 1745–1824* (2nd edition 2010).

ISABEL MACKENZIE

Libindx NM183497.

Gaffney, Victor, *The Lordship of Strathavon* (Edinburgh 1959).

Hall, Rev. James, *Travels in Scotland by an Unusual Route* (London 1807).

Sinclair, Sir John, (Ed.), *The Statistical Account of Scotland*, Vol. XII, Kirkmichael Parish (Edinburgh 1791–99).

MARGARET DAWSON

The Gordon Highlanders Museum, Aberdeen.

Libindx; NM182495; spouse: NM182492; son: NM035645.

Bartlam, W, *Evolution of a North East Scottish Woollen Mill* (2000).

Bulloch, JB, (Ed.), *The Gordon Book* (Fochabers 1902).

Gordon, Archie, *A Wild Flight of Gordons* (1985).

Gordon, George, *The Last Dukes of Gordon & their Consorts* (Aberdeen 1980).

Harrison, EP, *Estate Tweeds* (Elgin 1995).

Henderson, Margaret Hay, *Thomas Dawson of the 92nd Regiment* (2002).

Sinclair-Stephenson, Christopher, *The Gordon Highlanders* (London 1968).

Venning, Annabel, *Following the Drum* (London 2006).

BARBARA SIMPKIN

Family papers of Michael and Alexander Simpkin.

Libindx NM207904; mother: NM089054.

Wireless School, Colwyn Bay.

Grant, Eileen, *Service of Life* (Aberdeen, 2002).


CHAPTER FIVE – ESCAPING POVERTY

NOTES

1 *The Forres Gazette,* 23.12.1863, p3/5.

2 *The Dufftown News* 10.07.1937, p4/1.

3 *The Elgin Courant* 11.01.1867.

4 Boardman, Steve, 'Wright, Christian Edington Guthrie', in Ewan, Elizabeth, Innes, Sue, Reynolds, Sian, (Eds), *The Biographical Dictionary of Scottish Women* (Edinburgh 2006).

5 McDermid, Jane, 'Stevenson, Flora Clift' and 'Stevenson, Louisa', in Ewan, Elizabeth, Innes, Sue, Reynolds, Sian, (Eds), *The Biographical Dictionary of Scottish Women* (Edinburgh 2006).

6 *The Elgin Courant* 09.01.1877, p3/2–4.

7 Moore, Lindy, 'Educating for the "woman's sphere"', in Breitenbach, Esther, and Gordon, Eleanor, *Out of Bounds* (Edinburgh 1992) p28.

8 Begg, Tom, *The Excellent Women* (Edinburgh 1994) p58.

9 Libindx SB004862.

10 Carter, Ian, *Farm Life in Northeast Scotland 1840–1914* (Edinburgh 1997).

## MAIN SOURCES

### ANNIE RAMSAY

Family information from Iona Kielhorn, great granddaughter of Annie Ramsay.

Libindx NM149918; mother: NM150175; son: NM001958; daughter-in-law: NM102908; Ishbel Macdonald: NM139550.

Cox, Jane, *A Singular Marriage* (London 1988).

Keith, Agnes, *The Parish of Drainie and Lossiemouth* (1975).

Marquand, David, *Ramsay Macdonald* (London 1977).

Marquand, David, 'Macdonald, (James) Ramsay', in *DNB* (Oxford 2004).

### MARGARET STEPHEN

Elgin Girls' School logbook, Aberdeen City Archives ZCMn SR Elg 79/1

Libindx NM178618; parents: NM176063, NM176694; siblings: NM178962, NM176395; Girls' School: PN007463.

Various articles from *The Educational News,* especially 4 March and 27 May 1905.

*The Northern Scot* Christmas Number 1912, p14.

*The Northern Scot* Christmas Number 1913, p33.

### HELEN LESLIE MACKENZIE

Cairney School logbook 1874–1925, GR6s/67/1/1 Aberdeen City and Aberdeenshire Archives.

Skene Street Public School, Infant Department logbook, GR6s/A66/1/1 Aberdeen City and Aberdeenshire Archives.

Libindx NM108494; parents: NM174182, NM173960; spouse: NM111062.

Begg, Tom, 'MacKenzie, Helen Carruthers', in Ewan, Elizabeth, Innes, Sue, Reynolds, Sian, (Eds), *The Biographical Dictionary of Scottish Women* (Edinburgh 2006).

Begg, Tom, *The Excellent Women* (Edinburgh 1994).

Begg, Tom, 'Mackenzie [née Spence], Dame Helen Carruthers', in *DNB* (Oxford 2004).

Browne, Sarah F, *Making the Vote Count: the Arbroath Women Citizens' Association 1931–45* (Dundee 2007).

Levitt, Ian, 'Mackenzie, Sir (William) Leslie', in *DNB* (Oxford 2004).

HELEN ROSE

Family records.

Libindx NM155663; parents: NM155957, NM155631.

Cameron, Isobel, *Helen Rose and Child Welfare in Elgin* (Elgin 1923).

*New Statistical Account of Scotland*, Vol. XIII Elgin Parish, (Edinburgh 1842).

*The Northern Scot* Christmas Number 1924.

ELLA MUNRO

Personal communication from Stella Sievwright, wife of the late Munro Sievwright – Ella's grandson; and from Ann Sinclair and other islanders of the George Waterston Memorial Centre, Fair Isle.

Annual Reports of Queen Victoria's Jubilee Institute for Nurses, Scottish Branch, and other archives in the Royal College of Nursing Edinburgh. (There is no mention of Ella Munro but a reference to one queen's nurse on Fair Isle.)

Libindx NM107748; spouse: NM140003; children: NM140004, NM139733, NM277165.

*Daily Record and Mail* 10.06.1938.

CHAPTER SIX – EDUCATION AND POLITICS: FINDING A VOICE

NOTES

1 Leneman, Leah, *A Guid Cause* (Edinburgh 1995) p20.

2 Ross, Margaret, 'The Royal Medical Society and Medical Women', in *Proceedings of the Royal College of Physicians Edinburgh* 1996; 26: 629–44.

3 Leneman, Leah, *A Guid Cause* (Edinburgh 1995) p276.

4 Ibid p277.

5 *The Forres, Elgin and Nairn Gazette* 08.11.1871.

6 *The Forres, Elgin and Nairn Gazette* 26.11.1873, p3/4.

7 *The Forres, Elgin and Nairn Gazette* 17.11.1909, p2/5.

8 *The Banffshire Advertiser* 01.09.1910, p8/6.

9 *The Banffshire Advertiser* 07.04.1910, p2/1.

10 *The Banffshire Advertiser* 01.08.1912, p8/2.

11 *The Forres, Elgin and Nairn Gazette* 06.09.1911, p3/2–3.

12 Leneman, Leah, *A Guid Cause* (Edinburgh 1995) pp76–77.

MAIN SOURCES

LAVINIA MALCOLM

Carolan, Janet, *Lavinia Malcolm: First Woman Town Councillor in Scotland 6 November 1907 and First Woman Provost in Scotland 1913*. Published by Dollar Museum, 1997, and revised in 2007 for the centenary of Mrs Malcolm's election to Dollar Town Council.

Carolan, Janet, and Leneman, Leah, 'Malcolm, Lavinia (1847/8–1920)', in *DNB* (Oxford 2004)

ISABELLA MITCHELL

Elgin Museum letters archive.

Libindx NM132760.

ALICE KER

Letters of Rosa May Billinghurst and Dr Alice Ker Vol. XXIX, GB 0106 9/29, Box 7 V 28 (B) – V30 (D), Letters from Holloway Prison from Alice Ker to her two daughters, Women's Library, London.

Libindx NM086373.

Cowman, Krista, 'Ker, Alice Jane Shannan Stewart', in *DNB* (Oxford 2004).

Helmond, Marij van, 'Ker, Alice Jane Shannan Stewart', in Ewan, Elizabeth, Innes, Sue, Reynolds, Sian, (Eds), *The Biographical Dictionary of Scottish Women* (Edinburgh 2006).

Helmond, Marji van, *Votes for Women: The Events on Mersyside 1870–1928* (Liverpool 1992).

Ker, Alice, *Motherhood* (Manchester 1891 and 1896).

Mitchell, Ann, *No More Corncraiks: Lord Moray's Feurs in Edinburgh's New Town* (Edinburgh 1998).

ETHEL BEDFORD FENWICK

Hector, Winifred, *The Work of Mrs Bedford Fenwick and the Rise of Professional Nursing* (London 1973).

McGann, Susan, *The Battle of the Nurses* (London 1992).

Main, Jenny, *The First Nurse* (Kinloss 2003).

NORA MACKAY

Libindx NM103892; father: NM102019; sister: NM102251.

*The Elgin Courant* 30.10.1931; 1.11.1946; 21.3.1952.

*The Northern Scot* 22.08.1952.

*The Northern Scot* Christmas Number 1937.

*Elgin Town Council* minutes 1931–34; 1964.

NANNIE KATHARIN WELLS

Libindx NM192429.

Bateman and Kerrigan, (Eds), *An Anthology of Scottish Women Poets* (Edinburgh 1991).

Cruickshank, Helen B, *Octobiography* (Montrose 1976).

McCulloch, Margery Palmer (Ed.), *Modernism and Nationalism* (Glasgow 2004).

McCulloch, Margery Palmer, and Purdie, Bob, 'Wells, Annie Katharine (Nannie Katharin)' in Ewan, Elizabeth, Innes, Sue, Reynolds, Sian, (Eds), *The Biographical Dictionary of Scottish Women* (Edinburgh 2006).

McMillan and Byrne, (Eds), *Modern Scottish Women Poets* (Edinburgh 2003).

Wells, N Katharin, *Diverse Roads* (Edinburgh 1932).

JOHANNA FORBES

Joseph Ross Collection, Ref. CSCNWW3 1/10, GB237, Coll-577, Centre for the Study of World Christianity, University of Edinburgh.

Documents and minutes of the Foreign Mission Committee of the Church of Scotland, National Library of Scotland.

School of Oriental and African Studies (London), Ref: GB 0102 MS 380570.

Libindx NM186976; brother: NM055755; spouse: NM186957.

*Aberdeen University Review*, Vol. xxx, 2, No. 89, summer 1943.

*Alma Mater*, 21 (1903–04) p17.

M'Lean, Douglas G, *Fordyce Academy* (Banff 1936).

Moore, Lindy, *Bajanellas and Semilinas Aberdeen University and the Education of Women 1860–1920* (Aberdeen 1991).

Roberts, JAG, *The Complete History of China* (Stroud 2003).

Watt, Theodore, *Roll of the Graduates of Aberdeen University 1901–1925* (Aberdeen 1935).

GRISELDA DOW AND HER SISTERS

Personal communication from Griselda Dow's daughter, Marjorie Whytock.

Libindx: NM070232; parents: NM043097, NM043147; sisters: NM250575, NM024183, NM057684.

*Alma Mater* Supplement 10.03.1921.

Moore, Lindy, *Bajanellas and Semilinas* (Aberdeen 1991).

Watt, Theodore, *Roll of the Graduates of Aberdeen University 1901–1925* (Aberdeen 1935).

BEATRICE SELLAR

Personal papers of Dr John Caldwell.

Libindx NM166394; father: NM078440; brother: NM167099.

*The Northern Scot* 06.04.1985.

ISOBEL DUNCAN

Libindx NM044543.

*The Northern Scot* 14.03.1986.

Elgin Town Council Minutes 1960–04.

## CHAPTER SEVEN – TWO WORLD WARS

NOTES

1 Adam, Ruth, *A Woman's Place 1910–75* (London 2000).

2 McKenzie, William J, *Morayshire Roll of Honour* (Elgin 1921). Most of the women mentioned in this introduction can be found in this volume.

3 Libindx NM040364.

4 Libindx NM211295.

5 Libindx NM003589.

6 Libindx NM012731.

7 Bartlam, Bill, and Keillar, Ian, *World War II in Moray* (Moray 2003) p73.

8 Sackville-West, V, *The Women's Land Army* (London 1944).

9 www.bbc.co.uk/ww2peopleswar.

10 Taylor, Pauline, *The People's War* (Moray 2005) p46.

MAIN SOURCES

AMELIA AND CHRISTINA CULBARD

British Red Cross Museum and Archives, London.

Leneman, Leah, *In the Service of Life* (Edinburgh 1994).

Leneman, Leah, *Elsie Inglis* (Edinburgh 1998).

McKenzie, William J, *Morayshire Roll of Honour* (Elgin 1921).

ISABELLA (GUGU) GRANT

Grant Papers 1780–1922, Elgin Museum.

British Red Cross Museums and Archives.

Libindx NM065970.

Farmborough, Florence, *Nurse at the Russian Front* (London 1974).

Harmer, Michael, *The Forgotten Hospital* (Chichester 1982).

McKenzie, William J, *Morayshire Roll of Honour* (Elgin 1921).

ANNABELLA RALPH

Libindx NM147426.

Royal Navy Museum.

Royal College of Nursing Archives.

Census 1891.

Birth Records for Rothes 1884.

HMHS *St Margaret of Scotland,* courtesy of Royal British Legion (Roll of Honour)

McKenzie, William J, *Morayshire Roll of Honour* (Elgin 1921).

TIBBY GORDON

Personal communication from Jean McLatchey, great niece of Tibby Gordon, and from Hugh Robertson, nephew of Tibby Gordon.

Libindx NM019916; parents: NM069203, NM069200; sisters: NM154308, NM152160.

*The Elgin Courant and Courier* 31.12.1915 p5.

McKenzie, William J, *Morayshire Roll of Honour* (Elgin 1921).

McLaren, Eva Shaw, *The History of the Scottish Women's Hospitals* (London 1919).

Leneman, Leah, *In the Service of Life* (Edinburgh 1994).

Catford, EF, *The Royal Infirmary of Edinburgh 1929–1979* (Edinburgh 1984).

CLARA MAIN

Libindx NM118338.

*MAST,* the magazine of the US Maritime Service.

*New York Times* 5.12.1943.

OLGA BYATT

Personal papers and letters owned by the Byatt family.

Libindx NM287957.

*The Elgin Courant and Courier*: 01.09.1939 p5/1–2; 08.09.1939 p4/4 and p5/6; 06.10.1939 p1 /4–5; 29.03.1940 p5/3–4.

Murray, Flora, *Women as Army Surgeons, Sept 1914–October 1919* (London and Edinburgh 1920).

HELEN CATTANACH

Family information.

NHS Grampian Archives.

Libindx NM020972.

*The Northern Scot* 13.05.1994.

*The British Journal of Nursing,* June 1939; February, March, June 1940; September 1941.

*Creag Dubh* 1995, Number 47.

## CHAPTER EIGHT – ACROSS THE WORLD

### NOTES

1 Stoddart, Anna, *The Life of Isabella Bird* (London 1905) p115.

2 *The Banffshire Herald* 02.06.1894 p5/1.

3 Cormack, Alexander Allan, *From Banff to Hanoi* (Peterculter 1966).

4 *The Moray and Nairn Express* 25.12.1886 p8/1.

5 *The Moray and Nairn Express* 03.09.1887 p5/1.

### MAIN SOURCES

#### GEORGIANA MCCRAE

Cowper, Norman (Ed.), *Australian Dictionary of Biography* online edition.

Keillar, Ian, 'From Moray to Melbourne: A Duke's Daughter in the Bush', in *Moray Field Club Bulletin* (Moray 1996).

McCrae, Georgiana, (Higgins, HB and B, Eds), *A Commonplace Book: Compiled at Gordon Castle, Scotland, and in Edinburgh and London During the Years 1828–1837* (Kensington, 1996).

National Trust of Australia (Victoria), *'Our Mountain Home': The McCraes of Arthur's Seat* (Victoria).

Niall, Brenda, *Georgiana: A Biography of Georgiana McCrae, Painter, Diarist, Pioneer* (Melbourne 1994).

#### PENUEL HOSSACK AND HELEN FINDLAY

Libindx NM049594.

Gardner, Sir Ronald East, *The Kiel Family and Related Scottish Pioneers* (Victoria 1974).

Pownall, Eve, *Australian Pioneer Women* (Victoria 1959).

#### EKA GORDON CUMMING

Gordon-Cumming archive, Deposit 175 in National Library of Scotland, Edinburgh.

Libindx NM034937; parents: NM039801, NM006641; siblings: NM034849, NM040196, NM040206, NM064925, NM040302, NM039993, NM039797; stepmother: NM039807; brother-in-law: NM061705.

Baigent, Elizabeth, 'Cumming, Constance Frederica Gordon', in *DNB* (Oxford 2004).

Finkelstein, David, 'Gordon-Cumming, Constance Frederica', in Ewan, Elizabeth, Innes, Sue, Reynolds, Sian, (Eds), *The Biographical Dictionary of Scottish Women* (Edinburgh 2006).

Birkett, Dea, *Off the Beaten Track: Three Centuries of Women Travellers* (London 2004).

Gordon Cumming, CF, *Memories* (Edinburgh 1904).

McMillan, Dorothy, *The Scotswoman at Home and Abroad* (Glasgow 1999).

Napier, Elma, *Youth is a Blunder* (London 1948).

Obituary, in *Geographical Journal* Vol. 65 (1925) p87.

Roth, Jane and Hooper, Stephen, *The Fiji Journals of Baron Anatole Von Hügel, 1875–1877* (Fiji 1990).

University of Cambridge, Museum of Archaeology and Anthropology.

MARGARET AND JEAN CHRYSTIE

Fochabers Heritage Centre.

Peter Dawson, researcher Fochabers Heritage Centre.

Scottish Geographical Society.

Libindx NM023854.

ELSIE WATSON

Family papers belonging to Lorna Glendinning.

Libindx NM113039; father: NM185435; siblings: NM202104, NM201701, NM202840, NM202830, NM073641.

*Daily Express* September 1903.

*New York Times* 14. 09.1913.

ISABELLA KERR

Personal communication from Lis Smith, University of St Andrews regarding LLA classes.

Collection of Joseph Ross, GB 237 Coll-577, Centre for the Study of World Christianity, University of Edinburgh.

Libindx NM086673.

Monahan, Dermott, *The Story of Dichpalli* (London 1938).

MARGARET HASLUCK

Personal communication from Margaret Woodward, great niece of Margaret Hasluck.

Libindx: NM075034; parents: NM074884, NM074983; sisters: NM074989; NM088867, spouse: NM075030; uncle: NM074402.

Unpublished Reports to the Trustees of the Wilson Fellowship, Marischal Museum, University of Aberdeen.

*Aberdeen University Review,* Vol. XXXIII, 2, No. 101, autumn 1949.

Allcock, John B, and Young, Antonia, *Black Lambs and Grey Falcons* (Oxford 2000).

Bailey, Roderick, 'Hasluck, (née Hardie), Margaret Masson', in *DNB* (Oxford 2004).

Bailey, Roderick, *The Wildest Province* (London 2008).

Hasluck, Margaret, *The Unwritten Law in Albania* (Oxford 1954).

Lock, Peter W, 'Hasluck, Frederick William', in *DNB* (Oxford 2004).

Mackenzie, Compton, *Greek Memories* (London 1939).

Manning, Olivia, *Friends and Heroes* (London 1965).

www.europeana.eu.

www.rgs.org.

SYLVIA BENTON

Personal communication from Ian Shepherd (late Principal Archaeologist, Aberdeenshire Council), Jennifer Shaw (Sheriffston), David Marshall (formerly, Hopeman) and the late Dr John McConachie.

Girton College Archive, Cambridge, Personal Papers of MV Wallace (GBR/0271/ GCPPWallace, MV) and card indexed notes on Sylvia Benton.

Libindx NMO13256; parents: NMO12434; NMO12838; sister: NMO12442.

Benton, S, 'The excavation of the Sculptor's Cave, Covesea, Morayshire', in *PSAS* 1930–31,177–216.

Benton, S, *Man* 1933 Article 28, 24.

Benton, S, Sylvia Benton papers in the Beazley Archive, Ashmolean Museum, Oxford.

Cook, Professor John, 'Obituary' *BSA Annual* Vol. 81 (1986).

Duke, Alison, 'Obituary', in *Girton College Newsletter*, 1985, pp30–31.

Waterhouse, Lady Helen, 'Sylvia Benton', in *Women in Old World Archaeology* (Cincinnati).

ANNE HARDIE

Personal communication from Andrew Johnson, Anne's son, and Margaret Woodward, Anne's great niece.

Libindx NMO88867; spouse: NMO89055 (*see also* Margaret Hasluck).

Allardyce, Mabel Desborough (Ed.), *University of Aberdeen Roll of Service in the Great War,* (1921).

Pernau, Margrit, *Female Voices: Women Writers in Hyderabad at the Beginning of the Twentieth Century* – www.urdustudies.com.

www.Mahbubia.com.

ELMA NAPIER

Personal communications from the family: Michael and Josette Napier, Patricia Honychurch, Daphne Agar and Jane Gordon-Cumming; and from Polly Patullo.

Gordon-Cumming archive, Deposit 175, National Library of Scotland.

Libindx NMO66406 and NMO39813; parents: NMO38899; NMO06641; uncle: NMO40300.

Brereton, HL, 'Review of *Youth is a Blunder*' *Gordonstoun Record* Christmas 1947.

Clarke, Sir Edward, *The Story of my Life* (1918).

Fermor, Patrick Leigh, *The Traveller's Tree* (London 1984).

Honychurch, Lennox, *The Dominica Story* (London 1995).

JAOF 'Afterthought on *Youth is a Blunder*', in *Gordonstoun Record*, Easter 1949.

Napier, Elma, *Youth is a Blunder* (London 1948).

Napier, Elma, *Winter is in July* (London 1949).

Napier, Elma, *Black and White Sands* (London 2009).

Shore, WT, (Ed.), *Notable British Trials: The Baccarat Case* (Edinburgh 1932).

Waugh, Alec 'Typical Dominica', in *The Sugar Islands* (London 1958).

## CHAPTER NINE – RUNNING A BUSINESS

### NOTES

1 Rampini, Charles (Ed.), *The Lintie of Moray* (Elgin 1887) p74.

2 Watson, WE, (Compiler), *The Convenery of the Six Incorporated Trades of Elgin* (1960).

### MAIN SOURCES

#### ELIZABETH CUMMING

Cardhu Distillery archives.

Libindx NM030712.

Barnard, Alfred, *The Whisky Distilleries of Scotland* (Gartocharn 1887).

Lodge, Christine, 'Cumming, Elizabeth', in Ewan, Elizabeth, Innes, Sue, Reynolds, Sian, (Eds), *The Biographical Dictionary of Scottish Women* (Edinburgh 2006).

#### ETHEL BAXTER

Family and Company background information supplied by Gordon Baxter.

Ethel Baxter's Diary of 1914, written retrospectively in 1948.

Baxter, Ethel, *From Small Beginnings* (1963).

Carden, Susan, *Scottish Memories: The Ethel Baxter Story* (1997).

Pallister, Marion, edited by Charles Walker, *A Legacy of Scots* (Edinburgh 1988).

Scott, Judith G, *Four Hundred Years of Ups and Downs: The Gordon Chapel, Fochabers*.

#### ISOBEL BROWN

Personal communication from Fochabers folk.

Fochabers Heritage Centre.

Libindx NM015031.

CHAPTER TEN – BREAKING INTO SCIENCE

NOTES

1 Gordon Archive, Elgin Museum, 65.19.

2 Collie, M and Bennett, S, *George Gordon: An Annotated Catalogue of his Scientific Correspondence* (Aldershot 1996); Gordon Archive, Elgin Museum 65.36.

3 McCallum Webster, Mary, *Flora of Moray, Nairn and East Inverness* (Aberdeen 1978), p3.

4 Andrews, SM, *The Discovery of Fossil Fishes in Scotland up to 1845* (Edinburgh 1982).

MAIN SOURCES

ELIZA GORDON CUMMING

Personal communication from Dr Mike A Taylor.

Gordon-Cumming archive, Deposit 175 in National Library of Scotland.

Geological Society of London MS Library.

Libindx NM039801; spouse: NM006641; children: NM03489; NM034834; NM040050; NM039791; NM034937; father-in-law: NM040040.

Act of Parliament 11° GEORGII IV. Cap.27 17th June 1830 (microfiche copy, Elgin Library L348.41022).

Andrews, SM, *The Discovery of Fossil Fishes in Scotland up to 1845* (Edinburgh 1982).

Andrews, SM, 'Altyre and Lethen Bar, Two Middle Old Red Sandstone Fish Localities?', in *Scottish Journal of Geology* Vol. 19 (3) 1983.

Campbell, Beaujolais, *A Journey to Florence in 1817* (London 1951).

Creese, MRS, 'Fossil Hunters, a Cave Explorer and a Rock Analyst: Notes on some Early Women contributors to Geology', in Burek, CV and Higgs, B (Eds), *The Role of Women in the History of Geology* (Geological Society London, Special Publications, 281 (2007) pp251–64.

Dick Lauder, Sir Thomas, *The Moray Floods* (3rd edition, Elgin 1873).

Rolfe, Julia Rayer, 'Gordon-Cumming, Lady Eliza Maria' in Ewan, Elizabeth, Innes, Sue, Reynolds, Sian, (Eds) *The Biographical Dictionary of Scottish Women* (Edinburgh 2006).

Gordon Cumming, CF, *Memories* (Edinburgh 1904).

Hay, Robert, *Lochnavando No More: The Life and Death of a Moray Farming Community, 1750–1850* (Edinburgh 2005).

Kölbl-Ebert, Martina, 'British Geology in the Early Nineteenth Century: A Conglomerate with a Female Matrix', in *Earth Sciences History*, Vol. 21, No. 1 (2002) pp3–25.

Miller, Hugh, *The Cruise of the Betsey with Rambles of a Geologist* (Edinburgh 1888).

Miller, Hugh, *The Old Red Sandstone* (Edinburgh 18th edition 1873).

GRACE MILNE

The Falconer Museum.

Boylan, Patrick J (Ed.), *The Falconer Papers, Forres* (Leicester 1977).

Libindx NM112939.

Mather and Campbell, 'Grace Anne Milne (Lady Prestwich): More than an Amanuensis?', in Burek, CV, and Higgs, B, (Eds), *The Role of Women in the History of Geology* (Geological Society London, Special Publications, 281 (2007) pp251–64.

ANNA BUCHAN

Private communications from the family: Irene Beanland, Sheila Dick, Diana Chadwick, and Alexander Buchan; and members of the Apostolic Church.

Libindx NM179465, NM015095; father: NM014817; spouse: NM179466.

Elgin and Moray Literary and Scientific Society Minutes 1921–52, 1952–55.

Buchan, Anna, *Investigation of the Glacial and Postglacial Deposits of Spynie,* University of Aberdeen Libraries Th 1935 Bu.

Hoppen, Alison, 'Notes on the life of Anna Buchan' (Elgin Museum Archive 2000).

Peacock, JD, 'The Pre-Windermere Interstadial (Late Devensian) Raised Marine Strata of Eastern Scotland and their Macrofauna: A Review' in *Quarterly Scientific Reviews* Vol. 18 (1999).

Suckling, Anna, 'Lamps through the Ages', in *Aberdeen University Review* Vol. XXXII.2 No. 97, summer, 1947.

Southwood, Helen, *A Cultural History of the Marischal Anthropological Museum in the Twentieth Century* (Aberdeen 2003).

ISABELLA GORDON

Natural History Museum Archives DF208/52; DF208/94; DF256/1–17; department of zoology, by permission of the Trustees of the Natural History Museum.

Libindx NM276039.

Datta, Ann, 'Fraser, Francis Charles', in *DNB* (Oxford 2004).

Rolfe, Julia Rayer, 'Gordon, Isabella', in Ewan, Elizabeth, Innes, Sue, Reynolds, Sian, (Eds), *The Biographical Dictionary of Scottish Women* (Edinburgh 2006).

Gordon, Isabella, (revised by McConnell, Anita), 'Calman, William Thomas', in *DNB* (Oxford 2004).

Holthius, LB, and Ingle, RW, 'Isabella Gordon, D.SC, OBE 1901–1988', in

*Crustaceana* 56 (1) (1989).

MARY MCCALLUM WEBSTER

Personal communication from Ian Suttie and Bridget Whyte.

Libindx NM115384.

McCallum Webster, Mary, *Flora of Moray, Nairn and East Inverness* (Aberdeen 1978).

Marler, Peter, and McCallum Webster, Mary, 'A Contribution to the Flora of West Sutherland', in *Watsonia* Vol. 2 No. 3 (1952).

McCallum Webster, Mary, 'Natural History', in *A History of the Parish of Dyke and Moy* (Dyke 1966).

McCallum Webster, Mary, *Checklist of the Flora of Culbin State Forest* (Elgin 1968 and 1977).

*Moray Field Club Bulletin*, December 1985.

Omand, Donald, (Ed.), 'Plant Life', in *The Moray Book* (Edinburgh, 1976).

Stewart, OM and Sell, PD, 'Tribute' in *Proceedings of BSBI*, April 1954.

LESLEY SOUTER

Personal communication from Lesley's sister, Phyllis Titt.

Libindx NM172759; parents: NM038053, NM04335; sister: NM263130.

Clayton, Robert and Algar, Joan, *The GEC Research Laboratories 1919–1984* (London 1989).

*The Illustrated London News* October 6 1945, p381 (explaining flying bombs).

*Rugby Advertiser* 14.11.1980.

*Coventry Evening News* 22.04.1981.


CHAPTER ELEVEN – THE CREATIVE LIFE

NOTES

1 Woolf, Virginia, *A Room of One's Own* (Chapter 1) (London 1929).

2 Cumming, CF Gordon, *In the Hebrides* (opening paragraph) (London 1886).

MAIN SOURCES

SOPHIA DUNBAR

Personal communication from the family: Sir Archie Dunbar and Alexander (Sandy) Dunbar.

Libindx NM009154; spouse: NM040026; stepdaughter: NM039497; brother-in-law NM041909.

Aberdeen Art Gallery collections.

Royal Commission for the Ancient and Historic Monuments of Scotland archive.

Anon, 'Notice of donations: Six Water-colour Sketches of Portions of Sculptured Stones Found at Burghead...' in *PSAS*, 1860–61, Vol. IV Part I (1862) p166.

Anon, 'Notice of Donations: Stone Cist Found Under a Cairn at Roseisle, near Elgin...' in *PSAS*, 1860–61 Vol. IV Part I, 52 (1862).

Clayton, Ellen C, *English Female Artists* Vol. II Tinsley 1876.

Dunbar of Northfield Papers, Moray Council Archives NRAS65 (uncatalogued, but including transcript of Agnes Dunbar's memories).

Dunbar of Northfield, Lady, *A Family Tour Round the Coasts of Spain and Portugal During the Winter of 1860–1861* (Edinburgh 1862).

Dunbar, Sophia, letter to Sir James Young Simpson, Royal College of Surgeons, Edinburgh 1176:1866, May 22nd.

Innes, Cosmo, 'A Note of the Excavation of a Cairn at Roseisle...', in *PSAS* III Session 1859–60, Part III (1862) pp374–75.

Innes, Cosmo, 'Notice of a Tomb on the Hill of Roseisle, Morayshire...', in *PSAS* III Session 1857–58, Part I (1860) pp46–47.

Napier, Elma, *Youth is a Blunder* (London 1948).

Stuart, John, *The Sculptured Stones of Scotland* Vol. 2 Spalding Club, 1867 XCIV.

MARY SETON WATTS

Libindx: NM039962; parents: NM241734, NM035957.

Bills, Mark, *Watts Chapel, a Guide to the Symbols of Mary Watts's Arts and Crafts Masterpiece* (London 2010).

Cumming, Elizabeth, *Hand, Heart and Soul* (Edinburgh 2006).

Cumming, Elizabeth, 'Watts, Mary Seton', in Ewan, Elizabeth, Innes, Sue, Reynolds, Sian, (Eds), *The Biographical Dictionary of Scottish Women* (Edinburgh 2006).

Gould, Veronica Franklin, *Mary Seton Watts* (Watts Gallery 1998).

Jekyll, Gertrude, and Weaver, Lawrence, *Gardens for Small Country Houses* (London 1912).

Watson, J and W, *Morayshire Described* (Elgin 1868).

*New Statistical Account*, Forres Parish 1842.

www.wattsgallery.org.uk.

MARY SYMON

Manuscripts Catalogue Acc. 7534, National Library of Scotland.

Libindx NM112678.

Milton, Colin, 'A Sough o War', in Hewitt, David (Ed.), *Northern Visions: The Literary Identity of Northern Scotland in the Twentieth Century* (East Linton 1995).

Milton, Colin, 'Symon, Mary', in *DNB* (Oxford 2004).

Symon, Mary, *Deveron Days* (Aberdeen 1933); *Deveron Days* 2nd edition (Aberdeen 1938).

EMMA BLACK

Personal communication from Jennifer Shaw (née Black).

Libindx NM002882.

ISABEL CAMERON

Personal communication with Elizabeth Macpherson's daughter, Jane Yeadon.

Libindx Isabel Cameron: NM032540; John Cameron: NM036203;

Olson, Ian, 'Isobel Cameron and The Doctor', in *The Scots Magazine* (2008).

Young, Douglas, *Highland Search* (Kinloss 2002).

DOROTHY BROWN

Personal communication from Sir James Dunbar-Nasmith, Dorothy Brown's nephew, and from Mr and Mrs Hugh Munro (d).

Libindx NM014254.

MARGARET WINEFRIDE SIMPSON

Libindx NM003568

KIM MURRAY

Information from former pupils John Mustard and Sandy MacAdam.

Elgin Town Council minutes.

Programmes and articles held at Elgin Museum.

Libindx Kim Murray: NM002578; Sister Mary Winefride: NM168271; Ella Taylor: NM002579.

ELIZABETH MACPHERSON

Libindx Elizabeth Macpherson: NM068522; Ian Macpherson: NM114447.

Young, Douglas F, 'Macpherson, Ian', in *DNB* (Oxford 2004).

Young, Douglas, *Highland Search* (Kinloss 2002).

JOHN AUBREY

Personal knowledge of William Smith.

Libindx NM022021.

Christie's Scotland, *Catalogue of the Studio Sale of John Aubrey* (1986).

Jacobs, Michael and Warner, Malcolm, *The Phaidon Companion to Art and Artists in the British Isles* (Oxford 1980).

*Medical Registers* (London 1897–1935).

VERONICA BRUCE

Personal communication from Lorna Murray, Education Manager, Scottish Ballet.

Libindx NM140522; parents: NM015858, NM015438.

Russian Ballet History: Diaghilev's dancers.

JESSIE KESSON

Libindx NM002998; mother: NM213534.

Gifford and McMillan, (Eds), *A History of Scottish Women's Writing* (Edinburgh 1997).

Murray, Isobel, (Ed.), *Somewhere Beyond* (Edinburgh 2000).

Murray, Isobel, (Ed.), *A Country Dweller's Years* (Glasgow 2009).

Murray, Isobel, *Writing her Life* (Edinburgh 2000), (2nd edition Glasgow 2011).

Murray, Isobel and Tait, Bob, *Scottish Writers Talking* (East Linton 1996).

Murray, Isobel, 'Kesson (née Macdonald), Jessie Grant', in *DNB* (Oxford 2004).


CHAPTER TWELVE – SPORTING SUCCESS

NOTES

1 *The Northern Scot* Christmas Number 1910, p16.

2 *The Daily Telegraph* 5 February 2009.

3 Libindx SB000547.

4 Main, Jenny, *Elgin People*, (Stroud 1998) p60.

5 McConachie, John, *The Moray Golf Club at Lossiemouth 1889–1999* (Elgin 1988) p4.

6 *The Northern Scot* Christmas Number 1912, p32.

7 *The Northern Scot* Christmas Number 1910, p16.

8 McConachie, John, *The Moray Golf Club at Lossiemouth 1889–1999* (Elgin 1988) p85.

9 Ibid p87.

10 Helme, Eleanor, *Family Golf* (1938).

11 McConachie, John, *The Moray Golf Club at Lossiemouth 1889–1999* (Elgin 1988) p87.

12 Ibid p47.

MAIN SOURCES

MARGARET (MEG) FARQUHAR

Personal communication from W Farquhar Thomson.

Libindx NM054048; sister: NM047593.

John McConachie, *The Moray Golf Club at Lossiemouth 1889–1989* (Elgin 1988).

*Scotland on Sunday* 21.06.2009, article by Kate Foster.

*Press and Journal* 19.01.1988, article by Colin Farquharson.

CHAPTER THIRTEEN – TRADITION AND MEMORIES

NOTES

1 London Morayshire Club, *Old Morayshire Characters* (Elgin 1931) p67.

2 Libindx SB007796.

MAIN SOURCES

CHRISTINA MUNRO

Douglas, Robert, No. 18: 'The Curse of the Lairds', in *Lays and Legends of Moray* (1939) pp47–49.

Mackenzie, William Ross, *A Century of Wit and Wisdom* (1888) pp37–41.

JEAN CARR (OR KERR)

Fochabers Heritage Centre.

Libindx NM155454.

Dawson, Peter, *The Little Fochabers Facts Book* (1999).

LUCKY JONSON

Dallas, Reverend, *Queer Folk of Taockburn* (c.1880)

JEANNIE SHAW

Oral tradition

JANET LEVACK

Libindx NM010090; NM008927; NM011114

*Stories of Old Lossiemouth as Told by Mrs Levack* (Elgin 1927)

*Papers Past: Daily Southern Cross* 3 June 1870, 6 July 1870, 21 July 1970, 7 October 1870.

JESSIE POZZI

Libindx NM149080, NM149076, NM149083

*The Elgin Courant and Courier* 03.09.1943, p3/3

*The Forres Gazette* 08.09.1943, p2/6

McDonald, Jean, 'Recalling a Notable Elgin Personality... Custodian of the "Northern Lanthorn"', in *The Northern Scot* Christmas Number 1955.

Family Search, International Genealogical Index v.4.01

CHRISTINA MACDONALD (JOYFUL)

Libindx NM189777

*The Northern Scot* 12.02 1927, p6/2.

BETSY WHYTE

Close and extended members of the Thom, Wilson and Williamson families.

*The Ross-shire Journal.*

Census records etc, Moray Heritage Centre.

The National Archives of Scotland.

JOANNE MCCULLOCH

Oral tradition

IDA MCPHERSON

Family records.

Descendants of Ida McPherson.

The Scottish Fisheries Museum, Anstruther.

# Index of Women

A

Adam, Elizabeth 96
Adam, Elizabeth 232
Adam, Ethel (*see* Baxter, Ethel)
Addison, Aunt 157
Alice, Princess of Athlone 223
Allan, Isabella 82, 83, 86
Allardyce, Miss 88
Allfrey, Phyllis Shand 224
Anderson, Bess 311
Andersone, Marion 39
Anderson, Marjory 65, 66, 67–69
Anderson, Miss 299, 300
Anderson, Tibby (*see* Gordon, Tibby)
Andrews, S Mahala 244
Angus, Marion 129
Anne of Denmark 24
Argyll, Agnes, Countess of (*see* Keith, Agnes)
Asher, Margaret 196
Aubrey, John 268, 297–301

B

Baillie, Joanna 51
Bain, Miss 132
Bannerman, Kathleen 301
Barlow, Mrs 112
Batchie, the 318
Bate, Dorothea 215
Baxter, Ethel 225, 226, 229–33
Baxter, Fanny 317
Bedford Fenwick, Ethel 105, 119-24
Bell, Vanessa 300
Benton, Mary 216, 311
Benton, Sylvia 14, 180, 212–17, 249, 252, 271, 311
Birch, Ann 284
Bird, Isabella 192, 195
Bisset, Edith 107
Black, Emma 268, 284–86, 300
Black, Helen 147, 149
Black, Rene 293
Blair, Magdalene 58

Blair, Stewarts of 318
Bodger, Eleanor 215
Bodichon, Barbara 273
Bowyer, Miss 97
Braco, Lady 225
Brander, Janet (*see* Levack, Janet)
Breadheid, Janet 44
Breckinridge, Mary 95
Bremner, Elizabeth (*see* Macpherson, Elizabeth)
Briggs, Mary 261
Brodie, Elizabeth 181, 182, 183, 184
Brodie, Emelia 48
Brodie Emilia
Brodie, Margaret 43
Brodie, Mary (*see* Ker, Mary)
Brodie, Mary (*see* Sleigh, Mary)
Brown, Christian (Chrissie) 233, 234
Brown, Dorothy 268, 288–90, 300
Brown, Isabella 316
Brown, Isobel 226, 233–37
Brown, Laura 288
Brown, May (*see* Dunbar-Rivers, May)
Bruce, Ida 293
Bruce, Ursula 303
Bruce, Veronica 268, 269, 301–03
Brunton, Mary 51
Buchan, Anna 217, 239, 249–52
Buchan, Anna 251
Buckland, Mary 244
Byatt, Olga 148, 149, 150, 169–76

C

Caldwell, Christian 42
Caldwell, Magdalene 141, 142, 143
Cameron, Elizabeth (*see* Macpherson, Elizabeth)
Cameron, Hilda 311
Cameron, Isabel 268, 286–88, 294
Cameron, Julia Margaret 274
Campbell, Agnes (*see* Keith, Agnes)
Campbell, Eliza Maria (see Gordon Cumming, Eliza)
Campbell, Olga (*see* Byatt, Olga)

Carr, Jean (or Kerr) 320–21
Carswell, Catherine 129
Cattanach, Helen 176–178
Cattanach, Marjory 176
Chalmers, Isabel (see John Aubrey)
Christie, Jean 61
Chrystie, Jean 180, 196–98
Chrystie, Margaret 180, 196–98
Clayton, Ellen 271, 272
Clayton, Josephina 179, 180
Collie, Mary 42
Corbet, Isabella 52, 54, 57
Craigen, Jessie 107
Crawford, JG 90
Crompton, Alice 107
Cruickshank, Helen B 129, 131
Culbard, Amelia 148, 151–53, 164
Culbard, Christina 148, 151–53, 164
Culbard, Edith 125, 151
Cullen sisters 51
Cumming, Elizabeth 226–29

D
Davidson, TD 287
Davison, Emily Wilding 107
Dawson, Elizabeth 50, 51
Dawson, Margaret 65, 66, 71–74
Dean, Annie 318
Dickerman, Marion 171
Dow, Dorothy 138, 139, 140
Dow, Elizabeth (Betty) 137, 138, 139, 140
Dow, Griselda (Grisel) 105, 137–40, 141
Dow, Margaret 137, 140
Dow, Marjorie 137, 140
Dow, Marjorie Johanna Macpherson (Mam) 137, 140
Duff, Ella Wharton 147, 149
Duff, Isabel Wharton 147, 149
Duff, Margaret 57
Duffus, Euphemia of 20, 25–26
Dunbar, Agnes (see Randolph, Agnes)
Dunbar, Agnes 270
Dunbar, Catharina 148
Dunbar, Elizabeth 21, 28–30
Dunbar, Ethel 147, 148, 149
Dunbar, Janet 28
Dunbar, Janet 28
Dunbar, Jeanie 270

Dunbar, Lilias 148
Dunbar, Margaret 28
Dunbar, Marjorie 148
Dunbar, Sophia 268, 269–74
Dunbar, Lilias 148
Dunbar, Sophia 268, 269–74
Dunbar, 'Tihi' 317
Dunbar-Rivers, Beatrix Justina 289
Dunbar-Rivers, May 288, 289
Dunbar-Nasmith, Evelyn 290
Duncan, Isabella 278
Duncan, Isadora 216
Duncan, Isobel (Sybil) 108, 127, 145–46
Duncan, Margaret 160

E
Eardley, Joan 301
Edgar, Beatrice Gordon 263
Elder, Isobel 42
Erskine, Margaret 33
Esslemont, Mary 138

F
Falconer, Louisa 245
Falconer, Louise 248
Farquhar, Christina (see Macdonald, Christina)
Farquhar, Margaret (Meg) 17, 311, 312, 313–19
Feld, Margaret 38
Fife, Duchess of 114
Findlay, Helen 186–89
Findlay, Penuel (see Penuel Hossack)
Fitzgibbon, Elizabeth 299
Fletcher, Elizabeth 50, 51
Forbes, Johanna 14,15, 106, 131–37, 138
Forsyth, Josephine 90
Fraser, Helen 107, 108, 128
Fraser, Rita 311
Froster, Margarat 21, 22

G
Garner, Elizabeth 224
Garner, Florence 220, 221, 222
Garrett Anderson, Elizabeth 105
Garrett Anderson, Louisa 169
Garrow, Jane 128
Gibbs, Daphne 222, 223

Gibbs, Elma (*see* Napier, Elma)
Gilbert, Isobel 43
Gill, Mary (Nanny) 289, 290
Gilzean, Jean 68
Gilzean, Marjory (*see* Anderson, Marjory)
Gordon, Alice 160, 165
Gordon, Clara (*see* Main, Clara)
Gordon, Georgiana (*see* McCrae, Georgiana)
Gordon, Isabella 239, 253–58
Gordon, Jane, Duchess of (*see* Maxwell, Jane)
Gordon, Jean 160, 164
Gordon, Lady 192
Gordon, Mary 165
Gordon, Tibby 148, 160–65
Gordon Cumming, Cecily 222
Gordon Cumming, Constance Frederica (Eka) 180,190-96, 241, 268, 269
Gordon Cumming, Eliza 190, 138, 239, 240-44, 269
Gordon Cumming, Elma (see Napier, Elma)
Gordon Cumming, Helen 269
Gordon Cumming, Ida 66, 242
Gordon Cumming, Nelly 190, 196
Gordon Cumming, Anne (Seymour) 190, 241
Gordon-Duff, Mildred 150
Gourdon, Marie 40
Gowdie, Isobel 41, 43–46
Grant, Anne 51
Grant, Elizabeth 61
Grant, Elizabeth 316
Grant, Isabella (Gugu) 147, 153–57
Grant, Ladie 40, 41
Grant, Mrs 286
Grant, Penuel 187
Gregor, Griselda (see Dow, Griselda)
Gregor, Marjorie 139, 140
Grey, Norah 259
Grey, Sybil 154
Gruoch, Queen of Scotland (Lady Macbeth) 22–25
Gunn, Isabella (see Kerr, Isabella)

H
Hair, Mollie 214

Hamilton, Cecily 117
Hamilton, Elizabeth 51
Hardie, Anne 148, 217–19, 206
Hardie, Margaret (*see* Hasluck, Margaret)
Hardie, Mary 148
Harper, Isabela 56
Harrison, H 310
Hasluck, Margaret 14, 148, 180, 205–12, 217
Hay, Jean 225
Helena, Princess 121
Helme, Eleanor 312
Hepworth, Barbara 298, 300
Holloway, Dr 161
Hood, Miss 311
Horne, Janet 41
Hoppen, Alison 252
Hossack, Penuel 186–90
Hudson, Alice 288, 289
Hughes, Miss 221

I
Inglis, Elsie 94, 148, 152, 160
Inkson, Jane 226
Innes, Barbara 42
Innes, Mrs 225, 226

J
Jacob, Violet 281
Jamieson, Miss 107
Jekyll, Gertrude 261, 276
Jex Blake, Kits 213
Jex Blake, Sophia 105
Johnson, Anne (*see* Hardie, Anne)
Johnson, Barbara (*see* Simpkin, Barbara)
Johnson, Hilda 74
Jones, Ida (*see* McPherson, Ida)
Jones, Katie 331
Jones, Nellie 331
Jones, Sarah 331
Jonson, Lucky 321–22

K
Karsavina, Tamara 268, 301
Keith, Agnes 20, 21, 33–37
Keith, Margaret 33
Kelman, Jeannie 149
Kennedy, Janet 21, 30–33

Kennedy, Marcelle 127
Ker, Alice 105, 106, 115–19
Ker, Ann 46
Ker, Margaret 116, 117, 118, 119
Ker, Mary 41, 42, 46–49, 54
Ker, Mary 116, 117, 118, 119
Kerr, Isabella 14, 202–205
Kerr, Isobel 203, 204, 205
Kesson, Jessie 252, 268, 269, 303–09, 329
Knight, Laura 300
Kynoch, Janet 109
Kynoch, Magdelene 141
Kynoch, Minnie 110

L
Laing, Abigail 109
Laing, Grace 109
Laing, Lavinia (see Malcolm, Lavinia)
Laing, Margaret 109
Laing, Mary 109
Lamb, Margaret 253
Lambton, Lucinda 276
Lee, Mally 53, 54
Leslie, Margaret 217
Levack, Annie 324
Levack, Ethel 150, 324, 325
Levack, Jane 324
Levack, Janet 150, 318, 323–25
Levack, Margaret 324
Levack, Thérèse 150, 324
Levingston, Isobel 32
Lindley, Mary Katherine 301
Livingstone, Mrs (see Edith Scott)
Longden, Anne 273

M
Macbeth, Lady (see Gruoch)
McCall, Grace (see Milne, Grace)
McCallum Webster, Mary 240, 259-63
McCrae, Georgiana 14, 180–85, 267
McCulloch, Joanne 317, 330-31
Macdonald, Catherine 87
MacDonald, Elizabeth (Liz) 303, 304, 305
Macpherson, Christina (Joyful) 82, 327
McDonald, Flora 117
Macdonald, Ishbel 86
MacDonald, Jessie (see Kesson, Jessie)

MacDonald, Jessie 303
Macdonald, Kathleen 312
Macdonell, Mary Scott 92
McGeagh, Chrystal 314, 315
McIntosh, Janet 316
McKay, Joan 327
Mackay, Nora 108, 124–28, 150, 151
Mackenzie, Helen Leslie 14, 81, 92–95
McKenzie, Helen (see Munro, Helen)
Mackenzie, Isabel 65, 69–71
McKibben, Anna 250
Mackintosh, Nora 310
Macleod, Mrs 69
McLeod, Jane 313
McNeill, F Marian 129, 131
Mcphee, Georgina 327
Macpherson, Elizabeth 268, 288, 294–97
Macpherson, Elizabeth 296
McPherson, Ida 331–35
McPherson, Isabella 332
Macpherson, Jane 296
Macpherson, Marjorie 137, 140
Macrae, Kate 107
Mactaggart, Euphemia (see Euphemia of Duffus)
Maggach, Margaret 132
Main, Clara 150, 165–68
Main, Meg Farquhar (see Farquhar, Margaret)
Mair, Mary 332
Malcolm, Lavinia 106, 107, 108, 109–13
Mallat, Margaret (see Dawson, Margaret)
Manning, Olivia 211
Manson, Ethel (see Bedford Fenwick, Ethel)
Manson, Henrietta 119
Margaret, Princess 224
Mariota 19
Mary Winefride, Sister 293, 294
Maxwell, Jane 52, 58–63, 64, 71, 180, 238
Miller, Margaret (see Dawson, Margaret)
Milne, Grace 239, 244, 245–48
Milne, Mona 14
Mitchell, Agnes 38
Mitchell, Isabella 106, 114–15

Moray, Agnes, Countess of (*see* Keith, Agnes)
Moray, Agnes, Countess of (*see* Randolph, Agnes)
Moray, Elizabeth, Countess of (*see* Dunbar, Elizabeth)
Morris, Margaret 302
Morrison, Elspet 148
Morrison, Gertrude 148
Munro, Christina 317, 318–20
Munro, Ella 79, 81, 82, 99–104
Munro, Jessie 107
Murchison, Charlotte 244
Murray, Flora 169
Murray, Ida (*see* McPherson, Ida)
Murray, Isobel 303, 304, 305, 306, 309
Murray Kathleen Ida (Kim) 269, 292–94

N
Nadezdinova, Maria (*see* Veronica Bruce)
Napier, Elma 14, 214, 220–24, 273
Napier, Patricia 222, 223
Naughtie, Isobell, 38
Neill, Elizabeth 216
Nightingale, Florence 66, 121, 123
Noble, Isabel (*see* Cameron, Isabel)
North, Marianne 195

O
Onlie, Lady 225
Orred, Sophia (*see* Sophia Dunbar) 269

P
Paget, Muriel 154
Pankhurst, Christabel 106
Pankhurst, Emmeline 107, 117
Paterson, Jessie (*see* Pozzi, Jessie)
Pavlova, Anna 301
Pease, Evelyn 289
Peddar, Effame 39
Petrie, Janet 178
Plummer, Mrs 318
Pozzi, Jessie 325–26
Prestwich, Grace (*see* Grace Milne)

Q
Queen of Scots, Mary 33, 34, 35, 36, 38

R
Rae, Elsie S 281
Ragge, Isobell 38
Ragge, Janet 38
Ralph, Annabella 147, 158–60, 177
Ramsay, Annie 81, 82–86, 341
Ramsay, Peggy 312
Randolph, Agnes 19, 21, 26–28
Randolph, Isabella 27, 28
Reid, Isabella 233, 235
Richardson, Louise 310
Richmond, Charlotte, Duchess of 64
Robertson, Elizabeth (*see* Cumming, Elizabeth)
Robertson, Elspet 227
Robertson, Miss 238
Rose, Annabella 145
Rose, Elizabeth 59
Rose, Helen 81, 96–99, 287
Rose, Jane 212
Ross, Euphemia of 19
Ross, Johanna 151

S
Scott, Edith 284
Scott, Nan 302
Sellar, Annie Maude 14
Sellar, Beatrice 105, 141–45
Sergison, Emilia 191
Seton, Margaret, 28
Shaw, Jeannie 322–23
Shearer, Moira 302
Shepherd, Alexandra 216
Simpkin, Barbara 67, 74–77
Simpson, Margaret Winefride 268, 286, 291–92
Sleigh, Mary 52–57
Smith, Annie Katherine (see Wells, Nannie Katharin)
Smith, Flora Ellen 108
Somerville, Mary 246
Souter, Lesley 149, 239, 263–66
Souter, Phyllis 264
Souter, Tresta 264
Spence, Helen (*see* MacKenzie, Helen Leslie)
St Barbe, Etheldred 274
Stephen, Margaret 79, 80, 81, 87–91, 93, 106, 125

Stevenson, Flora 80, 81, 115
Stevenson, Louisa 80, 81, 115
Stevenson, Margaret Miller 115, 116
Stewart, Christina 33
Stewart, Isabel 26
Stewart, Maggie Anne 85
Stopes, Marie 116
Stout, Ella 102
Stuart, Margaret 291
Suckling, Anna (*see* Anna Buchan)
Symon, Helen (*see* Findlay, Helen)
Symon, Mary 106, 267, 268, 278–83

T
Taylor, Ella 269, 293, 294
Taylour, Miss 107
Terry, Ellen 274, 275
Thom, Eleanor 330
Tillyard, Phyllis 213
Titaua, Princess 193
Tocher, Agnes 134, 135
Tocher, Johanna (*see* Forbes, Johanna)
Trewavas, Dr 255
Tudor, Margaret 31, 32
Tulloch, Katie 215
Tytler, Mary Seton Fraser (*see* Watts, Mary Seton)

V
Varden, Cristen 21, 22
Victoria, Queen 192, 198, 269, 316

W
Walker, Ethel 300
Wallace, Winnie 108
Watson, Elsie 14, 106, 180, 198–202
Watts, Mary Seton 267, 268, 269, 274–78
Webster, Teenie 318
Wedgewood, ML 259
Wei Chen, Margaret 137
Wells, Nannie Katharin 106, 107, 128–31
Wellwood, Edith 148, 149
West, Rebecca 207
Whyte, Betsy 327–30
Whyte, Elsie 330
Whyte, Jane (*see* Whyte, Betsy)
Whyte, Jeannie 330

Williams, Emma (*see* Black, Emma)
Williamson, Betsy (*see* Whyte, Betsy)
Wilson Betsy (*see* Whyte, Betsy)
Wilson, Helen 136
Wilson, Mary 149
Wink, Elspeth (Elsie) 198
Winslade, Rosina 265
Woodville, Elizabeth 269
Wright, Christian Guthrie 80, 81

# Index of Places in North-East Scotland

A

Abbeyside 245
Aberdeen 13, 50, 59, 77, 92, 93, 106,
107, 114, 115, 128, 129, 132, 137,
138, 139, 154, 158, 176, 188, 196,
199, 203, 205, 215, 216, 229, 230,
231, 232, 239, 249, 250, 251, 252,
253, 254, 262, 270, 271, 278, 279,
281, 296, 301, 304, 305, 311
Aberdeen Church of Scotland Training
College 196
Aberdeen Music Hall 105
Aberdeen Practising School 196
Aberdeen, Royal Infirmary of 158, 229
Aberdeen, University of 88, 131, 132,
138, 149, 141, 203, 205, 206, 207,
209, 217, 249, 294, 308
Aberdeenshire 11, 88, 202, 273, 294,
304, 306, 328
Aberlour 40, 94, 105, 141, 143, 144,
157, 169, 175, 190, 290
Advie 150
Albyn School, Aberdeen 139
Altyre 190, 191, 220, 221, 239, 240,
241, 242, 243, 244, 247
Alves 83, 109, 147, 148, 158, 303,
304, 318
Archiestown 51, 144, 186
Ashley Road School, Aberdeen 106
Asliesk 48
Auldearn 43
Aviemore 61, 232, 311
Avon, River 144
Avon, Loch 311

B

Ballindalloch 69
Balmoral 317
Balnageith 164
Banff 60, 107, 261, 320
Banffshire 13, 14, 17, 115, 128, 160,
202, 328
Begrow 160
Bellie 59, 61, 128, 196, 234, 236
Benrinnes 285

Birnie 74, 231, 238
Bishopmill 100, 101, 146, 284, 304,
318, 327, 330
Blackhills 186
Blelock 140
Bogfearn 186
Boharm 149
Bothgowan 23
Botriphnie 15, 136
Braemar 260, 311
British Restaurant 126, 127
Brodie 41, 42, 43, 46, 47, 48, 49, 52,
53, 54, 55, 56, 57, 181
Buchan 33, 217, 239, 249
Buckie 81, 107, 225, 262, 291, 317
Buinach 289, 290
Burghead 165, 190, 271, 272, 316
Burgie 44

C

Cabrach 235, 278, 282, 283, 321
Cairney (Cairnie) 92
Cairngorm Mountains 144, 311
Cantray 43
Calcots 284, 305
Campdalemore 70
Cardenhill 303
Cardockhead 137, 140
Cardow 227, 228
Carron 228
Castle Bridge 112
Cathedral Lodge 325, 326
Cawdor 23, 35, 238, 243
Chanonrie Kirk 39
Chapelton 206
Claggan 226, 227
Claydales 83, 90
Cloddy Moss 55
Cluny Hill 23, 42, 288
Cocoa School 98, 99
Cokstoune 40
Conicavel 44
Connagedale 160
Cornhill Mental Hospital 305
Coulardbank 305

Cove 205
Covesea 69, 190, 212, 214, 220, 249,
 271, 318, 327
Coylumbridge 311
Craigellachie 158
Craighead 69
Craigmoray 82, 304, 305
Cranloch 236
Crofts Farm 178
Cromdale 236
Culbin 44, 45, 261, 262, 263, 359
Cullen 80, 81, 105, 106, 107, 115, 131,
 132, 133, 134, 136, 139, 202
Culloden 54, 60, 65, 66
Culreoch 295
Cummingston 229, 230
Cygnet Ballet Dancing School 301, 302

D
Dallas 137, 211, 212, 219, 242, 303
Darnaway (Ternway) 20, 26, 28, 30,
 31, 32, 35, 36, 44
Darnaway Castle 20
Dava Moor 150
Deskford 105, 115, 116
Deveron 282
Dipple 38, 233, 234, 235, 236, 237
Downie Hill 44
Drainie 67, 83, 165, 217
Dr Gray's Hospital (Elgin) 78, 101,
 125, 126, 164, 251, 285, 344
Drumblade 206
Drumdewin 43
Drywells 278
Duff House 62
Dufftown 92, 94, 95, 219, 267, 278,
 283, 294, 310, 327
Duffus 20, 25, 26, 35, 158, 160, 190,
 229, 269, 270, 273, 318, 328
Duffus Church 108, 273
Duffus House 20, 269, 271
Dundurcas 285
Dunkinty 199
Dunnottar 33, 34, 35
Dunphail 206, 301
Dyke 55, 57, 259, 261, 262

E
Edinkillie 150, 296

Elchies 147, 153, 154, 157, 169, 175,
 186, 227
Elgin 13, 19, 21, 23, 25, 26, 28, 38,
 39, 40, 41, 42, 45, 47, 48, 55, 57, 64,
 67, 68, 69, 71, 73, 74, 77, 78, 79, 80,
 81, 82, 87, 88, 89, 90, 91, 93, 94, 96,
 98, 99, 100, 102, 105, 106, 108, 114,
 115, 119, 124, 125, 126, 127, 128,
 132, 137, 138, 140, 144, 145, 146,
 148, 149, 151, 153, 157, 160, 161,
 164, 165, 170, 174, 175, 176, 183,
 186, 193, 195, 198, 199, 202, 206,
 213, 215, 225, 226, 229, 230, 234,
 236, 238, 239, 249, 250, 251, 252,
 262, 263, 264, 269, 270, 271, 273,
 284, 285, 287, 288, 290, 291, 292,
 293, 294, 299, 301, 303, 304, 305,
 306, 308, 310, 311, 314, 315, 316,
 318, 319, 320, 321, 322, 323, 325,
 326, 327, 329, 330, 334, 340
Elgin Academy 88, 89, 106, 138, 145,
 146, 176, 198, 202, 206, 234, 238,
 264, 294
Elgin Cathedral 19, 21, 26, 28, 39, 41,
 67, 91, 153, 325, 326
Elgin Dairy 310
Elgin Free Library 114
Elgin Girls' School 87, 93
Elgin Girls' Technical School 90, 125
Elgin High Church 249
Elgin Institution 67, 68
Elgin Library 285, 358
Elgin Lunatic Asylum 114
Elgin Museum 148, 68, 79, 114, 157,
 213, 215, 226, 238, 249, 251, 252,
 262, 271, 293, 294, 299, 323
Elgin Public Library 114
Elgin Town Hall 114

F
Falconer Museum 243, 247, 248
Findhorn 13, 110, 111, 129, 190, 220,
 238, 239, 242, 243, 245, 247, 268, 316
Finlarig 303
Ford Cottage 231
Fordyce 128, 132, 133, 136, 138, 139
Foresterhill Hospital 252
Forres 23, 29, 42, 47, 56, 78, 100, 106,
 107, 109, 110, 112, 154, 164, 165,

190, 191, 195, 206, 220, 238, 243,
244, 245, 247, 248, 259, 274, 275,
288, 293, 301, 302, 303, 331
Friars House 291

G
Gallows Green 319
Garioch 320
Garmouth 148, 160, 164, 302, 316
Glasterim 160, 161, 164
Glen Grant Distillery 74
Glen Rothes 289
Gollachy 202
Gordon Arms Hotel 263
Gordon Castle 49, 51, 52, 58, 59, 60,
61, 70, 181, 182, 183, 184, 236, 316
Gordon Chapel 233
Gordonstoun 54, 140, 160, 174, 190,
196, 214, 220, 221, 222, 241, 242,
244, 269, 293
Grange 43, 177
Grant Lodge 114, 269, 285
Grantown 70, 295
Gray's School of Art (Aberdeen) 301
Greyfriars Convent 293

H
Headis 43
Heathfield 186, 188
Hell's Hole Cave 328
Hempriggs 109
Highfield 230, 231, 270
Hillhead 312
Hillocks, The 86, 322, 323
Holy Trinity Church 290
Hopeman 150, 158, 231, 286, 288, 294,
295, 316, 328, 331, 332, 334, 335
Huntly 29, 30, 60, 92, 180, 181, 188,
206, 280, 297, 314

I
Inshoch 44, 47
Inverugie 33
Inverurie 251, 305

K
Keam 229
Keith 20, 21, 33, 35, 36, 37, 92, 94,
132, 136, 138, 141, 179, 196, 212,

253, 270, 291
Kilnhillock 202, 203
Kilravock 35, 57, 59
Kincraig 216
Kingussie 52, 58, 61, 137
Kinloss 25, 44, 128, 131, 150, 270
Kinloss Abbey 131
Kinrara 61, 62
Kintessack 55
Knockando 137, 140, 147, 176, 178,
180, 186, 226, 227
Knoll, The 100

L
Lady Lane 87, 327, 329
Laggan 51, 295, 316
Lairig Ghru 144, 311
Lesmurdie 330
Lethen 41, 47, 243, 358
Lhanbryde 40, 67, 96, 147, 149, 212,
284, 286, 303, 317, 325
Linksfield 305
Linkwood 322
Littlehaugh Cottage 289
Lochindorb 19, 20, 26
Lochindorb Castle 19, 20
Lochloy 44, 45
Loch Spynie 20
Logie Coldstone 140
Lossiemouth 67, 69, 82, 83, 84, 85, 86,
108, 127, 148, 150, 165, 168, 187, 188,
195, 214, 215, 216, 219, 249, 264, 297,
298, 299, 305, 311, 312, 313, 314, 315,
323, 324, 325, 327, 330

M
Macduff 107
Mackie Academy 140
Marischal College 59, 138, 251
Marywell 38
Meadowhillock 229
Michael Kirk 196, 244
Milne's Institution 128, 196, 197, 234
Monymusk 51
Moray, Earldom of 20, 26, 29, 31
Moray Golf Club 216, 311, 312, 313,
314, 315
Morayshire Brick and Tile Works 249
Morayshire Union Poorhouse 78, 79,

82, 327
Mortlach 95, 278, 283, 327, 328
Mosstowie 303
Mosstodloch 237
Moy 190
Munro Home 100

N
Nairn 43, 126, 140, 149, 190, 236,
 240, 259, 261, 262, 286, 288, 291,
 310, 311
Nethybridge 294, 295, 297
Newmachar 239
Newmill 73
North College 174, 175
Northern Nursing Home 158, 229, 230
Northfield 99, 269
North Lodge 92, 151
North Lodge Industrial School 92

O
Reformatory School, Aberdeen 232
Oakbank 284
Oldmills 151, 153
Over Deanshaugh 77

P
Park 55, 274
Peterhead 231
Pitgaveny 23, 193
Pitsligo 59
Pittyvaich 278, 282, 283
Pluscarden 77, 148, 206, 217, 292
Portgordon 160, 164, 202

Q
Quarrywood 71, 114

R
Rafford 125, 149, 303, 321, 325
Red Kirk 231
Rosehearty 239, 249
Rosemount 251
Rothes 48, 74, 147, 158, 160, 289, 290
Rothienorman 305

S
Sanquhar House 220, 274, 275
Sculptor's Cave 212, 213, 214, 216,

217, 271
Sheriffston 96, 97, 149, 212, 325
Silverhills 160
Skene 62, 92, 117, 138, 304, 305, 306
Slorach's Wood 321
Sluie 243
South Church (Elgin) 126
South College Street (Elgin) 101
Spey 13, 20, 38, 58, 65, 144, 151, 152,
 184, 230, 231, 233, 236, 295, 317, 321
Spey Bay 151, 152, 317
Speymouth Church 235
Speyside 38, 142, 150, 153, 229, 285
Spynie 20, 56, 57, 86, 105, 114, 119,
 140, 165, 249, 250
Spynie House 119
Stonehaven 140
Stotfield 69, 312, 313, 327
Strathspey 58, 61, 295, 312
Strichen Senior Secondary School 294
St Sylvester's 77, 293
Stynie 231
Sweethillock 83

T
Tamdhu Distillery 176
Thornhill House 238
Tombain 296, 297
Tomintoul 14, 69, 70, 71

U
United Free Church (Elgin) 125, 127,
 268, 286
Urquhart 38, 237, 284

W
West End Mission Hall (Elgin) 97, 98
Wester Elchies 153, 154, 157, 169, 175,
 186
Westerton 206, 217
Westfield 28, 345
Whitehills 132
Windyridge 249
Woodend Hospital 176
Woolmanhill 158

## The Prisoner of St Kilda

Margaret Macaulay
ISBN 978 1906817 65 7 PBK £8.99

*The true story of this lady is as frightfully romantic as if it had been the fiction of a gloomy fancy.*
JAMES BOSWELL, 1785

Married to a Scottish law lord, Lady Grange threatened to expose her husband's secret connections to the Jacobites in an attempt to force him to leave his London mistress. But the stakes were higher than she could ever have imagined. Her husband's powerful co-conspirators exacted a ruthless revenge. She was carried off to the Western Isles, doomed to thirteen bitter years of captivity. Death was her only release.

Based on contemporary documents and Lady Grange's own letters, *The Prisoner of St Kilda* looks beyond the legends to tell for the first time the true story of an extraordinary woman.

*It's a stunning story and Margaret Macaulay has done it full justice.*
THE HERALD

## Women of Scotland

David R Ross
ISBN 978 1906817 57 2 PBK £9.99

In a mix of historical fact and folklore, 'biker-historian' David R Ross journeys across Scotland to tell the stories of some of Scotland's finest women. From the legend of Scota over 3,000 years ago to the Bruce women, Black Agnes and the real Lady Macbeth, through to Kay Matheson – who helped liberate the Stone of Destiny from Westminster Abbey – and Wendy Wood in the 20th century, these proud and passionate women shaped the Scotland of today.

Leading his readers to the sites where the past meets the present, this is a captivating insight into some remarkable tales of the Scottish people that have previously been neglected, a celebration of and tribute to the women of Scotland.

*Women of Scotland, it is you who will bear and nurture our future generations. Instil in them a pride in their blood that will inspire the generations yet to come, so that our land will regain its place, and remain strong and free, defiant and proud, for the Scots yet unborn.*
DAVID R ROSS

## The Spey: From Source to Sea

Donald Barr & Brian Barr
ISBN 9781906307 35 6 PBK £12.99

'The River Spey means something to most Scots, and to many people from elsewhere. For some it is the great salmon river, summoning up images of chaps in tweeds and waders casting prodigious distances. To others the Spey is synonymous with whisky. And others yet think of it as a fearsomely fast and dangerous river.'
DONALD BARR

Donald and Brian Barr consider this multiplicity of identities as they affectionately explore the river, whose presence flowed through their childhoods, from its source to the sea. From the small brown trout of Loch Spey to the Dolphin pods of the Moray Firth, from a meagre burn in the Monadhliath Mountains to a powerful waterway nearly 100 miles later, the Spey is a truly unique river. Also included are easy-to-follow walks, notes on local wildlife and historical sites, as well as the distilleries, golf courses, tourist attractions and, of course, the fishing. The book also offers information that only a lifetime of living near the Spey can offer, with surprises even for those who know and love the Spey.

## Women of the Highlands

Katharine Stewart
ISBN 9781906817 92 3 PBK £7.99

The Highlands of Scotland are an evocative and mysterious land, cut off from the rest of Scotland by mountains and developing as a separate country for hundreds of years. Epitomising the 'sublime' in philosophical thought of the eighteenth century, the Highlands have been a source of inspiration for poets and writers of all descriptions.

Katharine Stewart takes us to the heart of the Highlands with this history of the women who shaped this land. From the women of the shielings to the Duchess of Gordon, from bards to conservationists, authors to folk-singers, Women of the Highlands examines how the culture of the Highlands was created and passed down through the centuries, and what is being done to preserve it today.

## Cattle on a Thousand Hills: Farming Culture in the Highlands of Scotland

Katharine Stewart
ISBN 978 1906817 44 2 PBK £7.99

'One cold spring morning I had a lovely surprise. As the first drops of milk spurted into the pail a blackbird, who had taken up residence in the byre over the winter, began to sing his little inward song, in rehearsal for the full-throated version he would sing from the branch of the rowan later on. This was a moment of delight which will be with me always.'
KATHARINE STEWART

Infused by the author's own experiences of small-holding at 'the end of the crofting era', this book offers an excellent insight into the social history and colourful customs associated with tending cattle on crofts, on shielings and on the drove roads of old, in an account that is populated by legendary figures, mighty beasts and characters larger than life.

Perhaps most importantly of all, however, this is a history that looks to the future – a recent revival in cattle and traditional practices could pave the way for the truly sustainable agricultural practices so crucial to the fate of the planet at large.

## Bodysnatchers to Lifesavers: Three Centuries of Medicine in Edinburgh

Dorothy Crawford and Tara Womersley
ISBN 978 1906817 58 9 HBK £16.99

From dissecting bodies 'donated' by murderers to developing lifesaving treatments, the Edinburgh medical community has always been innovative and challenged entrenched medical ideas. This has ranged from setting up an inspirational public health system to discovering chloroform as an anaesthetic, which was fiercely opposed as pain relief for women during labour.

*Bodysnatchers to Lifesavers* gives a fascinating insight into the development of modern medicine and the leading role that Edinburgh played on the medical stage.

The tale of Edinburgh's medical past is told through the stories of colourful characters including the bodysnatchers Burke and Hare, the evolutionist Charles Darwin, surgeons Joseph Lister and James Syme as well as Sophia Jex-Blake, who headed the campaign for women's right to study medicine, and 'James Barry', Britain's first female doctor.

# **Luath** Press Limited

*committed to publishing well written books worth reading*

LUATH PRESS takes its name from Robert Burns, whose little collie Luath (*Gael.*, swift or nimble) tripped up Jean Armour at a wedding and gave him the chance to speak to the woman who was to be his wife and the abiding love of his life. Burns called one of the 'Twa Dogs' Luath after Cuchullin's hunting dog in Ossian's *Fingal*.
Luath Press was established in 1981 in the heart of Burns country, and is now based a few steps up the road from Burns' first lodgings on Edinburgh's Royal Mile. Luath offers you distinctive writing with a hint of unexpected pleasures.
Most bookshops in the UK, the US, Canada, Australia, New Zealand and parts of Europe, either carry our books in stock or can order them for you. To order direct from us, please send a £sterling cheque, postal order, international money order or your credit card details (number, address of cardholder and expiry date) to us at the address below. Please add post and packing as follows: UK – £1.00 per delivery address; overseas surface mail – £2.50 per delivery address; overseas airmail – £3.50 for the first book to each delivery address, plus £1.00 for each additional book by airmail to the same address. If your order is a gift, we will happily enclose your card or message at no extra charge.

## **Luath** Press Limited

543/2 Castlehill
The Royal Mile
Edinburgh EH1 2ND
Scotland
Telephone: +44 (0)131 225 4326 (24 hours)
Fax: +44 (0)131 225 4324
email: sales@luath. co.uk
Website: www. luath.co.uk